JANE POLLER

OATH

OF

REDEMPTION

By Jane Poller

Royal Oath

Oath of Rebellion
Oath of Revenge
Oath of Redemption

Vinci Books

vinci-books.com

Published by Vinci Books Ltd in 2025

1

Copyright © Jane Poller 2025

A CIP catalogue record for this book is available from the British Library.

Paperback ISBN: 9781036708023

DWARVES

RINEHOLD

HARTSGROVE

FERAL
FOREST

SIDRANO

OLIVE'S

DEMEREE

BUSPARIA

GROWLERS

OVERHOLD

MYRRVANE

GLATHEN

CAPITOLS OF
DOPHIAS

Chapter One

Seven Months Ago...

Leopol's spirit stirred, a wisp of consciousness coalescing amidst the rubble of what was once the grand ballroom. Dust hung like a shroud over the remnants of opulence, the air thick with the scent of charred wood and magic turned sour. His form flickered, translucent and unstable, as if he were but a breath away from being whisked into oblivion.

Again.

This feeling, the reforming–it was familiar and yet not.

The skeletal dragon, a monstrous relic that brought faint memories, lay in a pile of bones in the jagged opening where a wall had collapsed. Beyond it lay the forest where Knox had ridden away, Eirwyn cradled in his arms. Leopol's gaze, however, was drawn downward, to the fractured mirror that lay prostrate at his feet.

A sense of urgency gripped him as he hovered closer, the broken glass reflecting his spectral visage in disjointed fragments. This form... he remembered this form but not from his time on Celawyn–from his time *before*.

His head pulsed as he tried to remember more of the before, more of his time with the dragons here. The gaps in his knowledge grated on his nerves, making his headache worsen. How could a spirit have a headache if he didn't have a body? It defied logic.

The golden apple tree stood nearby, once vibrant and heavy with fruit, trembling under an unseen assault, almost in time with the pulsing in his mind. With each pulse of nekros magic that seeped from the mirror's cracks, the tree's leaves curled inward, turning to ash upon their branches, weeping golden tears that evaporated before they could touch the earth.

Nekrotic was wrong, soul sucking, opposite of his own. It–like all magic–could be used for good or harm, but this reeked of darkness, evil, and something more. Something familiar.

As Leopol's eyes locked with his own shattered reflection, the mirror became a gateway to the past. Memories surged forth like floodwaters breaching a dam–images of an ancient library, a place of infinite knowledge where he had been in this humanoid form but also more than a mere wraith, where he had served a purpose greater than himself. Illustros, the celestial god resplendent with light and wisdom, flashed through his mind as he walked beside Leopol through the rows of shelves. A woman smiled at him proudly from the other side of the all-father god–a goddess in her own right, and her features so reminiscent of those that stared at him from the broken mirror.

Yet her name was out of reach, beyond the memory. All that remained was the feeling she'd instilled within him, even all those years ago before he had come to this realm.

The memory shifted. Another mirror materialized within his recollections, this one whole and gleaming in another part of Hartsgrove Castle, in another time. A wizard stood before it, a figure both formidable and familiar, weaving spells that echoed through the ages. And there he was, not as the apparition he was now, but majestic and powerful—a dragon whose scales shimmered with the very essence of magic.

Yet the clarity was fleeting. As the dark magic faded from the mirror and the apple tree in the center of the broken ballroom withered, doubt clouded his newfound awareness, leaving him adrift in a sea of fragmented truths. He sensed a connection to Knox, a thread woven between them by the enigmatic tapestry of lost magic. But the certainty of kinship eluded him, leaving only questions in its wake. Knox was his cousin, but also... not.

Leopol lingered in the shattered ballroom, a spirit haunted by echoes of what once was, determined to reclaim the scattered pieces of his existence. Knox and Eirwyn had said he was a ghost, which meant he was dead.

But he wasn't, not really. He couldn't be dead when he'd never really been alive. Ghosts were untethered, but he *knew* this place.

The truth of that was the most real thing he knew. Of all the scattered memories, visions, and dreams that had haunted him the past few days since awakening in this corporeal form, he knew two things to be true. He'd never really been alive, and he still had a body somewhere.

Magic hummed through this castle, calling to him to search every nook and cranny, read every book and spell, find the construct of his body that the gods had given him.

Leopol felt something tugging at the edges of his spectral form—a subtle vibration that spoke of hidden pathways and forgotten connections. Each shard of the broken mirror reflected not just his translucent image, but glimpses of landscapes and moments that seemed both familiar and alien.

One fragment showed a stone archway carved with intricate runes, another a spiral staircase descending into darkness, and a third a library shelf lined with scrolls that seemed to breathe with their own strange life. The magic coursing through Hartsgrove Castle was not merely ambient; it was sentient, deliberate, watching him with an intelligence that felt almost... calculating.

His ethereal hand hovered over the largest mirror fragment. As his translucent fingers neared the surface, the glass began to ripple like liquid mercury, its reflection shifting like a living entity. The magic within the castle walls seemed to pulse with an ancient rhythm, drawing Leopol closer to the mystery that lay just beyond his spectral perception.

A whisper, soft as a breeze yet sharp as a blade, cut through the stillness. *Not yet*, it seemed to say, the words forming not in sound but in the very essence of the magical currents surrounding him, running through him.

That voice was familiar, like a homecoming in its own right. A whisper of wind carried fragments of an ancient dialect, words that seemed to pulse with forgotten power, the translation just beyond his reach.

The mirror fragment trembled, its surface now a kaleidoscope of shifting images—glimpses of battles long forgotten, arcane rituals performed in chambers hidden from mortal eyes, and fleeting shadows of figures whose identities remained tantalizingly out of reach.

Something ancient moved just beyond his perception, a presence that felt simultaneously familiar and alien.

A sudden tremor rippled through the ballroom—not of physical movement, but of magical resonance. The broken mirror pulsed with a dim golden light, its fractured surface reflecting nothing and everything at once. Leopol felt the magic surge around him, a living thing that breathed and shifted with its own consciousness.

Threads of golden magic–gossamer-thin yet strong as steel–began to weave around his translucent form, pulling, probing, searching. Something was coming. If only he could remember, could recognize it...

The withered golden apple tree's remaining branches creaked, responding to the energy that pulsed through the castle's stone foundations. Its branches now brittle as old bones, a single golden leaf detached, spinning through the air in defiance of natural laws.

Leopol drifted closer to the tree, his ethereal form wavering like smoke caught in an imperceptible current, like the exhaled breath of some forgotten hope of the world.

Another memory flickered–broken images of arcane rituals, of power exchanges that transcended mortal under-standing.

Each breath of magic seemed to pulse with recognition, as if the very stones of Hartsgrove Castle remembered him and urged him to remember in return. Leopol extended a translucent hand toward the withered golden apple tree, feeling the residual energy that still trembled within its dying branches.

It quivered, its leaves releasing a final, desperate breath of magic that intertwined with the emerging energy. Threads of golden magic swirled around him, filling him with light, hope, a vibration of knowing something important...

He blinked slowly, feeling through the magic, following the threads back to the source. The magic filled his soul, knitting his memories back together, the magic transferring out of the dying tree and into him.

A sudden tremor rippled through the ballroom floor, causing fragments of the broken mirror to shift and realign momentarily. His eyes widened where he stood next to the tree. In that fractured reflection, Leopol glimpsed movement—something darker than his own spectral form, something that did not belong. The shadows seemed to breathe with a malevolent intelligence, watching, waiting.

The nekros magic that had been seeping from the mirror's cracks began to coalesce, forming tendrils that reached out like seeking fingers. They probed the edges of Leopol's ethereal form, and he threw his hands up, the golden tendrils of magic forming a shield.

The tendrils recoiled, hissing like serpents burned by sunlight. Something ancient and malevolent pushed against the golden shield, probing for weakness. Leopol felt the magic surge through him—not just defensive, but sentient, almost hungry.

His spectral form flickered, solidifying momentarily as the nekrotic energy tested his ethereal boundaries. The shadows that breathed at the edge of his perception seemed to pulse with recognition, as if they knew something about him that he had not yet remembered.

A piece of memory surged forward—a ritual binding conducted in a chamber within this castle where time warped and contorted. The golden magic within him vibrated in sync with this hazy recollection, blending with the image he had seen in the shattered mirror earlier. This fusion produced harmonic vibrations of truth within him. It triggered the fragments of the broken mirror to emit an unearthly resonance, as though they too recalled the traumatic event.

The shadows retreated, but not in defeat. Their withdrawal felt calculated, like a predator biding its time before the next attack. Leopol understood–or rather, felt–that something was gathering strength, preparing for a more calculated assault.

He had to be ready. Somehow, he was the best hope of defeating it.

The golden magic within him pulsed, like a living thing that remembered pathways and connections long forgotten. He remembered the first time this magic had flown through his dragon body, bringing him to so-called life after the–the memory failed him.

The magic tugged at him, urging movement, exploration instead of introspection. Each fragment of the broken mirror now seemed to vibrate with potential–portals waiting to be understood, memories waiting to be unlocked.

A distant rumble echoed through the castle's stone corridors, like the deep growl of some ancient, awakening beast. The last of the shadows disappeared–and with it, the images in the broken pieces of glass. For the first time since awakening, Leopol was truly alone.

Chapter Two

Present Day...

Bella followed Eirwyn into the sunroom, fingers flicking as she concentrated on holding the spell to animate the potted rose. The golden sunlight that bathed the space brought no warmth to her translucent skin. The rose petals brushed her cheek, though she couldn't feel them—only the memory of touch remained.

She hadn't held anything physical in seven months. Not since the wizard stole her body, tethering her soul to this single fragile rose. If it died, she died. Simple as that. It was her curse, her punishment, her prison.

Eirwyn's voice broke through her thoughts. "Isn't it wonderful, Bella? To have you here—it's like the old days, reborn from ashes."

Bella nodded, the corners of her mouth twitching upward. "We never just sat in a sunroom in a castle, Eirwyn. The good old days involved the tavern, spilled ale, stinky peasants, and your light shows entertaining the masses. Not this..."

"Peacefulness?" Eirwyn smirked, waving to a table by the window. "It doesn't seem real to me either, and I grew up in the palaces! Here, put your rose here before you tire out your magic carrying it around."

Bella floated toward her and assessed the room, thinking about their shared history.

She'd been catching up with Eirwyn all day as if no time had passed between them. As if Eirwyn's brother, Gastone, hadn't created a rift between them when he'd married Bella. As if Bella herself hadn't set aside their friendship for her new husband in her quest for knowledge. As if Eirwyn's mate, Knox, hadn't battled Gastone on the castle roof, triggering the events that led to Gastone's death and Bella's widespread curse on the land.

Eirwyn didn't seem to care how many mistakes Bella had made. She'd been welcomed with open arms by both Eirwyn and her mate, Knox, both of whom were apparently ruling the Feral Forest as king and queen.

It didn't surprise Bella, though. Eirwyn was born to rule; the princess never should have sought refuge in Bella's tavern as a child. But her father and Lailant had insisted that Eirwyn's presence was not going to bring about their ruin, so Bella had taken the little girl under her tutelage. It had been the last request he'd made before being called to war, leaving her to manage the tavern.

Now they were both all grown up, both queens, even though Bella hadn't had a chance to rule and prove herself. That was why she was here, after all, to fix the curse and make it up to her people.

The sunroom was beautiful, quiet, untouched. And maybe, just maybe, it could serve as a sanctuary to begin her work undoing the damage she'd caused—a place to weave magic and unlock secrets from nature's depths.

"Are you sure this space isn't already in use?" she asked.

Eirwyn laughed. "Hardly. It's a glorified sitting room. Empty and waiting for you."

Bella stepped further in, scanning shelves and tables, her mind already spinning with ideas. It was a suitable location for her to set up a makeshift laboratory. She would need to get supplies and ingredients, but that was a challenge she was ready to face. Her years of training and experience had prepared her for this moment.

"I have some old shelves in the storage room that we can use," Eirwyn offered, eager and helpful as always. Her friend knew Bella would want books everywhere. "And I can start gathering some herbs from the inside garden for you. Unfortunately, the long winter has kept us from spring planting."

Eirwyn had explained her concerns about the lack of food being planted for the growing nation of forest people, but there was little they could do to make the lingering winter end and force spring to arrive.

Bella smiled gratefully at Eirwyn's offer. Having a friend like her was truly a blessing Bella didn't deserve. "Very well, if you're sure I won't be intruding here."

"Never an intrusion," Eirwyn said, running her finger over the top of the central table near the chaise to inspect the layer of dust. She held up her finger. "See? No one uses this room. But with the garden doors, it's easy access for when the garden does start producing."

Bella carefully used her magic to set the budding rose down on a small table behind the glass double doors that led outside. Eirwyn was right, the furniture in this room was slightly dusty from disuse.

The glass door flew open with a gust of wind, banging into the table.

"Eirwyn, where is the—?"

The movement startled her and her hand jolted, the pot slipping—shattering on the floor.

"No!" Her cry echoed, vibrating the walls. The earth shook, soil scattered, and petals fluttered.

Bella dropped to her knees, hands trembling above the broken rose. Her entire being ached, torn as though she'd been physically struck. Her soul strained to reach the damaged tether.

The once-beautiful flower now lay ruined, mirroring the state of her life. Clusters of soil clung to the twisted roots, and the vibrant orange rose drooped with the weight of its own petals. Some lay fluttering on the ground around it, while others still clung to the stem, barely holding on.

"I'm so sorry," the man said, stepping forward. "Are we turning this into a conservatory now? I wasn't aware we were adding new gardeners before the eastern wing was finished."

Bella's head snapped up. His calm voice rubbed like sandpaper against an open wound.

"It's not just a plant," she snapped. The furniture behind her shuddered an inch across the floor.

Eirwyn raised her hands, her eyes wide. "Bella—"

The man lifted a brow, the bright light masking his features. "My apologies. Shall I call it a specific type of rose? Are you the new gardener, then?"

Magic crackled in the air, pulsing in time with her rage. "I don't know what type of rose it is. All I know is it's the tether to my soul."

The man stiffened. "Tether? Wait, let's talk this through rationally—"

"Rationally?" Her hands clenched into fists. "You nearly killed me, and you want calm discussion?"

Before he could answer, her father Wulfric entered the room. "What's with all the rattling and yelling? Who's upsetting my daughter?"

Wulfric's wolf-like features—ears, nose, tail—hadn't changed the comfort she found in her father's presence. But he couldn't touch her, hold her like he used to when they'd lost her mother.

He prowled toward her, his frown of concern making her feel like at least one person in the land still had her best interests at heart. It made her feel less alone after half a year of being so lonely in this form.

"Just a klutz who's going to get me killed," Bella cried, blinking furiously to keep the tears at bay. Logically, she knew she was overreacting, but she struggled to hold in her emotions.

Her father's eyes softened, and the tears grew bigger.

The man in the doorway to the garden tugged on his jacket. "Wait, who said anything about killing—"

"I did, you idiot! The evil wizard took possession of my body and tethered my soul to that rose. It dies, I die. Understand now?" The air crackled around her, charged with the force of her indignation.

Wulfric crouched to inspect the rose while Bella bit her lip, unsure if she should cry or scream.

The man's gaze returned to her. "Daughter? Then you must be—"

"Bellatrix," Eirwyn said. "Queen of Busparia. Lord Leopol, meet my dear friend Bella. Bella, this is Leopol, our royal advisor and right-hand man."

The tension in the room shifted, becoming something more profound, a recognition of invisible threads that knew something she didn't. The man rubbed a ring on his finger and stepped forward, bending into a deep bow. "Your Majesty, forgive me."

Guilt raced up her spine, and she twisted her hands in her skirt with a loud sigh as she waved her hand. "Oh, none of that majesty business. I haven't done anything to earn that title. Until I fix this curse on the people, just call me Bella."

She had a mission to accomplish before her soul descended into the underworld for judgment—before the last petal on the rose fell, that is. She was in a race against time and didn't have, well, time for titles of grandeur like your majesty.

The moment her pot shattered, something inside Leopol twisted, freezing him to the moment while he analyzed and assessed.

He hadn't felt anything in months. But the crack of the pot, her broken cry—and the powerful tether of golden magic linking her to the flower—it all sent a pulse through him.

Leopol's chest tightened as the gravity of his carelessness settled upon him like chains. He watched, horrified, as Eirwyn cradled the fragile rose in her hands, her fingers working with delicate urgency. Leopol whispered a simple spell, much easier to do now than when he'd first woken up seven months ago.

A yellow-orange smoke-like line of magic flowed from Bella to the rose. The air hung heavy with tension, and within it floated an unspoken truth that Leopol could no longer ignore—the rose was more than just a plant; it was an anchor to Bella's very soul.

Tears clung to her lashes, and he walked toward her, his feet not making a sound in this form. There was something about her that drew him inexplicably closer.

"I'm so sorry, Your Majesty. I didn't mean to hurt you or your tether," he said softly, reaching for her hand and bowing, an outdated habit that he'd been unable to break these past few months. It'd always brought a stab of pain, a reminder that he was no longer who he once was.

He froze as his hand contacted hers.

Contact.

The touch sang through him, burning into his core. A connection he hadn't known he craved until now. For the first time in months, his soul ached for something other than his own body and memories. A shadow phantom feeling of his draconic form hit him like a punch to the gut, heat and desire flooding his psyche. Even in that draconic physical form, he hadn't ached like this. Emotion, heat, and desire threatened to overwhelm him.

He breathed deeply, slowly, trying to maintain control as his spirit vibrated with *something* he didn't know how to identify.

He frowned, eager to puzzle out this feeling and why she triggered it. She was in spirit form, like him, but it couldn't just be that.

She turned sharply, her hazel eyes widening as she met his gaze, her fingers gripping his tightly in shock. Her lips were full and curved in a perfect bow, inviting and tempting even as they parted in surprise. Her gasp was like music to his ears, echoing in his mind as he drank in her beauty.

Their magic swirled around them, crackling with recognition.

Her oval face was filled with surprise and her wide hazel eyes sparkled with wonder. Her skin was smooth and glowing, highlighting her high cheekbones, delicate features, and the light dusting of bronzed freckles across her nose.

Her lips parted, light from the window falling on her pert little nose, the light seeming to gather around them as their magic danced, testing each other on a plane most people couldn't see.

The shaking fingers of her other hand reached up as if in slow motion, settling on his chest.

"You're a ghost like me," she whispered, awed.

Leopol swallowed. "Not a ghost. Not exactly."

Their fingers remained locked, and he covered her other hand on his chest, just over where his heart had been. Light glowed faintly from her rose, the golden tether pulsing between them as her magic flared.

Her hand trembled. "I didn't know... I thought I was alone."

"You're not," Leopol said, fiercely. She wasn't a ghost or alone.

He knew she was a spirit; if she was a ghost, she wouldn't be tied to the rose. He didn't know why they were both in the same place at the same time. But they were together now, bound by more than accident and more than magic.

The pieces of her story, her soul, the sorrow in her gaze—they drew him in, and he would not let her go. Lightning shot through him with a rush of heat, magic, and belonging.

His hand shook, and when his thumb caressed the back of her hand, her breath hitched. The castle, his body, his memories, the curses, the war—all of it faded beneath the sheer force of this moment, this touch, this woman.

Mate.

The word slammed into him, unbidden and undeniable.

Nonsensical. Mates were for the living. Not for him. Not for a spirit construct like him or a spirit tied to a rose like her.

Yet he couldn't deny how his lips tingled with a desire to feel the softness of hers against his own. Imagining the warmth and plumpness of her lips under his, he lifted her fingers and kissed the soft skin of her knuckles. Magic and need flared between them, flowing through them, swirling together for one brief, intense moment that should've brought him to his knees.

Bella gasped, swaying closer as their magic swirled around them faintly. "What—what is that?"

Eirwyn hmmed where she kneeled. "Interesting."

"Very," Wulfric said, but Leopol couldn't look away from Bella to see what they were talking about.

Bella had no such problem. Blinking swiftly, she looked down at their hands but didn't step away from him. Her eyes widened as she gasped again, and he nearly groaned at the way her mouth bowed up.

"What is that?"

At her words, he finally glanced down to see the rose flickering on the floor, its petals glowing faintly. A tether of golden energy pulsed between her and the flower.

His jaw clenched as memories of spells and books swam in his mind, as if touching her had released some of what had been withheld from him. Some of the puzzle pieces of who he was slipped into place, forming a hazy picture.

He blinked, focusing on her, always her. "You're tied to the rose, you said?"

She swallowed hard and nodded. "If it dies, I die. But it's never pulsed before. I've never been able to see the threads of magic before..."

A sharp possessive fury burned through him at the thought of her dying for real. Unacceptable.

His hands curled into fists. He didn't know her, had no claim on her. But every instinct in his soul rebelled at the idea of her slipping away.

The fates had bound them together. He would not even let death tear them apart. If he admitted it now, though, it'd scare her away. She appeared human, fragile, delicate, graceful, and beautiful.

Bella stepped away, crouching to inspect the rose. As she released him, some of the brightness of the magic swirling around them faded.

He tugged on the hem of his blue dinner jacket and stepped back, using magic to close the glass doors as softly as he could.

"Wait, why is it no longer glowing? It looked like it was getting healthier, didn't it? Or was that just a wish?" Bella asked, questions flying. She was clearly intelligent, inquisitive, everything he'd hoped for in a mate.

He had a hard time reconciling her with what he knew of her.

This was the evil queen Scarlet had been so angry with. Wulfric's daughter and Eirwyn's friend, a former tavern owner who had kept her safe from the evil king Gastone. The same king who had married Bella before sending Scarlet to kill Eirwyn.

The same king who had wrought nekrosan magic through the mirror, animating the skeletal dragon to attack Knox and Eirwyn when they'd reached Hartsgrove, wakening Leopol from wherever his spirit had been slumbering.

The same queen who—when the king had died—had made an illegal blood magic potion from his heart, releasing a curse and wiping out an entire city on the edge of the forest.

No wonder he'd felt such power. The tendrils of his magic probed the edges of hers, almost like a taste on his tongue. She didn't feel like a nekromancer. She was an enigma, an anomaly that he wasn't sure he'd ever come across in however many hundreds of years he'd been on this world.

"No, I saw it too, although I didn't see any magic threads. Just the faintly glowing rose as it seemed to perk up," Eirwyn said.

"Right, well, looks like we need a better solution for the rose. I'll hunt down a better pot," Wulfric said, standing.

Leopol stepped forward, almost in a clumsy lurch, eager to impress his mate. "I can fix it. Here," he said, waving his hands and kneeling. With a frown of concentration, he wove the threads of magic and knit the pot back together, the seams glowing.

"How are you doing that?" Bella asked, but Leopol ignored her as he fixed her pot, weaving in a protection spell while he was at it, carving the runes into the pot itself like a hot brand.

"Leopol is the strongest, most knowledgeable sorcerer I've ever met," Eirwyn said softly. Bella gasped, and Eirwyn continued as if she'd spoken. "Exactly. Even among all the years of formal schooling and the best tutors the kingdom could buy, Leopol out magics them all. He just can't touch anything living."

Bella seemed to vibrate, the furniture in the room shaking along with her. "Just like me," she whispered.

At that moment, he breathed a sigh of relief. "There, all fixed. It should withstand being dropped now. Wulfric, would you care to test it before one of you re-plants the rose?"

Wulfric picked up the plain brown pot and dropped it. It bounced, so he picked it up and stood, dropping it from higher, then again with as much force as he could muster. Still, it held up, and Leopol breathed a sigh of relief as he stood.

Eirwyn beamed up at Leopol as she gathered up the plant. "Excellent, I know that was weighing on your mind, Bella. Thank you, Leopol."

Wulfric helped Eirwyn plant the rose, but Bella stood and launched herself into Leopol's arms. He gasped, gathering her tight against his body in his first hug since waking. It felt... like coming home.

The moment her arms wrapped around him, Leopol's breath caught in his throat. Her ethereal form pressed against him, cool and light as mist, yet with a surprising solidity he hadn't expected. His hands instinctively splayed across her back, fingers tracing the delicate lines of her spirit-form.

"Thank you," Bella whispered, her voice trembling. "For saving the pot and helping me protect the rose. Thank you for... understanding."

Wulfric cleared his throat. "I see you two are... becoming acquainted."

Bella pulled back, her translucent cheeks flushing a soft golden hue even though she didn't drop her hands from around his neck. Leopol noticed how the magic threads between her and the rose pulsed differently now—stronger, more vibrant.

"I apologize," she mumbled. "I'm not usually so... physical."

Leopol wanted to reassure her. "No need. It was pleasant."

Her cheeks turned pink, even under the translucence of her spirit form. "I just—I haven't been able to touch anyone in months."

Leopol's fingers hovered on her waist, uncertain. "Neither have I."

Wulfric cleared his throat, watching them with a mixture of curiosity and something deeper—a protective father's careful observation. "Perhaps we should discuss how you two seem to interact when neither of you can typically touch physical objects."

Eirwyn's eyes sparkled with intrigue. "Exactly. Something's different here. The rose perked up when you touched—both times, actually."

Bella dropped her arms and stepped back, turning to the potted rose now in Wulfric's hands. He set it on a small, low table next to a settee in the middle of the room—still where it could get light from the tall, glass windows, but not where it could be knocked over by someone opening the garden door.

Eirwyn's knowing smile suggested there was more happening than a simple embrace, her eyes darting between Bella and Leopol. Something unspoken passed between them—a recognition of the magical connection that had just sparked to life.

Bella stepped toward her rose and tapped her chin as the magic swirling around it faded. Still strong, but it no longer pulsed. She muttered under her breath, and Leopol watched, waiting to see what her brilliant mind would deduce.

"Leopol has been searching for answers about his own condition for months," Eirwyn interjected. "Perhaps you two might find more together than apart."

Leopol nodded in a soft bow, murmuring, "It'd be my pleasure."

Bella blushed again, and Eirwyn chuckled. "I'll leave you to discuss the details then, so I can get ready for the council dinner tonight."

Leopol knew this was a bigger meeting than the normal monthly meetings with the council. The new leaders in the Feral Forest—Robins, druids, and elected villagers who reported to Knox and Eirwyn—would want to know about the battle at the Winter Palace. Scarlet and Wulfric were supposed to report tonight on what had happened, but he wondered if Bella would attend.

After all, spirits didn't need to eat dinner.

Eirwyn smiled and reached for Bella's hand before she remembered they couldn't touch. She cleared her throat and said, "Bella, I'm so glad you're here. I know this is a chaotic time for you, but I want you to think of this castle as your home, and Leopol knows every inch of this place better than anyone. I've assigned you to the Rose Room, obviously. Leopol, can you escort her there when you're done showing her around the sunroom?"

Leopol nodded, his gaze connecting with Bella's once more.

"Wulfric, come with me, please."

"But—"

Eirwyn paused in the doorway and gave the Growler a heavy look. "We need to prepare what you're going to report tonight."

He just sighed and narrowed his eyes on Leopol. Leopol lifted his chin and held the man's gaze. Finally, he just snorted and followed Eirwyn toward the door.

Eirwyn chuckled, her footsteps fading as she smiled. "I'll see you both at dinner, then."

Then he was left alone with the only other spirit he'd ever met. His mate.

Chapter Three

"Come, sit and talk with me," Leopol said, settling on the velvet settee, his voice sending a shiver down Bella's spine. "Tell me your story so I might know how to best help you."

"Why would you help me?" Her voice was a whisper, and her eyes narrowed, studying Leopol with a mixture of suspicion and intrigue. She'd never met anyone like him, much less another spirit. Her fingers traced the edge of her golden gown—a nervous gesture that betrayed her carefully constructed composure.

She couldn't help but stare at him, this spirit who had so thoroughly captured her attention since he'd walked through the door like he owned the place.

The man was almost as tall and muscular as her father, Wulfric. Indeed, they both had hair that was too long by society's standards. Leopol's hair was tousled, as if he had been running his hands through it in frustration and fell just above his ears. Her fingers tingled to brush it out of his eyes.

Her fingers tingled. She hadn't felt anything in months,

nothing but grief and heartache and anger. But he made her feel so much more.

Leopòl matched her calculating gaze, ever watchful with those brilliant blue eyes that were so bright, they could be ice or gemstone. Colors were muted in this form, and she could almost see through him. But those eyes were as vivid as if she were still living.

"Let's call it mutual curiosity. I've searched every grimoire, every ancient text and spell book in this castle. I know things about magical curses that most scholars would kill to understand, and your magic is... unique. I'd like to get to know you."

Her hazel eyes narrowed, her foot tapping where she stood. "You mean to study me."

He arched a brow. "Study, examine, inspect, probe—call it what you will, but I promise not to harm you. It's just, I've not been able to...touch...anyone else since I woke like this last year. Yet somehow, I can touch you..."

His words drifted into the space between them, teasing them both with the promise of more touching, more exploring. The tension and magic flared along with his eyes. She was as attracted to him as he was to her. She felt it as surely as she could see their magic swirling in the air earlier while they were touching. That alone led to so many questions, and curiosity—the need to know everything so that she could best help save others—had always been her downfall.

She licked her lips. "And what makes you think your knowledge applies to my particular curse?"

Her heart seemed to race as his gaze dipped down to her lips, a phantom fluttering feeling in her stomach at his smile reminding her of the first crush of her youth.

The sharp angles of his face, the prominent jawline and cheekbones that hinted at a life of intensity and purpose, it all painted a heart-stopping package that made her lick her lips in surprise and anticipation. She hadn't expected to meet someone who made her entire body sit up and take notice. Not even Gastone had done that; she'd been more attracted to his power and what he could offer her than the actual man himself.

"We won't know if we don't try, now will we? Aren't you just a little bit curious? What do you have to lose?"

Her eyes shuttered at his words, and she finally sank onto the settee, frowning slightly.

"Everything," she whispered, her voice catching. "I have everything to lose."

"You saw a sampling of what magic I could wield earlier. I can teach you to protect yourself too, even in this form. Tell me your story. Let me help," he whispered, his fingers along the back of the couch playing with her hair.

Normally, she was very protective of her space, but when he was near, when he touched her, it was as if her soul settled into a soft hum of peace.

Leopol's clothes were outdated but of fine quality. She hated judging people by their clothing, but she'd learned a lot by doing so during the decade she'd managed the tavern. Despite the fatigue on his face, determination shone through, giving him an air of strength and resilience. This man was no ordinary noble, to still be hanging around as a spirit.

Ghosts were rare, the things of myths and story books. Spirits even more so. She'd done enough research after her own incident that left her in this damn incorporeal form. She knew she wasn't a ghost, but people just saw a semi-transparent being and lumped them all together.

For him to be a spirit, he had to have been powerful or experienced a powerful death to be here like this.

She took a deep breath and leaned her head back further into his touch even as she decided to test him. She closed her eyes and tried to feel the magic around her.

"The magic you used earlier. What was it, and how did you do it?"

"Synthara for the protective barrier around it and vitas to preserve the flower itself, using ancient runes to bind it all together into a permanently enchanted object. As a dragon, my magic is inherent, and something I just feel. I don't need spells, although they certainly help."

Her eyes widened. "You're a dragon?"

He ran a hand over the back of his neck and smiled sheepishly as he turned and placed his hand along the back of the couch. His eyes turned guarded, though, and she wondered what he was hiding. "Yes, Knox and I are both full-blooded dragons. From what Eirwyn tells me, we might be the only two dragons left on the continent, if not the entire world."

Bella's mouth opened and closed, then she turned away from him to process. Eventually she said, "That sounds lonely."

He nodded, tilting his body to face her, his other hand resting on the velvet between them. He ran his fingers over it, and Bella wondered if he could actually feel it. "Not as lonely as being a spirit."

They shared a commiserating smile before she continued, touching the velvet fabric near his hand. She couldn't feel it. She missed such simple things in life.

"I used to think it would be amazing to be born with magic instead of learning it. I was never happy with what I had and always wanted to learn more. Since becoming a ghost, my magic has gone all wrong."

Leopol's chuckle filled the room like a gentle melody,

revealing straight white teeth and deep dimples. His transparent form seemed to glimmer and sparkle in response to his joy, making him look even more ethereal.

As Bella looked at Leopol's mischievous, smiling face, she couldn't help but reach out and lightly touch his arm. His skin felt cool to the touch but also oddly comforting, like soft silk against her fingertips. A warm sensation spread from her hand throughout her whole body, causing her stomach to flutter with excitement.

"You're a spirit, not a ghost, but let me guess. The more emotional you are, the harder it is to control?" His grin was like the first sip of a sweet and potent potion, filling her with a heady and electrifying rush. She could quickly become addicted to him.

Her eyes widened in surprise, and she leaned forward. "Yes! How did you know?"

He settled his hand along the back of the couch as he talked. "When I first arrived, my father taught me to channel magic through meditation and breathing exercises. But when I woke up like this, I found my emotions all over the place. It was like I was a youngling learning to fly all over again, and my innate magic fluctuated with my emotions."

It was a weird way to talk about being born, but she sighed, letting the thought go as her shoulders slumped against the settee.

"That's exactly how I feel about it. It's more difficult to learn how to control this magic inside of me than it was when I first learned spells as a child."

Humans weren't typically born with innate magic. Those who were often became healers like her mother. Drakin, shifters, and others had magic, but humans? Not so much.

One of his brows dipped in confusion. "But when you were emotional earlier, you seemed to have a decent control on it. None of the tables flipped over or anything."

Bella chuckled and leaned her head back on the couch. His hand brushed her neck, but she didn't pull away. It was like her body craved his touch, after almost a year without touching anyone. She'd come a long way from waiting tables and being sick and tired of people touching her without her permission.

"If that's the measure of having control, then yes, I'd say I'm learning slowly but surely. Doesn't change the fact that if I could go back, I'd do it all differently."

"What kind of magic do you wield as a human? I've studied for months about the curse on the people, but I still haven't figured out the mechanics of it." He paused, tilting his head. "Is that what you would do differently? The curse on them?"

She nodded as she thought, frowning. His spell on the pot and rose had been more complex than a simple binding; she could sense that when he'd done it. She sat up, and his hand dropped away. With eyes closed, she felt the magic fade, grow more muted somehow.

She sat back, his hand brushing against her shoulder, and the magic flared.

Why could she sense his magic? It would need more experimentation, but the strength of magic when they touched was—abnormal. What did it mean?

If she wanted to find out, if she wanted to experiment on this bond and the magic between them as much as he did, then she would have to trust him, at least a little.

"The curse is just one of the things I'd change."

Her mind drifted to all the mistakes she'd made. Each memory felt like a blow to her being, leaving bruises that would never fully heal. Her thoughts became tangled like a thorny vine, each misstep and regret looping together until it formed a dense and impenetrable barrier in her mind.

"What do you mean?" The smoothness of his voice was calming, and she opened up to him like a blossoming rose.

She rubbed her forehead and closed her eyes. "What do you know of my story? What has Eirwyn told you?"

The silence stretched, and the faint echo of birds chirping outside drew her eyes to the window.

She was going to be upfront and honest about her mistakes. If he was to be an ally—and she desperately wanted an ally who knew what she was going through—then she wanted to have everything laid out in the open.

"Not much. They've been preoccupied with the dragonling egg's delivery and before that, the restoration of the castle. I've attended all the monthly council dinners, and there are a lot of complaints about you. But there's two sides to every story. Tell me everything," he said, his fingers winding into her hair.

She laughed, a brittle sound. "Everything is a very long story. And trust does not come easily to those who have been betrayed as thoroughly as I have."

It was because of her trust in Gastone that she hesitated to trust Leopol now. Logically, she knew it. Eirwyn trusted him, so she should too.

He laid a hand on hers, and she froze before her eyes swung to his. The electric shock of being able to touch someone confirmed that he was integral to her survival. The magic that she could somehow see now—but only when they were touching—showed the rose pulsing with strength and magic and vitas.

"Tell me anyway," he growled low and deep. Her eyes widened at his words. Something in his tone—a blend of command and compassion and raw need—drew her forward. Finally, she nodded.

"My entire existence is bound to this flower," she continued, her voice raw with a vulnerability she didn't intend to reveal. "One wrong move, one miscalculation, and I could vanish forever. Forgive me if I'm not eager to trust another magical being with my fate. I'm more nervous than I care to admit that you wove magic anywhere near it, much less such powerful magic."

"I'll never hurt you, Bellakari. I swear it on the gods," Leopol said. The fervency in his words made her turn to him.

His gray-blue eyes pierced into her soul as he listened unlike any man ever had before, not even Gastone. None of the men who had frequented the tavern had ever sat with such an enraptured, intense expression as he listened and asked clarifying, insightful questions about her story.

His stare was like a caress, and her spine straightened under his scrutiny. With such a deep and soothing voice, he calmed some of the chaos that has consumed Bella's mind, and she paused, taking a deep breath to control her rioting emotions.

Half of her was distracted by him, but the other half was cataloging all the questions and experiments she wanted to complete with him, with their combined magic, and more.

Bella's breath hitched as memories clawed their way to the surface—a torrent of anguish and longing that pushed away her fascination with Leopol. She looked away, her gaze finding the sunlit plant lifeline standing proudly on the small table in front of her.

"Magic... has always been a double-edged sword for me," she started, her voice quivering like the delicate petals of her counterpart. "When my husband was murdered, a voice urged me to rip out his heart and make a potion from it. And yes, I know that nekrotic blood spells and potions are forbidden. But grief drowned out my consciousness, rationality...humanity. It was almost like I was in a trance as I drank it."

He sucked in a breath. "It sounds very traumatic."

"Oh, it was. It transformed my body into a drakin of some sort. The spell twisted my body so much—there was so much pain—and somehow I cursed thousands of innocents, knocked my spirit out of my body, and found myself tethered to this rose, which grew from Gastone's ashes."

The walls of the chamber pulsed with her anguish, slight tremors that sent whispers through the tapestries. Leopol, ever attentive, caressed the back of her neck, offering comfort without being pushy. She wanted to turn away from him; she didn't need him. But oh, it was so good to finally have someone to talk to, someone who understood, someone to touch. She couldn't bring herself to push him away like she'd done with all the men before.

"That's a lot of pain and change all at once. Overwhelming," he said.

Bella choked out, her laugh as bitter as wormwood. "Every day, I am reminded of my failure, of my need to fix it before it's too late. I've worked tirelessly ever since to find a spell or potion or combination that will separate the living from the non-living objects they've been cursed to become."

"What have you done so far to find a solution?" he asked.

The storm of regret lashed out from her core, and Leopol's hand fell from her neck as she sat up straighter on the couch. Without his touch to anchor her, the emotions swept through her like a malevolent tornado.

Her body itched, and she wanted to scratch under her skin.

Experience had taught her to jump up and move. She paced around the table toward the windows as the room shuddered more violently, a mirror to Bella's inner turmoil.

"I started experimenting on the plants around the castle that had merged with objects, but the plants all died. I thought I'd gained progress, and a servant tried one of my potions on a kitten—it didn't end well."

"The kitten or the servant?"

Bella snorted, her magic flaring at the memory and the glass doors rattling open. "Both. All the kittens died, one by one. Then both the servants that had been trapped with me..."

She caught her reflection in the glass of the window—a ghost of a queen, haunted by specters of her own making.

"There's no changing the past. All I can do is try to make the future better, and it's all up to me. But I only have as long as the rose lives," she said, tears streaming down her cheeks as the emotions inside her built.

Her form wavered, ethereal in the sunlight as she looked around for escape. "I—I need air, space to think... to breathe. Excuse me."

Without another word, she whirled around and fled from the room, her dress a swirl of yellow and red silk. The garden called to her, promising a reprieve from the intensity of the past. As she moved, the castle itself seemed to groan in sympathy, the stones no match for the force of her sorrow.

Chapter Four

Leopol's breath hung in the air, a visible testament to the tension that had settled over the room like an uninvited specter. As Bella fled through the glass door, a shadow in the hall paused, then Wulfric stepped inside.

He walked toward the table and asked, "What's upset her this time?"

Leopol's lips twisted as he sighed and stood. Hands behind his back, he walked to the windows, giving the big Growler room. He still had so many questions about how her spirit was tethered to a rose. It was a spell he'd only seen in one book in all his studies, and the rareness of it made him wary.

"She was explaining what caused her to be in spirit form and tied to the rose," Leopol said.

He watched as Wulfric crossed his arms in the doorway to the garden, watching protectively over his daughter. "Did she tell you it wasn't her fault? Because it wasn't," the man said gruffly.

"I didn't think it was," Leopol said, holding his ground to stand shoulder to shoulder with him.

Wulfric scowled. "Scarlet blamed her for a long time, and I'm assuming a lot of people in Vidrland and here in Hartsgrove blame her too. But it was an accident, plain and simple."

The gravity in Wulfric's words anchored Leopol. His hand instinctively sought the dragon ring on his finger, twisting it back and forth as he absorbed the unspoken truths lurking beneath the surface of Bella's tale.

"One she aims to rectify though," Leopol said, his thoughts neatly cataloging every spell he could remember or had read about in the past year of being a spirit.

"Her heart grieves for her husband, but even more for every soul ensnared by this wickedness," Wulfric continued, his eyes pools of sorrow in the afternoon light. "She carries their pain, their hopelessness, and it torments her. Even when she was a child, she wanted to heal her mother's fever so badly. Being powerless then is what made her seek as many spells, books, and learning as she could get. Then she'd see some creature hurting or sick, want to fix it, and practice her magic and heal them. But now that she sees it as her fault?"

Wulfric shook his head and sighed, his shoulders drooping as he rubbed the back of his neck.

A spark ignited within Leopol, a fierce determination that eclipsed his own personal goals. Bella's distress took precedence. The trembling of the castle in the wake of her emotional storm might have triggered her to run outside until she could gain control of her emotions.

But he was the one quickly losing control of his own emotions, deep and repressed though they may be. He was already obsessed with her. The feel of her skin under his hand still left a tingle that he couldn't deny. He would help her lift this curse that bound her so tortuously. He would be her knight in shining armor and solve this problem for her.

A thought made him pause.

"And if the rose dies, she dies?" Fear gripped him by the throat. She'd panicked when it had fallen, had said it plain as day, but surely that wasn't possible.

Light filtered through the glass windows, casting colorful patterns across the room and illuminating Wulfric's features. His canine-like appearance was both eerie and fascinating to behold, but in this moment, all Leopol could see was the weight of sadness in his eyes.

"That's what she says," Wulfric replied, the bitter truth of his words like a blade to the heart. Leopol's world spun with finality, and he drew a deep breath.

Almost as an afterthought, Wulfric added, "And any hope for a cure of the curse dies with her."

"I will help her," Leopol murmured, his voice laced with newfound resolve. "If you'll excuse me, I'm going to track her down and start right now."

Wulfric exhaled, and a weight seemed to lift from his shoulders.

Leopol took a step toward the door but looked over his shoulder. "I might miss the council dinner tonight. If I do, will you tell them what our plan is? That I'm helping her break the curse and reverse engineer the spell combination?"

Wulfric grunted, but Leopol didn't wait for a further reply. Without another word, he strode from the room, his deep blue and silver tailcoat billowing behind him as he made his way to the garden.

The tendrils of anguish and solitude wove through the air like thorns seeking skin, and he followed the oppressiveness toward her.

The garden greeted him with open arms, its greenery vibrant against the backdrop of the encroaching dusk and the snow littering the ground. On a stone bench nestled among the winter blooms sat Bella. Her figure seemed smaller amidst the foliage, her shoulders hunched as if bearing the weight of the world.

But there was something about her that drew him like a moth to a flame.

Mate. Could it really be? It was new, alarming, and wildly fascinating. Who'd have ever thought that he—a dragon construct—would have a *mate*.

He approached softly, his boots not even whispering against the icy ground. She looked up, her brown eyes reflecting a tumultuous sea of emotions. Sitting beside her, Leopol took her hand gently in his, the warmth of his skin a stark contrast to the cool evening air.

How ironic that he'd not been able to feel the cold since he'd woken up, but when he touched her, all of his senses came flooding back. He could even smell the evergreens around them.

"Can you smell that?" he asked.

Her eyes widened as she looked around, her nostrils flaring. "I can... smell it. And is it really that cold here?"

She shivered, and he slid along the stone bench, wrapping his arm around her shoulder. "It is. This damn winter is lingering unnaturally long. But even though the skies are gray, and it seems like spring will never come, it will. Don't lose hope. You're not alone, you know."

She sighed, and he turned his head, so his nose took in the scent of her hair. He took a deep breath, trying to commit the scent to memory as he continued. "I want to help you break the curses, including the one that ties you to the rose."

Bella's eyes widened in surprise as she leaned her head back to stare at him. "How can you possibly help me? I've tried for almost a year with no success."

"Two heads are better than one. We'll make steady progress if we work together."

Bella's gaze fell to their entwined hands, and she drew a shaky breath. "Progress is a fickle friend. Spells that should offer salvation end in death. My attempts so far have cost lives—not just the innocent animals, but servants who became dear friends," she confessed, her voice a quivering whisper that tugged at Leopol's heartstrings.

He closed his eyes, remembering the losses he'd experienced as well. "Sometimes we must lose something to gain something greater," Leopol murmured, his thumb tracing soft circles on her translucent hand. "And I believe what we'll gain is worth the risk and heartache. If I didn't believe in that, the weight of loss would crush me."

Bella's ethereal form trembled, not from cold, but from emotion. Her eyes, deep pools of sorrow and hope, met his. "You sound so certain, like you've lost people too."

"Because I am and I have," he said firmly, not expanding on who. "The library holds secrets. Ancient texts. Forgotten spells. Between my knowledge and your intimate understanding of the curse's origins, we might unravel this."

A fragile hope flickered in her expression, like candlelight dancing against shadows. She leaned closer, her spectral form momentarily solid against his warmth.

"Each misstep, each death, weighs upon me. I'm afraid to hope and try again, even though that's the entire reason I came with Scarlet and Da to this place." Bella's admission unraveled in the space around them, raw and pained.

He also felt the pain of failure, but the only one who suffered in his case was himself. Her pain and desperation would be a hundred times worse than what he'd felt over the past few months, what he remembered from his life as a dragon.

Leopol felt the press of her despair as palpable as the evening breeze. In the dance of shadows and whispers of leaves, they shared a moment that transcended time—a dragon and a queen, both haunted by ghosts of their pasts, finding solace in the silent understanding of shared burdens.

"Bella," he began, her name a prayer of supplication. If he could help her, if there was hope for her, then there was hope for him too. In helping solve her problem, perhaps he'd find his own redemption.

His grip on her hand was firm, yet gentle. "I don't know what tomorrow will bring. While this spirit form is limiting, I'm not without skill and knowledge. I can be useful. Let me help."

The sun sank below the tree line, and light glinted off his dragon ring as it lay against his knee—a symbol of his noble lineage now intertwined with her own fate. The warmth of her touch seeped through him, a comforting presence in the coolness of the night.

Bella turned more fully toward him, her eyes now curious. "Your kindness is unexpected, and I do appreciate it," she murmured. "However, I'm hesitant to accept. The lives of so many people hang in the balance, and I cannot—will not—endanger them further with reckless actions and under-developed spells and potions."

"I understand," Leopol said, his voice resonating with

respect for her caution. "But isn't it worth a shot? We can forge a fresh path, one that leads to redemption rather than ruin. Allow me to stand with you, Bella. We can succeed where solitude has failed. I'm so tired of being alone in this quest..."

He trailed off, frowning as he glanced toward the helrose hedge and the ever-present giant eagles circling in the west. Then his eyes drifted to the boulder with the struggling apple tree in its center, the oak grove a tight circle around it. Since he'd woken up all those months ago, he'd worked hard to restore the castle to its former glory. He'd had the apple tree replanted and the bones buried. He'd organized the workers in the main castle and then the west wing.

All under the guise of searching for his body. He'd thus far been unsuccessful, finding neither his body nor a way to fix the curse that plagued so many of the new residents of the castle.

His heart beat a rhythm of regret and yearning. He needed a win, needed to succeed at something after so many months of failure. If she accepted his help, they could share the load.

"Quest? You've been trying to solve the curse too? What progress have you made?" Bella asked, her eyes lighting up.

He opened his mouth to correct her, then paused. He nodded slowly, "I have gone through hundreds of ancient spell books and lore in the past few months. I'm almost done researching."

She cleared her throat and sighed. "So, you haven't crafted anything yet. I see. The thought of more innocent blood makes me want to say no. If we fail—"

"But what if we succeed?" Leopol asked, turning his eyes back to her.

She searched his face as if looking for answers, and he didn't know what she found there. He was just a dragon stuck outside his body. Whereas before, all he wanted was to find his body and rejoin the fight, now he was just looking to make a difference in the world, her world.

She bit her lip, then asked, "How can I trust you? What do you get out of this?"

He hesitated to tell her of his predicament. He'd kept the secret from everyone all this time, and he wasn't sure how to talk about it.

He finally shrugged and said, "How do I know I can trust you? How do we trust anyone in this world?"

She pursed her lips, but her expression softened. She didn't move away or tug her hand from him. Her touch was a lifeline, grounding him in this reality in time and space.

"If we are to do this, you must promise me—no action will be taken without thorough consideration. Every step forward must be measured, Leopol. No rash actions or being led by emotions." Her voice was a whisper, carrying the gravity of her fears across the stillness of the garden.

"Of course," he vowed, his assurance a bond to them both. "Every precaution will be taken. We'll document every potion, spell, and attempt. Perhaps we can even publish our findings in a spell book when this is all over."

Bella chuckled, and her eyes brightened. "You're a fellow book lover, then?"

In the shelter of the dusk softened garden, surrounded by the whispers of nocturnal winter blooms, they found an accord. Her willingness to let him help and a shared love of literature sparked a tentative trust within—a trust that might just bloom into something greater, something as fragile and precious as the rose that held her life force in its petals.

"Some would say books are my entire life," he said, memories flying through his mind like a dream.

He was more afraid to trust that bud of attraction than he was their partnership to end the curse. The garden's growing shadows danced around Bella and Leopol, their bodies still entwined as if afraid to sever the fragile connection they'd just begun to forge.

With each passing moment, the air between them thrummed with a quiet longing, an unspoken acknowledgment of the solace they found in each other's presence. The cold seeped into his soul even as the warmth of being pressed against her side set a flame of burning desire to light within him.

Leopol's voice was soft, a mere breath in the darkening sky. "What type of books do you love most? Which ones inspire passion and thaw the ice of solitude?"

In the brown depths of her luminous eyes, he saw flickers of a fire long suppressed. "There is something to love in every book," she confessed, her fingertips tracing the veins on the back of his hand, a tentative exploration that sent ripples through his very soul. "Books of other worlds intrigue me. Worlds unmarred by my mistakes with a future where the laughter rises higher than the wails of pain."

Leopol leaned closer, drawn by the gravity and vulnerability of her words. "And what of your own laughter, your own desires?" His thumb brushed across her cheek, a touch featherlight yet laden with meaning.

She hesitated, her breath catching at the intimacy of the question, the closeness of his body to hers. "I've forgotten the sound of it," she murmured, a tremor in her voice betraying the ache within.

"We can rediscover it together," he whispered, the

promise hanging between them like a sacred vow as he leaned in.

Their gazes locked, hearts beating in sync as the space between them charged with the potential of what might be. The coolness of the night was forgotten, warmth spreading from where their bodies touched, a tangible testament to the burgeoning bond they shared. Her lips glistened in the pale light, and the need to kiss her grew louder in his head.

Then she blushed and leaned back, not breaking their locked hands, but severing the moment. "After the curse is broken. But what do we do now?"

He remembered the loss of her husband and swore silently. He shouldn't push her into something she might not be ready for, no matter how powerfully strong this pull toward her was.

With a control that fortified his every fiber, Leopol stood, pulling her gently to her feet. "Come," he said, his tone laced with determination as he tucked her hand into the crook of his elbow. "I will show you the library, then the workshop. It's the perfect spot for our experiments, where your brilliance will shine brightest. You'll craft potions and spells and finally break the chains of this curse."

Bella's lips twitched in the faintest of smiles, and she allowed herself to be led, her steps matching his as they traversed the verdant labyrinth of the garden. She glanced up at him, and his heart dared to hope that she may be the one who held the key to his freedom.

Chapter Five

Bella paused, her skirts flaring as Leopol used a wave of magic to open the double arched door. She passed under the arch and gasped. The scent of old parchment and wax lingered in the air, a teasing hint that always settled her nerves.

Three stories high, the ceiling disappeared into shadows. Books climbed the walls like ivy, while globes of enchanted light floated lazily between the rows, casting a warm glow over everything.

Rows and rows of books sat along either side of the grand arched doorway. Two grand circular staircases wrapped up each wall to her left and right, providing multiple reading nooks, couches, and writing desks around the room.

"Do you like it?" Leopol asked softly, his voice reverent in the grand room. Curtains let in plenty of light along the back wall, and between the two massive windows sat a stone fireplace.

Her hand trailed along the spines of books etched with

gold lettering, each title promising its own world of mysteries and magic.

She stepped free of the rows of books to a main sitting area in the center of the room and spun in a slow circle.

"Oh gods, I love it! It's bigger than the Winter Palace library. Maybe bigger than it and the Cathedral combined."

She caught Leopol's grin and nod of satisfaction. "It should be. This was King Feralt's personal library, centuries of tomes gathered and preserved with spells."

The pride in his voice was obvious.

Leopol stepped toward a large desk under one of the large staircases as he spoke, and she went to the other staircase, inspecting the spines.

"You can read whatever you like. Consider it yours."

"Oh, I couldn't possibly–"

"Bella, I highly doubt you'd destroy any of these precious books. I feel like I can trust you to respect each one as if it'd been written by you."

She made her way to where he stood over a table strewn with scrolls and parchments, his blue coat catching the light like midnight made cloth and emphasizing the strength and confidence that radiated from him.

"Of course. I would never knowingly damage a book." She frowned.

He looked up at her and smiled, taking her breath away. "Exactly. So I'll share every book that I've been entrusted with to your care. Help yourself."

She looked around, so awed. "I–I don't even know where to start."

He chuckled, the sound drawing her eyes back to him. "Ah yes, I should explain the filing system and the spell to put whatever book you take down back where it belongs."

Her spine straightened at the promise of learning a new spell, and her spirit naturally drew closer to his.

Hours later, Leopol re-entered the library to find Bella. She had been so obsessed with the library that he hadn't wanted to show her the workroom yet. He wanted to let her have this simple joy of exploring an ancient library.

He had fond memories of exploring a similar one, but it was as if he'd explored in his dreams. He didn't remember the library of his dreams as one he'd ever visited while in dragon form.

Doubts plagued him on whether his memories were real or dreams. He had no one to ask either, except Lailant, and she'd been so cryptic with her comments when he'd seen her since waking in this form.

Instead of taking Bella away from the simple joy of exploring the library, he'd gone to the council dinner for a few minutes. He hadn't wanted to leave her for too long.

After giving his assurances that he and Bella were working on the cure for the curse, the meeting had been much of the same as every other month. Grumbling from the priests and nobles about the lack of deference to their station, complaining about the curse and lack of resources in the two small villages that supported the refugees in the forest. Knox and Eirwyn had done their best to alleviate fears, but Leopol felt the energy growing more tense with each monthly meeting.

Bella sat reading on one of the couches in the middle of the room. Her beauty gave him pause once more, but when she looked up and smiled, it was as if the floating lights in the room glowed brighter.

She always caught him off guard—but it was her mind that drew him closer. Every time he looked deep into her eyes, he could see the gears working, her thoughts spinning with intelligence and connections that surpassed those he'd met since waking.

"Are you settling in alright?" he asked.

She nodded, nearly bouncing on her toes with excitement as she leaped up. "It's all I've ever wanted. You have a Bone Ledger from the founding of the Dragon Dynasty, and an original Primer of Lost Languages with a section on actual Celestial Script." Her fingers trembled as she turned the delicate page. "These are the oldest texts I've ever touched."

He took the book gently, skimming the first page and sidestepping the question. Alarm flared in his mind, urging him to be cautious. What if she accidentally activated something by reading it?

"Do people know Celestial Script now?" he asked instead, walking toward his desk. "When I was alive, no one even agreed if it was truly the gods' tongue."

"No one really knows. That's why I asked." Another book fluttered in front of her and opened itself. She frowned and tilted the book sideways as she floated after him. "Oh, but look at this. Is this supposed to be a book? It's just pictures. What am I supposed to do with this?"

He chuckled. "Those are Moonstone Glyphs—the original language of the Founding Age. Not really meant to be read so much as... experienced."

She leaned in, teasing his senses. "Are you sure that's what it is?"

He grinned. "I'm sure."

She twisted her hands in her skirts as she came closer. "I guess it doesn't matter that I can't read it, but it's so elegant.

Sacred. I wish I could read it—read so many of these amazing books in your library."

He took her hands in his, pulling hers from her skirts.

"It's alright. No harm done. I didn't consider the language barrier though. Let me fix that."

She frowned and opened her mouth to protest, but before she could speak, he murmured a spell in High Elvish—the magic shimmered as it wove into her aura.

A translation spell. Not common. Not exactly legal, either, at least, not outside of the High Elfaeren court.

When he finished, he reached for the book on the edge of the desk and opened it to a random page. "There. What about now?"

Her eyes flicked down to the book, then widened. She leaned in as though pulled by gravity, her hands going to the book and letting him go. When they touched, his world became so much sharper. Colors, scents, sound—every detail surged around them.

"I—I can read it. What—how did you—?" she whispered, stunned. "Wait, it references the Celestial Codex? I thought that was a myth and why they removed the Celestial Script from all the history books!"

His eyebrows lifted. Her words sparked something familiar, something ancient and painful—a flicker of alarm under the surface of his awe. "You know the Codex? I didn't think anyone remembered it. There is only one original and no copies."

"I've only seen mentions," she said breathlessly. "Vague references in textbooks about the eras of Celawyn history. The Codex was always treated as legend."

He hesitated then, her excitement brushing up against something dangerous. The easy trust he'd offered began to harden into cautious edges. Something warned that the Codex was to be kept secret.

"The Celestial Codex contains the earliest divine histories and spells," he warned, gently setting the book down between them. "Not all texts are meant to be read—some reshape the reader. Like the Moonstone Glyphs. That's why many were sealed. Or burned."

She stilled, her expression sobering. "I know. The priests warned us even about reading the Writ of Ashborne when I was growing up. We might read it, but that doesn't mean we understand what we read or what spells we might unleash."

His brows drew together. "What is the Writ of Ashborne?"

She lowered her gaze. "A necrotic blood-magic text. They said it combined spells from the Age of Aurelic with Moonstone Glyphs and potion recipes from Soltharin. The devastation it caused supposedly led to the outlawing of nekromancy. I'm surprised you don't know it."

Recognition stirred behind his eyes, flaring alarm in his soul. He reached instinctively to the base of her spine, grounding himself with her presence. "Ah, we called it the Aethermor, back before the kingdoms burned their copies."

She blinked, stunned. "The Great Burning of the Archives? You were there? That was... over a thousand years ago. How old are you?"

"Old enough," he said with a crooked smile—though truthfully, he didn't have a number he trusted.

Still, her nearness centered him. Whatever he was, however old he was, a few fractured pieces of his past remained, but touching her made it easier to stay in the now.

She looked away, her voice quieter now. "As terrible as it

is to destroy any text, they were probably right. After what I accidentally created with Gastone's heart..."

She sobered, her face drawn in a frown that he didn't like to see. "I guess I understand why the priests used the fear of those texts and forbidden magics to keep us from researching or reading about them. I just wish they hadn't always told me no, that they hadn't made knowledge feel like something forbidden."

His head tilted. "Told you no about what?"

"Reading." Her eyes locked onto his again, full of something bitter and bright. "The priests gatekept everything, even non-magical books. I spent years scrubbing cathedral floors in exchange for reading scraps of parchment. 'Not fit for girls like you,' they'd say."

He inhaled quickly, anger at them sharpening his voice. "They were fools not to see how brilliant you are."

She swayed a little at the words, and he ached to kiss her. She licked her lips, and his eyes dropped to them. The need to act on the mate bond was something his psyche wrestled with.

She looked away, blinking rapidly as she blushed. The moonlight had deepened around them, silver and soft, the magical orb lights casting warm halos in the library.

She glanced up at him again, a tremble in her voice.

"That's why it meant so much when you said I could read anything I wanted. And now you've granted me the ability to read all of these books, even the ancient ones... Thank you. I won't abuse this gift, I swear."

The words hit him like a blade. Guilt speared through him. He *had* hesitated, doubted. But she was his mate. If he couldn't trust her, how could he expect her to trust him? And without trust—without unity—they had no chance of fixing any of this.

He leaned back slowly against the edge of the desk, studying her, letting his floating body settle.

"I meant what I said. You're welcome to read anything here. Just..." He let a small smile tug at the corner of his mouth. "Be careful. With your magic tied so tightly to your emotions, I'd rather not have the castle explode because the wrong book pissed you off."

She laughed at his semi-crude words, the sound filling the room and making the dancing lights glow brighter. "Oh, I'm fully aware of how volatile I am. I take it the events at the Winter Palace were discussed at the dinner tonight?" She sighed and shook her head, hunching her shoulders slightly as if disappointed with herself.

"I reported on our plan to cure the curse. Scarlet and Wulfric had already reported on how they found you before I arrived at the council dinner," he said.

She turned wistfully to the library, eyes flicking over books as if searching for answers. "I don't know how long it'll take to find the information we need."

"I don't know either, but don't be daunted by the sheer number of texts in the library. I've already read them all."

He watched the tension in her shoulders ease, and her eyebrows lift as if impressed, only for her expression to sharpen again with renewed curiosity. That fire in her eyes— the hunger for knowledge—was something he recognized all too well.

"I'd love to read the Codex and the other forbidden texts, but I have no interest in practicing such magic. Nekros has never appealed to me. I've always been more interested in vitas and healing, but understanding nekros would help me better understand the opposite of it, don't you think?"

He sighed in relief and stood, taking her at her word. With Eirwyn vouching for her and her open expression, he felt like he knew her more deeply than anyone else he'd ever met. Then again, that could easily be the mate bond talking.

He stretched, somehow feeling the stiffness of muscles when she was around. "Would you like me to retrieve them?" he asked, already knowing her answer.

Her eyes widened as she leaned forward. "You have one? The Codex or the Writ of Ashborne?"

He arched a brow and leaned forward, dropping his voice to a whisper. "Both."

Her eyes grew impossibly wider as she gasped. "No, you do not."

He tugged on the hem of his jacket in mock outrage. "Your Majesty, I will never lie to you. Here, let me prove it."

Leopol floated from the desk and past the couches to the other side of the cavernous library, the air thick with the musk of ancient tomes and whispered secrets. Each step was a silent pact of trust, and a blend of anticipation and trepidation twisted his stomach. Underneath one of the grand staircases was a curved wall of shelves.

He reached out, fingers brushing against the spine of an unassuming leather-bound volume.

"Watch closely," he whispered, voice barely louder than the earlier rustle of parchment in the room.

With precise care, the book tilted forward, and a soft click echoed off the walls, more felt than heard. A section of the bookcase shuddered before swinging inward, revealing a passageway bathed in the soft glow of enchanted sconces.

Bella stepped closer to him. He slid an arm along her waist, drawing her to his side. The hidden door was a relic of his past diligence, etched with symbols that spoke of protection and knowledge—a sanctuary for one who had forgotten so much.

"Leopol, this is... incredible," she breathed, her voice tinged with awe. Leopol swelled with pride as he grinned at her even as his arms felt bereft when she stepped into the hallway away from him.

"Indeed," he replied, allowing a rare smile to touch his lips as the warmth of shared discovery began to overshadow the insecurities and empty holes in his mind and memories. Two bobbing lights followed them into the hallway, illuminating the books.

All he saw was the tilt of her face, the way her body seemed to vibrate with excitement.

They stepped into the concealed wide hallway, dust heavy all around them. Here lay the scrolls and artifacts that even the revered Growlers of the Feral Forest sought knowledge from. Yet, despite the grandeur, it was also a place of intimate vulnerability, a reflection of the fragments of memories he yearned to piece together.

He gestured with a sweep of his arm, the shimmering silver and blue fabric of his coat reflecting the chamber's light. "Everything you see here is a part of who I am... or who I was."

He watched her eyes roam, alight with curiosity and respect, and for a moment, he could feel the weight of uncertainties lift, replaced by the quiet strength of their burgeoning connection.

Bella's feet slowed, her gaze swinging to the shelves on either side of the hallway.

"Oh gods, there's so many, and the preservation magic is extraordinary." Her voice was a whisper of wonder at the shelves of arcane books, her touch barely tracing their spines.

Leopol's fingers traced the dragon ring on his hand, a

nervous habit he'd developed since waking in human form. Something about her enthusiasm reminded him of forgotten memories, like whispers just beyond his comprehension.

"I come from a long line of dragons who've collected hundreds of spell books over the generations."

It wasn't exactly a lie—but it wasn't quite the truth, either. He didn't *know* he was one of them or not. All he had to go on were dreams, flashes of memory. A hunch, really, but something deep inside him said he was so much more than a dragon.

He led her down the hallway of books into a circular stone room lined with shelves carved directly from the earth itself, each cradle holding countless jars and bottles filled with swirling mystical concoctions. In the center were three long tables, one covered in stacks of books with pages worn from use. The room was organized chaos, with papers scattered haphazardly and quills and ink bottles placed strategically around the tables.

Here, in this sanctuary of old, lay the heart of their quest. Bella drifted deeper inside. She trailed her fingers over the rough texture of the wooden tables.

"So, this is your workshop?"

Nerves made him shift, and he went to the table to straighten the books. "Yes, my sanctum. Knox has been in here, but no one else. Eirwyn has been too busy, which might be why she showed you the sunroom earlier."

She chuckled. "No one? It seems we have more in common than just being spirits who love books. I rarely let anyone into my spell room, either."

He shrugged but wanted to offer something of himself to her. This place was special, and though he hadn't spilled all his secrets, he wanted to show her that he was worthy of her trust. "Before I... became a spirit, this room was only used by the royal family of dragons."

Her eyes turned to him, curiosity clear. "You're royalty?"

His chin tipped up even as his ears burned. He didn't want her to trust him because he was royal. "Something like that. Knox's father was my closest friend. We were raised as brothers."

A pang filled him at the memory of the dragon falling outside the castle. He hadn't been there to stop it, too busy doing... something. His memory failed him, making him even more frustrated.

She frowned. "I'm confused. I thought his father died years ago?"

"He did," Leopol said, glancing away before meeting her gaze once more. "Three hundred years ago, actually, in a battle outside this very castle."

She gasped, drifting closer to him. "And you've been a spirit this whole time? Dear gods, I'm so sorry."

He opened his mouth to tell her the truth, but her hand on his forearm made him pause. He slid his hand over the top of hers and breathed in her essence. The faint trace of jasmine and rosemary made some of the tension in his chest ease.

She was extraordinary. She had so much heart. The way she selflessly sympathized with him and offered comfort from her own strength... it was rare to have someone so beautiful have a beautiful soul as well.

A face soft and delicate, yet strong with a stubborn tilt to her chin that intrigued him. With high cheekbones and a warm smile that lit up the room, was it any wonder he was so smitten?

And then there was her hair. The rich chocolate brown fell in soft waves around her shoulders, half back in tiny braids held by a pearl clip. Her pale-yellow silk dress accented her curves, but it was the elegance and grace in her posture that drew him closer.

Leopol released her hand, only to brush a stray lock of hair from her face, his fingers lingering against her cheek. "Yes, but it's irrelevant for now. What matters is finding a solution to the curse problem. This is where we will begin."

Her eyes reflected the faint glow of his ethereal form and something more—something raw and undisguised. This was where their relationship might begin too. A bud of hope blossomed inside him.

She stepped closer as if drawn by an invisible force, her gaze exploring every crevice, every shadow of his face. The air around them pulsed with potential, with power and anticipation that beckoned to his very soul.

He cupped her cheek and leaned in, holding his breath as he drew within a hair's breadth of her lips. His heart hammered in his chest, the anticipation building for the kiss he'd craved all day—perhaps even for centuries before meeting her.

Chapter Six

Bella pulled back, regret and shadows in her eyes as she sighed and turned away. Disappointment slammed into Leopol, but he couldn't rush her. She wasn't even widowed a year yet. If she felt for her husband the way he felt for her already...

She drifted to a table and traced her hand over an open spell book.

"Do you really think your books hold the answer to reversing the curse?" Her voice was filled with genuine concern, like she was afraid to hope. Leopol's lips twitched, the feeling mutual.

"Yes, I do," he said, moving to a sturdy oak table at the center of the sanctum. "We'll combine our strengths. Your knowledge of spells and healing potions, my command of ancient lore and texts. You said you've made some progress before you came here?"

She nodded and turned to one wall. Drifting closer, bottles and vials glinted like jewels, each containing untold promises. She reached out, her fingers brushing against a flask filled with swirling mist. It reacted to her touch, glowing briefly before settling once more.

"I did, but then I ran out of supplies and people to help. I think my notes and books were taken up to my room, though."

"Well, we can grab those tomorrow, if you'd like to see the research I've done on the subject tonight?" Leopol asked, his voice a low rumble that echoed off the stone, excitement building within him at the new challenge, at sharing this piece of himself with her.

She turned to him, her chin hardening as she walked to the table with the most books. "I'd love to. What have you found?" Her determination was a beacon in the darkness, unwavering even as doubt whispered from her expression.

Leopol spread out a series of ancient manuscripts, their edges crinkled and worn.

"I focused on the villagers' curse—I didn't know you were still bound to a rose or left in this state. After interviewing several of the cursed villagers—Scarlet, Knox, and Eirwyn too—I traced the lineage of curses similar to the one you unleashed. I searched the Codex, the royal dragon records, even the Aethermor—sorry, the Writ of Ashborne. There was even a report of a curse in the Whaletid Isles. Most of them described spectral bindings, especially those involving objects with emotional resonance, to inanimate objects."

She leaned forward as he explained what he'd found, the scent of jasmine mixing with the ancient parchment and herbs. He didn't know how much he'd missed the simple act of smelling until he could suddenly do so again, when she was close enough to touch.

She drew the scroll closer, unrolling it carefully. "That

matches what I've seen. The villagers—most of them were merged with items tied to their daily lives, not magical items. Everyday things."

He cleared his throat, trying to stay on topic despite the distraction that was Bella. "Right. That may be why traditional potions and spells haven't worked. But your case is unique because the binding object isn't inert. It's a living rose—formed in the moment of death, grief, and love. It's not just an anchor. It's a vessel, holding your emotions."

Her expression faltered. "A vessel?"

"When a magic user wields emotion like a secret ingredient, it preserves the emotions and trauma from that moment. Your spirit, your trauma, and maybe Gastone's too. It's more than a tether. It's preserving the moment of your breaking—and it's changing. Blooming. Becoming something else. Some texts suggest living vessels like that can evolve to change function."

Bella's form flickered slightly, the air thickening with unspoken pain. "Trauma. Such a clinical term for something so personal."

His hand settled at the small of her back, offering comfort even as he carried on his explanation.

She looked down, voice quiet but resolute. "So even if we destroy it... it wouldn't set me free."

"No, it might destroy you instead. We'll need a ritual that untangles all of it—spirit, memory, magic. Something that honors the loss, without anchoring you to it. If you want, I'll work on that while you—"

"It's not just about me," she said, her eyes flaring with purpose. "The villagers come first. Solving their curse will go faster if we're both working on it."

He hesitated, frustration pushing against his restraint. "Their curse is terrible, yes—but they aren't tethered to a rose that's counting down with every petal. Without you, we can't fix them. I–I think you're the key." He hesitated, but held her gaze, imploring her to work with him on this.

Bella blinked, her shoulders stiff before they softened with a sweet exhale of her breath. "I'm sorry. You're right. I shouldn't downplay my part."

Leopol offered a small smile. "We'll fix all of it. One curse at a time."

He moved to the next scroll, his mind a whirl of thoughts all connecting like stars in the sky to make a constellation. He knew there were pieces of her story he was missing, and he understood her reluctance to dive deeper and excavate the painful memories that bound her spirit to the magical rose. But he couldn't solve any of the problems if he didn't have all the information. It would be like a puzzle missing pieces.

A soft rustling from the sanctum's far corner interrupted their discussion. Leopol's hand moved instinctively to his hip, missing his sword not for the first time since waking like this.

His magic flared, a burst of gold light flooding the shadows and pressing them back into the corners of the room.

"Did you hear that?" he murmured, his eyes scanning the room.

Bella's form flickered. "Didn't hear it... but I felt something. What was that?"

He didn't answer right away, unease creeping through him. "I'm not sure. Possibly just a rat. I'm going to need to renew the protective wards."

He downplayed the strangeness of it for her sake, not wanting to alarm her. The dragon ring on his finger caught the light, casting fractured rainbows across the nearest scroll. Something tugged at him—a sense of déjà vu.

His gaze dropped to the parchment beneath the rainbow, and his fingers brushed across symbols that shimmered faintly under candlelight.

"I've seen this before," he murmured. "I must have, but it meant nothing to me then. I think I've transcribed these before because they stir some of my memories. They could be a key, or just another dead end. I've been re-reading everything, hoping something would click."

She sighed. "Just because we can read it with the spell doesn't mean we understand what it's talking about."

He closed his eyes, willing the memory to surface. A flash of light on water. The smell of jasmine and burned leaves. A voice, female, speaking in a language he couldn't place.

Nothing more, but it was enough. He opened his eyes and rubbed his chin, staring at the symbols. His brows rose as realization settled in his stomach like a weight.

"These Moonstone Covenant glyphs are some of the oldest I've seen, but I think I understand now. It could be interpreted two ways though."

Bella gasped, moving beside him. "Are you sure? I've never known anyone who could read the glyphs. Hells, I've never even seen them before coming here. The priests certainly didn't have any texts with them. What are the two interpretations?"

Leopol barely heard her. His fingers traced the edge of the symbol, the paper suddenly too familiar, and the parchment shimmered again. A memory teased him, and he closed his eyes, trying to mentally chase it. Words from books he'd read over the years jumped out at him, and his chest grew tight with a single thought.

"It's talking about a vessel but this symbol here? It could mean transmission," he whispered, opening his eyes and staring at her.

Bella leaned forward to peer closer. "You mean like a beacon?"

He shook his head and stroked his chin. "No, not a signal. More like a message, possibly to another realm, if this symbol here is what I think it is."

"The only other reference to realm messages was in the histories in the northern archives, and those are long gone. Although one of the history texts at the Winter Palace mentioned technologically advanced dwarves that facilitated messages among the realms. Of course, they also mentioned how those messages led to the fall of Illustros, so it was all presented as a warning."

He startled at the mention of the dwarves and wondered if the ones at the northern town were descended from those from her textbooks. "You know your history—and its consequences."

Her blush returned, blooming across her spectral cheeks. "History isn't just facts. It's... alive. It whispers secrets if you're quiet long enough."

Leopol nodded absently, still half in the memories and thinking through previous books. "Whether it's a vessel or a message, a warning or instructions… that's what I'm not sure about. There are too many possibilities here."

Bella drifted closer, her fingers hovering above the parchment. The glyphs shimmered faintly, responding to her presence. "Well... you said you might have transcribed it before. Why don't you do that again, now? I'll keep reading—maybe between the two of us, we'll figure it out."

The tightness in his chest eased. To work side by side

with his mate was something he didn't think would ever happen for him.

She smiled faintly. "Moonstone glyphs, Leopol. I can't believe you can actually read it. That spell from earlier helps me read some of the basics but there are several that don't translate in my head. The symbols are too much like pictures and not enough like words, but you..."

She shook her head like she still couldn't believe it. He smiled at her excitement and wanted to impress her. He nodded and pulled a pen and inkwell closer.

Hours passed. Candles burned low, their wax pooling in brass holders, casting soft flickers that danced across the walls like shadows from another realm.

Leopol found himself distracted—not by the scrolls, but by the curve of her neck, the way her lips moved silently as she read. The magnetic pull between them grew stronger with each passing moment, a tether he hadn't expected but couldn't ignore.

Bella's eyes narrowed with concentration, absorbing every detail. The sanctum had gone quiet save for the occasional rustle of parchment or the soft murmur of his voice answering her thoughtful questions. Her initial hesitation had melted into focused intensity. She moved with purpose now, tracing connections between texts he hadn't noticed—her spectral fingers hovering, her thoughts moving faster than his own.

Then she paused.

Her breath caught as her gaze landed on a worn, crumbling page. She looked up at him, catching him staring not for the first time, but he didn't look away.

"Leopol, what does this mean?"

He moved beside her, inhaling the now-familiar scent of jasmine and something wilder. His eyes followed her gesture. In the dim candlelight, a faded illustration emerged—a ritual circle, two entwined figures, and hovering just beneath them, the faint outline of a dragon, its eyes glowing like embers.

A chill prickled across his skin.

"What does it mean?" Bella asked, awe and uncertainty bleeding into her voice.

Leopol bent over the page, turning it slightly toward the light. "I'm not sure. I'm fluent in Elfaeren but my High Elvish isn't as strong as I'd like. They speak in so many circles and riddles," he admitted. "But this—this looks like a bonding ritual."

She leaned in closer, her breath warm against his cheek, grounding him even as the air around them seemed to thrum with magic.

"These glyphs," he murmured, finger brushing the faded ink, "usually represent unity, like with fated mates... but here, this symbol. It means eternal binding."

His throat tightened. A ritual like this could mean many things: power, fusion, love—or complete surrender of self. The idea of that kind of bond—with her—both thrilled and terrified him.

"An eternal binding," Bella echoed, her voice faint. "That can't be right. The villagers don't need more binding. They're trying to break free, not merge further with objects."

She sighed, already pulling a new book toward her. "Still, it's fascinating."

Leopol lingered over the illustration, his thoughts spiraling. The script tugged at something just out of reach. He began mentally translating it, but the words came too slowly. With a frustrated breath, he moved to the other table, grabbed a loose sheet of parchment and a quill, and began a rough transcription, humming as he went.

"What are you doing?" Bella asked without looking up.

He rubbed his eyes. "Translating. The spell to read it doesn't mean we can comprehend it. Sometimes the sentences in one language are rearranged, so I need to translate it to understand. Based on this, it's definitely a binding ritual. But not just physical. It binds souls—essences—together with a third force. In this case... the dragon in the glyph."

She turned, curiosity sharpening. "Would that mean shared powers?"

Leopol hesitated. "Possibly. Or... a sacrifice. One essence offered to empower the other."

Her eyes widened. "Like what I did with Gastone's heart. He died, which could be classified as a sacrifice, then when I drank the potion, I absorbed his fire powers, his essence. Before being kicked out of my body, that is."

Leopol nodded slowly, tension coiling through his limbs. He'd thought the ritual meant something symbolic, offering a part of oneself for strength. But no. She had enacted the ritual fully—blood, sacrifice, power. It wasn't theoretical at all.

She turned back to her book, flipping pages absently. "That must be why the wizard whispered to me."

The quill in Leopol's hand stilled. The air in the sanctum grew heavier, thick with something old and ominous.

"What wizard?"

She paused, her translucent form flickering faintly. "Oh... I mean, I didn't realize at the time. I thought it was just... part of the magic. But the whispered voice–the one that told me how to rip out his heart, how to make the potion, even the exact words for the spell–it was him. The wizard. He whispered it all, filling my mind and making me think it was my thoughts, my idea."

Leopol straightened slowly, his entire being focused now, vibrations of pent-up magic building with his emotions. "You never said anything about another person. You think it was a wizard who had you complete the ritual?"

Bella hesitated, then met his eyes, voice steady despite the tremble in her form. "Yes. I didn't know what was happening when I was first knocked from my body, but then... my body began moving without me. I watched it walk, speak, cast. He used my voice. My transformed face. And then he created the rose–anchor, tether, whatever it is– and walked out."

His breath caught. "In your body?"

She nodded once, her expression tightening, the glow of her magic dimming like a flame caught in a draft.

"And he has all of it now–my body and its magic reserves. When the ritual finished, I felt it. My spirit was torn loose, tethered to the rose, but... its not just my body missing. A third of my magical power vanished the moment he completed the merge. He didn't just steal my body–he used Gastone's heart as a catalyst to create a vessel strong enough to hold all four sources: his own mind and spirit, plus my body and Gastone's strength. It was blood magic at its most refined... and most grotesque."

The table between them felt like a chasm. Leopol stepped back, mind racing, fragments of memory and dusty scroll lore colliding in his thoughts. A wizard powerful enough to manipulate a soul-binding ritual. One who orchestrated the death of a king. One who twisted the spell to steal Bella's body—and with it, her power.

It was a targeted attack, deliberate.

"Your condition isn't an accident," he whispered. "The curse on the people wasn't some tragic byproduct of grief or something you did. Someone did this to you."

Her silence was answer enough. He paced, blood roaring in his ears.

He thought out loud to process all the new information. "The wizard's curse on you released a magical wave of energy. The nekrosan spell was meant to merge you, Gastone's body, and the wizard's soul and mind. That spell exploded out, which is why all the villagers were merged with things too."

Why? Why her? Why that ritual? The ancient texts spoke of soul fusion and spectral anchors, yes—but few had the knowledge to use them like this. And fewer still would dare. Unless they were trying to siphon power. Control a bloodline. Or... raise something ancient.

Ancient texts warned of spells meant to anchor gods. Now he feared those warnings had been real.

A line in the Codex explained how Illustros bound Asmoroth to the hells. If the wizard used an anchoring spell that was meant for gods, it explained how it leveled a city and cursed them all.

"This changes everything," Leopol said, voice low and hard as fear filled his soul. "If a wizard took your body, then he's ruling in your stead. That's why Scarlet and the villagers think *you're* the evil queen at the capitol."

His fist slammed into the table, rattling the scrolls. "We need to find out what he wants—before he finishes whatever he started."

Bella's form flickered, her expression darkening. "I know what he wants."

He stilled, the air suddenly thinner.

"When Scarlet and Da came to the Winter Palace to rescue me, we had an incident with him. He said he has a new plan and–"

She froze mid-sentence, her eyes going wide. "A message..." she whispered, horror dawning on her face.

Something ancient stirred in Leopol's soul, deep and cold. Frantic, he grabbed his earlier transcriptions of the Moonstone glyphs. The words seemed to leap off the page at him, suddenly making sense.

"These glyphs, the rose, a transmitter of emotions or energy... A message, possibly to another realm. Is that the wizard's plan? He's using you to send a message?"

She gripped her skirts and licked her lips. Her spectral chest moved in short, anxious bursts–pure instinct, not necessity.

"The wizard made a deal with Asmoroth," she whispered, voice low and bitter. "And when the rose dies... I carry the invitation. He wants the god of death to rise."

Leopol took a step back, heart hammering. His mind spun–scrolls, prophecies, half-remembered warnings from the Celestial Codex.

This wasn't just possession of her body or reversing a few curses.

This wasn't even about power.

This was about gods, war, and the end of this mortal world.

A vibration shivered his soul–another memory, not whole but sharp, like glass in fog. The world tilted beneath him.

He practiced the meditative techniques his dragon

father had taught him. Closing his eyes, he gripped the edge of the table, anchoring himself in time and space.

Finally, he opened his eyes and said slowly, "He's using your body to bring back the god of death."

She nodded, the glow in her eyes burning hot with fury. "And I'm the bait. The message, the transmitter, as you said."

Leopol stared at her, shaken to his core. He wanted to roar, to smash every cursed scroll in the room, to tear through the veil of the world and destroy the one who'd done this to her. But all he could do was breathe—slowly, carefully—and reach across the table.

"We will stop him," Leopol said, voice raw with promise. "We'll break the curse. Get your body back. And if he wants war with the gods..."

His grip tightened on her hand, the promise solidifying into an oath. "Then we give him a reason to fear dragons again."

He met her eyes, soul to soul, and gripped her hand. Magic flared, brightening the room and pushing back the shadows. Her expression wavered between fury and fear.

"I swear to you, Bella... you're not alone in this fight."

Her expression crumpled, eyes shining with a grief so deep it cracked something open in him.

Leopol didn't hesitate. He stepped around the table and pulled her into his arms, holding her like she might vanish. Her spectral form was cool and warm all at once, magic and memory and longing. His hand slid up to cradle the back of her head, anchoring her to him, and maybe him to her.

She didn't resist.

Her arms slipped around him, and she buried her face

in his chest as magic pulsed between them in a soft, steady rhythm–two hearts trying to beat as one.

"We'll fix this," he whispered into her hair. "All of it."

He pulled back, his hand cupping her face and pushing her hair back. She looked up at him with those big, brown eyes so full of misery, and he just wanted to make her feel better.

No, it was more than want. It was a primal need he couldn't prevent.

His lips descended to hers, and finally–*finally*–their lips connected.

Chapter Seven

Time stopped. Magic swirled around them like liquid silver, and Leopol's soul shuddered. Her spectral form pulsed against his touch, flickering between solid and ethereal as their lips met.

The kiss sparked like lightning—wild, reverent, undeniable. Her fingers clutched at his shirt, anchoring herself even as her form threatened to dissolve. Their magic surged together, twining deep like ancient roots, primal and sacred.

This wasn't just a kiss. It was a collision of soul and spell, a bond echoing through lifetimes. Leopol felt it resonate in every part of him. Not a choice, but a cosmic truth.

His mate.

Outside, thunder rolled. Wind battered the stone walls as if the world itself recognized their union. But nothing matched the storm inside him.

There had been kisses during his life as a dragon. He'd studied dragons, drakin, humans—learned their courtships like lessons in a book. But nothing prepared him for this.

Their magic pulsed—ancient, primal, undeniable—as her tongue teased his, their mouths finding a rhythm that was urgent, electric, alive. It was already changing him. He could feel it swirling, reshaping, marking.

Her fingers tangled in his hair, tugging him closer as he gripped her tighter, magic sparking along every nerve.

She gasped against his lips, then kissed him harder, clawing at the back of his neck like she couldn't get enough. The need between them surged, wild and consuming. If he'd had his dragon body, his scales would've flared in instinctual response.

As it was, magic poured through him—hot, liquid, relentless—coiling around their hearts like a vow. The ache to touch her skin-to-skin pulsed through every part of him.

The stone chamber seemed too small, too confining for the raw energy erupting between them. Leopol's hands slid down her back, tracing the dip of her spine and the curve of her hip.

Their spectral forms flickered between solid and ethereal, their bond too powerful for physical boundaries. And in that moment, Leopol understood everything.

Bella wasn't just a woman. She was the missing piece of his soul, the one he'd searched for across lifetimes.

The other dragons had always talked about how rare mates were, how the bond snapped into place, how some dragons don't really have a desire to fuck anyone until they meet their mate.

He'd always just assumed because of how he came to Celawyn that he'd never actually experience it himself, construct that he was.

But here she was, fulfilling all his hopes, dreams, and hidden secret desires just by being her charming self. He groaned, wanting to consume her, deepening the kiss once more and leaving them both breathless.

A fresh rumble of thunder shook the stone walls, and Bella tore her lips from his, breath ragged. Her eyes shone with awe, confusion, and heat—and Leopol couldn't look away. She brushed trembling fingers along his jaw, the contact crackling with cold energy.

Then, as if reality had slammed back into her, she stepped away. Her hands flew to her mouth. "We can't," she whispered, voice raw. "Not yet. The curse—"

He silenced her with a fierce kiss, swift and desperate. "The curse will break," he said as he pulled back. "We'll find a way. And while we work—"

"No." She slipped around the table, putting space between them. The loss of her touch stung. "Not until we reverse the curse. Not until the wizard's gone. I don't have time for this—not with the rose blooming faster every day and—"

She sucked in a sharp breath, chest heaving. Her eyes were wild.

Leopol froze. The ache of rejection twisted through him, but he forced himself still. Of course, she needed space. After everything she'd been through... pushing now was selfish. Even knowing they were fated didn't make her ready.

Their connection pulsed between them, an unfinished promise, a spark that wouldn't—couldn't—be denied for long. Magic still shimmered in the air, aching to close the gap.

Slowly, cautiously, he stepped around the table. She shifted as if searching for a way out. He stopped just short and raised one hand, brushing his thumb gently along her cheek.

"We'll break the curse. Defeat the wizard. Get your body back," he said quietly. "Then we'll talk about *us*."

Her gaze dropped. She hugged herself, magic still crackling faintly in the air. So close—and yet so far.

He started to speak again, to ease the tension tightening between them—but the grating scrape of stone interrupted him. Knox stepped into the hallway, his frown already heavy.

"Leopol, the storm knocked out scaffolding in the west wing. Do we have anything to plug the hole? That room was just re-floored."

Leopol scrubbed his jaw with a sigh. "Yeah, I'll take care of it." He cast a glance toward Bella, who bit her lip but said nothing. His chest tightened. "I'll be back to escort you to your room," he murmured.

He followed Knox out of the sanctum, up the stairs that creaked beneath their feet.

Knox glanced over his shoulder. "What was that tension back there?"

Leopol exhaled sharply. "I–I don't fucking know. She's scared, hurt, and I might've come on too strong."

They paused as lightning flashed through the tall window, throwing Knox's profile into stark relief as he asked, "What makes you say that?"

Leopol hesitated, then said it aloud for the first time. "She's my mate."

Knox stopped mid-step. "Seriously?"

"Yeah." Leopol nodded. "Everything I told you—all that mate bond lore in your office? It's real. Not just theory or fuzzy dragon memories. I feel it in my soul. We're... meant to be."

Knox frowned and resumed walking. "Okay, but...

you're both ghosts. What happens if she gets her body back, and you don't?"

That stopped him cold.

Shit.

He hadn't thought of that.

Another lightning flash rattled the windowpane. At the end of the hall, a maid wrung her hands in the open doorway. Knox moved toward her, but Leopol remained rooted. The shock of even thinking of losing her had triggered a revelation.

His memories.

They were back.

Hundreds of years—flashes of wings, temples, voices, the wind over mountaintops. He blinked hard, breathing like he'd been punched.

The mate bond. It had triggered the release of his memories.

He clawed through them, trying to pinpoint the location of his body. He saw Feralt—Knox's father—soaring through smoke and fire above Hartsgrove castle. On the ground had been an enemy. He'd followed someone into the castle—someone dangerous. He had to stop them.

Then—

Nothing. A blank where the most crucial memory should be, still locked away from him. Gratitude for the memories gave way to frustration. The most vital piece was still locked away.

"Leopol, if you've got ideas, we could really use them," Knox called from the room.

Leopol jerked into motion, shoving his personal chaos aside to focus on the kingdom.

Bella's jittery magic flipped the pages too fast to follow. Research kept her grounded, logical—safe. And she needed that now.

She opened a book she'd already skimmed, hoping she'd missed something, and her eyes narrowed on a passage.

"...and thus, shall the karinth speak the True Name of the Star-born, for the soul's memory hides in the syllables of origin: names not spoken in ages, but known only to the bond."

She scowled, the passage of dragon history making her think of Leopol and that kiss.

With a frustrated huff, she set it aside and scanned the nearby shelf. One book shimmered faintly, and her magic reached for it without thought. The tome thumped onto the table, fluttering open to a page as if guided.

"To awaken the bound flame, the soul-chosen must speak the name he forgot but never lost. The fire-touched Starborn, marked by oath and breath—"

The ink smudged halfway down the page. Someone had scrawled notes in the margins, barely legible. Only one word stood clear: *Raelion*.

She rubbed her forehead, trying to focus—but her mind betrayed her.

His mouth had been the perfect mix of soft and demanding. Just the right pressure. Like they were made for each other and just... fit.

By Borga's blade, it had been the best kiss of her life.

"Bella? Are you in here?"

The muffled voice echoed through the stone walls. Bella went to the little hallway and activated the mechanism, making the hidden bookcase creak open. She stepped out from the sanctum's hallway into the library's warm glow.

"I'm here," Bella said. "Are you alright?"

Eirwyn's jaw dropped as her head spun to the now-open

bookcase. "What in the world? I've lived here half a year and didn't know that was there. What is it?"

"It's Leopol's sanctum—meant for the royal bloodline," Bella explained as she stepped aside. "He said only Knox had ever seen it before. He didn't want to intrude on your grief over losing Gastone or seem like he was pressuring you to step into something you weren't ready for."

Eirwyn hesitated in the doorway. "But will he mind that I'm here now?"

Bella shook her head. "Not at all. He considers you family, Eirwyn. The door was never closed to you—it was just waiting for you to walk through it."

Eirwyn gasped softly, eyes wide as she stepped through the hidden passage. "I've heard of such secret places, but to see one..." Her gaze flitted over tapestries and glimmering artifacts. "Most royal families have them. I wasn't allowed in the sanctums, though. Gastone said they were only for the heir."

"That's bullshit and you know it," Bella muttered.

Eirwyn gave a crooked smile. "I know."

Bella sighed. "He hid the sanctum at the Winter Palace from me too. I didn't find it until after everyone was gone. Ignot showed me."

Eirwyn's eyes misted. "It's good to see you again. Like this, I mean."

Bella wanted to take her friend's hands—but she couldn't. "Eirwyn, I should've listened to you about Gastone. When you came home from Glathen, I wasn't myself. The wizard was already whispering through the mirror. But that's no excuse for how I treated you. I'm so sorry. I hope you know that."

Eirwyn's smile wobbled as she nodded. "I do. I didn't

know how to tell you how afraid I was. I should've been louder."

"And what would you have said? 'Don't marry him, he's evil'?" Bella snorted. "Yeah, I doubt I would've listened. But I should've. You've always had my back, and I–I treated you like shit."

Eirwyn wiped at her eyes. "It's alright. Sometimes friendships are hard. But we grow through them–or move on and try to find new ones. Personally, I'm glad we're fixing things. I don't want to find new friends. It's hard, as a queen, to make friendships that *last*, you know?"

Bella arched a brow. "You realize how that sounds, right?"

Eirwyn groaned and waved her off, laughing. "Ugh. Don't even say it."

"I love you, Eirwyn. You're the little sister I never had. Thank you for not giving up on me."

"Damn it, Bella, stop being all mushy." Eirwyn sniffed, dabbing at her cheeks. "Kind words *and* you're glowing– what's going on with you?"

Bella blushed and tucked a stray curl behind her ear. "I– uh. Thank you?"

Eirwyn narrowed her eyes. "Bella. Are you blushing?"

"What? No," Bella said, ducking behind a book. "I'm just happy to be here. All these books, the research–it's good to feel useful again."

"Hmm. If you say so."

"I am," Bella insisted–too quickly. She winced. "I just... I'm feeling more like myself. Less tired. More in control of my magic."

Eirwyn stepped into the main room of the sanctum. "I wonder how much of that has to do with being near Leopol today."

"Leopol? What does *he* have to do with it?" Bella asked—even though she had a feeling what was going on, she wasn't quite ready yet to admit it, even to herself.

He'd shared meditative techniques his father taught him when she'd grown overwhelmed earlier. He was an excellent listener and had worked tirelessly alongside her to help the villagers. His care was evident in every curated shelf and how the servants had constantly sought him out throughout the day.

"I noticed how your magic pulsed when you touched," Eirwyn said. "And he's clearly smitten."

Bella remembered that first spark—how their magic had flared like kindling at a single touch, awakening something she hadn't dared name.

Bella smiled before she could stop herself. The way he'd ushered her in here, shared this hidden part of himself—intimacy not lightly offered. He hadn't just granted access to the library—he'd given her the means to unlock their secrets, even if she didn't yet understand them. But then that kiss...

"Leopol must think highly of you," Eirwyn added. "To share this sanctum on the very day you met."

A shiver danced along Bella's spine. She'd felt his spirit press against hers in perfect sync. Their combined magic had set her ablaze alongside the kiss to end all kisses.

Bella gave a small, dismissive snort. "Doubtful."

Eirwyn teased, a playful glint in hers, "Come now, even I noticed how he can't take his eyes off you. You should've heard how he talked about you at the council dinner tonight. It was clear he admired you."

Bella scoffed to brush off the observation, despite the flutter in her chest. "I'm sure it's merely the novelty of my... condition that intrigues him."

"Or perhaps it's simply because you're enchanting,"

Eirwyn countered. "Don't let Gastone taint what could be, Bella. You deserve someone who sees your worth."

Her words stirred something deep within, a hope Bella had locked away since her wedding day to Gastone. Yet, with each whispered jest, each stolen glance shared with Leopol, the lock rustled loose, inviting thoughts she dared not entertain.

What had started as comfort had become something soul-deep. His presence, a fortress. His touch, an unexpected vow she hadn't known she craved until that moment. Her lips still tingled, the memory of his kiss blooming like warmth through her chest.

"You're blushing again," Eirwyn said softly.

Bella straightened, jaw tight. "It doesn't matter. There's no time to explore what might be between us. We have curses to break."

Even as she said it, images of Leopol drifted closer in her mind. His presence haunted her—warm, undeniable. There was no time for fantasies about what could be, no matter how many pages she'd re-read after losing herself in thoughts of him. Facing the wizard had been easier than resisting him.

"Have you discovered anything?" Eirwyn asked, glancing at the stacks of open books.

Bella shook her head, translucent fingers trailing across a crinkled page. "Not yet, but I can feel it's here somewhere." Her voice carried both determination and frustration. "The Northern Archive texts hint at a ritual that might reverse curses, but the translations are a mess."

Eirwyn gasped. "The Northern Archives? I thought those all burned."

"So did I! But Leopol visited the region decades before the war. He'd copied a number of tomes himself. Honestly, it's fascinating. Did you know he's even been off continent?"

Eirwyn crossed her arms and raised a brow. "Oh really?"

Bella looked up. "What?"

Eirwyn grinned. "You like his big brain. Admit it."

Bella scowled, cheeks heating. "We're just working together."

"Uh-huh. And has *he* found anything?"

Bella fiddled with a scroll. "He's been combing through the Moonstone Covenant glyphs. He thinks there might be an overlap between the different magic types and dragon transformation rituals from the pre-kingdom era. Things we haven't explored yet."

Her voice softened at the mention of him. Was Eirwyn right? That kiss... And the way he explained things—gods, he was brilliant.

Before Eirwyn could comment, a knock echoed through the hall. Leopol appeared a moment later, his stride confident, cloak fluttering like a shadow behind him.

"Good evening, Your Majesties," he said, voice smooth as velvet and sending a shiver up her spine.

Bella's breath caught. "Good evening," she murmured, clenching her skirt to hide sweaty palms.

"Hope you don't mind me in your sanctum," Eirwyn said.

Leopol bowed slightly. "Of course not. You're Knox's mate—and family. My apologies for not showing you this space sooner. Technically, it's your sanctum, not mine."

"Did you patch the roof?" she asked, saving Bella from having to speak.

He nodded. "We did. Knox went to check on the hatchling. Claimed the room was a breach in the defenses."

Eirwyn chuckled. "I swear, I love that man, but he needs to stop raising our son like he's preparing for war." She moved to the exit. "I'll see you both at breakfast?"

Bella hesitated. "I think I'll just research—"

"No." Eirwyn's voice was gentle but firm as she glanced back. "You need normalcy. You need time with your father. Just come sit with us. I won't take no for an answer."

Bella caught the stubborn tilt of her friend's chin and sighed. "Very well."

Eirwyn grinned. "Excellent. Leopol, would you show her to her room?"

"Of course," he said with a bow, stepping forward as Eirwyn disappeared down the hidden passage.

Chapter Eight

Bella followed Leopol up the stairs, nervously grabbing her skirt to avoid tripping. The silence between them pulsed with unsaid things.

"This is your home now," he said gently, matching her pace. "I hope you'll be comfortable here."

She nodded, clearing her throat. "Thank you. Hopefully, it doesn't take long to find a cure for the curse and defeat the wizard–but it's already been half a year, so..."

"Seven months, three weeks, and four days," he said quietly.

She glanced over. "How–how do you know that?"

He shrugged, rubbing his jaw. "That's how long I've been awake. I think the curse hit just after."

Her mind spun. "So, you were... dead? Or asleep? How does that work?"

He chuckled, and it sent a thrill through her. "I'm not dead," he said with certainty.

She paused on the stairs as his gaze found hers, steady

and deep. When he took her hand gently between his, she didn't pull away.

"Please don't mention it to Knox or Eirwyn," he said. "They have enough to worry about."

She frowned as he tucked her hand into his arm and continued up the stairs.

"What do you mean, though? That you're not dead?"

He sighed. "I was here when Knox's father died three hundred years ago, but I don't remember dying. I'm certain my body went into hibernation. I've been trying to find it."

She wanted to press for more, but they reached the landing, and he gestured left. "That's the west wing. It's not safe yet—structural issues. The north wing's the family wing, but your room is in the east. It's the warmest wing in the castle."

She smirked. "Not that it matters when I'm like this."

He gave a soft laugh. "Still, I want you to be comfortable. Tell me what you need. I'll do anything for you, Bella."

Her breath caught. They stopped beside a carved wooden door bearing a rose motif. He glanced at her lips, and her heart raced.

They were both thinking of that kiss.

Still... what would it be like to invite him in?

Her body hummed with anticipation—until the cruel reminder hit: she didn't *have* a body. That ghostly ache of wanting, but being unable, twisted inside her.

He cleared his throat. "I—uh, I'll see you at breakfast?"

She nodded slowly. He opened the door and stepped back, dropping his hand as she entered.

"Is everything to your liking?" he asked from the door.

She scanned the cozy furnishings—the pink damask walls, oversized bed, roaring fireplace, and vanity beside a curtained window.

Her gaze locked on the vanity, and her pulse jumped. She swallowed hard and ignored it, spinning to smile brightly at him. "It's lovely. Thank you."

"Very well," he said softly. He stepped in as if unable to stay away from her and took her hand again. "Sleep well, Bellakari."

He pressed a kiss to her knuckles, eyes never leaving hers as surprise filled her from the unfamiliar term. Magic shivered through her, and the chair beside the fire shifted. She inhaled sharply, focusing hard to contain her magic—and her reaction, her need at his touch.

The door clicked behind him. Alone, she let out a breath.

How could he unnerve yet steady her all at once?

She used her magic to toss a blanket over the vanity mirror. It wasn't enchanted, but simply wood and glass. Still, she didn't trust it.

Sleep was useless in this form, always accompanied by nightmares of that night. Settling onto the rug in front of the fire, she tried the breathing exercises he'd shown her, but her thoughts spiraled back to Leopol.

The way he thought—his mind was as fascinating as his trim, lean frame. She could still feel his gaze burning into her. She imagined him hovering above her, all heat and reverence.

She groaned and rubbed her temples. *It was going to be a long night.*

She gave up on meditating and grabbed her books. Work would have to be her distraction.

Leopol walked into the breakfast room and paused. Bella immediately took his breath away. In the same yellow and red dress as yesterday, she glowed under the soft morning light.

Her hands waved as she told her father a story, her face light with laughter. She was so beautiful, so carefree. So different than yesterday where she'd been reserved, tense, and worried about the curse.

Wulfric threw his head back and laughed. Scarlet smiled and leaned back in her chair, sipping a steaming mug as she watched her mate. There was a peace in her eyes that hadn't been there in their last visit. Leopol assumed she'd finally accepted the mate bond.

He glanced at Bella, wondering when—if—she'd ever accept him. A thought made him pause. What would happen if she never did? The books had explained that various species had different consequences for denying the mate bond, but he couldn't remember what they'd said about dragons.

Damn it, he'd need to brush up on that research.

"Leopol, join us," Knox said from the head of the table, his voice filling the room.

Bella's head shot up and her back straightened. Her mouth opened in surprise, and he wanted to—gods, he wanted to do so many things to her, with her, for her.

Way too many dirty things to be thinking with her father sitting right next to her.

He cleared his throat and smiled. "Good morning, everyone."

He sat next to Scarlet, and they both stared at Wulfric and Bella, probably with similar besotted expressions on their faces.

A soft smile played at the corners of his mouth. She

shimmered slightly when she met his gaze, a reaction she couldn't quite control. Did she even realize she did it? Did she think of him last night as much as he thought of her?

She glanced down, reminding him of the leather-bound manuscript beneath his arm. He set it on the table, and said, "I've been reviewing some texts in the eastern wing. There might be something here about spectral binding."

Bella nodded and bit her lip, swaying toward him across the table before turning back to her father.

"Great. We can dive in after breakfast?" she asked.

"Absolutely," he said, setting the book to the side. "I'll meet you in the library later, and we can get to work." He turned to Knox to discuss the day's agenda, but never quite let her out of his sight.

Wulfric's brows pulled together as he looked between them, but right when he opened his mouth, Bella turned to him with an overly bright expression.

"Did I tell you about the time that Old Mitch tried to catch one of Eirwyn's light and shadow characters from one of her stories?"

Wulfric's eyes narrowed on Leopol, then he turned back to Bella, his face smoothing, relaxing into a smile.

"No, what happened?"

The conversation at the table flowed, breaking into smaller conversations here and there. Bella reconnected with her father, and Leopol was happy for her. He didn't begrudge this time with her. Instead, it made him think through all the interactions he'd had with his own father.

If he could even call him that. He sighed, his shoulders sinking at the memories, now solidified. They were almost all back now, thanks to the start of the mate bond process.

He needed to talk to Knox about this new understanding, but it was insignificant in the grand scheme of things. Between the wizard and the curse, they were rather booked.

Breakfast flew by as he made plans with Knox for a more permanent repair of the west wing roof. Knox and he eventually stood and went about their work repairing the castle, ordering supplies, and talking with the staff.

They left Wulfric and Bella in deep discussions. It seemed like she was trying to catch him up year by year of all he'd missed in their village. Scarlet sprawled on the chair, picking at her nails with one of her daggers, listening quietly.

It was hours later when he found his way to the library, unable to stay away from her for longer. Bella was already in the sanctum, reading through the manuscripts on the table.

She looked up at him, her expression guarded even as she smiled. "Hello."

"Hello, Bella. How was your morning catching up with Wulfric?"

She smiled wider, relaxing her shoulders. "Oh, it was so nice to talk with him. It reminded me of when I was a child. He'd be making his world-famous ale, and I'd sit at the table and just chat his ear off."

Leopol's brows rose. "World famous?"

She grinned mischievously as she shrugged. "According to him."

Leopol chuckled as she grew quiet.

Her smile wavered. "Talking like that was how we got through the tough times together. Like right after we'd lost my mother, and the silence was sad."

Leopol set the book from earlier on the table next to her. "The silence in the castle was deafening after Knox and Eirwyn left. I barely lasted the week until they came to see if I was still here and awake."

She nodded, and he felt her eyes on him. "The Winter Palace was like that too. Deafening silence is so oppressive. You're wearing different clothes today."

The sudden shift in topic made him blink. "Uh, yes, I am. Is that alright?"

He needed her approval on a fundamental level, and he'd never questioned his clothing before.

She frowned and clutched at her yellow and red skirt. "Yes, but how did you do it? I've been in this dress ever since the incident."

He shrugged and thought about it. "Meditation and spell work, I believe. There's not really any book about how to be a successful ghost, but the mind remembers what the body's supposed to look like."

She crossed her arms, drawing his gaze to her chest. "So, you just what–think up something new to wear?"

"Let me show you." He chuckled and stepped closer, turning her gently and wrapping his arms around her waist. She stiffened in his arms, then relaxed as he crooned softly into her ear. "Sh, it's alright. It's easier to feel the magic when we touch."

She could pull off this type of magic, he knew, but if they'd learned anything yesterday, it was that their magic was more powerful when they were touching.

He pulled her to him until they were front to back, and he fought back a groan at the way her ass nestled his now hardening dick. She wiggled slightly, and he closed his eyes and focused on keeping his breath steady.

He whispered, "Close your eyes. Do you remember the breathing exercises?"

There was no missing her sudden shallow, panting breaths as he held her. He didn't draw attention to it, too obsessed with holding her tight. The melody of magic propelled him to sway like the softest of dances, her ass moving against him in the most delicious of ways.

His voice was low, and his breath teased her ear. "Think of your favorite dress. Remember the texture of it, how it felt against your skin, the way it flowed around your ankles...the way it cupped your breasts."

His hands on her waist slid up, his thumbs caressing the underside of each and teasing them both.

The tingle of magic swirled around them, and the scent of jasmine filled him. The unsung melody grew louder in his mind, and she began to hum. The darkness behind his eyelids grew brighter with a flash.

But instead of her dress changing, she now stood naked in his arms. He groaned, his fingers digging into the skin of her sides. She was so soft, the light falling on her and highlighting the most perfect breasts that had ever existed.

She gasped and cupped them, trying to cover herself. "Oh gods, what happened?"

He swayed side to side, and with a flash of magic, he too was naked. He stroked her side, not daring to move higher or lower until she gave consent. She swayed toward him, wiggling her ass again where his cock nestled hard and aching against her. It encouraged him, made him think that she *wanted* to be in his arms.

"The mind remembers, and your magic is powerful. You didn't remember your favorite dress, but being naked." He took a deep breath, the scent of jasmine mixing with something deeper, something more primal.

He groaned and kissed under her ear. She shivered, and her hands tightened on her breasts.

"How—how do I fix it?"

"Think of the dress," he growled, kissing down her neck to the sensitive part where her neck met her shoulder. He pleaded with the gods. "Fuck, you feel so good. Gods, Bella-vore, think of the dress before I lay you on this table and feast. Hells, I can smell you. I want to lick up your slit and taste you, suck on your—"

A pop of magic, and she was clothed, stepping away from him and scurrying around the table. He stood naked, unashamed of how she made him so hard that his dick bobbed. Her eyes widened, and her mouth dropped open in surprise, her hands cupping her cheeks.

His magic flared, and he was back in his regular blue waistcoat, white shirt, gray pants, and black boots. A slight frown creased her forehead to see him clothed.

"Look how quickly you picked that up! Such a good girl," he said with a smile. Her breath caught on the words, and her eyes flashed up to his. "I knew you could do it. I like that dress. Blue suits you."

The dress was a cerulean ocean, its waves gently caressing her as she stood in the warm light, her eyes widening in awe as she glanced down. It clung to her curves, its simplicity highlighting her natural beauty. White embroidered edges of the sleeves and hem added a touch of femininity to the fabric.

The practical white apron had deep pockets with blue embroidery, suggesting she was ready for a hard day's work. He could imagine her confidently gliding through the tavern, her radiant energy filling the room as she effortlessly carried out her tasks.

She smoothed her hands down the front, the rustle of fabric and the smile on her face showing just how happy she was to have the new clothes.

"I did it. This is my favorite dress," she said in awe, her hand smoothing down the soft fabric. "I—thank you."

She looked up at him, her eyes soft with gratitude and–did he dare hope, something else?

He took two steps and–when she didn't move away–cupped her cheek, his thumb caressing her soft skin. "You're very welcome, Bellakari."

She swayed toward him, licking her lips before catching herself. She cleared her throat and glanced around. "Um, shall we get started?"

He nodded and pointed to the book he'd brought in laying open on the table. "This is what I was talking about earlier. See this?"

Bella leaned toward him, and he inhaled the scent of jasmine and old parchment. Underneath it lay the scent of her arousal, but her reactions showed that she was nowhere near ready to discuss their bond or even act.

The way his senses sang when she was near, when he'd held her naked in his arms. He wanted to experience that every day. But he wouldn't push her or scare her with his growing need for her. He had to be patient and wait.

Chapter Nine

His proximity sent tiny sparks of magical energy dancing across Bella's translucent form. Gods, he smelled divine. Her mouth watered, nearly desperate for another taste of him. And the way he'd felt, naked and pressed up against her back?

Fuck, she'd never wanted anyone the way she wanted him. She dragged her gaze from the flex of his shoulder and the lingering taste of his skin. Focus. This wasn't the time.

"These markings," Leopol murmured, his finger tracing delicate runes along the manuscript's edge. "See how they're similar to the binding runes we discovered?"

The way his hands moved across the page, so sure, confident and strong. She wanted his hands on her, teasing, touching, caressing her into oblivion.

Bella leaned closer, her arm brushing against his as they stood side by side. The magical charge between them intensified, a subtle dance of spectral energy that made the surrounding air shimmer with potential. Her translucent fingers hovered just above the text, careful not to disturb the fragile pages.

She focused on the words and whispered, her voice carrying a hint of excitement. "You're right. We saw something like that in the translation you made. There were fragments that suggested a similar linguistic pattern."

Bella's magic rippled suddenly, reacting to a flash of fear she couldn't quite name. The rose, time slipping through her fingers without straightforward answers. Her pulse sped up, and she turned away, hands shaking.

Leopol's blue eyes lifted, meeting hers with an intensity that made her translucent form flutter. The proximity was both dangerous and compelling—each moment together seemed to unravel another layer of the mysterious connection between them.

It was more than just a physical need, and the possible significance of it scared her.

His spirit wavered toward her, and her heart raced with need and desire. She wanted him, and not just physically because he made her feel alive. It was him, his soul, his essence, his caring touch and constant belief in her.

No, she couldn't give in to whatever this was between them. Not until they saved everyone who'd been cursed. The memory of the rose this morning made her mentally push aside the memory of his nakedness, the feel of him. She was running out of time, and panic licked at her heels.

She turned to the far table, rapidly flipping through book after book using her magic. Her rapid page-turning created small magical eddies around the manuscripts, causing loose papers to flutter and float. Leopol's gaze made the hair on the back of her nape stand.

"Bella, slow down. Your agitation is changing the delicate texts."

She paused, her translucent hand hovering mid-turn. He was right. Her desperation to solve the curse was causing her magic to destabilize. She watched in horror as the open book in front of her morphed, the writing inside shifting, flowing like liquid.

She dropped it and stepped away, shaking her head as sweat beaded her lip. "No, no, no, not again."

The book's ink writhed, its words swimming off the page. Just like the last time. Just like when she lost control and a bookshelf in the Winter Palace had exploded.

"Again?"

"I thought I had more control on it than this." Tears pricked her eyes, and she squeezed them shut, hoping against hope that she wasn't ruining the manuscript with her volatile magic. A sharp tremor ran through the sanctum. The manuscripts trembled, their edges curling as if alive.

Leopol's hand instinctively reached for Bella's forearm, fingers brushing her ethereal form. His proximity made her magical energy pulse, once, twice as he pulled her into his embrace. It was protective, comforting, and somehow more intimate than their earlier naked embrace.

Then the magical charge between them exploded, golden light settling around them like dust. Runes along the walls began to glow, pulsing with an ancient rhythm that seemed to breathe with its own consciousness.

His hands slid up her arms, rubbing in a slow rhythm that soothed her emotional outburst. "Breathe with me now. In, two, three, out, two, three. There you go. Again."

The runes continued to pulse, their golden light casting intricate shadows across the sanctum walls. Bella's trembling slowly subsided, her translucent form stabilizing under Leopol's gentle touch.

"I'm sorry," she whispered, her voice barely audible with her cheek against his chest. "This happens sometimes when my emotions get too intense."

Leopol's fingers continued their soothing rhythm, never breaking contact. "Don't apologize. Your magic is powerful–it's learning, just as you are. Each manifestation of your magic is a clue, Bella, not a failure."

A sudden warmth spread through her, different from the magical charge. His understanding felt like a balm to her fractured spirit. The manuscripts around them settled, their edges smoothing back into place as if nothing had happened.

Except runes on the stone walls began to shift, their ancient symbols realigning themselves in patterns that seemed almost purposeful–like they were responding to her.

Dread filled her at the idea that her magic had ruined another book, another manuscript, scroll, or text. She hated the idea of disappointing him and not taking care of the books within his care.

Leopol's grip tightened as one particular rune seemed to glow brighter than the others. He frowned, muttering, "The golden apple."

Bella's hands fluttered to Leopol's waist, the fabric of his coat soft beneath her fingers. She wanted to touch more, but her mind latched onto his words. "Golden apple? What does that mean?" she echoed, the phrase tingling with recognition.

Scarlet and Eirwyn had both mentioned a golden apple tree, but it wasn't producing fruit. She hadn't really thought something so simple could be such a powerful thing.

Leopol stepped toward the rune, but it shifted back to its original form and stopped glowing. He frowned, then waved to her. "Come here for a minute. Let's test a theory."

She floated over to the wall, and he slid his arm around her waist. She slid her arm around his as well. Touching him felt natural, was so easy and... right.

Pressed together from thigh to side, each with an arm around the waist of the other, the rune pulsed again, casting a soft golden light across the sanctum's stone walls. Shadows danced around them, seeming to whisper ancient secrets. Bella felt a tremor run through her—something about this symbol resonated deep within her spectral essence.

"It's an ancient symbol in draconic lore. Not just a fruit, but a metaphorical representation of transformation magic. Although, the druids believed it was a gift from the goddess that would reveal truth and cure all sickness. For example, when Growlers aren't able to shift back after going Feral, it's a blocked transformation. The golden apple was supposed to realign those pathways in the body."

Bella's eyes widened. "That's why Knox was told to seek it out? So he could finally shift into a dragon?"

Leopol nodded. "Yes, the seer Lailant had told him it would reveal his true form, but I'm not convinced it worked. I think he could finally shift into his full dragon form because he completed the mate bond with Eirwyn."

Bella frowned, thinking through everything her friend had told her about how she'd come to this castle. "Eirwyn bit the golden apple too, but by then, the fruit had been cursed, right?"

Leopol nodded, his grip tight on her as he growled, "By Gastone."

Bella frowned, a hazy memory coming to her mind. "No, Gastone was simply the puppet. The wizard orchestrated it."

Leopol stroked his chin with his free hand, drawing her

gaze from the glowing rune that still pulsed like a heartbeat. Gods, he had the sharpest jaw she'd ever seen.

"That makes sense, but I can't quite identify why. It's like the knowledge is right on the tip of my tongue. Much like some of these texts, it's a fragment that never quite reveals its full meaning. Damn it, I wish I knew what was missing."

His burst of disappointment made the rune pulse erratically, and a book flew off the shelf next to it.

Leopol let go of her and caught the book before it hit the ground, his reflexes swift despite the magical disturbance. The tome landed softly in his palm, its leather binding creaking open as if responding to his touch.

"Curious," he murmured, turning to the table as he scanned the pages. His fingers traced a series of intricate diagrams, each more complex than the last. The golden rune continued to pulse behind them, casting shadows across the sanctum walls.

Bella floated closer, her translucent form brushing against Leopol's arm. "What is it?"

"A map," he said, his voice low and measured. "But not of any territory I recognize. These markings–they're older than the dragon kingdom's oldest records. But they're not druidic or pre-kingdom glyphs either..."

She waited, her heart seeming to race as he flipped a few pages then back again. The book's pages seemed to shimmer, ancient symbols bleeding into one another like watercolors. Bella's spectral energy rippled, responding to the magical resonance, and she tried to stay away from it. She didn't want to get too excited and her magic spaz out, turning the words into gibberish again.

He sucked in a breath, his finger tracing a shimmering symbol that moved under his finger. "This matches the carvings in the temple I woke in. The place I became a dragon."

Bella's heart skipped. "Where you woke with no memories?"

He nodded, flipping pages, faster now.

"I've never found a single record of those symbols until now. They bleed together when we're not touching, like they're resisting being fully seen. But with our combined magic, I can see it more clearly... this could be it. The place where my story began, where I might find answers to how I came to this realm... maybe even where I come from."

"Still no memories from before?"

He shook his head. "No, but I'm grateful for my dragon memories to be mostly restored now. It's progress."

The golden rune on the wall pulsed again, drawing Bella's gaze from the book to its rhythmic glow. The symbol seemed to hum in response to their magic, as if it too had recognized something.

Her eyes narrowed slightly. A pattern was forming, runes reacting to their touch, memories surfacing, transformation linked to touch and magic...

Her voice dropped to a murmur. "What if we're looking at this wrong?"

She let go of his forearm, and the runes faded. When she touched him again, magic flared gently between them and over the runes on the wall.

"What if the golden apple isn't just about realigning transformation pathways, but restoring someone to what they're supposed to be?"

The rune on the wall flickered beside them, as if responding to her hypothesis. Her grip on him tightened imperceptibly.

"Restoration," he repeated, the word rolling off his tongue like an incantation. "Not just physical transformation, but magical healing. A reset, of sorts. Yes, if it works, it could be the key to reversing the curse on the people."

She vibrated with magic and excitement. "What if it's the missing ingredient?"

Maybe it could help him too. If the golden apple truly restored people to who they were meant to be, could it restore his forgotten past? That is, if they could figure out how a spirit could absorb a potion.

His eyes widened, and he nodded. "Yes, let's shift our focus on the research to anything dealing with a golden apple and see what we come up with."

Excited once more, the rune still glowing behind them, she reached for another book.

The hours passed as Leopol pulled all the books, scrolls, and manuscripts he could remember mentioning the golden apple. They lost themselves in research until a servant came to get Leopol for dinner. Bella declined, waving a hand as she turned a page, too engrossed in their progress.

The clink of silverware and hushed murmurs filled the long hall. Wulfric sat stiff-backed at the edge of the council table, the flickering light of the sconces throwing shadows against the ancient stone walls of Hartsgrove Castle. The scent of roasted venison and sweet root soup hung thick in the air, but his appetite had vanished the moment the grumbling started.

"–ought to be locked away," one of the lords was saying. "It's madness to let her roam about like some holy, untouchable ghost."

"She cursed us," a councilwoman hissed, her too-tight

necklace bobbing with her pulse. "And now she thinks she can just waltz in and play hero?"

Wulfric's grip on his goblet tightened. Beside him, Scarlet's jaw ticked. She caught his gaze and gave a subtle shake of her head, but the tension in her shoulders said she was just as close to snapping.

He wouldn't let them talk shit about his daughter though, their former queen.

Wulfric leaned back in his chair, goblet in hand as he tried to appear at ease. His voice, when it came, was quiet but firm.

"She didn't waltz in. Scarlet and I found her trapped in a cursed rose at the Winter Palace, where she'd been held hostage by a daemon. The wizard that took her body and is the real reason for the curse showed up when we killed his guard dog. He summoned a tornado of shadow magic and nearly tore us all to shreds."

The table fell quiet, but the looks on the council members' faces told him they weren't convinced.

"She tried to stop him," Wulfric said. "Tried to sacrifice herself again to stop him, even though she was half-spirit and barely here. She was protecting us—all of us—trying to stop him herself. I nearly died fighting beside her in that magical vortex of death."

A few of the councilors shifted uncomfortably.

Others rolled their eyes, murmuring about how convenient healing potions and natural Growler quick healing was. He glared at the fiend.

"She's dangerous," spat a woman in fine silks from the merchant's guild. "She may've been fair when she ran the tavern, but that was *before*. Power changes people. She isn't the same girl."

"She's not a girl anymore at all," Wulfric said tightly,

reining in his growl. "She hasn't been for years. And if we're talking about the tavern—did any of you have complaints then? Did she cheat you? Threaten you? Refuse aid when you were sick or drunk or hungry?"

No one answered. A few of the regulars he remembered from the tavern avoided his challenging gaze.

Wulfric snarled, "She ruled Demerel fairly long before Gastone ever put a crown on her head, taking care of her people—any who crossed the threshold of that tavern."

"That was before," another muttered. "Now she's a ghost with a cursed rose and too much magic. No control and little sense. It's not safe."

Leopol leaned forward at his seat next to Knox at the head of the table. "You're a fool if you think she has little sense. Have you even talked to her—ever? The woman is more brilliant than everyone in this room combined—including me!"

Eirwyn laughed and tried to diffuse the situation. "You're right about that. She's always been brilliant, even without formal schooling."

"Gastone gave her all the tutors she asked for. That's what I'm saying. Being queen changed her, and the dungeon is the safest place—for her and for all of us."

"It didn't change who she is at her core, in her heart," Wulfric said, slamming his goblet down so hard it sloshed ale to the linen.

Leopol glared down the table. "If you want the cure, she needs access to the library. She needs the royal sanctum. She needs time to work a miracle that's never been attempted before. She can't work from the dungeons."

A flicker of something fierce in the ancient dragon's eyes—resolve, maybe—made Wulfric pause. Resolve to do right by his little girl. Wulfric took a shallow breath, his claws barely sheathed.

"She should never have been queen to begin with," one man muttered under his breath. "Lowborn, no drakin blood to speak of. A tavern girl."

Wulfric snarled, his claws flashing with fangs bared. He pushed back his chair and stepped to where the man now slunk low in his chair.

"You think I'm proud of how things went down between me and Bella?" he said, eyes burning. "I wasn't here for her when she needed me. I chose to become a Growler rather than die, foolishly thought I'd be able to take care of her, come back and help—somehow. Losing those years with her after the change—that's my burden to carry. But don't you dare call her unworthy because we come from humble roots."

Scarlet reached out and gently touched his arm. He met her eyes and inhaled slowly, fur still bristling.

"She's not the same girl," he said, softer this time, less confrontational. "You're right. But not because of a crown. Because she's lived through hell and is still fighting."

Leopol met his gaze across the table and nodded, his chin sharp and eyes ever sharper as he used his gaze like daggers at the disgruntled dining guests. "She's not asking for your forgiveness—she's trying to *fix* what went wrong. You'd rather lock her up than give her a chance to save you?"

The silence was sharp now.

Eirwyn laid her hand on Knox's on the table, her voice demanding respect in a way only a born princess could command.

"She's the Alpha's daughter," Eirwyn said. "But she's also the queen of Busparia and my closest friend. I trust her.

The only questions that matter are... do you trust me? Do you trust Knox to protect this little forest kingdom? Do you trust Leopol to work with Bella to find a cure?"

Wulfric's fur still stood, and he shifted on his feet in the silence.

I don't think I can handle this nonsense for much longer, he warned his mate through the mate bond.

Scarlet snorted and stood, tossing her napkin on the plate, her voice steady as she added, "She's not your enemy. The one who stole her body and unleashed the curse still sits on the throne in Demerel. If you want vengeance, aim your rage in the right direction."

Wulfric walked out, heart pounding. The council's chatter resumed behind him, quieter now, tinged with uncertainty. He had to trust Knox, Eirwyn, and Leopol to handle the dinner now, because if he stayed a moment longer, he'd be out for blood.

Bella wasn't there to defend herself, but maybe—just maybe—they'd heard enough.

Come on, Wolfie. Let's go for a run and grab a drink to cool off, Scarlet said into his mind. Immediately, his feet moved toward the front door of the castle.

A run through the dark, dangerous forest was exactly what he needed. And he'd never turn down a drink with his mate.

Chapter Ten

The wind nipped at Scarlet's cheeks as she and Wulfric walked the narrow path from Hartsgrove to the village beyond the outer gate. The council dinner still simmered in her chest, but the crisp air and forest run had cooled the worst of it.

And her anger wasn't even as bad as Wulfric's had been.

His fur had flattened, but tension still clung to his shoulders. He was still worried about his daughter.

She sighed, her voice low, "If I can get over my need for revenge on Bella, then the rest of the cursed will come around too. Especially when she fixes it."

Wulfric's eyes softened as the wind ruffled his coat. "She's always been good at fixing things. Damn near lit a fire in her soul to save everyone when her mother died. She just had to read all the books and learn all the spells and potions to heal people."

He spoke softly as they passed under the wooden archway into the village square.

The scent of baking bread reached them first, warm

and buttery, nearly masking the raw newness of the village. There was no tavern yet—the village too small, too fresh—but the bakery stood proud and glowing with lantern light.

They stepped inside, greeted by the golden warmth of the oven and a smattering of locals. There were a few cursed among them—one with twisted iron coat hooks branching from his scalp, another with stained-glass shards instead of skin—but all of them nodded respectfully at Wulfric's presence.

The baker's assistant, a round-cheeked man with a flour-dusted apron, looked up eagerly. "We've got spiced mead or spiced mead. What'll you have?"

Wulfric chuckled. "Hm, spiced mead it is. Thank you."

As he poured, Wulfric leaned casually on the counter, chatting easily with the baker and a few wide-eyed villagers about brewing techniques and tavern management. Scarlet watched him with an odd pang.

He wasn't just a warrior. He was good with people. Maybe it had just taken him longer to remember who he'd been before.

He was right. Despite all that had happened, they were still the people they'd always been at their core.

She scanned the shadows and stiffened. A man sipped a pint, quiet with eyes like sharp stones. A reminder of what she used to do. The man didn't belong in this friendly village, yet he blended into the background better than anyone.

Scarlet stepped a few feet away from Wulfric and slid onto the bench beside the Hunter's Guild leader. "You're far from home," she said, leaning against the wall and mirroring his stance. Feet kicked out like his, arms crossed instead of holding a pint to show she wasn't about to reach for her daggers.

"So are you," he replied, lifting his chin. "But you walk like you own the place."

"Bad habit, that, I know." She leaned forward, voice quiet. "You're not here to discuss my new situation, though. You've just returned from Busparia?"

The man's expression darkened. "We've seen the Dragon Claws. They performed a ritual and brought a daemon from a portal. It spread another blizzard–this time moving north."

Knox would want to know. Scarlet's jaw tightened. "Where?"

"Venshire. Seven leagues west of the capital." He hesitated, then added, "The insignia on their cloaks... it matched the queen's."

Scarlet froze. Wulfric did not, his Growler ears picking up the conversation easily in the tiny room not even big enough to hold two tables.

"Like hell you say," Wulfric growled from behind her, pushing off the counter and crossing the room in three long strides.

Conversations halted. Eyes turned. Scarlet sighed, placing a steadying hand on his arm. "Easy there, Wolfie."

Wulfric's voice dropped to a deadly quiet. "Bella's been locked in the Winter Palace–cursed, imprisoned, barely a spirit. She's never even been to Venshire or commanded the Dragon Claws. Hells, she's never been to the capital either. Remember Bella? She grew up in Demerel. Coming to Hartsgrove is the first and only time she's ever left."

The Hunter met Wulfric's eyes. "I know what I saw."

Scarlet stepped between them. "And we don't doubt your report. But the woman you saw isn't our Bella or the real queen. There's an impostor–someone stole her body and throne. A wizard of unimaginable strength and power who uses forbidden magic."

The villagers began murmuring again, unsure, frightened. Words like nekromancer, sorcerer, and warlock were heard in the small room.

Wulfric's growl simmered. She nudged his shoulder toward the door and flicked a dagger between her fingers, lazily walking behind him. She glanced at each of them in the room as she did, staring just long enough that they blanched or looked away.

Scarlet paused at the door, raising her voice. "The Bella we know from the tavern–the Alpha's daughter–is trying to fix all this. She's not the enemy. But the one using her face? He's the one spreading this war, the winter, commanding the daemons and Dragon Claws–all of it. If you're going against Bella, the one here in Hartsgrove, then you're siding with the wizard and all the evil he's brought–including the fucking curse. Think about that, why don't you."

She slammed the door shut and pocketed her dagger, turning to find Wulfric shifted and running to the edge of the village. She sighed and gathered the clothes that were strewn about the street before following him.

Half an hour later, they were shivering and putting their clothes back on beside a tree. The village lights had dimmed and the dark helrose hedge back to the castle loomed dark and dreary. Yet she wasn't afraid. She was never afraid.

Once dressed, Wulfric rubbed a hand down his face and sighed, his shoulders low. "Sorry, I just... I can't listen to them twist it. Not when I know the truth."

"I know," she said. "But we need to be smart about this. Let the truth unravel on its own. We've planted the seeds to flame up the rumors and get people talking."

They followed the path back to the castle in silence,

boots crunching through frost. He was processing and would probably talk when they got back to their room. She knew he was worried–about the wizard, the winter, feeding his people, but most of all about his daughter.

As they neared the north wing of the castle, a warm glow shone through Knox's office window. Scarlet paused and said softly, "We should tell Knox what the Hunter said."

Wulfric nodded and knocked once before nudging the door open.

Knox looked up from his desk, maps and reports spread around him. "Back already? What time is it?"

"Past midnight, but we got some intel," Scarlet said. "Dragon Claws performed a ritual in Venshire. Another daemon blizzard, but this one is moving north."

Eirwyn, curled up on the couch with her egg cradled in a new wrap, looked up sleepily. "The capital's close to Venshire."

Scarlet nodded. "The queen commanded the Dragon Claws and brought a daemon."

Knox hissed a breath between his teeth. "Damn. Can you confirm this?"

"I want to investigate it," Scarlet said, then paused. "But I do trust the one who saw it. As much as I trust any Hunter."

Knox rose and pulled something from a drawer–a small circular pocket mirror with glowing runes on the sides. "Take this. Call if anything goes wrong."

Scarlet snorted. "Yeah, it doesn't exactly work like that."

"Scarlet–" Knox warned, gas floating from his nose to the desk.

She held up a hand and took the talkie. "You planning to leave your mate and egg and fly across the continent?

That would take hours. We'd have the problem dealt with by then."

Knox said reluctantly, "Still, be sure to check in. *Regularly*. So, I don't worry about you."

Wulfric laughed under his breath. "She's not great at the whole 'regularly' thing."

"I'm standing right here," Scarlet muttered, taking the talkie and stuffing it into her cloak.

Knox just smiled. "Exactly. Be safe, Red."

She rolled her eyes at the nickname and walked out. There was a mission to plan.

———

The sun's first light filtered through the tall windows of the library, casting a glow on the rows of ancient tomes. Using magic, she lifted a large, leather book from the shelf and placed it on a couch in the library, then sat down.

Bella's fingers trembled as they traced the ancient script. The spell, elegantly inscribed like the many others she had poured over for a week now, spoke of the enchanted golden apple tree. This book was similar to the others, but it said the fruit held the power to break even the most malignant of curses.

Her heart pounded with the possibility. The castle's hidden sanctum and this library had been her refuge since she'd arrived. She'd stayed away from most of the others, only joining them once a day for a stroll through the garden or to sit with her father at breakfast. She had just gotten her father back and did not want to lose him again.

But he and Scarlet had left yesterday for Growler territory to check in with the other alphas before going to Busparia on a reconnaissance mission. She'd felt lonelier yesterday, like her father wouldn't just pop into the library to talk with her or she wouldn't hear his laugh booming through the castle at any moment. She wasn't even sure she wanted to go to breakfast this morning, but she knew Wulfric would want her to.

For a week, she'd poured herself into researching and testing her last recipe. She had completely ignored the fact that Leopol hadn't made any further moves.

Despite his silence and their halted progress, she craved him—his touch, his voice, the impossible comfort of his presence. Even now, her body remembered the feel of his against hers, and she hated how much she wanted more.

She'd been with men, sure—what tavern owner hadn't? But she was usually the one deigning to give the time of day to a man.

A bird tweeted a greeting as it flew past the window, and she shook her head, glancing down at the forgotten book in her lap.

The room was thick with dusty silence and the musty scent of ancient knowledge. It seemed to press in around her, as if eager to witness the unraveling of this long-guarded enigma. Her reading glasses slid down the bridge of her nose, and she pushed them back up, a habitual motion that grounded her in a surge of determination.

Bella's translucent fingers traced the embossed runes that spiraled across the heavy, leather-bound spine. Her mind wandered as she read, searching for what, she wasn't sure. They'd gone over every single tome about the golden apple that they'd found, but they were stalled. Without the apple, she couldn't test it on the working recipe she'd developed thus far.

"Can I fetch anything for you, Bella?" Eirwyn's voice danced through the silence like a gentle breeze, her presence a comforting warmth against the chill of her ghostly existence.

Bella turned toward the door of the library, the slight rustle of her gown echoing softly as she set the book down and stood, floating toward her table.

"Good morning, Eirwyn. Not fetch, but could you mix these ingredients for me? My hands can't manage."

"Of course," she replied with a smile, approaching the small table Bella had taken as her own in the vast library. Hidden in the corner, natural light fell on the desk throughout most of the day.

She didn't have the magical apple, but she still wanted to test the recipe, although she was loath to test it on a live subject. Losing Sharlo and Ignot were still too sharp a pain in her chest.

She'd spent days in research, various vials and pouches lay scattered along with a few key texts she'd found. Like other mornings, Eirwyn's nimble fingers worked deftly, measuring powders and liquids with practiced ease.

As she poured a pinch of shimmering dust into the delicate glass beaker, Eirwyn said, "We missed you at dinner last night."

Bella sighed and leaned forward, watching the mixture. "There's no point in going when I can't eat. My time is best spent finding a cure for the curse. It would go so much faster if I could do precise measurements like this."

She waved a hand to Eirwyn, her voice laden with wishful longing.

"Say no more," Eirwyn assured, her concentration unwavering as she continued her precise work. "I'm here to help with whatever you require. But your spirit form isn't all bad, is it? You're not really sleeping, for instance. Feels like I have to take multiple naps a day just to keep from falling asleep at the dinner table."

Bella smiled, a pang in her chest. "That's because you just birthed a dragon egg. Your body is still recovering. Give yourself some grace. Are you taking the herb mixture Lailant left you?"

Eirwyn's nose wrinkled. "Every morning. It's awful. Why can't potions taste better?"

Bella laughed. "Don't even get me started. I still can't stomach the scent of cinnamon. Not after that last potion that—"

She cut off her words abruptly. Eirwyn glanced up, both of their smiles falling.

"The one that was made of Gastone's heart?"

Slowly, Bella nodded. "I—I'm sorry again."

Eirwyn blinked and shrugged, turning back to the task even as she frowned, and her shoulders sagged. Bella knew her actions had hurt her friend.

"It wasn't your fault, Bella. We've talked about this. It was the wizard."

Bella stepped closer to the edge of the table, pushing her hand to flip the pages of the book. Magic flared, and words blurred. Her hand dropped. Even though her chest was tight, the emotions as strong as ever, they weren't as over-whelming as they'd been when she'd first come to Hartsgrove.

"Logically, I know that, but it doesn't absolve me of guilt. I should've known better than to trust your brother, after all you'd told me through the years."

Eirwyn put the bottle on the table and looked at Bella, her blue eyes sparkling in the early morning light. "We learn from our mistakes, Bella. That's all we can do in life.

Perhaps when I tell you to trust Leopol, you'll actually listen, though?"

Bella rolled her eyes and blushed. "Perhaps. We're growing close, but I wish we were making more progress. Without the golden apple, we have nothing to experiment with."

Eirwyn frowned, her lips pursed. "If the winter would dissipate, we'd be able to see if the transplanted golden apple tree survived or not."

Bella blinked in surprise. "Leopol explained about the golden apple tree's destruction in your battle with the bone dragon. I saw the skinny little sapling when I arrived, but Scarlet said it's not really growing. Is that what you're talking about?"

Eirwyn's head tilted to the side. "We replanted what we could, under the bone dragon in the center of the oak grove outside the castle."

Bella remembered seeing it upon her arrival, but she didn't realize its significance. A flash of magic filled her, and she nodded as she connected the pieces in her mind.

"So, we need to stimulate the plant growth or reverse the winter's effect, perhaps create a greenhouse around it?" Bella mused.

Eirwyn's eyes widened as she smiled. "Oh, that's a great idea. Let me take you to the gardeners before we go to breakfast. You can ask them what they've already been doing."

Eagerly, they left the library. It felt good, like they were on the right track.

Chapter Eleven

Leopol pushed open the heavy oak door to Knox's office, the familiar scent of ink and parchment greeting him like an old friend. Morning light spilled across the cluttered desk where Knox hunched over a tangle of maps and supply lists, his brow furrowed in concentration.

"Trouble with Vidrland again?" Leopol asked, his voice echoing slightly in the expansive room.

Knox glanced up, a weary smile tugging at his lips. "No, not Vidrland. The druids have that bustling town under control. No, this is the northern town."

When the curse had spread from the Winter Palace, the citizens of Demerel had fled into the Feral Forest under Knox and Eirwyn's protection. They'd gone to the Robin's camp of Vidrland, and Knox had used his magic to grow trees into living houses and buildings. It was the only way the people had survived the harshness of winter.

Once that work had been completed, Knox had gone north to the dwarves with a group of the hardiest men and families to establish a new town there. They were to help the dwarves mass produce magical items to use as trade goods with Glathen and someday, even with Busparia and the rest of the world.

"Ravrgard? What of them?" If the new outpost was having a major problem, the dwarves would've used their new pocket talkie device to tell Knox of the emergency. With a letter, Leopol wasn't as concerned with whatever problem had cropped up.

"They're eating through supplies faster than we anticipated," he admitted, gesturing to the documents that lay scattered before him. "At this rate, we'll lose workers in the mines to starvation before we can even get a spring crop in the ground."

Leopol nodded, his gaze sweeping over the papers as he walked toward the towering bookshelf behind Knox's desk. He had spent countless hours studying the intricacies of their lands, and the solution came to him as naturally as breathing.

Leopol said, "There's a surplus from our biggest Glathen importer. The mayor of Talma is desperate for income to revitalize the dilapidated town, and the daemon-induced long winter hasn't affected Glathen as much as Busparia and the Feral Forest yet."

"It's definitely spreading that way though," Knox murmured.

Leopol nodded and pointed to the town on the map hanging beside the desk. "It is, yes, but if we can reroute some of that stockpile before it reaches them, Ravrgard will have enough food without taking from Vidrland or here at Hartsgrove. It would mean adjusting trade routes temporarily, but it should tide them over until the treaty with Glathen is finalized."

"Brilliant," Knox murmured, already reaching for a

quill to make notes. "Now to just focus on securing the actual treaty."

"And ending the curse, stopping the daemons from dragging out winter, defeating the wizard, getting Bella her body back..." Leopol's voice trailed off as he heaved a weary sigh.

Knox groaned and rubbed his temples, sitting back in the chair. "Exactly. So many things to do and not enough time in the day."

"Tell me about it," Leopol said, sliding the tome on dragonology back into its rightful place on the shelf. He liked solving problems and helping his new king, but it did seem like they were never ending. Still, helping solve a simple trade supply issue made him feel less useless in the grand scheme of things.

The weighty leather-bound book felt cool under his fingers, a stark contrast to the fire that seemed to perpetually simmer within him ever since he'd first touched Bella. He let his hand linger on the spine for a moment longer before turning back to face Knox, ready to tackle the next challenge.

Knox's eyes trailed after Leopol, noting the book he placed back on the shelf. "What are you doing with that one?" he inquired with a hint of curiosity coloring his voice, his chin propped on his hand with an elbow on the arm of the chair.

Leopol rubbed his chin thoughtfully, the rough scrape of stubble under his fingers grounding him momentarily, triggering a faint memory of before Celawyn. This spirit form was what he'd been before he'd come here, but he couldn't remember anything of that time—where he'd been, with who, or even what he'd been doing. He shook it off and focused on his cousin.

"Bella," he said, the name rolling off his tongue, heavy with emotion.

Knox leaned back, his expression going sympathetic. "Ah, you still haven't told her she's your mate?"

Leopol shook his head. "No, we kissed, but it freaked her out."

Knox frowned. "Why?"

Leopol shrugged and leaned against the bookshelf, crossing his arms. "Damned if I know. Maybe the intensity of it scared her off? If she felt half as much as I did, she was probably shaken to her core."

He glanced at the rising sun out the window, the giant eagles circling the western wall. Knox didn't say anything, just allowed Leopol time to process his thoughts.

Leopol finally sighed. "I thought it best not to push her about this chemistry between us. But this past week, every attempt to maintain distance from her has only drawn me closer. The more I'm with her, the more I'm consumed by this primal urge to claim her, mark her as mine. It's unlike anything I've ever felt before."

A knowing chuckle escaped Knox, a resonant sound that filled the room with warmth as he shook his head. "Ah, the call of the mate bond. Eirwyn definitely took me by surprise too."

His laughter was one of camaraderie, making Leopol feel a closer kinship than he had before.

When Knox and Eirwyn had stumbled into Hartsgrove and woken up Leopol's spirit, Knox hadn't known he was a full-blooded dragon. Leopol had told him as much as he could remember in those few days before the bone dragon's attack and their subsequent departure for help and healing.

Now they were mated, happy despite the chaos of

leading a fledging nation, and expecting the first dragonling in centuries.

Leopol shifted his weight from one foot to the other, his gaze settling on Knox with a mixture of hope and apprehension. The morning light filtered through the office window, illuminating his dragon cousin. "Any helpful relationship suggestions? It's my first time navigating this type of thing."

Knox leaned back in his chair, the creak of the leather and the solid thump of his boots hitting the floor underscoring the gravity of the conversation.

Knox snorted. "Advice? Don't you remember when I came here last year? We pored over every book about dragon biology we could find just to make sure I wasn't going to hurt Eirwyn with my gas or poison. Hell, I'd been a virgin until her."

Most dragons who eventually found mates didn't feel desire at all, but Knox's tone made Leopol want to laugh and tease.

He smirked. "Yet within days, you two were fucking on the front lawn for anyone to see."

Knox's cheeks darkened, and Leopol laughed outright.

"I blame the mate bond," Knox said, his mulish expression making Leopol's chest feel lighter. He'd missed this type of friendship, missed Feralt, Knox's father. These teasing exchanges helped him feel more like himself, more normal.

"I know," Leopol said softly. "But that's why I'm asking you for advice. You've experienced it. Somehow you convinced Eirwyn to accept the mate bond, and I have no clue how to do that with Bella."

Leopol sighed, running his hand through his hair in a gesture that reminded him of a time from before Celawyn.

Those memories were still fuzzy, no matter how hard he meditated and tried to remember.

"Finding a mate is not something we take lightly. I'm not sure how rare it was when you were alive, but today?" His gaze held a certain reverence, a respect for the rarity and sanctity of the connection Leopol was grappling with. "It's a rare gift, one that comes once in a lifetime, if at all. It changes everything."

Leopol felt the weight of Knox's words settle over him like a mantle. This was more than just a fleeting romance or a passionate entanglement; it was the potential forging of a bond that would span centuries. Knox's serious expression served as a reminder of what was at stake—a mate for a dragon was a treasure beyond measure.

He waited, feeling the *but* hovering in the air.

"But you can't learn how to form and maintain a relationship from a book. It's something you have to feel your way through, doing what's right for you and your partner. What worked with Eirwyn and I might not work for you and Bella."

The gentleness in his voice contradicted his gruff, serious expression.

"Eirwyn had no problems jumping into the mating rituals, but Bella is a different woman. What's holding her back?"

Aside from the fact he hadn't told her they were mates? Leopol sighed and stared out the window behind Knox, knowing it was probably her experience with Gastone that had her so hesitant.

The birds chirping, the sun rising over the trees, the calm, everyday morning was deceiving because inside, he was a raging storm of tumultuous emotions about Bella.

Turning from the peaceful scene outside, he looked at Knox, his expression a mix of frustration and admiration for Bella.

"She insists on focusing on one thing at a time," Leopol said, pacing slowly before Knox's desk. "First is fixing the curse. Then it's defeating the wizard and getting her body back."

Knox's eyes followed Leopol's movements, nodding once as if in affirmation of Bella's strategy. "That's a good plan," he said, the tone of his voice conveying both approval and a hint of caution. "Can you hold off that long on claiming her?"

Leopol's hand clenched at his side, the knuckles whitening as he turned to face Knox squarely. "I don't know. I won't force her to accept me, though. I'm not a savage like our ancestors of the past. I have to somehow convince her to take a chance, but she's still dealing with the emotional trauma from her marriage to Gastone. How do I fight something like that?"

His eyes bore the intensity of a storm yet to break, his voice laced with an urgency that betrayed the calm he tried to exude. "Plus, I can't stop thinking about what you said."

"What I said?" Knox asked, his brows rising.

"Yes, you. What if she gets back in her body, and I still can't find mine? What if finding my body has a time limit too, like with her rose, and I just don't know it?" He paced in front of the desk, lost in the what ifs.

Knox, who had been leaning back in his chair with an air of nonchalance, straightened abruptly. His fingers stilled atop the stack of papers, and his expression shifted from mild interest to stark confusion. He stared hard at Leopol, the lines of his forehead deepening into a frown. "What the fuck are you talking about? What body?"

Leopol froze in front of the desk, then raked a hand over his face. "Lights above, I didn't tell you about that."

"Tell me what, Leopol?"

"I... lied to you," he said, his chest tight. "When you left Hartsgrove when Eirwyn was injured, I told you I couldn't leave because I was tied here as a spirit. But the truth is... I wasn't ready to admit the truth because I wasn't sure if it was real or just wishful thinking on my part."

"Wishful thinking? What truth?" Knox asked.

Leopol nodded. "She anchors me with this mate bond. I can do more than I ever could drifting alone as a spirit. Not just with magical manipulation or interacting with objects, but my memories came back. Everything from my time with the dragons." His voice was soft, hesitant. "I *do* have a body in the castle... somewhere."

"A body..."

Leopol turned to pace again, each step measured and deliberate even though his words tumbled forth like a fountain.

"There was a battle," he began, his gaze trailing along the ornate patterns of the rug beneath his feet.

"The one that killed my parents," Knox said.

Leopol waved a hand as he glanced at his cousin. "Yes, that one. Except I was fighting someone else in the drawing room. I don't remember dying–but I know I didn't."

His eyes grew distant as he visualized the scene. "I remember everything up to stepping into the drawing room to face the enemy. I know that once I find my body, the rest of that battle will come back to me. It's why I've been searching in every hidden nook and cranny, every forgotten corner since you woke me from that darkness when you came to Hartsgrove."

"But you haven't found it."

Resolve had his shoulders straighten behind him. "I will. I'm certain it's here, within these walls... somewhere." His voice held a note of conviction, a deep-seated belief that was unshakeable, but several notes of doubt gnawed at him.

Knox leaned back in his chair, fingers gripping his chin as he scrutinized Leopol with a mix of skepticism and curiosity. "Really? Are you certain, or are you just hopeful?"

The words cut through the morning stillness of the office, sharp and direct and so reminiscent of Feralt, it made a pang settle in his chest.

Leopol met Knox's gaze squarely, his jaw firming with unwavering determination. "I'm as certain of that as I am that Bella is my mate," he declared.

It was more than conviction; it was an intrinsic knowledge that resonated within him, as clear and true as the magic that once danced along his scales.

Knox's expression shifted from skepticism to resigned understanding, his hand absentmindedly reaching up to scratch at the place where his human flesh met the toughened scales at his temple. Leopol's gaze lingered on the motion, a pang of nostalgia flooding him as he remembered the sensation of his own scales—how they would bristle with emotion and prickle in response to the changing winds.

He tucked his hands into his pockets, the weight of unspoken secrets tugging at his conscience. He still hadn't told Knox everything, and now was as good of a time as any.

There was so much more he could share about his fragmented past, about the mysteries that seemed to unravel and twist with each moment he spent as a dragon in Celawyn.

But he held back, biting down on the truths that might

only burden Knox further. His cousin had his own dragons to slay, metaphorically speaking.

Knox sighed. "Well hells, it looks like we have a body to find."

Leopol exhaled sharply, running a hand through his hair before letting out a sigh that seemed to carry all his frustrations and uncertainties.

"You believe me?" he asked, half surprised.

Knox straightened the papers on his desk and nodded once. "Of course. You're my cousin, but you've also proven yourself these past few months. If you say it, it's the truth. You're honorable, Leopol. We all know you're a man of your word."

Leopol blinked rapidly, relief and pride and gratitude filling him to know that the last dragon, his last family, believed in him.

"How can I help?" Knox asked, switching to fix-it mode.

Leopol shuddered a ragged breath and turned to pace once more. "I'm repeating the search of places I've already looked. It's just all kinds of fucked up, and feels pointless, and I don't know what to do about it," he confessed, his voice low and tight with emotion.

He turned on his heels and strode in the other direction. "I can't think or concentrate on anything when I'm with Bella. All I want to do is…"

His words trailed off, unfinished, but the longing in them echoed loudly in the silence of Knox's office.

Knox leaned back in his chair, the leather creaking under his weight as he regarded Leopol with an expression that was part amusement, part sympathy. "Yeah, yeah, I get it," he said, the corner of his lips quirking up in a knowing smirk. "Maybe give her some space? It'd do you both some good, I think."

Leopol's brow furrowed as he stopped in front of the desk again. "What do you mean?" he asked, genuinely perplexed. How could distancing himself from Bella help when every instinct roared for closeness?

"If you can't think with her around, then don't be around her for a day or two. It'll let you think so you can find your body, and it might help her want to be closer to you too."

Leopol frowned, still confused as Knox continued.

"Absence makes the heart grow fonder and all that," Knox said, his voice taking on a reflective note as he leaned forward to lean on the desk. "When I left Eirwyn at the dwarves, she came flying off after me. It... hurt... to be separated from her even by a day, to think that she was going to die, but it really showed both of us how much we wanted to be together."

Leopol's hand drifted up to scratch at his chin, the stubble there a testament to the days spent in anxious contemplation rather than grooming. The notion of absence was like a foreign spell—one he had never contemplated casting, especially not when every fiber of his being wanted proximity, to be near Bella, to ensure her safety and succumb to the pull of their bond.

But if it worked for Knox...

He nodded slowly, his mind's eye picturing Bella, her fierce concentration, her single-mindedness. He could give her space to focus on breaking the curse, on reclaiming her body from the wizard's twisted enchantments. And perhaps, in doing so, allow her to feel the absence of his presence, to ponder the depth of their connection without the distraction of his constant nearness.

It might grant him clarity on where to find his body too.

"Alright," Leopol conceded, his resolve firming with the

decision. Turning on his heel, he strode toward the door, pausing just before opening it. "In that case, if you see her at breakfast, tell her I'm working on the west wing project today and wanted to get an early start."

The words felt strange on his tongue, like a spell he wasn't sure he had mastered. But they held power—the power to test the strength of their fledgling bond, to give Bella the room she needed, and perhaps to stir within her the same restless longing he felt every moment they were apart.

Leopol's hand hesitated on the doorknob, the cool metal grounding him as he sought to steady his heart—a wild drumbeat in his chest. He couldn't really feel it, but he held on to the memory of the sensations, which became increasingly harder each day. With a deep breath that did little to calm the tempest within, he pushed the door open with a blast of magic and stepped through the threshold.

Leopol could feel Knox's gaze heavy on his back, carrying with it the weight of shared understanding and unspoken encouragement.

"Will do, cousin," Knox called out, the laughter clear in his voice. It was a warm sound, one that seemed to linger in the air even as Leopol used magic to open the door. "Good luck."

The words echoed after him as he closed the door behind him, following Leopol like a whispered spell. Good luck—simple words, yet they held a multitude of meanings. They were a benediction, a hope, and perhaps even a small spell for success in this unconventional strategy he had agreed to undertake.

With each step down the hall, the distance between him and Bella grew, tugging at his insides like invisible chains. Yet, he walked on, the determination set in his jaw, his stride purposeful. Today, he would immerse himself in tasks and distractions, burying thoughts of her beneath the weight of duty.

But even as he turned the corner, Leopol couldn't shake off the feeling that he was not just walking towards his work in the west wing but also, somehow, towards an inevitable crossroad of their fates.

Chapter Twelve

The frostbitten wind stung Scarlet's cheeks as she crouched on a snow-laden ridge, watching the Dragon Claws move across the frozen field below, following a small, frozen creek. This land should've been bursting with late spring wheat and golden barley, but the frost clung unnaturally thick, creeping like rot from the capital. Nothing grew, making the Buspartans hungry and desperate. A dangerous combination.

She shifted and glanced at Wulfric, who kneeled beside her near the top of the ridge, his Growler eyes glinting in the dark as they watched the three below.

Odd. There should've been more.

A branch broke behind them, loud in the stillness, and she whipped her head around.

"Ambush!" she yelled, launching toward their back as Dragon Claws burst from the shadows like arrows loosed from a bow. Scarlet sprinted at them, blades flashing. There were no screams—just snarls and shifting, magic and steel flying as the clash began.

It was a brutal, bladed dance.

Scarlet ducked under a swipe from a Claw with spiked gauntlets, slashing his hamstrings as Wulfric slammed into another, claws raking down the man's chest. She heard the crack of bone, the wheeze of breath, the cry of one of their own.

She twisted—but not fast enough to save Bren, the youngest of their squad. His body hit the snow, blood blooming like ink in water as two Claws stepped away from him.

Rage sparked, but beneath it, shame cut through. She was the best Hunter in Busparia, yet *they'd ambushed her.* Crept through her blind spot, their auras undetected.

Scarlet twisted again, blades flashing with the rage of pain, grief, and failure. She carved through a Claw's throat without slowing. Minutes—maybe less—and it was over. Blood steamed on the snow. The wounded moaned.

The last Dragon Claw tried to run. Scarlet shifted into a deer to catch him quickly, then tackled him in her wolf form.

She straddled his chest, shifting back to normal with her blade against his throat, naked and cold but not caring. "Where's your master marching?"

The Claw spat. "Long live the Queen."

Wulfric crouched beside her, bleeding from a gash down his arm. "You want me to hold him, or do you want to have fun first?"

Scarlet smiled darkly in anticipation. These bastards had given the forest Growlers a terrible reputation and two of her pack mates lay dead nearby. "Fun for me, but not for you, Claw."

Hours later, the Claw moaned where he sat tied against the tree, skin blotched from truthleaf extract and frostbitten appendages. Scarlet leaned in, clothed now, and calmly cleaned her bloody dagger on the Claw's fur.

"Now tell me the truth. You serve the monster queen in the capital of Busparia?"

"Yes," the Dragon Claw ground out, lips barely moving as he tried to keep his mouth shut. He gagged as if to vomit, but she grabbed his muzzle and held it closed.

"None of that," she said. "Throwing it up won't help. Tell us what we want, and you'll get the antidote."

Wulfric kneeled beside him, hands on knees. "Tell me what the false queen plans to do."

"Going to Glathen," the Claw rasped. "The Queen calls the daemons... forging bonds with death, winter, shadow, and more."

"Who leads the Dragon Claws?" Scarlet asked.

"Always the ruler of Busparia." The Claw tried to bite his tongue, but it didn't stop him.

"What is the plan in Glathen?" Wulfric asked.

"Raise an undead army, secure the continent, and bring back Asmoroth." The Claw bit down on his tongue, blood running down his lips. The truthleaf had him in its grip now.

A chill went through her, and it had nothing to do with the weather. The ancient god of death was involved in all this? *Fuck.* They were all fucked.

Wulfric swore and kicked a stone across the field. "We need to warn the others."

Scarlet rose, wiping her blade on the man's cloak as she got a grip on her panic. "We need to split. You warn the tribes and prepare them. They'll try marching along the Southern Road, so I'll go along that route before meeting you at the Growler camp."

Wulfric growled and grabbed her wrist, spinning her

into him. His arm around her waist was like fur wrapped steel. "I'm not splitting up from you. Where you go, I go."

Some of her chill melted at his words, and she reached up to stroke his soft cheek. "Fine, we'll go together along the Southern Road and send the rest of our pack back to camp with the wounded."

He nodded and turned from her. "We'll all leave at dawn. Call Knox?"

She pulled the talkie from her satchel and pressed the runes. "Knox? Come in. This is Scarlet."

His voice crackled through. "What happened? Are you safe?"

"Ran into the Dragon Claws. One dead. Five wounded. Captured a Claw and truthleaf forced him to talk."

"And what did he say?"

"The wizard is going for Glathen with his daemons. We're heading back to prepare our people and gather reinforcements. Warn Eirwyn. Another war is coming, with Asmoroth at the root of it."

A pause, then Knox sighed heavily. "We'll be ready."

Scarlet clicked the rune and tucked it into her pocket. Wulfric moved from pallet to pallet, checking the scraped, bruised, and bloodied Growlers.

Scarlet looked down at the Dragon Claw, his tongue swelling. Wulfric glanced at her as the Claw began to convulse.

"Still got that edge, bunny?" he murmured.

"Only when I need it," she said.

He nodded toward the Claw. "What happened to the antidote?"

She growled, "Did Bren get an antidote? Will Clark live?"

Wulfric exhaled through his nose, shrugged, and turned back to work.

Her need for vengeance had shifted in the months she'd learned to love and be loved by him—but mercy had never been part of her job.

It was hard, but someone had to do it. Might as well be her. The next morning, they vanished into Busparia, snow trailing in their wake.

The wind rushed past as another screech split the sky.

Eirwyn flinched just in time to see one of the newer riders—a broad-shouldered mountain boy—go somersaulting off a giant eagle's back. His scream was high and frantic, flailing as the ground rushed toward him.

She gripped the egg tightly, fear starting to rise—but before it took hold, a flash of green cut through the air.

Knox dove after him, catching him with one powerful arm. His wings snapped open to slow the descent, both of them landing on the frozen ground of the clearing near the newly erected village outside Hartsgrove Castle.

The eagle trilled happily as if it had been a planned maneuver.

Eirwyn pressed her hand against the dragon egg satchel slung across her chest, instinctively shielding it as she stalked forward. The strap dug into her shoulder—the awkward angle made her lopsided—but she didn't dare let go.

The dragon egg inside pulsed faintly with life and magic, and any time she left it in a nest or cradle too long, her skin itched like wildfire until it was back in her arms.

"Again?" she glowered at the amused eagle still circling overhead.

Knox stood, shifting into his normal hybrid form and dusting snow off himself and the shaken rider, murmuring something soothing before sending the man off toward the mess tent.

"They're testing us," he said, strolling toward her with that prowling, confident gait of his. "I think they're genuinely amused by how worthless humans are at balance."

"They're *playing*, doing this on purpose," she snapped. "They understand me—I know you do," she shouted up at the eagle. She turned back to Knox. "But they're treating this like a game."

"You *are* carrying an egg like a satchel of stolen pastries," he said, eyeing the awkward sling across her chest.

She snorted. "It's the only way I can keep him close."

"A flight might help settle your nerves," Knox said, stepping close and running his hand up and down her spine.

She shivered and stepped closer to his warmth. "I haven't flown since the birth. I can't focus on my magic and keeping my wings stable while worrying about carrying him."

Knox's smile softened. "I know you miss it. I'll hold him if you want to take a quick lap around. You know how my skin itches when I don't shift and fly. Perhaps you need the release."

"I know I do, but it's not as intense of a feeling as I feel when the egg isn't close enough to touch," she admitted, running a hand over the thick leather strap. "A quick flight on your back still gives me some of that peace of the wind, the speed, the quiet freedom in the air..."

"It's not the same," he said softly, pulling her into a soft hug, the dragon egg between them. Safe, warm, and pulsing. She sighed in relief as some of the stress of eagle training lifted.

"No," she agreed, leaning into him. "But it's close enough for now."

He kissed her temple. "I don't like seeing you out of sorts, especially when I can't fix it, and you won't let me carry him. Are you sure Leopol's right?"

She laughed and nodded, pulling back to look up at him. "Yes, Leopol said it's normal for mothers of dragons to feel the bond physically, not to want to let go of their egg and protect it at all costs. He even showed me the book where it explained it."

Knox sighed and adjusted the satchel slightly to ease the weight off her sore shoulder. "Then let me at least take you to the tailor later. There *has* to be a better way to carry a dragon egg than this."

"If they can make something that doesn't make me feel like I'm going into battle with a coconut strapped to my chest, I'm in," she muttered, rolling her shoulder carefully.

"I know your back's screaming by the end of the day," he said, his hand warm and steady against her spine. "Come on, let's get back to the castle and get ready for dinner. Perhaps you can lay down for a bit. Take a hot bath to ease the sore muscles?"

She groaned and turned to walk beside him. "Gods, twist my arm, why don't ya?"

He chuckled, green gas flowing from his nose as they left the eagle field behind. Knox barked a few dismissing orders to the straggly band of rebels who were brave enough to attempt an eagle ride. A few of the birds gave playful chirps as they flew loops overhead, but Eirwyn ignored them.

Soon they reached the edge of the helrose hedge. Its twisted, thorny branches bristled with pink blossoms despite the freezing temperatures, pulsing faintly like breathing hearts. The hedge pulsed with old magic and impossible memories.

"They bloomed again last night," Knox said, brushing a flower with the back of his hand.

Eirwyn slowed. The helrose blossoms had opened fully—lush and pink despite the frost—pulsing like tiny hearts.

"I noticed," she murmured. "It's Bella. Her magic's waking the land, even without trying. She doesn't even realize it."

Her voice softened with awe, but the warmth faded just as quickly. "And still, our people fear her."

Knox sighed, his fingers trailing a thorn. "Some say she should be dead or imprisoned. Others still think she's cursed. Dangerous."

"She *is* cursed," Eirwyn admitted, shifting the egg against her aching shoulder. "But not dangerous. Not to us or anyone in the forest—or Busparia. She's a friend. If they'd just accept her as she is, they'd see that."

Knox's shoulders dipped with another sigh, like the weight of the entire kingdom pressed down on his spine. "The fear around her isn't just political. These people—many of them were cursed by that magic blast. They're scared this is permanent, that they'll never be whole again."

"I still don't think *she* did it," Eirwyn said, her fingers curling protectively around the satchel strap. "Not really. She was so... cold, totally unlike herself those last few weeks in Demerel. Gastone twisted her—put something in her head. Maybe it was the wizard speaking through him like she says, but it definitely was a spell of some kind. Either way, that woman who married my brother and wore the crown? That wasn't really her, you know?"

Knox glanced at her, one brow raised in gentle skepticism.

"She's back to herself now," Eirwyn added quickly. "I don't care if she's half-dead, cursed, or haunted. The Bella we have now? She's the one I remember. She's trying to save everyone, fix everything, like she always does."

Knox stepped closer and laid his hand against her back, rubbing slow, grounding circles. "She's more the person I remember from the tavern, that's for sure. Even ghost-tethered and helpless as she seems, she's stronger than any of us realize. The forest knows it. I know it. Soon, the others will too."

Eirwyn's brows furrowed. "Not sure how they'll see that when she's holed up in the library all day. She won't even come to dinner."

"It's probably hard for her," Knox said. "To sit at a table and not eat. To be surrounded by people who flinch when she walks by. For someone who ran a tavern with ease to become a queen who exploded with magic and cursed a kingdom... it's a lot. People have forgotten she's got a soft heart under all that steel. They'll remember that, eventually."

Eirwyn arched a brow at him. "She used to navigate the tavern with ease, but when she got engaged to Gastone and we had all those fucking balls and political dinners, it was like she froze. Like she thought she wasn't enough... I wouldn't put it past Gastone to plant those seeds of doubt."

Knox's grin curled as they kept walking. "She has a tough-as-nails exterior but a secret fluffy core. Don't tell her I said that, or she'll sic a chair army on me or that fork and spoon. Vicious little things."

Eirwyn snorted. "Why Knox, that's quite perceptive of you."

His gaze turned warm, molten, the kind of look that always curled heat through her veins. "What can I say? Being king teaches a guy how to observe, think, and make a plan before acting."

"Taking after Leopol, are we?" she teased. "Though from what Ashur and the Robins say, you were pretty strategic before Hartsgrove."

He shrugged, raking a hand over the scaled side of his head. "I'm just saying... don't worry about Bella. Our people will come around—especially once the cure works."

Eirwyn's expression faltered. "*If* it works."

Knox glanced at her but didn't press. He just took her hand, warm and steady, as they walked in silence.

Ahead, Hartsgrove Castle rose above them, its bright banners snapping in the frigid wind. Side by side, they moved forward—quiet, hopeful, and together.

Chapter Thirteen

Later that evening, Bella stretched and left the sanctum. After being holed up in the library for days, trying to find the elusive solution, it had been nice getting outside with Eirwyn earlier.

Talking with the gardeners hadn't gone the way she'd wanted, though. They'd seemed to vibrate with anger when Eirwyn had introduced them earlier. They obviously blamed her for the curse, which was understandable.

Their angry gazes had quickly sent her back into the library for the rest of the day. It had been downhill from there. She hadn't seen Leopol at all. Usually, he stopped by for a few hours here and there in between his other duties helping Knox run the forest kingdom.

Her tension had grown higher the more time she'd gone without seeing him, though. She had only been here a week, but she'd already gotten attached. Just one day without seeing him, and the loneliness had crept back into her heart. And that scared the shit out of her.

That kiss played on repeat in her mind, especially at

night when she was alone in her room. Her emotions were so strong in this incorporeal form. That must be why she was so obsessed with that kiss, why it had been so good.

Unable to concentrate on her research, she slipped down the hall and out a side door. With dinner almost ready, she knew the gardeners would be done working for the day. She wanted to investigate the apple tree without the suspicious glares of others around. Perhaps she'd find something she'd missed.

When she passed the sitting room windows, she paused. The memory of the journey through the Feral Forest last week was still vivid in her mind. The gods had given her a vision in the fire that night with Scarlet. A dragon in hybrid form had fought inside that sitting room, but the vision hadn't shown the victor. It had just jumped to the dragon, injured and bleeding, going into a cave and passing out. Possibly dying.

Not a day passed that she didn't think of that gorgeous, dangerous silver and white dragon. She wondered if he was a vision of the past, present, or future. Without answers, she continued to the circular oak grove. Emerging into the open air, she followed the castle walls.

The very earth beneath her feet seemed to hum with latent energy, guiding her steps toward the grove's center. The anticipation thrummed in her veins, each beat of her heart echoing the rhythm of a world veiled in mysticism as she slipped through the narrow space between the trunks.

There it stood, amidst a ring of towering oaks—a solitary tree gleaming with stark, empty branches. It was barely a sapling and obviously hadn't produced fruit before.

Bella's breath caught in her throat as she approached, her eyes wide as the glimmer of hope faded. Even if it could shatter the wizard's spell, it'd take years to bear fruit on its own. She *had* to find a solution.

As twilight approached, casting elongated shadows across the land, Bella knew she was on the cusp of something monumental. And yet, despite the thrill of potential victory, a shiver of foreboding crept along her spine.

She drew closer and reached out to brush the rough bark with the tips of her fingers. She pressed into the bark, not feeling it in this ethereal form, her hand passing through it.

And yet the touch sent a jolt through her, a connection igniting between the essence of the grove and the magic coursing within her. A faint memory of standing beside Gastone tickled her mind like a long-forgotten dream. They'd stared into the mirror, and he'd raised the dragon skeleton of Knox's father to kill Eirwyn once and for all.

Bella stepped back in surprise, her gaze locked on the tree that was just a few inches shorter than herself. She crossed her arms and tapped her fingers on her elbow as she thought.

The wizard had used Gastone and herself to attack with nekrotic magic, animating the skeleton.

What if the wizard already knew of the tree's existence? What if her discovery led not to salvation, but deeper into his evil web? Did he know of the tree's purpose?

She couldn't remember if Gastone had used the magic mirror that had trapped the wizard or if it had been just a regularly enchanted mirror.

Her head ached along with her heart. How many times had Gastone manipulated her in the short time they'd been married? Only now was she able to realize he'd been siphoning her magic, fuzzing her memories, and alienating her from Eirwyn.

Eirwyn. Her spine straightened as the hair lifted on the back of her neck. She needed to ask Eirwyn and Knox how safe they were here. Had the wizard ever attacked this place? Or had the protections of the forest kept him from pushing inside at all?

There were too many questions that she couldn't answer alone. Bella turned and strode back toward the castle, the weight of the unknown heavy on her shoulders.

A shadow above drew her gaze, and she paused.

The earth trembled underfoot as Knox landed near the fountain in the main driveway. His wings unfurled like the sails of a ship in the books she'd read as a child, catching the last rays of sunlight before folding against his colossal form. The sight of him—a dragon of legend—sent a ripple of both awe and unease through Bella's chest.

He was so much larger than when she'd first seen him like this. He'd been the size of a few horses then. As he landed, his form seemed to shrink to fit onto the drive. His four claws sent dirt scattering, then he shifted into his hybrid form and raked his hands along the sides of his head, stretching as he turned toward the front steps. He paused as Bella strode closer, straightening the cuffs of his sleeves.

"Didn't expect to see you out here," she said, her voice steady despite the memory of his fiery clash with Gastone.

"Nor I, you," Knox rumbled, his voice reverberating through the air. "You haven't joined us for dinner at all since you've arrived. I figured you were hiding away, working on the cure for the curse."

Guilt made her flush, and she stopped a few feet away from him. He smiled, but she was still wary of trusting anyone after the past year. She owed it to Eirwyn to try, though.

"How are the training and taming of the giant eagles

going?" Bella asked, the corners of her mouth lifting at the thought.

"Stubborn and pigheaded creatures," he grunted, a plume of green smoke escaping his nostrils in frustration. "There's no reasoning with them. They're smart as can be, but their will is all that matters."

"Sounds familiar. Hopefully, your offspring won't inherit that thinking," Bella smirked, her fingers absentmindedly tracing the lines on her palms, wishing for lines of a different kind—the creases of a tiny hand clutching hers.

"Ah," Knox let out a groan that shook the branches above, "they probably will. Between Eirwyn and I, they'll be a handful, no doubt about it. Has she always been so stubborn?"

Bella barked out a surprised laugh, the sound rusty from disuse. "Oh yes, from the first day Da brought her into the tavern. She was a handful, even at ten."

"I can't imagine a child in a tavern," he said, tilting his head.

Bella smiled and glanced at the cloudy sky, breathing in deeply as the memories of a sweeter time filled her. "We knew who she was, of course, but Da wouldn't send her back to the castle when she was cold and hungry. The plan was to feed her in the kitchens, no one the wiser that she was there. If the king didn't know, then he couldn't burn the tavern down."

Bella frowned, reconciling her long-held belief about the temperamental king with the king she'd married. They were the same drakin, but when it was just she and Gastone alone, he'd differed from what she'd expected.

"I take it she didn't stick to the plan. She never sticks to the plan." Knox's lips twisted wryly, and Bella snorted a laugh.

"Got that right," she said. "She was dancing on the tables, telling stories, and throwing shadowy figures on the ceiling by the end of the night. Had everyone eating out of the palm of her hand, including my father."

Knox's eyes pierced her soul, seeing too much. "But not you?"

She reached up to brush away a stray strand of hair from her face before she looked to the sky. "I was annoyed when she kept coming back and following me around. She was the little sister I never wanted."

Her chuckle was bittersweet, and her sigh held a hint of regret. "Then when Da left for war less than a year later, she was the joy that kept me going. In a sense, we grew up together in that tavern."

Eirwyn hadn't left her alone to run that tavern or her grandparents' shop. She'd still been a child, and Bella had barely been fifteen, but somehow, they'd made it work. When Eirwyn had gone on the diplomatic mission to Glathen last year, Bella had known that big changes were coming. She'd felt it in her soul, as if warned by the goddess herself.

Things were still changing. Eirwyn was a wife and mother, even though her egg hadn't hatched yet. Bella had watched Knox and Eirwyn this past week at breakfast. It had been a stark reminder of what lacked in her own life.

She'd thought it was possible with Gastone, had hoped that it would finally give her a genuine family. What could be better than the annoying little pseudo-sister becoming her actual sister? A pang of longing surged within her, an echo of the love and acceptance that seemed to elude her grasp and the reason she'd avoided the dinners this week.

"You sound wistful," he said.

Bella's brows rose in surprise at the insightful words. She

shrugged, fingers running over the smooth fabric of her dress. "Wouldn't you be? Now she's grown up and living the dream while I'm decidedly not."

"You're making progress, according to Leopol. The curse can be broken, and then you'll rejoin your body." He sounded confident, but she wasn't so sure.

"It's not just about getting my body back," she said, unsure of why she was talking with him so freely like this. Eirwyn had always been her confidant. She met Knox's gaze and lifted her chin. Perhaps after so long of having no one to talk to, she was now more open with people.

"Is it foolish to want something so... ordinary? Someone who loves me, a home, a family?" Bella murmured more to herself than Knox. Her gaze drifted to the horizon where the last light fought against the encroaching shadows.

"Ordinary?" Knox's form shifted, his reptilian eyes softening. "What's ordinary about yearning for a legacy and arms to welcome you home? Love isn't ordinary. It's extraordinary."

Their raw exchange hung on the brink of vulnerability. Words flowed freely, weaving a tapestry of common wants and secret anxieties. Knox shrugged, shoulders stiffening as if the open conversation was uncomfortable.

"Once this is all over and you're back on the throne of Busparia, what will you do?" He certainly sounded confident enough for the both of them.

Amusement and sadness warred within her, and her eyes darted away from Knox's penetrating gaze. "I'm not so certain I'll be on the throne. I fear I'm not cut out for that—I wasn't born to rule Busparia like Eirwyn. I was barely Queen for half a year before it all was ripped out from under me. I never even left the Winter Palace."

"Sometimes leadership is thrust upon us, even if we

don't desire it. Perhaps because we're the best person for the job, whether we believe ourselves worthy or not," Knox intoned, his gaze piercing through her defenses. "Occasionally, we are exactly what the world needs."

Her breath hitched at his words, the raw honesty binding them in a moment of unexpected kinship. As the stars began to prick the canvas of the dusky sky, his words were a soothing salve to her wounded soul.

She ducked her head to the side and wiped the corner of her eye, her voice breathless and self-deprecating as she said, "Thank you, Knox. Eirwyn is blessed by Borga to have you as a mate," she said, stepping away from the comfort of their shared solitude. "Now go on. You'll be late to dinner with your lovely wife."

Knox grinned, his teeth flashing white in the growing dimness. "Come join us. You know we'd love your company. You know *Leopol* would love your company."

Bella shrugged self-consciously. "I–I see him every day. Missing dinner doesn't make a difference. Besides, I have much to do if I'm to break this curse before the rose dies."

Knox opened his mouth to argue, but Eirwyn stepped onto the steps by the front door. She smiled when she saw them and called down from the landing, "Oh, there you are. Dinner's getting cold."

Knox turned to his wife, his face lighting with joy that sent a pang through Bella's chest. Someday someone would look at her with such longing and contentment, as if her mere presence improved his life.

"Coming, love. Was just trying to convince Bella to join us," Knox called as Eirwyn briskly walked down the stairs.

Eirwyn turned to Bella and smiled. "Of course you'll join us. Lailant is back from Vidrland and would like to see you in the drawing room first. Then you'll join us for dinner?"

Bella's brows rose and her heart raced, even as a knot of anxiety settled in her stomach. Her mentor, the woman who practically raised her after her mother died, was back. She would have a lot to say about Bella's actions and the subsequent curse.

Bella groaned, and Eirwyn grinned as she took Knox's arm. Together, the couple walked up the stairs, and Bella dragged herself after them.

Glancing over his shoulder, Knox gave her a reassuring nod. His support, though it shouldn't mean much, made her feel a little less alone in this foreign land.

She turned to the drawing room and stepped inside, a blast of magic opening it. Lailant, the medicine woman, healer, shaman, and mentor who had molded her into the woman she was today, possessed a knowledge of the arcane that seemed as vast as the oceans themselves. Bella had always tried to live up to her strict, high expectations, but the more she learned, the more she realized there was so much more to know. And it was time to face her and admit all the failures she'd made in the past year.

Chapter Fourteen

The woman stood in front of the roaring fireplace, her gnarled dark hands spotted with age held tightly behind her back. The flickering flames of the fire pit cast an eerie glow across the floor. Bella's heart raced as she recalled the countless evenings spent hunched over tomes and scrolls just trying to make any sort of magic work the way it was meant to.

When Bella floated closer, the woman turned her piercing emerald eyes and seemed to penetrate the depths of Bella's soul. Her white curly hair in several braids pulled into a messy bun atop her head was a soft halo of wisdom. Her body appeared old and frail but as always, she radiated a quiet strength born of endurance and resilience.

"There you are, child. I would hug you, but you're more fragile than I am these days, eh?" Lailant snickered, and some of the tension inside Bella melted. She smiled slowly and drifted closer.

"It's good to see you, Lailant."

Lailant's eyes softened, and her smile wavered. "You too,

child. You too. I'm sorry I didn't stick around when you arrived last week. I had pressing business in Vidrland. But you've settled in nicely?"

Bella nodded and twisted her blue skirts as she strode to the windows overlooking the garden. She gave a frustrated sigh. "This place... do you know if there was a battle here between dragons?"

The question tumbled out, something she'd been thinking of for over a week now. If anyone were to know, it'd be Lailant. She knew the most random things that defied all reason or explanation.

Lailant's soft footsteps were slow but firm as she joined Bella at the window, closing the garden door gently. Lailant tapped the glass, pointing to the oak grove with the apple tree inside.

"You already know the answer to that question, child. The boulder being the bones of Knox's father, the oak grove his mother. Feralt was a force of nature—fiery and unyielding," Lailant's hand dropped, and she sighed. "He stood alone against the drakin coup, their claws sharp with betrayal. He fought, not just with tooth and claw but with all the fire in his soul."

Bella whispered, her heart in her throat. "It wasn't enough."

Somehow, she knew. Between the vision in the fire and what she'd learned the past few days from Leopol and Eirwyn, combined with her history lessons as a child, she knew. The drakin had taken over the continent, defeating the last dragons on the planet. How Knox had survived as an egg for hundreds of years still amazed her.

The silence that followed was thick with reverence. Lailant's eyes flickered to the oak canopy. "His mother had the purest druidic magic, strong enough to weave the protection through those very trees. She stood guard over his dying corpse and kept the drakin from doing unspeakable things. With her last breath, she bound her life force with the forest, transforming into the sacred oak grove to safeguard us all."

Bella exhaled a trembling sigh, the ethereal edges of her form quivering like leaves in a silent gust. "That's why the Feral Forest tried to destroy any intruders for so many years, isn't it? Why we were always warned to stay away from the forest growing up? She was protecting it."

Lailant nodded. "Her protections are weakening, but thankfully Knox is here to pick up the mantle of responsibility."

The silence wasn't cloying or oppressive, but just enough for Bella to process the information. Eventually Lailant said, "They gave their lives for this land, their people, their homes. It's beyond noble–it's the kind of love that writes legends."

"Legends don't ease the burden of living up to them," Bella muttered, scowling as she glanced at the stars above.

"Feeling the pressure of queenship?"

Bella knew that weight, the suffocating cloak of expectation. "When I was crowned queen of Busparia, the crown felt like thorns upon my brow. I thought it would give me resources to help the people, the ability to spread more knowledge and heal the sick. But every decision, every whisper at court cast doubt. I don't belong there, Lailant."

"Yet there you need to be," Lailant countered, a smile tugging at the corner of her mouth as she turned to face Bella. "A queen without a kingdom should still fight for the future of her people."

"Of course, I'm fighting. I've been working non-stop to find a cure for the curse that haunts them. Just because I don't belong there doesn't mean I'm not going to do the right thing. Really, what else is there?" Bella responded, her words hanging between them like an unvoiced oath. "We fight, we bleed, we love with everything we have—even when it feels like we're grappling with shadows."

Bella nervously brushed the hair away from her forehead. She looked up at her mentor, her eyes pleading for guidance and support.

"The curse will be broken and all will be as it should be," Lailant said softly.

Bella crossed her arms and tapped her elbow with her fingers. "You have to bring vague platitudes into this?"

Lailant grinned. "Even the most cryptic psalms unravel in time. You're not alone in this."

She turned to face the room, turning away from the windows and pushing off her reverie. "I know, but it's hard to shake the feeling that I should be moving faster, doing more. I had almost figured out the spell and potion combination that would work."

Bella poured the pain of the past year out to her mentor, explaining how she'd had two servants with her at the Winter Palace in Demerel and how they had also been cursed. Merged with inanimate objects, they'd both taken potions before they'd been ready, resulting in their deaths.

Lailant listened patiently, not interrupting even as she walked slowly to a chair near the fire and sat. Bella drifted closer, arms waving as she explained about the cats and the plants.

"I was so close, Lailant, yet still so far from a cure," Bella said, staring into the fire.

"And what has Leopol said of your efforts? His knowledge is bigger than this castle."

Bella's heart thundered against her ribcage as Lailant's

words sliced through the haze of uncertainty that had shrouded her thoughts. "I–I haven't shared my potions with him. We've been buried in spell books and research. Our latest theory revolves around the golden apple tree, but since it isn't anywhere near blooming and bearing fruit, I can't incorporate it into the recipe to see if it's the missing ingredient," she confessed, a thread of weariness weaving through her resolve.

"Maybe it's time Leopol saw everything you're capable of," Lailant said.

Her breath caught in her throat. She'd clung to the research like a shield, afraid of revealing the chinks in her armor to Leopol. But Lailant was right; she couldn't afford to let pride hinder progress–not when so much was at stake.

"Gods, I'm terrified he'll think I'm an idiot." The words spilled from Bella, raw and unguarded. Her fingers twitched on her nose, reaching for glasses that weren't there–a phantom gesture betraying her inner turmoil. She patted her pocket, confirming their presence. Gus and Jaq had been exploring the castle, and she hadn't seen them all day.

"Leopol's not the type to mock genuine effort. And neither am I." Lailant's gaze held her own, steady and unwavering. "You have a destiny that requires you to be more than you think you are. You have to trust him and your friends and family if you're going to fix all that's broken before it's too late."

A wry chuckle escaped her lips, the sound brittle over the crackling of the fire. "Blast it, sometimes I hate when you're right."

"Of course I'm right," Lailant said, making Bella laugh before she continued. "What's the worst that can happen? He sees your failures and... what?"

Bella shrugged uncomfortably. "We start over?"

Lailant beamed and pushed herself up from the chair. "Exactly. Sometimes the best way forward is to acknowledge where we stumbled."

"Thank you, Lailant." Gratitude flooded her senses, warmer than the fire. If she were still in her body, she'd hug the old woman. Her hugs had always filled her with peace and comfort, restoring her soul when she'd most needed a mother figure.

"Anytime, Bella. Now go find Leopol in the library and set things right. I smell dinner somewhere, and I'm starving."

With a resolve forged anew, Bella followed Lailant out of the room and strode in the opposite direction down the hallway. Jumping at the permission to miss dinner, each step was a defiant drumbeat, echoing her determination and nerves.

Her thoughts tumbled over themselves, each one snagging on the undeniable allure of Leopol—his intense gaze that seemed to strip her bare, his hands that could as easily wield a sword as they could tenderly turn the fragile page of a spell book.

A flush heated her cheeks at the memory of his touch during the past week—he was always touching her, yet she didn't mind—and she cursed herself for allowing such feelings to surface now.

"Focus, Bella," she reprimanded, adjusting her glasses onto her face like a shield before battle. "There's more at stake than your damn heart."

Her pace quickened, as she navigated the familiar yet foreboding corridors through the fortress. Shadows clung to her like whispers of regrets she longed to undo. Every tapestry along the wall seemed to echo an old story, none strong enough to pull her focus from the dread coiling in her chest. Dread at confessing her failures.

It warred with anticipation at the thought of seeing him again, touching him. The day had dragged on without a glimpse of him, and the absence made her skin itch with unease.

Chapter Fifteen

Bella stepped into the open door of the library. A low humming noise reverberated through the shelves, breaking the stillness, and she smiled. Leopol often hummed when no one was around.

As she approached his desk, his eyes lit up, and a smile spread across his face. Her chest tightened. Was it just her or was that look very similar to the way Knox looked at Eirwyn? No, it couldn't be. It was just because Knox and Leopol were cousins that caused them to look alike.

Her fingers tingled with anticipation as she drew closer, and her hand brushed against his back as she came around to stand next to him. A jolt of electricity seemed to shoot through her body at the contact, making her breath catch in her throat.

"What are you reading?" she asked breathlessly, glancing down at the table. It was as if an electric current ran through the air, crackling with a magnetic energy that drew them closer.

She had tried so hard to ignore it, but her resistance was

weakening by the day. Every hour she spent in his presence distracted her from the task at hand. She'd thought being without him today would ease it, but it'd just made her want him more.

"I brought one of the spell books up here for a change of scenery. That way I'm within hearing distance if they need me at dinner."

Bella sighed and turned around to lean her ass on the edge of the table. Her hands gripped the table as she said, "I miss food. More than I miss sleep, that's for sure."

His brows rose. "You don't sleep?"

She tilted her head. "Too many nightmares. You do?"

Leopol's fingers brushed against hers, sending a jolt up her arm. She caught the flicker of something deeper in his eyes. "So different yet so similar," he said.

Her heart pounded faster at the sound of his voice, a deep baritone that resonated within her. She could hear the slight catch in his breath as he caressed her hand, and she didn't pull away.

She forced herself to stay still and not insist on this separation between them. Eirwyn and Knox thought he hung the moon. Lailant had said to trust him, and that meant trusting that his touch wasn't going to hurt her. She had seen nothing in the countless hours she'd spent with him that warranted this hesitation on her part.

She knew it was just past trauma making her cautious, but it was a hard habit to break, no matter how much she craved his kiss.

"Trust," she said, the word bursting out to hang between them like a promise.

"Trust what?" he asked, his brow furrowing.

She cleared her throat and hooked her finger with his, avoiding his gaze. "Trust you. I need to trust you."

He pulled back, breaking the contact between them. "Do you not trust me?"

She shrugged, crossing her arms and picking at the fabric on her elbow. "I do, yes. But I haven't shared the formulas for the potions I was working on at the Winter Palace. We've been researching the binding spells, the runes, the apple, but perhaps—maybe you should look at the potion formula? I—I think it's time you look over my research and tell me what you think."

Leopol stepped closer and settled his hands on her elbows, stopping her fidgeting. His eyes met hers, their electric blue color sparking something deep within her. The curve of his lips as he smiled sent her body into overdrive. Or rather, she had phantom feelings, since she was bodyless. Her breath caught and a warmth spread through her soul.

"I'd be happy to, Bella. You know that. I've not wanted to push you too fast and have just been waiting for you. I never want you to feel uncomfortable because you *can* trust me. Whatever it is, we'll handle it together."

"Together... that's what I'm most scared of," Bella drew in a deep breath, her resolve solidifying as her hands settled on his hips. She licked her lips and closed her eyes, his nearness intoxicating and clouding her senses.

"I know," he said, brushing her hair back from her face. "But you don't have to fear me or be alone anymore. I won't let anything happen to you, Bellavore. I swear it."

She whimpered and squeezed her eyes tight, her breath catching at his words, too afraid to believe him, to trust that this was real. He caressed her cheek and pulled her into his arms, cradling her tight into a cocoon of safety. She was a fool for limiting their touches this week to mere accidental grazes of the hand when his arms around her felt so right.

He cupped her face in his hands, a fire in his eyes that soothed her nerves. She was tired of being alone and afraid.

"What does that mean? You've called me that and Bellakari all week."

He paused, his eyes growing sharper, more predatory and sending a shiver down her spine. He licked his lips and glanced at her own before answering. "Bellakari is draconic for my beautiful treasure. Bellavore is the one I hunger for or my consuming beauty."

The air between them crackled with electricity, and her heart raced. "You hunger for me?"

Before she could think, Leopol leaned in, slowly closing the distance between them. Bella's breath hitched, but she didn't pull away even as papers on the table behind her rustled with unbridled magic.

She had spent too long running from love. This wasn't love though, but an exercise in trust. Trust that she could control her magic. Trust that she would be alright, even if she fell for him and something terrible happened.

She held her breath, eyes closed as she waited. His breath teased her lips, anticipation racing through her body like lightning.

"Like a starving beast, I hunger for you. It consumes me until you're all I can think about day in and day out," he said, each word sending his lips caressing over hers.

She shivered, his words a balm to her soul and his touch a match to kindling. She groaned, and his lips settled more firmly on hers, his tongue immediately sweeping inside to take advantage. It was as if he could read her mind, knew her every hidden desire.

What she really desired was him and how he made her feel. Being without him today had left her feeling self-conscious and the self-doubt in her ability to solve all these problems had skyrocketed her anxiety over the entire situation.

But when she was in his arms—hell, even when they were just in the same room—he made her feel confident, like she could take on every problem because she was badass. She saw it in his eyes, in the reverent way he touched her, in the burning hunger in his gaze.

Their kiss deepened, and she curled her hands up into his hair, the silky texture making her feel alive. He growled, sending a vibration straight to her core. Then he picked her up and set her on the table. The books crashed to the floor but neither of them paused to take stock of the mess, too absorbed in each other to care. Her knees spread as he grabbed her hips and pulled her to the edge of the table.

When his hard length met her, they both groaned. Her hands gripped his hair, tugging him closer. She wanted to consume him, inhale him until there was only this undeniable heat. She'd never felt anything like it.

The slide of his hand up her calf made her jerk, but there was no more hesitation or need to pull away from him. She was done running. Perhaps all she needed was a mindless orgasm to relax her enough to think through how to solve the problem of the cursed villagers.

His hands stroked the back of her knee, and she shivered. There was nothing mindless about Leopol though. He had shown how focused he was on her this week. How many times had she felt the weight of his gaze tracking her as she researched or moved around the sanctum or library? Even at the breakfast table while he'd been deep in conversation with Knox, his eyes had eaten her up.

It was a heady feeling to be the obsession of such a powerful man. None of the tavern patrons had ever appealed to her half as much—and a few of them, she'd slept with.

What was stopping her from giving in to this temptation that was so much stronger than anything she'd ever known?

Nothing.

She spread her legs wider as his hands traced the seam of her leg, making her shiver in anticipation. He broke the kiss and leaned back, his eyes searching hers as his thumb traced too softly across her pelvis to the other leg and back again.

"Bellavore, I—I don't know how much longer I can hold out." His voice had deepened, and his eyes blazed with a white-hot heat that seemed familiar somehow.

She thrust her hips, trying to get his thumb to stop on her clit. "Then stop playing and take me."

His eyes widened, and his features seemed to shimmer into something more dangerous, monstrous, beastly. But she barely noticed as his thumb finally—finally—stopped on her clit. Slowly, he applied pressure. Not moving, caressing, or stroking like she wanted. Just pressing on her.

Her eyes fluttered as her hips bucked, nearly desperate for more. "Please, Leopol," she begged.

For the first time, she was reduced to begging for more. She didn't have time to analyze why as a slow grin spread across his face. Goosebumps broke out across her skin right before he circled her clit, once, twice.

Then two fingers traced up her slit. He licked his lips—had his mouth shifted into something more beastly—before he said, "So slick and wet."

"Yes," she gasped, two fingers sliding inside and making her eyes flutter. "Gods above, yes. More."

His eyes flashed white again, glowing now as he sank to

his knees and pushed her skirts up around her waist. "I'll gladly feast on you, Bellavore."

Her breath hitched as she watched him, his gaze dropping to her bare pussy wide open for him. She'd been with plenty of men before, but none of them had—oh gods. His breath teased her, sending goosebumps again as his mouth settled around her clit.

Two fingers thrust inside, and her body went taut. She screamed and bucked, pulling him closer with a hand on the back of his head. Oh gods, when he said he was hungry, he wasn't kidding.

His mouth worked her into a sloppy, incoherent mess. She thrust against his mouth, moaning nothing intelligible with each swipe and suck. The pressure inside her built, and the books remaining on the table began to rattle with her magic.

She didn't even care if her magic fritzed out. There was no stopping the build up. Her body grew tighter, her thrusts more frantic.

"Leo, Leo, Leo, please," she drew out the last syllable on a gasp as his fingers shifted their angle.

He hummed as if happy about her reaction, and the sound, the vibration, the suction, the fingers hitting that sweet spot inside that no one seemed to know how to find—it came crashing around her in a flash of sizzling sparks.

She cried out, gripping his hair and holding him in place as she rode his face. Eyes closed, she shook, lost in the pulsing release of tension within her.

Slowly she eased her grip on his hair and looked down. His eyes glowed, his entire being seemed to shimmer as he stared at her with such intensity, she sucked in a stuttered breath. He hummed and lapped at her pussy.

"So, fucking delicious," he said, whispering praise with

every swipe of his long tongue. "I want to eat this pussy every damn day, mibella."

Another swipe, another ragged breath as her hands stroked his hair out of his face. "Now that I've had a taste, I can't go without. Say I can have you every day and every night. Be mine, forever."

The mention of the word forever made her pause. Blinking rapidly, their reality crashed around her, and she sat up, pushing her skirts down. He stood and licked his lips as he leaned into her, his hands on the table on either side of her hips.

The sight made her flush, but her mind was latched onto the new problem.

They were spirits. Neither of them had a forever. The complications and variables swirled inside, and she opened her mouth to point them out.

A loud slam of a door made them both jump, but instead of jumping away, she clung to the lapels of his coat. His arms tightened around her, his head snapping up as he listened. A commotion near the front door distracted them both. Shouts echoed through the castle, and Leopol pulled back, his blue eyes intent on her once more.

He leaned down to peck her cheek, her scent filling her nose. "Stay here where it's safe. I'll be right back."

Then he rushed around the table, through the library, and to the door. She cupped her cheek where it tingled. Her whole body was on fire in a way she'd never felt before. Books rattled on the shelves around her. Had he really meant it? What would forever look like? Was it even possible?

Perhaps it was best not to give in yet to these temptations, at least not until they thought through some answers.

She glanced around, surprised her magic hadn't burned down the library.

That had been... incendiary. Who knew what would happen if they took things further? Still... she wanted to try. She might not have much time left to experience love on this world.

Besides, if he promised orgasms like that every day, she'd be a fool to say no, and no one had ever called her a fool.

Chapter Sixteen

The commotion outside drew her attention from thinking about the incredible orgasm with Leopol and all the questions that had resulted. Bella's heart raced as she floated closer, pausing in the doorway of the library at the panicked servants racing by.

"What's going on?" she asked.

"We're under an attack!"

She stiffened, her body growing cold.

The wizard?

No, he couldn't have found her so quickly. She raced toward the main hall to find Leopol and Knox throwing orders left and right, organizing the servants into groups. She found Eirwyn a few steps up the stairs, the sling bag holding the dragon egg across her shoulder. Her hands clasped the egg satchel tightly as she surveyed the organized chaos in the foyer.

"Eirwyn, what's going on? Who's attacking?"

Eirwyn's gaze swung to Bella as she approached, her eyes wide. "I don't understand. The villagers who've settled outside Hartsgrove to the east–they're marching through the helrose hedge with pitchforks and axes and torches."

Knox's voice rose above the chaos. "Alright, everyone ready? I'll go out and see what the fuss is about. There has to be some sort of explanation for this. If I can't calm them down, protect the queen and the egg."

Eirwyn's voice was soft. "The villagers were perfectly fine yesterday morning when I visited. What could've upset them so?"

Perhaps it was the wizard. Perhaps he'd somehow bespelled the villagers to attack, causing confusion so he could then launch an attack from a different angle. He'd manipulated the bone dragon to attack. This was no different, although then he'd needed Gastone to make it work.

Then again, the gardeners had been so angry today. Maybe they had instigated a riot?

Ideas and explanations flew through her mind as Knox opened the door and stepped onto the large terrace. Eirwyn's hand flew out, as if to pull him back into the safety of the castle, but she took a deep breath and drew herself up to her full height. It wasn't much, but it reminded Bella that her friend–the one who used to sing and do dishes in the tavern while she cooked dinner–was now truly a queen in every sense of the word.

Bella floated toward the door just as Leopol went through after Knox. Through the crack in the door, she watched as about a dozen villagers stopped at the foot of the stairs. Knox raised his hands, and green gas sank from his nose to curl around his feet.

"What's this all about?" he demanded, his voice bellowing in the cold air.

"Give us the evil queen!"

"Kill the queen!"

"She's ruined us!"

Bella gasped, and the door shook as her magic flared. They wanted *her*. Leopol sensed or perhaps heard her because his head whipped to the side, his blue eyes piercing into hers. The ferocity on his face sent a thrill through her, and he shook his head at her, silently telling her to stay back.

She didn't listen, floating through the door to confront those she'd once called friends. She recognized so many from the village who used to visit the tavern daily. She'd grown up around them, valued their insight.

The mob startled as she stepped beside Leopol. The weak winter sun had already set, and their torches burned bright, casting shadows along the frozen ground.

Leopol's chin lifted. "As you can see, you can't kill her if she's already a spirit."

Angry whispers echoed as the crowd seemed to pause at the words.

"We're doomed," someone yelled from the crowd.

Bella hovered at the top of the stairs. "No, I'm working on a cure. I've worked every day, but the recipe isn't ready yet."

A man stepped forward, his torch casting flickering shadows across his weathered face. "You've cursed us all! Families are torn apart! We've lost our homes, our livelihoods."

Bella's translucent form trembled. These were her people—the same villagers who'd once welcomed her, shared meals, celebrated festivals together. Now they looked at her with pure hatred. It broke her heart, and her hands clenched in her skirt.

"I'm working to break the curse," she said, a waver in

her voice. "I swear on everything I hold dear. I came here to help."

Knox stepped forward, his dragon magic crackling around him like green lightning. His voice resonated with ancient power. "What would you have us do, throw her in the dungeons? What good would that do? She needs the freedom to work on a cure."

Leopol's hand moved subtly, positioning himself slightly in front of Bella as he took her hand. "It's the truth. We've been working together day and night since she arrived. We've already made progress, and we think we know what's missing. Be patient."

"I'm tired of being cursed!" came a woman's cry from the back, holding up her hand that was joined with a watering can. The rest of the crowd mumbled, their anger rolling like a wave. Behind them, she felt more than saw Eirwyn and Lailant step through the door.

The tension crackled through the crowd like lightning, each villager's desperation more palpable than the last. A young man near the front, his face twisted with grief, suddenly lunged forward.

"My entire family was turned to monsters! My children can't move, merged with chairs! We had to carry them on our backs as we fled into the woods. How much longer must we wait?"

Bella's spectral form wavered, her energy flickering with the raw emotion of his pain. She understood their suffering more intimately than anyone. These were not just nameless villagers—these were her people, her community.

"I know you're suffering. I know the curse has taken everything from you. But you must believe me—I'll fix this."

The angry faces of people she knew sent dread through her. They didn't believe her.

"There are reports in Busparia of the evil queen controlling the winter."

"With daemons! Winter daemons! Shadow creatures."

Leopol drew her to his side, wrapping his arm around her waist. "That's not Bella. It's the wizard inhabiting her physical body. But is she trying to find a cure to her own curse of being separated from her body? No, she's solely focused on fixing the curse on *you*, her people, her friends." He snorted, his nose snarling. "Some friends you are."

The way he stuck up for her made her warm and tingly.

A rumble of uncertainty passed through the crowd. Some villagers shifted uncomfortably, their torches wavering.

"Lies. The queen cursed us, and she must be stopped."

"Kill the queen!"

Their faces hardened in anger, the torches raising as their murmurs grew louder.

Knox's dragon magic continued to swirl around him, green tendrils of power dancing between his fingers. "You will not threaten her," Leopol growled. "She's Eirwyn's friend. Have you forgotten her time serving all of you at the tavern? Don't you remember who she really is? She's not an evil queen. She's just Bella."

Knox's voice was low, measured, green smoke curling from his nose. "Stand down. Violence won't solve this. Listen to reason. They just need a little more time."

But reason seemed in short supply. The mob surged forward, torches raised, pitchforks gleaming in the moon-light as they yelled in time with each step up the stairs. "Kill the queen!"

Leopol's grip on Bella's hand tightened, and he pulled her back toward the front door, his arms protecting her. Her heart raced in fear.

Knox stepped forward into a defensive stance, his dragon magic swirling around his feet like a living green mist, tail sweeping up behind him with barbed tip pointed toward the villagers.

A stone flew from the crowd, arcing through the air toward them. Leopol's hand shot out with a flash of gold, silver, and blue, and the stone disintegrated into dust before it could touch her translucent form. The crowd gasped as Lailant stepped to the top of the stairs.

"You dare challenge my mate?" Leopol's voice was low, dangerous but projected strength for all to hear.

Bella stiffened, her breath catching in her throat as his words settled in her mind, pulsing with every breath. *Mate?*

Mate. The word echoed in her mind, unwanted and dangerous. She couldn't afford the distraction, not when lives were at stake.

Mate. Her heart twisted at the word as it reverberated on repeat within her. She couldn't afford to hope, not when she'd hoped for love before—and Gastone had died in the end. Energy crackled around him, his spirit form shimmering brightly like a torch, his form growing hazy and shifting. His blue eyes blazed with an intensity that made the nearest villagers pause on the steps.

The villager's hands raised again, and the chant continued. "Kill the queen!"

Lailant flicked her wrist, sending magical dust around the villagers. The scent of the sleeping dust made her sneeze.

A silence fell over the crowd as the magical sparkles settled around them, broken only by the crackling of torches and a distant screech of eagles through the helrose hedges. Bella trembled, caught between anger and profound sorrow. These were her people—the same villagers who'd once shared bread with her, celebrated festivals, mourned together.

One by one, they sank to the steps, yawning and stretching before curling up in whatever sleep position they preferred. One spread arms and legs wide on his back. Another still on the ground level curled onto her side and stuffed her thumb in her mouth. The woman with the watering pot hand curled around it and held it like it was the most precious thing.

Lailant harrumphed and shook her head. "Humans. Serves them right."

Eirwyn stepped up behind Knox and placed her hand on his back, soothing the tension from his shoulders as she asked, "What was the dust? It smells familiar."

"A sleeping dust, a more powerful one than the ones the druids or Hunters have. They'll be out until tomorrow night."

"We can't just leave them there," Eirwyn said.

Knox turned and pulled her into his arms. "They dared to march on our family."

The mention of family–of her being included in that– brought tears to her eyes. She sniffed, and Leopol pulled her into his arms and squeezed tight. "Are you alright, Bella?"

She ignored the emotions and focused on the villagers.

"Why didn't they lower their weapons?" she asked, her voice carrying in the stillness as they fell asleep before them. "I've known most of them since childhood. Do they truly believe I would intentionally harm them, that I could've spread these curses?"

The young man who had spoken of his family, his face etched with grief, sank to the ground last. His torch wavered as it fell. "My kids," he said, his voice cracking as he yawned and joined the others. "Save my children."

Leopol's grip on her waist tightened, a protective gesture that sent tiny sparks of magical energy dancing between them.

"Do they think I haven't been working every day to do just that?" she asked softly.

"I don't know," Leopol said. She sank into the safety of him with a sigh of relief.

Eirwyn frowned as Knox and Lailant went down to check on the sleeping villagers. "I bet it was the gardeners. I didn't like how they looked at you earlier," Eirwyn said.

Bella sighed and nodded against Leopol's shoulder. "I'd assume so, but I'm working around the clock."

"We both are," Leopol said, kissing her temple.

Her eyes fluttered closed. It was so... natural to be held like this by him. She'd never wanted to rely on a man like this before, preferring to stand on her own two feet and make her own way in the world. It was the only way she'd been able to run the tavern at fifteen when her father had left.

Eirwyn glanced at them and sighed. "Leopol, take her back to the library. I'll get some servants to bring them inside, so they don't freeze."

"Put them in the green parlor," Leopol said. "It's mostly empty and the fireplace will keep them warm."

"Good idea," Eirwyn said.

She stepped out of his arms. If they went inside, she'd have to address the *mate* comment, and she just—she couldn't do that right now. It was too life altering, and she'd had enough life altering events to last a lifetime.

She paced on the terrace, staying out of the way as servants came to gather the sleeping villagers. Lailant and Eirwyn directed them while Knox stood with arms crossed. Leopol's eyes followed her with every step.

"We have to find a solution," she muttered. "Tonight. Or at the very least, tomorrow before they wake up. It's the only thing that won't make it worse. If they wake up and find that there's been no progress and they've been knocked out for so long, they'll feel helpless. Cornered."

She turned and paced the other direction. "Like scared rabbits."

That thought triggered another about Scarlet's curse and all the things she'd tried to solve it.

She glanced up at Leopol. "There was a text that mentioned the Growlers' ritual to transform. Can you find that text for me?"

He frowned but bowed slightly. "Anything for you, Bella."

He turned and followed the last servant inside, all the villagers now moved to the green parlor. Eirwyn and Knox followed him, talking softly.

Lailant paused in front of her, gaze critical as ever. "What are you thinking, Bella?"

Bella took a deep breath, the puzzle pieces clicking in her mind. "I am going to grab my spellbooks and meet with Leopol to figure out the spell, potion combination, but I need you and Knox to work your magic on the golden apple tree."

Lailant's eyes narrowed. "How so?"

Bella's chin tipped up. "Make it grow, flower, and bloom. I want to experiment with a golden apple. I think it's the key."

"I'm not sure that's possible, child. It's barely a stick in the ground."

Bella sniffed and walked around her, skirts swishing. "Don't play games at a time like this, Lailant. I know you have power that I've only glimpsed. I know you can do it, especially considering Knox's specialty with growing trees."

Lailant sighed as Bella crossed the threshold. "Fine, I'll go find Knox."

"Great. When you have a golden apple, bring it to me in the library."

Lailant's laugh cackled in the still night, and Bella glanced back at her with one brow raised. The old woman waved her hand. "You may not have been born a queen, but never doubt. This *is* who you're meant to be, child."

Bella's stomach twisted at the pressure. Failure was not an option. They had to succeed, and it had to be done tonight.

Chapter Seventeen

Leopol flipped through the book as quickly as his eyes could process, searching for the text chronicling the Growler ritual. He'd shouted from the metaphorical rooftop that she was his mate, but she'd ignored it, ignored him.

His skin itched. No, not his skin, since he didn't have any in this form. His entire soul itched and ached with something that was deeply uncomfortable and fundamentally wrong. Time was running out in more ways than one, but they had to focus on one problem at a time.

His thumb stopped, the words practically jumping off the page, and he breathed a sigh of relief at finding the Growler information.

Just then, Bella floated through the door of the library with two books in her arms. She bit her lip as their eyes met, and a worried wrinkle marred her forehead. She held up her books nervously.

"These are my spell books. Can I show you what worked and what didn't?"

Leopol opened his mouth to speak, but what could he

say? That her voice made the ache in his chest worse? That being near her was both balm and torment?

He just nodded, swallowing everything he wanted to say under the weight of everything they still hadn't spoken aloud.

His now thick tongue prevented him from saying anything about the fact that they were mates. She floated to his desk, books still scattered on the floor from when he'd set her on top of it earlier.

She set her books down and launched into nervous chatter, explaining every page with rapid fire words.

Leopol listened intently, watching her fingers trace the delicate symbols and incantations, her nails sharp against the yellowed pages. Each gesture seemed calculated, yet her voice trembled with an undercurrent of anxiety that he could sense like electricity crackling between them.

"This sigil here," she said, pointing to a complex geometric design. "It didn't stabilize the transformation sequence as I'd hoped. I tried to modify the binding spell, but the resonance was all wrong. See how the sigils collapse inward?"

He remained silent, absorbing not just her words but the subtle shifts in her energy. The mate bond hummed between them, a living thing neither could fully ignore nor completely acknowledge. His declaration hung unspoken in the air—a tension more complex than mere magical research.

He finally cleared his throat and focused. "Sigils are tricky to get right. It's why most academies only teach standard runes instead of how to create personalized sigils. The outer rings are slightly misaligned on this one. See? Right here."

She frowned and glanced down, peering closer at the

JANE POLLER

page where he pointed before nodding slowly. "You're right. I just don't have enough precise control on my magic in this form."

Bella shifted her weight, fingers now trembling slightly as she turned another page.

He leaned closer, careful not to crowd her. The proximity made her breath catch, a tiny hitch that sent a tremor through his spectral form. She was trying so hard to be professional, to ignore the electric current of their connection.

But he knew. And she knew, even if they weren't talking about it yet. She needed time to think and process. If he'd learned anything from studying her this week, it was that.

By the time Knox and Lailant came into the library close to sunrise, they had a working theory. Some of the awkwardness had fallen away as they worked, even though the underlying tension was undeniable.

Lailant held up the golden apple and Leopol and Bella glanced at each other before looking back at the apple. Bella licked her lips, her eyes wide.

"By the gods, it–it worked?"

She lit up like sunrise through storm clouds, and for a moment, Leopol forgot how to breathe.

He wanted to touch her. To call her to him. To say what burned in his throat every time she was within touching distance.

But she wasn't ready, and he wasn't selfish enough to demand it. Not yet.

Lailant laughed, her eyes nearly disappearing into the wrinkles. "You said it would."

Bella blinked in surprise, and Leopol pointed to the desk across the library under the window where Bella and all her potion supplies lay.

"We'll need to cut it into pieces so we can test different combinations and recipes," Leopol said, knowing she had a few base potions already completed from her last test batch.

"Are you certain this will work?" Knox's voice cut through the thick silence of the chamber, his skepticism a stark contrast to Bella's confident movements. The apple yielded to his blade, each segment falling away like petals from a bloom. Twelve pieces lay on the table, equal in promise and peril.

"Not at all. But we don't have a choice," she replied, directing Lailant in the making of the sigils and runes on the beakers while directing Knox to take one of the apple slices and grind it with the pestle and mortar to make a paste.

"We have a good baseline that worked before. I've already made a few this week, thanks to Eirwyn's help with the precise measurements." She pointed to the three cork-capped bottles on the windowsill. "They should have the moonlight absorbed from last night's full moon too."

"That will help," Leopol said, shifting back and forth on his feet. There was an idea on the edge of his mind, percolating, waiting to come to fruition. Fruit...

Bella's voice grew quiet as she frowned. "We don't really need the multiple pieces. If we take the entire apple and turn it into a paste, we can then add drops or a spoonful to the base potions before testing the strength of each."

Lailant stopped working, the lack of movement drawing Bella's gaze. "Ignot and Sharlo's deaths were not your decision, child. For this to work, we will need test subjects. We'll ask for volunteers from the villagers when they wake up tonight. If none of them will take the risk, then we'll go into the village or to Vidrland to find volunteers."

"There will be plenty of people willing to take the risk," Knox said.

Leopol took Bella's hand as she sighed, barely looking at him as she glanced between Knox and Lailant. "I know, but what if we fail?"

Her hand didn't move in his, didn't squeeze him back. She just lay limply, not registering him at all. It grated on his nerves, but he had to focus on helping her and not on the need to make her sit up and notice him. He fought back the need to throw her over his shoulder and find the closest flat surface.

Lailant smiled softly, her eyes kind but with an edge of steel underneath. "There is no progress without failure. You know that."

Bella drew away from him, focusing on the sigil that Lailant had drawn in the magical ink on the first bottle. She pointed and shook her head. "No, Leopol thinks the sigil isn't quite right. Where are the books?"

"I'll get them." Leopol used his magic to bring the three books from the other table to their work area, spreading them out so Lailant and Knox could see the various symbols.

After a few minutes comparing the images, Lailant picked up the sigil maker and tweaked the markings. Afterwards, she added the standard runes on either side of the sigil, including the transformation runes they'd rediscovered in the sanctum.

When Knox was done, he uncorked the first container, ready to pour the apple paste inside. Leopol shook his head and rubbed his chin.

"No, wait," he said, turning to stare out the window at the rising sun. The eagles already soared, but he barely paid them any attention. "Just pouring the apple paste in won't work. It needs to be more palatable. A syrup maybe? Then the syrup can be mixed with the base potion?"

"A syrup?" Bella asked. Her voice called to him, but he couldn't look at her and think clearly. He almost had the idea ready to go. Just a few more moments. He continued staring out the window as he talked out loud.

"These potions will work for testing the ritual, but if we plan to administer this to an entire village eventually, we'll need something more... refined. Stable. Repeatable."

Bella arched a brow. "But a syrup?"

He gave a short nod. "I know, but did Sharlo or Ignot mention anything about how drinkable the potions were?"

Knox leaned over to Lailant and whispered, "Who the hell is Sharlo and Ignot?"

Lailant just hushed him, staring intently at them.

Bella wrinkled her nose and ignored the other two. "Sharlo mentioned it a time or two."

Leopol rubbed his chin again. "So, it needs to be drinkable. Potions are difficult to standardize in bulk—temperamental and generally foul tasting. But Growler rituals worked because the delivery method was consistent with a liquid base made at a specific temperature. It was the catalyst for the ritual spell and oath that caused the transformation."

"So... you're saying it needs to be a regular drink, like a tea or something? Isn't that what Scarlet and Da said the Growlers love to drink?" Bella asked slowly, her eyes narrowing with thought.

"Yes, but not quite. The Growlers ritual is transforming the dying to a new, hybrid creature, and that's not our end goal. We want to separate the living from the non-living objects, returning them to their original structures."

He turned to face them, but he only had eyes for Bella.

"The potion must enter the body as something the body accepts. If the soul resists the medium, the transformation could fail. That's likely what happened before."

Bella blinked, then her face lit up with an idea that made her eyes sparkle. "Well, if we're making it a drink, it might as well be a damn good one."

Lailant looked up from the next beaker she was carving. "You're thinking what I think you're thinking, aren't you?"

Bella grinned. "My father used to make the best ashplum ale in the county. I helped him every fall—watched him blend the spices, smoke the barrels, steep the cinnamon sticks. The whole village used to come to the tavern just for a taste of his autumn brew. When he left for war, I continued it. It helped me miss him a little less."

Knox's brows rose. "I know that drink." He lowered his voice into a deeper tone. "Ashplum Gold: Brewed in fire, aged in love. Drink ashplum ale by the hearth, and you'll forget your sorrow—unless it's worth remembering. Only available at the Bloomin' Brew."

Bella laughed, her form glowing with joy. "That's the slogan we had printed up in the paper each year. Did you ever try it?"

Knox grinned. "Oh yeah. Three drinks, and I made a fool of myself, crying and wailing like a widow. Ashur had to carry me out of the tavern before I threw off my hood and scared everyone with my scales and horns."

Bella laughed. "Yeah, it's dangerously potent. My father used to say ashplums are stubborn and taste like heartbreak unless you treat them right. Thus, our proprietary brewing process. Then they taste like coming home."

"So, we can take the golden apple and turn it into a ritual drink," Leopol mused. "Symbolic. Magical. Potent enough to change everyone back to normal."

Bella paced in front of the table. "We could make a reduction syrup from the golden apple first. Let it concentrate the magic. Then infuse the base with something herbaceous—maybe starleaf or godsage for stability?"

Knox straightened, shaking off the fatigue. "There are old barrels in the cellar made of oak. Might still be good. I think some were used for moonwine based on the smell."

"Perfect," Bella said, grabbing a glass vial. "We'll need to test a small batch first. One blend with just apple, one with honey added, and one with bitterroot."

"You're making three versions of the ale?" Lailant asked, amused.

Bella laughed softly. "No, I'm finding the right flavor for redemption. The one that sticks and is most stable. The apple alone might not be strong enough to be a permanent solution to the transformation curse. Honey will smooth the edges of the potion and hopefully smooth the transformation process back to normal. But bitterroot should make it more durable and long-lasting."

"So, the plain apple version will be the control test, then we'll have two other versions. But maybe a third that combines the honey and bitterroot?" Leopol asked.

Bella's forehead wrinkled in thought as she nodded slowly. "Yes, I think you're right. Knox, if you can go ahead and ground the rest of the apple—core included—into a pulpy paste, then you can go get some rest. Lailant, if you'll help carry the apple paste to the kitchens, then Leopol can convince one of the cooks to help me make the syrup reduction... we might be able to have a test batch done by tonight when they wake."

The nervous anticipation on her face made his own chest tighten. For her sake, he hoped she was right. For his own sake, he prayed he could keep himself together long enough to see it through.

The longer he went without finishing the mate bond, the harder it was to maintain control of himself. He fought the primal need to claim her. Every minute with her was soothing but also grating because of the unfinished business between them.

Lailant and Knox murmured on the other side of the table, gathering the rest of the ingredients and tools, but for a moment, Bella stayed. Just her and him in the quiet.

He stepped closer, unable to help himself. The scent of magic and golden apple clung to her like a promise. His fingers itched to touch her, to pull her close, to remind her she didn't have to carry this alone.

"Bella," he said, voice rougher than he meant.

She turned halfway, her eyes uncertain, guarded—but open in a way that made something inside him nearly snap.

"I meant what I said last night, but I didn't say it for them," he whispered. "I said it for you because it's time you knew the truth. You're my mate. We belong together."

Her breath caught, and for one fragile heartbeat, she didn't move. Her gaze flicked to his lips, then to his eyes—like she wanted to speak, wanted to close the space between them, wanted to hope. The bond hummed, live and restless between them.

"Leopol..." Her voice was soft, almost tender, and he drew closer, unable to stay away from her.

She blinked, then pulled back like the moment had burned her. She shook her head. "We can't—" She looked down at the books and potions on the table. "We have too much to fix. One thing at a time."

He nodded slowly, but the fire under his skin didn't dim. "I'll wait. I'm not a patient dragon, but I'll wait for you."

It wouldn't be long now. After the way she'd given in to his hands, fingers, and tongue on the table yesterday, she'd start thinking and—even better—yearning for more.

She didn't answer but just turned and floated back to the table and the promise of the distraction of the ritual.

She didn't look back, but she knew he was watching. She always knew when he watched her; her breath hitched, and her pulse jumped erratically at her throat.

Even when he whispered her name, a plea for more that burst forth from his soul and vanished into the quiet, she didn't look at him. But the way she tucked her hair behind her ear and her cheeks flushed in awareness had him looking forward to tomorrow.

They all scattered to their tasks, the scent of dawn clinging to the air. By nightfall, they would know if hope was enough. And tomorrow? Perhaps she would be ready to talk about the inevitable bond between them.

Chapter Eighteen

Ashur's labored breaths mingled with the crisp winter air as he trudged through the frozen forest. The giant eagles had finally retreated and flown away, their massive wings disappearing into the horizon. He paused, catching his breath from the exertion, but he couldn't stay still for long. The eagles were supposed to be training to protect the forest, but all they were good at was playing and toying with anyone who got too near the castle.

No matter how much the forest called to him with its beauty, he had to keep moving quietly and avoid making any loud noises. The Feral Forest was a dangerous place, and he couldn't risk drawing attention to himself, especially not this close to sunrise.

Every step he took left deep imprints in the stiff grass beneath his feet. The curse that had transformed him into this monstrous form also heightened his strength and caused him to destroy more than he wanted to. As second-in-command of the Robins, he had always taken pride in leading his fellow outcasts alongside their dragon king,

Knox. But now, he felt like more of a liability than an asset.

He snorted, his breath curling white from the cold. Under his wing. That was funny.

He slumped his shoulders, gritting his teeth against the pain spreading throughout his body. The sun was creeping up on the horizon, and he knew he had to move quickly if he didn't want to be trapped outside the castle once again.

The fucking birds had left so much crap on him that day. He sighed and dodged around trees. He picked up his pace, weaving through the trees with practiced precision.

A fluttering in the trees had him glancing up. Damn it, they were back. Hadn't they had enough playing around the first time around?

He could feel their piercing stares and hear their screeches growing louder. His heart raced as he pushed harder, desperate to reach the safety of the wall of thorns before sunrise.

But his joints were becoming increasingly stiff, and it was a struggle to keep going at such a frantic pace. The birds swooped down closer, their large wings creating gusts of wind that nearly knocked him off balance.

He ducked to the right, and a bird narrowly missed him, screeching in anger. His joints were growing stiffer with each minute that passed.

Finally, he broke free from the thick forest and reached the edge of the wall of thorns, relief washing over him.

The birds circled above as he dodged, his joints locking up and making him stumble like a drunkard as he followed the thorny wall. Come on, where was the break that led safely through?

The birds dove, their sharp claws reaching out to grab onto his shirt. He grunted in pain and fought against the stiffness in his joints. With a sudden burst of strength, he flexed his muscles and spread his wings, causing one bird to flail and rip his shirt.

He landed on the ground with a thud, leaving a deep gash in the frozen dirt from his weight. Gasping for breath, he quickly scanned his surroundings and spotted the break in the wall.

Legs pumping too slowly, he ran toward it even as the pull of the sun caused him to slow. Almost there, just another dozen feet.

They dive bombed him again, and he instinctively raised his wings to shield himself. His body lurched forward, carrying him parallel to the wall as he struggled to maintain balance. Through the small opening between his wings, he saw a deep rift in the ground ahead, with trees on one side and the wall on the other.

From the rift, dirt flew up like a geyser. He tried to stop, but his momentum was too much. The dirt settled, but his feet were still running.

He frantically pumped his wings to slow his momentum, but the small gulch was too close. He was going to fall in and drop like a stone.

Haha, he grimaced. This was no time for jokes. If he wanted to avoid falling, he'd have to speed up and try to glide again.

The gargoyle's feet pounded against the rough terrain, his wings spread wide as he raced faster towards the edge of the rift. The air whipped past him, making his eyes water and his heart race.

As he started to go over the edge, a clawed hand grasped onto the rim of the embankment. A black and red creature with horns pulled its multi-eyed head up. The thing paused in surprise, staring at him as Ashur kept barreling down on it.

Ashur's instincts kicked in, and he used the creature's head as a stepping stone to propel himself forward over the crater. As he flew over it, he saw a swirling mass of red and black below, filled with grotesque hands, feet, and strange heads.

Before he could fully process what he saw, something slammed into his side, knocking him off balance.

A feminine squeal and the softness of flesh and silk pressed against him as they tumbled across the frozen ground. As they rolled in a jumbled tangle of limbs, birds screeched above and disappeared over the trees.

Ashur gasped for breath and tried to make sense of what had just happened. His heart raced, and a sharp pain in his back made him wince as they came to a stop.

He had landed on top of the strange woman, shielding her from harm with his large wings. The warmth beneath him was soft and unexpected, a startling contrast to the harsh, icy ground they had collided with.

Breathless and bewildered, Ashur scrambled to his hands and knees, taking his heavy stone-filled weight off the poor woman.

The sudden closeness sent a jolt through his body; it was as though bolts of lightning had replaced his veins. The woman beneath him was an enigma wrapped in silk and mystery. His mind raced with questions, yet there was an odd sense of familiarity about her—the curve of her cheek, the fragrance of her hair.

She was like a delicate dream come to life. Here he was, a creature of stone and nightmare to many, cradling something so fragile in a world that seemed perpetually on the brink of chaos. The absurdity of the situation struck him—a gargoyle and a mysterious woman entangled by fate on the edge of a hellish abyss.

Her bow shaped mouth opened in surprise, but no sound escaped. Confusion swirled within him, mingling with a budding sense of wonder.

Her eyes fluttered open, revealing irises like molten gold that seemed to pierce right through him, shining with a mixture of terror and awe. Her eyes, wide and luminous even in the shadow of his wings, held a universe within them—starry and deep. Despite their perilous situation and the oddity of their meeting, Ashur felt an inexplicable pull, an attraction and protectiveness that seemed as mystical as it was immediate.

Her white hair was a tangled mess, the silver circlet askew on her head revealing pointed ears. But the press of her body was the shock that made him freeze more than any sun ever could.

Ashur paused, his words catching in his throat as he absorbed the sight of her, this ethereal being under him. He cleared his throat, an unnecessary act for a gargoyle but one that bought him a moment to gather his thoughts. "Are you hurt?" he finally managed, his voice gravelly with disuse and concern.

She blinked at him, processing his question as if the words were foreign. "I... I don't think so," she whispered, her voice lilting like a melody played on the breeze. She shifted slightly under him, wincing just a bit. "Just a little shaken."

He nodded slowly, staying motionless over her for a moment longer, ensuring she felt no immediate pain.

"I'm Ashur. What's your name?"

Her mouth opened to respond, but a deafening roar from the pit beside them made them both jump. She pushed at his chest, and he rolled to the side, afraid he was crushing her but also overwhelmed by the shock that ran through him at that small touch.

In a flurry of white silk, she scrambled to her feet, leaving behind only a faint trace of her scent.

She yelled in some language he'd never heard before and pointed at the gap as more monsters crawled out. Light from her palms shot out and illuminated them.

Ashur pushed himself up, his muscles aching as the sun rose. White spread from her hands to the hole as she strained. He stumbled over to where she stood, her hands still emitting a bright white light as she struggled to close the rift. Despite her efforts, more of the slimy monsters continued to wriggle through, avoiding the piercing rays of light.

One of the blood-red creatures lunged at her, and Ashur quickly stepped between them. He swung hard, his fist of stone slamming into the thing's face with a satisfying crunch. The creature flew to the thorn wall and was impaled with a shriek.

The next creature tried to attack, but Ashur swung first. He slammed his rock-hard fists into its body, breaking bones with sickening snaps as he protected her from harm. One after another, he fought off the dark creatures, using his strength and brute force to push them back or throw them back into the pit.

But then one of the winged bat-like creatures swooped down towards him. His hand was too slow to block it, and its sharp claws left stinging scratches on his face before he grabbed hold of its scrawny neck and squeezed tightly.

He felt time running out as the sun rose and his body slowed. He couldn't keep this up for much longer.

"Hurry," he yelled, struggling to grab onto another one

of the slimy black creatures with tentacles that were wrapping around his legs.

The rift was closing. Slowly, but it *was* closing even as he threw the tentacle creature back into the hole and stomped on its head to shove it down. Another flying bat with horns dove at him, but this time he reared back and punched it out of the air with a loud scream, sending it flying into the wall.

"Just hold them," the woman shouted over the chaos of the battle.

He didn't look back, too focused on protecting her. He ripped a small daemon in half and tossed it back in the rift, feeling his body grow stiffer and slower as he battled on. The creatures were getting smaller now, some only the size of foxes. Another horned creature dove at them, swooping too close to the woman.

Jumping in front of her, he caught the thing in midair, then glided over the rush of energy and magic coming from her hands. He landed on the other side and adjusted his grip on the flying creature in his hands.

Ashur used it like a club as he swung wildly at any remaining creatures. More of them were pushing at the edges of the crater as it grew smaller than a carriage wheel.

He swung the monster in his hand and hit those trying to escape the crater, stomping on their hands and claws. They screamed in pain and let go, falling back into the swirling abyss.

As the sun rose, his feet slowly stiffened in place. Still, he bent, hitting the monsters with his demon club, blood flying as the skin ripped.

When his knees froze, he swung the body from side to side. One more swing and his makeshift club split apart, pieces of it flying into the trees.

His hips froze as he panted. He shivered, spreading his wings as the last of the rift closed. A ripple of dirt was the only sign it had ever existed.

Well, that and all the blood and daemon pieces lying around. With a shiver, he spread his wings and looked around at the destruction they had caused.

He wiped his hands on his shirt and turned to the woman in the white dress as her knees buckled. He reached for her but couldn't help as she braced her hands on her knees.

The scent of death and fear lingered in the air, causing her to shiver. She wiped her hands on her blood-stained white dress and met his gaze with a mix of terror and gratitude as she stood back up, shaking.

His stone chest heaved as he panted, trying to catch his breath. A shiver of awareness ran through him as their eyes locked. Above them, giant eagles circled, squawking menacingly.

He pointed through the gap in the tall, thorn-covered wall. "The eagles will attack if you stay here. If you go through the hedge wall, it'll take you to Hartsgrove Castle. You'll find safety there. Tell Leopol that Ashur sent you. He'll feed you and provide shelter."

She panted and held her side with a shaky hand as she looked behind her. "Through the wall of thorns? What about you?"

As if to answer her question, Ashur's chest began to turn to solid stone in the early morning light. "I'm cursed...a gargoyle," he explained. "I can't leave until nightfall."

But the woman's face softened, and she took a stumbling step towards him, reaching out a trembling hand. Ashur tried to reach for her, but his stone feet kept him rooted in place. He frowned, his heart beginning to slow. Why was he so concerned with this pint-sized woman?

"I don't think I'll make it to the castle," she said weakly, coughing up blood. "I can't even see it from here. I–I think I'm going to pass out."

Ashur panicked, and with a burst of determination, he fought the stony shift. He spread his wings as the eagles screeched and swooped closer.

He motioned her closer. "Come here and rest under my wings. If you wake before nightfall, you can wiggle out and make a run for the castle."

She took a step toward him, and her knees buckled. She fell hard to the frozen ground, and he lurched to help, but his feet had already turned to stone.

"Come on. You can do it," he said, his heart aching as he watched her, feeling an overwhelming need to protect her. It was unlike anything he had ever felt before, as if his entire purpose in life was to keep her safe.

"Alright," she said, crawling to his feet. She looked up at him with big, grateful golden eyes. "Thank you for the shelter, and for your help with the daemons."

His chest ached for her, and he nodded, arching his wings to form a cocoon around them. "Anything for you," he said softly.

He meant every word. He was used to protecting people, but not with this deep-seated need of desperation. It was a strange feeling, like he'd die if anything were to happen to her. Ashur prayed that she would stay safe until he woke from his stony slumber.

She curled up on the frozen ground with a sigh. "Still, I appreciate it, Ashur. Ashur..."

She sighed his name and tucked her hands under her head. "Such a nice, strong name."

He felt his shoulders turn to stone. He wanted to keep talking with her, needed to know everything about her so he could protect her. "What's yours?"

She yawned, then said sleepily, "Cerci."

His neck turned to stone and his blood slowed, his heartbeat growing louder in his ears. No, she couldn't be—

"Named after the goddess?" The incredulity was obvious in his voice, and he winced in embarrassment.

But she just closed her eyes and smiled. "Actually, I *am* the goddess."

His mind whirled furiously, trying to think about what this meant. The goddess only appeared during times of great transition.

She yawned again. "Well, demigoddess, anyway."

His breath was still puffy white, but it was slightly warmer within their dome of safety. An opening on either side of his wings would allow Cerci to crawl out when she was ready.

But for now, Ashur prayed that she would stay safe inside their cocoon until he fully woke from his slumber. With that thought in mind, he descended once again into a deep sleep, knowing that the goddess herself was watching over him as he watched over her.

Chapter Nineteen

Lailant walked beside Bella, carrying the bowl carefully in her wrinkled hands, the amber paste inside glinting with dawn light. They stepped out into the corridor, the castle hushed and still around them, unusually so for the breakfast rush. Even the walls seemed to hold their breath.

Lailant sighed heavily, and Bella paused, hands hovering. Before, she would've taken Lailant's arm to help her walk, but without her body, she was helpless. She hated this feeling.

"Are you alright? Can I help with anything?" Bella asked as Lailant shuffled down the hall.

"I'm fine, child. Probably more so than you," Lailant said softly, her eyes piercing in the early morning light. "We all heard what Leopol shouted last night. How are you feeling about the mate bond?"

Bella's breath caught, but she didn't stop walking, even as the tapestries on the wall shivered in the ripple of her magic.

"You don't have to answer yet. I know you need to think

192

it through," the old woman added. "But when a handsome scholar-warrior bellows to the heavens that you're his fated mate, it's the sort of thing that sticks in the air. Hard to breathe around, if left unspoken for too long."

How many times over the past few years had Lailant asked her about finding a husband to settle down with? They'd had conversations for years about love, fated mates, and partnerships that could help the tavern grow and prosper. Then Lailant's pilgrimage trips every few months started growing from a few days to a few weeks. She was gone for most of Gastone's courtship, and Bella had foolishly thought—well, it no longer mattered, did it.

"I don't have time for a mate. I have to focus on solving the cursed villagers," Bella said, maybe a little too sharply. "One problem at a time."

Lailant gave a soft hum. "Of course. But hearts—much like curses—rarely follow a schedule. Don't leave him waiting for too long, or you'll regret it."

"He doesn't even know me. We just met last week," Bella said, keeping her voice low so it didn't carry in the hall. Leopol and Knox had already disappeared into the corridor to the kitchen, but she didn't want him to overhear as it might hurt him.

"Fated mates are an immediate understanding, simply a knowing," her mentor said with a far-off look on her face. "He stood for you when the others forgot who you were. That kind of deep understanding of who you are at your core—the essence that is Bella—that's what fated mates are all about. It's not something you'll be able to ignore for long, child. I'm surprised you two haven't finished the bond by now."

Bella didn't reply. She couldn't. Not when her chest felt tight and hollow all at once. Is that what she wanted? To finish the mate bond, to know that he would be by her side for the rest of her life…

A sense of dread filled her, because she knew her life was ticking away daily. The rose was nearly blooming, the colors of the bud now visible. How cruel were the gods to show her a mate when she was going to die so soon?

She frowned as they reached the turn toward the kitchen, and Lailant paused, offering the bowl to the pastry chef as she left the breakfast room and turned in front of them. "Take this directly to Leopol. Do not let anyone else touch it. Do you understand?"

The petite woman's eyes widened as she curtsied, taking the bowl reverently. "Aye, Seer. As you say, so it'll be."

Lailant's eyes narrowed as she watched the woman walk away, but still she said, "I'll rest a while now. Wake me if you need help stirring the second reduction."

Bella nodded, following the servant and not letting the bowl out of her sight. She floated through the swinging kitchen doors.

Inside, she found Leopol in full command—directing the kitchen staff like he'd done it all his life. Servants scurried between tables, and Knox was bent over a table on one side of the room, arranging the bottles and glass flasks, each now covered with carefully crafted runes and sigils.

Bella's heart stuttered as her gaze naturally went back to Leopol. Her awareness sharpened on him, always on him.

Was it because they were mates? Was it true? Was that why she was so obsessed with him this past week, constantly thinking about him and wondering what he was thinking about every little topic?

Leopol looked her way, and she took a deep breath.

It was the underlying thought that bothered her the most—mates were special, fated. And she… she wasn't worthy of that kind of bond. Not after Gastone. Not after being lied to, manipulated, and tossed aside as if she were something delicate and disposable.

Surely if she were as smart and worthy as she thought she was, as much as she wanted to be, she wouldn't have fallen for Gastone's bullshit.

She'd told Lailant the truth. There was no time to figure this out. The curse had to come first.

"Thank you," she said, nodding toward the preparations. Leopol had already commandeered half of the kitchen and three servants to help, including the pastry chef who now sat the bowl of golden apple paste on the table.

Leopol gave a slight smile. "They've been briefed. What do you need to make the syrup?"

Bella moved to the central table and gestured for the servant to bring over the crushed apple paste. Together, she and Leopol directed them to heat the stove, the pastry chef adjusting the flame beneath the pot to simmer the syrup slow and low.

After a half hour, she dropped in a sprig of godsage, watching the golden mixture swirl and bubble. It would help with binding everything together and give it a smoky taste.

She didn't speak to Leopol or he to her. They worked side by side in an easy rhythm, but the feelings inside her bubbled along with the syrup. They didn't talk about the bond or about what it meant.

They focused on the potion, which was exactly as it should be.

So why was she growing more antsy as time passed?

After several hours, the syrup had thickened, the scent warm and spiced. But the longer they stood there waiting, the more restless Bella became—pacing between stations, checking and rechecking their notes in the spell book. Her energy was coiled tight.

Leopol leaned against the counter beside her, arms and ankles crossed as he stared at her critically. "You're nervous. Don't worry, Bella, this will work."

Her cheeks flushed, but she twisted her skirts and licked her lips. "It *has* to work. I just hate the waiting."

He paused, then said, "We should start a batch of ashplum ale."

Bella blinked at the topic shift. "Now? That'll take weeks."

"Exactly," he said. "We'll need just as long to monitor the potion's effects, so why not? It'll take at least one full moon cycle before we know if the transformation holds. Why not prepare something useful while we wait?"

She hesitated, then slowly nodded. "We do need time to see what the side effects are. And if it works, the ashplum ale will make the potion go down easier."

He smiled, and the room seemed to brighten around her. "And when we're ready, we'll throw a party. One that even cursed villagers will want to come back to life for. Drinking, dancing, the works."

Bella huffed a laugh. "You're not wrong. Maybe if they're drinking, they'll loosen up a little, make it easier for their souls and bodies to let the ritual do its job."

With that plan in place, Leopol sent a servant to the cellar to fetch a moonwine oak cask. She didn't point out that it would take a long time to get to the point of needing a cask, but they could clean and prep it at least.

Bella followed the kitchen boy through a side door and

into the small garden beyond the east wall. She trusted Leopol to keep an eye on the syrup, and she paused at the realization. She trusted him.

Perhaps the question of if they were mates or not could be boiled down to that simple statement. She trusted him.

They wouldn't know for weeks if the first potion worked, but she couldn't stand still, not with everything inside her restless and aching for answers. So she returned to what she knew best—fire, fruit, and patience in the kitchen.

The ashplums came from the garden behind the east wall. Twisted trees from the winter and years of neglect, but the fruit was perfect. Just like her father liked them: ugly on the outside, but worth the wait.

She plucked one and turned it over in her hands. The skin was dull, almost bruised-looking, but the scent—sharp and sweet and full of memory—hit her hard.

And... she could *touch it*. She was still using magic, but it was much easier to interact with the physical object than it had been when she'd arrived a week ago.

She frowned, her mind shying away from the questions on that puzzle and why this was happening. Soon, the questions would bubble up in her mind. She needed to add them to the ever-present list in her spell book, but her gut told her Leopol had the answer.

Hours later, as Bella adjusted the heat under the now-glossy syrup, a gust of wind and the squeak of a swinging door announced Eirwyn's arrival.

She burst into the kitchen with a braid half undone and excitement crackling in her magic. She had the freshly loved and deeply satisfied look that Bella had seen so often the past week. It sent a pang through her chest, and she wondered yet again if she'd ever have the chance to experience something so pure and raw and beautiful.

"I smelled something sweet and possibly dangerous," she announced. "Are we making magical cocktails or just getting drunk for fun?"

Bella chuckled under her breath, remembering past nights at the tavern where they'd done just that. "Both, if we're lucky."

Eirwyn peeked into one of the simmering pots, then leaned her elbows on the counter, watching while Bella stirred the syrup.

"Knox getting some rest?"

Eirwyn nodded. "Yeah, curled around the egg. You gonna pretend you didn't hear him call you his mate, or are we saving that meltdown for after the potions?"

Bella froze, spoon in hand.

Eirwyn sighed dramatically. "Fine, saving for later it is. Eventually you won't be able to deny you two are perfect for each other."

Bella scowled down into the syrup. Eirwyn danced away to the other side of the kitchen, humming as if completely unaffected.

"I was there. Half the castle heard it. And anyone who's seen you two in the same room will agree that there's something between you. Something powerful and romantic and... primal..." Eirwyn's voice trailed off, her eyes going dreamy as she no doubt pictured Knox. She always wore that expression when she talked about him.

"I'm not talking about that," Bella muttered, glancing back to the pot. "Not until this is all over."

"Fine, fine. Let's pretend he didn't risk ghostly combustion to defend your honor." Eirwyn held up her hands, then grinned wider. "But if he proposes in the middle of a potion test, I'm going to cry. Just so you know."

Bella rolled her eyes, but a reluctant smile curved her lips. "If he proposes in the middle of a potion test, you have permission to throw something at him."

"Gladly," Eirwyn said, and reached for the finished syrup. "Time to pour this into the potion bases?"

At Bella's directions, Eirwyn moved gracefully between stations, decanting the golden syrup into four separate bottles—each one a different test version: apple only, apple and honey, apple and bitterroot, and the fourth, a blend of all three.

Leopol entered just as she finished, a servant behind him carrying two overflowing buckets of more ashplums. The scent hit Bella immediately—like nostalgia and firewood, summer and heartbreak. She swallowed hard and kept working.

That evening, they gathered in the parlor.

The sun dipped low, staining the windows amber. Villagers blinked sleepily as they emerged from the enchanted slumber Lailant had cast on them the night before. Confusion quickly turned to tension—until Knox cleared his throat and raised his hands.

"All right, settle down. Food's coming. Drinks too. And no one's going to be cursed further—at least not tonight."

Eirwyn swept into the room behind him with platters of bread, roasted vegetables, and warm cider. The mood lifted slightly as they ate and chatted.

After half an hour, the villagers seemed to grow nervous. Leopol stepped forward.

"The last two villagers who attempted the ritual did not survive," he said. No preamble. Just truth. "But thanks to months of research, Bella's adjustments, and the use of the golden apple Lailant and Knox grew last night, we believe we've created a version that will work."

He gestured to the table where the four potion bottles stood, their contents shimmering faintly.

"I wanted to test it on animals and plants, which is what I did at the Winter Palace," Bella said, glancing at Leopol who nodded in encouragement. She turned back to the villagers as they stared at her, keeping their distance. "But I don't think you want to wait that long?"

"No, we're ready to go back to normal," came a voice by the window.

Leopol's hand settled on her lower back, steadying her nerves.

"Then we'll need volunteers," Bella said. Her voice was calm, but her hands trembled at her sides. "We've tested the magical components, but not the long-term effects with this latest batch. This will be the first live trial. If you step forward, you do so willingly, knowing the risks."

Silence followed. Then five villagers stepped out from the crowd. They drew straws to see which four would take the potion, then Leopol handed the four a vial each. They'd decided on only one version at a time. If this didn't work, they'd try a different variation.

Bella met their eyes as she directed them to say the oath of transformation, of her redemption, reading from the spell book that she and Leopol had tweaked earlier.

"Repeat after me," she said softly, her voice carrying in the stillness so full of anticipation.

"I drink to the gods, I drink to the flame,
To shed the curse and speak my name.
I call my soul from shell and clay,
To breath, to flesh, to life today.

Let form be freed, let fractures mend,
Let what was lost return again.
By apple's heart and honeyed breath,
I rise anew from living death.
My form is mine, no curse shall bind–
By blood, by soul, by will, by mind."
She couldn't breathe as the echoes of their words rang through the room.

Then, one by one, they lifted their vials and drank.

Chapter Twenty

Cerci's body trembled, plagued by dark and torturous nightmares of her time in the Deep. She couldn't escape the memories haunting her, his face and hands burned into her mind.

The cold seeped into her bones, reminding her that she was no longer in the burning Deep. She shivered under the protective stone dome that was Ashur.

Her savior. No, she couldn't burden him with that title. He was a gargoyle, a valiant warrior. She gazed up at him towering over her.

The stone-cold calm of his face in repose as she looked up at him tugged at something deep within her—a mixture of gratitude, hero worship, and a budding affection that bewildered her. Throughout the ages, her body had often sought companionship. But she'd held herself aloof, encasing her heart in a hard gemstone of practicality and survival.

Her human half made so many mistakes, and while she

had fought back to back with Ashur, she didn't *know* him. She only knew what she felt in her soul.

But her soul could be such an idiot. In all her thousand years, she'd never been so stupid as to be tricked by Asmoroth. Even if Mother had assured her it was all part of the Grand Plan in those one-way dream messages she'd sent.

And here she was, shivering her buns off, finally back on Celawyn where she belonged but without any idea of how long she'd been gone or even what continent she'd crawled onto.

Despair threatened to consume her, but it was nothing compared to the horrors she'd endured in the Deep of the Hells. The sounds of the forest comforted her as birds chirped happily, relieved that the giant eagles had given up and flown away.

She shivered, finally giving up on sleep and wiping the exhaustion from her eyes. Based on the shadows, hours must've passed while she'd recovered. She touched her nose, sighing in relief that it was no longer bleeding.

Peering through the small gap between his wingtip and feet, her nose wrinkled at the destruction around them.

Carrion birds feasted on the dead daemons, the magic of their blood long gone. Her own stomach growled, long used to dining on raw daemon from the years spent away. She licked her lips and shook her head, refusing to give in to the conditioned response to jump on the meat, snatch her portion, and eat it before it was gone.

It was time to get some answers, real food, and plan. Somehow, she had to contact her mother and let her and the aunts know of the coming war.

Slowly crawling out of the shelter of Ashur's wings, Cerci stretched and took in her surroundings. The sun was setting but not quite ready to dip below the horizon. The towering trees loomed over her, casting a menacing darkness and obscuring the sun. She turned away in dread.

To the right was the wall of thorns just as tall as the trees. They too seemed to block out the sky, but it was enough for Cerci to take a deep, satisfying breath. For once, the smell of ash, soot, and burning flesh was gone.

She stared at the pink and gold clouds above. Snow would fall soon. Tears stung her eyelids, and she blinked them back. She'd despaired of ever seeing the sky again, and now it was here, so beautiful. She took another breath of the cold air and blinked away her emotions.

There was a narrow gap in the thorny wall only a few feet wide, winding slowly to the right like a river or path. It wasn't a never-ending maze like those in the Deep, and Cerci took that as a sign of hope.

This was her way out of the nightmare, a way to stop the impending doom over them all. Yet, she hesitated and turned back to the stone man, his majestic form still and silent, yet so protective even in slumber.

Ashur's unexpected entry into her life when she'd finally escaped her nightmare caused a chink in the armor around her heart. She was too emotionally, physically, and mentally exhausted from the Deep to resist.

She crawled back into the cocoon of his arms and raised her own. Resting her head against his chest, she sighed. He was solidly a stone, yet he still smelled of sweat, man, earth, and dirt.

The way he'd shielded her with his own body, morphing into an immovable stone sentinel just to protect her from those relentless daemon attacks—it awakened a warmth in her chest she had thought long extinct. His silent, stoic nature might seem cold to others, but Cerci read it as the quiet depth of a still lake, a soothing and steadfast rock amidst her turbulent sea.

She touched his wing gently, the texture familiar and oddly comforting. Memories of how he had shielded her with these very wings, wrapping her in safety as they escaped the daemons, flooded her mind. She owed him her life, yet it was his unwavering kindness that ensnared her heart more tightly than any debt could.

As she traced the lines of his chiseled features softened by shadows, a longing stirred within her—a longing laced with fear. Fear of what might be lost should Asmoroth achieve his goal.

She stepped back and ducked out from the shelter of his arms. Without a backward glance, she walked through the gap in the wall, her limbs heavy from the change in gravity. Each step was painful, her lungs freezing, her breath wheezing, her entire body growing cold the further she went from him.

The birds weren't screaming. The wind didn't carry pain. She wasn't hiding or fighting. She was walking like a regular woman, like herself once more.

Her lungs burned from exertion as she rounded the corner of the wall and came to a stop, hands on her knees. A wide, shimmering pond surrounded by neatly trimmed bushes was to her left.

Two gardeners worked side-by-side, their laughter floating towards her. Behind them, a magnificent castle with spires seemed to touch the sky. She took a deep breath and tried to slow her racing heart before standing straight, hand still holding her side.

She was so weak, it was pathetic. She had to build her strength; otherwise, she'd be useless in the future war.

But for now, she needed food, water, and answers. She

walked around the pond on a well-worn path, each step causing pain through her body. The sound of crunching gravel drew the attention of the gardeners, who turned to look at her with surprise.

One turned and ran for a side door of the castle while the other stood defensively, holding his garden hoe tightly as she approached. She smiled and held her hands out, palms up.

"Hello," she said in the same language that Ashur had used. "Ashur the gargoyle said I might find shelter here?"

Movement from the door drew her gaze, and she stumbled to a halt in surprise. A semi-familiar man strode across the frozen ground toward her, followed by the other gardener. He was dressed in tall boots, fitted breeches, and a jacket over a waistcoat adorned with intricate patterns.

But he was incorporeal and floated like a ghost. No life, just the gray lifeless color that she was all too familiar with.

Panic surged through her body as she took a step back, her hands lighting up with magic. "No! You can't make me go back!"

The ghost frowned and looked down his straight, regal nose. "My lady, I have no intention of making you do anything. *You* are the one who's come to *my* home. Who are you, and what do you want?"

The wheezing of her breath, and his stern tone of voice gave her pause. She wavered on her feet, the use of magic and the fear combining as she saw spots.

As she struggled to catch her breath, she felt a wetness under her nose. She wiped at it and asked hesitantly, "You–you're not from the Hells? He didn't send you to bring me back?"

The man crossed his arms, and she could faintly see the castle through him shifting like a mirage. "I'm glad to say

I've never had the displeasure to go to hell yet, although I'm sure there's still time."

He paused and tilted his head as he watched her. The light on her hands flickered and then fizzled out. She looked at them in surprise, then wiped her nose. Bright red on the back of her hand made her blink. It had been eons since she'd used so much magic she depleted herself.

Blood from her nose dripped down onto her hand, matching the stains on her once white silk dress.

The edges of her vision dimmed, and she swayed on her feet again. The power left her fingers like sand slipping through a broken hourglass. Her nose bled starlight-red, the telltale mark of divine depletion. When she fell, it was not with a crash, but like a leaf lost to the wind.

As if from a tunnel, she heard the ghost yelling orders to the gardeners.

"Oh gods, catch her! She's going to pass out, hopefully not to the Edge."

Then everything went black once more.

———

As the sun disappeared, Ashur came slowly awake. The chill of the stone made him shiver, but he couldn't move yet.

The first breath hurt. Always did. Like life clawing its way back into lungs that had forgotten warmth. His ribs ached. His skin prickled. His eyes stung against the light. But the pain was proof he was alive.

He took shallow breaths, the stone creaking as his body grew warmer. Finally, he flexed his muscles and slowly moved, shedding the stiffness. He threw his wings wide, relishing in the satisfying stretch.

At the rise of every dawn, he hated this curse of stone.

But every night, when he drew that fresh, clean breath and spread his wings... he didn't mind being a beast so much. With a pull on each arm, he stretched and yawned.

There were carcasses pinned to the thorny wall, already picked clean by carrion birds. He frowned at the blood-stained grass and memories trickled into his mind.

The gaping hole that led to the underworld. The menacing daemons that emerged from it. *The girl* who had bravely faced them alongside him.

Now she was nowhere to be seen. He strained to remember her name and the last few moments before sleep had claimed him. He must've told her to go to the castle.

He stretched out his neck, relishing the crack of joints. The familiar itch on the back of his neck made him wince as he reached behind him to scratch.

His hand came away wet, and he glanced at it. Damn birds, always pooping on him when he was caught out in the daylight. A normal sized bird flew down and perched on the thorny wall, chirping as it picked at the leftovers.

Ashur wiped his hand on his pants, cursing all birds and striding for the opening of the wall. Surely, she had gone inside and gotten help from Leopol. Curiosity hounded him with every step.

He remembered something about a goddess. Why had she been in the Hells?

By the time he made it through the wall to Hartsgrove, it was fully dark, and the sleepy memories had returned. That was one good thing to come out of this gargoyle change. He could now see clear as day in the dark.

He strode through the gardens to the castle door, glancing at the lights inside. His friend Knox had spent the past six months building up Vidrland for the refugees from Busparia. But the closer his queen had grown to delivering the first dragon egg in centuries, the more Knox had retreated to Hartsgrove Castle. Now the egg was here, and Knox wouldn't leave his wife or future hatchling. As second-in-command, it was up to Ashur to go to Vidrland and put out fires and help the people.

Thus, Ashur's trip from Vidrland to Hartsgrove, to report back to Knox. He stomped the mud off his boots and pushed open the door to the kitchen. His breath caught in his throat.

At the table sat the goddess, bathed in the glow from the fireplace. She held a steaming mug in her hands and smiled up at Leopol who was pacing, arms gesturing wildly as he told some story.

He hadn't seen her smile before. It captivated him, with a dimple on one corner and a freckle at the corner of her mouth on the other side. It provided an odd sort of symmetry that took his breath away.

One of the servants walked toward the cook at the stove and saw him standing in the doorway. "My lord," the young man said, bowing quickly and continuing on his path.

The smirk on the young man's face said he knew how that title would grate on Ashur's nerves, and he made a mental note to take Reggie outside and teach him a lesson.

All under the guise of training him to protect the castle, of course.

The others in the room fell silent as Ashur stepped forward, his gaze fixed on Cerci.

Leopol rushed to open the door. "Lord Ashur, so glad you made it. I was just telling Lady Cerci here about the time I helped King Feralt settle an argument between his father and his brother using a pig's intestine ballooned up into a ball."

He stood tall, his head almost grazing the ceiling. "Is that so? I take it Lady Cerci is recovered then?"

Cerci blushed, her mouth dropping open as she saw him. Her eyes widened as they raked down his body. Judging by how her back straightened and her blush deepened, she liked what she saw.

Ashur pushed down the hope. What goddess could ever hope to love a beast like him? He stepped inside and shut the door against the cold.

"Not quite," she said softly, her voice a melody that spoke to his soul.

He didn't take his eyes off her. "Leopol, when are you going to have one of these servants write down all your exploits and stories, hm? I think the continent could do with an updated version of the history books."

Leopol waved a hand. "Oh, you flatter me. Lady Cerci, *are* you recovered enough for me to escort you to your room to freshen up?"

"I–I'd like to stay for a late supper with Ashur, if that's alright. I'm still starving, and I doubt he's eaten." She looked away, nervously twirling the end of her long, white hair as it cascaded over her shoulder.

He hated seeing her so submissive. Just hours ago, she had stood strong and fearless in the face of danger. He longed to see that same determination in her posture, with her head held high and a fierce glint in her eyes. Maybe she'd look like that as she rode him.

The thought made him jerk in surprise, but no one seemed to notice as the cook turned from the stove and pointed a spoon at them.

"Perfect timing, my lady, as supper is served," Hank said.

Leopol clapped his hands. "Excellent, excellent. Lady Cerci, are you quite warm enough?"

"Oh yes, Sir Leopol, I've quite recovered my body temperature, thank you."

"Then let's adjourn to the formal dining room, shall we? I'll introduce you to the king and queen of the Feral Forest, as well as the queen of Busparia, and the Seer. Lord Ashur, wash up and join us. Tonight, we're celebrating!" Leopol waved to the swinging kitchen door and floated toward it, his feet not grazing the floor even though he walked.

Cerci stood, her mug shaking in her hand. She cupped her other hand around it, holding it steady as she glanced at him, blushing furiously. He wanted to know her every look, wanted to read her expressions like a book. But he had no idea what she was thinking as she nodded and followed Leopol through the door.

When she was gone, Ashur turned to the sink and took a deep breath. It felt like he'd not been able to gather enough air into his lungs since he'd stepped inside. She took up all his spare oxygen, all the space in his heart and mind. He had no claim over her, yet he couldn't shake the emotions she evoked in him.

"Good to see you again, Lord Ashur," the cook said.

Ashur scoffed. "Hank, I've known you since before the Feral Forest became a kingdom and Knox gave me that ridiculous title. How many times must I tell you Ashur is fine?"

The greasy cook grinned, revealing relatively clean teeth, even if a few of them were missing. "I'll call you Lord Ashur as long as I please. It's the least I can do for getting us out of the dungeon before the whole castle collapsed. You'll have my gratitude forever."

Ashur felt his ears heat as he dried his hands. He said gruffly, "Well, I don't need it. Just keep yourself safe and take care of the missus. How are you both liking Hartsgrove?"

The cook regaled him with their comfortable sleeping quarters and the news that they were expecting. A pang of longing went through him, but he punched that feeling down too.

He forced a stony smile and clapped the cook on the back. "Congratulations," he said.

The cook winced at the touch, and Ashur withdrew, pursing his lips as he backed toward the swinging door. "Sorry, I keep forgetting my own strength. Are you alright?"

The cook nodded as the bus boy put a pot on a tray. "I'll be fine. Will you get the door for Reggie?"

Ashur stepped forward and grabbed the tray. "I'll take it. Reggie needs to build his strength. He's more likely to drop something this heavy."

"Hey," Reggie whined, his mop of curly hair bobbing as he punched Ashur in the arm. He sucked in a breath and shook his hand in pain. "Ow, damn it, why'd you have to be turned to stone. Why did everything have to change for the Robins? Ugh."

Ashur neatly juggled the silver tray laden with three bowls of stew and mini loaves of bread. "Good to see you're adjusting to Hartsgrove well, Reggie. Have you kept up with your training?"

Reggie grinned and said cockily, "How 'bout I meet you outside after dinner, and I'll show you?"

Ashur chuckled as he backed toward the door. "We'll see."

The door swung behind him, and he strode down the short corridor to the dining room. Their voices were muffled so he didn't stop to snoop. Instead, he turned and backed into the swinging door, spinning into the room as gracefully as he could while carrying a tray of food.

None of those inside looked up at him as he set down a bowl in front of Leopol to the right of the head of the table. He winced, was he supposed to serve the goddess first?

Damn his country roots. He set the bowl in front of her, then the loaf of bread before circling back to Leopol.

"Where's everyone else?" he asked, setting the last bowl in the center of the plate in front of his chair, adding bread beside it. The scent of ash clung to her, but he wanted to get closer.

Silver glinted on the crisp, white tablecloth, the dragon crest embroidery glinting with green and gold thread. The white porcelain plates were rimmed in gold and green.

Leopol frowned and shook his head. "They're telling the last of the villagers goodbye. I'll go tell them dinner is served. But please, Lady Cerci, eat. We're not going to keep a goddess from eating her first real meal in hundreds of years. I'll be right back."

Leopol smiled and bowed before leaving the room toward the main hallway. Ashur put the now empty tray on the sideboard as Reggie came into the room and set a pitcher on the table next to him.

Ashur sat down beside Cerci, unable to leave her side. Her delicate hand was pale against the white fabric as she picked up her crystal glass filled with dark, amber mead.

The shadows under her eyes betrayed her exhaustion and fear. Her nails were torn and the tips of her fingers were raw. She'd washed the blood from her hands and face, but the evidence of where she'd come from made his chest ache. The blood splatters on her dress, the smell of daemons clinging to her, tangles in her hair.

She should've gone upstairs and soaked in a long, hot

bath. He snapped the napkin and put it on his lap as Reggie poured his mead.

"Eat, gorgeous," Ashur said softly, nodding to the soup.

The tension in his shoulders tightened as he observed her every movement, the way she flinched slightly at the clink of silverware, how she scanned the room with wary eyes that spoke volumes of her prolonged isolation and recent traumas.

It was pain he felt echoing in his own heart, magnified by his inability to shield her from it. The weight of his feelings for her—complex and burgeoning beneath his breastbone—seemed to expand with every breath he took in her presence.

As Cerci hesitantly brought the spoon to her lips, the broth likely alien to her refined but long-untested sense of taste, and he wished he could carry her up the stairs and take care of her.

He wished he could strip away the horrors of her time in hell alongside every layer of clothing. Then he'd kiss every inch of skin until her mind and body were healed of that place.

Chapter Twenty-One

The last echoes of laughter faded as the heavy wooden door closed behind the volunteers and their guards. Bella lingered in the hallway, still processing the past few hours. Relief washed over her like a gentle tide, bringing with it a cautious sense of celebration.

When the volunteers hadn't keeled over dead immediately, the entire room of villagers had broken out in applause and excited chatter.

Leopol had spoken with authority, his words carrying in the room as he organized guards for the volunteers. They needed to be observed around the clock for the next month. All the side effects needed to be documented.

Bella bit her lip, worrying about when they would separate from the inanimate objects. If their research and notes were accurate, it should be between the twenty-four- and forty-eight-hour mark.

Leopol had instructed the volunteers to return before sunset tomorrow so that they could observe the transformation process—and provide healing potions if necessary. After the initial transformation period, they'd be sent home. While regular guards had been sent with them tonight, Leopol would curate a group of people to rotate following the volunteers around the village as they went about their daily lives.

She frowned, remembering how healing potions had been no help to Sharlo or Ignot.

Almost immediately after the thought, she sighed in relief at how different this test trial was. No one was vomiting blood. No one had collapsed. No twisted limbs or unnatural shifts.

Her shoulders, which had been bunched tight with dread, began to relax, the tension unspooling slowly. She exhaled, only then realizing she'd been holding her breath.

They were alive. They were whole—still cursed, yes. But there was time yet before the next phase of the plan. Time for the potion to work its magic, time for the curse to loosen its grip.

They might actually solve this problem. The thought was a delicate thing, fluttering in her chest like a bird too afraid to take flight. It was a dangerous thing to hope, to let down one's guard when the battle was far from won.

But in that moment, as the darkness enveloped the castle outside, she couldn't help but feel it—relief, that sweetest of emotions, tinged with the prospect of victory. She was so afraid to hope, but she was undeniably human.

Eirwyn and Knox went into the dining room, and Lailant paused to peer at Bella from too-sharp eyes.

"You're on the right track, child. Stop fretting. It'll turn out alright in the end. You'll see," Lailant said as Leopol paused by the dining room door and smiled at her.

That smile said it all. He was proud of her tonight. He hadn't said it but she could feel it deep in her soul. It was in the bright shining eyes, the tilt of his chin, the width of his grin.

He held out his elbow for her to take. "I know you don't eat dinner in this form, but tonight, we have cause to celebrate. Will you join us?"

It was a command and a question, cajoling and pleading, all rolled into one. She could no longer deny him.

As she stepped toward him, something in her chest hitched. The way his eyes lingered on her, warm and unguarded, made her stomach flutter. The world seemed to fade around the edges, softening, narrowing to the heat in his gaze and the sudden, traitorous awareness of how badly she wanted to feel his arms around her again. The bond between them thrummed low and hungry beneath her skin.

The moment stretched. Bella's steps slowed, a surge of emotions rising to the surface—uncertainty, desire, fear, hope. Her soul knew before her mind did. She needed him. Wanted him. And maybe, just maybe, she could trust herself again and take the chance on him.

Her mate, if he was to be believed.

They entered the dining room, her gaze assessing those inside as she made her way to her seat. The sturdy chair received her weight, a solid comfort compared to the fluttering uncertainty within her. It wasn't as hard to use her magic to stay on the chair as it had been last week.

Leopol stroked the back of her arm, and she shivered, turning away from him. They were mates, but could she trust that bond, trust him? She'd thought she could trust Gastone.

Her eyes found the woman seated next to Ashur. Bella's healer instincts surged to the front. The woman was worn and tattered, exhausted to her very bones. Yet she sat with poise and was clearly something—or someone—special.

"Are you hurt?" Bella asked gently, patting her pockets to find a small healing vial. "This should help with any pain or fatigue." She floated the vial down the table to the woman.

The woman accepted with a grateful nod. "Thank you. Leopol's already given me several, though."

Before Bella could ask anything more, Lailant sat next to the newcomer. She frowned and leaned into the woman's personal space.

"Cerci?" Lailant whispered, voice trembling.

Cerci turned, eyes wide. "How do you know my name?"

The room stilled. Lailant slowly reached out to cup her cheek, hands shaking. Then she spoke in another language Bella didn't recognize. The spell Leopol had used apparently didn't work for spoken languages, just written.

The melodious tones and sounds were familiar though, like a dream that one doesn't quite remember on waking.

Bella could hardly believe her ears or her eyes as Cerci's eyes welled with tears, and she threw herself into the old woman's arms.

Lailant crooned softly, patting her hair just as she'd done so many times for Bella herself. A pang flowed through her of...not jealousy but an ache for a simpler time.

Ashur hovered behind Cerci as she shifted, laughing self-deprecatingly as she wiped at her tears. He offered her a napkin and barely restrained himself from touching the woman.

Leopol cleared his throat. "Lady Cerci, I see you know Lailant, the Seer. This is King Knoxious and Queen Eirwyn of the Feral Forest, and this is Queen Bella of Busparia. Everyone, this is the demigoddess, Cerci."

The rest of the table froze in surprise, except for Ashur and Lailant. Bella hadn't expected a goddess to show up before the soup course, but there she was—in a blood-stained dress, seated beside Ashur like she belonged there. And maybe she did.

Cerci's too pale cheeks flushed as she nodded first to Knox, then to Eirwyn and Bella.

"It's a pleasure to meet you. I apologize for dropping by unannounced and in rags."

"Nonsense," Eirwyn said, her smile tight as she struggled to keep the confusion off her face. "Tell us how you came here. How did you survive the Feral Forest alone?"

"She didn't. She crawled out of a hole in the ground." Ashur shifted slightly in his chair, voice deep and matter of fact. "She nearly died fighting off a horde of daemons from a rift by the helrose hedge."

Cerci shot him a look, weary but with such hero worship, it made Bella ache. "He protected me with his own body, wrapped his wings around me and turned to stone mid-fight. The daemons clawed and slashed at him, and he didn't even flinch. I barely had the strength left to cast the seal on the rift."

Ashur's brow furrowed. "I only did what any decent warrior would do—held the line so you could finish the spell to seal it. I just slowed them down."

"You saved me," she said simply. "I wouldn't be here without you."

Cerci shared pieces of her harrowing tale from the Deep, each word sending tremors down Bella's spine.

As Cerci spoke of horrors beyond comprehension—of darkness without end, of whispers that drove the mind to madness—Bella's breath caught in her throat. A chill crawled down her spine, not from fear of daemons, but from the echo of helplessness that sounded so familiar.

What if the same fate awaited her people? What if all

their effort had only delayed the inevitable? What if even Leopol couldn't stop what was coming?

Her fingers curled tightly around the edge of the table, knuckles white. This wasn't just a story. It was a warning—and they were already running out of time. Dark forces stirred after centuries of silence. It was a war long coming, if the history books were to be believed.

Knox scratched the side of his head. "Let me get this straight. You crawled out of a rift to the Hells?"

"I created the rift. It was time to get out."

"But how did you get there?" Bella asked, leaning forward.

Cerci glanced at Lailant out of the side of her eyes, then tipped her chin up. "I went into the Deep willingly, but Asmoroth thinks he tricked me," Cerci explained, her voice quiet but firm. "I was on a mission from my mother to learn what Asmoroth was planning. I found out more than I bargained for. He's created several sin lords on Celawyn. They're helping him build him a path out of the Deep."

Gasps and sharp inhales filled the room.

Leopol leaned toward her, whispering softly, "That aligns with what we know of the wizard."

Bella nodded, her relief from the ritual's non-side effects forgotten as another worry took its place.

"Once he escapes, he'll use Celawyn as a staging ground—amass his army here. And from there, he'll do what no other god has tried. He'll rise... and challenge the gods themselves." Cerci swayed on her chair, and Ashur's hand squeezed hers.

Cerci looked up at him with total trust and faith, the type that shouldn't be there without a long, solid foundation.

Ashur said, "You're exhausted. Let's get you washed and in a proper bed. You need to rest."

Cerci yawned and nodded. "I think you're right. It took far too much of my magic reserves to crawl out of the Deep."

"She's had enough excitement," Ashur said as he stood and offered her his hand. "Leopol, can you have someone send up a hot bath to my room? And clothes?"

Leopol nodded, but said, "We've prepared–"

Ashur interrupted, firm and unshakable. "No, she'll stay with me. She's mine." He blanched and turned to look down at her with a slight panicked expression. "I mean, if you want to, I'll take care of–"

Cerci smiled up at him, her hand on his forearm stopping him mid-sentence. "I'd prefer not to be alone right now, yes."

The tension in Ashur's shoulders immediately lifted as he swept her into his arms. She leaned into him, peaceful and content with a soft smile on her face. The room remained silent as he carried her out the door, his heavy steps echoing up the stairs.

Bella stared, her heart full and aching. The way Cerci melted into Ashur's arms–utterly sure, utterly safe–left a raw scrape across Bella's chest. It shouldn't have been possible. They'd just met. No long conversations, no careful planning, no weighing pros and cons or setting boundaries. Just instinct, certainty.

That's what it looked like–to just know. No more hesitating, no endless weighing of risk and reward. Just trust, love.

Bella had spent her whole life thinking, planning, calculating. Her mind was her sharpest weapon, her best shield. But watching Cerci and Ashur now, she wondered if she'd been wielding it like armor instead of a tool.

Could she let herself leap like that? Let herself trust the pull she felt to Leopol, that soul-deep gravity that had terrified her since the moment he'd touched her hand? It had built with their kisses and touches but had all coalesced with him claiming her as his mate in front of everyone.

Was it so foolish... to want something that simple? To believe that maybe, just maybe, she didn't need to *earn* love this time–she just had to accept it?

Leopol stood, his movement unhurried as he stepped to the servant hovering nearby. After speaking to him, he turned and nodded at the others before bending closer to murmur in her ear, "We have much to discuss and plan for the test subject's arrival tomorrow. Would you like to get started on that now?"

He stood and looked down at her, an unspoken question in his eyes. His hand extended toward her, open and steady, Bella hesitated, heart thudding against her ribs. Her mind screamed caution–memories of past betrayals, of Gastone's empty promises–but her soul... her soul whispered something else.

That here, in Leopol's quiet strength, was a different promise. One not demanded but offered. Slowly, she reached out, her fingers trembling as they slipped into his. His warmth grounded her, the touch sparking a thousand thoughts all at once.

Bella stared up at him, the quiet reverence in his eyes clear. She placed her hand in his and offered her good nights to the others. He didn't release her hand as they walked out of the dining room, and she rather liked it.

"Would you like to go to the library to plan or do you want a few hours rest? Have the meditations I taught you been helping you sleep?" Leopol asked, tucking her hand into the crook of his elbow.

She licked her lips, knowing what she wanted but unable

to come right out and say it. So, she took the coward's way out.

"Yes, I'd like to meditate for a while. Would you escort me to my room?"

As he had every night, they walked up the stairs side by side. Usually, she filled the quiet with questions, theories, anything to keep from thinking about how close he was.

But tonight, silence lingered between them like a held breath. Her heartbeat echoed in her ears, each step a silent countdown. Perhaps it was still the shock of an actual demigoddess showing up. Her mind went through every story she'd ever read about the portal and transformation demigoddess, all the books on the old religion.

At her door, she paused, no longer able to distract herself from the spirit beside her.

His hand tightened on her elbow, a silent offer. A question without words, the same one he'd silently asked since she'd arrived.

Bella stared at the worn handle of her door. She could say goodnight and slip into her routine again. She could pretend that the fire between them hadn't flared in the dining room, hadn't been stoked by every glance, every moment of understanding and trust between them this past week.

Her fingers hovered near the door handle, heart hammering against her ribs. Gastone had used sweet words too. Promises and smiles that made her feel seen—until they didn't. Until they shattered her. Was she making the same mistake again?

Leopol wasn't Gastone. He had seen her broken and helpless, and still stayed. Still wanted her. Maybe... maybe that was worth the risk.

She turned, searching his face. "Would you like to meditate with me?" she asked, voice soft but steady.

Leopol blinked, startled at the change in their routine, then nodded. "I would love to spend more time with you, Bella. You know that."

She flushed and stepped inside. He stepped inside, quiet and steady as always, but the moment the door clicked shut, she could feel the space hum with unspoken want. The space around them shifted—charged with possibility, with something raw and infinite.

Bella's breath caught. This wasn't just another evening. This was a turning point—one she'd chosen. No more running. No more walls. He'd followed her into the room, and she knew it was time to face him and what they could be together.

Heart hammering, soul trembling, she stopped in front of the fireplace and turned to face him. Her fingers curled slightly at her sides as doubt and longing warred inside her—twin storms battling for control. Was this foolish? Reckless? Or was it finally brave?

The warmth of the fire echoed the heat rising in her chest as she met his gaze, all the things she'd feared finally brought into the light. She was ready to choose him. No more questions. No more waiting.

For the first time, she didn't feel like a ghost at the end of her life, running out of time. She was on the edge of a new start, a new relationship, a new adventure... and dare she even think it? A new love.

And this time, she wouldn't run from what they were becoming. Not anymore.

Chapter Twenty-Two

Leopol shifted on his feet, obviously nervous. She smiled, finding it endearing that he seemed to not know what to do with himself.

She waved to the pillows on the floor in front of the fire. "Would you care to sit?"

He cleared his throat and strode the few steps over, sinking to the plush carpet and crossing his legs, hands resting gently on his knees. The flames cast faint shadows over his face, highlighting the soft blankets and brocade pillows scattered around them.

She sat on her favorite one, a flick of the wrist using her magic to interact with it. She found it easier to interact with things these days, which was probably a result of the meditations she'd been doing nightly.

"I don't think so," Leopol said. "I think it's a result of the mate bond changing us."

She blinked, not even realizing that she'd been speaking aloud. The scent of burning wood filled her nostrils, reminding her that she was human.

Her mouth went dry as she frowned, straightening her skirt to cover her legs as she crossed them. When she was finally facing him on her pillow, she processed his words.

"What do you mean, the mate bond changes us?" Her breath caught in her throat.

She wasn't ready for more changes. There was so much that had happened the past few days—and her entire life had been turned upside down less than a year ago. She wasn't sure how much more change she could handle.

He frowned and shifted onto his knees, taking her hands in his. "Hey, it's alright. Breathe with me just like I taught you."

The crackling of the fire and the soft, steady sound of their breathing calmed her nerves. His hands anchored her, bringing comfort and intimacy that made her soul tingle.

His presence stabilized her flickering energy. It had been doing that all week, but was it really a result of the mate bond?

His thumb grazed the back of her hand, and everything in the room sharpened into focus.

Their souls were close, their knees almost touching, their joined hands grounding them in the here and now. They stared into each other's eyes, his thumbs going back and forth, their breathing flowing together like a harmony and melody of a song their souls knew on a fundamental level.

In this quiet space, their energies began to merge and swirl, creating a bond of a different kind. Leopol had been steady and strong all week, balancing her in a way that was both comforting and exhilarating.

This connection was more than just physical attraction or the fact that they could actually touch each other. Cerci was a powerful demigoddess, if the history books were to be believed, yet she had trusted Ashur and leaned on him when she needed help.

Perhaps this deep sense of peace and understanding she felt with Leopol was what she had been searching for all along.

It wasn't just lust or fate—it was peace, knowing that whatever this was between them was real, that she could trust it and trust him. Not just with her body or soul but with everything.

She bit her lip, worrying about how to actually take that step of trust.

Leopol's eyebrow rose, and his lips quirked on one side. "Stop thinking," he said.

She sighed and rolled her eyes. "I'm sorry, it's just hard to do when so much is going on."

"Close your eyes," he whispered, voice like velvet soaked in thunder even as his blue eyes blazed with a depth of emotion she was afraid to explore. She took the coward's way out and obeyed.

"Let yourself just feel. Let go of all the thoughts blasting in your mind," he said, his breath caressing her cheek.

Bella's breath hitched again, this time because he let go of her hands and trailed the backs of his fingers up her hand to her forearms. She obeyed, because gods help her, she wanted to trust him. For once, she wanted to stop thinking, stop calculating, stop controlling.

His fingers found her cheek, brushing the line of her jaw with a reverence that made her spirit form shiver.

"That's it," he murmured, his breath warm against her lips. "You live in your head. Let me guide you back into your body."

"I don't even have a body."

"You have a soul. And right now, it's everything." Each

word was a barely-there caress against her lips. She leaned forward, closing the distance between them.

He groaned and slanted his head, so their lips slid together like a key in a lock. They just fit.

The kiss was slow, deliberate—a careful exploration that spoke more of tender discovery than passionate urgency. His lips moved against hers with a reverence that made her soul tremble, each touch a whispered question seeking permission.

Tentative at first, as if they were both afraid of breaking something delicate, but then Leopol's hand slid into her hair, anchoring her, and the tentativeness dissolved into something more primal. His magic swirled around them, creating a cocoon of warmth that made the firelight seem pale in comparison.

Bella felt herself falling into him, not just physically but energetically. Her spirit was liquid, merging with his in ways she had never experienced. This wasn't just a kiss—it was a conversation without words, a promise without sound.

When they finally pulled apart, her breath came in short, ragged gasps. Leopol's eyes were darker, more intense, filled with a hunger that went beyond physical desire. His thumb traced her lower lip, and she saw something vulnerable in his expression—a mix of wonder and fear.

He sighed, his forehead resting against hers. Their breath mingled, creating a shared warmth that seemed to pulse between them. The firelight cast amber shadows across his face, revealing the vulnerability etched in the lines around his eyes.

"We don't have to do anything more if you're not ready," he murmured, his fingers still tracing delicate patterns on her cheek. "We have time to figure out this mate bond together."

Those words—simple yet profound—settled between them. Bella realized she'd never been offered time before. Every interaction in her past had been transactional, calculated, with an expected outcome. But here, with Leopol, time stretched between them like silk—soft, deceptive. And untrue.

They didn't have time. The rose on the side table behind him pulsed brightly, and with him touching her, she could see the thin golden tether tying her to it. Fainter now, thinner. But the rose seemed to shiver in anticipation at what their kiss meant, reflecting what her soul yearned for.

She blinked up at him, his thumb caressing her cheek while his other hand tucked a piece of hair behind her ear.

"I—I want you, Leopol."

The words tasted foreign on her tongue—honest, raw, terrifying. Her breath caught as silence fell between them. For a heartbeat, she almost took it back.

What if this ruins everything? What if I break him too?

But then he looked at her—like she was the answer to a question he hadn't dared ask in centuries—and the fear cracked open into something softer. Trust, desire, hope—it all coalesced into a burning knot in her stomach.

His eyes widened as he froze, glancing down at her with eyes burning with desire.

The moment hung suspended between them, charged with an electricity that made the fire's flames seem tame by comparison. Leopol's breath caught, his fingers still tracing the delicate line of her jaw. For a heartbeat, neither moved.

Then, with a deliberateness that spoke of restraint and raw emotion, he shifted. His hand slid from her cheek to the back of her neck, fingers splaying against her skin. Not demanding. Not pushing. Just present.

"Are you certain?" The words were a whisper, barely audible above the crackling fire.

Her soul trembled at the reverence in his voice. This wasn't just a physical wanting–it was something deeper. Something that resonated in the marrow of her being. *Mate.*

She nodded, answering him and acknowledging what her soul had known all along as her fingers traced the line of his jaw. The firelight cast dancing shadows across his skin, revealing the vulnerability beneath his strength. Every touch felt like a revelation–delicate, charged with potential energy.

Their magic swirled around them, soft tendrils of azure and silver weaving through the firelight. The rose behind them trembled, its golden tether flickering like a distant heartbeat. Time seemed to compress and expand simultaneously, breathing with their own synchronized rhythm.

Bella understood now what her soul had been whispering all along: this moment was inevitable, written by the gods in the stars. They had each been created for the other.

Her rose pulsed bright behind her on the table, the tether between them glowing... then snapping, not fully, but fractured and redirected.

Somewhere beneath the castle, a pulse of gold light echoed through the earth–unseen, unfelt by most.

Bella's heart stuttered.

Fire. Stone. A staircase spiraling down. A cave of treasures. The vision she'd had by the hearth weeks ago came rushing back, sharper now. A cave filled with a dying dragon and a hoard beyond her wildest dreams.

She clutched Leopol tighter. "Did you feel that?" Why did she think of that fire vision now, when they were on the precipice of something that could change their relationship forever?

He stiffened, eyes going unfocused. "Yes," he said hoarsely. "Something just... woke up."

She gasped, light bursting behind her eyes. "What–what was that?"

"Perhaps it's the bond," Leopol rasped, trembling with restraint, only their hands gripping each other's arms. "The mate bond changes us both. One of the seals binding you to the rose just... broke as a result of us taking the next step in the mate bond."

"The next step? Seals? There's more than one?"

"Yes." His mouth moved lower. "And I intend to unlock each one. You are everything I never dared to hope for. There's nothing I wouldn't do for you, Bella."

He dipped his lips to hers once more, and her eyes fluttered closed so that she could finally lose herself in him.

He kissed her like a scholar discovering a lost language– slow, methodical, devout, promising more than she ever thought possible. Their magic crackled around them, threads of gold and violet and silver weaving between them.

He reached for the button on the back of her dress, and she moaned, shaking her head slightly. She focused and a split second later, she sat before him naked as the day she was born.

He froze and sat back on his haunches, his eyes hungrily devouring her, glancing over every exposed inch.

Leopol's breath caught, a tremor running through his hands. "You're breathtaking," he whispered, the words laden with something deeper than mere physical appreciation.

A slight flush crept across her cheekbones. She was unused to such unguarded admiration, having spent years protecting herself from genuine connection. His eyes tracked the blush, a small smile playing at the corners of his mouth, his breath catching. "I... I've never done this before. Not like this. Not with someone who matters."

Bella's breath caught. "Wait—you mean you've never done this ever or—?"

"Not in this form. Not with this much magic in the air. Not with someone I..." He cut himself off and looked away, flustered. "It doesn't matter."

But it did. The words hung between them like a sacred thread. She reached for him, heart thudding. "We'll figure it out together."

His gaze was reverent, almost worshipful, with a raw intensity that made her skin prickle with anticipation. She felt exposed, vulnerable, but not afraid in her nakedness. Instead, she felt powerful, seen completely without judgment or expectation.

He leaned forward, pressing a soft kiss to her collarbone. His lips were warm, deliberate—each touch a careful exploration.

His magic flickered around them, azure tendrils dancing with her own violet energy and creating a cocoon.

She reached forward, her fingers tracing the line of buttons on his shirt. Each movement was deliberate, charged with intention. She didn't rush, didn't fumble—her touch was a question, an invitation.

When the last button slipped free, she pushed the fabric from his shoulders. A flash of magic, and his boots, socks, shirt, and evening jacket disappeared, leaving him in nothing but his pants.

His skin was marked with intricate tattoos she hadn't noticed before—swirling runes and delicate symbols that seemed to pulse with their own inner light. They weren't just decoration. She recognized a few of the runes and sigils.

The tattoos told a story—ancient magic etched into his skin, each line a testament to generations of power and lineage. Her fingers traced the intricate patterns, feeling them pulse beneath her touch. Some were familiar runes from old texts, others looked like symbols she'd never encountered.

"What are these?" she whispered, her breath catching as one particularly complex symbol near his heart seemed to shimmer with an inner luminescence.

Leopol's muscles tensed beneath her exploration. "Ancestral markings, among other things" he murmured. "Protection spells. Binding contracts. Memory records. I don't..."

His voice trailed off as his raw vulnerability was exposed. she waited as he swallowed and looked into the fire, his eyes growing vacant as he looked inward.

He licked his lips. "I... don't know what they all mean." His voice broke on the last word, and he suddenly stood, pacing barefoot across the soft carpet before the fire as he raked a hand through his hair.

"I told you how I woke up—really woke up, I mean—it was in a temple. Marble floors cracked with dirt and overgrown grass. Stars etched into the ceiling. My dragon parents found me there, fully grown, no childhood, no history. But I remember... *other things*."

He paused, fingers tangled in his hair, frustration radiating off him in waves as his soul flickered, glowing and pulsing as he turned to pace the other direction.

She slowly stood up and magically brought her favorite dressing gown around her shoulders, tying it with the blue belt. The hem was frayed but so soft, and the pale blue almost matched his eyes.

She sank into the chair to the side of the hearth and listened as he mumbled.

"Sometimes I see flashes. Not dragon memories—*human ones* in this form. I see these hands holding books in a place of light with rows and rows of books, endless books, mountains of them. More books than anyone could ever read in a lifetime, so I know I was endless, not mortal—because I know I read all of them. I *knew* those books. Books on every subject ever studied by every author who ever set pen to paper. And these tattoos?"

He thrust out his arm, the glowing runes dancing in the firelight. "Some of them I know, like a record of some of the most special books. Others I *feel*, deep in my bones. They're older than this planet, Bella. Older than the gods here."

He looked at her then, raw and wide-eyed. "It's like I lived a whole other life before the dragons gave me this one. And I don't know who I was. Or if I'm still him. Or if I'm just crazy and these memories aren't real or—"

Bella stood and wrapped her arms around his waist. He stiffened, then pulled her into his arms, resting his chin against her hair.

"Breathe in with me," she whispered, mimicking his breathing exercises from earlier.

Together they regulated their breaths, restoring the harmony and melody they created when they were together.

She understood this was more than just skin art—these were his history, his bloodline's secrets mapped across his body. Each mark represented a story, a connection to something larger than himself, and not knowing what all of them meant must be so hard for someone like him.

"Some of these markings I recognize from being a dragon. I know they were on my dragon body, which didn't look like this human version. Am I a dragon? Or something else? What if–"

"Whoa, slow down, professor," she said, leaning back to stare up into his too-serious face with a teasing smile. "You're spiraling."

She leaned up and gave him a quick kiss on the lips.

"You're brilliant. Maddening. Broody." Each word she punctuated with a kiss before she said, "I know you need to know all the things, understand the workings of people, places, everything you encounter so that you can make it better and help people."

She stroked his spine slowly and relished in the feel of his skin beneath her hands, of his intense gaze solely focused on her. She recognized that about him because she did the exact same thing. He was a kindred spirit.

"But give yourself some grace. You saw how I struggled to find the right recipe, spell, potion, and ritual to fix the curse, but all those sleepless nights of hard work are finally paying off. Be patient, professor. It doesn't matter so much who you were before. Whoever you are, whatever you are..." she paused, hesitating to give words to what she was feeling.

She licked her lips and leaped into the metaphorical unknown. "You're mine now."

His eyes darkened as a flare of magic pulsed between them. Arms locked around each other, he dipped his head until his lips hovered softly against hers. Then he growled. "And you're mine. Forever, Bella. You're my mate, my heart, my everything."

Then the rest of his clothing disappeared. She gasped, her hands sliding down his spine to the rise of his ass. Her eyes widened, and her magic flared, shaking the furniture around them as her dressing gown disappeared.

Both naked now, standing wrapped in each other's arms

in front of the fire still as statues, they stared into each other's eyes. He licked his lips and glanced at hers. "Close your eyes," he said softly.

Her eyes fluttered closed. She didn't know if it was because she couldn't deny him—or just didn't want to. For once in her life, she wanted to just feel her way through this.

He tucked her head against his shoulder and stroked the back of her hair slowly, soothingly. Her nerves settled, even as her awareness of him increased.

She wanted him, wanted this physical connection between them when nothing else was quite physical enough.

Bella licked her lips, nestling her head into the crook of his shoulder. "Do—do you think it's always like this with mates?"

Leopol smiled. "Perhaps, if Knox is to be believed. But I can't imagine any other fated mate pair in the history of the universe ever felt quite this good."

She giggled softly, burying her head in his shoulder.

"What?" he asked, leaning back to tip her chin up with one finger.

The grin spread on her face, her soul light for the first time in months. "Nothing. It's just—we haven't even done anything yet, but you're right. It does feel unbelievably good to just..." A blush swept up her chest and over her cheeks as she glanced away.

"Just?" he encouraged, stroking her jaw with his thumb and sending a shiver up her spine.

She met his blazing blue gaze. "Just to be held, seen, known."

Slowly, his smile spread, and he shifted slightly against her. Her nipples hardened, and she gasped at the length pressed against her.

"I'd like to know more of you, Bella, if you're willing."

She licked her lips, something clicking in her mind. When you're known by someone on the soul level, there's safety, hope, belonging. An acceptance of who you are exactly as you are. There was no need to pretend to be anyone but herself.

In the cradle of his arms, with the firelight flickering across their skin, Bella finally understood what it meant to be *chosen*. Not for power or prophecy—but simply... for love? Was this love?

Love didn't always go hand in hand with fated mates. The history books were full of stories of it going wrong.

But this didn't feel wrong. This felt right on every level.

Slowly she nodded and lifted onto her toes, pressing her lips to his.

Chapter Twenty-Three

Leopol's world condensed to the space where their bodies met, a tumultuous tempest of desire and connection that defied the very laws of physics.

He cradled her face between his hands, thumbs caressing her cheeks with the gentleness of a whisper, lips descending onto hers in a kiss that spoke volumes of how much he worshipped her. It was a kiss that held the softness of a thousand tender moments and the promise of a million more.

He had never felt so strongly for another person before. He wanted to protect her, love her, stand by her side for eternity. He poured all of his hopes and dreams into the kiss, circling her tongue with his until she went liquid in his arms.

Her reaction was immediate, tightening her grip on his hips, pulling him closer as if she could meld them into one entity. He knew exactly how she felt; he, too, wanted to burrow into her and never leave.

She shifted against him, her restlessness a silent plea for

more, her moans a not-so-silent demand for relief. Her breaths came fast and shallow, each exhale a symphony to his senses. Leopol felt the rhythm of her heart against his chest, a pulsating drumbeat that guided him through their intimate waltz. He savored the ebb and flow of her every sigh, attuned to the language of her body as though it were his own.

In that instant, they were more than two beings; they were the very essence of unity, messy and magical, tender and explosive—just like them.

Leopol's hands, emboldened by desire, traced the curve of her spine in a descent that was both possessive and reverent. Finding purchase beneath the softness of her flesh, he lifted her with a strength honed from centuries of yearning. Her legs instinctively coiled around his waist, her essence clinging to him as though their souls were entwined by invisible threads.

A primal need surged through him when her slick slit cradled his dick, trapping him against her. Her legs held him tight, and he lifted her by the ass, her moans molding with his growl into a song as ancient as the gods.

With stumbling steps, he crossed the threshold to the silken sheets, eager to claim her, bury himself in her, and show her how he felt. Gently, he laid her upon the bed, a temple altar for their primal rites.

His hand, glowing with the subtle light of magic, traced down her sternum, each fingertip drawing concentric circles upon her skin. The touch left a wake of magic, summoning goosebumps and shivers that danced across her like ripples on a moonlit pond.

He thanked the gods for his years studying the mating rituals of dragons, silently using his magic to paint temporary runes on her skin that would heighten her desire.

Her eyes widened, glowing brightly as she threw her head back against the bed. "Gods, yes. I don't know what the fuck you're doing, but don't stop, Leo. I need you."

Music to his ears, he smiled under her words. She shifted on the bed, her body chasing his touch like she craved him as much as he craved her.

Her movement inexorably drew his gaze to the dusky rose of her nipples, now taut with arousal. They beckoned him—a silent siren call that stirred a deep thirst within. He lowered his head, lips parting with a reverence befitting the worship of a goddess, his goddess, his mate.

The first brush of his mouth against her skin was a revelation. His tongue teased and caressed, learning what she liked and what she didn't.

That was the good thing about being a forever student who craved knowledge. He wanted to read her like a book, memorize the rush of her breath, the arch of her back. As he gently drew her into his mouth, exploring, testing, teasing them both—all while determined to bring her so much pleasure, she'd come back for more.

If he could learn what she loved, perhaps she would keep him and stop holding him at arms' length.

She gripped the sheets on either side of her hips, and he slowly unhooked her hands and put them on his head. He released her nipple and moved to the other.

"Show me what you want, mibella, what you need." Then his tongue circled her nipple until she gripped his hair tight, pressing him closer with a throaty moan that made his dick weep with need.

Leopol marveled at the flavor of her skin, a shadow of what she'd tasted like on his tongue. Delicate and intoxicating, the scent of jasmine filled the air around them, making his mouth water.

His hand drew up her hip and his other tweaked her other nipple. She squirmed beneath him on the bed. Each breath, every sigh and moan that escaped her lips—it was the most beautiful symphony he'd ever heard. It resonated in the deepest chambers of his soul, and he knew he wanted to hear it every day of the rest of his life.

His tongue teased her nipple, before capturing the peak with a tender tug of his teeth. Her spine curved like a drawn bow, her legs parting to welcome him closer into her embrace. His hand, guided by the magnetic pull of her desire, traced the contour of her side, closer to the heat of her but not nearly close enough for either of them.

She responded with a restless shift upon the bed, her movements suggesting an insatiable hunger for his touch—an echo of the yearning that coursed through his own veins.

His fingers gave a feather-light touch across her clit, and her hips bucked, chasing a deeper touch.

Her fingers tangled in his hair, nails scraping delicately against his scalp, sending electric shivers down his spine.

"Leo, please," she gasped, using her hands to push his head lower.

He grinned, his mouth trailing molten kisses down her stomach as he settled on the floor on his knees. He pressed her knees wider and glanced up at her. Eyes glowing with passion, she licked her lips in anticipation.

Her breath caught in her throat, a trembling gasp that betrayed her anticipation.

His thumb grazed her clit again, the smell of her filling him and making his body hum with need. "What do you want, mibella? Use that pretty mouth to tell me."

She sucked in a shaky breath, her hands pushing his hair out of his eyes. "Make me come like you did in the library."

He kissed her thigh, the seam of her leg, a whispered promise of what was to come. "I can't wait to taste you again. I smelled you all day. I have no idea how I functioned because all I could think in the back of my mind was how delicious your pretty little pink pussy tasted and how I wanted more. Always more..."

He kissed the other thigh, then used his thumbs to spread her wider, opening her to his gaze, his lips, his touch. She moaned, then cupped her breasts.

Gods, it was one of the most erotic things he'd ever seen.

"You're my goddess," he growled. "A creature of pure desire and raw power. And I am utterly, completely yours."

He lowered his mouth and licked her clit, flattening his tongue and pressing hard on the little bundle of nerves. Her flavor, her essence burst on his tongue, and he paused as they both moaned. Her hands gripped his hair.

The magic runes he'd drawn earlier began to shimmer, casting a soft ethereal glow across her skin. They pulsed in rhythm with her heartbeat, amplifying every sensation until the line between pleasure and magic blurred into something transcendent. She arched against him, whimpering and wild, her body speaking a language more profound than words could ever capture.

Leopol knew he was treading a dangerous line— between possession and worship, between claiming and surrendering. His touch continued its deliberate exploration, each caress designed to unravel her, to make her understand that this was more than mere physical connection.

Her restlessness beckoned him, a siren call he could not—would not—resist. His fingers, slick with magic and desire, traced the delicate landscape between her thighs.

She was wet, impossibly so, as he slid first one then a second finger inside her.

Her muscles trembled beneath his fingertips, squeezing him so hard, his dick bobbed in his pants. He ached to replace his fingers with the real thing, stretch her wide, finally feel her wrapped around his thickness.

But first, he wanted to see her completely undone, unable to think or even mumble words beyond, "Yes, gods, yes, Leopol!"

It was the most beautiful music, a prayer of supplication, a demand for release that he was more than willing to give her.

He explored her with the reverence of an archaeologist uncovering an ancient, sacred text—every curve, every sensitive nerve a hieroglyph waiting to be deciphered. Every lick and suck of her clit, every thrust of his fingers making her gasp, turning her noises into less prayer and more profanity.

Her inner walls clenched around him, silk and fire and raw, unbridled sensation. He moved slowly, deliberately, watching her face transform with each careful stroke.

"Leo, please," she gasped, thrusting her hips to meet him. When he twisted his fingers slightly to hit the soft, hidden spot deep within her, she jerked.

Her body trembled, muscles quivering as she approached the precipice. The magic runes on her skin pulsed brighter, casting prismatic shadows across the bedchamber. Leopol watched her unravel, mesmerized as her body tensed, muscles coiling like a spring about to release.

He knew precisely the moment she would break. A few more thrusts... Just before her climax, he sucked her swollen clit while curling his fingers deep inside her, hitting that secret spot that shattered her completely.

She came with a primal cry that seemed to echo through centuries—a sound of pure release. Her back bowed off the bed, muscles clenching rhythmically around his fingers as waves of pleasure consumed her.

The magic runes on her skin pulsed brighter, synchronizing with her trembling muscles, amplifying every quiver and gasp. Her release was a tempest—wild, uncontrolled, and magnificent.

When she finally collapsed back onto the bed, breaths ragged and skin glistening, he knew he had claimed something far more precious than her body. Her vulnerability lay exposed before him, raw and beautiful.

He moved with the fluid grace of a predator who knew how to bide his time and play the long game. He lay on his side beside her, one hand drawing lazy patterns across her trembling abdomen.

Her breath was still uneven, little aftershocks of pleasure rippling through her body. He watched her, fascinated by every small reaction. The runes on her skin faded like watercolors bleeding into silk, leaving behind a faint shimmer that spoke of their shared bond.

She looked at him, eyes half-lidded and glazed, a soft smile playing across her lips.

"Mibella," he whispered, his voice rough with emotion, "are you alright?"

Her gaze didn't waver as she looked at him, and he half feared she would start overthinking this again. But instead, her fingers reached out, tracing the line of his jaw with unexpected tenderness. No words were necessary between them in this moment—their bodies had already spoken a language more profound than speech.

Something flickered in her eyes. A shadow. A hint of vulnerability that made his chest ache.

He wanted to tell her how much he cared for her, that she had nothing to fear. For once, words failed him.

Instead, it was she who spoke, not words of sweet nothings but a simple, "Come here."

Her voice husky with spent desire had his dick bobbing.

He moved slowly, deliberately, until he hovered above her. Her legs parted instinctively, welcoming him into the cradle of her hips. His hardness pressed against her, and she reached down, her palm wrapping around his length, her touch both reverent and possessive.

He froze, his breath knocked from his soul by her hand.

Chapter Twenty-Four

A growl rumbled deep in Leopol's chest, a sound that was part desire, part warning. He wanted—no, needed—to claim her. The pressure to hold back and give her time to process what they were to each other was like a corked bottle. It was long overdue, and he was slightly worried he was going to blow this up.

Her hand guided him, her eyes locked with his. With shaking arms, he held himself still as she positioned his tip at her entrance. There was something primal in her gaze—a challenge, a dare. She wanted him to take her, to claim her completely. She trusted him, and he held onto his control with everything he had.

When he felt the wet heat of her on his tip, he paused. She licked her lips and blinked rapidly. "Leopol," she demanded, her hands now on his biceps and tugging him closer.

The first thrust was deliberately slow and measured. Inch by agonizing inch, he watched her face transform with each incremental slide deeper. Her breath caught, muscles tensing as she thrust up, drawing him as deep as he could go.

She gasped, her back arching, muscles clenching around him in a velvety embrace that made him see stars. Their two souls had been searching for each other across lifetimes.

He paused, fully seated inside her, giving her time to adjust but him as well. He needed a moment because this—she... it was more than he ever thought possible.

Forehead pressed against hers, magic rippled between them, invisible threads weaving their energies together. The runes from earlier had faded, but they didn't need them anymore. She was ready for him. Now they were joined without any barriers, each of them finally finding home in the other.

Her breath came in short, sharp pants against his lips, her nails digging into his shoulders.

"Move," she whispered, a command and a plea.

He withdrew slightly, slowly at first, each stroke designed to make them both savor every single inch of their joining. Her hips rose to meet his, matching his rhythm, demanding more. The bed creaked beneath them, a rhythmic accompaniment to their primal dance.

His movements became more urgent, less controlled, more desperate, as though he could somehow merge their very essences through sheer physical connection. The careful precision gave way to raw, animalistic need. Her legs wrapped around his waist, heels digging into his lower back, urging him deeper. Each thrust sent tremors through her body, magic crackling between them like invisible lightning.

She arched her back, changing the angle, and suddenly he was hitting a spot that made her cry out—a sound between a moan and a scream. The slick slide of his cock inside her, gripping him so tightly, black began to edge his vision.

Her nails raked down his back, leaving trails of heated sensation, making him thrust harder. He growled in response, a sound so primal it seemed to come from something beyond human.

"Gods," she gasped, her fingers threading through his hair. "Right there—don't stop—"

Her words dissolved into a moan that seemed to reverberate through the very walls of the chamber. Leopol felt her beginning to tighten around him, her body preparing for another release. Yet he sensed her holding it back, dragging it out.

"Breathe, *mibella*," he whispered, thumb brushing her lip. "You don't have to hold back."

He thrust harder, searching for release with her, racing toward the edge right beside her. His balls tightened up, his body bowing around her like a supplicant at prayer. All rational thought fled until all he knew was the feel of her beneath him, the need to feel her come around his cock.

"Bellavore... simi dravak," he groaned, his magic flaring as the bond surged between them.

Shadows danced on the walls, responding to their rhythm, to the pulse of their joined bodies. Runes that had faded earlier flickered back to life, casting ethereal light across their skin. They were more than lovers now—they were a ritual of their own right.

"Leopol, I—I" Her eyes fluttered, then her entire body shuddered.

He dipped his head to the curve of her neck, kissing and nipping with every breath.

"Simi velkarinth, mibella, come with me," he begged, biting her shoulder.

She jerked, her climax rolling through her like thunder made liquid, the world lighting up around them.

She screamed, "Raelion!"

The rose bloomed. Magic surged. Her spirit flickered solid for a breathless heartbeat, and as he crashed their mouths together, Leopol swore her lips had never tasted so real.

She squeezed him like a vise, and he thrust once, groaning as he froze, hovering, pulsing within her.

Her word echoed in the chamber, growing with power even as their bodies slowly came down from their orgasms.

Leopol's breath came in ragged gasps, his forehead pressed against her collarbone, heartbeat thundering in synchronicity with hers. He'd known that finding his mate—if she existed—would change everything, but he'd underestimated just how much.

For several moments, neither moved. The chamber remained suspended in a fragile quiet, punctuated only by their mingled breaths and the distant whisper of wind against stone walls. Magic still hummed between them, gossamer threads of energy that seemed reluctant to dissipate.

The rose pulsed across the room. Her skin shimmered like starlight, her spirit briefly solid against his own. Then everything cracked open inside him.

Raelion.

The word kept echoing in his mind, keeping pace with every fading squeeze of his cock, every pulse of him inside her.

Her fingers traced lazy patterns across his back, nails

skating over the raised welts her earlier passion had left. Tremors still coursed through his muscles, aftershocks of their profound connection. Her lips brushed his cheek, a gesture both tender and possessive.

He moved onto his side, his hand on her stomach, his leg twisting between hers, needing her closer.

They didn't speak. There was nothing to say. Their bodies remained tangled, breath slowing in shared rhythm, magic still humming faintly beneath their skin.

Leopol blinked, watching the firelight dance across her shoulder. Something was shifting in the quiet. Something inside him.

Light coiled around them both, divine and ancient, laced with stars and memory.

Then, as the last of her word faded into the night, he saw it—*everything*. The castle halls, the fight, the cave, the sleep.

Everything from the time before too, of his time in the library, of his mission from the dawn of time itself, of his mother, his true mother.

He sat straight up on the bed, staring at the fireplace across the room in shock.

She frowned, pushing up onto her elbows. "What is it? Did I do something wrong?"

"What? Gods, no, it's not that. You were—are—perfect in every way, Bellavore. It's just... what was that word you said?"

He glanced at her, needing to see her expression. Confused and frowning, a blush staining her cheeks as she tucked her hair behind her ear and raised the blankets over her chest, she bit her lip. "Raelion?"

She whispered his name—his true name—and the world shifted. Her voice reverberated inside him like a bell struck in a cavern of memory. It didn't hurt. But it opened something. A door. A star. A wound.

The name echoed like a thunderclap through the hollow places in his soul.

His jaw dropped, and he tensed. She misunderstood his reaction, launching into an explanation as she twisted the bedsheet in her hands.

"I–don't know exactly. I think I read it in a book, maybe. It just–came out somehow. It felt right to say it, so I said it. Oh gods, did I unleash another curse? What does it mean?"

He blinked. *Raelion*. The voice of another woman in another time and another place.

"It's... my name. From before. I remember," he whispered, reverent, wild, broken. "Oh gods–I remember *everything*."

Bella blinked up at him. "What?"

"You did it. You unleashed my blocked memories of before I came to this world. And now–oh gods, my body," he said, eyes wide with growing panic as he raked his hand through his hair. "It's beneath us. I know how to find it. It's here. I have to see it–oh gods, my dragon body..."

He jumped to his feet, dressing in a blur of magic and breathless words. "Come with me. You have to see it too. I–I can't explain, but I *need* you there."

She clutched the blanket tighter as she sat up, disheveled and gorgeous. He leaned over and kissed her hard, sweeping his tongue inside to remind them both that what they had was still there. He needed her with him, always, especially now.

When he paced away from the bed, she slid to the edge, a flare of magic, and she settled her favorite blue dress around her shoulders.

"Leopol–slow down. You just–"

"I know. I know. But it's real, Bella." He reached for her hand, eyes fierce and alight with purpose. "I have a body, and it's *here*."

Magic surged. Memories flooded him. He couldn't breathe—

"Raelion," she whispered again, stroking his hair, her voice calm while he trembled. "Breathe with me."

She grounded him when everything around them was out of sync. He closed his eyes and breathed deeply, slowly letting the peace find its way back inside him.

And just like that, the memories weren't terrifying anymore. They were... home.

He licked his lips and took a deep breath, pulling back to look down at her.

She smiled softly. "Better?"

He nodded, his throat tight. "Thank you," he said, voice dark and gravely with emotion. "Will you help me? I know where it is, but I don't know what I'll find when I get there. I–I don't want to be alone."

She cupped his cheeks and stood on tiptoe to kiss him softly. Relief surged through him. He hadn't fucked this up between them and thank the gods for that.

He needed her more than he needed to get back into his body. When the kiss broke, she hugged him tight and said, "Of course, but do you want me to call you Leopol or Raelion now?"

He shuddered at the word and held her tight. "Um, let's only use Raelion in the bedroom. I–I don't want anyone else to know it right now."

The echo of another woman saying it wasn't something he wanted to explore right now. Not when there was already so much information spinning through his head.

She stepped back, beaming up at him. "Your secret is safe with me. Now, let's go find a body."

She paused, then giggled. "That sounded creepy, didn't it?"

He chuckled, his magic swirling around them like a cloak as he tugged her from the room, already using magic to open the door. She strode with him down the hall, side by side. She didn't fight him or hang back to walk behind him like she'd kept doing for the past week.

Something had shifted between them. He felt it, knew that she trusted him now, that she knew they were together in whatever the world would throw at them.

The stairs to the library were cold, worn from centuries of secrets. Each step echoed with destiny as he opened the secret passage to the sanctum.

"It's down here? Really?" she asked skeptically.

"This is why the runes on the walls shifted when we touched that first night. You were always meant to find me," he said, breathless as he pushed the wall where the rune had glowed after their first kiss. "Even when I forgot myself, I recognized you as my mate, my other half."

Her quickly indrawn breath alerted him to the tension in her shoulders, but he didn't look over at her. He filed away the conversation of mates to have with her later and drew several sigils over the runes from before, his magic flashing and mixing on the wall. Then the grating shift of stone on stone echoed in the quiet.

The wall moved, swinging in and revealing another stone staircase going down into the dark.

Bella gasped, grabbing his hand tightly. "That's the door the silver dragon went through."

His gaze swung to hers. "What dragon?"

"The one who fought a battle in the parlor. I saw it in the fire on the way here, in the Feral Forest. A message from the gods. I told Lailant about the battle I saw, the silver or white dragon stumbling down the stairs. I'm not sure if it's a vision of the past or the future—"

"It's the past," he said. "It was a memory of... of me."

Their gazes held, both of them realizing what this moment meant. If he was right, this could change their future together.

Chapter Twenty-Five

Bella's steps echoed behind him, her fingers still laced with his. "You said you remember everything. What does that mean, exactly?"

Leopol paused at the top of the stairs, fingers brushing ancient stone. "It means... I wasn't born a dragon like the others. Not even like Knox."

She frowned, drawing closer. "You're not just a dragon?"

He gave a low laugh—half wonder, half disbelief. "I'm afraid to admit what I am, Bella. I woke in that ruined temple with those parents waiting for me, a completely different creature than I'd been before. I have a purpose in this realm."

"What purpose?"

"When I came to this world, I was given a dragon body, one of the most powerful beings on the planet, so that I could protect and guard. But with my past and where I was before, I guarded knowledge. Here, I was to guard—I'm not sure. People? My family?"

He paused and half-turned to stare at her a few steps above him.

"So not *all* of your memories have returned?" she asked, her hand resting on his shoulder—her brow furrowed, her confusion clear. But she held him steady, truly listened. And gods, it was heady, having someone offer him that in return.

He was so used to being the one who listened to others, who helped solve all their problems. It's what he'd done for centuries on this planet, and for centuries before that.

He licked his lips, taking her hand in both of his as she stepped down closer to him, analyzing the memories. "Not all of them, but the puzzle is coming together now. I originally was meant to protect the library. So many of my fragmented memories were tied to books, ancient knowledge that none of the other dragons could explain."

Despite the dark, he could see her clearly from the faint glow of their spirit forms. She didn't push him for more, just waited, trusting him to reveal what he needed to.

He took a deep breath. "But now that you're here... I've been waiting for you for centuries."

She didn't answer—but her hand tightened on his arm. Her eyes widened and a faint blush covered her cheeks as she shook her head. "No, that can't be it. I'm just a working girl from a small village."

"You're the queen of Busparia," he said. "No matter that you're out of your body, you're still the queen, my queen."

She pursed her lips but didn't deny it. "Technically, yes, but I'm not Eirwyn, born into this. Or you, raised to advise kings for generations. You're powerful, strong, and the most brilliant person I've ever met. I saw that during our first bump in the sunroom."

He grinned. "You mean when I pissed you off and sent you running into the garden?"

Her nose wrinkled adorably as she shrugged. "Not my finest moment. I'm glad you didn't let my terrible first impression scare you off."

Pausing on the stairs, he gathered her close, tipping her chin up so he could hover over her lips. "I knew from the first touch that we were mates, Bellavore. You may not want to talk about it yet, but it doesn't stop it from being true."

Their kiss was tender and slow, filling him with heat and wonder. He thought their time together would soften the need coursing through him, but it wasn't so. He wanted her more now than he did yesterday.

When he pulled back, her eyes were heavy with desire and her cheeks flushed. She took a deep breath and stepped back on the stair, nearly toppling over. He held her elbow steady as she shook out her skirt in a nervous gesture he'd come to recognize.

"What did you think when we could touch that first day?" he asked, trying to distract her and make her more comfortable.

Her eyes softened as she looked up at him. "I was suspicious."

He laughed, and she placed her hands on her hips. "What? It's true. I knew you were hiding secrets. You still are."

"But you're not going to pry?" he asked, curious and always wanting to know more about what her thought process was.

She shook her head. "No, I won't pry. I figure you need time to think and process like I do. When the time's right, we'll talk about it, and perhaps you'll tell me what other secrets you're hiding."

He smiled softly and tucked a strand of hair behind her ear. "Just like you'll share your own secrets with me when the time is right."

Her lips spread into a mischievous grin, but she avoided his eyes for a heartbeat too long. "Perhaps. Perhaps not. I guess we'll just wait and see, won't we?"

He laughed and tucked her hand in the crook of his elbow. "I suppose we will. I want to share this part of me with you, though. I wasn't lying before when I said I didn't want to face whatever's down here alone."

Her face softened, and she leaned her head on his shoulder as they walked down the stairs side by side. "I know, and you don't have to. I'm here now."

His chest burned brighter at her words. In all his centuries of existence, no one had ever stood beside him like this.

"Thank you," he said, his voice deeper and rougher with emotion. "I've never shared these things with anyone before. I'm not used to it, but I appreciate you just being beside me through it."

After a few steps of silence, she said softly, "Does Knox know about your body?"

He sucked in a deep breath, his shoulders tight. "Sort of. I told him that my dragon body is here somewhere but not that I came here fully grown. What would I have said? Knox, you're my cousin, but also not really."

He changed his voice to imitate Knox. "And why do you say that?"

He changed his voice to his normal one. "Oh, just a deep knowing in my psyche that I can't explain because I don't remember what happened."

He snorted. "Yeah, no one in their right mind would have believed me."

She pinched his arm through the sleeve of his shirt and jacket. "You don't give him enough credit. He looks up to you, is proud to call you cousin, and has never treated you like a majordomo or butler or any of the million roles you fill in this castle."

His throat tightened with emotion. After clearing his throat, he said softly, "I know, but perhaps I didn't want to lose that look in his eye."

"What look?"

He swallowed hard and squeezed her hand tighter in his like a lifeline.

"He doesn't have any other family. If he knew that I was just a dragon construct who arrived on this realm in a temple fully grown, how would that make him feel? Probably lonely, like we're not really family at all."

They reached the bottom of the stairs and paused. He was afraid to look at her, to see what she thought of that pronouncement of his past. What kind of being came here fully grown? She'd been trained in magic; she knew what a construct was. Knowing her, she'd ask a million questions, once she had time to process it.

"Family isn't only about blood, Leo. It's more than that. For an ancient dragon, I'd expect you to know that by now."

The teasing tone eased some of his fear, and he looked down at her with a smile. She lifted on her toes and kissed him softly, her lips a balm—comfort and awareness wrapped in a single breath.

When she pulled back, the fear in his gut was gone, replaced by the hum of desire and something deeper. Longing for something more than physical.

"Come on," she said, her voice warm and sure as she tugged his arm. "Let's see what's behind the door."

A long hallway opened up before them, and the faint

drip of water echoed. An old stone door lay ahead, and fear gripped him over what he'd find on the other side. What if his body wasn't there after all? Or worse—what if it was, but it was beyond saving?

She never let go, and neither did he, clinging to her like a lifesaving potion. He pressed his other hand to the stone wall, magic coiling at his fingertips as he triggered the hidden latch.

The stone shifted with a sound like metal grinding bone—slow, heavy, ancient—and the door swung open.

A rush of stale air billowed out, carrying the scent of dust and something else—something metallic and sharp that made Leopol's nostrils flare. Bella squeezed his hand, their spirit forms casting a soft luminescence into the darkness beyond the threshold.

The chamber was larger than he remembered, its ceiling lost in shadows that seemed to breathe and shift. Massive stone columns rose like petrified sentinels, their surfaces etched with intricate symbols that danced at his memories. He remembered etching them.

Bella pressed closer to his side, and together they walked through the cave toward the center, closer to the thick pull of ancient magic.

Leopol's magic instinctively pulsed outward to test the space before them. Something ancient and watchful pressed back against his probing energy—not hostile, but cautious. Calculating. Waiting.

The room grew brighter with each step until they rounded the last column. They both paused, Bella gasping and her hand tightening on his.

"Oh gods, that's it. The dragon from my vision. It really is you."

The stone slab before them was massive, easily twenty

feet long and half as wide. More of a bed than an altar, stretched across its surface lay a figure—not human, not a dragon like Knox. Crystalline silvery scales glimmered like fractured moonlight, covering a body that seemed both fragile and impossibly strong.

Leopol's breath caught in his throat. The body was his.

Not a representation or a memory, but his actual physical form—suspended between life and death, trapped in some impossible magical stasis. Thin tendrils of silver magic wove through the crystalline scales, pulsing with a rhythm that matched his own heartbeat.

"It's me," he whispered.

Bella's fingers traced the edge of the stone slab, her spirit form casting a soft glow across the immobile figure as it glowed brighter at her nearness. "Looks like you were right. You're not dead."

His chest tightened as he stepped closer, drawn inexorably toward the crystalline form. Each step felt like walking through layers of memory, fragments of forgotten moments pressing against his consciousness. The silver tendrils of magic seemed to pulse in recognition, reaching toward him like curious tendrils.

He snorted. "Not dead, but not fully alive either. Otherwise, I wouldn't be in this form."

Bella's hand remained locked with his, anchoring him. Delicate fracture lines ran through the crystalline scales, like a map of impossible journeys. Mostly healed, others were scars telling stories from centuries on this realm.

A low humming began to emanate from the stone slab, vibrating through the chamber. Not sound, exactly, but a song that seemed to bypass hearing and sink directly into bone and spirit.

"What do we do now?" Bella asked.

Leopol stretched his neck and gritted his teeth. "Now, we figure out the correct spell combination to get my spirit back into my body. I'm going to work on every spell I can think might work. While I do, can you analyze the texts under the stone slab?"

Bella bent slightly at the waist and gasped. "It's a bookshelf!"

He smiled at her eagerness to explore more ancient texts. She was perfect for him. Was it any wonder the gods had put them together as mates?

The gods... he frowned, a faint memory of one god and a few goddesses flitting through his mind. They were nothing more than smiling, regal faces, but they didn't look like a painting in his mind. They felt like a memory, like he knew them.

He snorted at the ridiculousness of it and began to draw intricate sigils in the air above his slumbering body. Bella lit a few candles and torches, while Leopol kneeled beside the slab. Magic coiled at his fingertips—old magic, deeper than instinct. He took a steadying breath, and the sigil began to burn gold against the shadows.

"Kah'sithar meval drakon'vir," he whispered, voice low and reverent. *I summon the soul to the vessel.*

The symbol shimmered, hovered for a breath—then hissed and unraveled into smoke.

He clenched his jaw and tried a different spell. Tracing a second symbol above the heart, this one more intricate, with loops that echoed wings and flame, he whispered,

"Essar vol tu'karin. Ashael mirak vor." *Spirit to flesh. Bind the will to essence.*

The symbol sparked against the silver tendrils crisscrossing his form—but again, it faltered, rejected by some unseen shield. The air hummed with resistance.

"Come on," he muttered. "Let me in."

He dipped his fingers into the glowing magic again, this time dragging the sigil across the crystalline scales of his chest.

"Sareth vel mora'thei. Vahlen tri'kaar." *Break the veil. Let truth pass through.*

The moment his spell met the body's surface, the lines evaporated. A surge of invisible force snapped his hand back. Leopol stumbled, panting with frustration. The barrier wasn't just magical–it was guarding his body like a sleeping god's tomb.

His voice trembled now. "Why won't it work?"

He steadied himself, pressing both palms flat to the slab. "I am the flame, I am the breath, I am the spark reborn."

Golden light flared beneath his hands as he whispered another spell, drawing the sigils on the slab this time. "Veythar kin dravok, melith solun." *By blood and fire, awake the body.*

Nothing.

Anger burned in Leopol's chest, an ache even a spirit could feel. He had studied countless books and practiced every ceremony until he knew them by heart, yet his body lay empty and still. Seven months of searching, learning, and failing hadn't prepared him for the deep hopelessness that now threatened to swallow him.

Frustration broke through the reverence, sharp and bitter. "This body–it knows me. It *is* me. Why won't it let me in?"

Bella moved beside him, silent and supportive, her presence grounding as her hand settled on his back. "We knew it wasn't going to be a simple thing to rejoin a spirit and body though. Be patient."

Be patient? Seven months of searching, learning, and

failing hadn't prepared him for the hopelessness that now ate at him. He drew another sigil and muttered a spell under his breath.

The sigils sparked—then *bounced off,* like water on oil. The barrier shimmered again, resisting him.

"No," he growled. "No, damn it."

His hands trembled. He tried a different combination—more desperate now.

"By breath and blood, I claim what is mine. Solvena. Erinth. Vettar!"

Nothing.

The wards didn't even flicker this time.

He clenched his fists, turning away. "Why now?" he whispered. "Why *this*? I can feel my heartbeat. I should be able to do this."

He had waited *centuries* for a mate, for a purpose like this. He'd fought battles, whispered in halls, guided kings. He'd earned the right to go back to the land of the living—to *become real* for the first time and live with his mate. And now, when he was *this close,* the magic denied him.

He turned back to the slab, whispering like a prayer. "Shael drak'en vol ankar. Velasir tru'mar." *By ancient oath, I claim what was meant to be.*

Still, the magic coiled back from him, refusing to bind.

He met her eyes with a flicker of despair, and she reached up a hand, cupping his cheek and kissing him softly. The kiss slowed his spiraling worry and fears, calmed him and grounded him unlike anything he'd ever tried before, even meditations.

When she pulled back and broke the kiss, her eyes were soft yet reflected a confidence in him that he didn't feel. "You can do this, Leopol. Just because we had a tentative success creating the transformation potion for the villagers—

which we still don't know is going to work, might I remind you—doesn't mean that you can do this in just a few minutes. This level of magic takes time. We both researched the cure for the curse for months."

"I don't want to wait months more to come back to life!" he cried.

She stroked his chest, and the hairs on the back of his neck settled. "I know, neither do I. But I need you to do this slowly, methodically, right, because if you do—*when* you do—it'll give me real hope that I can do the same. Please Leopol, don't give up, don't stop. Just keep going, keep testing..."

He sighed, pulling her into his arms and hugging her tight. He wanted to give her hope. Rejoining his body and spirit was a proof of concept. He'd never seen it referenced as possible in any of the Celawyn texts, but something in his soul told him he'd seen this happen before. He knew it was possible. Perhaps in one of the texts that haunted his dreams at night, from his time prior to coming to this realm.

Leopol's shoulders trembled with pressure and expectation as he reigned in his thoughts. "There's a protective ward, a similar signature as the one I put on your rose's pot. So I think... I think I put it there, but I don't remember how to undo it."

Bella squeezed his waist and leaned back to meet his gaze. "Then we'll find a way. Together."

She kissed him softly and let go, just as he was about to take the kiss deeper. She smiled then turned, gathering a few texts from the slab's base and sitting on the floor at the foot of the altar bed as she talked. "Slow and steady wins the race, right? So do what you always do, Leopol."

He frowned, his chest tight. "And what's that?"

She looked up at him and smiled brightly, even as her intelligent eyes pierced his soul. "Methodically go through all the spells you can remember. Then all the sigil rune combinations. Then we'll progress to potions. Hells, maybe the golden apple potion will work on you too."

He growled and settled both fists on the slab, breathing deeply through his nose. "Can't force a potion down my dragon throat if we can't penetrate the barrier."

"Then focus on spells that will do that, instead of merging your spirit and body spells."

A light went off in his head, and he nodded, hope flickering in his soul.

Hours later, the flickering candles cast long shadows on the cave walls, almost as if they were laughing at his failed attempts to bring himself back. With every soft spell, he begged his spirit to return to the flesh that once held his bright soul, but the magic sputtered out, leaving him a restless spirit. He'd already gone through all his saved memories of spells to penetrate the magical barrier, and he'd circled back to trying to merge his spirit and body.

But none of it was working.

No warm rush of blood, no twitch of fingers or toes; just the cold fact that he was still locked outside his body.

In the corner, Bella's soft breathing broke the silence—a reminder of the life he longed for. She'd stayed by his side through it all, her trust never wavering even when his own hope faltered. Now she lay at the foot of the altar, her eyelids fluttering shut as sleep claimed her, surrounded by old tomes. Spirits didn't need sleep, but it definitely helped refresh the mind. He'd taught her to meditate, but she'd said she hadn't really slept.

Yet completing the physical part of the mate bond process had finally allowed her to sleep. Leopol was glad she could finally rest and dream, finally escaping the endless hunt for answers.

He had no such relief. Turning back to the shelves, he let his see-through fingers brush over the leather-bound books he hadn't touched since becoming a spirit.

Each book opened under his touch, pages full of hidden magic, Bella's eyes flitting behind closed lids with every turn of the page.

Her dreams must be alive with these secrets, her mind as hungry for them as his own.

For Leopol, every word was a possible key—or just another dead end. Time slipped away as he pored over the pages, praying for a spell or cure that would pull his spirit back into his body.

As the candles burned low and the night turned to morning, his anger settled into firm resolve. There had to be a way. He would find it—or remain a half-ghost forever.

"Invoket cor meum. Nexara tuon vel esten." *Let my heart awaken. Let this construct know me.*

The symbols hung for a heartbeat—then unraveled with a flicker, dissipating like ash on wind.

Leopol cursed under his breath, voice tight.

"It's not you," came Bella's voice behind him, quiet but certain.

He turned, startled to find her yawning as she stood and stretched. Rubbing sleep from her eyes, she hovered at the edge of the barrier near his dragon's heart.

She blinked as the barrier seemed to pulse brighter at her presence, then tilted her head. Her nose scrunched up in that cute way she had when she was thinking, and he waited. Eyes narrowing, she studied it—not with frustration, but with curiosity.

"I think it's waiting," she said, reaching out a hand slowly.

"For what?" His voice cracked, his heart unexpectedly going faster as she grew closer.

She looked up at him, something tender in her expression. "You're trying to force your way in like it's a fight. But maybe it's not about force. Maybe it's about... alignment."

She stepped forward, her hand brushing the air above his chest. The barrier shimmered—but didn't repel her. When she pushed forward, it *welcomed* her touch.

Leopol's breath hitched. Her spirit glowed brighter, pulsing in sync with his body's dormant rhythm.

"If I'm your mate," she whispered, her eyes locked on where her hand went through the shimmering barrier. "Then maybe I'm part of the key."

He couldn't speak. Could only watch as she pressed her palm to the scales—and the ward flared *inward*, not out.

Something deep within his chest trembled. *It's her. She's the piece I was missing.* The reason he was made and put in this world. His mate, his hope, his entire life was hers.

Chapter Twenty-Six

She hadn't meant to drift off, but the endless waiting—the silence, the failure—had pressed heavy on her chest like ash. Combined with the previous night of staying up to make the potions for the villagers, she was exhausted.

Even in sleep, doubt had crept in, whispering that maybe he'd never return to that body. That maybe *this*—a half-life of spirits and memories—was all they'd get. It combined with visions of the symbols and spells she'd read in those ancient books at the foot of the stone slab. Then one of the dreams showed her how to help him.

He was still trying when she woke, still whispering spells like prayers. The sight of him lit something fierce and aching in her heart—he was frustrated, vulnerable, afraid.

She might not be able to accept the mate idea yet, but she couldn't deny that he was *hers*—and she wouldn't let him carry this burden alone, dragon or not.

He hadn't given up. So, neither would she.

Bella stood beside the dragon, the cold stone biting into her thighs through her skirt.

She studied the crystalline lines of his sleeping body, the shimmer of magic like frost webs across its surface. There was something familiar in the sigils he'd used. Not the shape, but the feeling. It was *protective* magic. Deep, soul-bound, and laced with a grief she recognized.

It was the same feeling she'd had when she'd lost Gastone and unleashed a curse. His method of channeling that emotion was much more productive than hers. Her magic wasn't nekrosan, but she'd definitely done harm with it.

She shook off the disappointment in herself and focused on the present and him. She had to step up and help him.

"You're very good at protective sigils and spells," she murmured.

He snorted and rubbed the back of his neck. "Too good, if I am even keeping myself out. How are you doing that?"

Her hand stroked along the side of his dragon scales, the rough, leathery texture fascinating her. She could feel it as well as if she were in her body.

"I don't know," she said, shaking her head. "After the battle in the drawing room, you were trying to keep yourself safe. You sealed yourself inside so you could heal."

Leopol looked up sharply. "I'm healed now, so why isn't my magic working? Why are you able to touch me?"

She smoothed her hand over the scales, palm pulsing with her own magic. It reacted—not with rejection, but *curiosity*, the shimmer on the dragon pulsing brighter.

"I can't break it," he said in a defeated whisper. "It doesn't respond to me."

"Maybe because you're trying to force your way in like a stranger. But if we're mates, the body must recognize me." She reached for his hand with her free one, heart thudding.

"Our magic is stronger when we're touching though. Maybe the magic will recognize us together."

He hesitated—then nodded, slowly, and took her hand. As always, tingles went up her arm, and she could see the barrier and their magic so much more brightly than before.

Bella let her magic rise, calling on the warmth of the gods. "What spells do you want to try first?" she asked, smiling up at him encouragingly.

He seemed to perk up as he took a deep breath. On the exhale, he said first in draconic and then in the common tongue, "Valen'kari seran drathai. *By bond and trust, I ask admittance.*"

The barrier pulsed beneath her touch—then shimmered and rippled but held strong.

Hope flared in her chest. "Wakey, wakey, sleeping beauty. Come on..."

She laid her hand on Leopol's chest—his spirit form—and then pressed her other hand to the body's heart. "We'll try together. One more time."

Leopol joined her, holding his hand over hers on his chest as he tried another spell.

"By soul and spark, return the flame. By blood and breath, remember your name."

Bella's mind flared with a memory, and she added, "Let the ward know love, not fear. Let what waits within draw near."

The magic *glowed*—then abruptly shuddered, sparking violently before breaking in a shower of light like something thrown into a fire. Bella gasped and fell back, and Leopol caught her.

"You did it. You broke the barrier," he said in awe. "But those spells weren't to break the barrier. They were meant to merge my body and soul. Something's still missing."

Bella stared down at the sleeping dragon, safe in the cocoon of his arms. "It needs more than spell work. More than logic or words."

No longer touching the dragon, it remained safely asleep, faintly glowing even without the barrier. "But first, I want to check for injuries. Let's make sure your body is fully healed. Looks can be deceiving, after all."

He snorted. "Three hundred years should be plenty. But go ahead. My body is your body."

She ran her hands over his scales where she could reach, a flare of heat in her chest at his words. Slowly, she gloried in the texture, wondering how it could be both soft and rough.

She climbed up onto the stone slab, and heard Leopol behind her breathlessly ask, "What—what are you doing?"

"Checking for injuries," she said primly, inspecting every scale. She had to climb onto his rear haunches to get onto his back, not having mastered the floating aspect of her spirit form.

She wobbled on unsteady feet on his spine, and suddenly Leopol was there, his hands on her upper arms and holding her steady.

She met his gaze, and the tension between them went from simmer to full boil instantly.

It was the mate bond, she knew. The soul-deep tie that had begun the moment they touched. The one she'd resisted, feared, needed. Hells, she was still resisting, still just as fearful.

But she couldn't deny that she needed him.

He licked his lips. "I need you too," he said.

She blinked, not realizing she'd spoken out loud. But as his lips descended to hers, she didn't care. His arms encircled her, holding her tight. Their lips met and clung, and the dragon beneath them seemed to shudder.

She ignored it, barely registering the feeling as everything was solely focused on their lips, the press of his chest to hers.

The kiss was like lightning, raw and electric, burning through her fears. His spirit form flickered, magic humming between them, warm and urgent. When they parted, she was breathless and somehow straddling him as he sat on the back of his dragon body.

Skirts up around her waist, his hands roamed up her back and across to her breasts, cupping gently but thumbs tweaking her nipples with an urgency that fanned the flames of her own desire.

"Oh gods, Leopol," she gasped, rocking against the hard length of him pressed against her core, separated by too much material.

He stared at her with hungry eyes, but for the first time, she understood what that other, deeper look meant.

This wasn't just about magic or mating. This was about vulnerability. About letting go of every protective wall, every carefully constructed defense to seize something beautiful from a life full of too few beautiful moments.

Everything else fell away. The magic thrummed between them, electric and alive, transforming the cold stone chamber into something intimate and charged. Leopol's spirit form pressed against her, not quite solid but undeniably present, his essence wrapping around her like a protective cocoon.

She cupped his cheeks tenderly and focused her magic, disappearing her clothes in a moment. His eyes flared, his magic sparking around them like flames, then he was naked too.

Safe in his arms with hands on his shoulders, she ground against his naked cock.

His breath caught, a low growl rumbling through his chest. The sound vibrated between them, primal and urgent. Her skin tingled where his hands touched, magic sparking like tiny lightning bolts against her flesh.

She positioned herself, feeling the hot length of him pressing against her entrance. Their eyes locked–his molten blue with a golden glow, hers burning with desire. No words were needed. Their bond hummed between them, ancient and powerful, transcending language.

As she slowly lowered herself onto him, they both gasped. The connection was more than physical, souls intertwining, magic merging, centuries of longing crystallizing into this singular moment. His hands gripped her hips, steadying her, trembling slightly.

"Bellavore, mibella, simi velkarinth," he murmured, kissing along her jaw with words she didn't understand. They sounded like a prayer or a promise.

She didn't care, too enraptured by the feel of him filling her inch by slow inch. When she took all of him, they both groaned, his hands pinching her nipples with just enough to make her clench.

She began to move, rolling her hips with a rhythm that made stars burst behind her eyelids. His magic swirled around them, iridescent and wild, creating a cocoon of pure sensation. Each thrust sent ripples of pleasure through her body, her magic responding in kind, weaving around them like molten silk.

Leopol's hands moved from her hips to her back, pulling her closer until their foreheads touched. His breath was hot against her skin, little gasps escaping with each movement. The dragon beneath them seemed to pulse in rhythm, ancient magic resonating with their intimate connection.

"More," he growled, his voice a mixture of spirit and flesh, demanding yet tender. His fingers dug into her skin, not painful but possessive, marking her in a way that transcended physical touch.

She complied, increasing her pace, feeling him deeper with each downward motion.

Her orgasm built rapidly, a gathering storm that she chased with open abandon. She arched against him as the beginning spasms teased her, her own magic rising to meet his.

Leopol's lips found the curve of her neck, teeth grazing her skin. "Mine," he whispered, the word both a claim and a benediction.

She whimpered, and the sound drove him wild. He flipped her onto her back, the dragon scales biting into her skin. Magic swirled and sparked, but she didn't care. Looping her arms around his neck, she held on as he pounded into her relentlessly, her orgasm approaching so fast, she thought she was flying to the edge of a cliff.

Then she tumbled over.

Her body arched, muscles trembling as waves of ecstasy crashed through her. Leopol's rhythm never faltered, drawing out her pleasure with each powerful thrust. Magic erupted around them in brilliant cascades of azure and silver.

His thrusts became erratic and still she clenched and spasmed on him, the wave slowing enough to allow her three short breaths before she flew higher and fell harder.

When she came the second time, it was with a scream that echoed through the stone chamber, her back arching off the scales as waves of pleasure crashed through her.

"*Raelion!*"

Her magic erupted simultaneously, a wild burst of golden light that intertwined with Leopol's blue-silver essence, creating a storm of raw, primal energy.

Leopol tensed above her, shouting his own release and triggering a pulse of magic so intense it made the very stones beneath them tremble. They flew through a landscape of pure sensation—their magic creating worlds between heartbeats, spinning realities where only they existed.

The stone chamber disappeared, but Leopol just gathered her into his arms and held her tight. Her eyes fluttered against the burst of light.

For several breathless moments, they remained tangled together, their bodies and spirits merged in a way that transcended physical connection.

When she could finally breathe and opened her eyes again, she blinked in surprise.

Above her was a ceiling of constellations. A tilt of her head, and she saw they were still on the stone slab, but now in a temple that felt familiar from the way he'd described it.

And he and the dragon body... they were no longer separate, but something entirely new—something powerful and ancient and inevitable.

She looked up at the dragon above her, eyes a solid glowing blue and silver. He was on his knees and elbows, cradling her under him.

His cock had filled her with warmth, but when their eyes met, and they realized that he'd finally been joined with his body, his cock pulsed again.

She licked her lips. "We—we did it. You're... you, right? Leopol? Raelion?"

He shuddered above her at the name, and his hips rocked forward, pressing into her even deeper than before.

"Yes," he whispered, his voice a blend of human and something ancient, a resonance that vibrated through her very bones. "I am both. Always."

"Both?" she gasped as something hit her clit with each slow thrust inside her.

His hand traced her cheek, scales glimmering where skin met magical essence. "Raelion was my first name. Leopol, the name I carried through centuries of exile. Now... now I am complete. Home with my mate."

His fingers traced delicate patterns across her skin, each touch leaving a faint shimmer of magic that danced like liquid starlight. Her nipples pebbled as the magic increased her desire.

She didn't tell him she didn't need the runes. She was already so hot for him, for this quiet warrior scholar who cared for her so deeply.

The temple around them seemed to breathe with their magic, constellations shifting overhead like living paintings. Ancient runes along the stone walls flickered in recognition, as if awakening from a long slumber.

Her fingers traced the line of scales at his neck, feeling the pulse of magic beneath. Something fundamental had changed—not just in his body, but in the very fabric of their connection. The mate bond hummed between them, no longer a tentative thread but a blazing cord of power.

"We need to understand what happened," she gasped, even as he thrust again.

"Later," he growled, a flash of magic making his body shift to a hybrid form.

His spine moved with a series of sharp, crackling pops, vertebrae shifting and reshaping into a sinuous, powerful structure. Massive leathery silvery white wings unfurled from his shoulder blades, membranes stretching translucent and veined like ancient parchment between razor-edged wing spears.

Where human hands had been, razor-sharp talons now gleamed, each digit ending in a curved scimitar of bone and keratin that could slice through a steel plate.

His face elongated, jaw distending into a reptilian muzzle lined with serrated teeth that could slice through steel. His serpentine neck arched with muscular grace, crowned by a wedge-shaped head adorned with crystalline ridges that caught and refracted light like prisms.

Where human eyes had once been, now burned molten gold irises ringed with electric blue. No longer human but predatory and slitted, they blazed with an inner fire that spoke of ancient, primal magic.

The hybrid form was neither fully dragon nor completely human, but a terrifying fusion that carried the intelligence of one species and the primal ferocity of another.

Still, he towered over her. Still, he could touch her, and she breathed a sigh of relief.

Still, he remained hard inside her, gently rocking as they both got used to the changes. A sliver of fear at the ferocity on his foreign face slammed into her with his next thrust, but it felt too good to stop.

"Don't stop," she begged, her hands stroking over those leathery soft scales of his shoulders, stroking his chest muscles, then sliding down to tug his hips to hers. "Harder."

He growled, the sound deep in his chest and making her body vibrate.

She screamed as something pressed on her clit while his cock filled her over and over. She saw stars, constellations overhead shifted and swirled, celestial patterns dancing in rhythm with their joining. The heavens sang, gaining with a crescendo that was unnatural.

It was too close after the back-to-back previous orgasms. She couldn't.

"You can, and you will," he growled, his razor-sharp teeth scraping along her neck and making her shiver. She felt no fear of him, just of the strength of their bond.

He thrust harder, and her pussy spasmed on him, trying to hold him in longer.

The magic sparked between them, electric and wild, transforming each touch into pure sensation.

"Raelion," she gasped, the name feeling like a spell on her tongue.

His hybrid form shuddered above her, wings spreading wide and casting prismatic shadows across the stone floor. Each thrust now carried a precision that spoke of centuries of controlled power—controlled until this moment of complete surrender.

"Mine, my mate, mibella, simi velkarinth." His growly voice vibrated through her bones, something between a human sound and a dragon's rumble.

The next thrust, the vibrations, the thing on her clit, his thick dick filling her—it was too much.

Her body arched involuntarily, and she screamed his secret name again. Muscles trembled as waves of pleasure crashed through her. Her legs tightened around her hips as her pussy clamped down on his cock.

The dragon's rumble turned into a roar as he stiffened above her, muscles tensing. Then a hot flood filled her, making her spasm and shake and cry his name over and over.

As they both slowly relaxed, the transformation continued–not just in his physical form, but in the very essence of their connection. Memories flickered between them like fragments of forgotten dreams: battles centuries old, landscapes burned and reborn, magical languages that predated human speech.

When her trembling finally subsided, Raelion–no, Leopol–shifted slightly, his hybrid form gradually lifting from her as if he never wanted to leave her. His head lifted, and she finally processed his new features.

He only faintly resembled the human form she'd known over the past week.

She traced the line of his jaw, feeling that hard, soft, leathery texture.

"Are you alright?" The words felt inadequate after what they'd just experienced.

He nuzzled against her neck, a gesture both intimate and protective. "Better than all right. I'm finally whole with my mate in my arms."

His voice was a low rumble that vibrated through her chest, but a sense of unease crept through her. She still wasn't so sure about this mate thing. Her biggest fear?

What if she couldn't get her body back and went to hells, but he was now alive and here?

Chapter Twenty-Seven

Leopol panted heavily, his body curled around Bella. His heart slowed. She was his mate. *His*. His cock still pulsed inside her, surrounded by heat and tightness like a glove. Amazement filled him. She had accepted this part of the mate bond—more than he'd ever expected or dared hope for.

A chill seeped under his scales and the stink of lichen tried to crowd out the smell of jasmine from her hair. The smells were his first clue, the chill the second. The air held that cold weight, dense and unmoving, of being in the cave under the castle, and the stone under his claws and knees were the same.

But the sound of waves crashing and the chirp of birds were his final clue that something had changed. Slowly, he leaned back and stared down at her. Her beautiful pale face was slack with post-orgasmic bliss and peace. Pride filled him, that he'd put that look on her face. Her hair stuck out at wild angles over the stone, a rat's nest of brown and gold, as if she'd fallen asleep in a sunbeam instead of nearly dying in a magical disaster.

Claws next to her head made him blink in surprise. *His claws*, in hybrid form now.

Then he remembered the way his bones had snapped and realigned as he'd fucked her. He was alive, restored to his previous draconic form... but very, very different.

He slowly left the comfort of her body. He had to protect his mate, and taking stock of the situation and their surroundings was his priority right now.

The sky above him was not a sky at all, but a ceiling: massive, domed, and cracked, its ancient paint peeling away in long strips. Faded constellations tracked across the arch, points of gold set in blue, most of them worn down to memory. Between the cracks, actual sky bled through. Judging by the faint color, it was just past dawn.

Bella stretched and hummed as if waking from a dream. "Do we have to get up now?"

He grinned or tried to; it felt wrong on his face. He raised a hand to touch his face, expecting the usual slender, human fingers, but paused to see a scratch and blood on his hand.

His hand... it was not even human, and his grin faded even as relief filled him. The back was covered in fine white scales, each edged in silver. Instead of fingernails, he had matte black talons, curved and sharp as a butcher's hook. The palm looked normal enough–callused and lined in familiar patterns, though the light blue skin was thicker, almost leathery–but the claws did not retract, and the whole thing was comically large, like a child's drawing of a man's hand. He turned it palm up, palm down, flexed the joints.

"If we want to figure out what happened, yes," he

growled, and the sound bounced off the ruins and came back as a deeper, more resonant version of itself. It took him by surprise, and he moved to sit up, but his tail—oh gods, he had a tail, didn't he—caught on the edge of the altar and threw off his balance.

The slab was bigger than a king's bed, carved from a single block of gray marble, pitted and worn by centuries of his dragon form resting on it. He braced himself and slid off the side, boots scraping over the grit. No, not boots. Right.

He looked down at his feet: four large, even toes, each tipped in black talons, and a wicked looking back claw. His legs were bare save for a pair of gray leather pants, tight enough to be indecent, and spattered with something that looked suspiciously like blood.

He took inventory like a soldier checking gear after battle.

Head? Still attached, thank the stars—though a bit foggy, like waking up underwater.

Chest? Broad and armored in white scales that shimmered faintly in the dim light, familiar and alien all at once.

Heartbeat? Present. Pounding like a drumline in a storm.

Spine? Still straight, but it curved at the base now, pulled slightly sideways by the weight of a tail that flicked of its own accord.

Genitals? Definitely accounted for—eager, aching, and probably more enthusiastic than was polite.

Honestly? It was more than he'd expected, and yet so achingly familiar to wake up here, like this again.

He ran a hand down his chest, marveling at the texture—smooth in some places, pebbled in others, like the surface of a river rock. Now that he looked closer, a faint webbing of scars and shallow bloody scratches crossed his chest. He wondered if they were decorative or a souvenir from the rebirth.

He rolled his shoulders, testing the restored alignment. No, not restored. Altered. Everything felt both wrong and right, as if his body had been replaced with a better copy and then reinstalled at a crooked angle. Well—maybe not better. His muscles and bones ached like he'd been rebuilt by someone who'd run out of parts halfway through and finished the job with magic and madness.

Bella groaned behind him. Her eyes fluttered open, brown and clear. She blinked at the ceiling, then at him, then back around them.

"Are we dead?" she rasped.

"If we are, I want a refund," he said, looking down at the pants again. "This isn't what I asked for."

She snorted, then winced. "My head is ringing. Where are we?"

Leopol glanced around, taking in the rest of the chamber. The altar stood at the center of a ring of ruined columns, each one twisted by centuries of storms. Along the western wall, black scorch marks stained the stone where candles had burned for generations, probably as offerings.

Above that, a faded artwork mosaic stretched nearly the length of the wall, but half the tiles had fallen out or been replaced by moss. The rest of the temple was open on three sides, but the outer perimeter was crowded with trees—some alive, some just rotting trunks. Beyond that, he could hear the crash of waves, though the water was hidden by the thicket.

"At the temple where I was born," he said as he helped her sit up, his body heavy and ears ringing.

She was lighter than he remembered, almost insubstantial, though that might have just been the new strength in his arms. She steadied herself with a palm on the altar, then caught him staring at her gloriously naked breasts swaying gently as she looked around. When she noticed his gaze, her cheeks flushed, and a flash of magic made him blink. Bella muttered something under her breath, a word that fizzed with power but felt homey rather than dangerous.

When he opened his eyes, she was settling the blue skirts of her favorite dress around her knees, sitting on the edge of the stone altar bed. Her feet were still bare, and her hair still did its best impression of a frightened squirrel, but at least she looked more like herself, more confident and ready to tackle this newest challenge.

He sighed, "Pity to cover such beauty."

She blushed a deeper pink, and he purred at the sight before he looked up at the ceiling again, trying to see if any of the constellations were familiar.

Bella smoothed her hair, glancing at him sidelong. "You're very... white and blue," she said, as if breaking bad news. "But at least your rune tattoos are all still here. And some new ones!"

She reached out a hand and traced some of them on his skin. Thank the gods, they could still touch, even though she was still a spirit.

Standing before her on the altar, he hissed a breath at her touch, tensing at the sensation, at the pleasure of it. He wanted to spread her out and worship at the junction of her thighs.

He swallowed hard and kept tight rein on his primal need.

"Better than polka dots, I suppose. Or plaid." He didn't

point out the silvery edges of his scales or the pale blue undertones of his chest or the blue ink all over him.

She grinned and looked up at him, opening her mouth to say some smart comeback. Instead, she started laughing. A real laugh, unguarded, so loud that birds took flight in the treetops.

"What is it?" he said, fighting the urge to join her.

"Your ears," she said, pointing. "They're... well, they're not really ears anymore. You look like a lizard and a wolf had a very regrettable child."

He reached up and found that, yes, his ears were now just ridges of bone with little holes in them, swept back and covered in fine, downy fuzz, protected by two horns going back around his head.

He tried to be annoyed with her laughter at him, but she sounded just so joyful and young. He purred at giving her a moment's happiness and grinned. It felt a little more natural this time.

"Better than the alternative, which is being dead," he said, raking a hand through the hair at the top of his head, following it as it tapered to nothing at the base of his skull. "Or worse, waking up as myself but somehow balder."

Bella snickered and leaned into him, her hand finding his. She ran her thumb over the back of it, tracing the scales.

"It suits you," she said. "I don't mind a bit of a monster in my bed."

He grinned, the sparkle in her eyes giving him ideas as she squeezed his hand. The warmth of her skin felt real enough to anchor him, and the glinting tease in her eyes settled him.

"I'll gladly play the part. Whatever my queen desires."

She blushed and rolled her eyes as she patted the space

beside her. Leopol, careful not to step on his own toes or tail, joined her.

"Tell me about this place. What do you know of it?" she asked.

He took a deep breath, but it wasn't enough to prepare himself. She was strong to face all this head-on, though. He glanced up and counted the constellations on the ceiling, each one subtly different from what he remembered: angles sharper, lines straighter, the stories written in new constellations.

After a moment, he said, "This temple is the one I originally woke in last time, but it's different now. They're not right."

"What isn't?"

He pointed to a gold fleck shaped like a bow. "The stars. That one should be further east. Either the roof shifted or we're in a different hemisphere than I remember."

Bella stared at the ceiling for a while, then shrugged. "If the biggest problem we have is star maps, we're doing alright."

He let go of her hand, only a little reluctantly, and checked the rest of the chamber. The sun was still climbing, and shafts of pale light began to creep over the walls, highlighting the scars and the moss and the very obvious lack of any other people.

Unlike last time when he'd awoken here, his draconic adoptive parents were nowhere in sight.

He felt for his heart again, the pang of loss heavy. It thumped in his chest, steady and strong. He was alive. He was new, but he was alive. It occurred to him that, aside from Bella, he might be the only living thing for miles.

He should feel lonely, but for the first time in a thousand years, he was not alone in his heart and soul and spirit.

He looked at Bella and tried to say something profound, but all that came out was, "You're bleeding. On your face."

She touched her cheek and made a face at the dried blood there. "It's not mine," she said. "Probably yours. I think your claws got caught in my hair."

"Oh mibella, I'm so sorry," he said, the ache in his chest turning to guilt and the need to fix it. He leaned forward and licked her face, his long hybrid dragon tongue slowly cleaning her cheek. She froze at the first touch, then sank against his side, tilting her head for better access.

When he slowly made his way to her lips, her breath was short. He paused, giving her time to pull away. If he was too monstrous for her like this, it would kill him—but he wouldn't push himself on her. His body hummed that sweet melody of the mate bond as he waited.

Two breaths later, she pressed her mouth to his with a groan of need that sliced through him like fire, burning away his fear of rejection. Kissing was different like this, his elongated jaw and muzzle making their angles change.

But she grabbed his cheeks and steered him closer. The kiss deepened, but not enough to suit him. Too soon, she was pulling back, a hazy smile of desire on her face.

She ran her hands over his cheeks. "Thank you, Leopol. And before you start worrying about it, I love your hands. Both the old ones as a human spirit and these claws. A little scratching doesn't hurt me at all. And if that's the care I get after, feel free to do it next time too."

She winked, and he laughed, elated that she wanted a next time. His smile felt fully natural now. They sat together on the edge of the slab for a long minute, holding hands, just breathing and listening to the crash of waves through the forest, each trying to process the impossible thing that had just happened.

Her sweet voice penetrated the silence softly. "How much do you remember?"

He started to answer, then realized he remembered *all* of it—but not in the right order. The memories came like chapters torn from a book and shoved back at random.

Some memories were crystal clear; the moment he'd seen his parents for the first time, the feel of the stars pulling at his bones, the last look on his true mother's face as she—

He blinked, not ready to face the pain of that yet.

"More than I expected," he said at last. "Some of it doesn't make sense yet, but I remember enough. And with each minute, I'm remembering more and more, even my memories of before I arrived here last time."

"You said you last came to this temple fully formed?" she asked, her hand grounding him. He clung to her like a lifeline.

He exhaled slowly, eyes drifting up to the ruined constellations overhead. "Yes, I wasn't born, and I didn't hatch. Before I ever had this physical dragon body, before I was sent to Celawyn..."

She gasped, squeezing his hand. "You remember?"

He nodded slowly. "I served in the heavens as a librarian of the gods. A keeper of truths too dangerous to speak aloud. That spirit form I took? That's what I was there in the heavens. Honifery shaped me, and Illustros breathed life into my soul, but I wasn't truly alive. I thought I'd forgotten all of it—but I can still feel the shape of that silent library in my bones."

Bella blinked. "You were a divine librarian?"

"An Archivist," he said, a wry edge to his voice. "I kept records of the celestial contracts. The laws of death. The bindings of spirits and the oaths of old gods. When Illustros fell and Asmoroth was trapped in the Deep, I... I was sent here."

She gasped again, her jaw dropping in surprise. "That was over a thousand years ago! There were still falling pieces up to three hundred years ago."

He nodded. "I know. I was here, lived through it all."

She breathed deeply, her brow creasing with thought. "But... why were you sent here?"

He paused, jaw tightening. "The library vanished in the fall, and I failed to protect it from those who wanted to steal the gods' secrets. I was left in limbo, ripped from my home and the only existence I ever knew, the only purpose I had. I was sent here to protect something..."

His voice faded, his memories settling into sharper focus the more he let himself feel them. "And maybe to stop what's coming. I remember now, everything."

"Does that make you a demigod?" she asked, tension creeping into her posture.

He shook his head. "No. When they made me in the heavens, I wasn't alive. I was a construct, a spirit of duty. When Honifery sent me here, I was given a dragon's body— but it never worked quite like theirs."

"In what ways?" she asked, watching him closely.

He shrugged, gaze distant. "I didn't need to sleep. Didn't get hungry." Then he turned to her, eyes burning with something deeper. "I never had a mate."

Her eyes widened, and she licked her lips. "But now you do. And you're back in your dragon body."

He nodded slowly, reverently.

She nudged him with her knee. "Then I'm glad I helped you get back in it," she said softly.

"I never doubted you were the key," he murmured, brushing a kiss to her temple.

"You know," she said, gesturing vaguely, "with the barrier and whatever was keeping the spells from combining you, I could feel you getting pulled between spirit and dragon forms, and I just–"

She broke off, her cheeks coloring. "It's hard to explain. But I think the mate bond *did* something. It wasn't just instinct–I could feel it happening. Your magic... wrapped around mine. Or maybe mine wrapped around yours. Either way, it felt right, like everything clicked into place, and I refused to let you go."

"Yes, your pussy and legs and arms held me tight, grounded me in the way life should be," he said.

She elbowed him, and he grinned at her. It didn't feel strange at all this time.

"As a Dreamscale dragon, I've always been able to walk through the Veil and see ghosts and spirits. I've only met a handful in all my travels, but none like you. In all my studies, none have ever been able to rejoin their hibernating body before."

She grew quiet, then she said, "Somehow I dragged you out of the Veil by sheer force of will?"

"That was probably part of it, but the mate bond is a powerful thing and not to be underestimated. We're probably going to keep changing until we finish the process and solidify our bond to one another. Assuming we can get you back into your body too."

She tilted her chin up, cheeks still blazing. "We damn well better. I don't let go of things that matter to me."

A slow warmth spread through his chest, a feeling as unfamiliar as the rest of his anatomy.

He lifted her hand and kissed her palm, her fingers threading over his razor-sharp teeth without hesitation. She smiled, and his chest purred again.

After a beat, Bella's expression clouded. "Do you think it'll work the other way? For me?" She tapped her sternum with her other hand, as if searching for a heartbeat. "Or am I stuck being a spirit until the rose dies?"

Leopol frowned and lowered their joined hands to his meaty thigh. He'd been so focused on his own state that he hadn't considered the reverse. The curse that had bound her was designed to keep her alive but only barely—half in the world, half out. If the mate bond had jump-started his return, could it do the same for her?

He wasn't sure. And he didn't want to lie. He blinked, switching on his magic sight. There was a faint line of magic trailing from her toward the south, but a stronger line of magic between them.

He didn't want to give either of them false hope, though.

"I don't know," he admitted. "But if there's a way, we'll find it. I won't—" He broke off, realizing he was about to make a promise he might not keep. He started again, softer as if making a reverent oath. "I'm not leaving you. Not after all this."

She studied his face, searching for cracks, but he held her gaze. Apparently satisfied, she squeezed his hand and smiled, even as a frown of worry marred her brow. "Good, because I don't want to do this alone, either."

He reached up—slowly, deliberately—and brushed her cheek with the back of his hand, careful not to scratch her with the talons. The touch made her relax into it. He'd never been this gentle before, never needed to be.

"Neither of us are alone anymore. You're my mate, my heart, my everything. I will burn the world and the wizard in it if that's what it takes to save you," he vowed.

Her eyes shone brighter with tears, and he stroked her cheek.

"I don't know what this means for us," she said, tapping her chest again. "But I'm not waiting around to fade or disappear into the hells. Even if I'm half-dead, then I'll do everything I can with the half that's still here."

They rested their foreheads together and just breathed. For a moment, her worries stilled, and so did his. But outside, the wind picked up, rustling the trees and bringing the sea's roar a little closer—as if time had merely paused, not stopped.

Something in the air stirred, subtle but charged—enough to lift the fine hairs on the back of his neck. She straightened like she'd felt it too.

Her brow furrowed, her eyes darting across the room as if cataloging every exit and potential hazard. "The air's shifting."

He nodded, not taking his eyes off her. Magic was a fickle mistress, and her hands spread as if feeling for threads of it.

She sucked in a breath, worry furrowing her brow. "Something's... moving."

He nodded. "Cerci's arrival is always an impetus for change. It can even impact the threads of magic itself."

She bit her lip. "I need to get back to the rose. I'm nervous about leaving it too long. Oh, and the villagers! They're coming back tonight, and we have to track their progress."

Leopol pushed off the altar and offered his hand again. "You're right. Let's explore the temple and see what memories tell me on how to leave this place. See if you like the rest of me in this form as much as you did in spirit human form."

Bella rolled her eyes but took it, and together they staggered to their feet. He towered over her, her head barely coming to his heart. He could probably pick her up with one arm, and he internally vowed to protect her no matter the cost.

The temple groaned around them, ancient and battered but still, in its own way, alive.

Chapter Twenty-Eight

They walked around the edge of the altar, Leopol's new feet making soft, scratching sounds on the stone. Bella's own bare steps barely registered, but her presence was a warm spot in the chilly dawn. They circled the open floor, passing the wall of blackened candle stubs and the faded stretch of broken glass tile mosaic. Even ruined, the temple bore the marks of something sacred, and if he analyzed his memories, he could almost see the place as it had been back then.

Bella tapped the wall where the tiles arched up into a rough outline of a winged figure. "Is this supposed to be you?" she asked.

Leopol traced the figure's outline, feeling the tug of familiarity. The curve of the wings. The stylized sun behind the head. The subtle little notch in the stone where the artist's chisel had skipped. He'd seen it before, but when it was newer, more colorful. A lot had faded after a thousand years. His mouth went dry.

"It's who I was supposed to be..." He paused, the misfiled memories clicking into place in his mind.

She pursed her lips. "You ever going to explain that? Or am I just supposed to keep guessing?"

He tried to smile, to answer, but the words tangled up. For a moment he just stood there, eyes on the mosaic, letting his mind trip over the ragged edges of memory. The air inside the temple felt heavier now, each breath tinged with dust and something older.

"Alright, guessing it is. This is a temple, and if that's you—does that make you the god of this temple? For drake's sake, if they worshipped you—"

"Hardly." He laughed, a sharp bark that bounced off the empty walls. "More like the harbinger, a prophecy yet unfulfilled."

He reached out and pressed a claw to the winged figure's chest, where the heart would be.

She gave him a look, the kind that meant she expected a better answer.

Leopol shut his eyes, letting the memories flood in. The lost library: endless, spiraling, filled with books that pulsed with life. He remembered tending them, cataloguing not just words but the stories behind them, the raw memory of worlds both real and imagined.

His mother's voice, stern but warm, echoing through the stacks. The hush of other gods, debating philosophy or just talking shop, always one argument away from upending reality.

He opened his eyes and looked at Bella. "I was the librarian of the gods," he said, and the words tasted true. "To understand the mosaic, you must understand where I came from."

"The lost library of the gods?"

He nodded, throat tight with emotion. The weight of the memories pressed at him from all sides, but it was a good pressure, like the feeling of being wrapped in a thick blanket on a cold night. Still, the details frayed at the edges—names, faces, whole events just out of reach.

He paced away from the mosaic, his mind spinning with memories as he tried to explain.

"When I was in that library, I had no body, was nothing but a spirit of raw protective power. The woman I called my mother created me, but Illustros breathed life into me, making me more than a construct. I still wasn't alive with a body that could die, though. They wanted me to act as the eternal leader of the sentinels, a protector of knowledge."

"Protector from what?" Bella asked, fear making her voice echo in the chamber. "What would the gods fear that they needed a bodyguard?"

He touched one of the pillars and prowled to the next, the scratching of his claws on the tile loud in the stillness, blending with the crashing waves.

"I wasn't guarding a body. Only knowledge. Some of the secrets of the gods couldn't be allowed to fall into the hands of the wrong people."

He glanced back at her, her frown of confusion still clear in the morning light that filtered in from above.

He sighed, pausing with a hand on another pillar. "Imagine if the monsters from the Shadow Realm knew how to open portals to the others. What destruction would they bring to other worlds? Imagine if vampires weren't limited by their weakness to the sun. Imagine if nekromancers could truly resurrect the dead without consequence or raise armies of true undead instead of shuffling corpses. The library held knowledge that could unravel entire civilizations, destroy entire realities."

Bella's breath caught. "And you were supposed to protect that?"

"Not just protect. Curate. Preserve. Some knowledge is too dangerous to exist, but too important to destroy." He tapped a talon against the pillar, leaving a small scratch. "I was the guardian of impossible truths."

"With no one but the gods for company," she said softly, her hand tracing the mosaic of his dragon form.

"I remember the loneliness most of all. The Dreaming whispered lullabies before I had a name. She was my first mother—the goddess who gave me shape and trained me as the Archivist."

"Your mother was a goddess?"

He shrugged. "I called her mother, though I knew she wasn't. But in those early days, when magic was all I understood, she was the one who fed me knowledge and warmth."

"And your father?"

He shook his head. "The closest father figure might be Illustros, whose laughter filled the silence with something like hope. He came to the library often but never fulfilled that father role. Sometimes Guiana came, too, but she always kept her distance, as if she were a guest in her own life."

The difference now was staggering. He had a body—a monstrous, patchwork thing, but his own. He had Bella, who saw him clearer than anyone else ever had. And he had the memories, sharp as knives, filling in the gaps of who he was and why he'd been made.

He looked up at the painted dome. The constellations were wrong because they'd moved; time here passed differently, faster, and the sky itself had shifted, different from a thousand years ago.

Bella looked at the other images on the mosaic, then glanced at him with her deep eyes that saw too much. "You look like you just found out your favorite bar burned down."

He snorted. "It's more like..." He trailed off, searching for the word. "Grief, but also relief. Like I lost myself for a while and just got picked up from lost and found."

Bella considered that. "I always hated the lost and found at the tavern. It smelled like cheese and old sweat." She glanced at him, then floated toward him with a smile. "You smell better, for what it's worth."

"Gee, thanks," he said, arching a brow. "Come on, let's explore."

Outside the temple, the ground sloped down toward the sea. Dew-soaked grass squished under Leopol's toes, and his tail dragged furrows in the mud. He still wasn't used to how heavy it was—or how, every time he shifted his hips, the world seemed to rebalance itself around the extra limb.

Before, he'd woken up a full dragon, and his adopted parents had to teach him to shift into a hybrid form. Yet, that hybrid form had been smaller, more human like, than this one. This one felt larger, more likely to fulfill the prophecies and omens.

Bella kept glancing at him out of the corner of her eye, like she was waiting for him to do a trick. When he finally caught her, she pretended to be looking for rocks to skip.

"You know," she said at last, "for someone who's never been truly alive before, you walk like you own the place."

Leopol snorted. "I had a body before. This is just... an upgrade."

She squinted at him, then at the broad stretch of muscle running down his forearm. "That's what all the ex-wrestlers at my tavern used to say when they lost weight and grew a beard."

He looked down at himself, trying to see what she saw.

The scales were smooth and fine, reflecting the sunrise in a thousand miniature suns. The rest of him was larger, more angular—his hands in particular had doubled in size. But it was still him, somehow. The shape of the face, the arch of the brow, the way he hunched his shoulders when he was uncomfortable.

Bella came to a stop at the edge of a flat rock. She planted her feet and looked up at him, serious now.

"You're not just alive," she said. "You're real, solid." She stepped closer and poked him, hard, in the chest. "Do you know what that means?"

Leopol considered. "It means I can actually eat food for a purpose, instead of just doing the motions. Or that I'll need to find pants that fit and won't be able to just magic my clothes on and off."

He wiggled his heavy brows, and she blushed even as she laughed.

Eventually, when her laughter died down, she said, "If you're fully alive now, then you're able to die now. And I don't think that's happened before, has it?"

He shook his head, the realization landing heavy. "No, last time, I was... merely a sentient construct, a shadow, a whisper. This body is definitely alive. Only the living get fated mates."

She tapped her chin, thinking. "Knox is a dragon and has poison, venom, and darts. If you're alive and a real dragon, what else can you do?" Her eyes sparkled with mischief.

He grinned at the challenge. "Oh, I can't wait to show you the things I can do with my tail."

She laughed, her cheeks blooming bright pink. "Plenty of time for that later. At a minimum, can you sprout wings and fly us home, or are you just going to stand here and look pretty while I find a solution?"

"Make up your mind, woman. Am I pretty or a monster?"

She arched a brow and crossed her arms, sassily tossing back, "Can't you be both?"

Leopol grinned, the corners of his mouth pulling back further than he remembered being possible. "If you're asking if I can change into the full dragon you saw under the castle, the answer is yes."

He took a deep breath, gathering the energy from somewhere behind his ribs. It was easy—much easier than when he'd first appeared with a dragon form. With a thought, his skin rippled, scales shifting and enlarging, bones stretching and popping. His hands folded in, claws elongating, and his tail whipped out behind him. His face lengthened, teeth sharpening, eyes going from gray to a bright, metallic blue.

The change took only a second. Where Leopol had stood on two legs, there was now an imposing ancient dragon of legends. White and silver scales gleamed in the morning light, and the wings, folded tight against his back, shivered with latent power.

He looked down at Bella, who was staring with the same rapt attention she used to give particularly complex books in the library at Hartsgrove.

"Well?" he said, the voice deeper now, a basso growl that reverberated in his own chest. "Impressed?"

She walked a slow circle around him, one hand trailing along his flank. "I'll give you this," she said, "it's a good look." She stopped in front of him and craned her neck to see his eyes. "Does it hurt? To shift?"

He shook his head, sending a shower of dew from his horns as he settled into a crouch so she could touch more of him. "Not at all. Feels... right, actually. My adoptive parents gave me this ring when they taught me how to do it."

Bella nodded, then pressed both hands to his soft, light blue chest. His runes glowed faintly. The touch was gentle, almost reverent, and Leopol shivered despite himself. She leaned in, examining a scale, then traced the line where it overlapped with the next near his shoulder.

"Like a focus item. That makes sense. I always thought dragons would be cold, but you're not," she said.

He blinked, startled. "Should I be?"

She grinned. "No, I like you warm." She moved down his side and ran her hand along the spine to his tail, careful not to touch the sensitive tip. "You're soft, here."

Leopol tried not to purr, but when she gently squeezed the tip, the sound escaped anyway. He glared at her, but she just laughed.

After a moment, she asked, "Can you fly?"

He spread his wings experimentally. They were heavier than he remembered, the membranes translucent and shot through with veins of silver. "What kind of question is that to ask a dragon?"

Bella took a step back to watch, curiosity written all over her face. "You said you never quite fit in with the other dragons, so I wasn't sure. Just don't break anything. Or me."

"I would never harm you, Bellakari," he swore. She flushed as he flexed the wings again, feeling the muscles bunch and release. With a tentative hop, he cleared the rock and landed a few feet away, claws digging furrows in the wet ground as he stretched. The motion was awkward but exhilarating.

Bella clapped, grinning like a fool. "You're so graceful, muscular. I thought you'd be lumbering around like a behemoth, but you're not."

Leopol preened under her praise and shifted back to his hybrid form, the change now as easy as breathing. He blinked, finding himself face-to-face with Bella, who had not moved.

She reached up and touched his cheek, fingers lingering on the line of his jaw. "You're really here, alive and well," she said, not a question.

He nodded. "I am."

She pulled him into a hug, strong and sure. He wrapped his arms—and tail—around her, holding tight.

After a long moment, Bella leaned back, searching his eyes. "We're going to have to tell the others, you know."

Leopol grimaced. "I know. I should've told Knox long before now what I thought my past was, even without the proof I sought."

She shrugged. "Yes, you should've. If we're mates, I expect you to never keep things from me just because it's only a hunch and you have no proof. Do you understand?" Her tone was light, but he saw the seriousness behind it.

He didn't answer right away. Instead, he looked out over the sea, the rising sun casting everything in gold and silver. For the first time, he felt not just alive, but present, anchored to the world in a way he'd never been before.

Like always, he turned to smile down at her. "As you wish, mibella."

Bella smiled, and the world felt new. "With that in mind, will you tell me what happened at the lost library? I know what the history books say about the fall, but were you actually there?"

His scales rippled, a shudder that seemed to come from somewhere deeper than his skin. "Yes, along with Asmoroth."

Four words, but they held the weight of the cosmos. A

distant crash echoed from outside the temple—waves against rock, or something else entirely. Neither of them moved.

"Oh, Leo, I'm so sorry," she said, wrapping her arms around his waist. "While the rest of the realms were reeling with the death of Illustros, you were kicked out of your home and thrust into this realm, this body—gods, and I thought I had it rough with the missing body and tether to the rose."

She laughed bitterly, and he wrapped his arms around her, holding her tight. The sun had risen just enough to send a band of gold across the forest floor, lighting up the dust motes and the tiny green leaves that had begun to sprout in the cracks. The temple behind them, even ruined, still had a pulse. So did he, perhaps for the first time, he was truly alive... and had something worth living for.

"What do we do now?" Bella asked softly.

"Now," he said, his voice low and rough, "I'm here with you, and I know everything will turn out alright in the end. We just—"

A sudden scraping sound interrupted them—something metallic dragging against stone from deeper within the temple. Leopol's ears—those strange new ridges—twitched. His tail swept behind him, positioning protectively in front of Bella, buzzing with premonition.

"We need to leave. We're not alone," he growled. "We're not safe here. This temple... it feels like a waypoint, a transition space, perhaps a powerful leyline where portals can open easily."

She pressed against his back, her hands finding purchase on his scaled lower spine. "And now that Cerci is back, the portals could be too."

The scraping grew louder, sending vibrations through the trees.

"It's the most likely explanation for how we got here, yes," Leopol muttered. "And if other things are opening long-closed portals... they might not be friendly."

The first hint of movement appeared in the temple's shadowed far corner. A glint of metal caught the light—something large, sharp and angular. Leopol's muscles tensed, scales rippling with an electric readiness.

The shadows seemed to pulse and contract, revealing first a gleaming mechanical limb, then another. Something mechanical was emerging from the temple's darkness. Not a creature, but a machine.

"Stay behind me," Leopol growled, positioning himself fully in front of Bella. His tail swept a protective arc, claws digging into the stone floor.

The figure revealed itself, definitely a construct, and he breathed a sigh of relief that at least it wasn't one of the daemons. Metallic joints clicked and whirred, steam hissing from hidden vents. Where a face should have been, there was only a complex arrangement of lenses and geared mechanisms that seemed to be studying them with an unsettling, inhuman intensity.

"Identification protocol initiated," a voice said—if it could be called a voice. Mechanical and precise, it emanated from no clear source, reverberating through the temple's stone walls.

Leopol's scales bristled. His claws scraped against the stone floor, leaving thin furrows. "Bella," he whispered, "whatever happens, do not move."

The mechanical construct took another step forward. Its movements were fluid yet unnatural—each joint calibrated with impossible precision. Steam continued to hiss from its joints, carrying a metallic scent that made Leopol's nostrils flare.

"Guardian protocol recognized," the voice continued. "Librarian construct sequence activated, designation incomplete. Biological match: eighty-seven point three percent confirmed. Partial recognition protocols engaged."

The mechanical voice carried no emotion, only clinical observation.

Leopol felt something shift inside him. Memories flickered at the edges of his consciousness—fragments of conversations in languages long forgotten, technical specifications for devices more complex than anything in this realm.

This was no random machine, but something purposefully designed. Something that knew him. Or at least, knew of him.

Recognition flared like a struck match, and Leopol's breath caught.

"I know this construct," he said. "It's a Sentinel—part of the original perimeter network around the library archives. They were built to protect the gods' knowledge, not roam free."

His brows drew tight. "But its presence here... it shouldn't be active, not this far from the library. This isn't a malfunction—it's a desecration. This thing was holy once. The Sentinels were my only company when the gods weren't visiting the archives."

A memory surfaced—this same design, once polished and gleaming, allowing only gods through the archive gates. Now its joints sparked, and its lenses glowed with the wrong red color.

"Who sent you? Why are you here?" he demanded, positioning himself more firmly between the construct and Bella. The construct triggered his training as an Archivist, and he quickly analyzed the situation from every angle, estimating every possible outcome.

The mechanical being tilted its head—a gesture so human it was unsettling coming from something so clearly not alive. Steam hissed from its joints, and for a moment the temple filled with a mechanical whisper. "Sender: Unknown. Primary directive: Locate. Verify. Protect."

The lenses shifted, focusing and refocusing on Leopol with an intensity that made his scales prickle. One metallic hand extended, fingers unfolding like precise instruments, each joint moving with impossible smoothness.

"Guardian," the construct said again, the word sounding less like a greeting and more like a command.

Bella gasped and pointed to the joint at its wrist. "That mark—Leopol, look!"

Etched into the metal just beneath the elbow joint was a jagged rune, crudely carved and blackened at the edges as if scorched into place.

"That's from the Writ of Ashborne," she said, voice tight. "Volume three, page one-forty-six."

Leopol's eyes widened, his grip on her growing tighter. "Fuck, you're right. It's a nekrotic binding sigil—meant to override a construct's original directives." And hadn't been there in the original library.

Bella's hand pressed against Leopol's back, her touch warm against his scales. "This wasn't just corrupted. Someone reprogrammed it. Bent it to their will."

Before Leopol could answer, the construct took another step forward. The stone floor trembled beneath its weight, dust rising in small clouds around its mechanical feet. Steam continued to curl from its joints, carrying the sharp scent of old machine oil and something else—something ancient and alien.

"Partial memory restoration detected," the construct

continued. "Incomplete guardian protocol requires restoration."

It stepped out of the temple and onto the grass, but it wasn't built for such terrain. Its clunky feet were more like hooves, and it slipped on the soft, dewy forest floor. It tumbled down the hill toward them, and Leopol swept Bella into his arms and out of the way.

It crashed against a tree and spasmed. Bella trembled in his arms, and the mechanical being twitched, repeating in that monotone voice, "Error. Error. Error."

The mechanical construct's lenses flickered, cycling through rapid pulses of white, then blue, then deep crimson. Its limbs jerked and twisted in angles that screamed of violence and violation.

Sparks shot from its joints–then something worse.

A thin line of black ichor began to leak from beneath its chest plating, hissing as it hit the stone. The scent was foul–burned copper and rotting leaves–and Leopol instinctively pulled Bella further back.

The ichor moved like it was alive, pooling and then writhing on the ground before seeping into the forest floor like ink into parchment.

"Nekrotic energy," Bella whispered, eyes wide. "That's not just anyone's magic. This has the wizard written all over it. With those sigils and runes? He hasn't just corrupted it. He infected it, twisted it for his own purpose. This is his work–the same rot that cursed me and the villagers."

The construct's lenses dimmed to darkness. "Guardian... corrupted... sequence... failed... Malfunction detected," the voice crackled, more static than speech now. "Recalibration required."

Its voice sputtered one last time before its limbs

collapsed in on themselves, metal groaning as the entire body seized and went still.

Leopol set Bella down but kept one protective arm around her. His scales bristled, reflecting the morning light in sharp, warning glints. Whatever this thing was, it clearly knew something about him—about his past in the lost library.

The construct's head swiveled, each rotation accompanied by a grinding screech of metal. Its lenses zoomed in and out, focusing on Leopol with an intensity that felt more like a scan than a gaze.

"Guardian protocol compromised," it announced. "Partial memory match. Incomplete restoration sequence. Malfunction, error, malfunction, error."

Its lenses blinked red, then it stilled, no movement other than the blinking red. Leopol frowned and breathed a sigh of relief.

"What the fuck is going on?" Bella asked, her voice wavering with a cross between anger and fear.

A tremor pulsed through the earth beneath their feet—faint, but unmistakable.

Leopol looked at Bella, voice grim. "Scout or assassin, either way... we're out of time. We need to fly home."

Bella's voice was barely a whisper. "If this was a warning, what's coming next?"

Chapter Twenty-Nine

It's a good thing that Leopol's dragon body was so warm because it was fucking cold to fly through the clouds on his back. She tried to talk as they flew south, Leopol following the faint pulse of magic that tethered her to the rose while juggling the Sentinel in his claws.

"Can you change colors? Like a chameleon?"

"Not unless I'm on fire."

She ran her hand over his scales, unconvinced. "What do you eat, then? Normal food, or do you need, like, whole goats and cows?"

He cocked his head, pumping his wings to keep them airborne. The back-and-forth went on for a while. As they flew, Leopol grew tense under her thighs. His responses became shorter and more succinct.

When he growled at her speculations on the aerodynamics of dragon wings, she sniffed and leaned closer over him.

"Someone sounds hangry," she snapped back.

"I'm not hangry. I don't get hangry."

"You didn't before, as a construct, but you're alive now. Of course, you're hungry, when you haven't eaten in three hundred years."

He grew quiet after that, and she stroked his side. They flew over the skyscraping mountains, snow on their peaks. The temple had sat in the secretive northern lands, the terrain a balmy deciduous forest at first, but growing progressively colder as they went south toward the mountains. The same mountains that none of the Buspartans ever wanted to cross.

She sighed, a touch nervous as they glided between two cold peaks. "Are you alright, Leopol?"

"Just tired, I think. And you're right. Hungry too," he said, his dragon voice low and deep. "I'm changing, Bella, and I don't just mean my body—I mean everything. The way I see things, the way I think. It's like... I'm a different animal. Literally."

She nodded, as if she'd already guessed. "That's not a bad thing, is it?"

"I don't know," he said, honest for once. "Maybe."

The mountain air bit harder as they crossed the mountains, and their conversation stalled. Leopol glided more and more, obviously tiring from being unused to flying. He'd only got his body back this morning, and now he was traversing the continent.

Admiration welled within her. Pride too, but also worry. She didn't want him to overly tax himself. As the sun set in the west, she bit her lip, pulling her fur-lined cloak tighter around her. Leopol had encouraged her to magic it up, and she'd called forth the pretty red one with the white lining that Gastone had given her.

Except he hadn't given it to her. He'd simply provided the funds and told her to order a fully stocked wedding trousseau of clothes that would be fit for a queen. She blinked back tears, keeping her eyes on the snow-capped peaks as they passed.

She realized now that Gastone had never been the man of her dreams. She'd wanted him to fulfill all her fantasies, but being rich and a king did not a hero make.

Leopol, on the other hand... no, it was wrong to pin all her hopes on him too. She didn't need a man. She could be her own hero and take care of herself. Hells, she'd been doing so for a decade, ever since her father went to war.

She could take care of herself. But who would take care of Leopol? The sweet man didn't even realize she could feel his stomach growling in hunger.

"We can make a camp for the night," she called into the wind, knowing he'd hear it anyway.

His head bobbed as they went between two more peaks. Another rose in front of them, and they banked slowly around it. The terrain changed slowly, the mountains not quite so tall or imposing. Still bigger than the rolling hills around her hometown of Demerel, these mountains had less snow and more trees.

Leopol called out. "I see lights ahead."

Bella leaned slightly around him and thought of the geography and their direction. "Is it the new village? The one by the dwarves?"

Leopol angled toward it, purring beneath her before he nodded. "I think so. Let's find out."

White glare ricocheted off the peaks and shivered across the shallow bowl of the valley, settling on the wedge-shaped cottages stitched to the cliffside like teeth in a jaw. The village was small, but it bristled with activity: huddled figures stomped pathways through the drifts, voices rising in thick, foreign syllables that rumbled like spring avalanches.

The dragon's shadow swept the slope first, low and wide, then Leopol hammered the ground with the force of landing in front of the largest and oldest looking of the buildings.

The snow compacted beneath him in a deep, concussive thud; powder flew outward, and a few startled goats skittered away, bellows muffled by the sheer vastness of the mountain silence. Bella, arms numb and face raw from the wind, did not dismount gracefully. She slid, half fell, boots punching through the frozen snow to land beside the crumpled Sentinel at his feet.

Thank the gods she'd magicked boots on earlier.

The village had paused, frozen at the sight of the dragon as if caught mid-breath. Then the crowd on the small, open village green—twenty, maybe more, some with tools gripped in gloved fists—began to edge in. The furs they wore were patched from wolf, deer, bear, and strange animals Bella could not name. They reeked of tallow and warmth, a direct challenge to the freeze.

She noted, as she had been taught to note all her life, how no single villager stepped out in front. They moved as one body, united and implacable, and reminded her of the angry mob at Hartsgrove. Her spine straightened, and she sucked in a nervous breath to gather her courage.

Leopol rumbled, the sound something between a threat and a reassurance. He shifted into his hybrid form—still only wearing the dirty, gray pants—and searched the crowd as he put his arm around her waist. At their feet lay the mechanical device where he'd dropped it.

An older dwarf with glasses appeared at the doorway to one of the larger buildings—a compact shape in dark leathers, hood thrown back, face alive with red windburn and intelligence. He walked to the front, steps careful but unhurried, the crowd parting in his wake.

They all stared, but it was the dwarf, the first of many who followed him out the door, that spoke.

"Hail, welcome to Ravrgard, home of dwarves and under the protection of King Knox of the Feral Forest. Who are you?"

She swallowed hard, half afraid to look at the villagers. She kept her gaze on their leader, but it was Leopol who stepped forward and bowed slightly.

"Well met, Kris. Perhaps you don't remember me. I look quite different than before, but I'm Leopol, Knox's dragon cousin."

Kris frowned in confusion. "You've come from the wrong direction. And last time I checked, Leopol was a spirit like her."

Leopol nodded. "This is Queen Bella of Busparia. She helped me find my dragon body and rejoin my spirit with it. In the process, we were sucked through a portal to a temple in the north. May we shelter here for the night?"

A grumble from the crowd began at her name, and a few voices rose in discord.

"That's the queen! From the Blooomin' Brew tavern!"

"No, the evil one's still on the throne—this can't be her."

Kris sliced the air with one sharp gesture. "Enough."

Bella straightened. She was no stranger to tavern stares, the kind fueled by ale and whispered rumor. But this was different. These people weren't drunk. They were afraid. Grieving their past lives, ripped from their homes.

To them, she was both monarch and monster. She didn't know which was worse.

Before she could respond, Leopol's lip curled into a fierce growl. "She's not evil."

The villager holding the axe, white-knuckled, stared at her with a morbid fascination. "The queen is in Busparia. How can she be here?"

"I heard she was cursed too."

"If she's cursed like the rest of us, why isn't she stone?"

"And why does she look like that? No one else is a specter."

Bella held onto Leopol's waist and stepped slightly forward. Her voice rang through the tension.

"My spirit was trapped by a wizard, who wears my body like a cloak. The thing ruling in Busparia is a puppet, nothing more."

A hush spread like frost.

The butcher, arms crossed over his bloodstained apron, growled, "So you're not the reason our kin are walking broomsticks and scythes? Why some were turned to stone in the village by the ash, unable to escape the curse?"

"No, she's not," Leopol said, his hand splayed on her back, voice thick and raw. "It's the wizard's doing. Your queen was replaced—usurped—by the wizard who stole her body and uses it to command the daemons. This winter? His doing. She's as much a victim as your family."

The tall villager's lip curled. "Some victim. She's here, and my brother isn't."

Bella raised her hand, and the axe the man held twitched in his grip.

"I'm not asking for your forgiveness in my part of these problems," she said. "Just the chance to fix what's been broken."

The axe stilled. The crowd went silent again.

Kris stepped in again, hand raised like a blade. "I said enough. No one's in the ground yet. She helped Leopol, and that's why they're here now. If there's a way to undo this curse, we're going to hear it. I've heard you have a plan?"

Bella took a deep breath and nodded. "We've finalized the potion and ritual and administered the first trial test on four volunteers in Hartsgrove yesterday. We need to get back and track their progress and changes. If they return to normal, we'll go to each of the villages and do the same for everyone."

The villagers murmured, the words fraud and test subject thrown around like darts.

The tall villager demanded, "How long until we know if this works?"

Bella glanced at Leopol, then answered, "One full moon cycle. Maybe less, if the symptoms show sooner. But that's the minimum."

The butcher piped up. "And if it fails?"

"We regroup," Leopol said. "We try a different approach. But we believe this will work. All the evidence points to a consistent spell craft—even the Seer agrees—which means it can be undone in the same way for everyone."

The butcher crossed his arms, chewing on the idea. The tall villager, not entirely mollified, grunted and jerked his chin at Kris. "You trust these two?"

Kris shrugged. "I trust Knox, and the communications this week have shared their efforts. This either works or it doesn't, but there's no use in you browbeating anyone tonight. Now what is this interesting contraption you've brought with you?"

The crowd's tension ebbed a notch—Bella felt it, the way a hunted animal senses a pack losing interest. The villagers withdrew, returning to their tasks.

Bella met Leopol's eyes, her lips firming as she gave him an encouraging nod.

Leopol took a deep breath and met Kris' gaze. "We think it's a Sentinel of the gods, but the wizard used nekrotic magic and corrupted it, sending it after us. Can you fix it? If I remove the nekrotic sigils?"

Kris kneeled on the cold ground and turned the thing over onto its back, poking and prodding as the villagers dispersed now that the newness of their arrival had faded.

Kris held up the device by the hand, inspecting the sigil on the wrist. "Aye, we'll take it apart, see what code is running inside. If it's as you say, we'll know. If not, we'll deal with that, too. Boys?"

Several other dwarves stepped forward, quickly carrying the thing inside. Bella and Leopol followed, the heavy weight of his hand keeping her grounded.

"Do you have anything to feed Leopol? He's just woken from hibernation and is starving."

Kris looked over his shoulder, bushy brows high as he held the door open for them. "Really? Tell me more of that while I fix you a bowl of stew. Do you need anything, Your Majesty?"

Bella paused but shook her head with a murmured thanks.

Inside the cottage, the air was saturated with woodsmoke and the yeast-sweet smell of bread. The walls were hung with maps and clockwork tools, some of them ticking or vibrating gently in their racks.

The door shut behind them. Kris said, not looking up as he puttered around the kitchen, "So, how'd you get it here without tripping the failsafe?"

"It fell down a hill and slammed into a tree," Bella said, sitting in a chair at the table.

Leopol nodded in Bella's direction. "She disabled the targeting and bypassed the proximity rune on the shoulder. I was too busy inspecting the nekrotic sigils to even see it."

For the first time, Kris gave Bella his full attention. The focus was so intense it felt surgical, as if Kris might dissect her on the spot to see how she worked. Bella's pulse spiked. She raised her chin, determined not to flinch.

Kris set a bowl of stew on the table along with a loaf of bread. "The workroom is through that door. If you need a washroom, it's through that one. Help yourself to as much as you'd like to eat while I check on the boys and see if we can crack it open without killing ourselves. Then I'll be back to get the story from you."

"Story?" she asked.

"Of how you left Hartsgrove," he said firmly before he disappeared into the workshop.

Leopol scarfed down the stew, shoulders hunched with exhaustion. Bella hovered, feeling restless. She needed to do *something* useful.

She stood and said softly, "I'll remove the nekrotic sigils while you eat."

He didn't even look up, and she swiftly went into the workroom to fix it. Even doing this one small task made her feel more competent.

When she rejoined Leopol, he was slumped at the table, hands on head and bowl empty, visibly depleted. She took his bowl and refilled it, using magic to move it to the stove and back again. Then she refilled his mug of ale with tea from the stove and grabbed another loaf of bread, setting both in front of him. Her control of magic, her ability to manipulate objects, was better the longer she was with Leopol. *Mated.*

She blushed, but his words pulled her from that spiral of thought.

"We didn't make it back to Hartsgrove," he said softly, glancing up with his brilliant blue eyes that took her breath away every time.

Bella sat on the stool at the end of the table and nodded to the bowl of stew on the table. "Eat. There's no sense in flying through the night, not when you're so exhausted from the long day today. You've just woken up, Leopol."

"But the villagers—"

"Will still be there tomorrow. Lailant is there if they need healing. I know Knox and Eirwyn will take care of them too. There's nothing we can do right now."

He picked up the spoon and dipped it into the bowl with so much dejection it made her chest ache. She sighed as another dwarf walked from one hallway, through the large living and kitchen area toward the workroom, holding an armful of instruments.

"Is that a—bone saw?" she asked, frowning.

The dwarf paused and bobbed his head bashfully. "Aye, need to pry her open and see what's hiding under the metal. She's got the same metal as you, Leopol, so that's interesting."

He disappeared into the workroom, leaving Bella with eyebrows raised and Leopol with the spoon halfway to his mouth.

"What did he say?" Leopol asked.

Bella rubbed her forehead. "You have metal? Like, inside you?"

He frowned and gave a weary sigh. "I don't fucking know what's up or down or sideways anymore."

She chuckled, the fire crackling and casting warmth through the room. It was funny. They weren't touching anymore, but her sense of smell and feeling was growing stronger the longer she was... mated with Leopol.

Was that the proper term? Were they mated? Had they completed all of the steps for the mate bond? The books on the subjects were fascinating, things she'd read years ago but had quickly moved away from when her life had gone to shit and her father had left.

She glanced down and saw his bowl was empty, so she used magic to bring the large pot of stew to the table, setting it down in front of him. He quickly scooped another portion while she found another loaf of bread and brought it over.

After five bowls and nearly as many loaves, Leopol sat back and stretched. Her eyes grew wide at the sight of his chest and arms, muscles rolling, firelight flickering over runes. It was almost like they were carved into granite.

She stared at the webbed scar on his chest—spiraling gold, threaded like veins across the skin. The runes along it glowed faintly, pulsing with a rhythm that didn't match his heartbeat.

Bella reached out, fingertips brushing the edges of it. "What happened here?"

He stilled. "An old wound. I think it's from the battle that sent me into hibernation. I remember flashes... blood, a drawing room, pain. Then nothing."

She traced a curve of gold thread. "This looks like a rune. A binding?"

"I don't know," he whispered. "But it burns when I get close to that thing," he nodded toward the workroom.

The firelight cast shadows across his skin, making the golden rune-scars shimmer. She realized he was still trying to figure out his past, and she sat back down as he refilled his mug. He'd flown the entire day holding the Sentinel, and it had been burning his chest. All because she'd asked him to bring it?

320

Her chest grew tight at the realization.

A door creaked open, and Kris emerged from the workshop, wiping grease across his already-stained leather apron. "We've got something," he announced. "You're going to want to see this."

Leopol's hand instinctively found Bella's, fingers intertwining, as they followed Kris into a room cluttered with mechanical devices along the back wall. To the right was a sort of stables with several elk stinking up the place.

She just smiled, grateful to smell anything at all.

The Sentinel was spread open on the worktable, its wrist panel fully dismantled.

Kris rolled up his sleeves. "This won't take long," he said, not looking at any of them. "But if it goes sideways, hit the deck."

"What does that mean?" Bella asked with a frown.

"It means drop to the ground and take cover," Leopol said off-handedly.

She looked up at him in surprise. "How do you know that?"

He shrugged. "Had to take ships a few times when I went to study on other continents."

The artifact thrummed, its core light swelling, and Kris's hands moved over it, quick and decisive.

Bella stared, but also, without knowing why, held her breath. The Sentinel clicked as if with chirping squirrels or birds.

Kris pulled back more of the chest panel, revealing golden light sparking in its chest, and Bella felt the hairs on her arms rise.

Kris leaned in, frowning as he pointed to the glowing wires inside. "Strange alloy in the core. Not iron. Not gold. Something purer." He tapped a glowing thread inside its chest cavity. "I think this is refined Illustrite, wrapped around–"

Leopol stiffened. "Illustrite?"

Kris blinked at him.

"I thought it was powered by Orythium," Leopol said slowly, voice low and reverent. "It's Illustros' essence–his blood turned into Illustrite when he fell, so how could this have Illustrite? This construct wasn't just divine tech. It was sacred with an Orythium core, built before Illustros ever spilled any blood. Not Illustrite."

Kris shrugged. "All I'm saying is what I see."

The Sentinel's core throbbed, a pulse in time with the glowing scars on Leopol's chest.

Bella licked her lips as she traced the golden pulsing lines on his chest. "That's–that's the same as you. Are you saying you have Illustros' essence *inside you?*"

The Sentinel's core throbbed again, low and steady, and the same golden glow flickered through the web of runes on Leopol's chest as he nodded.

Bella's fingers hovered just above the glowing lines, but she didn't touch them. The heat coming off them wasn't just warmth–it was memory. Power. Purpose.

"It remembers you," she whispered.

Leopol didn't answer. His gaze was locked on the construct's exposed chest, and for a heartbeat, he looked... haunted. Or maybe reverent.

The light between them pulsed once more–his scars and the Sentinel in perfect rhythm.

Bella exhaled slowly, her voice barely a breath. "So why does it feel like it's remembering more than just you?"

Chapter Thirty

"Hmm, it might help to play back its last memories. Then we can see what exactly it's remembering," Kris said.

Bella's brows rose in surprise, and Leopol stiffened beside her.

"What do you mean?" Leopol growled.

She squeezed his hand, hers so small in his, but knowing he needed grounding.

Kris stood back from the worktable, wiping a line of sweat from his brow. "If my theory's right, this thing has more than muscle memory. It should have visual memory stored in its core."

Leopol's scars pulsed golden in rhythm with the Sentinel's faint inner hum. "It's responding to me. I think I can activate the recall protocol."

Kris hesitated and then shook his head slowly. "I don't recommend it. Bella may have removed the nekrotic sigils, and there's no nekrosan magic detected inside it, but it'll still be better to use the magic mirror."

He motioned toward a long mirror on wheels as another

dwarf rolled it from a back corner. It looked like a normal, battered-looking mirror, framed in etched runes and mounted between two thick metal rods.

Bella groaned, tired of all the magic mirrors. First Gastone's spying mirrors in Demerel, then the wizard trapped in one, and now this? Ugh.

"We used this on Knox, when we needed to pull a memory to save Eirwyn," the other dwarf explained. "If the Sentinel holds a visual record, this should pull it, even though it's not a living thing."

Two dwarves stepped forward, pushing both rods into the Sentinel's pseudo-hands. The mirror shimmered once, then stilled. Nothing happened.

"Hmm," Kris said, hand on chin. "Perhaps we should sync the mirror, the Sentinel, and Leopol. The way you both have Orythium and pulse together—it's worth a shot."

The dwarves hooked up two more rods to the mirror and then handed the handles to Leopol. He still faintly trembled from fatigue, and Bella worried for him. He needed to rest soon.

"Focus," Kris said, frowning. "Center yourself and breathe."

Leopol's brow furrowed. "I will."

The Sentinel gave a faint chirp. Its fingers flexed slightly around the rods. The mirror rippled again, and a gray haze appeared.

Bella hovered near Leopol, eyes locked on the golden lines threading through his chest and half-afraid to look at the damn mirror. Her fingertips tingled, and the back of her neck prickled—like something ancient was whispering just beyond understanding.

Magic—she could almost taste it, felt it vibrating through her soul.

"Let me help," Bella said before she could think.

It wasn't knowledge—it was a deeper understanding of how intricate pieces fit together. The same tug she felt when her magic aligned for a spell or a ritual followed all the expected steps and outcomes. She didn't understand it, not fully. But her magic *did*.

Kris blinked. "You know how this works?"

"No," she said, standing behind Leopol and placing one hand over the back of his, the other over his shoulder where the golden rune glowed strongest, "but I think I can feel what it's trying to show us."

The moment she contacted his chest and the Orythium, the mirror flared.

Light burst across the glass, scattering shadow against the walls—and an image sharpened. A cold, sterile workshop came into focus, lined with dark stone and lit with green-purple flame.

A figure hunched over the Sentinel's lifeless form, but it wasn't clear who from this angle.

Runes—familiar, foul, necrotic—glowed as he carved them with a hooked stylus into the metal body. His voice echoed, distorted but clear enough to chill the blood.

"Find the spirit. Find the dragon. Both slipped through my grasp. Both need eliminated."

Bella's grip tightened on Leopol's chest. He stood rigid, staring at the mirror.

The rune carver stepped back from the Sentinel, and the flickering flames still shielded his face.

"They can't be allowed to complete the mate bond."

Bella flinched, but didn't release Leopol as the image in the mirror shifted. The wizard stood in a dark stone hallway. Growlers stood in front of him, clearly soldiers in formation as they took new orders.

"There's a fucking dragon's egg?"

The Growlers mouth moved, but no sound came through the projection. Then, *"Well, fucking find it! I don't care if you're discovered. Be as brutal as you want. Just find me the fucking egg."*

Then the wizard strode angrily down the hall, passing the Sentinel as he murmured, *"I will claim the egg and forge a stronger body—one powerful enough to finish the ritual that will bring my liege back from the hells. If I have to raze Glathen in rot and freeze out Busparia and the Feral Forest to do it, I will. When the gates crack, even the gods will kneel—especially the one who locked me away."*

Leopol exhaled like he'd been punched. "That voice—"

The wizard turned fully toward the mirror projection. The face came into focus. Pale. Sharp-boned. Familiar. A pale gleam. Sharp jaw. Eyes like hollow stars.

The hair on Bella's arms lifted. She looked at Leopol—and froze.

His hand had dropped from hers, but her other remained anchored on his chest. His breath was shallow, eyes locked on the mirror, unblinking.

"That's him," he whispered in horror.

Bella blinked. "Who?" But she already knew.

Leopol's voice dropped, hoarse and broken. "That's him. The one I fought in the drawing room. The one who instigated the riot that led to Feralt and Analise's deaths. The one I—"

His voice cracked.

Sister. Hanzel. Death. The puzzle fell into place in Leopol's mind.

Xander the Red had received a report once about a witch named Grettel who had eaten dragonlings to absorb their power. Xander had quickly killed her, but her brother had gotten away. No one knew his name or what he'd looked like but Hanzel... Hanzel must be him.

Bella took his hand again.

Kris looked between them. "You're saying this is the same one—?"

Leopol spoke louder now, teeth gritted. "He was searching how to break a binding spell. His sister Grettel was executed for stealing children and siphoning their magic. This was before nekromancy was outlawed, and she was bound to the hells so none could raise her. He wanted to undo it and bring her back, so I stopped him. I see now that it was a temporary solution."

"You're the one who forced him into a mirror, trapping him in a smaller, similar ritual as the one that bound Asmoroth?" Disbelief colored her voice, but she didn't care. The magic that did that spell was powerful, perhaps the most powerful she'd ever seen. He nodded, but before she could question him more, the projection flickered.

A new scene showed the Sentinel standing in shadow, watching the throne room from behind a pillar as the wizard—wearing Bella's body—gave orders to a daemon.

"Find the egg, the spirit, and the dragon. Break them before the bond can form or bring me the egg before it can hatch."

Bella's stomach flipped. Leopol jerked back, eyes wide.

"He knows us, knows what we are. That's why the Sentinel was hunting us."

The light from the mirror flickered, casting shadows across his face as he turned to her.

"He's not afraid of me, Bella," Leopol said, voice low and broken. "He's afraid of *us*."

The image began to distort—warping around the edges like melting wax—before the mirror cracked down the center with a sharp snap.

Silence.

"Hells below," Kris said. "You just synced with a corrupted divine artifact like it was a music box built just for you. You shouldn't have been able to do that."

Bella's head throbbed, and something wet dripped from her nose. Her pulse raced—but more than that, there was a humming at the base of her skull.

Silence rippled through the workshop like the moment after lightning strikes—too bright, too loud, too much. She looked at the Sentinel's core, then down at her own shaking hand.

Bella staggered back a step.

"Bella?" Leopol caught her by the elbow, steadying her. "Are you—"

Her hand brushed her upper lip, and when it came away, there was blood. Not a lot, just a thin line, vivid red against her pale skin, but it was enough to scare her.

"I'm fine," she said, wiping it away on her sleeve. "Just... that took more out of me than I expected. I didn't realize I was using so much magic."

"It's a *corrupted divine construct*," Kris said, running a hand through his hair. "It's a miracle the thing didn't bite back harder."

Leopol's arm slipped around her waist. "That's enough. We're done for the night."

"But we have to get back to Hartsgrove. If that projection was right, he's planning a siege on Glathen—and he wants the dragon egg," she started.

"Then we'll stop him tomorrow." His tone was low, firm, final. "You've pushed yourself like a soldier instead of pacing yourself like a queen. Now you're bleeding from your nose while trying to interface with a relic that doesn't belong to this world. We rest. Just for tonight."

Bella opened her mouth to argue—then closed it again. He was right. She was tired, so tired, the kind of bone-deep, soul-sore tired that made her want to step into the Edge and never come back.

"Alright," she said softly. "But only if you promise you'll rest too."

His fingers laced with hers. "I will. I swear it."

She didn't fight him this time. Even queens needed someone to say *enough*.

He just held her tighter, as if anchoring them both to the present as they helped each other upstairs.

Later, when the room fell still, they lay curled together beneath a thick wool blanket, the fire burned low to embers. Bella wasn't sure when Leopol had stopped talking about the wizard or when he'd stopped responding to her touch. At some point, he'd just... slipped into sleep.

His breathing was deep. Steady.

She pressed her cheek to his chest, listening to the slow thud of his heart. It was new. All of it—his weight, his body, the dragon warmth curled around her like a shield.

She'd never felt so safe.

She'd never felt so scared. Bella's last thought before sleep made her wonder. Why is he so afraid of us?

———————

He jerked awake, breath catching like he'd surfaced from drowning.

The darkness pressed close, hot and heavy, like smoke that hadn't cleared. Sweat dampened his chest. His heart thundered against his ribs.

A hand touched his shoulder.

"Leopol?" Bella's voice was soft, blurred by sleep–but laced with concern.

He didn't answer. He was already on his feet, crossing the cold stone floor in long, silent strides. The room was dim–just the faintest embers glowing in the hearth behind him–but he could see clearly. Too clearly. The memory hadn't faded, and for once, he wished he could forget.

He stopped at the shuttered window and pressed a hand to the cold wooden frame, grounding himself as the images rolled through him like aftershocks.

"I saw him fall again," he said. "Not the wizard–Illustros. Forgetting those memories for a thousand years... it was a mercy I didn't know I needed."

Behind him, Bella shifted in the bed, covers rustling. He heard her stand but didn't turn.

"He fought Asmoroth. Was dying–or changing. I don't know which. There was fire, screaming. The archives were gone. The sky cracked open, and I fell through it, holding something in my hands–"

He held them out in front of him, but all he saw was his own scarred skin. "Something made of light. It was humming like it was alive."

Bella came to his side, barefoot and silent as she took his hands, anchoring him in the present.

"You were dreaming," she said gently.

He shook his head once. Not hard. Just enough. His voice was low and rough. "No, I was remembering."

Silence stretched. She didn't press him, just waited.

Leopol closed his eyes and let the weight of it settle. The dream had clarity no dream should. And the feeling in his chest–that slow, inevitable pull and pain and burn–was the same he'd felt when he touched the Sentinel.

"Illustros didn't just trap Asmoroth," he said. "He could

have killed him, but instead he *bound* him. To something older than them, something sacred. It wasn't destruction or a spell of death or even banishment, really."

He turned toward her. Shadows flickered over her face, half-lit by the coals behind them.

"It was containment. A prison with a purpose. That Sentinel—Bella, it's not just divine tech. It's a cage. And it might still be holding something—maybe more than one thing—that could help us against Hanzel... and maybe, one day, against Asmoroth."

Her eyes widened, and a breath hitched in her throat. "You—you think there's going to be a battle against Asmoroth?"

He squeezed her hands, grounding himself again. "I know there will be."

"How in the hells do we fight a god? We're mortal."

"The prophecies at the temple—the images in stone—gave clues to the final battle. But it might not be anytime soon, perhaps not for centuries."

She sighed in relief. "Let's focus on the wizard then, one step at a time. Do any of your memories help us defeat Hanzel?"

"Yes, I know what to do," he said. "When I fought him last time, he was already a well-known mage almost two hundred years old—older than a human should live to be, even one with drakin blood. His magic sustained him, so I don't think killing him is the solution."

"What are you saying?"

"I'm saying we need to *bind* him, like Illustros did Asmoroth."

Bella swallowed hard, fingers tightening around his. "But you bound him to the mirror, remember? It was a temporary solution, and it didn't work. He broke free and trapped me to this spirit form, remember? So how do we bind him for good?"

He nodded slowly, his body practically vibrating at the ideas flooding his system, chasing the high from the nightmare, his heart speeding.

"If the Sentinel has Orythium, we can create a new binding device... and then take that device—and him with it—directly to the Deep. That way if he escapes again, he's already in Hell. It's how they executed and trapped his sister, so I know it'll work."

She sighed and leaned her forehead on his chest. He pulled her into his arms, holding her safe and tight.

"Then we're going to need that Sentinel," she whispered.

He looked out the window again, toward the distant mountain shadows as the first rays of dawn lightened the sky.

He whispered, "I will fix what Hanzel has fucked up."

Guilt licked his spine. Hanzel had found a way to escape his binding spell to the mirror. If he had done a better job of solving the Hanzel problem three hundred years ago, Bella wouldn't have had all these problems and be facing death with each day.

Bella stirred her tea absently, letting the steam sting her nose as she leaned into the warm mug. Her fingers still trembled slightly from the night before—not fear, not really, just the lingering ache of magic used too deeply, too fast. Across from her, Leopol nursed a thick, bitter dwarven brew that looked like it had been mined rather than brewed.

At his wince, she asked, "Would you prefer some tea?"

He shook his head and sipped the bitter brew. "Dwarven coffee hasn't changed in centuries. Still tastes like coal water."

She grinned, even at something as simple as that little domestic complaint. It humanized him, made him being alive more real. Her grin faded, worry still licking her spine at the idea that he would live, and she would die.

They hadn't said much since the nightmare an hour ago, but her own dreams had been full of him leaving her behind, the rose fading and her with it.

Kris entered the small side room off the forge floor and paused just inside the doorway. "You two look like you've stared down the void, and it blinked first."

Leopol gave him a dry look. "We have a plan."

Bella set her mug down with more force than necessary. "Two, actually."

"Two?" Kris asked, arching a brow.

Leopol nodded. "We're going to bind the wizard, like a magical cage," Leopol said, eyes glowing faintly. "Like the one Illustros used to trap Asmoroth."

"And we need to disrupt his nekrotic influence," Bella added. "We need the Sentinel's core, or the Orythium, to bind him, but we also need a weapon. We suspect Hanzel will be using nekrotic magic. We need a way to nullify that, whether that's with a bomb that will cover a large area and take away the nekrotic magic so we can confront him, or an arrow that will affect him directly."

"But an arrow won't work because we don't want to hurt or kill Bella's body," Leopol added.

Kris's expression didn't change, but his head pinged back and forth as each of them spoke. It was somewhat comical, but she paused to give him a minute to process.

He blinked then pulled off his glasses to clean them with

his shirt. "You're talking about taking apart one of the most advanced divine machines we've ever seen—using it to build a cage *and* a bomb?"

Bella nodded. "Exactly."

He exhaled a long breath, then ran a hand through his beard. "You're either a genius or absolutely mad."

Leopol offered a faint smile, meeting her gaze. "Bit of both."

They were in this together, and it felt so good to not be alone. She'd worked by herself for more than just the past cursed year. But now, she had a mate.

She shook her head, the smile not even slipping from her lips as Leopol turned to Kris once more.

"Do you have your talkie? I'd like to apprise Knox of the situation."

"Of course. I let him know you were both here last night. Let me grab it," Kris said, walking into the work-room. They sat in silence.

Kris slid the palm-sized communication mirror across the table, the gilded edges catching the morning light. Bella hesitated, her tea forgotten, then took it in her hand with a flash of magic. It was definitely easier to interact with objects now, taking less magical output than before.

The polished mirror sat heavy in her palm, warm from Kris's workshop and layered with expectation. She hesi-tated—just long enough for her nerves to spike.

She didn't even realize her fingers were trembling until Leopol's larger hand covered hers, steadying her.

"Go ahead," he said quietly.

She tapped the rim on the rune that connected to the device at Hartsgrove.

The surface shimmered, flickered, then resolved into the familiar sharp lines of Knox's face. Shirtless, damp-haired, and squinting against the early morning light, he looked more like he'd been hauled out of bed than the seasoned king of the Feral Forest.

"Bella," he rasped, stepping out of his bedroom and shutting the door behind him softly. "Thank the gods, you're alright. Eirwyn was beside herself yesterday when you and Leopol disappeared."

Leopol rubbed her back and slid closer. "There was an unfortunate mishap with a portal."

He remained out of sight for now, and she leaned in slightly, her heart thudding. "The villagers. Are they... are they stable? Have any transformed yet?"

Knox exhaled through his nose, scrubbing a hand over his face. "Stable as cursed villagers can be. One of them tried to brush a goat with her forked hands. Another's learning embroidery from Lailant using her teeth. The two men were picking more ashplums. I think they're almost as excited about the Ashplum Gold ale as they are about ending their curses."

"So, they're alright," she said.

"Eirwyn's running it like a fae wellness retreat. Herbal soaks, lullabies, honey cakes. I'm worried she's going to unionize the cursed before you get back."

Despite the tension still thrumming in her chest, Bella let out a tight laugh and relaxed slightly. "No deaths?"

Knox paused, then said softly, "No deaths. No transformations either. Holding steady over here."

Bella sighed. "Not sure if I should feel relieved or not."

"Honestly, based on our calculations, the peak transformation timeline is forty-eight to seventy-two hours. So as long as we're back home by tonight, we should be there in time for everything," Leopol said.

Knox's humor faded. "Then I'll be ready. What's the

plan? How are you going to get back? Cerci said she felt a portal activate, and when we couldn't find either of you, we just assumed you'd been sucked into it."

"We were," Leopol said. "I'll explain more when we get back, but how long does it take for you to fly from here to Hartsgrove?"

"Fly? As a dragon? A little under five hours. Longer if winds are bad or you're hauling a passenger. Why?"

Leopol stepped into view beside her, his hand going around her waist as his thick thighs bracketed her on the chair. "Because I found my body and can fly again."

Knox's eyes went wide, his jaw dropping. "Holy shit."

Leopol's lips twisted. "Hello, cousin."

"We'll fly out this afternoon," Bella said. "I want to arrive before the forty-eight hour mark."

Knox gave a short nod. "Good. Just—come back in one piece."

Bella touched her fingers to the mirror in farewell. "We'll try. I'll let you talk to Leopol now while we go work on the Sentinel."

"Sentinel?" Knox asked as she put her hand on Leopol's thigh, squeezed, then followed Kris into the workshop.

"What's a Sentinel? How did you find your dragon body?" Knox demanded, using his kingly voice. Bella smirked, having heard that exact same tone from Leopol over the past week. Gods, had she only known him a week?

She rubbed her forehead. It felt like a lifetime already.

Chapter Thirty-One

Leopol didn't look away from the mirror.

Knox's image shimmered faintly in the glass, jaw clenched tight, eyes shadowed with worry—but it was the kind of worry a dragon wore just before sinking his teeth into a threat. Good.

Bella had handed Leopol the mirror moments ago, and now Leopol took a deep breath before reporting all to his cousin.

He launched into a succinct explanation of when they'd arrived at the temple and how the Sentinel had been discovered, their flight to the dwarves, and the discovery of the wizard.

"So the man who caused the rebellion—the one who got my parents killed—is the same wizard who controls Bella's body?" Knox said, his jaw slack as he sank into a sturdy chair in his sitting room.

Leopol nodded, the words tasting like iron in his mouth. "I failed your parents, and they died because I wasn't strong enough, didn't know enough."

Knox paused, then quietly said, "They died protecting their people, their kingdom—and me. That's not on you, Leopol. You stopped him once before, and you'll stop him again."

He paused, his throat tight as he vowed. "I will not fail you."

"I know you won't, but you have to understand that it's not all on you, Leopol. We're in this fight together."

Leopol's jaw tightened. "We intercepted a memory of Hanzel's plan. He means to claim your egg. Use it somehow, perhaps to siphon the magic from it like his sister used to do. I'm not sure exactly."

The screen went silent.

Then Knox's voice dropped to something darker. "If that bastard comes near Eirwyn or my dragonling, I'll cut him in half with my teeth and let Eirwyn string his bones like windchimes."

Leopol almost smiled. "Good. I'd like to see that. Has there been any word? More portals or rifts opening? Unusual daemon activity?"

Knox's brow furrowed. "Nothing new since the last report. Lailant and Cerci sealed the castle with sigils. No portals in or out without our knowing."

"Good, very good. We're going to take apart the Sentinel this morning, but we'll leave right after lunch."

Knox gave a curt nod. "Then I'll have the western wall cleared and brief the others. Bye."

The mirror shimmered, dimmed, and went black.

Leopol set it down gently, then turned to the workroom, ready to build a cage strong enough to trap Hanzel for good.

Bella oversaw the deconstruction of the Sentinel like a conductor with a silent baton, catching subtle vibrations in the magical lattice and calling out adjustments when energy fields twisted wrong. Her mind worked faster than her fingers could follow.

"Wait—pause there. That crystal fragment's catching too much resonance from the silver band. Try rotating it thirty degrees. I can feel it dragging sideways." She leaned in, hands hovering, not touching.

One of the dwarves adjusted the piece, then nodded in satisfaction. "That fixed the pulse distortion."

But when Bella reached to anchor a new filament of crystal to the lattice netting, her fingers trembled. The strand hissed and flickered out.

"Damn it," she whispered.

"I've got it," a dwarf said gently, taking over with steady hands and a calloused confidence.

Leopol worked nearby, frustration radiating off him in waves. His hands were too large, his muscles too tight in all the wrong places. A tool slipped, and he hissed. Bella's hand settled him, and he stretched his neck, popping it.

"You're still adapting to this body," Bella reminded him, voice low and even. "You're still brilliant. Let me do the impossible-sensing part—you explain the theory and walk us through it. We'll meet in the middle."

One dwarf snorted as he scribbled a rune. "The two of you are like the perfect fusion of madness and method. I'm not sure which is which."

"Your greatest weapon has always been your mind," Kris said. "And if you're right about this cage, we'll all need to remember what we used to be in the good old days."

Kris and Leopol's eyes connected, both of them remembering the past.

Bella looked at them both and frowned in confusion. "You know each other?"

Leopol glanced at her and smiled. "A story for another time. I'll tell you about it as we fly back to Hartsgrove." She frowned, but Kris spoke up before she could.

"This'll hurt like hell," Kris said, double-checking the runes. "To the wizard, and to anything else twisted by nekrotic residue, including you, Bella."

Bella paled. "So, it's a reset button. Just one more thing that could kill me."

Leopol wrapped an arm around her, offering silent support.

Kris let out a breath that might've been equal parts awe and dread. "You don't have to use it. It might bring divine chaos into the Feral Forest."

"If we're right," Bella said, "we're going to save it, the continent, and perhaps the world."

They documented everything they could—rune placements, alloy fusions, crystal responses—leaving notes and diagrams in case the dwarves needed to refine or replicate anything.

By lunch, the skeletons of their two devices began to take shape. The binding regulator—made from the Sentinel's inner frame—rested like a half-formed idea on the forge table. It was almost wand-like, but shorter than any wand he'd ever seen, and pulsed with Orythium.

The resonance pulse bomb was smaller, more precarious, designed to disrupt the necrotic frequency he could sense. The dwarves had taken the Illustrite and melted some of it down, then wove it into a circular puzzle that would break apart on impact. Leopol had created a series of intricate runes and sigils inside, and it now pulsed with magic too.

Leopol, once finished eating, inspected the supply houses and asked pointed questions about parts distribution and heat-source regulation—somewhere between a general and an engineer. He stood outside, speaking with the logistics head dwarf, when Bella stepped into the icy afternoon light.

His eyes lifted when he saw her, and he smiled—not like a warrior or a dragon or a savior, but like a man who couldn't believe his mate had chosen him.

She fastened the cloak she'd magicked into being as she approached, her breath curling in the air.

He would've pulled her into his arms, if they weren't already running behind. They were always running behind.

She hadn't left him, had been nothing but a support and comfort to him over the past few days. With so many changes, she hadn't faltered but seemed to grow stronger.

Even now, after all the chaos of the past week, she chose to stand by his side. That—more than the egg, more than the war—was what gave him strength to keep going and find a permanent solution for Hanzel.

He wanted to show her how much he appreciated her, but it would have to wait. They'd been so tired last night, they'd both fallen into sleep within minutes of laying down.

He hoped the villagers transformed tonight, but he also hoped they didn't. He would like a night at Hartsgrove to just breathe and be with his mate in her bed.

Bella smiled at him as she stopped, then smiled at the dwarf next to him. He tuned back into the conversation, and then they quickly said their goodbyes to all the dwarves.

When he shifted into his full dragon form, golden threads of light faintly glowed under his skin, pulsing out from the scar on his chest. Those outside paused, their jaws dropping, and he preened slightly as he crouched for her to climb up his tail to the small dip between his wings.

The winds were bitterly sharp, but the sky was clear.

"We'll reach Hartsgrove before nightfall," Leopol said, lumbering onto all four feet, his voice deep and resonant in her mind.

Bella looked toward the horizon. "Then we might still be in time."

He launched into the wind. Below them, the forest unfurled like a tapestry of green and silver.

She pressed a hand to his warm scales and whispered into the wind, "Forty-eight hours. Please let it be enough."

The sky roiled with clouds the color of ash and bruises, bleeding orange at the edges—the last light of day clinging to a promise it couldn't keep. Hartsgrove rose from the trees as the spirit came home. Even the giant eagles kept their distance as the ancient dragon flew closer.

Every wingbeat beneath Bella tightened the knot in her chest. They were almost there.

Its towers were cloaked in shadow, windows lit with flickering firelight that cast the courtyard in molten gold. The familiar silhouette pierced something deep inside her. It had been home for barely a week, but she felt more comfortable there than she ever had at the Winter Palace with Gastone.

She tightened her grip along Leopol's back, pressing herself as close to him as she could.

She gripped the ridge of Leopol's scale harder than she needed to, not for balance, but to stay grounded. Each breath tasted of ice and something acrid, like anticipation laced with guilt. She had left those villagers behind, even if she'd never meant to. She was responsible for fixing this curse, and now they were changing. Because of her.

Please, she begged silently. *Let us be on time.*

The moment Leopol touched down, the wind stilled–and her body didn't. She slid from his back, boots hitting the packed dirt harder than expected. Her knees wobbled–not from the flight, but from the truth waiting in the flickering shadows ahead. Leopol shifted and quickly pulled her into his arms. She shook as they clung to each other, both of them staring at the door to the ballroom.

Knox was already moving toward her with Lailant at his side, torchlight catching the edge of their eyes. Bella tried to steady her breath but failed. Her heart felt like it had been packed in ice and expectation.

The world hadn't ended while they were gone, but that didn't mean it wouldn't tonight.

"Are we too late?" she asked as they drew closer.

Knox shook his head, but it was Lailant who answered. "The magic's pulsing now, like it's crawling under their skin. We'll be lucky if we get another hour."

Knox held the torch high, the same unreadable tension in his jaw she'd seen when he'd stared down Gastone in their battle. "They're stable, for now," he said. "Lailant gave them a dose of sleeping dust after dinner, but two started murmuring in their sleep."

Knox paused, stepping closer to Leopol. His lips pressed into a hard line, and both men looked like they were holding back the tide of emotion.

For seven months, Knox had known Leopol only as a voice in the halls, a spirit tethered to the castle. Not touchable. Not fully real.

Now he stood before him–scarred, solid, alive.

Leopol looked almost wary, like he wasn't sure if he deserved the welcome. Hope flickered in his eyes, edged with the fear of rejection.

Then Knox crossed the last few feet and wrapped him in a tight, brutal hug.

There was no ceremony in it, no words. Just the thud of two hearts and months of unspoken weight crashing together.

Leopol's hands gripped Knox's back like he didn't quite trust the moment to last. Like maybe he was afraid to let go.

This was the first time she saw him fully *received*. No barriers. No magic. No need for him to fix this or solve that. Just family accepting family.

For a moment, her chest ached with something more than guilt or anticipation. A hollow space she hadn't even known was empty. This is what it meant to be home.

Bella couldn't look away, her heart so full for him. She was glad he had this, had family, a body, a life. But a sliver of fear snuck into her at the idea she might never have this again. Sure, she'd gotten her father back, but there was no hug like this.

She wanted what they had—a big, messy, loyal family that wrapped around each other like roots around a wounded tree.

Perhaps that's why Hartsgrove felt more like home than the Winter Palace. Before, she could touch anyone before the curses, but she'd been so alone, a queen in a gilded cage surrounded by all the books and tutors she could want.

Here, she could only touch Leopol, but they had so much more than just touch. They had genuine connection, affection, a fated mate bond organized by the gods. And her friends were here, her mentor. Even if she couldn't touch them, they were as much a part of ending this curse as she was.

She blinked back tears as Knox and Leopol patted each other's backs and stepped away, neither talking, but both their eyes shining bright.

The torchlight behind them caught on the gold threading faintly through Leopol's skin, pulsing in time with his heartbeat now. The hug wasn't long, but it was everything.

A reunion. A reckoning. A promise.

Knox cleared his throat like it was the only way to keep from shattering.

Bella looked away—just for a moment—to give them their moment. Her breath shook as she turned toward the ballroom doors, mentally girding herself to face what lay inside.

When she felt Leopol's hand on the small of her back, Knox's eyes rose. "Even with his body back... you two can still touch?"

She looked at Leopol and knew her brows were as high as his. It hadn't even occurred to either of them that they might not with his new form.

Lailant smiled softly and turned to go back inside, leaning heavily on her cane. "The fates make no mistakes. It is as it should be. Come, let's check on our patients."

A stab of guilt speared her as she walked beside Leopol. She'd been thinking of them as test subjects, volunteers, villagers. She'd never once thought of them as a patient—and she'd studied under Lailant for many years as a healer. Once, that was all she wanted to be, to save people like she couldn't save her mom.

She took a breath—long and anchoring—and stepped through the terrace doors. The castle ballroom didn't look like a ballroom anymore.

Four narrow beds were lined in soft linen and thick quilts, each one set up near the enormous fireplace yet spaced apart. If there was thrashing, there needed to be space to move.

Tables stood nearby along the wall next to the fireplace, stacked with potion vials, bandages, enchanted restraints, and more. A single steaming kettle was on the hook above the fire, filling the room with the sharp scent of mint and something more ancient, wild, and primal.

The click of her boots echoed in her ears. Her gaze flicked between beds as she rushed forward. All were breathing deeply through their sleep.

Relief hit her like a wave—and vanished just as fast.

Cerci didn't look up from where she crouched beside a young woman's bed.

Bella moved closer, catching the sheen of sweat on the villagers' faces—no, the patients. One woman's arm was wrapped in gauze, but even beneath the bandage, she could see the *wrongness* of it, the fork tines still visible, and for the first time in days, she remembered Jaq and Gus. She hadn't worried about them, was no longer lonely enough to crave their company and want to keep them in her pocket.

The flesh beneath the woman's gauze pulsed faintly with a sickly silver light, and her stomach turned as a ripple shimmered across her skin. It had begun.

"Thank the gods," she whispered. "We're not too late."

She felt more than heard Leopol's answer. A quiet *not yet* that pulsed through their bond like a promise as he stepped in behind her, silent but warm, solid. She didn't turn, but she felt his hand on her back. The golden thread of his magic brushed against her own—reassuring, grounding. *She wasn't alone.*

"They each have a bed," Lailant said smoothly as she

passed Bella and Leopol where they'd stopped. "Restraints are prepped. Healing potions on the left. Ritual chalk and sigil infused water on the right."

Bella's throat tightened. "Has anyone screamed yet, started to transform?"

"Not yet," Knox said, too calm, stopping beside them. "But it's close."

Bella stepped up beside the man with the watering can hand. She pressed two fingers to his wrist—felt a heartbeat beneath the cursed skin and twisted flesh and metal.

Fast. Erratic.

The air was changing. Growing heavier as the woman with fork hands stirred in her bed, Cerci wiping her damp hair. The silence cracked. The first cry split the silence—sharp and human and full of pain. It hit her like a memory of Sharlo, and her anxiety snapped taut. It was time.

Chapter Thirty-Two

The woman with the forked hands shifted first—just a twitch of her fingers, a furrow of her brow, a broken whimper in her throat. Her pulse had gone erratic beneath Bella's fingers, and the magic under her skin flared brighter for a heartbeat, like someone had stoked a fire beneath her flesh.

But it wasn't her who screamed.

Bella leaned in beside Lailant, startled, scanning the others with rising dread.

Another scream tore through the air—sharper, louder. Her gaze snapped toward the sound.

The man with the watering can hand convulsed, his back arching off the bed like lightning had struck his spine. His eyes flared open—but they didn't *see*. His scream cut off sharply, gasping in as he prepared for another. His mouth stretched wide in a scream that echoed louder than the others.

Bella ran to his side, her boots levitating slightly on the polished stone as she crossed to his bed. Heart pounding, she pressed her hands to his chest, reaching with her magic even though she wasn't sure it would help. His body seized again, and the metal on his hand cracked open, splitting like a seedpod.

"Oh gods, oh gods–" she muttered, grabbing a vial of golden healing tonic with magic, her other hand over him as she tested the magic within. He bucked on the table.

"Let me help." Leopol kneeled beside her, calm but quick, and together they held him as the violent transformation began in earnest.

Skin peeled back in silvery flakes, bone reshaping under blood and muscle. Magic rippled through the room like a pulse, setting off the nearby woman–fork-hands jerking, twisting, her mouth opening in a raw, keening wail.

Bella turned just in time to see Cerci join Lailant to help the woman.

"They've got her. Focus on this one first," Leopol said quietly. He grounded her with his presence, but he didn't interrupt or try to direct. He was just *there*–solid, warm, watching her with concern but trusting her to lead.

She tried to focus. Tried to remember the training. Healing came in three parts: weave through the pain to identify the problem, stabilize the magic, then rebuild the body. She could do this. She *had* to do this.

But the moment she swiped a bandage along his hand, she froze at the blood on the bandage. The shape of the hand was wrong, and blood seeped into the sheets. Instead of his watering can split open with ropes and wires of metal-like veins, she saw her mother's hands instead.

Burned fingers split open with stringy tissue. A still chest. Fevered wet hair plastered to her too pale forehead. The memory was always there, waiting under her skin like its own kind of curse.

Her breath hitched. For a moment, she couldn't move.

Lailant's voice came quietly from across the wails of the nearby woman. "You've trained for this, Bella. Focus now."

She didn't look up.

"You are doing what your mother only prayed for." The Seer's voice echoed like a prayer itself, and Bella nodded. She shook off the memory and reached for the magical salve.

She didn't cry. She didn't scream. There was enough of that already with these two. Instead, she got to work. Her magic faltered at times, but her hands didn't. She applied poultices, whispered spells, braced broken limbs and trembling hearts.

Leopol followed her, not hovering, not commanding—just anchoring her and assisting where needed. A hand on her shoulder when she paused too long. A look when her breath caught. Anticipating when she needed another salve. It was more than enough to know she wasn't alone like she'd been when she'd lost her mother.

She wasn't alone.

And neither were these patients. She would get them through this. They wouldn't end up like Ignot or Sharlo or the cats.

Over the next few hours, they went back and forth between the woman and the man. The ballroom stopped feeling like a room of broken people, stopped smelling of the stench of death. Now it was a battlefield, a sanctuary, a test that Bella refused to fail.

But she was tired and weak. Since mating Leopol, she'd actually begun to sleep—needed sleep when she hadn't before in this spirit form. When the two were stable enough, she stepped away from the bed, hands shaking and chest heaving like she'd been running.

She made it to the table of supplies and leaned on it,

breathing deeply. A movement from the corner of her eye drew her gaze, and Jaq and Gus hopped up to the surface. They chirped at her, and she drew a soft comfort from their presence.

They'd been there when the last patients had died from the transformation back at the Winter Palace. Since Lailant had arrived, they'd stuck to the Seer like glue.

Leopol leaned a hip against the table and turned to stare at the patients, arms crossing over themselves.

"Are you alright? How are you holding up?" His voice was soft and gentle.

"I'm making it, slowly but surely," she sighed, wiping her forehead with a sleeve before staring unseeing down at the table.

"You're very good at this, at healing and just intuitively knowing what to do next. I feel like I only know what I've read in books, but you have an instinct like nothing I've seen in a thousand years on this planet."

His words sent a spike of heat through her, her cheeks flushing. "Thank you. That means a lot, but you're probably just saying that because I'm your mate."

He nodded. "Mate or not, I wouldn't say it if it wasn't true."

The truth of that settled over her like a cleansing rain. She'd known him less than two weeks, but she did know he spoke true. He'd always been a gentleman, despite her teasing him about being a monster. He was loyal, patient, and treated everyone—servants included—with respect and dignity.

"Why did you train with the Seer as a healer?"

Bella's eyes remained fixed on her hands as she flexed them, the ache in her knuckles echoing a deeper exhaustion.

She didn't answer him at first.

Then, quietly, like it had been waiting in her chest this whole time, she said, "Because I couldn't save my mother and failed her."

Leopol didn't respond, didn't push. Just waited, the way he always did–with that impossible patience that made her feel safe enough to continue.

"She got sick when I was young. Something in the lungs. My father brought every doctor, every alchemist from out of town. Spared no expense. But nothing worked. I sat by her bed every night for weeks, holding her hand, reading her stories, bringing water. I was almost five." Her voice broke, just slightly.

"Oh, Bella, I'm so very sorry. That must've been so hard to see," he said, placing a comforting oversized hand on hers on the table.

She swallowed hard and kept talking. "Very. I kept thinking–if I just knew the right potion or spell, I'd find the thing that saved her. Some herb, a spell or miracle. Instead, I failed."

She looked up at Leopol then, eyes shimmering but dry– not because she didn't feel it, but because she'd already cried those tears long ago. "Lailant moved to town right after she got sick, and I visited her shop often to ask questions. I stole several potions and herb mixtures from her, but looking back on it, I feel like she wanted me to. She always explained every potion in detail–never talked down to me, never treated me like a child. Then she'd turn her back with a wink, so I–I stole from her. Imagine, the queen–a petty thief."

She snorted, but Leopol shook his head fiercely. "Life drives us to do strange things for those we love. Often, they don't make sense. I find no fault in your actions. You loved your mother. Who's to say I wouldn't have done the same in your shoes?"

She smiled softly and shrugged. "Looking back on it, I feel like she wanted me to. Each potion and herb mixture she taught me was good for my mother's condition. For example, she never taught me in those early days about things like tooth pain or wart remedies—only the ones that eased the lungs, cooled fevers, calmed the heart. "

"She's a good Seer. The best I've ever met in all my years on Celawyn. It's good that she's here with us now."

The silence was broken by the little whimpers and groans of the two patients who had finished their transformations. "You didn't fail your mother, you know," he said softly.

Bella swallowed down her tears. "She—she died gasping for air, and I couldn't do a damn thing but cry. I swore I'd never be that helpless again."

He exhaled, slow and heavy. "You have never been helpless. You have an uncanny ability to look at something and problem solve it. You don't see an impenetrable brick wall and give up. You find solutions. Definitely not helpless."

She huffed out a laugh that wasn't really a laugh. "I still feel like that little girl, though. Still chasing an impossible cure, still thinking maybe if I do enough, I'll fix everything."

Leopol picked up her hand and kissed her palm. "You're not that little girl anymore, and you don't have to fix everything by yourself. I'm here with you. You just have to keep going and not give in to the defeated feeling that tries to suck us under."

Her eyes widened as she realized he knew that feeling. A silence stretched between them, warm and quiet, comforting.

Bella blinked, then reached for another salve. "Thanks for staying beside me tonight."

"I will stand at your side, my queen, my mate, mibella," he said. "For all eternity. I'm not going anywhere."

His warm claws slid around her neck, and she turned to face him, hand hovering over the jars. His gaze was intense as he leaned forward and kissed her, softly and oh so tenderly, it made a tear spill down her cheek.

When he pulled back, his thumb brushed it away. "You're doing great work here. Whether this works or not—it's not a reflection on you. It won't make you a failure if it doesn't succeed. Life is a series of choices and chances. All we can do is face the next one."

Bella exhaled slowly and nodded once, her hand cupping his on her cheek.

A low moan echoed from one of the beds, then the sound of something shattering. Like stone cracking under unbearable pressure. Her head whipped around, heart dropping.

The third patient seized violently in his bed. Stone-spiked legs jerked, the jagged rock spreading up his thighs like frost claiming a branch. The veins in his neck bulged as he arched, the restraints at his ankles groaning under the strain.

"Time to face the next one," she whispered. Her hands were already moving, sleeves pushed up, magic swirling as she grabbed supplies from the table. "Let's get to work."

Bella shot forward before she could think, already mentally reaching for her magic even as her spirit wavered under the strain of the night.

"Lailant!" she said, pointing in horror. He'd twisted the sheet off his legs.

"I see him," the Seer replied, hobbling fast despite the cane. "The curse isn't breaking. It's spreading."

Bella dropped the supplies beside the bed and held her hands over his thighs. "It's like the transformation's going the wrong direction. Why now? Why him? The others stabilized—why is this different?"

The man thrashed again. One restraint snapped. Stone ground against metal, the texture harsh and brutal as the transformation reached his torso. His breathing came in shallow gasps. Blood seeped down his legs where skin gave way to stone like flesh through a grater. She saw it—his body splitting open under the strain, magic pulsing dangerously beneath the surface.

She pressed a hand to his knee, reached with her magic—and flinched at the resistance. It was thick. Coagulated. Violent. His skin radiated heat, acrid and sharp beneath the scent of blood and magic dust.

"This isn't a healing pattern. It's consuming him."

"We have to redirect it," Lailant said. "Balance the overload before it eats through his heart."

"I need the dark salve. The one with marrow root."

"I have it," Leopol's voice came from behind her, calm as a still pond in a storm. He passed her the jar, then moved to the opposite side of the bed.

Another restraint popped.

The man's arm flung outward, stone spreading over the elbow joint. Bella didn't even flinch as it passed through her—but Leopol caught it.

The sound of impact—flesh and rock meeting unyielding force—rattled her bones, even if it hadn't touched her.

Leopol grunted, holding the limb steady with both hands as the man thrashed. "I've got him," he said. "Keep going."

She nodded and pressed the salve to the raw, bleeding flesh just above the knee. Magic sang under her fingers, a discordant, screaming note that clashed with the pulse of life beneath it.

"Balance it. Focus," Lailant murmured beside her, weaving her own spells like threads through cloth.

Together, they redirected the flow–Bella using touch and intent, Lailant reinforcing with sigils etched in glowing chalk across the man's stomach. The spikes on his legs softened, stone turning from jagged obsidian to smoother granite, then to patchy, cracked skin.

Bella poured her magic into his ribs even as her eyes watered and her head began to ache, whispering spells in a voice she barely recognized–hoarse, exhausted, determined.

It took a long time. She didn't know how long. Things grew fuzzy at the edges of her vision, and wetness dripped down her nose. Yet she still didn't stop.

When the man finally relaxed against the bed–when the pulse in his neck settled and the rise and fall of his chest returned to rhythm–Bella slumped back, barely catching herself on her hands.

He lived. This time, they'd won.

Her muscles trembled as she pushed herself upright. Hands slick with blood and salve, magic sparking erratically under her skin like lightning with nowhere to go. She moved to the basin of clean water and dunked her hands, the sharp sting of her own raw skin grounding her back in her body.

She lifted her hands from the basin–only to see them waver. Not just with fatigue, but with magic. Translucent. Then normal spirit. Then not, see through and invisible. Her breath caught. She blinked, but the world blurred at the edges. This–was she so close to the Edge that she was seeing things?

She wobbled, and suddenly Leopol was there, his big arm protectively around her waist. "I'm here. You're alright. They're all fine now."

Bella took one more breath and looked over the patients. Cerci was already helping Lailant clean up. The thin light of dawn was filtering through the glass terrace doors.

Leopol helped Bella over to where the final patient lay still. His brows twitched in sleep, the muscles of his jaw tight even at rest. She brushed a lock of damp hair from his brow. The hair was so similar to her mother's in those last days—slick with sweat and fever, soft despite the sickness.

She swallowed down the ache in her throat and leaned closer.

"You're safe now," she whispered. "Rest easy."

Leopol watched her, not pushing, even as he handed her a handkerchief. She wiped her brow and nose to find blood. Her heart thudded unevenly in her ears—too much magic and too little left.

She took a deep breath and stumbled toward the doors to the garden, her steps uneven.

"Where are we going? You should rest while we wait for the final transformation," Leopol said, concern softening the gentle chide.

He opened the terrace doors, arm still firm around her waist, keeping her upright without making her feel weak.

Bella leaned into him, just a little—but it was enough to keep her standing, enough to keep going. The dawn bled through the glass, pale and gold and quiet. As they stepped through, it smelled like dew and blood and the end of an endless night.

It wasn't the end, though. They still had one to go. The

air outside slapped her cheeks with cold, pushing some of her brain fog away.

She stepped onto the balcony, boots dragging against the stone. Her shoulders shook with each breath. She didn't realize she was crying until the salt touched her lips—quiet, involuntary tears her body shed without permission.

Leopol caged her in against the balcony railing, silent and steady. He wrapped his arms around her from behind, cocooning her in warmth without smothering her. He didn't speak. Just let her *be*. Shaking. Breathing. Raw and emotionally and magically drained.

"If they all survive this..." she said at last, voice scratchy and low, "I might finally believe there's an end in sight to this nightmare curse."

Leopol didn't hesitate. "You have already succeeded. Three out of four is remarkable, especially for a brand-new ritual."

She hesitated. "Not brand new. I lost Ignot, Sharlo, and the cats, remember?"

He kissed her hair, and she relaxed back into his embrace. "But there was no ritual with them. You had no help and didn't know what to do. Now you have me."

She let out a soft snort that might've been a laugh. "Oh? And that's so special, is it?"

"I'm an ancient archivist with centuries of knowledge—your very own encyclopedia, body and soul, entirely at your service."

His voice dipped low as he kissed the side of her temple, a promise more than affection. "And you're not alone anymore, Bella. For as long as I breathe—and even after—I'll be here for you. Plus, you have Lailant and Cerci in there, too."

Her breath hitched. She didn't want to cry again.

"You can't burn yourself out. There's still one more. Rest—just for a moment."

But then—a low moan echoed faintly from inside.

Bella turned her head, vision swimming. The floor tilted beneath her boots. She blinked, tried to focus but her knees buckled.

"Bella—" Leopol caught her before she hit the stone. Her body sagged in his arms, breath coming shallow.

She gripped his leathery soft chest, wincing. "I—I'm fine. Just—need a second—"

"You've spent too much magic," he said. "You've been on your feet all night."

"I can still help with the last one," she whispered, eyes fluttering as her hands roamed his chest as if seeking warmth, love, acceptance.

"You *will* help," he promised. "But not if you collapse in the middle of it."

She pressed a trembling hand to his chest—right over the scar.

And *froze*.

Beneath her palm, magic pulsed. A steady, powerful rhythm that vibrated through her bones. Warmth flooded into her hand, and with it, her shaking began to fade.

Golden light flickered where her palm touched his chest, drawn into her like breath into dying embers. The threads of her own power, frayed and unraveling, began to tighten and reweave.

She gasped.

Leopol stilled, watching her. "Do—do you feel it too?"

She nodded in awe. "Your scar, the rune—it's pulsing, sharing magic, pouring strength into places I didn't know were hollow."

He didn't move, just tilted his head in awe. "Orythium is

Illustros' essence, and he is the All-Father, the creator of life. It's opened a pathway for me to share some of my essence with you, refill your magic and give you strength."

"Leopol..." her throat closed up in wonder. Her spirit steadied, and breath deepened. "You're saving me from burnout," she murmured, still stunned.

She glanced up and frowned at him, removing her hand from his chest. "I don't want to take too much and leave you weak."

He snorted, the breath tickling her hair. "As if I could ever be weak. *All* I have is yours, Bellakari. Take what you need, so we can save them, together."

Tears filled her eyes but didn't fall this time. "Thank you," she said, voice husky and low. "I think I can help now."

She tried to push out of his arms, half-hearted, but he ignored it and carried her bridal-style back inside. The last patient moaned, her limbs twitching beneath the sheets—but the curse hadn't surged yet. Not fully.

The ballroom glowed faintly in the dawn light. He set her beside the supply table, her feet solid now. "Just a moment to let the magic settle. Then we finish this."

Bella flexed her fingers. Magic still sparked beneath her skin, faint but steadying.

She wouldn't quit. Not now when they were so close.

She let him smooth the hair from her face, leaning into the touch. It was nice—being cared for, for once.

Chapter Thirty-Three

The tremors began softly–barely a rustle of fabric as the last woman on the beds shifted, her limbs twitching with growing violence. Leopol hovered behind Bella as she talked swiftly with Lailant, cataloging the changes for Cerci to write. He was used to archiving and could do the writing, but he'd been relegated to strength and muscle.

He didn't mind–he was here beside his mate, helping where he could–but it was still unusual. After so many months as a spirit to suddenly have this hybrid body–a bigger version of who he'd been before–he was still stomping around awkwardly and trying not to claw or shred things.

He stiffened as the metal cuff groaned at the woman's wrist.

In front of him, Bella swayed.

He reached instinctively to steady her, his hand at her back as her fingers shook over the patient. She didn't blink–just kept watching the patient with that same hollow-eyed

determination that had carried her through three excruci-
ating transformations already.

Then he saw it—a single crimson line slipping from her
nostril. *Again.*

"Bella," he whispered. "You're bleeding."

She didn't react. Her hands were already moving to the
next task, uncorking a healing potion with trembling
fingers.

"You need to stop." He caught her hand mid-reach,
steadying it. "Just for a moment. Let me—"

"No." Her voice cracked like a whip, sharp and immediate. "No, Leopol, I *can't* stop."

She yanked her hand from his grip and staggered closer
to the woman, already casting a diagnostic spell over the
woman's violently shaking body. The patient convulsed, skin
rippling like waves under her robe, magic flaring so hot it
made the air hum. One of her legs cracked outward with an
unnatural jolt.

Leopol clenched his jaw as Bella's hands shook, using
magic to pour the potion into the mouth that Lailant held
open. When she stood upright, bottle empty, she weaved.

He braced himself, catching her again before she
collapsed fully and slipping an arm around her ribs.

"I'm fine—"

"I *heard* you," he growled back, more worried than
angry. "But you're falling apart. Let me help."

Without waiting for her argument, he grabbed her wrist
and pressed her hand flat against his chest—right over the
scar where the Orythium pulsed like a living sun—the same
current that had refilled her less than an hour ago. His
magic, his essence. He willingly gave her what she needed,
no matter the cost.

Her eyes widened, but her spine stayed rigid. "No—

Leopol–don't. I told you, I can't take too much from you, and I can't stop, I *won't*. They need me."

"You'll die if you don't," he hissed, cupping her jaw as golden warmth surged from him into her, bleeding into her fingers like firelight. "What good is saving one more if it destroys *you*?"

The patient screamed–a horrible cracking sound–and Bella tried to surge forward again. He tightened his arms around her. Bella's neck twisted to look at the patient, but Cerci was there, helping Lailant.

"It's alright, child. She's not as bad as the last one," Lailant said, her hand steady over the woman's brow.

"I think she's through the worst of it," Cerci added, gripping the woman's waist as her leg twisted apart and began to re-form.

Bella's body shuddered in relief, and the glow of her hand on his chest sputtered out as her entire weight sagged into his arms.

"Bella–"

She didn't answer. Her eyes fluttered, lashes trembling, and she went still.

His heart stopped, worry sweeping him that she'd fallen to the Edge.

"Take her to bed," Lailant said softly. "She's done enough for one night."

Cerci nodded, tapping the notebook at the foot of the bed. "I'll record everything so you two can analyze the results. We'll handle it from here."

With a whispered thanks, he swept his mate into his arms and turned from the chaos. She was limp in his hold but still warm, still breathing. That would have to be enough–for now. She had pulled so many back from the Edge tonight. He'd be damned if he let her fall over it.

He took the steps swiftly, trying not to jostle her as he strode down the hall to her room. His breath puffed through clenched teeth, the weight of her limp form both grounding and unbearable.

At her door, he whispered the unlocking spell–but nothing happened. Instead, he felt a tug low in his gut, a static itch beneath his skin, just out of reach. The wards were active, and the spell rejected him.

He cursed under his breath, adjusting his grip on her body as his magic flared to dismiss the ward. Her shoulder slumped against his chest, and for a moment he closed his eyes. He couldn't wait. She needed rest now.

The ward fell, and his magic flared again. Icy breath curled around his spine, threading along his arms and down his legs as his heartbeat slowed.

Spirit walking.

He hadn't done it since before the cave hundreds of years ago and never like this, with a passenger. Logically, he knew it was possible, but he'd never tried it.

But now–now he didn't hesitate.

"Hold on," he murmured, tightening his arms around her as he stepped forward–through the world instead of around it.

The air went thin and sharp. The walls turned translucent for the space of a breath. Light bent, color bled, and then the world caught up.

He stepped into her room just as solid flame snapped in the fireplace. The warmth hit him first, followed by the faint scent of wood and jasmine soap. It shouldn't have surprised him, but it did–he hadn't walked that way in centuries. And she had come with him.

She'd followed him through the Veil. He stared down at her, breath caught in his throat.

Of course, she did.

He crossed the room and kneeled beside the bed, gentler now, tucking her under the quilt like she might slip away if jostled wrong. Her form wasn't quite solid—shifting faintly at the edges like steam—but she didn't float, either. She settled against the mattress as if gravity still loved her.

Perhaps he did too. He certainly didn't think he could live without her.

The faintest light brushed across Bella's cheek, catching on her pale lashes as he tucked the quilt around her. One hand hovering an inch above her sternum, he cast the same common diagnostic spell she'd used earlier.

The golden rune glow from his palm dimmed, signaling what he hoped for: her magic was low, but her life force steady. She was not slipping toward the Edge or fading into the Beyond—only resting. His shoulders dropped, relief sweeping through him and leaving him light-headed.

She had pushed herself to the limit again. He should have intervened earlier.

The door creaked behind him.

"Leopol? Is that you?" Eirwyn asked, peaking her head around the door frame.

He nodded and stretched his neck, waving her in. "Yes, I'm here. She's asleep."

Eirwyn opened the door wider, tiptoeing as she whispered, "I thought I'd find you here. How is she? I just checked on the volunteers below. All seemed quiet, but Cerci explained about Bella."

Eirwyn's maid followed in behind her, quietly shutting the door. Helga's tea leaf hair was pulled back into a bun at the base of her head, and she did a double take when she saw him. Her eyes widened as she gasped, "Leopol? You—you're—"

"Alive? Yes, I am. I guess Knox hasn't told everyone quite yet?"

Helga shifted hesitantly, but Eirwyn was the one who answered. "There's not been a lot of time. When we found out that Cerci had accidentally sent you through a portal somewhere–after searching the castle all day long–we were exhausted. Plus, there were the volunteers to entertain and prepare for the transformation."

He frowned as Eirwyn stopped on the other side of the bed and peered at Bella, using her magic to first flare light so she could see her friend, then to dim the light so Bella could sleep better.

"Yes, we made it back in time last night to help with the transition, but Bella nearly burned herself out. Damn well toed the Edge," he said, using a claw to push a piece of hair from her cheek.

"The Edge? Does she need a healing potion? Can she even take one like–"

"No, she can't, but she doesn't need it either. I checked, and she's just asleep. She'll take a while to wake up." He shifted on his feet and crossed his arms, staring down at her.

Then his stomach rumbled.

"Well, you can't stand over her all day. Might as well eat first, then you can come back and check on her," Eirwyn said softly.

"I don't want to leave her. What if something happens?" Leopol murmured, straightening. "I need to be sure she's safe."

Eirwyn crossed the room and placed a gentle hand on his elbow. "She's alive. You confirmed it yourself. Let her sleep and let Helga watch over her. She's competent–and nosy enough to call us if she even twitches."

Helga gave a short curtsy. "I'll see to her, my lord. You have my word."

Leopol hesitated only a second more before exhaling and nodding, raking a tired hand over the back of his head.

Eirwyn guided him out and down the stairs, taking his elbow.

"You look more beast than man now," she said, glancing sideways at him. "Compared to Knox, who at least keeps up the illusion of being mostly human. Does it bother you?"

Leopol paused on the next step, considering. "No, my body is honest now. This is what I am. I feel... more solid. And if it frightens my enemies and makes my mate feel safe, then I have no complaints."

She laughed. "Good answer."

The scent of hearth smoke and sizzling meat greeted them at the bottom of the stairs. The dining hall was warm, the stone walls reflecting the early morning glow of the sun over the tree line outside. Emberbread sat on a platter beside smoked meats, eggs, and boiled root vegetables.

Leopol wasted no time. He loaded a plate heavily–four emberbread cylinders, a pile of sausages, and a heaping of spiced potatoes.

Eirwyn sat and poured tea with far more restraint. "Knox will join us shortly. He was going to stop by the office first. We both talked with Lailant and Cerci earlier."

"You said they're all stable and well?" he asked, taking his normal seat and picking up a fork for the first time in centuries. His big, clawed hand struggled to hold it properly, and he growled, glancing up at the servant who stood by the sideboard.

"Reggie, will you please fetch the larger utensils in the second storage room? They're in the far back right corner, second drawer from the top. Thank you," Leopol said, the young man's eyes wide as he bowed slightly and took off through the swinging doors to the kitchen.

Eirwyn poured his tea and tilted her head. "Larger utensils?"

He held up the fork between his forefinger and thumb. "We have a set for dragon sized guests. Apparently, I need them."

Eirwyn nodded, her eyes bright as Leopol bit into the emberbread with gusto. The cheesy tang mixed with the smoky meat in a burst of flavor that left him groaning.

Eirwyn laughed with delight. "Is this your first meal in this body in centuries?"

He shook his head and swallowed quickly. "No, I ate with the dwarves, but it was hearty stew and jerkinola the next morning. A simple sandwich for lunch. Delicious, but not very satisfying. I was still hungry and afraid of eating too much of their reserves."

Eirwyn just rolled her eyes. "That doesn't surprise me, actually. Knox could eat a whole cow a day and still be hungry."

Knox entered and slapped him on the back as he walked to the sideboard to load his plate. "She uses too much magic in the transformations, and *you* look wrecked. You sure she's the one who collapsed?"

Leopol grunted. "She gave way too much of herself. She's asleep now and hopefully healing. She won't do that again—not while I live."

Knox sank down at the head of the table and nodded. "Bella's work last night was extraordinary. Cerci says the patients are stabilizing well. The effects of the curse are receding. Your mate may have changed the tide, Leopol."

He nodded, chewing slowly, but his eyes remained distant. Reggie returned with the box of utensils, and

Leopol plucked a larger fork, knife, and spoon out, directing him to store it in the dining room from now on.

When he turned back to the table, Knox had a brow raised. "If you're Bella's mate and she's queen, that will make you king of Busparia, assuming she gets her body back. How do you feel about that?"

Leopol shrugged, suddenly worried about his place here. Xander the Red had split the continent among his dragon children to avoid conflict, claiming that multiple dragons in one territory would lead to war. He didn't want to do that with Knox. He certainly hadn't done that with his father, Feralt. He'd been an excellent advisor, when he'd been home, but it was one of the reasons he'd traveled every few years.

"I was never meant to be king. That was always your father and uncles," Leopol said slowly, stabbing his potatoes with more force than they warranted.

Knox stabbed his own food. "You would make a far better king than I, no doubt about it. There's no way the castle would even be livable if it wasn't for your work over the past half year. We'll all need to adjust to your new body. But I'm damn glad you're alive, cousin, even if it means you'll eventually leave us to rule Busparia."

Leopol paused, then swallowed the bite. He hadn't told Knox he'd been adopted into the bloodline. Would it matter? Would it change how Knox saw him the way the other dragons he'd met had done?

Eirwyn cut in smoothly, "I'm glad too. I like having family around, but knowing that my people—well, former people—will be well taken care of with your experience guiding Bella's heart... I'm relieved, to be honest. Now for Bella to get her body back."

Leopol frowned, the food turning in his stomach. "Did

Knox tell you what all we found out at the dwarven settlement?"

Eirwyn nodded and frowned. "Yes, but what's our plan?"

"We're going to prepare the defenses here, protect you and our egg," Knox growled.

Eirwyn smiled and nodded at him before she continued. "I have no doubt that you will, but what about everything else?"

Both of them naturally looked at Leopol, and he wiped his mouth with a cloth napkin. "Yes, well, Bella and I talked on our long flights the past few days, and we have a plan."

Eirwyn chuckled and leaned back in her seat. "I knew you'd have one."

He smiled as he continued, "These four patients need to be monitored until the next full moon. Once we're certain they don't suffer long-term magical side effects, we'd like to have a ball here at Hartsgrove. Anyone who wishes to partake in the transformation ritual can do so at the ball. Bella and I have some casks of Ashplum Gold ale and a mocktail for the children curing now. It'll make the ritual potion go down smoother. Then we'll need to monitor their transformations, set up the ballroom the next day with beds to monitor everyone."

"Ashplum Gold! Oh my," Eirwyn said with a laugh. "We might need a few days to recover from that."

Leopol smiled.

Knox sighed and rubbed his head, "After their initial transformations are complete, we need to head to Glathen. I've already sent messengers to warn the king of the marching army, but we need to finalize this damn treaty."

"And make a final stand against Hanzel the wizard," Leopol growled, his hand turning into a fist on his knee.

Knox nodded. "I'd rather not confront him here in the Feral Forest. Too many civilians and I don't want the forest to be hurt. At least in Glathen, there are a few fields on their rocky coast."

Eirwyn twisted her goblet on the table, worrying her lip. "Very well. We'll have another council dinner in the next few weeks to go over all the changes so we'll finalize the treaty's rough draft there, then they'll tell both Vidrland and Ravrgard of the plan."

They grew quiet for a few minutes, only the clinking of forks on plates breaking the silence as they thought through the plan for the next month.

"We'll all be vulnerable during the transformation window, if everyone takes it at the same time," Knox warned.

Leopol nodded. "I don't want Bella to push herself into the Edge or the Beyond to help everyone have a smoother transition, either. It was very–hard last night, to see her so exhausted."

Knox gave him a look that said he knew exactly how Leopol felt, since he had his own mate to worry over.

Leopol rubbed his chest. Surprised, he glanced down and realized that he was still only in dirty, dusty pants. No shoes, no jacket or shirt. He blanched and looked up at Eirwyn, stricken. "Oh gods, why did you bring me here in such a state of undress? I need a bath, and clothes, and–"

She laughed and tilted her head to give him the look. "Leopol, you've had a trying few days. A warm, filling meal was more important than what you're wearing."

He glanced at Knox, who simply nodded to agree with his mate. Slowly, the knot of unease left his shoulders. "Very well. We have much to do in the next few weeks to prepare for our departure."

Knox froze, fork halfway to his lips. "To Glathen? You're going with us?"

Leopol shrugged. "You're family. I protect mine."

A silence settled briefly over the three of them—not awkward, but resolute.

"Speaking of protection," Eirwyn prompted, "how are the dwarves faring with food stores?"

Leopol set down his fork. "Very low. Their reliance on hunting has increased, but the deeper mining outposts are rationing. However—"

He looked at Knox. "It may be possible to imbue certain crystals with your plant-growing abilities. If you're willing, we could experiment. See if thermal caves or warm chambers in the mines can support crop growth."

Knox tilted his head. "Like portable greenhouses in a rock garden? I'm in."

Eirwyn leaned forward. "If it works, we might solve all our food supply issues. That winter isn't ceasing thanks to those daemons concerns me. We can't plant a vegetable garden or crops."

Leopol finally smiled, slow and small. "Then we have work to do. But first—I'm going to check on Bella."

They nodded. For the first time in days, a fragile hope settled at the table like steam rising from the emberbread.

Chapter Thirty-Four

Bella didn't move the rest of the day.

Leopol sat beside her bed, elbows resting on his knees, fingers threaded loosely together as if praying to gods he no longer served. The faint firelight from the hearth flickered against her face, softening the hollow under her eyes. She looked more ghostly somehow, too pale with no breath, flickering between transparent and just see through.

It scared him. He'd just found his mate, and he wasn't ready to let her go.

He'd tucked her, smoothing the blankets once more just for an excuse to touch her. Her magic was still low–dangerously low–but at least she was stable now. There were no signs of slipping toward the Edge. Even Lailant had come to check on her and verified his findings. There was no trace of that thin, unbearable hum that came before a soul faded from the body.

Still, he didn't trust sleep. That was where the dying went to feel safe before they vanished.

The longer she slept, the more his worry ramped up.

He'd had his meals delivered to the room the rest of yesterday and again this morning. He'd waved food under her nose, hoping to inspire her to wake. But there wasn't even so much as a twitch of her fingers.

He sank back into the chair he'd had brought in, one of the few that fit his now enlarged size. Rubbing his chest, his eyes felt dry and gritty, but at least Eirwyn had brought him a shirt.

Her breathing hitched.

He jerked upright, hands already outstretched, heart kicking against his ribs.

Bella stirred with a small, pained sound—then her eyes fluttered open, lashes damp and pale, mouth slightly parted in confusion.

"Leopol?" she rasped, barely louder than a breath, flickering between visibly transparent and invisible.

"I'm here." He leaned closer, voice low, anchoring. "You're safe. The transformations are over."

Her brow furrowed. "Are they alright? The woman—was she—?"

"She made it," he said gently. "All four live, so far."

She closed her eyes again, a tear slipping from the corner.

"How do you feel?" he asked, catching her tear with his thumb. Her skin was too cool. Not ghost-cold but depleted and burned out.

"I feel like I got ran over by a dragon. Did we... walk through the door?"

"I had to get you inside to rest comfortably, so yes. So I stepped through the Veil and you followed."

Her lips curved faintly as she turned onto her side, tucking her face against her palm, too tired to smile but too stubborn not to try.

"I always follow you," she breathed. "Even when I shouldn't."

His breath caught. There was so much weight in those words—trust, recklessness, affection. The ache in his chest deepened.

"How long have I been out?" she yawned.

"Just over twenty-four hours," he said, aching to lay down with her and curl his body around hers protectively.

"You stayed by my side?" she whispered, slowly forcing her eyes open as if she was already half-asleep again.

He smoothed her hair from her forehead, unable to stop touching her. "I wanted to, but Eirwyn made me eat. After that first meal, I stayed here and had meals delivered. You're my mate, and I... kept worrying."

"Why?" she asked, not sure she was ready for the answer.

His voice went rough with accusation. "You almost didn't come back."

She reached weakly for his hand, and he gave it to her, letting her squeeze his fingers with the last of her strength.

"I—I didn't mean to push so far," she murmured. "But I couldn't let them die."

"I know." He lifted her knuckles to his lips. "You did such a great job. You're an amazing healer, Bella."

They sat like that for a moment—his lips pressing to her palm now, hearts still finding their rhythm again.

Then she blinked, nose wrinkling. Her expression shifted from fragile to bemused. "Leopol... you smell like old blood and stanky men from the tavern."

He blinked. "Excuse me, I know I haven't bathed yet, but *stanky*?"

Her snort was soft, almost a laugh. "You need a bath, a

shave, and new clothes. Will a brush work on your hair? Gods, do you even have clothes for this body?"

His mouth twitched. "None that fit, no. Eirwyn had one of the maids cobble this shirt together from two of Ashur's."

She squeezed his hand again. "Go clean up before you scare the staff. Maybe find a tailor so you'll feel more like yourself."

He hesitated. How did she know he didn't feel like himself?

His free hand hovered just above her chest, fingers twitching like he might lay them over her heart again, just to be sure.

"I'll be here when you come back," she said quietly with a yawn. "You have to take care of yourself too, Leopol."

He squeezed her fingers before laying her hand down on the bed. "If I have to take care of myself, you have to too. Don't scare me like that again, do you hear?"

She gave him a tired smile and let her eyes fall closed. "Bossy dragon mate."

"I'm serious, Bella. If you're running low, I'll share my magic."

She rolled her eyes. "Fine, but how are the patients?"

He leaned down and pressed a kiss to her forehead. "They're resting the same as you. I'll share more details when your strength is back."

And then he rose, slow and reluctant as she sighed and turned onto her side on the bed. He looked back at the doorway, but she was already back to sleep.

Shutting the door quietly behind him, he went down the stairs to the library. If he wanted to show her the crystals plan, he needed to pull the books to show her the theory.

As he approached the library's double doors, Ashur appeared like a shadow in the doorway. Leopol's brow rose, still surprised that he was bigger than Knox's right-hand man now.

"Cerci sent this for you," the gargoyle said, stepping forward to place a thick leather-bound notebook in Leopol's hand. His gaze swept over Leopol, pausing at the dried blood on his forearm, the claw marks across his pants, the tangled mane of hair falling to his shoulders.

"You look... unlike yourself."

Leopol grunted in acknowledgment. No argument there. "Thanks for the loan of the shirts. I'll order you two more from the tailor."

"It's fine. Easy come, easy go." Ashur shrugged and left, his heavy footsteps echoing faintly down the corridor.

Leopol stood there for a moment, then walked into the library as he flipped through the notebook with one clawed hand. Most of it was Bella's notes on the past few months of tests. He'd seen the notebook before and read most of it with her.

The last few pages held Cerci's tight scrawl tracking every detail of the four transformations–the tremors, the timing, potion dosages, magical reactions, patient responses.

He skimmed, his gaze absorbing each line like a sponge. Midway through the second patient's notes, he slowed, then paused.

This was Bella's work, her method, her design, her potion. Every symbol, every potion combination–they carried her logic, her creativity, her heart.

He closed the book.

She should be the one to study this first. They should do it together, like they had in the sanctum. Leaning over ancient scrolls, whispering spells, arguing about theory and tracing runes, solving problems together.

Gods, he missed it. He missed *her*.

A flicker of doubt stirred inside him. What happened when all of this was over? When they reversed the curse, defeated the wizard, and Bella reclaimed her body?

Would she still want him?

He hadn't always belonged here–an ancient watcher, wandering between Hartsgrove and the mountains, serving when called, retreating when not. He'd lived in castles, caves in the mountains, and on ships across the seas. But the Feral Forest had been his home longer than most human nations had even existed.

Knox had recognized him as a dragon, as family, as Bella's mate. He would be at her side, whether as king or not. That meant a new home, because home was wherever she was.

He turned and caught his reflection in the mirror above her desk. He stepped closer, shoulders hunched, hand hovering like he might scrape the rune-glow from his chest still visible through the soft linen shirt.

Light blue skin marbled with white scales. Runes glowing faintly across his chest and neck. A savage scar down the center, golden light still webbing outward from the Orythium beneath. Broad shoulders hunched, tail twitching behind him. Feathered hair matted, tangled and wild.

A beast.

"I look like something she needs protection from," he muttered.

His chest burned with shame. Not because of how he looked–he didn't mind being monstrous–but because he felt unworthy of the way she'd looked at him, like he was something precious.

"If I'm to take care of myself like she wants and protect her like I need to," he growled, turning from the mirror, "then I need to stop looking like something that's been dragged through the hells."

He stalked from the room and down the back stairs toward the kitchen door, intending to take the lesser-known trail through the living hedgerow that curved toward the new village beyond the garden walls.

But the castle was too full of people, and his thoughts too full of everything else. Spirit walking. Crystal powered greenhouses. Their mate bond.

He could have flown, since that's what dragons did, but his wings still felt too heavy, his thoughts too loud. Magic stirred beneath his skin—and with a breath, he stepped sideways into the in-between.

In seconds, the village shimmered into view ahead of him, quiet and idyllic, outlined in the faint silver haze of the Veil. He spirit walked toward it like a ghost threading between two halves of a world.

No sense in bathing when he didn't have clothes to put on afterward.

Time to reclaim the man he'd been these past few months.

Time to become someone she could choose—not just the only one she could touch.

He took stock of the crude, new signs over the freshly built shops and slipped into the tailor's entryway—still half in the Veil. He shifted fully into view just inside, making the tailor jump.

An hour later, Leopol stood, arms out, while the village tailor—an older man named Thomar—clicked his tongue and tugged at the measuring tape around his bicep.

With pins in his mouth, he said, "You're lucky I have enough fabric. Getting supplies from Busparia has been hard."

Leopol grunted. The ceiling felt low and the walls too close. The entire shop, new as it was, had been twisted from living tree trunks–Knox's handiwork–but the space still was too small for his liking.

Thomar yanked the tape tighter across his chest. "Stop flexing."

"I'm not," he growled, tail thudding against the platform behind him.

Most customers stood on the platform to be measured, but Thomar stood on it now–otherwise, he wouldn't have reached Leopol's shoulder.

"Yes, you are. Now turn."

Leopol obeyed with a curse as his daughter, a teenager with frizzed hair and wide eyes, scrambled to write down the numbers he called out. Leopol took a deep breath at the sight of the girl's hands. They were grotesquely merged with a pen, her finger stained in ink.

The tailor pulled another pin from his hair, making Leopol shudder. The man's entire head looked like a pincushion–literally–thanks to the curse that had merged his profession into his body.

Soon he found himself in the bath at the barber's next door, the tailor's wife pouring scalding hot water on his head, making him hiss.

"Oh, don't be such a baby. We'll get you cleaned up in no time," the woman said.

"My thanks," Leopol murmured, arms crossed over his chest, soaked and scowling.

"Do you need help scrubbing beneath the scales of your back?"

He nodded mulishly, and she got to work with the effi-cient ease of a professional while he scrubbed his front with a soapy rag. When she reached the base of his tail, he jerked in the water, sending it sloshing.

"Sorry, didn't realize it was so sensitive," she said.

"I'll do the tail," he growled, glaring at her over his shoulder. He hadn't been this sensitive when he was just a dragon construct. Now that he was actually alive, it was like all his senses were heightened.

When he stood, he took the large sheet and dried as best he could. It wasn't a soft towel but was probably what Ashur used when he was in town.

He prided himself on taking care of others. Anticipating needs, being prepared.

Yet somehow, he'd missed this, and the oversight made him crankier.

He dressed in the new pants and shirt the tailor had delivered to the barber while he bathed. He flexed his toes and sighed, hoping the cobbler would know how to make dragon bracers. Since no dragons had been around for hundreds of years, he probably didn't.

He threw open the door and stepped into the front room of the shop, where he sat grumpily while the barber trimmed and cut his hair.

"These feathers are fused with hair," she muttered, awed. "Amazing texture. So many layers, and the way it all lies between your horns like Knox's? You're definitely a dragon."

He frowned, not sure why even his hair had to change with the transformation to life. His previous dragon body had no hair at all.

"You're a bit feral looking, but we'll get you sorted out," Gora said, deftly weaving a section of dark silver-feathered hair into a tight braid, despite the hindrance of the comb that was merged with the back of her forearm and the scissors that made up her thumb and forefinger of one hand.

Leopol sighed as she cleaned him up. If he was going to Glathen next month, he wanted to be presentable. Bella would hold her head high as she walked on his arm. Imagining it got him through the next few hours of torture.

After he left the cobbler with plans for foot bracers, he paused on the dirt-packed street.

The sunlight was bright but it didn't heat the snow to melting. The village was bustling in quiet, determined ways—stoneworkers shaping blocks at the edge of the square, gardeners trimming vines from the eaves of newly shaped homes, cursed engineers barking at each other over the newest aqueduct addition. Leopol knew the giant eagles had attacked the last one, but this one seemed to be holding up.

As he passed the edge of the training field where the eagle riders were doing crude formation drills, he spied Knox leaning against an outer wall.

"How's training going?" he asked as he stopped near his cousin.

Knox nodded with a shrug, arms crossed. "Better actually. I think it has something to do with Cerci's arrival, but they're actually taking riders now and not attempting to throw them off mid-air. It's been a rough few days, and they're still pissed, but they're not really fighting us like they were before she arrived."

Leopol tossed the shredded shirt aside and rubbed the bridge of his nose. "Makes sense. She is the goddess of transformations."

Knox snorted. "How's Bella today?"

Leopol exhaled through his nose. "She woke up this morning. Weak, pale, but mostly normal. Figured I'd clean up so I'm not so beastly, maybe convince her to fully accept the mate bond."

Knox breathed a sigh of relief. "Good, I know you were scared, although I didn't realize the mate bond wasn't completed."

Leopol sighed as they watched two riders on their eagles fly overhead. "I don't know that the bond can be completed without her body. I'll need to do more research in the next few weeks."

Knox glanced sideways at him. "You're not a one-man army anymore. You've got me, Eirwyn, Bella, Cerci, Lailant. Even that cranky bastard Ashur. We can help research too."

Leopol cracked a smile. "We're going to Glathen after the full moon, but we'll need someone to guard Hartsgrove."

"I know."

"You're not going without me. It'll have to be Ashur who stays. I know he manages Vidrland, but the druids can handle that village. He can guard Hartsgrove."

"I know that too," Knox said simply. "Eirwyn might be the one trained in diplomacy, but you're our shield, our memory. You carry more than just spells and runes, Leopol. You carry all of us, always anticipating our needs."

That silenced him for a few moments. His chest grew tight, then Leopol said quietly, "What happens after this? After Bella has her body back, after we kill the wizard? I don't... I don't know who I am anymore. I can't anticipate what happens after."

Knox didn't joke this time. "You're still Leopol. Dream-scale, stormborn, scholar of a thousand years. Doesn't matter if you walk in spirit or in skin—what makes you you is still there."

The itch started beneath his shoulder blades again, that now-familiar heat of too-long-contained power.

Knox watched him carefully. "You want to shift?"

"Yes," Leopol said simply.

Knox tilted his head. "Then let's give these eagles some test battles, shall we? Come on, cousin, let's fly."

On the edge of the village, Knox flexed his shoulders and then shifted in a puff of green gas. He launched into the sky, and by the time his wings beat twice, Leopol had shifted.

A deep breath, and he followed his cousin into the sky, his throat thick with remembered emotion. It had been a long time since he'd flown with another dragon.

Chapter Thirty-Five

Bella stopped at the base of the stairs, blinking against the bright light of sunset pouring through the castle's open front doors. The butler went to close the door, but Bella slipped through it first. She needed some fresh air, after being cooped up for two days now in her room.

Outside, two shadows descended beyond the threshold, a flurry of wings and wind echoing through the front courtyard.

Knox landed first, laughing, his green-scaled tail swinging as he turned. Leopol followed a breath later, the wind catching his feather-braided hair and sending silver-tipped strands dancing around his face. With twin thuds and a swirl of magic—Knox and Leopol stood at the foot of the stairs, windblown and grinning like reckless boys.

Taller than ever, he was cleaned up and dressed properly for the first time in days. Leopol's light blue shirt clung to his broad chest, clean, new, and open at the throat where the Orythium scar still glowed faintly.

His dark blue pants actually fit, even accounting for his

thick tail. His feathered hair had been pulled back into sleek braids, silver-tipped strands glinting like threads of moonlight.

He looked... dazzling. Alive, present, and definitely not the haunted, overburdened shadow who she'd met almost two weeks ago.

And he was smiling, laughing. It was a real, unburdened laugh with head thrown back that seemed to shake the dust off every stone in the castle.

Her heart cracked wide open, but then, he saw her standing on the steps to the castle.

That was the look. The one she'd seen Knox give Eirwyn so many times, the one she'd dreamed someone might give her someday.

It lit Leopol's entire face as he looked at her, his posture straightening, his grin turning softer, more tender. It should look ridiculous on his monstrous face, the scales going down his cheeks, the soft blue, white, and silver mixing on his face so much, she didn't want to look away.

But it was the most beautiful face with the most important expression of her life.

Was it love?

She hesitated. Maybe she was imagining it. Maybe it was gratitude or hope. Maybe he was just relieved she hadn't died. She had seen him nearly broken this morning, wan and drawn and worried about her.

She would wait and watch. She couldn't trust a moment like this. A single look could just be a mirage. She'd been fooled by a similar look before, after all.

"Bella! You're up," he said, taking the stairs two at a time, greaves wrapped around his clawed feet to form a type of open toe, open sole boot, leather covering up his calves.

Her heart jumped at the sound of her name on his lips—

too eager, too fast. She took the last step as he reached for her hand, his palm warm and rough where their fingers brushed.

"You look... better," he added, eyes sweeping over her face as if still confirming she was real.

"You look... bathed," she replied, arching a brow with a wry smile.

His laugh was rough and self-conscious. "Went to the tailor and barber then helped Knox with some eagle rider training. Not sure which was more violent."

They stood for a breath too long, close enough to touch but neither giving in to it.

Shyly, she gestured toward the doors. "Want to look through Cerci's notes with me? I was going to do that, then check on the patients."

His answering nod was too fast, too earnest. "I was hoping you'd say that."

He tucked her hand into the crook of his elbow, and together, they headed for the library—side by side, barely touching, like magnets resisting the inevitable pull.

Now that she was feeling more herself, despite her ghostly form, she couldn't deny the tug of the mate bond. It was too new and raw for her to hope it'd last, that it was real, though.

They retreated into the library, books spread across the center table as the sunlight slanted in through the tall windows. Leopol led her to her favorite desk and opened her notebook. Bella leaned over beside him, breathing in parchment and lemon oil, the quiet steadiness of him anchoring her as they worked.

"First patient is now sitting up," he said, flipping a page. "The second one requested eggs this morning. Lailant said he even laughed at something Cerci said."

Bella blinked fast, her hands trembling where they hovered over the open journal. She hadn't let herself hope. Not really. Not until now.

"That's... wonderful," she whispered.

"It's working, Bella, really working. A perfect fusion of ancient glyphs, Growler techniques, and grounded runes—yet it honors the boundaries between traditions."

"Of course I didn't cross any boundaries," she said with a frown.

He took her hand and shook his head. "I know that. What I'm saying is *you* built something no one else could. It honors every law regarding magic but merges multiple modalities to solve the problem. Even I couldn't have made something this practical, this elegant yet efficient."

Bella sniffed, her heart melting for this sweetheart of a beast, her own warrior scholar. He was so giddy with pride in her success, it made her chest ache.

She cleared her throat and took a deep, shuddering breath, blinking fast. "Thank you, Leopol. That—that means a lot to me."

Leopol studied her, concern softening the edges of his harsh features. "My words made you almost cry, but hearing the patients are improving didn't. You don't look relieved."

"I can't—" she faltered, then straightened. "I just need to see them with my own eyes. I'm afraid to hope, Leopol. I can't afford to be wrong again."

He closed the journal with one hand and cupped her cheek with the other. "You're not wrong or a failure. You've just created a counter to a curse blast, something I've never seen in a thousand years. You're healing them, Bella, saving them."

Her eyes watered at his words, and she leaned her forehead on his chest. She breathed in the new scent of him.

Still faintly of Leopol, but now of something more primal, more alive.

"Feels like I've been working on this for so long, it's hard to believe the end might actually be near."

He ran his hand down her back and just held her. "I can understand that. You have a good heart, Bella. You may not feel like a queen, but you lead with the heart. It's one of the things I love about you."

She froze, sucking in a breath at his words. It wasn't a declaration of love, but it was dangerously close. Gastone had claimed to love her so quickly, and this was almost as fast.

She eased back, separating herself by gently taking the book and tucking a stray curl of her hair. "I–I want to update the patient files, see them for myself."

He stepped aside, no protest in his gaze. Just steady support. "Then let's go, my queen."

Her heart reeled as they crossed to the ballroom, not at the results—but what it might mean. What came next, what it meant for *them*. Because the last time she'd had dreams for a family of her own...

They crossed the corridor to the ballroom, where four patients now occupied cleaner beds rolled into the sunshine through the glass doors. All of them were visibly improved. One smiled when he saw Bella enter, raising a shaky, normal hand in greeting.

Emotion swelled so fast in her chest that her breath hitched. She couldn't breathe, couldn't hold it together.

Leopol slid his arm around her waist. "I've got you," he murmured softly.

She swallowed hard and nodded, whispering, "I'm supposed to be the queen. Don't let them see me cry."

He nodded as their steps slowed as they drew closer.

With a shaky hand, she talked with each of them one by one. Leopol gently took the notebook from her hand and scribbled as she talked, asking questions here and there but mostly being a supportive presence beside her.

There were slow tears from a few of the patients, but the loud, jovial man kept the rest of them distracted and joyful for the most part.

One of the older women, her hair silver at the roots but dark from old dye, reached for Bella's hand with trembling fingers. Her skin was no longer stone-spiked, just wrinkled and warm and human, but her hand passed harmlessly through Bella's spirit form.

Bella smiled faintly as the woman didn't seem to notice the lack of touch. The woman simply dropped her hand and gripped the blanket tight.

"You're the ghost queen who didn't give up. You never gave up on your mother either. I don't remember everything these days, but I remember that, remember you."

Bella froze, breath catching, but tried to be practical. "You don't remember everything? Were you having that problem before the curse, or has it worsened with the transformation?"

The woman shook her head. "Prior condition. My mind's the same, as far as I can tell. But you've healed my body, Your Highness. I–I never thought I'd hold my granddaughter again. I thought I'd die a monster."

The woman used a well-loved handkerchief to dab at her eyes. "Thank you. Your mother would be proud."

That did it. Her composure cracked like frost under the sun. Her chin trembled. A sharp breath pulled through her nose, but it wasn't enough to stop the rush of tears that blurred the beds before her.

Leopol stepped in without a word and wrapped his arm

around her shoulders, murmuring their goodbyes and sweeping her out into the corridor. He didn't stop until they reached the shadowed hall between the library and the main stairs.

"It's alright," he murmured, wrapping her in both his arms. "You did it. You saved them, and they're alright."

She buried her face in his chest, the tears finally slipping free. She didn't sob—there wasn't enough air in her lungs for that—but her shoulders shook with the force of holding it all in for so long.

They were going to be alright. How many nights had she lain awake as a child hoping the same for her mother? She couldn't save her, but with these villagers—her people, people who'd watched her grow up, knew her parents, had been there to help with the shop and the tavern when she'd been left alone...

She could finally pay them back for all their support. She could finally heal them all, be the queen they needed her to be.

A sob escaped as she clutched at Leopol. He crooned softly, holding her tight, his hand tracing slow circles on her back.

The warmth of his body grounded her. His steady breathing reminded her she wasn't alone—she didn't have to be strong for everyone, not right now.

She clenched her fists against his tunic, her tears soaking the fabric as her heart cracked open in silence.

Then—so gently she almost didn't feel it—he pressed his lips to her hair, one hand on the back of her head. He held her so reverently, as if her tears hurt him and she was something precious to be cherished.

Her breath caught.

Another kiss landed on her temple, lingering just a second longer before moving to her cheek.

Her heart stuttered, a slow unfurling of realization blooming inside her chest. This wasn't just comfort from a sense of duty. This was so much more than anything she'd ever had before.

A clawed thumb stroked her neck, and she tipped her chin up toward him. His eyes searched hers, asking without words.

So slowly, he kissed her jaw, pulling back slightly to watch her with those reptilian eyes.

He hovered over her mouth, waiting, breath mingling.

She shuddered a tear-filled breath, almost a hiccup, and the sound pushed him past restraint. His lips crashed down to hers, and it wasn't gentle like when he'd been a spirit.

It sent a primal need racing through her, and she gasped, opening to him.

He pressed her against the wall, mouths locked, tongues dueling, their magic sparking wildly between them. He groaned as her hands slid into his hair, tangling in the feather-braided strands. When she tugged, his hips jerked, grinding his cock into her stomach. She moaned with need, her core hot and aching.

They slammed into a shelf, and his head jerked up, breaking the kiss with a growled, "What the hell?"

He froze, his head not moving as he looked down at her with wide blue eyes. The surprise on his face made her giggle.

He blinked and looked around, still holding her close. "We're in the linen closet."

Bella looked up and laughed softly again.

"I can see that. Hold still," she said, reaching up with both hands. "You're tangled in a loop of towels."

"But how did we get here?" he growled, holding his head still—even as his hands raked over her ass, his cock still pressed to her.

"I don't know exactly. The heat of the moment or—"

Bella's hands were still unweaving towels from around his head when the closet door opened.

Light spilled across them, and they both froze, heads slowly turning to look. Cerci stood there, hands on hips with a thoroughly confused expression.

"Um, do I want to know?" she asked.

Bella let out a small laugh and buried her face in Leopol's arm.

"Absolutely not," he said smoothly, grinning over her head.

Cerci arched her brows. "Actually, I *do* need to know. Something sparked in the aether just now, opening a portal, and it wasn't me. I followed the pulse here."

Bella peeked up. "You felt that?"

"You *ripped* a portal into the castle's linen closet. I thought someone was trying to attack the castle from the inside."

"Oh," Bella said weakly. "Um... no. Just, uh..." She glanced at Leopol. "A private moment."

"Very private," he growled, adjusting his horns and tossing the last of the towels to the ground.

His hand on the small of Bella's back was hot as he led her out of the closet. Cerci stepped aside, holding the door with a frown.

"We still haven't discussed the portal that sent you out of here. Knox tried to explain, but I need more details."

Bella groaned quietly and rubbed her temples, aching from the tears. "Do we have to?"

"Yes," Cerci said, closing the door to the linen closet.

"Because if this is going to keep happening, I need to rein-force the wards—or better yet, teach you how not to trip them like a pair of hormonal spell grenades."

Leopol's brow furrowed. "It's not like we meant to trigger anything."

Cerci cocked a hip and settled a hand on it. "Didn't you accidentally portal yourselves into a ruined temple while—"

Bella cleared her throat. Loudly.

Cerci grinned widely, "—while *reconnecting*?"

"We were having sex, yes," Leopol muttered, unfazed by the words. "We weren't exactly planning on getting sucked across the forest mid—"

"Thrust?" Cerci offered helpfully.

Bella flushed, glaring at the woman. "Don't encourage him."

Cerci shrugged, smirking. "Clear communication is helpful in these types of situations. So that's two confirmed surges triggered during heightened emotional... or physi-cal... stimulation. Until we control it, I don't recommend you—partake—in any more of those activities."

Leopol threw up his hand. "So, I can't even kiss my mate without risking a magical black hole to the laundry room?"

Cerci sighed, suddenly looking defeated. "I realize you wouldn't be having this problem if I hadn't shown up, and for that I'm sorry. But you're bonded, magically and emotionally, and you're unstable."

"Thanks," Leopol muttered.

"I mean it literally," Cerci said, unfazed. "You're still newly restored to life, still adapting to your physical form. Bella's tethered to a rose and barely stabilized herself. Add in a volatile mate bond, and any shared magical surge my presence here brings is going to punch through reality unless it's properly grounded."

Bella rubbed her arms. "That's why it only happens when we're... intimate?"

"Exactly. You're channeling too much through raw emotion. You need containment."

"Containment," Leopol echoed darkly. "Sounds like prison."

"Not a prison, a focus item perhaps, like a tuning fork," Cerci corrected. "Something to harmonize the frequencies between you. If your magic aligns too abruptly, they collide. That's when portals open, boundaries shatter, and you accidentally teleport into a closet."

Leopol crossed his arms, flexing his bare chest. "What happens when we finally have sex again? I don't want to end up on the dining table with my bare ass out for anyone to see."

Cerci pressed her lips together. "Honestly? That's a valid concern."

Bella made a choking sound, trying to hold back her laughter. "This is *not* what I imagined when people talked about fated mates."

Cerci sighed and gestured toward the hallway. "Come on. Let's go to the most heavily warded room, and I'll teach you how to control it."

The sunroom glowed with a soft blue light from the magical model of the castle in the center of the coffee table.

"Sit, sit. This may take a while," Cerci said, waving a hand over the image as Leopol and Bella settled on the couch.

Several flickering spots lit up—one near the ballroom, one in the library, and another pulsing red in the linen closet.

"This is a time stamp of earlier, and that's you," she said, pointing. "These are emotional surge echoes, where your magic overwhelmed the ambient barrier and tried to find release."

Bella peered closer. "So, how do we stop it?"

Cerci turned to them, her expression sharpening. "First, you need training. You have to learn how to ground your bond without breaking the wards around the castle. You'll also need to start designing ward keys—specific sigils you imprint onto the portal magic, like passwords."

"Great, anything else?" Leopol growled.

Cerci crossed her arms, foot tapping with growing impatience. "It's not just training. You'll need an anchor. A magical seal—something that physically ties your bond into this plane. Think of it like hard wiring your connection into a stable loop. And..." She hesitated.

Leopol narrowed his eyes. "And what?"

"A binding mark." She looked at Bella. "It's a ritual tattoo. Usually inked with blood, magic, and intent."

"Blood magic has been outlawed for centuries!" Bella gasped, her face draining of color as she thought of Gastone. "And with good reason."

"And yet here I am. Portals rupturing. Ghost queens falling in love. Magic unraveling at the seams. If there was ever a time for the old ways..." She lifted a brow.

Bella jerked at the love comment but didn't deny it. Instead, she rubbed her temples again, knowing the woman was right. Leopol's hand settled on her neck, brushing the hair to one side. She glanced at him, a worry line on her forehead.

He murmured, "She's the demigoddess of portals and transitions. She only comes in times of great change."

Bella blew out a breath. "I know that," she grumbled. "But I'm a spirit. You can't tattoo air."

Cerci stepped closer. "You're not air. Not anymore. Or at least, not entirely. Your soul is real. Your spirit's tangible. He can touch you and administer the tattoo. If we do this right, with his magic and your soul not fighting it... it *will* hold."

Leopol's hand tightened on the back of her neck, his expression shifting in concern. "You'd feel the pain and heat of it. It feels like a brand. But you have to accept it, welcome the pain and not fight the magic. It's a declaration, not just a tool."

Bella stared at them both, swallowing. "And if I don't?"

"Then," Cerci said gently, "you'll keep punching holes in the world every time he touches you."

Leopol reached for Bella's hand, claws careful. "We don't have to decide today, but I'll be here, no matter what."

Bella glanced at the magical map again. The little red glow in the linen closet pulsed brighter for a second, like a heartbeat.

She took a deep breath. "Alright, teach us how to stop tripping the wards first. Then we'll talk about the binding."

Cerci nodded. "Good. Because if you two keep using each other as arcane firecrackers, I'm going to need a bigger map—and sturdier linens."

Chapter Thirty-Six

The long dining table was crowded, not just with platters of mostly cold food and empty goblets, but with maps and scrolls too. The firelight crackled low in the hearth, casting shadows across wary faces.

Bella sat upright at the far end, tense and uneasy at the Council dinner. It wasn't like she could eat. Even if she wanted to, she was too nervous. Her father and Scarlet had arrived and were safe. The four test patients were having limited side effects, and they were ready to administer the full ritual with any who wanted to partake at the ball tonight.

Beside her, Leopol's claws tapped against the wood in a slow, thoughtful rhythm. Eirwyn had taken a seat next to Knox at the head of the other end. Her steady voice had been the only thing keeping the conversation from devolving into shouting.

"Two dead. Four wounded," Scarlet said grimly from the center of the table, her jaw clenched tight. "And a captured Dragon Claw Growler turned on his own. Gave up everything under truthleaf extract."

The murmur of voices filled the room as they continued their report.

"He confirmed it," Wulfric added. "The wizard, masquerading as Bella, is marching on Glathen. The Dragon Claws are gathering strength with the daemons and testing tactics."

"But the treaty—" one of the council members exclaimed.

Eirwyn licked a map using lights and shadows onto the ceiling. "Exactly, we must secure the treaty first, before the wizard invades. We won't survive another three months without food and supplies."

Leopol spoke beside her, voice even but rumbling, "The growth crystals are working. We've stabilized three chambers to sun-like heat in the past few weeks, but the crops are barely sprouting now. There's no food to spare."

"We're burning through our emergency stores in the Growler camps too," Scarlet said. "If the wizard marches along the Southern Road to Glathen, we can hold out a few more months. But if he secures Glathen and Busparia with the Feral Forest between, he'll apply pressure from both sides."

"He'll freeze or starve us out," Wulfric said grimly, crossing his furry arms and pulling the sleeves of his black dinner jacket tight.

Knox leaned back in his chair, raking a hand over the back of his head. "With Hanzel the wizard marching on Glathen, we need to prepare a full-scale extraction if something goes wrong during our visit. I won't have my mate in danger."

"We don't have enough Robins or refugees for a full

army," Eirwyn cautioned. "We cannot risk provoking Glathen into thinking we're invading either."

"The extraction team will have to be on standby until summoned by a talkie," Knox added.

Bella watched them go back and forth. They were in perfect sync. She had watched them banter, flirt, and lean on each other all month. She wasn't jealous exactly, but they made leading together look easy. It was nothing like what she'd had with Gastone.

She'd even helped Leopol with his project, made more of the Ashplum Gold, and trained with Cerci. But despite mastering the dome of silence, neither of them had become adept at creating a portal where they actually wanted to go. At least they could kiss in the dome and weren't thrown around the castle.

A councilman—one of the Druids—set his goblet down and said, "It sounds like you already have a plan in mind."

Knox met Eirwyn's gaze and spoke. "Yes, if it's necessary, we want to deploy the eagle riders. They're elite and can get in and out quickly. They could be a show of force if we need to get our queen back alive."

"Or queens," one of the older councilwomen said pointedly, glancing toward Bella and Scarlet.

"They could provide a distraction, at a minimum," one of the other councilmen said. "All in favor of keeping the eagle riders on standby and deploying them in an emergency?"

A round of ayes came quick, and none were opposed.

Eirwyn pressed her hands to the table. "Thank you. We'll make sure the meeting goes well. Glathen isn't the enemy. The king and queen were open to ending the war last year, and the prince and princess were nice enough. But reports say that the king has not been himself since the queen died."

"We can't rely on diplomacy completely," another Druid said. "They might not even accept that Bella is the queen."

One councilman, a thickset nobleman whose daughter had once vied for courtship with Gastone, said, "No offense, *Your Majesty*, but you're... still unstable. A ghost, bonded to magic none of us understand. Perhaps we send someone more likely to get us what we want."

A few of the dinner guests paused, some straightened, their eyes sharpening as wolves circling prey. Bella was used to it, after all her time in the tavern.

Her pulse spiked, but she didn't flinch. She'd heard worse in taverns with a bloody mop in her hand. *Still, this was different—this was personal, public.*

"If I'm unstable, it's because I've had to carry a nation's curse in my soul. I didn't want this curse on anyone, but I won't apologize for doing all I can to save people, including going into a country we've been at war with for ten years."

Her voice didn't rise, but the steel in it cut through the room. "I may not be the most stable option, but I will fiercely fight for my family, my friends, my people. That includes those here in the Feral Forest as well as those who still remain in Busparia, suffering an even stronger winter than us here."

His wife sipped her ale and murmured, "A demigoddess would lend our requests more weight, though."

Bella frowned, knowing that Cerci wasn't ready to face politics, not after so much trauma from her centuries in the hells. Cerci wasn't even at the dinner, preferring to save her strength for her appearance at the ball. Plus, her new friend wanted to stay here and help monitor the villagers post-transformation. They'd trauma bonded in the past few weeks.

The older councilwoman scowled. "You think two queens, two dragons—one a king, one who was alive during the founding dynasty—and the head of all the Growlers are not enough for them to take us seriously?"

The councilman nodded, his jowls swinging. "She's a ghost. You said yourself her ability to remain on this plane is tentative at best, not that her death would truly matter in the grand scheme of things."

Wulfric slammed his hand down on the table, making several around him jump. "Watch your tongue or I'll rip it out for you."

But it wasn't Wulfric who made the man go silent. She could feel Leopol's magic flare beside her, but he didn't so much as move a finger.

His eyes glowed, pale and glinting, and the air grew thick with magic. A crackling ripple pulsed outward from his body, and invisible threads of force wrapped around the councilman's collar, hauling him up as if by a fist.

After a month, Bella could now see the threads of magic, but everyone else gasped in surprise when the man rose nearly a foot off his chair, feet kicking, throat bobbing. The unseen hand gripped the collar of his soul and shook once.

Her hand slid beneath the table to rest on Leopol's knee. Not to stop him—yet—but to anchor him, remind him that she was here and needed him. She hated that she needed him, but after the past few weeks, she couldn't deny their bond.

"Say it again," Leopol growled, voice like distant thunder. "Say her life doesn't matter."

The man paled. The room stilled. Even the flames in the hearth lowered as if in fear.

Her heart pounded in her ears. She should stop him. Should want to stop him. But some petty, broken part of her liked that he was willing to burn the world down for her.

She squeezed his knee. "We're not tearing each other apart for the wizard to laugh at. If you can't control your emotions, step out of the room and collect yourself."

Leopol paused at the gentle rebuke but didn't look away from the man.

Eirwyn said, voice calm but sharp as steel. "This is a volatile time, but I won't have it in my home. We all feel strongly, but this is the dinner table, not a battlefield."

Bella's thumb stroked the back of his scaled hand. "They're not our enemies. The wizard is."

The magic faded slowly. The councilman dropped into his chair with a wheeze, red-faced and trembling.

Leopol didn't look away from him. "You want strength for Glathen? Then know this—Queen Bella has it in spades, and so do I. Together, we'll have Knox and Eirwyn's backs in a way that only family can. We're going to Glathen."

The man's wife scowled at him as if he was a weakling she wanted to squash under her boot. She'd been very catty at several of the events at the Winter Palace when Bella had been engaged and then married to Gastone. No doubt, the woman was still bitter her daughter hadn't become queen.

Knox nodded at Leopol as if he approved of the action though. "Family is important and not something I take lightly. We welcome the support from you both, Leopol. When this is over, I know you'll make an excellent king for Busparia."

Her pulse skittered. *King of Busparia?*

She hadn't thought that far ahead—not really. She was

still fighting to reclaim her own body, her own name. The idea of ruling again tightened something in her chest. She'd barely survived the last time—and that was before her soul had unraveled.

But when she looked at him—proud, loyal, terrifying and tender—and saw the surprise on his face, the reverence in his expression... something in her stirred.

He would make an excellent king. And maybe... maybe she didn't have to do this alone. Maybe it was alright to need him so much, to still want to be queen so she could help more people.

The table broke into an uproar over that, and she glanced at Leopol, who sat stunned. Bella's own heart raced at the thought. Would he rule by her side? Is that even where she wanted to be?

The councilman's wife grit through clenched teeth, "But she's a ghost. She can't rule as a ghost and a marriage between them wouldn't be legal or binding."

Bella winced, remembering that the woman had been the high judge of Demerel. It didn't matter that she was a spirit, not a ghost—not legally, anyway.

Eirwyn cut in smoothly, "We'll cross that bridge when we come to it. First, we have to defeat the wizard, end the winter, and feed our people. Questioning the Queen's right to lead—especially when she is the reason we're sitting here before the ball where we will end the curse instead of buried under rubble and ash..."

"That she helped cause," someone grumbled.

Knox let out a puff of green gas from his nose. "Enough. This dissension is beneath this council and not what we stand for. We must act as one body and all be in agreement."

She'd broken up a dozen bar fights over spilled ale and

stolen kisses—this wasn't so different. Power plays were common over a table. But she knew people, and she knew how to call their bluff.

Unease settled around the table, and Bella leaned forward slightly, her voice calm but clear. "If we go to Glathen, we do it with transparency and strength—not just force. We'll make them see we've already started to rebuild, both as the Feral Forest nation and as Busparia. We're stronger together."

Eirwyn frowned, impatience coloring her voice. "Let's focus on the here and now. Do you or do you not vote yes to this plan to go to Glathen?"

A round of various ayes echoed around the room, the nobleman's last.

"All opposed?"

Leopol glared, and Bella would've found it adorable if the tension wasn't so awkward.

Eirwyn sighed. "Thank you all. As you know from our letters, the ball tonight is a momentous occasion. Bella, Leopol, will you explain about the transformation process and how it's going to work tonight?"

Bella hesitated, her ghost-light form flickering slightly in the low hearth glow. Every eye was on her, judging and measuring. She was used to rowdy drunks and back-alley deals, not diplomats and drakin nobility. She lifted her chin anyway.

"This cure wasn't built on raw power or blood magic—it was built from notes, careful rituals, and practices most scholars forgot existed. It's not perfect, but it's working. And tonight, our people get to choose the life they want. We'll protect them either way."

Bella took a deep breath and launched into an explanation of how the ritual would work and the timeline of the night.

"It's not an easy transformation, but hopefully the Ashplum Gold will allow the body and soul to relax enough to accept the trigger to change," she said.

Excited chatter—and one or two groans—echoed from the table at the mention of the potent ale. Her father looked delighted, his grin mischievously wide.

Leopol, frustration now forgotten, beamed with pride. "Bella's brilliant. For all my knowledge, she was the one who found the solution."

Eirwyn smiled. "Tomorrow, the servants will turn the ballroom into a makeshift hospital for all who take part in the ritual."

Bella continued, "Gods willing, everyone will transition within the next two or three days."

Ashur nodded. "Lailant the Seer and Cerci will stay here to continue supporting the transformations."

"With Ashur in charge of defenses and Hartsgrove, Leopol, Bella, Scarlet, Wulfric, Eirwyn, and I will leave for Glathen." Knox cleared his throat, pushing back his goblet. "Now enough work. Tonight, we have one mission. Show the people we're united. Let them believe in the change that's coming. If we fracture here, Glathen will see it, and they'll use it."

Eirwyn nodded. "The ballroom doors open in thirty minutes. Let's give them something to believe in."

Bella looked around the table, lingering on the doubters, then on her friends—her allies, her family—those who had bled beside her, cursed and bound.

Tavern keeper. Healer. Spirit. Queen.

Leopol took her hand and kissed her palm, a soft smile of concern on his face.

She smiled back and nodded. "That went better than I expected."

He chuckled and together, they rose from the table and followed the others toward the ballroom.

Leopol escorted Bella through the castle to the ballroom. Servants bustled around, and they checked with the head butler about the Ashplum Gold and the mocktail. They had meticulously worked the correct runes and sigils onto twelve cups while Knox and Lailant had grown a few more of the golden magical apples. They'd cured them in the full moon last night, and tonight was the night.

It already felt like pure chaos.

This section was on a raised dais and roped off with six guards. They wanted to record every person's curse, their name, and their side effects before administering the dosage and saying the spell together. They'd work in small groups, in full view of everyone else in the ballroom, until all who wanted to change had participated.

Cerci stopped beside them as he and Bella checked each of the cups. "Do you two need anything?"

Bella shook her head and checked another cup. "No, we're fine. Thank you though. I'll be glad when this is all over."

Cerci smiled. "You've accomplished a lot in a short amount of time. It's quite impressive." The demigoddess had trained them both the past month, and he'd even had several good conversations about his memories over the past thousand years. Some of the events he'd heard about that she'd been part of and vice versa.

Bella blushed, the color quite captivating with her

sparkling yellow dress with the red trim. "Oh, no need for flattery."

"It's not flattery," Cerci said, her eyes piercing in a familiar way. "Not only about the ritual preparations, but your tattoos have healed and the portal training is progressing nicely. I always teach at least one person when I find myself in a new place, but you two?"

They paused their work with the cups to look at the demigoddess. "You're stronger than you give yourselves credit for, and much stronger together. You haven't opened any unintended rifts in four days."

Leopol growled. "We're running out of time. The rose bloomed this morning."

Bella's flush faded and her expression turned grim. They hadn't really talked about the rose. It just sat in Bella's bedroom now, a nightly reminder of the ticking timer they were working against.

Cerci shrugged. "It *is* your tether. The stronger your magic, the more dangerous it becomes. If you push too far—whether a portal or an emotional surge—you might rip yourself apart one petal at a time."

Silence fell between them, and fear spiked through him. He growled, taking Bella's hand. "Don't worry about that for now. We're here together, and that's what matters."

Ashur called for Cerci, and she went to him. They were so open together and obviously in love.

He looked at Bella as she bent over the cups again. He'd seen countless people fall in love over the years but hadn't ever thought it'd happen to him.

Not after failing his king. Not after centuries asleep, buried in stone and regret. He'd expected duty, vengeance, maybe a second chance at fixing his mistakes, but not her. She was completely unexpected.

She moved down the line of goblets with a concentration that stole his breath. She was precise, determined, unshaken by politics or prophecy—equal parts storm and salve, queen and tavern keeper—and it terrified him how much he wanted to protect her from everything. Even from herself.

He stepped in behind her, not quite touching, just close enough to share her space. Her ghost-light form shimmered faintly in the golden glow of the ballroom sconces, soft but steady.

What happens if I lose her?

The thought rose unbidden and lodged like a shard behind his ribs. The rose was blooming. Cerci's warnings echoed in his mind. Petal by petal, Bella might vanish.

And if she did—he didn't think he'd survive being alone again, not when the world had just started to feel whole.

He reached for the next goblet to check, the red trim of her dress sleeve brushing against his wrist, and every muscle in his body tensed.

Don't touch her. Not here. Not now. Not when one wrong kiss might tear the floor out from under them.

But gods, he wanted to.

Her fingers lingered on the rim of a cup, her profile bathed in the golden light. Her hair had been pinned up in some delicate twist, but a few loose strands had fallen near her neck. He stared at them a moment too long.

He stepped in closer—not touching, just near enough that the heat of her brushed against him like a memory.

He reached forward and straightened the goblet she'd just checked. It didn't need it, but his hands needed something to do.

"What are you doing? I already checked that one," she said, frowning as she concentrated.

"I know, I trust you," he said quietly, not because she needed reassurance, but because he did. "I just wanted an excuse to be close to you."

"Leopol," she murmured without looking.

She'd felt it too. Her body shuddered, and he silently begged her to look at him. She checked the next goblet, and he barely held back a curse.

His claws curled at his sides. He was going to break. If he had to watch her bend forward one more time, brushing past him with that curve of her hips in that damned dress—

He shifted behind her, barely grazing her hip with the back of his hand. Her breath hitched, and a throb of magic pulsed between them. It didn't create a rift or portal, and that was progress. He felt ready to explode from his need for her.

She reached behind her and brushed her fingers over his knuckles at her waist. The feather-light touch was just enough to acknowledge what hung in the air.

Just enough to promise: *Later.*

He exhaled slowly, trying not to imagine what *later* might look like. He'd asked Cerci every other day if they were strong enough with the protective anti-portal dome to mate again, but she'd just cryptically told him—repeatedly, every damn time—that he had to weigh the risks and decide for themselves if they were ready.

Fucking demigoddess couldn't even own up to cock-blocking him. Between the dome and the tattoos, they should be fine, right?

His claws bit into her hip, the feel of the lacy fabric scraping his skin.

When her eyes finally cut to him, one brow lifted slightly, she didn't move away. Didn't shy from the energy simmering between them like an unspoken promise.

Instead, she licked her lips.

He bent his gaze to taste, unable to stay away any longer...

Then the heavy doors at the far end of the ballroom groaned open, and the villagers stepped in, one by one. Bella placed a hand on his chest, and they both sighed in disappointment as they turned to see the crowd move in.

The villagers entered, hesitant at first. A wave of fur and feathers, scales and stone. Some limped. Some leaned on canes. Some carried small bundles wrapped in blankets—cursed infants, perhaps. All walked forward with the same expression of hope and excitement.

Bella straightened her shoulders and stepped off the dais to greet them. Before she moved too far, she looked over her shoulder and gave him one last look—equal parts queen and lover.

"Will you—stay beside me," she murmured, a flash of vulnerability flickering across her face so fast he almost missed it.

He was already hers, body, soul, and every aching breath. "Not even death can keep me from you, Bellavore."

Her eyes softened, then she squared her shoulders and faced the growing crowd.

"Then let the ritual begin."

Chapter Thirty-Seven

The ballroom shimmered beneath golden light, every sconce and crystal reflecting the warm glow of possibility. Musicians played softly in the corner, their songs weaving beneath the hum of voices. The terrace doors were shut tight against the icy night, but between the firelight and the finger foods on linen-draped tables, the guests were warm, laughing, and full of cautious hope.

"You're doing such a great job," Leopol murmured with a kiss to her temple, his hand warm on the small of her back. The contact was a balm–but also a reminder of how tightly wound she was. "Just one group left. Then we can mingle and dance."

Bella sighed and nodded, leaning into his slightly for support. Her cheeks ached from smiling for hours, but she forced another one for the sake of the crowd. She could rest later. They needed hope now.

Leopol stood tall beside Bella as the last family–mother and daughter, both part-spinning wheels and soft-eyed–

raised their cups. Four others stood next to them, each taking a rune-covered cup carefully off the table.

"Ready for the ritual?" Bella asked, schooling her expression to friendly openness. "Repeat after me..."

She led them in the spell, activating the runes on their cups, then the group drank together. When they lowered their cups, a few smacked their lips.

"That's it?" the mother asked, uncertain and worried.

"That's it for now," Bella said gently, tucking a strand of hair behind her ear. "You'll feel the change begin over the next day. It's not instant, but you'll feel out of sorts. When you come back tomorrow night, we'll help you through the hardest part of the transformation." Her voice carried no pomp, just honest reassurance.

The little girl clutched her mother's hand but stared at Leopol, eyes wide. "Are you gonna transform too?"

Leopol crouched down, grinning. "No, little spark. This is just my regular face." He crossed his eyes and stuck out his tongue. "Terribly ugly, isn't it? No ritual will help this."

The girl giggled, a bright bubble of joy that echoed around them.

Bella smiled, warmth tightening her chest. He was good with children. So naturally good, as if he'd done it a thousand times. A pang of longing bloomed sharp and quiet beneath her ribs. He'd be a good father—of that she had no doubt—but the world wasn't ready for dreams like that yet. Not with the rose blooming and death whispering at the edges of every spell.

The family bowed their heads in thanks, murmured blessings to them both, and then slipped off the dais to rejoin the gathering.

"I wonder if those who chose not to take the ritual will

choose to remain as they are forever," Bella said softly, scanning the records on the clipboard on the table. "A few said they're waiting for the next moon, but there weren't as many as I expected tonight."

"Choice is important," Leopol murmured. "It makes the healing real. And many of the cursed are still in the outlying villages—we'll have more full moons to come."

Bella nodded, eyes following the housekeeper organizing the used goblets. The clink of crystal against wood was oddly grounding.

"We've done all we can for tonight," Leopol said gently. "Are you ready to join the celebration?"

She wasn't sure she was. But she took a deep breath and stepped forward anyway.

A young man—Bella vaguely remembered him as the tailor's apprentice—stepped forward. "Sir Leopol, your new trousers are ready. Master Thomar said he'll bring them tomorrow."

Leopol nodded, his voice dry. "May they survive longer than the last pair."

Bella barely stifled a laugh, but the humor was short-lived. The baker's assistant leaned toward her next. "Is it true, Your Highness? That you and your da might open a tavern in the village?"

Bella blinked in surprise. Her heart stuttered at the idea—something as normal as opening a tavern still felt so far away. "We... hadn't talked about that, no."

"The queen doesn't have time," Leopol said, tone light but assured. "She'll be ruling Busparia after the wizard is dealt with, and Wulfric's leading the Growlers."

Her steps faltered.

Queen. Again, so easily spoken. As if her path was already set in stone.

The word wrapped around her neck like a too-tight ribbon. Choices were important, and it felt like she had so few.

"Oh, well if King Knox and Queen Eirwyn agree, I might open one myself then. Would love the recipe for your ale, if you're willing to share it." The baker smiled, finishing off a cup.

Bella laughed and shook her head. "Perhaps. Be careful not to drink too much though."

The baker grinned the open, lopsided, tipsy grin she was so familiar with at the tavern. "Aye, might be too late for that, lassie."

Bella giggled as Leopol tucked her arm into the crook of his elbow, and they made their way around the edge of the ballroom. They wove through dancers and chatter until they found Scarlet and Wulfric near a decorative pillar wrapped in moonvine.

Both wore matching green shirts and black, formal outerwear—Wulfric in a sharp dinner jacket, Scarlet in a red leather vest that complemented the braided crown of her hair. Her antlers gleamed, delicate and strong, and her wolf tail twitched as she laughed at something Wulfric murmured.

Wulfric shook Leopol's hand firmly, then nodded to Bella. "You look... radiant."

Bella smiled. She wished she could throw her arms around his solid shoulders like she used to. She still didn't know how to touch people. Either they passed right through her, or magic sparked, threatening a portal.

Leopol leaned toward her. "Will you be alright with your father for a bit?"

She nodded, grateful for the space since that queen comment. He disappeared toward the hallway, slipping through the crowd with the grace of someone who belonged both in every shadow and spotlight. Bella wished she felt that certain—like her place in this new world was more than borrowed light.

Scarlet smirked. "He's probably going to put out fires with the servants."

Wulfric grunted in agreement. "He's good at that, at taking care of what needs taking care of." He turned wolf-sharp eyes on her. "Including you, little girl."

Bella's cheeks flushed, but she didn't deny it. Instead, she turned to Scarlet.

"I noticed you didn't take the ritual to end the curse. I thought that's what you wanted?"

Scarlet's shoulders rose nearly to her ears, her rabbit's nose twitching.

For a breath, Bella feared she'd offended her—but then Scarlet glanced at Wulfric, and something shifted. The wariness faded, replaced with a steady warmth built on love and trust, a bond forged in fire and long nights and countless battles.

Scarlet arched a brow. "Eh, I think I'm about all trans-formed out for a while. Between the reversed Growler ritual and the fated mate bond changes, I'm actually alright with who I am now."

"I'm happy for you then. If you ever want to try it, you can always change your mind later," Bella said slowly, glancing at her father. He just shrugged, but the pride and affection on his face spoke volumes.

Leopol strolled through the crowd, his sharp-toothed grin clearly visible over the heads of the others. He stopped to talk with a few of the villagers here and there before making his way to her side.

Her tension eased the moment he drew near. What kind

of future could they really have? She was afraid to hope that they'd succeed against the wizard. Her rose had fucking *bloomed* today. If the wizard was right, when the last petal fell, so would she.

Each beat of the music felt like a ticking clock. When it struck midnight and the last petal fell, she felt like she'd go straight to the hells.

Lailant's beady gaze caught hers across the ballroom, the old woman standing alone in the shadows of a pillar. She'd looked at the rose earlier and had declared that it'd take at least a week for all the petals to fall.

She had one week left on this plane, and Leopol was talking about ruling Busparia, perhaps even together, if Knox was to be believed?

She sighed, her grip tightening on her skirt as Leopol stopped beside her. His warm hand on her lower back was reassuring, but he frowned as he leaned close.

"Are you alright?" he asked.

She pasted on a fake smile and nodded. "Yes, just tired. Nothing to worry about."

The music shifted again—brighter, fuller before the song came to an end. Then Eirwyn and Knox stepped onto the dais that she'd occupied most of the night. Knox raised his goblet, tapping against the side with a green claw.

When the crowd paused, Eirwyn said clearly, "We're so thankful to have our friends and family here tonight to celebrate the start of a new era. Tonight, we celebrate the hope for a brighter future. Thanks to Queen Bellatrix of Busparia, we have an antidote to the curse, a ritual spell that will bring forth transformations for our people."

"To Queen Bella," Knox announced.

The crowd's cheers drowned out the few remaining

grumbles, and Bella froze. Her breath caught, her stomach fluttering. The noise of clapping rose like a tide around her.

It wasn't the cold sneers of court from her time with Gastone. Those who stared at her now were smiling politely, but optimistic, not judging but hopeful. They weren't calculating or malicious like her engagement ball or the angry glares from nobles from her wedding ball. These gazes were... warm, trusting, and welcoming.

She wasn't born to be queen, but many of them looked at her like they had in the tavern, especially the ones she'd talked one on one with tonight or over the past month. Tonight, they looked at her with relief, like they were glad someone had done something to fix this damn curse.

She had done that. Her and Leopol, together, had solved this problem. She stood a little taller and nodded her head regally as the crowd clapped. Perhaps they could rule Busparia and provide a better future for their people.

When the noise died down, Eirwyn said, "After the transformations, we go to Glathen to secure the treaty."

"And defeat the wizard Hanzel who released this curse, the daemons, and the eternal winter," Knox said grimly.

The crowd whispered, the hopeful faces reverting to worry until Eirwyn's voice rose above them. "To spring, and a new year, new possibilities, and new friendships."

"Here, here," the crowd echoed. Then someone else in the crowd added, "To the death of the wizard!"

"Here, here," bounced off the walls once more.

Bella's heart raced. If the wizard was defeated—in her body—did that mean she wouldn't be getting it back? Did she even want that hideous body? He'd changed her, made her a monster.

She looked up at Leopol, who smiled down at her reassuringly. If that's what it took to stay beside him, it'd be worth the effort. The thought took her by surprise.

Knox and Eirwyn joined their small circle after the toasts, both grinning. After the initial excited conversations, Eirwyn beamed at Leopol.

"I'm so glad we had a big party for this. It was a great idea, Leopol."

"Of course it was a good idea. All of my ideas are great," he said with a grin and a wink. Their little group chuckled, but Eirwyn leaned closer to Bella and tried to take her hand.

Well, she tried to, but her hand passed right through. Bella reached down and grasped Leopol's instead, but Eirwyn powered ahead as usual.

"I love these balls and parties. Compared to those in the palaces in Busparia, these are so much more... I don't know how to describe it..." Eirwyn frowned, her hand going over the wide skirts of her formal red and blue gown.

She'd had it custom made so that she could carry her egg against her lower back, but the cut of the dress didn't make her look pregnant at all. Form fitted in the front, the material draped over a bustle. Draped from her shoulders lay a long train of material that fell to the floor, like a cape without the hood that only went from shoulder to shoulder in the back.

Wulfric looked around. "It feels more like a payday weekend at the tavern than a ball at a palace."

Scarlet pointed a dagger—when had she brought it out—and said, "Exactly what I was thinking."

In a blink, the dagger was gone, hidden away on the Scarlet's body somewhere.

"That's what's different, isn't it?" Bella said to Eirwyn, voice barely above the music.

Eirwyn nodded. "It took time to earn their trust. Mostly it was face-to-face visits to each of them in the village. But the more they saw me bleed, laugh, and cry, the less they saw me as royalty. Then I just became Eirwyn, their beloved queen."

Bella laughed, envy filling her. Her friend had found her place in the world, and it had a bright future.

Bella watched villagers sway to the music, fingers touching, cups clinking, laughter blooming in corners. The laughter faded. She wasn't so certain there was a bright future for her at all.

"If I live through this," she said quietly, "and take up the mantle of queen... I want this kind of rule. I won't be the palace's puppet again."

Eirwyn's look was full of emotion. "You're in charge of your own destiny now, Bella. When this is all over and you're back in Busparia as queen, you can make the changes you always talked about."

Bella's breath caught in her chest. Wasn't that why she'd married Gastone in the first place? She wanted to do good in the world and help her people. Perhaps Eirwyn was right. Perhaps this was her chance to make the changes she'd always wanted.

But first, they had to defeat a wizard and somehow deal with the blooming rose. Stop the god of death from coming back to the world.

She scoffed in her head. No big deal, right?

Over the next few hours, the ballroom lights dimmed to a soft golden hush, casting shadows like candle smoke across the polished floor. The music changed—slower, deeper, as if the melody itself carried a memory.

Many of those who had brought their children carried them to the courtyard, where wagons waited to take them back to the village. The ballroom wasn't even half-full now, and Bella was tired yet strangely wide awake. The image of the rose in full bloom was ever in the back of her mind.

Leopol stepped in front of her, his silhouette tall and sharp-edged in the glow, his clawed hand outstretched in invitation.

"May I have this dance, my queen?" His voice was velvet-dipped thunder, and her stomach fluttered.

She hesitated only long enough to feel the beat of her own heart, then placed her ghost-light fingers in his hand. "Of course."

They moved to the center of the ballroom as others stepped aside, giving them space. All around them, the world melted into a golden blur.

Leopol had learned the dance—clearly practiced the more modern style. His steps were steady, confident, his strength reined in just enough to guide without overwhelming. He held her as though she were solid, real, irreplaceable.

Her body remembered the rhythm even if her heart raced out of time. Each step was deliberate, every turn an echo of something deeper.

When he spun her beneath his arm, her translucent skirts flared like flame. Their eyes locked mid-twirl—and something inside her stilled.

Everything else fell away. All the worries about Hanzel, the transformations, and the rose blooming just disappeared.

He *saw* her. Not the spirit. Not the rose-tethered queen. Just *Bella*.

That moment was more powerful than fate. It was a promise, a choice, and a hunger wrapped in reverence that promised a future that she'd dared not dream of for so long.

The music swelled as she danced back into the safety of his arms, as if the very world exhaled in relief.

They danced until the last note shimmered into silence. And when it did, the applause around them felt like wind in the trees—distant, unimportant.

Only he mattered. With him, in this moment, she felt like they actually could defeat Hanzel, get her body back, and rule Busparia together.

Chapter Thirty-Eight

Bella stared up at him in the middle of the dance floor, his arm locked around her back and pressing them flush together from thigh to stomach. He held her hand to their chests, just over their hearts, and his Orythium scar glowed faintly.

The success of the villagers taking the transformation ritual, with a little assistance of the ale, let her relax further into the moment. The press of his body against hers amplified the simmering desire that had been building since their last time together a month ago.

Leopol's eyes were dark with need, not just lust but longing—the kind that felt carved into her soul. She licked her lips, panting from the dance or from him, she wasn't sure which.

"I—I need some fresh air," she whispered.

He growled, his hands shaking with restraint, but nodded without saying a word.

He led her out into the cold hush of the gardens, where moonlight painted the hedgerows in silver and the stars scattered above like spells waiting to be spoken. The echo of music followed them faintly through the open terrace doors before fading altogether.

Their steps slowed near the eastern fountain–frozen and ringed with frost-dusted petals. Winter still lingered in the soil, but spring should be well under way.

Not even the reminder of the wizard and his winter daemons could pull her from this moment, though.

Leopol turned to her. His hand lifted, palm glowing with familiar magic. With a careful breath, he traced the sigils Cerci had taught them in the air.

The pulse of magic warmed her ankle where he'd tattooed the rune sigil combination under Cerci's tutelage. Cerci had administered the matching one on his wrist.

They'd practiced daily for a month–how to create the protective dome that kept them from portal hopping when they kissed or fooled around. Too often, their passion was so great that the protective dome splintered and cracked.

But she wanted to kiss him now. At the end of this long, long night, she wanted him to hold her, kiss her, and dream of a future with him.

A *hum* filled the air–low, resonant, like a chord stuck in her chest.

A dome shimmered into being, encasing them in a half-sphere of quiet light. The garden outside dulled to watercolor and snow. Inside, the air warmed, the breeze stilled.

It was their cocoon of safety–one they'd been escaping to more and more with every passing day.

Since binding their sigil tattoos to stabilize the portal magic, the dome had held steady: warm and whole each time they tested it.

They'd pushed the boundaries of what their magic

could hold, stretching and strengthening it like a muscle. And now, it shimmered around them—strong as a vow.

Bella turned to him, heart in her throat. "I—I want to kiss you, but I'm afraid it'll quickly lead to more."

"I'm alright with more if you are," he said, his eyebrow arching slightly.

"I don't doubt it, but I want this so badly it scares me. And if we fail—if the dome cracks—I could vanish before I get to feel you again."

He didn't smile. Just stepped closer and lifted her hand to his chest, anchoring her. "We won't fail. When will you see that when we're together, we're unbreakable."

Her voice wavered. "Our joining could shake the rose so much the petals fall and... poof. I'm gone. What then?"

He growled and yanked her into his arms, holding her tight with a fierceness that betrayed his own fear. "Then I'll fix it," he said, low and hoarse. "Surely all this knowledge will be good for something."

Her hands curled into his coat. "You'd find me again?"

"In every world, every realm, every time."

"Even if I'm just a wisp of magic?"

He leaned down, brushing his lips to hers. "Then I'll become the wind that carries you."

His lips devoured hers, and magic rippled outward. His tongue tangled with hers—another pulse, stronger this time—but the dome held.

On the third kiss, his body curled around hers. She surged up into him, mouth needy, body aching for more. All the fears—portals, transformations, Glathen, the wizard—fell away, burned to ash in the heat of him.

This kiss wasn't desperate or driven by madness or magic. It was primal—wet, wild, and wholly hers.

He wrapped his arms tighter around her, one hand

buried in her hair, the other resting on her waist as if grounding himself. When they parted, breathless, she reached up and traced the golden rune pulsing at his collarbone.

"I can't just kiss you tonight, Bella," he growled, voice rough with restraint. "I need you. It's been a month. I ache for you."

He kissed his way along her jaw to the soft spot underneath her neck.

She moaned, her eyes fluttering closed. "Oh gods, I've missed you. I didn't know how powerful a simple touch could be until I went months without so much as a hug. Now? I'm addicted to your touch."

He growled and kept kissing down her neck, overwhelming her senses with his need *for her*.

"Thank the gods, it's not just me who feels this way. Simi velkarinth–All of you is mine. You belong with me, for now, for forever, whether in this form or another."

He tugged at the tight bodice of her golden gown–but it didn't yield yet.

She was his, and he was hers. His, hers, his, hers. It pulsed over and over like a drumbeat in her chest. She licked her lips, trembling, as his tongue traced her collarbone, then lower, teasing the edge of her gown.

"Yours?" she gasped as he jerked again, needing some last bit of reassurance.

"Mine," he growled, claws shredding the last of her dress until she was left in nothing but her dancing shoes.

He groaned, raking a hand down his face, his body shaking. "Gods, you're a vision, mibella. I want to savor you, but I–I don't know if I can be slow." His expression was fierce as he jerked out of his dinner jacket.

"I don't want you to," Bella said, cupping her breasts and pinching her nipples.

His growl deepened, and his own shirt ripped as he flung it away. "Damn it, stupid fucking clothes."

She laughed as her hand mimicked his in its downward trajectory. "Too bad you're not still a spirit—you were great at magicking clothes off."

As his hands shoved his pants down, getting stuck on his boots, she cupped her mound, fingers sliding over the wet bundle of nerves that made her toes curl.

"You tease me, luvien dravak. You make me want to shift and take you like a beast."

Her breath caught and her hand paused. "Is that even possible?"

"Oh, it's very possible among mates," he growled, kicking his boots to the side, where they bounced off the dome.

She shivered as his gaze roamed over her body in the soft light. "Do you—want to shift?"

His eyes glowed with an unnatural inner light. "Only if you want me that way," he said, wrapping his hand around his dick and stroking slowly.

She paused, but there was no thinking, no second guessing. Her body knew. It hummed in anticipation.

"I want *all* of you," she said, one hand tugging on her nipple and making her hips sway forward into her hand. "Please, Leopol."

Time seemed to stand still—a moment, a second—then she whispered, "Raelion, take me."

He roared, chest rising with power and glowing golden as he shifted. His form shimmered, expanded—limbs unfurling into white-tipped scales and ancient grace. When he came down on all four claws, wings grazed the top of the dome, yet it still held strong.

Before her stood a radiant, terrifying god-beast—ancient grace and raw desire wrapped in living scale. A beast with one thing on his mind, but his eyes still glowed the same: soft, reverent, hungry for her, his mate.

She shivered and stepped between his front paws, running her hands over the softer scales of his chest. He purred under her, folding his arms and wings to cradle her like a blossom.

"Touch me," he growled, the sound echoing in the dome. Who was she to deny such a simple request? Her hands explored like they had in the cave when they'd first found his body, smoothing over velvety leather-like skin and along tough as diamonds scales.

He shuddered with the glide of her fingers, but only barely shifted from his position. Sitting on his back legs, front arms extended, he was like a lion watching his prey come to him. It sent a shiver up her spine, and she knew how wet she was.

He sucked in a breath with a hiss. "I can smell your arousal, mate. I need to taste you. Please—" His voice caught on the word like it hurt to say it aloud. "Please let me have this."

She stepped out of the heated embrace and backed up, his glowing blue eyes following her every move. He frowned—how did she know he frowned with that elongated dragon face—and lay down on the soft grass. Melted frost from the dome made it slick and wet, and she lifted her knees, bending them as she spread her legs.

Bared before him, he lowered himself onto his front elbows and licked.

The dome around them pulsed with heat and magic, resonating with their shared desire.

His tongue was hot, ridged, and rough like silk-wrapped steel. She gasped, back arching as he explored her with an almost scientific precision—mapping her reactions, learning every sensitive spot. When he pressed the flat of his tongue against her, she moaned. He circled it over and over, driving her too fast toward the brink.

When his long, reptilian tongue pushed its way inside, she gasped and wound her hands around the hard, white and silver-tipped horns that curved up and behind him, anchoring herself against the overwhelming sensations.

His ridged tongue raked over her clit with every thrust inside, making her cry out with need.

Golden light rippled like heat waves, casting everything in an ethereal glow. Her body trembled, caught between pleasure and something deeper—a connection that transcended physical sensation.

The magical dome flickered briefly—a reminder of their precarious connection—but held steady as he set up a rhythm with his tongue. His tongue—hot and impossibly long—went deep, making her back arch, and every slide out bumped along her clit, making her shudder, making her want more, always more.

Unlike his human form, his dragon tongue could reach places that made her entire body tremble as she drew closer and closer.

"Raelion," she whispered, her voice trembling. "I—I need more. All of you. Want to come—on you."

His scaled head lifted slightly, blue eyes burning into her. Before she could blink, he'd gathered her into his arms, and the hollow beneath him radiated comforting heat. She burrowed into him, and—without warning—he launched into the stars with a rush of wind and glowing frost.

The soft watercolor garden fell away.

They flew weightless, like dreamers, moonlight catching the dome of magic that protected them even in the air, preventing them from accidentally triggering another portal.

In that quiet night sky, between stars and snow clouds, she rubbed her body along his chest, his stomach.

His claws were careful with her, and on the next down-draft, his body thrust up—and he slid inside her in one fluid, impossible stroke.

Stars exploded behind her eyes—not from the sky, but from the stretch and fullness of him.

His entry was smooth despite his massive size, her body welcoming him like she'd been made for this moment. When he pulled his wings up, he slid out inch by inch, and she gasped.

Oh gods, those ridges...

Her muscles clamped around him, desperate to keep him inside, wanting to hold him tight and never let go.

His wings pushed down, and he filled her again.

Her body arched as he filled her again, the stretch nearly too much—but she wanted more. The dome flickered, golden light dancing across his scaled shoulders as she gasped, fingers digging in to anchor herself against the intensity of each thrust.

He growled low, a sound that vibrated through her entire being. Not just a physical sensation, but something primal and ancient. His wings beat against the night sky, movements synchronized with his rhythm inside her.

The stars blurred. Wind rushed past them. And still, the

protective dome held—a fragile magical barrier against the vast darkness surrounding them.

Her body trembled at the aching recognition that she belonged here, with him, like this.

She wrapped her legs around his scaled body, feeling every ridge and curve of him, her ankles finding a gap between two scales. She used his own body to thrust up against him, encouraging him and driving herself wild in the process.

"More," she gasped, gripping his scales tight, feeling the beginning quakes deep within her soul.

Magic crackled between them, a living thing sparking with every stroke, every breath.

"Simi dravak. Mine," he growled, the word vibrating through scales and skin as he thrust harder, deeper.

They went higher and higher with every beat of his wings. A tightness hit the entrance to her pussy with every thrust, pressing on her. He grunted, then that tight ball pushed its way inside, making her scream. Her orgasm had built for too long, and that stretch was enough to send her over the edge.

When she came, it was like lightning splitting the sky—brilliant, unexpected, consuming everything in its path. Her magic surged, intertwining with his, creating fractal patterns of light that danced in the night sky. She cried out—pleasure blooming from her soul like spring bursting from frost. This wasn't just release. It was a rebirth into who she was meant to be. His mate, his queen, his... love.

He roared and froze, tucking his wings around them both, and for one weightless moment, they were suspending in mid-air like a sleeping bat.

Then they were falling, the pulsing warmth of his dick flooding her insides as he spasmed, holding her tight, her aftershocks milking him with every pump. She didn't register the fall, too busy locked in the overwhelming feel of him filling her pussy, the intense stretch. She clenched around him, as if her body knew he belonged there.

His purr vibrated through her, a sound both fierce and tender.

The wind rushed around them, cold and crisp, but inside their magical sphere, everything burned with impossible heat. Slowly, as if waking from a dream, the ground became less a wave of darkness. Her gasp echoed inside the magical barrier, mixing with the soft whoosh of his wings.

"Raelion," she said like a prayer, closing her eyes against the dizzying rushing doom.

He shuddered around her, his dick pumping more slowly inside her now. "Huh?" he grunted.

She smiled, feeling sleepy and not even a little bit worried. "Think you can get us safely to the ground? Because we're kind of falling right now."

He stiffened, and she felt his head jerk up, his wings beat once, then catch an updraft. "Oh gods, that could've been bad."

She chuckled softly, snuggling into the warmth of his chest and trying to maintain her grip on his scales. His hands held her safe either way, but she didn't want to tire him.

"Worth it though," she said with a yawn.

"You're mine, Bella. You've always been mine."

She smiled as they glided to the ground, curled together in the dome's light. Her head on his chest and his breath in her hair as he kissed her head reverently, the air around them thick with magic and meaning.

They didn't need to speak to know they'd chosen each other. Whatever came next—they'd face it as one.

Chapter Thirty-Nine

Leopol landed on the castle's highest tower, claws skidding across the flat stone roof as he checked that the dome still shimmered around them. Then he dropped to his knees—shaking, not from depleted magic, but something deeper.

This hadn't just been a knot-her-until-she-passed-out-and-his-legs-shook kind of orgasm.

This had been *everything*. She truly was his.

He felt the bond pulse at the completion of it—not just physical and magical, but woven between their essences, ancient and undeniable. The old gods had made him for this, for her. His mother, perhaps, or one of the Fates. Maybe even Guiana herself.

Green dragons like Knox were bred for fertility—Verdantfangs sowed forests and filled valleys with life.

But Leopol's original dragon construct body had been formed into a Dreamscale.

They were crafted for permanence, no matter that they could walk between realities through the Veil. He really was alive now, bonded and mated forever to the one perfect woman for him.

He eased down onto his side, keeping Bella safe in the warm cradle of his stomach. They were still locked together, his knot anchored deep. It would be hours yet before they separated—but he couldn't sleep. Not when so much needed doing.

If she reclaimed the throne, she'd need more than love and a mate. She'd need leverage, allies, maps and knowledge long buried. He would be her library, her sword, her shield. Whatever she needed, he'd *learn* it, *build* it, *become* it.

He'd failed before—failed Feralt and Analise, failed to stop the wizard, failed to rejoin his body in time to stop the curse from touching Bella at all.

He hadn't gone with Knox and Eirwyn to Glathen. But he'd been *here*, the day the wizard struck down his king and queen, his best friends, his closest family.

That memory still lived in him like a wound. And though remembering cut deep and vivid, he was still grateful to have all of him back. Remembering was a two-edged sword, but he was real, alive, here, whole.

But if he lost Bella, like he lost them?

He brushed a lock of her hair from her face. Her features were soft in sleep, glow-touched by moonlight.

There would be no second chance this time, no hibernating until he could strike again.

He had one week. One week before the last petal fell, and she was gone.

She curled against him, boneless and glowing, and he tucked his wings around them both like a vow. The tattoo on her ankle pulsed softly with shared magic—and something in his chest ached.

He didn't know when it had happened—sometime

between that first day in the quiet garden and the stars tonight—but the truth rang through him now like a bell.

He loved her.

Completely. Quietly. Fiercely. With heart, soul, body, spirit, and mind.

What happens if I lose her?

His jaw clenched. Sharp teeth clicked together, and the dome shimmered in answer.

If the gods or the wizard came to take her, he'd burn the world down and the gods with it.

Later that week, Bella leaned against the worn tavern bar, the wood sticky with age and charm. Laughter and fiddle music floated through the smoky air, but her mind hadn't landed with her. It still flew somewhere between shadows and the clouds they'd left behind.

Today, two dragons and their mates had flown together across the Feral Forest, skimming mountains and secret valleys with an overnight stop at the dwarven settlement, before circling down into Glathen's border town.

They'd landed at this trading post just past the forest as the sun disappeared over the horizon. It was a crooked village, where dirt paths crisscrossed between timber buildings and where the inn smelled like yeast and old magic. Scarlet and Wulfric had been waiting with their guard, cloaked in fog and relief.

She caught sight of her father at a corner table, lifting a mug high and waving his newly clawed hand for emphasis as he told the tale of how he'd become a Growler. He exaggerated it, of course, but she wasn't surprised.

His voice carried like it always had, no matter the tale.

Full of smoke and certainty. She'd seen him tell stories like this when she was small, tucked behind the tavern counter with a chipped mug of apple cider.

It was jarring to see it again after ten years of grief. It was beautiful, a relief, but it still hurt. They hadn't buried him after all. Instead, they'd buried the girl who used to sit beneath the counter.

Eirwyn sat near the hearth, conjuring a light show across the rafters while children squealed in delight. Knox and Scarlet flanked the room like silent sentinels—watching, waiting, and weary. Comfortable in their silence as only siblings can be. They drank little. Laughed even less. Just... stood guard.

Five other Growlers were scattered among the three Robins they'd brought—all grizzled veterans with cautious eyes. At first, the Glathenians had kept their distance, hushed and tense. But as the ale flowed, and the music surged, that invisible line began to blur.

Their group of Buspartans, Robins, and Foresters raised their mugs with strangers, former Glathen enemies—even the Growlers who hadn't trusted anyone outside their pack last year joined in. A bawdy song erupted from the center table, and suddenly, voices old and young joined in.

Bella blinked back tears, remembering the normalcy of nights just like this back at her father's Bloomin' Brew tavern.

This was what peace might look like, where the shifters and drakin and humans could all live in harmony.

And yet, she couldn't join in like she had at her own tavern. At Hartsgrove, they'd avoided her because of the curse.

Over the past seven weeks, she'd earned their trust and respect by finally ending the curse, though. She still wasn't sure if it was the ashplum ale or the way the rituals seemed to stabilize when Leopol touched her, but the transformations had gone much smoother when the villagers had returned to the castle the day after the ball.

Leopol's theory was that she'd been separated from her rose when they'd gone through the portal, which had left her weaker than normal when the first four patients had transformed.

Maybe it was a combination of all of it. It didn't really matter though.

The transformations this past week had gone smoother than expected. Too smooth. She felt like the other shoe was about to drop, and it all centered on their trip to Glathen.

Jaq and Gus had tried to take the ritual too, but they remained animated and refused to leave Lailant's side now. Somehow, she'd given them life and now they had latched themselves onto her mentor like she held the answers to the universe.

Now they'd finally made it into Glathen. No one looked at her with hatred. They just... didn't look at all. Not unless she passed too close. Then they flinched and avoided eye contact, creeped out by the spirit in the room.

Even with her father at the center of it all, surrounded by her family and friends... she was still the ghost queen, the one tied to a cursed rose, a ruined city, and a wizard bent on world destruction.

Her father had his ale and his stories. Eirwyn spun lights across the ceiling. Knox and Scarlet sat close, Wulfric nodding along to the beat of some bawdy tune. The Growlers had even started teaching Glathenians the words.

It should've made her heart sing with the fellowship, camaraderie... family.

Instead, it twisted in her ribs like something caged.

She slipped from the room before her emotions cracked too wide.

With the close of the tavern's back door, the laughter faded behind her like smoke. A chilly wind teased her hair, but it had become progressively warmer the further west they'd flown. Glathen had escaped the worst of the winter daemons—unlike Busparia and the Feral Forest. Somewhere nearby, an owl called.

She leaned against the tavern's worn wall and pressed the back of her head to the rough wood. The stars overhead were fractured by the twisted trees leaning in from the Feral Forest's edge. Even the constellations looked wrong from here, rearranged by branches she didn't recognize.

She was coming apart, running out of time. The rose had bloomed, and petals fell every day. Three days lost to transformation rituals. Two days more to reach Glathen. The wizard still marched, according to Scarlet and her father. Maybe he was already knocking at some other border town, past the breaches of Auckwald. She had to actually face him, and the idea of it sent her too close to panic.

She closed her eyes and breathed deeply, trying to get control of her emotions. In her mind's eye, she saw that cursed rose, withered and gasping, shedding its petals like tiny funeral processions. After landing, Leopol had carried it upstairs to their room at the inn. When he'd set it on the side table, another petal had fallen. One by one, her tether to this world unraveling.

The door creaked behind her. She didn't have to turn to know it was him.

Leopol stepped out into the night, boots crunching softly on frost-laced stone. His warmth radiated beside her like a quiet promise, but she didn't lean into it. Not yet, not when she was on the verge of emotional combustion. If she touched him, she'd give in, let him hold her, and cry for the little girl who'd once lived a life untouched by war and curses.

"What's on your mind, Bellavore?" he asked, voice low.

She let the moment stretch, weighing the silence between them. But in the end, she wanted to talk—needed to. Maybe if she said it out loud, the shadows wouldn't pull her under.

"I keep thinking back to before," she murmured softly. "Before I was queen, before the war, my biggest problem was trying to figure out how to keep drunken farmers from fighting in the tavern."

A beat of silence.

"You miss it?" he asked.

She laughed, but it cracked at the edges. "Yes, but it's not like I could go back. That girl doesn't exist anymore. She died with Gastone. Or changed with the curse along with everyone else. Now, they don't need me."

His head tilted, claws gently twisting a strand of her hair. "Bella—"

"My dad, Eirwyn, even Scarlet and Knox. They've all moved on, have their own lives. They laugh like I'm not even here."

Leopol reached up and brushed her hair behind her ear. "That's not death. That's growing up. Becoming something new—like a butterfly coming out of a cocoon."

She leaned into his touch with a bitter sigh. "A butterfly is useless in a war like this. They act like it doesn't matter that I have days before the rose dies and me with it."

He flinched, hand dropping from her cheek as he straightened.

She swallowed, arms wrapping tighter around her waist.

"Maybe that's best, though. All I've done is bring more curses, more danger, more fear. The wizard wouldn't have broken free of the mirror if it wasn't for my easily manipulated mind."

"You don't know that," he growled, crossing his own arms. "You don't know the wizard like I do. I knew Hanzel when he was just a power-hungry novice in the academy. I guest lectured at the hall and answered his questions, saw a bright potential in him... the same bright potential I see in you, Bella."

She snorted and tipped her head back up as if searching for answers among the stars. "Flattery will get you nowhere."

"It's not flattery. It's the truth. You stared down the entire council and didn't flinch. You de-escalated tensions like the queen you are."

She blinked against the tears, the stars blurring overhead. "What if it's not enough? What if we've gone through all this—and we still fail? What if I can't save the world?"

He rested his palm against her chest, above her still heart. "You already have. You've saved me, and you're my entire world. So I'm going to save you too. Don't count petals, Bella. We're not out of time yet."

"And what—think of a future as queen?" she snorted. "I don't know how to be a queen. I had mere weeks of training, and Gastone had me as a puppet on a pedestal the entire time."

He reached for her hands, lacing their fingers. "Then let me help you figure it out. You won't have to make any decisions alone. I'll be there. Every step. As your king."

She stiffened, and he noticed, his thumb stilling.

"I didn't ask for a king," she whispered. "I didn't ask for a crown either."

The air between them grew heavy with emotion, and his hand fell away, leaving her bereft of his touch. But she wouldn't—couldn't—reach for him, no matter that she wanted to cling to him with every second she had left on this world.

He took a shaky step back, eyes shadowed with hurt. "So you're just going to let the rose finish the job and disappear into the hells?" he asked, the anger in his voice making her tense.

She straightened her shoulders. "Right now, I'm holding everything together with spit and stubbornness, and when the last petal falls..."

"I'll catch you," he said. "Even if the world breaks, I'll save you and break your tether to the rose. Our mate bond is strengthening every day, and the tether to the rose is weakening. Can you see it?"

Her breath hitched, her eyes wide. "Is that why the thread of magic is fainter? I thought it was because the rose was dying."

He hugged her tight. "As long as we're together, it'll be alright."

"I'm afraid to hope, Leopol. I want to believe the worst is behind us, but it's not. The last petal is days away from falling. Somehow, we have to convince the king of Glathen to help us defeat the wizard. And I'm still a spirit."

"You're more alive than anyone I've ever known," he growled, frustration clear in his voice as he crossed his arms. "I won't consider an outcome where you go to the hells and I'm still here on Celawyn."

Bella's voice trembled with a new fear. "If I die... you can't follow me. I won't let you."

Leopol's hands dropped, forming fists at his sides. "Why not? Where you go, I go. My place is at your side, whether in life or death."

The words sent a chill through her soul. Somehow, she had to convince him to *live*, even if she couldn't.

"If I die, you'll need to live for me," she said. He made a noise—not a gasp of outrage, but close enough—and she placed a hand over the glowing scar on his chest, faintly visible under his shirt.

"No talking like that. We're going to stop the wizard and save the people, you included. Your tether to the rose will dissolve when the wizard dies. It's the only outcome I'll accept. I won't fail again and lose you," his voice turned gravelly as it deepened with emotion.

She shook her head. "We don't know what the future brings. Maybe I'll still vanish. Maybe I'll survive and finally get to live a life of my own."

He said, softly, "A life with me by your side?"

Silence stretched between them, but she couldn't talk past the knot in her throat. She didn't know how to answer. Did she want to live a happily ever after with him, changing Busparia into the nation she'd always dreamed it could be?

Yes, but she wasn't stupid or naïve. At least, not anymore. She had grown up since her world had fallen apart last year.

He stepped forward, taking both her hands in his. He held them to his heart and took a deep, shaky breath. "Bellakari, know this. You're not just my mate. You're my heart, my world, my treasure, my universe. Without you, I am nothing."

She opened her mouth to argue, to convince him to live without her, but he placed a finger against her lips. The tears that tracked silently down her cheeks were ignored by both of them.

"Sh, I'm not done. I know you're scared. I am too, but

we're in this together. Have faith. All will be as the fates will it."

He swallowed, his shoulders relaxing slightly. "And since the woman I called mother is one of the fates..." His smile was wobbly as he shrugged. "Since I'm alive now, I assume she wants grandbabies."

A chuckle bubbled up from his words, and she wiped her tears away, trying to compose herself. Thinking of babies made her think back to when they soared through the skies, locked together as one.

She shook her head sadly. "We make love like it will save us, but what if it just makes failing harder? I don't want to be your weakness, Leopol."

Leopol's thumb gently wiped away a stray tear. "Our bond makes us stronger. Alone, I fail–I'm weak. But with you, I fight harder. You're my reason, Bella. My reason to keep going, to never give up, to chase every solution until your dreams become real. Fight with me, *luin*. Fight for us."

"Luin? Sounds like luvien," she said.

His eyes burned bright as he said softly, "They mean the same. Love."

She sucked in a breath, but he didn't say anything else. Just pulled her into his arms slowly. There was no heat, no hunger, just comfort and partnership. Just strength and silence and the promise of someone who wouldn't walk away when things got tough, who wouldn't turn on her or accuse her of being the reason it all went to shit.

Have faith, he'd said. She sighed and hugged him tighter, not sure how to do that when she worried so much.

She wanted to believe him. She really did, but faith was hard when time was running out.

Chapter Forty

The weight of a thousand gazes pressed against Leopol's hide as he moved through the cobbled streets of Glathen, claws clinking against stone. The rose—half-wilted and fragile—rested in a satchel strapped across Leopol's back, nestled just behind where Bella sat. No petals had fallen yet today, even with their constant travel.

Bella's hands flexed nervously on the scales between his shoulder blades... Every cheer seemed to make her flinch, like she didn't trust the crowd—or the welcome. She was tense, her gaze flicking here and there—chin tipped up regally, yes, but not relaxed. Not safe either.

He scanned the crowd.

A shivering buzz of magic flared two rooftops down—a flare ward, harmless, but enough to trigger his instincts. He tracked its source to a nervous-looking adolescent in mage robes, who quickly ducked behind a building. No threats yet. Still, Leopol kept his wings loosely extended to the edges of the street, keeping the growing crowd at bay.

Leopol was ready to protect his queen, a shadow large enough to shield her from arrows, spells, or stares.

Knox walked just ahead of him, larger than usual in his biggest green-dragon form, his scales darkened in the afternoon light and shoulders nearly reaching the walkways on either side of the street. Mist curled from his nostrils in thin green tendrils, keeping the crowd away. They startled every time Knox so much as exhaled. He prowled down the street, Eirwyn on his back, like he was ready to fly her and the hidden egg somewhere safer.

His cousin wasn't made for cities, Leopol knew. Raised in the wilds of the Feral Forest, Knox tensed at every cheer like it was a battle cry.

Leopol paced himself to match Knox's wariness, keeping one eye on his cousin and the other on the crowd. Growlers and human Robins marched before and behind them, forming a cordon of muscle and magic. The citizens of Glathen had turned out in full force, crowding balconies and steps, craning for a glimpse of the draconic spectacle.

As they went through the castle gates, trumpets sounded.

A balcony on the castle's second floor unfurled its golden banners as a figure prowled forward on four legs. The winged lion, forged of golden scales instead of fur, paused and furled its wings, its eyes gleaming with ancient fire.

One roar cracked the air like a thunderclap, silencing the crowd in an instant.

Neither lion nor dragon, this descendant of his uncle Griffion still retained more of their shared features than Eirwyn did of her dragon ancestor. Leopol's theory was that the chimera-dragon offspring retained the genes for shifting longer.

Then he shifted into a tall, willowy man with gray hair, a stately beard, and beady eyes. The king of Glathen lifted his hands and smiled, his ceremonial robes moving slightly in the breeze.

Leopol stilled, his breath catching at the resemblance to his uncle. The older man moved like a seasoned performer—broad gestures, artificial warmth in his voice.

Leopol caught the subtle tremor in the king's hand, the way his smile didn't quite reach his eyes. Politics, he knew, were never as smooth as they appeared. Knox snorted a small puff of green gas, and it sank to the cobblestones before it dissipated.

The king's gaze flickered momentarily to Knox, then back to Leopol and Bella. "Distinguished travelers," he proclaimed, "Glathen welcomes you with open arms."

He welcomed them with polished fanfare and overly poetic declarations of peace, droning on about how glad they were for the war to be at an end.

Beside him, Knox rumbled low—a sound barely audible but vibrating with warning. Dragons understood subterfuge better than most. This welcome rang hollow.

Bella's fingers flexed tighter against his scales, her body going still with sudden wariness.

The king's speech continued, each word calculated, each gesture rehearsed. But beneath the pageantry, Leopol detected a tremor. Not of fear, but of calculation.

Knox shifted restlessly, green mist thickening around his shoulders. Eirwyn placed a hand on his neck, a restraining touch that spoke volumes about their bond and her understanding of his wild nature.

Finally, the king welcomed them inside, and the crowd roared behind them, clapping in excitement.

Behind his neck, Bella leaned forward, preparing to dismount.

"He acts just like Gastone did. I don't trust him," she whispered before sliding to the ground. His hand hovered, ready to catch her or help her down, but she stood on both feet and tipped her chin up.

His queen was ready for this fight, even if she doubted herself. He didn't respond, just lowered his head slightly in what looked like deference but was really sizing them up.

The king's advisors watched from alcoves, their eyes darting between Bella and the dragons with a mixture of fascination and wariness.

He stepped back and let the change ripple over him—scales softening into leathery skin, wings folding into his shoulders, bones shifting with a controlled snap of power. In seconds, Leopol stood in his hybrid form, watchful and battle-ready.

Wulfric stepped forward, golden eyes glowing, black hair raised with alert tension. "I'll take the backpack and the rose," he said. "You protect your queen."

Leopol swallowed hard as the Growler carefully lifted the satchel from his back and slung it over his own. It was a small moment—but coming from her father, it felt like being handed the honor of a lifetime.

Bella's gaze flicked to the pack, then to Wulfric—just for a second. A quiet acknowledgment passed between them, trust deep and absolute. She knew exactly where the rose was, hidden safely inside the bag Leopol had carried, and she trusted her father to guard it.

He stretched his shoulders before offering Bella his arm. Arm in arm, they swept forward, flanked by scaled might and the silent support of their family.

He'd faced kings, warlords, and gods—but this time, the

stakes were different. He wasn't just guarding a throne. He was guarding her.

A tall woman in silver-trimmed robes stepped forward, her posture rigid. "His Majesty will receive you in the throne room. Follow me," she announced, her accent crisp and western.

Her eyes flickered to Knox, then back to Bella, measuring and calculating before she turned on her heel and led them deeper into the castle. The castle's interior echoed with marble and gold, every surface polished to reflect artificial grandeur.

Bella's chin lifted slightly with each measured step—her posture rigid despite the tension coiling through her muscles. She moved like water—fluid, controlled, dangerous.

Leopol's heart thudded with anticipation, all of his years at court culminating in this diplomatic battle. Bella's warning was completely justified. It was good to be cautious because he had to protect them all. He would not fail this time.

Inside the castle, the air changed, and Eirwyn wrinkled her nose. The scent of polished floors and politics hit her as soon as she stepped through the arched doors.

Knox, now his normal hybrid self, leaned closer to murmur, "Are you alright?"

"All is well," she said, patting his arm. "Ready to win over a kingdom?"

"The sooner it's done, the sooner we go home," he muttered.

She chuckled. "That's the spirit."

The egg shifted in the special pocket sewn into the

bustle of her dress—a gentle pulse of reassurance or warning, she couldn't tell. The cape-like fabric fell from her shoulders, hiding the egg pouch and giving her a regal air that she quite liked.

The deference the servants were giving them as they walked through the castle had already improved from her time here last year. It gave her hope that they'd take her seriously this time...

She knew this court. She'd walked these halls, won smiles from nobles—and almost won a treaty, if the Buspartan Chancellor hadn't shut her down.

The throne room doors opened, and they stepped through, Leopol and Bella flanking to her left and Scarlet and Wulfric to their right. The room was more than big enough for their entire party to walk shoulder by shoulder, but the other Growlers and Robins pulled up the rear, silent and watchful.

This place reeks of secrets, Knox sent into her mind via their mate bond.

Eirwyn's smile grew wider, sending back, *I know. Don't be fooled by the polished floors. Their nation was built on the backs of pirates and corsairs. They're scrappy—but vicious.*

Why did I let you come here? Knox grumbled, a small green tendril of smoke sinking from his nose. *You should've stayed home, safe and sound.*

Eirwyn pinched his arm as they walked, reminding him without words that he wouldn't be going anywhere without her. It was sweet of him to be so protective. Sure he grumbled and worried, but he didn't try to keep her from doing her job. It was refreshing after how Gastone had treated her her entire life.

The bright stained-glass windows cast light on the opulent ceremonial armor of the guards on the edges of the room. Diplomats cloaked in Glathen's deep green and gold and nobles in varying colors of rich fabrics crowded near the pillars around the room. Last year, she'd been offered little more than polite smiles and perfumed platitudes from them, even at the ball they'd held in her honor.

But this time—

"Princess Eirwyn!" Prince Eryk strode forward, arms wide. He was barely older than her, jaw neatly trimmed, eyes sharp but welcoming.

Knox stiffened as the man folded her into a genuine hug. "Queen Eirwyn," Knox growled.

"Oof," Eirwyn said in surprise. "Well, it's good to see you too, Prince Eryk."

She met Princess Merida's warm gaze as she stopped behind her brother. Knox growled, a faint trail of green sinking from his nose before Eryk released her and Merida clasped her in a fierce, winged embrace. Their griffion skin shimmered faintly golden—strong with well-trained magic.

"Welcome back," Merida murmured. "I'm sorry about your brother, but I'm not sorry the war has ended."

"Me too, on both accounts. And I'm sorry to hear about your mother. She was a kind woman and an excellent queen," Eirwyn replied, her gaze drifting to Knox as she squeezed Merida in a tight hug.

When the woman pulled away, Eirwyn said, "May I introduce my husband, King Knoxious Clawson of the Feral Forest."

He bowed and kissed the back of Merida's hand, and Eirwyn stepped closer to him, sliding her arm through the crook of his elbow once more. With a courtly appropriate smile, she introduced the rest of their party.

"Queen Bellatrix is a ghost?" Merida said, brows raising in surprise as she and Bella exchanged curtsies.

Eryk frowned. "I thought you were marching on Glathen from the Buspartan capital?"

Bella winced, and Leopol put his hand on her back as he said, "No, the person in Bella's body is an evil wizard named Hanzel."

"It's a long story," Bella said, her tone apologetic.

Merida nodded. "Very well. We'll hear it over dinner then, I suppose. It'll be better that way–fewer prying eyes of the court."

Bella breathed a sigh of relief.

Merida and Eryk stepped back toward the throne as they bowed to the King of Glathen. Not too deeply to show submission, but not so shallowly as to offend either. She'd tried to teach them all the nuances of court over the past month, but there was no turning back now.

Chapter Forty-One

The King of Glathen prowled as the winged lion, crown catching the light as he paused by the throne. Then he shifted into his human form and descended the dais slowly, arms open. "So, the dragons are real. We'd heard rumors, but to meet two in all this glory... quite magnificent."

Knox shifted on his feet beside her, but Eirwyn smiled. "Yes, Leopol is Queen Bellatrix's fated mate, so he will help her rule Busparia when—"

She hesitated, unsure of how to phrase it with the king. He was older than her father, but still had sharp, beady eyes that missed nothing. Those eyes bored into hers, and she smiled, keeping her expression friendly and open as she continued.

"Well, that's really a conversation to be had over dinner, don't you think?"

The king simply arched a golden brow and turned his gaze to the rest of them. "Indeed, but I would be remiss if I didn't welcome the Growlers as well. Of course, Glathen has long been open for shifters of all types here. Everyone is equal and has a place. Unlike some kingdoms, we don't relegate them to bodyguard duty."

The jab landed with precision. Knox growled before he could stop himself, smoke flaring hot across the tiles.

"Dragons need no bodyguards," he snapped, green eyes flashing.

Eirwyn placed her hand on his arm, subtle pressure steadying him. She felt the egg shift against her back as she sent through the mate bond, *Don't fall for the jabs of court.*

He's trying to bait me, Knox sent back.

So don't fall for it. She glared at him, pleading and demanding all at once for him to behave. She could feel the low burn of his anger through the bond, the warning before the wildfire. *Don't do anything stupid,* she warned.

Knox sniffed but didn't respond, some of his anger shifting to a simmer.

Wulfric's tail twitched. "We're not here as bodyguards. We're here representing the Growlers of the Feral Forest. Our ranks have grown exponentially over the past years, and we are part of this treaty delegation."

Scarlet's eyes narrowed at the king. "Our alliance with the dragons is strong. Knox is my brother, and Bellatrix is Wulfric's daughter. We have a vested interest in the proceedings here and are equals in these discussions."

Oh dear, this passive aggressive conversation wasn't going to end well. The king had been just as eager for treaty talks last year as she'd been, but something in his expression—the tilt of his lips, the tension in his shoulders—gave Eirwyn pause.

"Forgive us, Your Majesty," Eirwyn said smoothly. "We've traveled far, and are not ready yet for the intricacies of court. Perhaps you could offer our party refreshment and rest before we discuss alliances at dinner?"

The king smiled, a little too wide. "Of course. I had

intended to give a symbol of goodwill, but now I'm not so certain I should."

"At the very least, accept our gifts, Your Majesty," Eirwyn said brightly. "They're quite rare and come straight from the dragon's hoard."

The king's expression darkened as one of the Growlers opened his pack wider and pulled out a small opal pink pearlescent vial. The size of Eirwyn's smallest finger, the Growler reverently held it up between thumb and forefinger.

Its surface was etched with intricate runes that caught the light. The sea-glass container was polished to a high sheen, clearly crafted by master artisans of one of the mer kingdoms.

The liquid inside shimmered like moonlight on water, luminous and faintly singing.

The king's eyebrows lifted, curiosity replacing his previous tension. "And what might this be?"

Leopol stepped forward, his white and silver-tipped scales catching the light from the stained-glass windows. His movements were precise, calculated—each step deliberate. "A symbolic gift of good health from the dragon nations. A vial of siren's tears, recovered from the hoard beneath Hartsgrove Castle."

The king's eyes widened. "The sirens are extinct. However did you find one and get tears?"

Siren's tears were worth more than entire kingdoms—their healing properties legendary, their acquisition nearly impossible. The king's fingers twitched, momentarily breaking his carefully constructed mask of diplomacy.

Leopol's eyes saddened. "Yes, I'd heard they'd gone extinct in the years I'd been hibernating. This vial has been untouched for centuries though, a relic even I had forgotten existed."

Eirwyn remembered when Bella had discovered the treasures under the castle. They had debated for hours over dinner one night about what gift to bring Glathen.

The king waved a hand forward, his sharp eyes tracking the Growler's movements as he went up the short steps to the throne, holding the vial out with a partial bow.

For a moment, the tension in the room seemed to dissolve, replaced by a scholarly curiosity that softened the king's previously calculating expression.

"Remarkable," he murmured, fingers hovering just above the vial but not quite touching. "The rune work is exquisite. If this is what you say—"

"It is," Leopol said confidently. "A rare gift from the sea to a kingdom of sailors, your majesty, from our people to yours."

Eirwyn caught Leopol's sideways glance—a look that suggested this was more than a simple diplomatic gift—and she nodded. The vial's presentation was calculated, a deliberate reminder of their shared past trade treaty. They had planned this, hoped it would smooth the way for the king to listen to them.

Glathen had always been the explorers of the sea, bartering goods from faraway lands for Buspartan goods and food. Glathen land wasn't as fertile as Busparia. Eirwyn looked at Bella in encouragement, hoping that her friend spoke up as they'd planned.

Bella took a deep breath and curtsied deeply, saying, "It's a token of good faith, and a reminder of our shared history. In our past, we were stronger together. The support our three nations can offer each other with this treaty could provide more than just stability for all three nations."

Eirwyn added gently, "It could be the start of a time of renaissance and prosperity."

Leopol's scales rippled slightly, a movement so subtle most would miss it. "Beware using the siren's tears, though. How the tears are collected changes the potency and effect. I found no details in our records of it—simply a log of its existence in the inventory."

"Rumors say you're an ancient dragon a thousand years old, yet you don't know how a siren's tears landed in your hoard?" the king asked skeptically.

Knox bristled beside her. *He baits us all, even my cousin.*

Leopol can handle himself. Bella too for that matter, Eirwyn replied.

Leopol shrugged but narrowed his eyes at the subtle dig. "When you have as big of a hoard as I, it's hard to keep up with such details. I did scour my books though, when I re-discovered it. Ancient texts warn that to drink a siren's grief is to gamble with your soul. It doesn't provide healing so much as...a return to the moment before the pain began. But that moment isn't always safe. It could be a powerful miracle or something worse than what you try to cure."

Leopol stepped back, meeting Bella's gaze as she watched him, her gaze sharp and calculating. They all understood precisely what was going on here: offering a gift so valuable it would be impossible to refuse, yet so fragile it demanded immediate respect.

The king shifted on his throne, sitting regally upon it as he said, "Very well. Thank you for your gift. It has been enlightening."

"If I may, Your Highness? We have two more gifts, one for each of your heirs," Leopol said with a slight bow of apology for interrupting.

The king's mask of diplomacy didn't crack—but it strained, his fingers tapping on the throne. Eirwyn watched carefully. Something was happening—a dance more complex than the simple diplomatic exchange she'd discussed with Leopol.

The egg against her back pulsed, almost as if it too sensed the shifting currents of power in the room.

Eirwyn smiled easily and waved to the other Growler, who proceeded to open his pack wider. "Prince Eryk, we know of your love of seafaring. We present to you a map crafted seven hundred years ago by our most respected navigators and diplomats. We offer this token of goodwill toward your continued success on the seas."

The Growler pulled out a cylinder, edged in silver and covered in runes and glyphs. The Growler handed it to Leopol, who explained the map's origins, the glyphs, and how the dragons came to have it—a relic from Xander the Red's own travels around the world.

As he talked, Leopol turned the end of the cylinder three clicks, and the end popped open. He slowly pulled the map from inside, opening it and holding it up for the prince to see. It was easily six feet wide, but he was so big in this hybrid form, he held it easily.

"As you can see, it's part of our great continent during the time of Xander the Red. It shows the dragon territories split among his sons."

Prince Eryk stepped closer, his griffion blood allowing him to recognize nuances that others might miss. "These territories... they're not just historical markers, are they? I don't recognize them, but they look like leylines."

Leopol's smile was thin, almost imperceptible. "Very good, your highness. Maps tell stories. Some stories are meant to be remembered, but some we'd rather forget. Some are meant to be a lesson to future generations, recording great events. Still others are warnings or invitations–it's up to *you* to learn to read the signs. If you'd like, I'll gladly teach you."

The prince's gaze traced the edge of the map, his keen eyes flickering between Leopol and the intricate parchment. "I definitely want to learn the stories this particular map tells us. Thank you for the gift."

The prince bowed to them, and a servant came forward to take the cylinder after Leopol rolled it back up.

Eirwyn smiled at Merida. "Now a gift for the princess of Glathen. As the heart of Glathen, you value strength as well as truth. We present this Whisperlens, a magical orb that will reveal truths and help you make decisions with wisdom."

Another Growler pulled out a small orb, barely the size of an apple. Leopol held it, making it look even smaller as he held it up to the light. It shimmered faintly with silver runes, pulsing with stored magic as he stepped forward and placed the velvet-wrapped orb into Merida's hands.

He arranged her fingers on the orb, his whispers meant only for Merida. Then he stepped back, his voice resuming at normal volume.

"One of the most delicate relics found in the ancient hoard beneath Hartsgrove. An orb of scrying–crafted long ago by Seers of the First Line. It now responds only to your voice command and reveals what is asked, so long as the subject exists on Celawyn."

He held it out–a smooth silver sphere no larger than an apple, etched with faint runes. The metal shimmered faintly as if it remembered being moonlight.

Merida accepted it reverently, eyes wide. "It speaks truth?"

"So long as the question is clear, it will show what is asked," Leopol said. "Ask to see something."

She turned, glancing to the throne, then down to the orb in her palms. Slowly, she said, "Show me... the Queen of Busparia."

Oh gods, Eirwyn thought, spine stiffening as cold sweat prickled at her neck. *We didn't plan for that question. Please, show the right queen. Don't show the wizard, not now, not when we're so close to finalizing the treaty.*

Knox squeezed her hand and said through their bond, *Breathe. You just said they could handle themselves. Have a little faith.*

She clenched his arm, heart hammering. *What if it only shows the wizard? What if the court turns on us—*

You taught me to trust my family, Eirwyn. Trust her now.

The orb pulsed.

And then, in mid-air, it projected Bella as she stood before the throne—radiant in ghost light, translucent but poised beside Leopol, her chin high and gaze unwavering.

Eirwyn exhaled shakily. Then the image turned fuzzy.

No.

Another image took its place.

The orb pulsed, and in its surface bloomed a shimmering image—Bella's body, regal and wrong, giving orders to a demon general. The wizard wore her face like a mask and rode an undead horse across a war camp flanked by cursed soldiers, some living and some not. Her eyes glowed red, and a black crown rested on her grotesquely twisted brow.

Gasps rippled down the table. Even the king leaned forward.

Leopol growled, "The wizard marches to Glathen. We

must secure the treaty and present a united force against him."

Eirwyn's stomach twisted. *No, that's not the plan. We weren't going to give them too much, too fast.*

Knox's calming voice echoed in her mind, steady as stone. *Too late now. We've shown them the truth. Tonight, we'll present the treaty and our trade agreement proposal. Let them decide what to do with it.*

She held his words like a lifeline.

The king stiffened. Prince Eryk muttered something beneath his breath. Merida's hand trembled, but she didn't drop the orb.

"You said it shows the truth, and it showed her, with the daemons..." Merida whispered.

"She has my face," Bella said softly. "But that's not me. I *am* the Queen of Busparia."

The king raised an eyebrow. "And yet... the orb you brought showed *her*."

Eirwyn pointed. "It also showed Bella here. They are both queens right now, but the wizard comes to destroy us all. This queen wants to unite us. Which would you really rather have?"

The crowd fell silent at her words.

Leopol's voice was steady. "That is why we've come. To save all three of our nations. To put the true queen back where she belongs."

Bella's smile didn't reach her eyes. She nodded politely, but Eirwyn could feel the fire building within all of them at his statement.

The king's gaze lingered on the orb, jaw tense.

"Interesting," he said, the word sliding like a blade between polite conversation and veiled threat.

"Interesting? No, it's more than that," Prince Eryk said reverently. "It's hope that this all finally ends."

Prince Eryk stepped closer, his griffion magic humming just beneath his skin, a low rumble of approval vibrating through the room. He recognized the significance of such an artifact—a treasure that represented trust, history, and potential alliance.

Merida stepped closer to him, showing the object, but the king's expression darkened at the comment.

The king snapped for a servant to accept the gifts and stood. "Thank you for your gifts. I suppose I will reciprocate after all."

He gestured, and a servant brought forth a lacquered box edged in gold. When opened, it revealed delicate silver bracelets of glass beads in Glathen's colors. Each bead was covered in runes, some she recognized—long life, health, prosperity—and some she didn't.

The faint hum of magic beneath the glass beads prickled against her skin. She didn't recognize the spell—but she didn't need to. It was a trap wrapped in ceremony. One they couldn't refuse.

She reached out and took one. "Oh, how lovely. Thank you, Your Highness. We're honored by your beautiful gift."

Wulfric, Scarlet, and the others each took a bracelet from the box. Even the eight Robins and Growlers received one.

Leopol hesitated, but after a look at Eirwyn who nodded with narrowed eyes and a frown, he took one too. Eirwyn didn't trust the bracelets either, but they'd figure out why when they retreated to their rooms to regroup.

Only Bella didn't take a bracelet.

Eirwyn watched her—watched the way Leopol tensed when Bella refused. The way Bella kept her hand tight on her golden gown instead, as if that were the only protection she trusted.

The king's voice boomed with barely controlled impatience. "Queen Bellatrix, you deny an old man the pleasure of gifting a beautiful woman jewelry?"

Bella jerked, then gave a slight curtsy. "I accept the gift, but I can't wear it, Your Majesty," she said, voice soft but firm. "Not until I'm whole again, which is a shame. It's very well made and quite beautiful. Thank you for the gift."

Knox said through the mate bond. *If that old snake was testing us, she just passed with fire. She sounds just like you, like a queen.*

She is a queen. At least two of us haven't pissed him off yet, Eirwyn sent back to him. The death of his queen and their own poor behavior had made this meet and greet a disaster.

"You're welcome. You may go freshen up now."

For a moment, the diplomatic tension seemed to ebb as the king stood and shifted back into his griffion form. As one, their party turned and strode the long gauntlet of whispering nobles back to the double doors.

That was tense, Knox said silently to her.

It could've been worse, she replied.

Four sets of guards stood next to the doors, hands a little too close to their hilts. A frisson of alarm went through her. The king hadn't made a gesture to order that. They were acting on standing orders.

The servant waited to escort them to their rooms. Eirwyn glanced back before they went through the throne room doors, though.

The king's eyes were narrowed and calculating. He had paused at the side door's frame to watch them but when he saw Eirwyn looking, he stepped into the darkness beyond. He didn't trust them—and Eirwyn didn't trust him, either.

The egg pulsed again, a soft thrum of life pressing against her spine—hope tucked beneath silk and diplomacy, a heartbeat from a future she would fight tooth and claw to protect.

Let the king posture and perform. Let the court whisper. She was no longer a hopeful princess with nothing to lose, but a queen, a mate, a mother. She would not let her hatchling inherit a world ruled by monsters like Hanzel.

Chapter Forty-Two

The corridors of the castle stretched before them, lined with tapestries depicting battles long past and servants who melted into the stone walls. Knox's hand remained on Eirwyn's lower back, just above the egg's hidden pocket, his fingers twitching with each step.

A faint hum filled Leopol, a warning but muted somehow. His skin itched, but it was beneath his skin, in his blood, his soul perhaps.

"Did you see how the king looked at the map?" she murmured, knowing Knox would hear her even in the bustling hallway.

"Like a predator sizing up potential prey," Knox growled softly. Green smoke curled from his nostrils, dissipating before any servants could notice.

Leopol, walking next to Bella, turned his head slightly. His scaled ear twitched—he'd heard everything. The dragon's tail swished once, a quick signal. "Sh," he said quietly. "Not here."

The party fell silent as they wound up the stairs, and

every step increased Leopol's unease.

Their assigned chambers were in the east wing, a series of interconnected rooms that allowed their entire diplomatic party to remain close. Their assigned chambers were grand–high-ceilinged rooms with intricate tapestries depicting Glathen's historical battles.

The head servant opened a double-doored room and stepped in with a bow. "This is for Queen Eirwyn and King Knox. Queen Bella, your room is across the hall. Growler Alpha, your room is next to hers." The servant proceeded to open the doors along the hall, directing them and their party to various rooms. They took up the entire hallway.

Eirwyn chatted smoothly with the half dozen servants, arranging snacks and winning them over with her bright smile. After the servants left, Leopol followed Bella across the hall to Eirwyn and Knox's room.

Wulfric and Scarlet were already there, Scarlet inspecting the room for traps.

As soon as Wulfric set the satchel down, Bella crossed the room without hesitation. Her fingers undid the latch with a pulse of magic, flipping open the top so Wulfric could carefully lift out the rose and set it on the table.

She brushed the edge of the rose's little magical barrier–checking and reassuring that it had made the journey. The bloom hadn't lost another petal. Not yet, but it was definitely dying.

The scar on Leopol's chest burned at the thought, and he rubbed it. He couldn't think about that now. All his hopes pinned on defeating the wizard, because that would make the rose a moot point.

First, secure the treaty. Hopefully within the day–then they could track the wizard and end this once and for all.

He activated his mage sight and frowned. The room's

enchantments were faint—less like weapons and more like toys.

"We need to examine these," Eirwyn murmured to Knox, tilting her wrist slightly where the beads caught the late afternoon light. "Something feels off."

Knox's green eyes narrowed, tugging at his own wrist. "Agreed. The king's welcome was strange, right? Like oil hiding the depths of the water."

Leopol stepped closer to Eirwyn, his mage sight still active. The beads glimmered unnaturally. Not just glamour—they pulsed in a rhythm, faint but too regular, like a heartbeat or a signal.

"Are we being watched? I can't tell," Scarlet said, turning with a frown. "I didn't find any physical traps."

"No poisons that I can tell, either," Knox said, sniffing the teapot the servant had left.

"Strange," Leopol muttered. "Not surveillance, not exactly."

Bella bent over his bracelet, inspecting it with him. "It's old. Bound magic, but bound to what?"

He grunted softly. "It's not a trap in the traditional sense—no explosion or curse—but the runes are layered, very complex and too malevolent for mere hospitality."

Bella crossed her arms, her gaze flicking from Eirwyn's bracelet to Scarlet's. "What purpose do they serve if not to watch us?"

Leopol said, jaw tight, "Perhaps it's meant to watch our emotions or track our intent. If you give me a bit of time, I'll translate these runes one by one and see if we can get a clearer picture."

Scarlet frowned, rubbing her wrist where the bracelet sat. "Then we shouldn't wear them."

"We can't remove them yet," Eirwyn said. "Not without

offending the king. If he's testing us, we have to pass the first round."

Wulfric growled low in agreement. "We'll wear them. But do they hear us talk like those communicator mirrors Knox is so fond of?"

Knox scowled at Wulfric, who just grinned and crossed his arms in response.

"Wrap them in iron mesh," Leopol added, sitting at the writing desk and pulling out paper and quill. "Dulls most passive spells."

He turned toward Bella, who still hadn't spoken much. Her expression was distant, calculating.

Her fingers brushed a petal from the table. They'd centralized the rose and the egg for protection—a single stronghold, easier to guard than many.

Her rose had definitely not taken the trip from Harts-grove well.

She caught Leopol's eye, and her lips flattened, barely perceptible, but it grounded him. She trusted Leopol to find a solution, and he would not fail her.

Eirwyn clapped her hands lightly. "Leopol will translate while we rest. Then tonight, we charm them at dinner."

Knox's tail thudded once against the plush carpeted floor. "Or we burn the castle down if they try anything."

Eirwyn couldn't help a faint smile as she rolled her eyes. "Let's aim for charm first."

The grand dining hall of Glathen Castle gleamed under the warm glow of enchanted chandeliers, their crystals pulsing gently like living things. Carved griffions perched high in the rafters, wings spread in frozen warning, their glass eyes fixed on the banquet table below—silent sentinels of a kingdom built on vigilance.

Leopol's gaze lingered on them as he entered, Bella at his side. The kingdom's symbol carved above them all, reminding every guest whose castle this was.

But they weren't the only beasts in the room.

Across the table, Knox caught his eye, then glanced up at the nearest griffion carving and gave a quiet snort. A curl of green mist slipped from his nostrils, subtle but deliberate. It dissipated before the nobles noticed—but Leopol didn't miss the message.

Let them keep their birds of prey on the rafters. The real predators had walked in through the front door.

Leopol entered alongside Bella, his stride measured, his perception wide. He didn't have to duck, as this castle had been built for dragons. His uncle Griffion had been a giant, golden dragon, but instead of having a hybrid form, he took on a lion's form to rule with strength and presence. He'd attracted a chimera mate, and his descendants kept their wings—and their welcoming attitude toward all shifters.

The weight of eyes—magical and mundane—pressed against his skin like static before a storm. Bella's hand barely brushed his arm, her posture regal and unreadable, but he could feel the thrumming current of her anxiety.

He scanned the crowd as they walked, but there were no signs of magical signatures that might be a threat. They sat at the head table, flanked by Wulfric and Scarlet. Eirwyn and Knox sat across from them with Merida and Prince Eryk beside them. At the head of the table, beside his son on one side and Wulfric on the other, the King of Glathen presided with a goblet in hand and a guarded smile that never touched his calculating eyes.

Leopol did not sit until Bella did. Once she did, he

folded into the chair beside her, every sense alert. Several small, polished silver griffion statues sat every few feet in the center of the tables like centerpieces—wings outstretched, beak open mid-screech.

The king raised his glass. "To peace—and the forging of something new."

"To truth," Eirwyn said lightly, raising hers in return. The crowd murmured as they all drank.

An awkward silence settled over them, then Merida turned to Eirwyn to ask, "You're going to tell us the story, right? Of all the changes that have happened since you were here last?"

"And then we'll get the story of the map," the king said firmly. Leopol nodded to him as the first course was served.

Light shimmered from Eirwyn's palm as she stood, casting the soft illusion of woven images into the air—a spell of visual storytelling, elegant and slow.

"Before I tell you of what happened last year, let's back up twenty years," she said. "The war between our nations did not begin as you believed. My father and mother were murdered, yes, but Glathen had nothing to do with it."

A gasp rang through the crowd in the long room and several paused with forks half-way to their mouths. Leopol watched every face, every expression, on high alert as Eirwyn wove images on the ceiling with her light magic.

She continued, her hands turning slightly as her voice rose. "My parents were on their way home through the Feral Forest when they were assassinated by a vampire... hired by Gastone, my elder brother."

A ripple of gasps spread through the table. Merida leaned in, her golden eyes sharp with interest.

"Gastone had been influenced from a young age by a wizard named Hanzel who was imprisoned in a mirror. His whispers twisted Gastone's mind until he orchestrated their deaths to take his place as king. After ten years solidifying his power, the wizard whispering every step of the way, he launched a war on a false pretense."

The light spell painted the scene of a mirror in a throne room, of a man pacing like a puppet tangled in invisible strings.

"While I was here, my best friend, Bellatrix, became engaged to my brother. When I found out, I was afraid–how could my brilliant friend fall for my twisted brother? The brother who threw fireballs at me regularly, who told me I was nothing but a pretty princess who would make a politically advantageous marriage someday..."

Eirwyn paused, and Leopol knew it was to control her anger. They'd discussed her brother in depth over the past few months, and he knew how much Gastone had hurt her. He'd come to treat Eirwyn as his own little sister, hoping to give her a better older brother figure.

"Last year, when I left Glathen, I'd wanted to see the Lone Road and the spot where my parents had died. The forest is dangerous though; many of you have lost people to its protective magic–magic put there by Knox's parents three hundred years ago."

She paused, letting them absorb this information. Then she said, "The forest attacked us, of course, but Knox and Scarlet saved my maid and myself. They escorted us to safety in Demerel, with no knowledge of who I was and no opportunity for reward. They did it simply because it was the right thing to do."

The magic shifted–an image of Knox lifting his head as forest light dappled his scales. A murmured exhale ran down the table.

"On the night of their wedding, Gastone hired the best

hunter, Scarlet, to kill me in the Feral Forest," Eirwyn said, smiling wryly at Scarlet, who gave a brief, unapologetic shrug. At this point, the crowd wasn't even pretending to eat. Instead, they ate from the palm of Eirwyn's hand.

She continued. "Instead, Scarlet took me back to the safety of Knox in the Feral Forest. She went back and told Gastone I was dead, hoping that he'd let me live out my life in peace inside the Feral Forest."

She showed an idyllic cottage in the woods with herself putting a pie on the table as Knox strode through the door. Her light character grinned at him, then threw her hands around his neck and kissed him.

The light burst apart, causing the crowd to cry out in surprise.

Eirwyn's voice turned bitter. "Gastone found out, though. He imprisoned half the town, including Scarlet, torturing them to find us. He grew increasingly unstable, the wizard whispering to him every day, until the last battle—"

Eirwyn's voice wavered along with her lip, and her eyes went glassy. She wove figures on the ceiling of Knox and Gastone fighting on the roof. Beside him, Bella tensed and sucked in a deep breath, but Leopol stood. When Eirwyn looked at him, sad and hopeless, he smiled reassuringly.

"Gastone set the forest on fire and kicked Knox off the roof, but in the process, Gastone was mortally wounded," Leopol added, his voice even but grave. He opened his mouth to continue as they'd planned upstairs, but Bella stood, her chair making a grating sound on the stone floor as it was activated by her magic.

He paused, and her hand on his arm was shaking.

But she tipped her chin up and said calmly, evenly, "I watched as Gastone tried to complete a ritual to save himself, but it didn't work. I tried to save him, but I heard a voice... It was the wizard speaking to me through the mirror. It was like drowning. I couldn't think, only obey."

Eirwyn wrapped up the illusion with the image of Gastone collapsing before the mirror's shards bled shadow.

Bella blinked and took a deep breath, but her resolve was firm, so he didn't step in or interfere.

"I tried to fight the effects of the spell, but I created a potion with his direction. When I drank it, my body changed into a beast, the mirror shattered, and the wizard escaped. His soul needed somewhere to go, so he took my body and left me a spirit."

The chair behind her rattled softly with her heightened emotions, and she squeezed his arm. He covered her hand with his and took back over telling their tale.

"The so-called Queen of Busparia that's been ruling for more than half a year? That's not the real queen. That's the wizard Hanzel in her body. *This* is the real queen of Busparia."

She smiled up at Leopol gratefully before sitting back in her chair at the table.

The king sipped slowly, but Prince Eryk's fingers drummed with interest. "And your people? We'd heard rumors of a curse destroying the border town and Winter Palace."

"The wizard's handy work. We've recently discovered the antidote to the curse and are having success with the victims." Leopol reached down and retrieved a scroll case from beside his chair, passing it forward. "The survivors of that cursed town now live in the Feral Forest. We've formalized their governance under this Constitution."

The king motioned for a steward to bring it. Unfurling the scroll, the steward stepped beside him, and several advisors on the opposite end of the table began to whisper to one another.

"And what of this treaty? I've read the missives over the past few months, but I cannot see how it would benefit my people," the king said.

Leopol passed forward a second scroll. "The treaty. A proposed agreement of formal recognition, trade, and peace."

The king didn't even look at it. "And what value is trade with a tiny forest people who can't even stay warm?"

Knox stood, slowly, and placed a small velvet-covered box on the table. When he opened it, he lifted the Wayfinder—a thick, compass-sized device that projected a glowing, animated map on top when activated. It shifted as he tilted it, terrain redrawing itself like flowing ink.

Slowly, Leopol explained what it did and how it worked while Eirwyn projected an image on the ceiling. "It would help with your maritime navigation, yes? Imagine using such a device to find your way, even on the darkest night where the stars are hidden."

Next, Knox pulled out a flame blade—slim, forged of etched silver. He pressed a crystal embedded in the hilt, and a white flame hissed to life along the blade's edge.

The crowd gasped. Several guards surged forward.

The king raised one hand, and the guards halted mid-step.

Leopol's voice was calm but commanding, "This is a Flame Blade, small, powerful, and not to be trifled with."

Knox gave a slight nod. Wulfric reached forward and lifted one of the silver griffion statues from the center of the table—no larger than a curled hand. Wulfric held steady. With a flick of his wrist, Knox brought the blade down. The griffion's head clinked onto the table beside its body.

Leopol watched the king carefully.

The monarch's jaw tightened. His wineglass lowered. His gaze locked on the severed griffion head, expression hardening like forged steel.

He understood the message.

Leopol didn't smile—but inside, he felt the turn of the tide.

Now, the king would truly listen.

"As you can see, it's the size of a knife, but can expand into a full blade. It's powered by dwarven technology. The crystal has a limited charge. It's less awkward to carry around than a full blade that clangs at the hip yet is very effective."

The crowd began to chatter in excitement, but they weren't done enticing their former enemies yet.

Finally, Knox pulled out a round, rune-etched disc no larger than a snuff tin.

"And this is another dwarven device we call the talkie," Leopol said, giving Knox the signal.

Knox pressed a sigil on the side, and a light glowed beneath it. "Ashur?"

The crowd paused as if collectively holding its breath. A voice echoed clearly from the device, "Yes, my king? Everything alright?"

The crowd gasped, but Knox answered anyway, "We've arrived safely at Glathen's court and are eating dinner with the king now. How are things at home?"

"Progressing. The new road to Vidrland is stable now. We're short on food supplies but holding."

"Aye, we'll check in later tonight, then." Knox clicked the device shut.

Merida leaned forward, nearly breathless. "And all of this was made... where?"

"In the Feral Forest," Leopol said. "Crafted by our smiths and enchanters and dwarves. These cannot be reverse engineered. They'll melt or explode if tampered with."

The king narrowed his eyes. "So, they are weapons."

"They are tools," Leopol countered smoothly. "But their magic fades without the proper crystal infusions—crystals only our dwarves know how to find, shape, or awaken. I've lived a thousand years. I've walked every continent, studied every known magical current. I've never seen anything like these crystals. Only the Feral Forest holds them. Only our people know their secrets."

Eirwyn smiled. "We offer trade—useful tools such as these in exchange for food, aid, and recognition."

The table was silent a moment too long, but the crowd was chatting with excitement. Finally, the king gave a thin smile.

"Enough bribery and politics," he said. "I'm hungry."

The feast continued, but Leopol sat, frustration dragging him down. He needed the treaty secured tonight—every heartbeat without the treaty signed was one petal closer to disaster. They had to find the wizard before it was too late.

Ever watchful, every scale under his skin coiled with warning as he stared at the king.

This was no simple dinner. This was war, dressed in velvet and lit by candlelight. And the silent signals the king was giving off? He knew something, something he wasn't sharing yet. Bella was right not to trust him.

Chapter Forty-Three

There were mornings when Scarlet fooled herself into believing all was well. This wasn't one of them.

The next morning, she sat stiffly at a long breakfast table in the Glathen palace's dining chamber, ringed by glass and a stunning view of the harbor. No one cared about the view. No one was talking. The table held thirteen dignitaries, dozens of dishes—and no appetites. Dread, dressed in silk and silverware, hovered in the air, thick as the humidity outside.

Through the window, Scarlet watched birds swoop near the harbor, and she longed for freedom such as that. Her fork clattered when it missed a potato; she cursed softly.

She wished, absurdly, for a crisp wind and a sunrise run through the forest, anything to thaw her out. Instead, she sat and glared at her food, stabbing it relentlessly.

"It's already dead. No need to maul it," Wulfric teased quietly.

She smirked—barely—and put the fork down, tension

crawling up her spine. They were all pretending things were normal, but something was wrong. Deeply wrong.

"Eat, bunny. You're too pale this morning," he added, nudging her plate closer.

Tension made her stomach clench. Nobody looked at anyone else. Leopol fidgeted with his teacup and sipped distractedly. Knox sulked so deeply into his green jacket that he resembled a bear at the end of hibernation, fur matted, mind unsteady.

The others picked at their food, tried and failed to find their voices. As they'd come downstairs, they'd all seemed out of sorts, as if they'd all just barely gotten to sleep only to be dragged awake for breakfast.

Even Eryk and Merida looked tired, both whispering with heads bent toward the other, their conversation stilted and worried frowns creasing both their faces when they looked at their father.

Only King Aldric seemed untouched by the tension, sitting straight-backed at the head of the table, his gray hair combed neat, and his eyes glazed in the peculiar way of men who had seen many, many more breakfasts than Scarlet had.

A servant, faceless and gaunt, entered and whispered to the king.

Their hushed conversations carried an edge of tension that made the silver cutlery seem to vibrate with unspoken dread.

The king's expression didn't change, but his left hand closed tight around the hilt of his butter knife.

"A messenger has arrived," he announced. The words made everyone pause.

The king's voice was not loud, but it filled the room, pressing in on Scarlet's eardrums. He inclined his head to the guard, who unlatched the dining chamber door and stood aside.

The messenger shuffled in.

Scarlet's first thought was that the man was a drunk. He staggered forward with arms loose and feet unsteady, his uniform soiled and too thin Buspartan red. The braid on the left side of his rust-colored hair. The hawk insignia—wings clipped short.

The messenger reached the center of the room and stopped.

Scarlet stopped breathing. Her fork hung in her hand, mid-air.

Her father's braid. Her father's crest. Her father's *face*—

But the eyes were wrong. Milky and unfocused, he scanned the table like an old lamp searching for oil. Scarlet thought she might vomit, or scream.

Instead, she raised her hand in a stupid little wave, a reflex that made her want to break her own fingers for their uselessness.

He didn't respond, didn't even pause as his rheumy gaze passed over her.

Bunny? What is it? Wulfric said through the mate bond.

The king stayed seated, one finger tapping rhythmically against the table.

Scarlet's heart thudded in her chest, hard enough she could hear it. She thought, *He's dead.*

Wulfric nodded slowly beside her, reaching for her hand where it now sat limply on her thigh. *I think he's undead. Not alive, but not dead. Animated by the wizard, perhaps?*

It's—he's my father.

Wulfric tensed beside her, and she squeezed his hand, holding on to dear life as her brain tried to wrap around this.

The silence stretched until it began to hum. Then the king cleared his throat. "We recognize your colors," he said to the figure. "What is your message?"

The mouth opened and closed twice before sound emerged. "For the king," it croaked. The voice was cinders and rope; Scarlet's memory rejected it.

This creature wore her father's face, but he wasn't in that body. He was just a vessel.

The king gestured, and the messenger placed a letter in the guard's left hand, a deep red wax seal visible even from halfway down the table. His hand shook, and the guard steadied it with his own.

For a moment, the blue-and-gold of Glathen's guard and the faded Buspartan red touched, and Scarlet wondered if the universe would shatter from the dissonance.

The king took the letter, broke the wax, and read. His face grew more haggard as he did but Scarlet ignored the king.

Her hands had gone numb as she studied the red-haired man's face. He had her father's broken nose and too-wide ears, but they were pink in her memory, the pink of the living.

Not this corpse gray ash pallor. She remembered his smile in the firelight, listening for deer in the thickets, the way he would gently flick her earlobe when she said something clever.

She thought, maybe, if she called out his name, he would snap to attention.

Her lips trembled as she spoke. "Dad?"

The messenger did not move.

"Dad, it's Scarlet."

His eyes did not register her, but she saw his hands flex

at the name, a tiny spider-crawl of nerve or memory, and her breath hitched.

That twitch–that tiny flicker–*had* to mean something. She stood, chair falling as she moved toward him.

"Dad, please," she whispered, louder this time, stepping forward. "Please look at me."

Nothing.

She surged closer, hand darting to her belt. One of her daggers cleared its sheath with a whisper of steel.

"Scarlet–" Wulfric lunged to block her, guards along the wall leaping forward to protect King Aldric. She slammed the dagger's hilt–not the blade–into the messenger's shoulder.

Remember, please, remember.

The force made the body stagger back a step, but it didn't react. No pain. No flinch. Just a slow, swaying return to stillness.

Her voice broke. "Say something. Gods, just say *anything!*"

She moved to strike again–this time higher, aiming for the face–but Wulfric's hand closed around her wrist mid-swing. He yanked her backward, catching her blade-hand in one fist and her waist in the other, pinning her to his chest.

"Stop. You don't want this," he whispered fiercely. "You'll regret it later."

She tried to twist free, and his hand dug in deeper, a warning.

"He's already gone!" she choked, struggling, but not fighting him. "What does it matter?"

"It matters to *you.*"

She remembered her father's hand on her shoulder after her first kill, how he'd said, *"What matters isn't only how it dies. It also matters how you carry the memory of its life."*

She crumpled against him, her free hand still fisted, knuckles white. He didn't let go.

"He's not my father anymore," she whispered, drawing a deep gulping breath as panic began to claw up her throat.

Wulfric said, "He's a mouthpiece, nothing more."

Her father didn't move, didn't blink. The stillness triggered a memory.

Kneeling in the mud beside her father, both of them were cloaked in shadow while a ten-point buck grazed only a few paces away. Her hands had shaken with cold and nerves, arrow nocked and heart in her throat.

"Stillness is the last mercy," he'd whispered, hand steadying her elbow. "If you feel your breath, they feel your breath. Still the forest in your chest."

She'd made the shot. Clean. Silent.

That lesson had carried her through ambushes and war. But this? This wasn't stillness. It was a storm.

She locked her knees and willed herself to stillness, gripping hard at Wulfric's shirt as he wrapped her in the safe cocoon of his arms.

Knox glared at the messenger. "That insignia," he said, "served in my uncle's unit. The second Infantry Division was wiped out in the war. He should be dead."

"He *is* dead," Wulfric replied, tone flat. Scarlet shook where she stood ramrod straight, staring in disbelief at her father.

King Aldric rubbed his temples and stared at the messenger. "This is not the first undead messenger we've had here, but if he's your father, I'm deeply sorry that you have to see him like this."

Scarlet sucked in a breath, fighting with tooth and claw to hold on to her emotions.

Mouth dry, she forced herself to speak. "That man—" She couldn't finish the sentence. She gestured helplessly.

"Yes," said the king. "The Queen of Busparia sent him as a token. Proof of her reach—and to unnerve us."

Scarlet wanted to scream, to claw at her own eyes and beg for five minutes of privacy to fall apart.

The king continued. "The Queen of Busparia doesn't just command daemons and Dragon Claws. She also has taken control of the dead who fell at Auckwald. She's turned them into an undead army."

Eirwyn gasped, "What? That's not possible. It takes blood magic to create undead."

Merida frowned, leaning forward in her seat. "Nekromancy has been outlawed on this continent for hundreds of years."

Leopol nodded gravely, "Since the great burning of the Northern Archives."

King Aldric banged his fist on the table. "And yet, here we are. The Queen of Busparia doesn't follow the laws and rules the way she should. She commands an army of the dead—and she marches for Glathen."

"She's not the queen. Bella is," Leopol growled, crossing his arms over his large chest and glaring at the king.

The king merely shrugged. "What would you have me do? Look at this man. We've seen a few others in the past few weeks. All messengers with clear missions. They follow orders mindlessly, don't care about pain, don't feel fear. How are we supposed to fight them?"

"With swords and arrows, the same as every other battle," one of the Robins said quietly.

Scarlet stared at her father. He stood there, thoughtless, emotionless, a shell of his former self. Scarlet never thought she'd see her father again, but to see him like this? It wasn't him at all. Not the strong, jovial but quiet man who taught her to hunt, to protect herself, to survive the Feral Forest.

"How do you kill something that's already dead? How do you destroy an army of them?" the king said in defeat. "The Queen of Busparia requests parley at noon. She... invites us to witness her new governance."

Eryk frowned. "What the hells does that mean?"

"The queen and the undead army will be here today." The king's voice was defeated and wooden, almost without feeling at all. He requested a quill and paper, and a servant brought it quickly forward.

Merida was shaking. "That's not possible. It takes a week to march from Auckwald."

"She has advanced farther than our intelligence allowed for, but the queen's demand is clear," the king said, tossing the letter to the table, where Eryk grabbed it to read. The king quickly scribbled a reply.

"Not the queen," Leopol growled. "The wizard Hanzel."

Eirwyn licked her lips, hands on her cheeks as the horror of it sank in. "What does Hanzel want?"

The king shook his head sadly. "Glathen will not be attacked if we surrender all foreign envoys to the queen. She claims she only wants to meet and negotiate."

Eryk straightened and his jaw dropped. Then he said, "It seems Hanzel has discovered a new method of travel. Or the undead do not tire as quickly as men."

King Aldric folded his letter and handed it to the guard, and the undead was led from the room, its feet scuffing the rug. Scarlet watched it go and tried to remember the last thing her father had ever said to her. She couldn't. The memory was gone.

Wulfric let go of her elbow, but she hardly noticed when

she turned into his arms. He wrapped her in the safety of his arms, and she stood there, watching the undead stranger shuffle away.

The table remained silent for a long, brittle minute. Scarlet felt as if a spike of ice had pierced her from throat to spine, freezing everything in place.

Eryk said, "Are we really going to turn them over to this wizard?"

Knox spat into his napkin. "It's a trap."

"Of course it is," the king said. "But we will answer, because not answering is worse."

Scarlet wanted to say something heroic. She wanted to summon up a speech about courage, or loyalty, or the unstoppable persistence of the living over the dead. But all she could manage was to sit, hands limp in her lap, and stare at the space where her father had been.

She did not feel tears, only cold.

Knox watched his uncle walk away, then turned back to Scarlet, worry making the scales on the back of his neck prick in awareness.

Gods, I can't imagine seeing my parents like that, Eirwyn said through the mate bond.

At least he's not fighting us the way my father's bones did, he replied.

The king rubbed his forehead, a gesture both regal and helpless. "I'm sorry it's come to this, but I'm going to ask that you remain in your rooms until the queen arrives. Would you care for more breakfast before the guards escort you back?"

Alarm shot through him, and Knox surged upright so

fast his chair clattered to the floor. He flung his arms wide and roared. "You can't keep us here!"

The guards beside the door stepped forward, but the king just held up a hand and sighed wearily.

"Not necessary," King Aldric said to his guards.

Knox froze, his muscles flexing... but no shift happened. He wrinkled his nose and snorted—then frowned at the normality of it.

What is it? Eirwyn said through their mate bond.

"I–I can't shift," Knox said. *No smoke, no gas, no poison.*

The king grimaced, as if he truly was sorry. "A side-effect of the bracelets, I'm afraid. It's slow-acting but should be fully in effect by now."

Knox lifted his barbed tail, but the barb wouldn't disconnect and fly to its target. Horror crashed into him. He'd only learned to shift less than a year ago—and now it had been taken. It felt wrong, like his birthright had been ripped away, leaving him raw and alone.

Eirwyn stood, her hand going to his arm. *Knox, it's going to be alright. We're together, and that's what matters most.*

He pulled her into his arms, holding her tight with hands on her upper back. *I need to get you two out of here to safety.*

We knew this might happen, that we might have to face the wizard.

But the babe—

Leopol grumbled, "That's why we feel so weak and out of sorts. Is it poison?"

The king shrugged. "I'm afraid I can't say. The effect is simply no shifting and no magic. Full suppression."

If he had access to his magic, he could identify exactly what type of poison it was. But even when they'd put the bracelets on yesterday, he hadn't felt that telltale nudge of magic. It hadn't been a true poison then. Whatever this magic was, it had been far more subtle than anything he'd seen before.

"But why?" Merida asked, her back stiff. She looked like a girl who'd just had her faith broken—stubborn, shocked, and hurting.

Eirwyn had talked about the girl for months. He knew they were friends, but for her father to betray them all like this... it had to hurt.

Eryk's disgust deepened as he replied, "Because the Queen of Busparia is on her way with the undead army. How can he turn over our guests to the Queen when they could just fly away to safety? Of course, he had to suppress their magic and shifting."

King Aldric just glared. "Don't take that tone with me, young man. I'm just doing what's best for the kingdom and our people. We won't survive another decade of war with Busparia and the queen—"

"She's not the fucking queen!" Leopol roared to his feet.

The king pushed back from the table. "A ruler is only as good as his ability to enforce his rule. She has an undead army at her disposal, so of course she's the real queen."

"You think this is all a trick?" Leopol snarled. "I'm the one who trapped that wizard in the mirror three hundred years ago. I know his magic—because I bled to bind it. And I swear to every god watching, *Bella* is the real queen of Busparia."

King Aldric's expression softened momentarily, a flicker of something—respect, perhaps, or old memory—crossing his weathered face.

"Your ancient memories don't change our current reality," the king said softly, dangerously. "We are facing an army that can't be killed, led by a wizard queen who knows no mercy."

The room trembled with unspoken tension, the king's words hanging like a poisoned blade between them.

Knox felt the weight of the moment pressing down on him, his inability to shift making him feel more vulnerable than he'd ever been. Eirwyn's presence through their bond was a constant, her fury bringing him back from the edge of panic. Her simmering rage threatened to overflow, and he held her tight.

Leopol slammed his fists on the table, cracking the wood in two places. "The wizard will not let Glathen escape. Even if you turn us over, he'll raze your land and enslave your people. Surely, you've heard the reports of Busparia. Release us from these bracelets, and let us face the wizard together."

A muscle twitched in Leopol's jaw, his ancient eyes blazing with a fury that seemed to transcend generations. The room grew thick with tension, the weight of unspoken history pressing against the stone walls.

King Aldric's composure cracked, just for a moment—a fleeting vulnerability that suggested he knew more than he was revealing. "Some battles cannot be won through valor alone," he muttered, more to himself than anyone else, his body seeming to deflate even as he said it.

"Father, don't do this," Merida begged, gently sliding back her chair and slowly approaching the king.

King Aldric straightened his shoulders and tilted his chin up. "We will parlay at noon. Would you like to wait here or in your rooms?"

Knox felt Eirwyn's presence surge through their bond, a mix of confusion and rising anger.

"I expected better from you, King Aldric. I'm very disappointed in our trip thus far," Eirwyn said with a glare.

Something fundamental was unraveling here, something far deeper than this moment, this room, this confrontation. The suppressed magic hummed beneath Knox's skin like a caged animal, desperate to break free.

Merida crossed her arms, her thunderous expression matching Eirwyn's. "As am I."

The king's lips flattened. "It can't be helped. This is the only chance we have at protecting our people. I suppose you can remain here until it's time. Now, if you'll excuse me, I have to start the evacuations before she arrives. We must get as many people out of the city as possible. Eryk, I'll need your help."

The king grabbed the letter where it had fallen to the table and turned on his heel to stride to the door. Eryk leaned in to say softly, "I'll see what else I can find out."

Merida reached for Eirwyn's hand and squeezed it. "As will I."

Together, they both turned to follow their father.

Only, the king had paused at the door. He turned slowly, eyes scanning the back of the missive. He glanced up, then sighed wearily as his two children reached him.

Pursing his lips in apology, he said, "I truly am sorry for this."

Then he blew shimmering dust into the air. Knox pulled Eirwyn to his chest, trying to shield her—but it was too late. They each sank to the floor or over the table, sleep stealing him into the darkness.

Chapter Forty-Four

Bella woke to silence—and the heavy hum of magic turned sour.

For a moment, she thought she was still seated at the breakfast table, hands folded in her lap and eyes on Leopol as she watched her worst nightmare unfold.

Instead, she was sprawled on the silver carpet, her skull pounding, mouth sticky with blood and fear. The air was thick and searing in her lungs. Somewhere behind her, a wall clock ticked, arrhythmic and fast, as if the event that felled them all had broken the very measurement of time.

All around her, others stirred. A groan here, a thud there. Then a scream, a raw, rending wail that shattered the air like glass.

Her vision blurred as her spirit re-anchored, pain sharpening in her chest at the sound. She sat up—or tried to. Her body flickered, insubstantial for a moment, then coalesced enough to move. She pushed herself upright. Her palms glowed faintly, as if the remnants of the spell were still at work, but her hands trembled too badly for her to weave any counterspells.

The dining room came into focus around her.

Three walls of glass, but everything was too still. The only source of light was the slanting morning sun and the ragged golden haze hanging in the air, leftover from the catastrophic magic discharge.

Another sob–this one fractured as Eirwyn gasped for breath. The same sounds Bella had made when the wizard had broken her world eight months ago.

Eirwyn lay crumpled in Knox's lap, her whole body shaking with grief. He rocked her slowly, gently, his massive arms trembling under the weight of her sorrow and his own exhaustion. Hollow bruises painted shadows beneath his eyes. His horns were dimmer, duller, and the scales on his temples had lost their usual luster.

She had to do something, fix whatever was breaking her best friend's heart.

Bella lurched forward, landing on her hands and knees, the rug's fibers digging into her skin. "Eirwyn–" she croaked, but her throat seized, unwilling to voice what she saw. Eirwyn was inconsolable, shrieking, rocking in Knox's arms, her entire form bent around an invisible center.

Eirwyn clutched at her back, where her bustle hid the egg beneath her dress. "He's gone," she sobbed in a register so high and ragged it barely qualified as speech. "He's gone. They took him! Gods, no–"

Knox tried to hold her, to soothe her, but his own arms were trembling, and his jaw was clenched so tight it was a wonder he hadn't bitten off his own tongue. "Eirwyn, it's going to be alright. We'll find him. We'll–" But he couldn't finish, and Bella understood. No one could lie convincingly, not with Eirwyn making those sounds.

Her friend's words penetrated the haze of unnatural sleep like puzzle pieces clicking into place.

"They drugged us—and took the egg while we slept?" Bella whispered, horror twisting her voice.

Bella's hands passed through Knox's shoulder, so she shifted her magic, refocusing until she could anchor just enough to touch Eirwyn's dress.

"That fucking king better not have harmed my drag-onling..." Knox growled, rocking Eirwyn even as he vibrated with rage.

Bella flinched. Even though he held her, his mind was elsewhere. Knox was instinctively ready to go to battle to recover the egg, his greatest treasure. Eirwyn, curled and keening in his lap, barely paid Knox any attention. The grief had already driven its wedge between them., Knox turning out for a solution and Eirwyn curling inward.

She had to get the egg back, safe and sound. Otherwise, this loss could tear them apart.

"No one will hurt your baby, I swear. We'll find him," Bella said, her chest growing tight. Tears streamed down Bella's cheeks as she watched her friend unravel. Gods, please don't let it be too late. Nothing in any of the realms could return what was already destroyed.

"I should have protected you better," Knox whispered, his voice frayed and brittle. "I should have insisted you stay safe at home. I shouldn't have—"

"This isn't on you, Knox," Bella said fiercely. "We were drugged. None of us could've prevented that."

Another scream cut through the room—higher, sharper.

Bella spun, heart lurching, to where Scarlet and her father had fallen under the sleep dust.

The guttural howl, half-human and not at all reassuring, made Bella's teeth ache. Her gaze flicked across the wreckage of the room, to where her father was sprawled over Scarlet, pinning her to the marble tiles. For a moment it looked obscene—her father's massive body crushing Scarlet's slight frame—but then she saw Scarlet's face, slack with terror, eyes rolling white as she fought against invisible restraints.

Scarlet was snarling like a wild thing, arms punching, legs kicking, completely lost in the grip of a nightmare.

Wulfric tried to hold her, his voice low and steady. "It's not real. Bunny, look at me. Open your eyes. It's not real—he's not here. It's just another nightmare."

But Scarlet didn't hear him screaming in words now, not syllables. "Stop, stop, no, please—" Her voice cracked, then jumped an octave, animal and primal. "Don't put me back—don't—"

She thrashed, landing a wild punch against Wulfric's ribs. The blow was hard enough to break most men's bones, but Wulfric didn't react. He simply held Scarlet there, massive arms unyielding as he protected her from herself, as she writhed and shrieked.

Bella pushed herself upright, the entire room slanting under her feet. She stumbled to them, pushing aside the dizziness. "Scarlet! Scarlet, you're safe, you're safe—"

She knelt beside them, ignoring her father, focusing on Scarlet's face, trying to anchor her to the present. "It's over, you're not there, you're not—"

Her fists landed against Wulfric's ribs again. He barely flinched, just kept smoothing the hair back from her face.

"No, Gastone, no. I don't know where they are, and I won't kill her, I won't!"

Bella clutched her chest as guilt filled her. Her magic skittered under her skin like startled birds, erratic and sharp, impossible to gather. She breathed through it, watching

Scarlet's horror bleed into the air like smoke from a burning memory.

She hadn't known what Gastone was doing in the palace dungeon. The man she'd trusted, the man she'd married. He'd been torturing Scarlet within the same walls where she'd sipped wine and read books and played at being queen.

A sob threatened to tear her throat.

Scarlet was still in the nightmare, lost in the memory, punching, clawing, and finally collapsing into a heap. She sobbed into the floor, shoulders shaking, voice ruined. Wulfric stroked her hair, his hands gentle for someone so monstrous. He looked at Bella, and there was no recognition in his eyes—just a bottomless, endless sadness.

The look on Wulfric's face wasn't empty. It was *grief*.

He looked like that the day Bella's mother had died. The same wounded, desolate stare. The same fear that the world was ending, and there was nothing left to protect.

She caught a glimpse of Leopol out of the corner of her eye and turned to him—for safety, for comfort. He was still unconscious, slumped at the edge of the carpet, an overturned chair pinning his legs. His skin was several shades too pale, but he was breathing. Bella struggled to her feet while reaching, trying to reach him.

Someone moaned behind her—a low, hollow note—and Bella looked back to Knox and Eirwyn. Eirwyn's screams had faded to soft, hiccupping sobs. Knox had her wrapped in both arms, rocking her like a child, eyes closed, mouth pressed against her hair. He looked up at Bella, and the rawness in his face was unbearable: he was begging her for something she could not give.

She glanced back to Eirwyn, who still clung to Knox like the air itself might turn to ash.

To Scarlet, who'd once been unshakeable and now couldn't even hear her mate's voice.

To her father Wulfric, who she'd thought had been dead for a decade—and yet, he was alive and hurting.

Then the light shifted through the windows, and she gasped.

That morning, before they came down to breakfast, only three petals had remained on her potted rose. There, in the middle of the dining table sat the saddest centerpiece floral arrangement in the nation's history.

Her dying potted rose, limp...and now with only two petals on it. Someone had moved it down here while they'd been drugged and lost a petal in the process.

Time was bleeding out like the air from their lungs.

Her fingers curled into trembling fists. She had to hold them together, all of them. If she didn't... everything was going to shatter.

Somehow, she was at Leopol's side, pushing the chair off his legs with magic.

"Leopol," she said, her voice fraying. "Wake up. Gods, wake up. We need to make a plan." Her hands were cold and unsteady on his face, but she slapped him lightly, urgency rising. "I need you."

He stirred, coughed, and opened his eyes. For a moment, he stared through her, as if looking at something far behind. Then focus returned, and he blinked. "Bella?"

Relief blinded her. She leaned into him, forehead pressed to his, and sobbed once. "I'm here. I'm alright, but everything's gone so horribly wrong, and I can't—I don't know what to do."

She was great at managing the tavern, but she didn't have a natural ability to just know how to fix things. She needed Leopol to wake up. This was where he thrived.

He tried to sit, but a spike of pain jerked through his body, and he collapsed back, panting. "What happened?" he asked, surveying the carnage. His hand reached for hers, and she let him hold it, both for him and herself, as she searched him for injuries.

"The egg is gone," Bella said in barely a whisper. "Eirwyn—she—" She couldn't finish. She looked over to Eirwyn and Knox, then to Scarlet, still trembling in her arms, and finally to her father, unmoving and silent. "We were drugged, the egg stolen, and everything fell apart."

Leopol's face hardened, and he pushed himself up, ignoring his injuries. "Is anyone dead?"

Bella bit her lip and squeezed his hand. "Not yet. They took the *egg*, Leopol. What if they destroy it? What if they try to siphon the power like Hanzel wants to do?" she asked, trying to get her mind back on track. It still felt like walking through fog.

The realization hit her like a punch; it was supposed to be Eirwyn's child. The last hope for a family line, for the rebirth of their kind, for any magic at all. Eirwyn's screams, Scarlet's nightmare, her father's vacant grief—all were symptoms of a world that had just lost its axis.

"They won't destroy it. It's still here, somewhere. They're probably going to turn it over to Hanzel or keep it as leverage." Leopol dragged himself to a sitting position, grimacing.

"How do you know that?" she asked, helping him sit.

He groaned, "Because I know Hanzel, and I know kings and how they think."

Her throat was tight as he rubbed his head and winced, looking around and ignoring the blood on his head. "We need to get them out of here and somewhere safe."

"Safe?" Bella laughed—or maybe cried, it was hard to tell

which. "There is no safe, Leopol. Not after this. Look at them—" She gestured helplessly at her friends, at her father. "We're shattering. And the rose—there's barely anything left of it... of me."

She pointed to the table, and his eyes widened.

Leopol looked at her, and for once, there was no cleverness, no smugness. Only bone-deep regret and determination. "I'm sorry."

She wondered if he meant for everything, or just for now. "It's not your fault."

He laughed, bitterly. "Wasn't it, though? If I had been stronger—"

Bella cut him off with a finger to his lips. "Don't. Please. We have to keep them together, or we'll lose them. It's time to problem solve and look forward, not backward." She gestured at Knox, who was now speaking softly to Eirwyn, his words too gentle to hear, and at Scarlet, who was finally breathing more evenly in Wulfric's arms.

Leopol nodded once. "Alright, we gather what's left. Are the Growlers and Robins awake yet? We need to find an exit."

"And if there isn't one?"

He smiled, determined and bright. "Then we make one."

Bella believed him. Not because there was evidence or hope, but because she had no other choice. She looked around the dining room, at the only people she had left in the world, and she decided. She may be a spirit about to go to the hells, but she would fight to her last breath to keep her friends and family from the same fate. They would not be reduced to ghosts. Not yet.

She stared at the morning light slanting through the window. If time was running out, then she would use every second, every drop of magic, every ounce of love she had left.

The words echoed in the wounded air, and the castle shuddered in agreement.

"Alright, I'll go check on the others," she said as she slowly got to her feet. Weaving slightly and shaking off the last effects of the sleeping drug, she went around the room, administering healing spells where she could.

Chapter Forty-Five

Leopol came groggily awake and groaned as he rolled onto his back, watching Bella as she moved to check on the others. She was efficient, moving silently with a delicate grace that belied her strength.

Leopol sat up and felt his head, dried blood pulling on the scales where it had caked between them. He glanced around and realized he must've hit the chair when he passed out. It was nothing but crushed wood beneath him.

"The Robins and Growlers are groggy, but fine," Bella said, walking back toward him. He wanted to smooth the worried frown from her face, but he had to take charge.

Dread settled in his chest, but he shoved it down and shifted into leader mode.

Wulfric and Knox were taking care of their mates, as they should. That left him to carry the burden of solving this.

The Growlers and Robins stumbled toward him, shaking off the drug faster than his larger frame. The Growlers' golden eyes gleamed with readiness, all muscle and menace. The Robins cracked their necks, stretching like predators about to be let off leash. Eight pairs of gazes bore into him, waiting for direction, for hope, for the leadership he wasn't certain he possessed.

He straightened his jacket and pressed a napkin to his head. "We have to find a way out of here. Split into pairs of two," he began, his voice steadier than he felt. The authority in his tone surprised him—perhaps years of solving problems for his king had prepared him for this moment more than he'd realized. "We're going to search systematically. Each team takes one wall, top to bottom, stone by stone if necessary. Check the windows, check the seams. Look for anything magical, mechanical, or weak."

They didn't bow but simply nodded and strode to a side of the room, leaving the royals congregated on the rug beside the dining table.

As the teams dispersed to their walls, Leopol found himself studying their methodical approach. The Growlers used their claws to trace mortar lines while the Robins tapped lightly on every inch of their assigned wall.

Their cooperation and automatic pairing spoke volumes. The Robins hadn't paired with Robins and avoided the feared Growlers. They'd split on their own and were using their strengths to complement the other. It felt like a turning point for the fledgling nation of the Feralt Forest.

Yet even as he watched their diligent work, an icy dread settled in his stomach.

What if there was no way out? What if the bracelet's magic had sealed them so completely that even with all his knowledge, they couldn't find an escape?

The thought clawed at him, and he pressed his palm against the rough table to steady himself. The texture grounded him momentarily but couldn't chase away the specter of failure that whispered at the edges of his consciousness.

"You're thinking too loudly," Bella murmured, drawing him out of his spiral with the ease of someone who'd learned how to read him too well.

She had moved closer, her ethereal form shimmering slightly in the chamber's uncertain light. "I can practically hear the gears grinding in your head."

Leopol managed a rueful smile, though it felt brittle on his lips. "Forgive me, I'm just worried. There are too many variables, and I don't know how to think through all the contingencies..." He trailed off, the weight of their situation pressing down on him like a physical force.

"We don't know what will happen when the wizard arrives," Bella said softly. Her understanding gaze made something tight in his chest loosen slightly. "We can't plan for everything. But you organize Hartsgrove like you were born to it. Look at them—they trust you, and we need you to do what you do best."

He followed her gaze to where the teams worked with focused determination. The Growler with the scarred muzzle had found something—a slight depression in the stone that he was investigating with intense concentration while his Robin companion offered encouragement. Despite their current predicament, Leopol felt a flutter of hope.

Bella's hand on his sleeve made him turn back to her. Her eyes were bright with hope and fear. "I trust you too, Leopol. I can't just wait around for the wizard to end me or the last petal to fall. Give me a task, something productive to do to make me think I'm helping us get out of here."

He pulled her into a tight hug, and the press of her body against his made some of the tension and worry dissipate. They would get through this. He spied the bracelet on his wrist as he stroked her back.

"Perhaps we should return our attention to the bracelet problem," he suggested, grateful for the excuse to focus on something concrete, something within his area of expertise. "The runes I transcribed last night—there might be something I missed."

Bella nodded, and they moved to the better light by the windows. The bracelet was tight against his scales, its metal beads seeming to absorb what little light touched it. Leopol had spent years studying ancient magical artifacts, but this piece held mysteries that made his scholarly instincts sing with anticipation even as his practical mind worried about their trapped state.

He lifted the wrist, turning it slowly in the light. "The outer runes say nothing of binding and containment," he murmured, more to himself than to Bella. "It feels like a classic ward structure, though more sophisticated than anything I've encountered in my research. I can't see the line of magic though, not with it suppressing me."

"You can't?" Bella asked, her brows raising. "Oh, but I can.'

"You can?" Leopol asked, his pulse beating harder in surprise.

"May I?" Bella extended her translucent hand toward the bracelet. When she held his wrist just above the bracelet, her form solidified slightly, as if contact with him anchored her more firmly to the physical realm.

She held him delicately, her fingers tracing the etched symbols with a familiarity that spoke of deep magical understanding. As she moved, examining each carefully carved line, her expression shifted from casual interest to intense focus.

"Leopol," she breathed, her voice tight with excitement or concern—he couldn't tell which. "There's something here, like a thread. It's small but glowing on the inside surface of the band. You can't see this?"

He leaned closer, close enough to catch the faint scent of roses that always seemed to surround her. "No, I can't—"

"Here." She gently turned his wrist, pressing the bracelet against his skin, the metal cold against his pulse point. "Now look."

Where the bracelet touched his flesh, gossamer threads of silver light writhed along the inner surface, forming patterns he hadn't seen before. The magic was so subtle, so perfectly integrated with the metal, that it remained invisible unless it contacted living skin.

"Extraordinary," he whispered, his scholarly fascination temporarily overriding their dire circumstances. "The enchantment must automatically block the wearer's ability to see it. A safeguard against tampering, perhaps. I can only see it because you're touching me."

They truly were stronger together.

Bella's eyes narrowed as she studied the emerging runes. "These symbols are from an older royal dialect. Not as ancient as the founding glyphs, but definitely ancestral."

She peered closer, and he held his breath.

"Can you read them?" Leopol asked, though he was already wishing for pen and paper.

Her brows knit. "Listen to this. 'Blood of the crown, key to the lock,'" Bella read slowly, her voice taking on the cadence of ancient incantations. "'Only the royal line may break what royal will has wrought. One blood to bind, one blood to free.'"

The words hit Leopol like a blade through his ribs. All at once, everything made sense—and none of it offered hope.

"Of course. These binding runes are tied to the royal bloodline, the king's family," he said, his voice barely above a whisper. "Only someone of the same royal blood that created these can unlock the magic."

"Which means we need either Eryk or Merida to return," Bella concluded, though her tone was grim. "And hope that they're on our side instead of their father's."

Leopol pressed both palms against his temples, trying to organize his scattered thoughts. The sleep dust was hard to shake off.

The discovery should have felt like progress, but it only emphasized their helplessness. They were locked in here, dependent on rescue from people who might not even want to help.

This was supposed to be just a simple diplomatic mission before they faced the wizard.

He'd gotten his body back—and yet he still couldn't protect his family, his people... his mate. Leopol wiped the blood from his brow and shook off the last haze of sleep.

He was supposed to help his king. To serve and protect the ones who mattered most.

But now he stood here, useless. Bound by poison. Weakened. No better than when he lay buried in stone, waiting for life to find him again.

"I wish I were still a spirit," he muttered, the words escaping before he could stop them. "At least then I could walk through these walls, find help, do something useful instead of standing here cataloging our problems."

The moment the words left his lips, he felt Bella's attention sharpen. When he looked up, her eyes were wide with a realization that made the air between them crackle with possibility.

"But I can," she said, her voice filled with wonder and dawning hope. "Leopol, I can walk through walls."

They stared at each other in the chamber's dim light, the weight of the revelation settling between them like a bridge across an impossible chasm. The others continued their methodical search of the walls, unaware that salvation might already be within reach.

"You're right," Leopol breathed, his mind racing through the possibilities. "Your spirit form—you're not truly solid."

Bella's expression shifted through a rapid succession of emotions—hope, fear, determination, and something that might have been relief. "I could find Eryk or Merida. I could bring them back. Maybe even find the egg."

"I don't want you to put yourself in danger," Leopol said, his scholar's mind immediately identifying the potential complications. "What happens if you're captured, and I'm not there to help?"

"How do you capture a ghost that's not bound by the physical world? They can't. They won't," she said, her ethereal form flickering slightly as if responding to her stubborn determination to succeed. "I'll be careful, Leopol. What other choice do we have?"

Around them, the chamber seemed to hold its breath. Even the searching guards had paused in their work, as if sensing the shift in the room's energy.

Leopol felt something fundamental change in that moment—not just the hope of escape, but a recognition that their survival depended on trusting in forces beyond his scholarly understanding.

Somewhere in the blur of crisis and chaos, it hit him.

He loved her.

Not just with loyalty or lust or fate—but with every

breath he'd fought to take back since waking in this cursed world. He had to trust his mate, the one he loved more than any text or ancient library.

"None," he said finally, his voice steady despite the fear and hope warring in his chest. "We might be out of options, but you're still the best person for the job."

———————

Bella pressed her forehead against the cold stone wall, she flickered like candlelight in a draft. The weight of their mission pressed down on her ethereal shoulders—she was their scout, their only hope of moving unseen, yet her nerves felt as fragile as spider silk.

Leopol's hands on her shoulders kneaded the tension, making her sigh. "You can do this. Just take a peek and report back. Nothing more. Baby steps."

The sound of distant whispers and hiccups from crying echoed in the dining room, and she flinched, her form growing more translucent with each spike of anxiety. She pressed her palms against the stone, feeling the ancient magic that coursed through these walls.

"Got it. I can do this," she whispered to herself, the words barely audible even to her own ears.

Gods, she hated this part of being a spirit.

Taking what would have been a steadying breath, Bella leaned forward and pressed her face against the wall. The stone yielded to her ghostly form like water, and she pushed through just enough to peer into the corridor beyond. Her heart—or whatever passed for a heart in her current state—hammered against her ribs as she surveyed the hallway.

Two guards stood at attention outside the dining room doors, their armor gleaming in the torchlight. They were positioned perfectly to spot anyone trying to move through the main corridor, their eyes alert and watchful as they stared toward that end of the hallway.

The end where she stood was near the windows. No one would attack from this angle—not this high up in the castle, with only rocky cliffs plunging into the sea below.

One guard shifted slightly, and Bella jerked back through the wall so fast she nearly lost her footing. Her form shimmered and wavered like heat haze above sunbaked stone.

Leopol caught her, his arms steady around her, his scent and warmth grounding her like a tether to the world she no longer fully belonged to.

She felt safe, protected, and—dare she think it—loved?

The word hovered in her mind, soft and terrifying, like a forbidden question. Unbidden, the answer came. Yes, she felt loved.

A flush crept across her cheeks, entirely irrational for someone without proper blood flow. She pushed the thought aside. This wasn't the time—or the place—to dwell on dangerous truths like that.

She squeezed her eyes shut, steadying herself against the rising panic. One thing at a time.

"Bella?" Leopol's voice came from behind her, low and concerned. "Are you alright? What did you see?"

She turned to face him, noting how his blue eyes immediately focused on her face, reading the fear there with unsettling accuracy. The others—the Growler and Robin—looked up from their inspection of the wall, their expressions expectant and tense.

"Guards," she managed, her voice barely above a whisper. "Two of them, right outside the dining room doors. They're watching the main corridor."

Her hands trembled as she spoke, and she clasped them together to still the movement. "I'll never get past them unseen."

Leopol's jaw tightened, and she watched him process this information with the same methodical calm that had drawn her to trust him. But even his steadiness couldn't quite quell the nervous energy that made her want to pace, to move, to flee from this impossible situation.

A sudden creak from somewhere above made her start violently, her form flickering so dramatically that she nearly disappeared entirely.

"Sorry," she breathed, forcing herself back to visibility. "I'm just—everything sounds so loud when we're touching."

Leopol's expression softened as he kissed the side of her temple, reverently and reluctant to let her go before he stepped back, severing the calming touch of his hands.

He traced her cheek and gave her a smile that had her soul melting.

"You're doing such a great job," Leopol said, his deep voice carrying that blend of command and compassion that had the power to anchor her scattered thoughts and send a shiver of awareness up her spine.

Instead of stepping forward and kissing like she wanted, he turned to the Growler and Robin, who had been working at loosening stones near what they hoped might be a potential escape route near the window and wall.

"Change of plans. I need you both to come with me to that corner by the window," Leopol said, jerking a thumb behind them.

The Growler looked up, dust from the ancient mortar streaking his weathered face. "What do you have in mind?"

"A distraction," Leopol replied, his eyes looking back at Bella. "Something loud enough to draw those guards' attention away from the corridor. Can you make some noise over there? Maybe work on that loose stone we spotted earlier, make it sound like someone's trying to break in from outside the window?"

The Robin nodded eagerly, already gathering the tools they'd been using–a couple of forks, spoons, and butter knives. "Aye, we can make a right proper racket if needed."

Bella's breath hitched as the plan took shape in her mind. "You want me to go through while they're distracted."

It wasn't a question–she could see the strategy clearly, and the thought of it made her stomach clench with nerves.

"Only if you feel you can manage it," Leopol said, but there was an urgency beneath his gentle tone that they both recognized. Time was slipping away from them like sand through an hourglass.

She glanced at the table where her rose sat in its pot. There were only two petals left.

She tilted her chin and nodded. "I–yes. Yes, I can do it." The words came out stronger than she felt, but speaking them aloud seemed to lend them power.

Chapter Forty-Six

Bella drew a deep breath and shifted her shoulders, trying to release some of the tension.

Leopol's presence was a steadying force, but he didn't touch her the way she wanted. "Wait for our signal. When you hear the commotion start, count to ten, then move. The guards should turn toward the noise, giving you a clear path."

The three men moved toward the window, their footsteps muffled against the stone floor. Bella watched them go, her anxiety climbing with each step. She wanted him to look back–just once. To kiss her temple again. To ground her with a word, a glance, a touch. She always wanted more with him.

Always would.

The familiar itch beneath her skin returned–that restless, magic-born tension that made her want to claw her way free of this cursed half-life. She needed to move, to release the energy pent up inside her.

But she had to wait, be patient, and focus.

The sound of metal striking stone echoed from the corner, followed by a tremendous crash as something heavy hit the floor. The Robin's voice rose in apparent alarm, shouting about loose stones and potential structural damage. The Growler added his own gruff commentary about the castle's deteriorating state.

Through the wall, Bella heard the shuffle of feet as the guards reacted to the disturbance. "What in blazes–?" one of them muttered, his voice fading as he moved away from his post.

"Ten," Bella whispered, beginning her count. Her form grew more solid as she focused, preparing for the crossing. "Nine, eight, seven."

The commotion continued, growing even louder as something else clattered to the ground. She could hear the guards' voices more clearly now, both of them moving toward the source of the noise.

"Three, two, one."

Bella pushed through the wall like a wraith emerging from stone. The corridor stretched before her, dimly lit by flickering torches that cast dancing shadows on the walls. The guards had indeed moved toward the disturbance, their backs to her as they hurried down the hallway.

Slowly, her ghostly form squeezed silently through the stone wall. Just as she reached the midpoint of her crossing, one guard turned slightly, as if some instinct warned him of her presence.

She froze, and time seemed to crystalize, each heartbeat stretching into eternity. The guard's eyes swept the corridor, passing over the exact spot where she stood frozen in terror. But her ethereal nature helped her this time–in the shifting torchlight and dancing shadows, she was nothing more than a trick of the eye, a wisp of air that might have been imagination.

The guard turned back toward the commotion, and Bella exhaled a breath. She continued forward on trembling legs, her entire being focused on remaining silent and unseen until she reached the safety of the far corridor.

Only when she had passed completely beyond the guards' line of sight did she allow herself to lean against the wall, her form flickering with residual fear and relief. The first part of their mission was underway, but the real challenges still lay ahead.

Bella hurried through the shadowed corridors, her ethereal form moving with desperate purpose even as every creak and groan of the ancient castle made her start. The stone walls seemed to close in around her, and she pressed one translucent hand to her throat, fighting the familiar surge of panic that threatened to overwhelm her completely.

The layout of the castle was confusing and new to her. Corridors that should have led to their quarters instead opened onto unfamiliar chambers filled with dust-covered furniture. Staircases she remembered as leading up somehow deposited her on lower levels, where the salt-tinged air from the nearby sea seeped through cracks in the foundation.

A distant crash echoed from somewhere behind her—perhaps Leopol and the others still maintaining their distraction—and she flinched so violently that her form flickered like a candle flame in a storm. Her breath came in short, sharp gasps she couldn't quite control, even knowing that breathing was more memory than necessity in her current state.

"Focus," she whispered to herself, pressing her palms

against a tapestry-covered wall to steady herself. "Use a locator spell."

She closed her eyes, trying to summon the simple spell she'd learned as a child. The guest quarters where they'd been staying should be in the eastern wing, near the chambers that overlooked the sea.

A faint sound of footsteps from a parallel corridor made her freeze, her heart hammering against her ribs. She waited, counting her panicked breaths until the sound faded, then forced herself to continue. Every shadow held potential threat, every whisper of wind through the ancient stones seemed to carry voices of pursuit.

Spell activated, she strode down the hallway, following the faint line of magic. She turned a corner and faced a familiar archway carved with sea creatures–mermaids and seahorses intertwined in an eternal dance. Relief flooded through her so powerfully that her knees nearly buckled.

The guest quarters lay just beyond, and she moved toward them with renewed purpose, though her nerves remained strung tight as harp strings. The door to Knox and Eirwyn's chamber yielded to her ghostly form, and she slipped inside, taking a moment to orient herself in the sitting room where they'd planned what to say at dinner last night.

Knox's belongings were scattered across a small table near the window–maps, writing supplies, and there, gleaming like a promise of salvation, the small mirror-like device he called a talkie.

Her hands shook as she reached for it, and for a terrifying moment, she feared her ethereal fingers might pass right through it. But the talkie felt solid and warm in her grasp, responding to her magic as if it recognized her desperate need.

She pressed the activation sequence she'd seen Knox use at dinner last night, praying to whatever gods might still listen that the device would work. The mirror's surface shimmered, then cleared to reveal two familiar faces—Ashur's weathered features and Cerci's sharp, intelligent eyes.

"Bella!" Ashur's voice crackled through the device, tinged with relief and concern. "Thank the gods. We've been trying to reach you for hours."

Words poured forth, as if his voice opened a floodgate within her. "You have to get here before noon," she said, her voice high and tight with panic. "The wizard—he's coming with an undead army. Everyone here is magically blocked except me, and I'm just a spirit. I can't fight. I can barely think straight, I'm so worried. The rose only has two petals too, and—"

Cerci leaned closer to her end of the talkie, her expression grave. "Before noon? That's impossible unless—"

She paused, and Bella could practically see the calculations running behind her eyes. "The only way would be to activate a large portal. Large enough for the war eagles to fly through. I'll need the Seer's help."

"Then do it," Bella pleaded, her form flickering with the intensity of her emotions. "Please, we're running out of time."

"It's not that simple," Cerci replied, though her tone remained gentle. "A portal that size requires massive amounts of coordinated magical energy. I'll possibly need others' help too. It will take time to gather them and prepare."

"We don't have time to wait!" The words tore from Bella's throat like a cry of anguish. "The dragon egg is missing—stolen. Everyone I care about is slowly dying from a magic block from these stupid bracelets. I'm the only one who still has access to magic, but what good am I? I'm trapped in this form, barely solid enough to touch things, jumping at every shadow like a frightened child."

She sank into a chair, her ethereal form seeming to collapse in on itself. "I can't fight an army of the undead. I can barely maintain my composure long enough to have this conversation. How are we supposed to survive until you arrive?"

Ashur and Cerci exchanged a look that spoke of shared concern and determination. When Cerci spoke again, her voice carried the kind of fierce conviction that had always made others believe in impossible things.

"Listen to me, Bella," she said, her eyes boring into Bella's through the talkie's surface. "Who's the one who found the right formula to reverse the curse that's been plaguing the people for eight months?"

Bella took a deep breath and frowned. "But that's different. That's–"

"It's not that different," Ashur said.

Cerci nodded. "You're stronger than you think. You're right that your magic is different, but that's a good thing! You can move through walls, scout unseen, go places and do things that none of the rest of us could manage."

"But in a fight–"

"In a fight like this," Cerci interrupted, "it's not always about who has the strongest sword arm or the most destructive spells. Sometimes it's about who has the brains to outmaneuver the enemy, who can think three steps ahead and turn the battlefield to their advantage."

Bella sighed. "That would be Leopol. He's always solving problems before we even realize they're problems."

She leaned forward, her expression intense. "It's you too,

Bella. Between you and Leopol, you have some of the sharpest tactical minds I've ever encountered. You understand magic in ways most people never will, and he has the strategic thinking of someone who's survived impossible odds. Together, your chances of holding out until we arrive are better than you think."

Bella wanted to argue, to list all the ways she felt inadequate to the task ahead, but something in Cerci's tone made her pause.

The familiar itch beneath her skin—that restless energy that had plagued her since her transformation—suddenly felt less like anxiety and more like potential. Like power waiting to be properly directed.

"How long?" she asked, her voice steadier now. "How long do we need to hold out?"

"Give us three hours," Ashur said. "Maybe less if everything goes perfectly. Can you manage that?"

She glanced at the gilded clock on the mantle. It would be cutting it close with the wizard. Three hours felt like three lifetimes, but Bella nodded. "We'll find a way."

"I know you will," Cerci said, and the absolute certainty in her voice was like a balm on Bella's frayed nerves. "Now go. Time is shorter than any of us would like. Make a list of problems and work through it methodically. Got it?"

Bella nodded, but the talkie's surface had already gone dark. She breathed a sigh of relief, but before she could exhale, the sitting-room door creaked open, sending Bella's heart into her throat.

She spun around, her form flickering wildly with shock, only to find Eryk and Merida stepping through the doorway to the bedroom. Their faces were grave, and she realized with a mixture of relief and dismay that they had heard everything.

"Gods above," she gasped, pressing a translucent hand to her chest. "You scared me half to death, and I'm already close enough to death as it is."

Eryk closed the door behind them with careful precision, his movements deliberate and quiet.

"We've been searching for a way to help," he said, his voice low but carrying the same determination she'd seen in him throughout this ordeal. "We heard voices and came to investigate. Forgive us for eavesdropping, but we caught most of your conversation."

Merida moved closer, her eyes bright with purpose despite the exhaustion that lined her features. "Three hours until reinforcements arrive, an undead army at noon, and everyone you care about slowly dying from a magical block." She nodded grimly. "We can at least solve the bracelet problem."

Bella felt a surge of gratitude so powerful it nearly overwhelmed her already fragile emotional state. "You'll remove them? Thank the gods. They'll need their magic if we're going to survive what's coming."

Eryk replied, "The locks are complex, but Merida has some skill with such things. She'll handle the bracelets. I'm sorry our father is an ass. We didn't know the bracelets weren't what they seemed. We'd hoped this visit would pull him out of the grief of losing our mother, but–" He shrugged, at a loss for words.

"And the dragon egg," Bella asked, her voice gaining strength as she fell into the familiar rhythm of planning and coordination. "Do you know where it is? It was taken from our rooms, and we need it back."

Eryk's expression darkened, a shadow passing over his features like storm clouds across the sun. "I know exactly where it is," he said, his voice tight with something that might have been shame. "My father keeps his most precious acquisitions in his private chambers, right beside his bed where he can see them when he wakes. The egg will be there, displayed like a trophy."

The bitter irony in his tone made Bella's heart ache for him. To have such knowledge, to be forced to work against his own blood—she understood that particular brand of pain all too well.

"Then we have our targets," she said, but Eryk held up a hand, his expression troubled.

"I hate to add conditions when lives are at stake," Eryk said, his voice tight with guilt. "But I have to ask. If we don't get our people out of the city, we'll be fighting on their corpses, possibly adding more dead to join Hanzel's army. We have to get them out of here."

Bella watched Eryk, who just straightened his shoulders and met her eyes, his frank, open, and earnest.

He pointed to the window and the view of the sea beyond the castle walls. "We're almost out of ships to evacuate the civilians. When word spread of an approaching undead army, panic set in. People made a run on the ships, and a few set sail too soon. Now we have people trapped with nowhere to run. Only the royal galleon remains."

Merida joined him at the window, her face reflecting the same concern. "Thousands of innocent lives hang in the balance. If your friends can truly create portals large enough for war eagles, could they make one large enough to evacuate civilians? Give people a way out before the battle begins?"

The question hit Bella like a physical blow. She hadn't considered the broader implications, had been so focused on their immediate survival that she'd forgotten about the city full of people who had no idea what was coming. The weight of all those lives pressed down on her ethereal shoulders like stones.

"I–I don't know," she admitted, her voice barely above a whisper. "I'll have to ask."

She reached for the talkie again, her hands shaking as she reactivated it. Cerci's face appeared almost immediately, as if she'd been waiting for the call.

"Bella? What is it?"

"The city," Bella said, words tumbling over each other in her haste. "There are thousands of civilians below the castle, and they're out of ships for evacuation. When the undead army arrives, they'll be trapped. Could you–is it possible to create a portal large enough for civilian evacuation too?"

Cerci's eyes widened as she grasped the scope of what was being asked. She turned away from the talkie, and Bella could hear her speaking rapidly to someone off-screen. When she turned back, her expression was grim but determined.

"It's possible, but it would require splitting our magical resources. A smaller combat portal for our forces, and a larger civilian portal that could stay open longer for evacuation. It's risky–we might not maintain both simultaneously."

"But you'll try?" Bella pressed, knowing she was asking for miracles upon miracles.

"We'll find a way," Cerci replied, and once again that absolute certainty in her voice was like an anchor in the storm. "Show us both locations–where you need us to arrive, and where the civilians can safely gather for evacuation."

Eryk stepped closer to the talkie, his noble bearing clear even in this desperate moment. "The main courtyard of the castle can handle your war eagles. For civilians, there's a large market square near the harbor—it's the traditional gathering place during emergencies."

"Noted," Cerci said, and Bella could see her making notes. "Anything else?"

"Time," Bella said simply. "We just need more time."

"That I can't help with. We'll just have to make every minute count," Cerci replied. "We'll see you soon."

The connection ended, leaving the three of them in the sudden quiet of the sitting room. Outside, the sound of waves against the castle's foundations provided a rhythmic counterpoint to their racing thoughts.

Merida said, breaking the silence, "So, we split up. Eryk takes you to retrieve the dragon egg, and I work on freeing the others from their bracelets."

Bella nodded, then held out the talkie to Merida. "Take this. You might need to coordinate with the others, and if something goes wrong..." She didn't finish the sentence, but they all understood the implications.

If her rose dropped the last petals, Bella would disappear.

Merida accepted the device with steady hands. "I'll handle the guards."

"Avoid them, if possible," Eryk replied. "But they're just following orders. Try not to hurt anyone who doesn't truly deserve it."

Merida smirked and arched a brow. "When have I ever hurt someone who didn't deserve it?"

Eryk rolled his eyes the way only siblings could and moved toward the door, his expression turning resolute by the time he reached for the handle.

"My father's chambers are in the tower overlooking the sea. It's an arduous climb of stairs, and there will be guards, but I know the way."

Bella felt her anxiety spike again at the thought of what lay ahead, but she pushed it down, channeling that nervous energy into determination. "Then let's go. Every second we delay is a second closer to confronting the wizard."

As they prepared to part ways, Bella caught Merida's eye. "Be careful," she said, the words carrying all the weight of her fears and hopes. "Tell Eirwyn and Knox that I'll find the egg and keep it safe."

"You too," Merida replied. "And remember what your friend said—you're stronger than you think. Go to my room first, Eryk."

The siblings gave each other a serious look that sent Bella's heart racing.

With that, they stepped back into the corridors of the castle, each carrying the weight of their crucial missions and the knowledge that the fate of thousands hung in the balance.

Chapter Forty-Seven

Bella floated through the bright corridors of the royal wing. Each step Eryk took beside her echoed with purpose, his boots striking the marble with a rhythm that matched her racing pulse—if ghosts could truly claim to have pulses.

The weight of their mission pressed against her chest like a physical burden. She would not let Eirwyn down, not after all she'd done during those short few months they'd both lived with Gastone. Bella owed Eirwyn, and if it was the last thing she accomplished before the petals fell, she would see mother and egg restored.

The air grew thick with anticipation as they wound deeper into the castle's heart, past portraits of long-dead monarchs whose painted eyes seemed to follow their journey. Windows were everywhere, sending beams of light toward the vaulted ceilings adorned with faded frescoes of maritime glory. Each flicker of light reminded Bella of her own tenuous existence—sometimes solid, sometimes shadow, always balanced on the knife's edge between worlds.

Eryk paused before a heavy oak door carved with intricate roses and thorns, his hand hovering over the iron handle as he glanced back at her. His expression held a mixture of determination and uncertainty that mirrored her own tumultuous emotions. Without a word, he pushed the door open and gestured for her to follow.

The chamber welcomed them with the warm glow of numerous candles and the sweet scent of lavender sachets tucked between silk cushions.

Eryk shut the door quietly behind them, saying softly, "This is Merida's room."

Bella nodded, but it wasn't the princess who stood beside a long table under the wall of windows.

The maid looked up as they entered, her face brightening with conspiratorial excitement.

"They're perfect," the maid whispered, her voice barely audible above the crashing waves outside. "Even I can barely tell the difference."

Bella drew closer, curiosity getting the better of her. Her gaze fell upon the two dragon eggs resting on the princess's workshop desk.

"Two?" Bella asked.

The craftsmanship was extraordinary; every scale, every subtle color variation, every hint of the otherworldly power that hummed within true dragon eggs had been replicated with stunning precision.

The maid, a woman whose weathered hands spoke of decades of intricate needlework and artistic endeavors, had somehow captured the essence of ancient magic in clay and paint. "Yes, two replicas," the maid said. "A practice replica and a spare."

"How did you manage this?" Bella asked, her voice carrying the awe she felt. She drifted closer to the desk, her ghostly form casting no shadow over the remarkable forgeries.

The maid smiled, pride evident in her lined features. "Years of painting miniatures for the royal family, my lady. I've learned to see the smallest details, to capture light and shadow in ways that fool even the keenest eye." She gestured toward the eggs with reverence. "The princess provided the measurements and descriptions using a snapshot replication spell, and we worked through the night to perfect every curve."

Bella frowned. "Through the night? But we weren't locked away until this morning."

Eryk stepped forward and lifted one of the replicas, turning it slowly in his hands before handing it to her. The false dragon egg felt appropriately weighty, its surface cool and smooth beneath her fingers. Even knowing it was a forgery, Bella could see how the torchlight played across its surface in ways that mimicked the subtle luminescence of the genuine article.

"My father was muttering after dinner last night. In his distraction, I read a few missives on his desk, ones with the Buspartan wax seal." Eryk's face grew dark as he crossed his arms.

"I told Merida, and we came up with a plan. Well, a plan to save the dragon heir, anyway. This will work," he murmured, more to himself than to the others. He gently took the replica from her and set it down gently.

The maid reached for a worn leather satchel on the edge of the desk. The bag showed signs of extensive travel—scratched buckles, softened leather, and the faint smell of sea salt that clung to everything in this maritime kingdom.

Bella watched as Eryk opened the satchel and began

removing its contents on Merida's bed. Ancient tomes emerged one by one, their leather bindings cracked with age and their pages yellowed by centuries of study. Maps followed, some depicting familiar coastlines while others showed territories she didn't recognize. A collection of correspondence, sealed with various noble crests, joined the growing pile on the blankets.

"What are those books? I don't recognize them," Bella said, her fingers itching to inspect the tomes.

"Father expects me to carry research materials," Eryk explained as he worked. "These books and documents provide the perfect distraction during long days at sea."

The maid handed over the carefully crafted replica, and Eryk slipped it into the satchel's main compartment, adjusting the leather flap to ensure it fit securely.

The prince moved closer, his black boots rustling softly against the stone floor. "So here's the plan. We'll go to my father's rooms, where he's keeping the real egg. Father is sharp-eyed, and any hesitation will raise his suspicions, but I'll distract him while you switch the fake for the real, alright?"

Bella felt a chill that had nothing to do with her ghostly nature run through her essence. The magnitude of what they were attempting pressed down upon her like a physical weight.

If they failed, if she was discovered, the consequences would extend far beyond her own fate. Eryk would face his father's wrath, the princess would be implicated in their scheme, and the real dragon egg—whatever power it truly held—would fall into hands that might use it for darker purposes.

"You must remain hidden," Eryk continued, his gaze finding hers across the chamber. "Can you sustain your invisibility long enough? Does it drain you?"

The question struck at one of her deepest fears. Her ghostly abilities were unpredictable at best, tied as they were to her emotional state and the mysterious connection to her rose. Her control over it had gotten better in the past few weeks, thanks to Leopol.

"I can manage it," she said, hoping her voice carried more confidence than she felt. "But what if something goes wrong? What if I can't make the switch or he catches us?"

Eryk's expression softened, and he stepped closer to her, close enough that she could feel the warmth radiating from his living form. "Then we'll face whatever comes with heads held high. If it were Merida with me like we'd originally planned, then I'd be worried. But Bella, you're the only one who can do this. Your ability to go invisible in spirit form—it's our greatest advantage."

The maid gathered the remaining materials, carefully wrapping the second replica in soft cloth before tucking it away in a hidden compartment of the princess's wardrobe. "For safekeeping," she explained. "Should anything happen to the first."

Bella nodded, drawing what comfort she could from their thorough preparation. She closed her eyes and reached inward, feeling for the threads of power that connected her to the physical world. The familiar sensation of dissolution began at her fingertips, spreading slowly through her ethereal form until she felt herself becoming one with the shadows that danced across the chamber walls.

"I'm ready," she whispered, her voice now carrying the hollow quality that marked her invisible state.

Eryk hefted the satchel, testing its weight and ensuring the straps sat comfortably across his shoulder. The leather bag now contained their carefully orchestrated deception,

and with it, perhaps the key to preventing greater cata-
strophe.

"Stay close," he murmured, speaking to the air where he
knew she hovered. "We speak to Father alone, and when the
moment comes, you'll know. I'll draw his attention away—a
sound, a movement, anything that gives you the seconds you
need."

As they prepared to leave the warmth and safety of
Merida's chamber, Bella felt the familiar weight of destiny
settling around them like a cloak. The corridors ahead
loomed like endless destiny, and she swallowed hard to keep
the nerves at bay.

Bella felt her essence shimmer as they approached the
massive oak doors that guarded the king's private chambers,
the strain of maintaining her invisibility pulling at the very
fabric of her being like fingers trying to unravel a delicate
weaving. It was harder to maintain this than to remain
transparent and visible. Leopol said it was a sign of how
strongly she was tethered to this world. Ghosts were naturally invisible and took effort to be visible, while spirits were
naturally transparent. It definitely took more effort to maintain invisibility.

Her heart hammered against her ribs with a rhythm
that threatened to shake her loose from the shadows
entirely. Each step down the marble corridor felt like
walking deeper into a trap of their own making.

Two armored guards flanked the entrance, their
polished breastplates reflecting the torchlight. Their eyes
were sharp with the vigilance of men who had served the
crown for decades.

Their presence sent fresh waves of anxiety through
Bella's translucent form. What if her invisibility failed?

What if they sensed something amiss in the air currents that swirled around her ethereal presence?

She took a deep breath and thought of Eirwyn, of Knox and Leopol. She knew Eirwyn wouldn't leave even if she could, not without her egg. It was up to her to save him.

Eryk's knuckles struck the heavy wood with three measured raps that echoed through the corridor like thunder. The sound seemed to resonate in Bella's bones. She pressed herself closer to the stone wall, drawing what comfort she could from its ancient solidity as they waited for permission to enter.

"Come," came the king's voice from within, carrying the weight of authority and something deeper—a weariness that spoke of burdens too heavy for mortal shoulders.

The guards moved aside, and Eryk pushed open the doors and stepped into the chamber. Bella slipped in behind him like a whisper of cold air.

The effort of maintaining her invisible state while moving through the doorway left her feeling stretched thin, as though she might dissipate entirely if she lost focus for even a moment. She pressed herself against the stone wall just inside the entrance, grateful for its support as she fought to steady herself.

The king's private chambers spoke of power tempered by melancholy. Candles guttered in iron sconces mounted along walls lined with faded tapestries depicting great naval battles of ages past—ships locked in combat beneath stormy skies, their crews frozen forever in moments of triumph and defeat. The flickering flames cast wavering shadows that seemed to bring the ancient conflicts to life, sails billowing and cannons firing in endless, silent warfare.

Heavy furniture dominated the space—a massive desk

carved from dark wood and inlaid with nautical charts sealed beneath glass, chairs upholstered in deep blue velvet that had once been the color of calm seas but now appeared almost black in the uncertain light.

Books lined shelves from floor to ceiling along one wall, their leather spines bearing titles in languages both familiar and foreign, speaking of a ruler who understood that knowledge was as vital as steel in defending his realm.

King Aldric stood with his back to them at the great arched window that overlooked the harbor, his silhouette etched against the sunny sky beyond. The bright light cast a lone beam along the floor, and Bella realized this room was the darkest of any she'd been in thus far in this castle.

Beyond the king, she saw a storm roll toward them from the sea. Lightning illuminated the churning waters where the fleet sailed up the coast—proud vessels that had once ruled the seas but now huddled together like beaten dogs seeking shelter.

"Father," Eryk said, his voice carrying across the chamber with studied casualness. He moved to stand beside the older man, dropping the satchel from his shoulder with a thump on the floor beside the desk. "The ships have evacuated all they can. Only the royal galleon remains. It's ready for you."

Bella remained motionless against the wall, watching as the king turned slightly to acknowledge his son's presence.

Aldric's face bore the lines that came from decades of tough decisions and sleepless nights, his beard streaked with silver and his eyes holding depths that spoke of wisdom earned through pain.

His hands gripped the windowsill with white-knuckled intensity, as though he could hold back the storms that battered his kingdom through sheer force of will.

"Look at them," the king said, gesturing toward the harbor where his ship rode the ever increasingly violent swells. "Once, those vessels carried our merchants to every corner of the known world. Our flags flew in ports from the Northern Wastes to the Whaletid Isles. We were the maritime superpower, Eryk. Every trade route, every valuable cargo, every exchange of goods between distant lands—it all flowed through our harbors."

The raw pain in his voice made Bella's chest tighten with unexpected sympathy. Here was a ruler watching his kingdom's glory fade like the ships disappearing beyond the horizon.

"The sea witch changed everything," Aldric continued, his words bitter as salt spray. "One day our captains sailed free across open waters, the next they found their paths blocked by walls of fog and monsters from the deep. She seized control of the oceanic routes as surely as if she'd conquered them with cannon and sword. Our merchants became prisoners in their own ports, our navy reduced to coastal patrols."

Eryk shifted his weight, and Bella caught the subtle movement from her position in the shadows. "The situation in Busparia might change things," he said carefully. "If the wizard is defeated—"

"Wizard?" The king's laugh was harsh as grinding stone. "Wizard, queen, sorceress—what difference do titles make when the result is the same? She demands tribute, Eryk, same as the sea witch. Demands the dragon egg as though it were some bauble to add to her collection. We give up the tribute, or it'll be taken from us like your mother."

Bella went rigid. The egg wasn't just a symbol of legacy or power—it was a key, a weapon, a bargaining chip. Hanzel wanted it badly enough to threaten war.

"The queen claims it's vital to her schemes," Aldric continued, his voice dripping with disdain. "More precious than any prisoner we might trade for it. It's your mother all over again, don't you see? The wizard-queen speaks of destiny and power, of magic that will reshape the very foundations of the world."

He turned from the window to face his son directly, his eyes blazing with frustrated fury. "No doubt she plans to siphon its magic, to add its power to her already considerable arsenal."

The weight of responsibility pressed down on Bella like a physical burden. She wished Leopol were here to ground her. He always knew what to say and how to keep her from unraveling. Hopefully the regulator and the anti-nekrotic bomb would be enough to level the playing field with Hanzel, but her gut warned otherwise.

Tears pooled in the corners of her eyes, but then she remembered Knox's words about the greater good and choices that transcend individual loyalties. She might not be the best to rescue the egg, but she was what the world had to work with. And she would *not* let them down.

"So, you're just going to turn over the egg?" Eryk asked, though Bella could hear the anger in his voice.

The king moved to his desk, his fingers trailing across the sealed charts beneath its glass surface. "What choice do I have? We cannot fight beings who command the very seas themselves. We learned that long ago, and this wizard queen is just as powerful. If surrendering one artifact might restore our trade routes, might bring prosperity back to our people..."

He shrugged, the gesture carrying the weight of capitulation as he sank into his chair in defeat. "Pride is a luxury we can no longer afford."

Bella watched from the shadows as father and son stood separated by more than the physical barrier of the desk. The satchel containing their deception seemed to pulse with its own significance where it sat on the floor.

Chapter Forty-Eight

The storm beyond the windows intensified, moving swiftly. Lightning illuminated the chamber in stark, violent flashes that made the tapestried battles seem to writhe with renewed life.

In those brief moments of illumination, Bella caught glimpses of her own reflection in the dark glass—a ghostly figure caught between worlds, about to help reshape the fate of kingdoms with a single, desperate switch.

She refocused, forcing herself invisible. Maintaining her concealment for their crucial deception felt like holding back an avalanche with bare fingers. Phantom pain ached through her non-existent muscles.

She watched the king's every movement with predatory focus, waiting for the perfect opportunity. The dragon egg nestled on the small table, tucked safely on a velvet pillow, seemed to radiate warmth and magic, its power a stark contrast to the masterful forgery waiting in Eryk's satchel.

The moment came when King Aldric called for one of the armored guards stationed near the chamber's entrance.

His attention fixed completely on the man as he marched inside. The king began issuing orders about harbor security and the positioning of patrol boats to watch for the wizard-queen's arrival.

Eryk waved to the window. "Are we sure they're coming from the south? It would be wise to surround us on three sides, and the wizard is no fool."

The king rose to his feet, and the guard followed him to the window, where the three argued on the best tactic to take for defense of the city.

His back turned, it was the perfect distraction.

She moved silently, gliding across the stone floor without disturbing a speck of dust. Maintaining her invisibility caused sharp pain, as if stretching her essence beyond its limits. She kneeled beside the desk and reached into the satchel, pulling out the replica dragon egg.

The artifact's surface was warm to her touch, pulsing with a subtle energy that would convince any casual holder that it was the real egg.

With movements so careful they barely disturbed the air around her, Bella reached toward the side table. With a quick glance at the three men by the stormy window, she picked up the real egg and replaced it with the replica.

The craftsmanship truly was extraordinary—even knowing it was false, even holding the genuine article in her other hand, she could barely distinguish between them in the chamber's flickering candlelight.

Then the power settled into her soul.

Ancient magic called to her, and for a moment she felt dizzy with the power that hummed within the egg's crystalline shell. The child within kicked, creating a hot spot where her hand lay, as if he knew Bella wasn't his mother.

This was no mere treasure. It was a wellspring of primal

force, old as the world itself, brimming with secrets king-doms would kill to possess. No wonder the wizard wanted this precious egg.

She shook her head and crouched back beside the table, opening the satchel to slide the real egg inside.

The entire exchange took perhaps three seconds—three seconds that felt like eternities as she fought to keep her invisible form from wavering under the strain of divided concentration. She flipped the top closed, securing the package just as King Aldric straightened from his conversa-tion with the guard and Eryk.

"We'll double the number of scouts on the east and north walls but keep the majority of the forces at the south entrance," Aldric said.

Shaking with effort and emotion, Bella slowly stood and backed toward the still-open door to the sitting room office. She paused as the guard saluted and went through the door.

"That's it? You won't evacuate?" Eryk asked.

Aldric walked to his desk and bent over the egg on the side table, his back to her. Bella dropped her invisibility and caught Eryk's searching gaze. She nodded once and then took a deep breath, focusing once more on activating and maintaining the invisibility.

The real dragon egg rested safely within his satchel, and when he bent to pick it up, casually slinging the strap over his shoulder, her shoulders released the weight of the world.

Relief flooded through her ghostly form like warm sunlight, followed immediately by exhaustion so profound that maintaining her invisibility became a battle of pure will against the growing darkness at the edges of her consciousness.

"I must be here to hand over the dignitaries and this egg," the king said, his voice weary and frail.

Eryk's soft sigh filled the sudden silence, a sound that carried more emotion than any shouted declaration. He moved to stand before his father, his posture straight despite the burden of their deception—or perhaps because of it.

He clasped his father on the shoulder, and Aldric turned his head to look up at his son.

"Sometimes doing what's right matters more than securing Glathen's future," Eryk said, his voice quiet but steady as stone. The words seemed to surprise even him with their conviction. "Sometimes we have to trust that the gods will judge us not by our victories, but by our choices. Are you sure this is your choice?"

The king's eyes flashed with something between anger and disappointment as he straightened to his full height. "The gods?"

His laugh was harsh as breaking glass, echoing off the chamber walls with bitter resonance. "The gods abandoned us long ago, Eryk. When the sea witch began strangling our trade routes, where were they? When our people started going hungry because ships could no longer bring food from the outer islands, what divine intervention did we see?"

Bella watched from her invisible sanctuary as the gap between father and son widened with each word. The king moved closer to Eryk, his chest puffing, his presence commanding and terrible in its authority.

"We are the only ones who can safeguard our people now," Aldric continued, his voice growing harder with each syllable.

"Father, be reasonable—" Eryk said, backing away slightly with palms up in supplication.

"Reasonable? The only pragmatic decisions in this world are those made by flesh and blood rulers who understand that survival trumps idealism every single time. You speak of righteousness as though it puts food on tables and keeps foreign fleets from our harbors."

The older man's hand fell heavily on Eryk's shoulder, a gesture that might have been paternal comfort in other circumstances but now carried the weight of a crown that demanded sacrifices. Eryk winced, but didn't look away.

The king told his son, "When you wear this crown, you'll see that moral certainty fades once you're responsible for millions. My choices aren't noble, but they are necessary."

From the shadows, Bella felt the weight of her actions: stealing hope from a desperate king and prioritizing her morals over his kingdom's survival. What made her actions *good* but his *bad*?

Despite the guilt, she recalled the greater evil they fought—Hanzel's power-hungry schemes endangered more than just Glathen. The wizard wanted to bring back Asmoroth, and that was definitely bad. Not just for Celawyn but for all the realms.

If Asmoroth gained control of the heavens, life as they knew it would cease to exist. All that would remain would be pain and suffering.

The chamber fell silent except for the storm's continued assault against the windows, lightning illuminating the ancient naval battles depicted in the tapestries—conflicts that now seemed to mirror the moral warfare being waged within these walls.

Eryk stiffened at his father's words, as though struck by invisible lightning, his muscles tensing with a burden Bella felt even from her hidden spot against the chamber wall. The weight of destiny and expectation bore down on him, threatening to crush him.

His jaw clenched, suppressing words of anger and frustration, while his hands formed fists. Father and son stood frozen—the king's hand on Eryk's shoulder like a shackle of duty, the prince trembling to contain emotions that threatened to tear him apart. Candlelight flickered, casting shadows on their conflicted expressions.

Then something inside Eryk seemed to snap. He glared, his fists clenching. The intensity in his gaze held both accusation and apology—and above all, sorrow for the fallout they would all have to face.

"I'm done pretending I can be the king you want," Eryk said suddenly, his voice cutting through the tension like a blade. "Keep the crown. I don't want it."

"The hells you say," King Aldric roared, his voice echoing off the stone.

But Eryk didn't flinch. His next words dropped into the silence like stones sinking in deep water.

"Mother gave us the freedom to become who we were meant to be. She and I both knew long ago that I would never be king. You thrust this role on me—but deny Merida the chance. It's as ridiculous and antiquated as your belief that Glathen should come above everything else... even our integrity."

Without waiting for a response, Eryk jerked back from the king and rounded the desk toward the door. He stalked toward the doors with long strides that ate up the distance in seconds.

The king called after him—"Eryk, wait!"—but the prince had already pushed through the heavy oak doors and into the corridor beyond. The armored guards stepped aside hastily as their future monarch swept past them, their faces carefully neutral despite the obvious tension radiating from the royal family's confrontation.

Bella followed in his wake, her invisible form slipping

through the doorway like a whisper of cold air before the guards could close ranks again. The effort of maintaining her concealment while moving quickly sent fresh spikes of exhaustion through her, but she gritted her teeth and pressed onward.

Only when they had moved down the marble corridor, around a corner, and down an entire flight of stairs did she allow her invisibility to fade. The release was like dropping a massive weight she had been carrying for hours, and she materialized against the stone wall with a gasp that echoed softly through the empty passage. Her ghostly form wavered for a moment before solidifying, translucent but visible once more.

Eryk stopped a few steps down, turning to look at her with one hand raised. "Are you alright?"

She nodded shakily before following him once more. "What happened in there?" she asked.

Eryk stopped walking at the bottom of the stairs, glancing sightless out the window where the storm was already receding. The satchel hung heavy from his shoulder, carrying their successful rescue like a badge of victory that felt more like defeat.

"I told him the truth," he said finally, his voice raw with emotion. "I can't be the king he wants me to be. I won't be like him. Mother may have died, but she made the right choice, unlike *him*."

The admission lingered in the torch lit corridor, amid portraits of proud monarchs. Bella felt a sharp understanding—another soul trapped by unwanted expectations and duties that felt like chains.

"What will you do?" she asked softly.

Eryk opened his eyes and looked directly at her, and she

saw something in his gaze that hadn't been there before—a freedom born of finally speaking an impossible truth aloud.

"The open seas call to me, Bella. They always have. I dream of horizons that stretch beyond sight, of winds that carry you to places no map has ever charted."

"I thought you'd already spent years exploring," she said.

His shoulders sank in defeat as they made their way down another corridor. "I have, but not to the extent I'd like, not with the sea witch still in power. I want to explore far off places, discover unique and rare treasures, have daring sword fights and break magical spells... live without the weight of a kingdom's expectations crushing my soul."

His words conjured images of sailing ships on endless blue waters, adventures free from politics and power struggles. She briefly envied him the dream of escape and choosing his own path, rather than being trapped by supernatural forces in an unchanging existence.

"I never dreamed of a crown either," she admitted, her voice barely above a whisper. The confession felt dangerous, as though speaking it aloud might somehow make her own chains heavier.

"When Gastone offered the chance to be queen, I thought, *this was it, the answer to how to help the most people*—the ability to protect those I loved and change our kingdom for the better. But the crown became a cage, and the responsibilities..."

She shook her head, memories of her failed rule and its catastrophic consequences washing over her like cold waves. "Sometimes leadership feels more like a curse than a blessing."

Eryk pushed himself away from the window and began

walking again, his steps echoing through the corridor with renewed purpose. "Then you understand why I have to leave, why I can't become what my father wants me to be."

Bella followed beside him, keeping pace with his determined stride as they moved deeper into the castle's winding passages. A memory surfaced unbidden from conversations in what felt like another lifetime.

"Knox once told me that sometimes leadership finds those who least expect it, those who are exactly what the world needs precisely because they don't want the power."

The words seemed to strike Eryk like a physical blow, and he stumbled slightly before catching himself against the wall. "You think I'm running away from my destiny?"

"I think your path is your own," Bella said carefully, "but destiny has a way of following us wherever we go. Sometimes the very act of running toward what we want leads us to where we need to be."

They had reached the grand staircase that swept down toward the castle's main levels, its marble steps worn smooth by centuries of royal feet. Eryk paused at the top, looking down into the shadows below where their escape route waited.

"Perhaps you're right," he said, and Bella heard in his voice the same mixture of fear and determination that had driven her own desperate choices in life and death. "But I won't put Glathen above doing what's right. My father may be king, but he's not right in this."

"Agreed. Let's find the others," she said, and they began another long climb down yet another set of stairs.

Their footsteps echoed through the empty corridors as they sprinted down the marble stairs, the sound bouncing off ancient walls and fading into the darkness behind them.

For now, the egg was safe, and Eirwyn would be reunited with her baby.

The chime echoed down the corridor like a warning bell. There were two petals left, two hours to act and prepare.

Then Hanzel would be here.

Chapter Forty-Nine

Leopol stood near the western window of the dining room, his pulse thundering like war drums in his ears. Below, the road curved toward the city gates, while off to the right, the market square bustled with movement. Near the harbor, the faint shimmer of a portal flickered like a mirage—visible only because he was searching for it.

The evacuation didn't hold his attention, too worried about Bella. She should've returned by now.

Every second she remained gone stretched tight across his chest like a chain ready to snap. He didn't care about the plan, the performance, or the poisoned bracelets that no longer held their bite. None of it mattered if she didn't come back.

Merida had arrived an hour earlier, breathless with urgency, laying out the new plan: she would disable the bracelets and free them while Eryk and Bella retrieved the egg. Eirwyn had fainted with relief. Knox had refused to budge without the child.

So, they waited—trapped in a careful performance of

weakness for the benefit of the guards outside. And Leopol waited too, the ticking clock drilling worry deeper into his bones.

Then—the door opened, and the guards stepped aside as Eryk and Bella entered the room. Thank the gods, the guards listened to Eryk and Merida instead of only their father.

A shimmer broke across the air as sunlight pierced the thinning clouds, casting a single golden beam onto her face.

Leopol exhaled for the first time in what felt like hours and strode forward, pulling her into his arms before the door even clicked shut behind them.

"What took you so long?" he murmured into her hair. But he didn't let go.

She sank into his embrace, her small hands clinging to his back as she sighed with contentment. "I had to bring back what matters most."

"You matter the most," Leopol said without hesitation.

Bella nuzzled into his chest, her nose catching on a button of his formal jacket.

"I'm two petals away from death, Leopol. I'm the least of us in this room."

"Not to me, you're not." His voice deepened with emotion as he tightened his hold. "You are—and always will be—the most important thing in my life, Bellakari."

Leopol felt it then—the subtle hum of magic pulsing near Eryk. He exhaled slowly. He hadn't realized how much comfort magic had given him until the bracelet had taken it away.

Eryk crossed to the low table where Eirwyn sat, her eyes open but dull with grief. Knox stood behind her, hands gently braced on her shoulders.

Leopol watched as Eryk opened the satchel at his hip and withdrew the egg.

Eirwyn gasped. She launched to her feet and cradled the egg against her chest. The shell glowed softly from within at her touch, responding to her voice as she murmured its name.

Knox pulled them both into his arms, his shoulders trembling with emotion.

The egg was safe. And Bella... Bella was safe too. For now. But now was all they had.

Eryk cleared his throat, dragging the room back to reality. "There's two hours left. Is Merida clearing the market square?"

Wulfric grunted, arms crossed but not taking his eyes off where Scarlet paced. "Yes, Merida is directing people into the portal, but Cerci can't hold it forever. You can just see them from the window."

Leopol held her a moment longer, breathing her in like a drowning man who'd broken the surface. The storm outside might have waned, but the real storm—the one that threatened everything they had left—was just gathering strength.

He couldn't let relief lull him. Not when they were this close to the end.

His mind turned to their bag upstairs—the pieces the dwarves had scavenged from the construct. The Orythium core. The regulator trap. The flame-conductive plating. Tools meant for war.

They'd have to reach them before the wizard arrived. They'd have to use them in the right moment too.

He glanced around the room—at Scarlet, still taut with fury barely leashed... at Wulfric, steady and quiet, always watching... at Eirwyn and Knox, clinging to hope now that it had a heartbeat again... at Bella, luminous but with the rose fading fast on the table behind her.

They were more than a cursed handful of rebels. They were the last line before the world bent to the wizard's will.

He let go of Bella just enough to look her in the eye. "We don't have much time. We need our supplies before we meet the wizard."

"We need a plan," Bella said, her jaw firming with resolve.

We need a miracle, he thought, even as she turned to Eryk.

"Do we know what will happen when the wizard arrives?" Bella asked.

Leopol laced his fingers with hers—as if anchoring himself to this moment, to her.

Eryk's expression was grim, but his voice remained steady. "You're to be marched through the city like prisoners, handed over in a parley just outside the gates. My father believes surrendering you—and the egg—might buy Glathen a future."

Eirwyn's cry of outrage lit up the air around her, sparks flaring like fireflies. "Never. They'll never get my baby."

Eryk raised his hands. "I know. I won't let that happen, either. Bella and I switched the egg with a replica upstairs—and Father doesn't know. He's going to hand the fake over, but you'll need to act devastated. Make it believable, alright?"

Eirwyn nodded, her arms tightening protectively around the egg.

"We need to buy Merida time," Eryk continued, "to get everyone through the portal with your Seer. Then, if we must, we fight. I won't see Glathen fall into the wizard's hands... or yours."

"We don't want Glathen," Knox growled, his voice low and sharp.

"Busparia doesn't either," Bella added. "All I've ever wanted was peace—for my people and for the ones we hurt."

Leopol squeezed her hand and locked eyes with Eryk. "The wizard doesn't just threaten our kingdom. He threatens every kingdom, every continent, every realm. If he wins, he'll free Asmoroth—and no one will be safe. Are you sure you want to stand with us?"

Eryk's jaw tightened. "My mother died trying to protect us from the sea witch's wrath. And if the rumors are true, that monster made her own deal with Asmoroth. I won't let my mother's sacrifice be in vain."

A knock interrupted them. Eirwyn dropped into a dining chair, slipping the egg onto her lap beneath the table's edge.

One guard cracked open the door and hesitated at the threshold.

"The king requests you prepare to depart. The rain is almost done, but he's granted permission to collect your cloaks and personal items from your rooms," the guard said stiffly, as if uncomfortable delivering courtesy alongside doom. He left the door open and stepped back into the hall.

"A final mercy," Knox muttered, helping Eirwyn secure the egg in the pocket of her dress at the base of her spine.

"Or a convenient excuse to make us walk slower to our deaths," Scarlet muttered, her hands twitching for daggers that were no longer there.

Eirwyn fluffed the faux cape of her gown, arranging the layers to hide the egg once more. How the king's spies had known where to find it, Leopol didn't know.

He tilted his head slightly, and Knox met his gaze. A

small shake—he had already thought of that but didn't want to discuss it here.

Leopol said nothing, already calculating to the next step. If they moved quickly, they could reach their packs and recover the supplies they needed. The bomb core. The regulator. The pieces the dwarves had salvaged were their last chance—if they used them wisely.

"Once we're in our rooms, we'll talk about strategy. I've got a few ideas—but we need the gear first. Meet back in Eirwyn and Knox's room?" Leopol asked.

They all nodded as they filed into the hallway, following the guards. A few hung back to bring up the rear.

As they passed, the younger of the two guards lingered, his eyes flicking to the cursed bracelet still wrapped around Eirwyn's wrist that Merida had disabled earlier.

"I—I hope the gods are with you," he whispered, barely audible.

Eirwyn didn't reply, just glared, but Leopol did.

"They're already here."

They filed quickly into their separate rooms under the watchful eyes of the guards, collecting cloaks, belts, satchels, and everything else they'd stashed away before their imprisonment. Within minutes, they regrouped in Knox and Eirwyn's room, the door shutting behind them like a final lock on peace.

Scarlet was the first to speak as she buckled a set of spare daggers to her thighs. "Finally." Scarlet exhaled. "Not the real deal, but at least they didn't check our bags."

Wulfric quirked a brow. "Those aren't *the* daggers."

"They're stand-ins," she grumbled with a shrug. "I'll make do."

"If we survive this," Wulfric said, fastening the straps on

his cloak, "I'm sure Prince Eryk or Princess Merida will ensure your babies are returned."

A beat of silence followed his words—heavy, uncertain.

Knox cleared his throat and turned to Leopol and Bella. "Can you open a portal?" he asked quietly. "Even a small one? Just enough to get Eirwyn and the egg out. Hartsgrove will be safer."

Knox's hands pulled Eirwyn's cloak around her shoulders as she glared up at him. "I'm not leaving you."

Knox glared right back. "You should."

Leopol glanced at Bella, his fingers curling slightly around hers. "We've spent a month learning how to *not* create a portal. Cerci is the only one who can control them. We can call on the talkie and ask."

"I'm not going to run away from this fight. Eryk and Merida are my friends. You're all my family. I'm not leaving you, Knox, but I'm not leaving them either," Eirwyn said, her hands going around Knox's waist.

"We can't just run," Bella added, her voice steady despite the tension in the room. "Hanzel will track us. And this—might be my last day. If I want my body back... I need to face him." She gestured to herself, her ghostly form faintly shimmering in the candlelight.

"See? If Bella is staying, I'm staying," Eirwyn said.

Knox's jaw flexed, his grip on Eirwyn's shoulder tightening. "Damn it."

"Don't worry," Eirwyn said, soft but fierce. She reached back to touch the egg. "We'll keep to the rear. I'll avoid the thick of it so you can focus, but don't ask me to abandon you."

A quiet moment passed between them while several of the Robins laced up leather armor and the Growlers checked their weapons.

Bella glanced at where the potted rose sat on the small table by the hearth. "If you're going to hang back, out of the battle, will you carry this for me? I'll be stronger with it nearby. I still don't know exactly how I'll fight as a spirit, but if the moment comes—I want to act. I'm a queen. It's time to act like it."

Eirwyn nodded and took the rose as reverently as she held the egg, holding it safely in front of her. "I'll keep it safe."

Leopol's throat worked as he stared at Bella. The idea of her going into battle in this fragile form—of her not return-ing—twisted something deep in his chest. He had to stay in control. If he lost her now, he'd never forgive himself.

"Eryk, what do you know of the wizard's forces?" Leopol asked.

Eryk shrugged from the window. "I know what I read in my father's missives... and what I can see. They're almost here."

They rushed to the windows, staring south as a black shadow came closer. Like the swift moving storm from that morning, it rolled like a wave.

"A shadow daemon," Bella whispered beside him.

He put his arm around her shoulders, more to ground himself than comfort her. "There will be other daemons probably too, on top of the undead he's collected along the route."

"And whatever magic allowed him to travel so swiftly," Eryk pointed out.

Leopol's voice was low but commanding. "We can't rush this. He'll expect brute force, not patience. We wait, strike when he slips, and disable the nekrotic field with the core. If we act too soon—we lose everything."

Bella squeezed his side. "Like we discussed back at

Hartsgrove. We use the scavenged core pulse bomb to disable the nekrotic field, trap the wizard's spirit with the regulator, and then Cerci will open the portal straight to the hells. "

His gaze swept over the room. "We only get one chance."

Knox nodded grimly. "Then let's make it count."

Chapter Fifty

The dull roar that shook the cobblestones beneath Leopol's feet came not from the sky, but from the throats of thousands of undead warriors massed beyond Glathen's walls. Their cries echoed off the limestone like the wails of the damned. Even through thick stone, the stench of rot and dark magic hung heavy in the morning air.

Leopol's jaw tightened. Citizens fled past him in terrified waves—mothers clutching infants, merchants abandoning carts, guards scrambling pale-faced to their posts. The city that had pulsed with life yesterday now writhed in chaos. Windows slammed, doors barred, and even the cobbles seemed to shudder with fear.

"There's a way out—go!" Prince Eryk shouted from the courtyard, directing people toward the harbor market. He pointed civilians through the inner gates, urging them away from the walls.

"Move." King Aldric's voice cut through the panic like a blade through silk—sharp and commanding, cold as stone.

He led the prisoners across the courtyard, his posture regal, his gaze fixed ahead.

Leopol forced his shoulders into a defeated slump, head bowed just enough to suggest submission. The bracelet on his wrist hummed with false magic, its silver links gleaming. Let them think him bound.

Knox strode beside him, jaw clenched, dark eyes scanning the street with lethal focus. His arm wrapped around Eirwyn, shielding her, even as her hands clutched the rose pot tight to her chest. Bella's lifeline. A fragile, vibrant thing nestled in a war zone.

The sight sent a spike of fury through Leopol's chest.

They were waiting, biding their time, letting their magical reserves strengthen from being bound this morning. The green vapor faintly curling from Knox's nostrils betrayed the effort it took to contain his power. The bracelets did nothing now.

Eirwyn's fear was real, but her posture matched Bella's and Scarlet's—chin high, shoulders forward, iron in their spines. They moved like prisoners but carried themselves like queens.

Bella drifted beside him, ethereal and glowing. She moved with purpose, her gaze pinned on the gates ahead—but he caught the tremor in her fingers where they gripped her skirts, the way her eyes flicked toward the wall where her stolen body waited.

He took her hand, anchoring them both, drawing strength from her even as he gave it.

"It'll all turn out alright in the end," he murmured, barely audible over the roar outside the gates.

She looked up at him, dark eyes solemn. Then she nodded once, her lips shaping a silent *we'll see.*

Behind them, Wulfric prowled like a shadow barely

leashed. His black fur bristled, his yellow eyes locked on every alley and window. He watched his daughter, his mate, his enemies. No leash in the world could hold the Growler's fury if they made the wrong move.

Scarlet's antlers caught the light. Her twitching nose and flicking tail made her look like some fey trickster, but her eyes were sharp as glass. Anyone fooled by her softness would die for their mistake. Her steps were light, her balance perfect, her gaze constantly measuring.

The servant behind her carried the gilded box with reverence. The egg within was treated as sacred—it was hope incarnate, or damnation for the entire world. Power rolled off Eirwyn's back, not the false egg in the box, humming in Leopol's bones like a second heartbeat.

As they turned from the courtyard onto the cobbled road, Eryk joined the procession. Leopol gave a subtle nod. The king's glare burned, but his son held his ground, meeting it with a stubborn stare.

He was brave and noble—but whether he was a hidden ace up their sleeve or a foolhardy, idealistic prince, time would tell. Leopol saw something of himself in the young man. Once, he'd taken a stand like that... and it had cost him his cousin, his king, his entire world.

Movement in the alley drew his eye. Flame-kissed hair flashed as Merida waved civilians into a small portal, blue rings of light swallowing families whole. Her hands never stopped. Her voice never faltered.

Their eyes met across the chaos. She recognized their group and froze like a deer before prey. Then her spine straightened, and determination settled around her like a crown.

Her gaze lingered on Leopol, and she gave a slight nod—acknowledgment, understanding, perhaps even encouragement. Then she was moving again, smiling reassuringly to a cluster of elderly citizens as they stepped through the shimmering circle.

Like Bella, she worked tirelessly to save lives while they marched toward potential doom. Fear and worry for them all twisted inside him—alongside a sliver of desperate hope. Maybe, just maybe, this game they were all playing would end with the innocent protected and the guilty punished.

He swallowed hard. Hope still lived, but so did danger, and it had grown more powerful in the three hundred years since he'd last faced it.

They marched on, and Leopol's thoughts churned with strategy. Too many pieces. Too many players. Aldric thought he was offering prisoners and treasure to buy peace. He had no idea he was handing the wizard everything he needed to end the world.

Leopol steadied his breath as they approached the massive gates, iron-reinforced wood standing as the final barrier between the city and the army of the damned. Soon, he would face the creature wearing his mate's face, speaking with her voice while harboring a soul black as the deepest pits of the hells.

He had to remain calm. Had to maintain the lie of weakness until the perfect moment. The bracelet pulsed with false energy, its magic designed to contain powers Merida had already disabled.

Let them think him bound and helpless. Let them believe their trap held firm. When the time came to act, their freedom would be the surprise that tipped the scales in their favor.

The truth would burn through every lie. And the gods wouldn't help anyone who stood in their way—not when Asmoroth was part of the equation.

A groan of iron shattered the silence, and the city held its breath. The gates of Glathen creaked open.

King Aldric commanded his guards and army to hold their positions, his authority echoing off the limestone walls. "Form ranks! Hold the gates! Let none pass without my command!"

Behind the opening gates, Glathen's forces snapped into position with practiced efficiency—archers nocked arrows atop the walls while pikemen and cavalry readied for the supernatural threat. Leopol doubted if conventional tactics would suffice against what approached.

Grotesque irony curled through him—the rightful Queen of Busparia was a spirit, while the wizard who had murdered her husband wore her flesh like a stolen gown. The thought made his hands curl into fists, the metal of the bracelet biting into his wrists as he fought the urge to let his true power flare.

Patience is a virtue. He snarled the platitude as they marched through the gates in their carefully orchestrated procession.

The formation was tight but deliberate: King Aldric marched at the front with six guards. Knox and Eirwyn came next, the rose cradled between them. Leopol walked beside Bella's spirit, followed by Wulfric and Scarlet, with the prince, the servant carrying the gilded egg box, and another guard detail bringing up the rear.

The enemy before him chilled his blood despite every ounce of confidence in dragon fire and magic.

The undead army spread across the field like a plague, their decaying bodies still clad in the crimson armor of once-proud warriors. Now, bound by dark magic, they stood in perfect formation. Their hollow eye sockets oozed congealed blood, and their swords, axes, and maces dripped with unspeakable substances. The stench was so overpowering that even the seasoned soldiers of Glathen retched over the wall and covered their faces.

Amidst the undead were living Buspartan soldiers, faces grim with the knowledge of their allegiance. These seasoned fighters moved with precision, their armor polished, and weapons sharp. Unlike their decomposing allies, they retained tactical awareness and individual thought, making them potentially more dangerous than the mindless dead.

Most terrifying were the Dragon Claws, exuding pure menace. Unlike the noble Growlers of Wulfric's pack, these were twisted, their natural ferocity turned into bloodthirsty savagery. Their fur was sickly green and yellow, eyes glowing with nekromantic magic. Even from afar, their constant low growling resonated in his bones.

At the head of this nightmare army rode three figures, and it was the middle one that filled Leopol with rage and anguish. Bella's stolen body sat on a black horse, transformed into something monstrous. Red scales coated her arms and neck, her eyes burning with malevolence. Twisted draconic wings sprouted from her shoulders, pulsating with dark magic.

It was the tilt of the head that confirmed he was Hanzel. The grip on the reins, the way the lip twisted on the left side in a permanent snarl. His hands twitched to wrap around the cocky bastard that had taken everything.

Eirwyn whispered to Knox and a faint line of green mist curled from his cousin's nose. He wasn't the only one holding on by a thread.

Every instinct screamed at him to tear the wizard from Bella's flesh and reclaim what was rightfully hers, but patience—deadly, calculating patience—was required now.

So he planned, thought through every spell he'd ever learned as both a dragon construct and as an Archivist in the astral library. As they drew closer to the enemy formation, Leopol studied the creature wearing Bella's face with the intensity of a scholar examining ancient texts.

"The General is on the left," Eirwyn murmured, her voice nearly drowned out by the tramp of boots and clink of armor.

Her fingers tightened around the potted rose as she nodded toward a figure flanking Hanzel. "Superb tactical mind, decades of battlefield experience. But the Chancellor..."

Her mouth twisted with distaste as she indicated the third rider. "He's just as formidable an opponent, though his weapons are political manipulation rather than sword and steel."

Knox's jaw clenched at his wife's words, and when he spoke, his voice carried the low growl of a protective mate. "Is that the bastard who kept pressing you for more even when you told him no?"

Eirwyn's nod was curt, her lips firming into a line hard as granite. The sound that emerged from Knox's throat was purely animalistic, a promise of violence that made several nearby guards glance nervously in his direction. Even bound in magical chains, the King of the Feral Forest radiated dangerous intent.

Behind them, Prince Eryk maintained his position despite his father's obvious displeasure, while the servant carrying the gilded box moved with the careful steps of a man bearing the world's fate in his hands.

Footsteps echoed behind them—Merida, hair tousled, green eyes sharp from the evacuation effort, slipped into step beside Eryk, her presence adding another variable to an already complex equation.

Her gaze lingered on each of them, assessing, calculating, preparing for whatever role she might need to play in the confrontation ahead. Leopol turned to face it too.

Carefully, he positioned himself behind Knox, using his cousin's broad shoulders as partial concealment without making it obvious. Hanzel probably realized he was alive—the Sentinel had almost proved it.

But just in case he didn't... the last thing they needed was for Hanzel to recognize him before the proper moment arrived.

The three enemy leaders urged their horses forward with predatory confidence, leaving the army behind as their group of prisoners with only a dozen guards strode beyond the safety of the gates.

Soon they would be face to face with the creature who had stolen everything from them—Bella's body, her kingdom, and the lives of countless innocents, including his own family years ago. Leopol's fingers flexed, magic coiled within him, hungry to strike despite the bracelet's supposed constraints.

The final game was about to begin, and he had to win this time.

Chapter Fifty-One

The gates groaned open, spilling sunlight—and dread—onto the road. The cobblestones ended in a dirt path through a field, meandering south. The low rumble of a thousand enemies coming to a halt made talk difficult.

The two forces faced off across fifty yards of packed dirt. On one side stood King Aldric of Glathen with political prisoners and a precious dragon egg, surrounded by disciplined soldiers on the edge of the cobblestone street.

On the other, chaos reigned: an undead horde, corrupted Growlers, and at their head, an abomination wearing Bella's stolen flesh.

Leopol held his ground as the three enemy leaders approached, their horses' hooves pounding like a funeral dirge. The General sat with military precision, his weathered face calm despite the supernatural army. The Chancellor's thin smile held no warmth—just the cold satisfaction of a scheming politician.

The creature at the center seized Leopol's unwilling

attention. It wasn't Bella–but her body had been twisted into a monstrous parody.

The stone streets behind them fell silent, leaving only wind, rot, and the soft clink of weapons awaiting command. King Aldric stopped where the cobblestone ended, his voice commanding yet slightly shaky.

"Here," he declared, pointing at the captives with strained confidence. "Take them, your army, and leave my lands as promised. Glathen has no conflict with you. Take them and leave us in peace."

Hanzel's laugh shattered like breaking glass, sharp and wrong from Bella's throat. The creature barely acknowledged the political prisoners, brushing off Knox and Eirwyn with a condescending sniff. His fiery gaze paused on Wulfric, sensing the alpha's threat, then skimmed over Scarlet to pause on Bella's spirit with barely concealed contempt.

"Your prisoners don't matter," Hanzel declared, his voice turning Bella's melody into a harsh command. "They're pawns in a game beyond your grasp. Where is the dragon's egg?"

The wizard's fiery eyes locked onto the gilded box in the nervous servant's hands. The container pulsed, the dragon egg inside bespelled to mimic the magical signature of the real one.

"The egg," Hanzel demanded greedily, his horse prancing closer to their group. "Hand it over, and maybe your pathetic kingdom will survive what's coming."

King Aldric clenched his jaw but kept his composure. "Why do you want a dragon's egg? What purpose justifies stealing a babe from its mother?"

The question hung like a sword mid-fall. Leopol sensed

the tension from both armies, anticipating the wizard's impending horrors.

Hanzel's scaled lips twisted into a predatory grin. "The dragonling's essence is raw, pure, and unimaginably potent. Draining it will give me the power I need to tear open the barriers between worlds and bring my sister back from the dead. Asmoroth will rise from the Deep, and this realm will burn in glorious flame."

The words dropped like stones into still water, spreading horror among the gathered forces. Several of Glathen's soldiers stepped back, while others crossed themselves or murmured prayers to their gods. Even the Chancellor's usual smirk wavered at the mention of summoning a demon lord.

Eirwyn whimpered, her hands gripping the potted rose tighter. The servant trembled violently, causing the gilded box to rattle, and Leopol feared it might be dropped.

With a low growl that barely teased his ears, Prince Eryk said, "They were right about the wizard."

King Aldric's face turned as pale as winter snow, his eyes widening. Aldric commanded, his voice hoarse with growing dread. "Show me this egg that's worth the destruction of the world."

Eirwyn jerked forward, but Knox's arm around her shoulders held her back as the servant hesitantly stepped forward, his hands trembling as he lifted the gilded box's lid. Inside, resting on silk, was an egg the size of a man's head.

Its shell glimmered with scales shifting through fiery hues—deep crimson, molten gold, and blazing orange, all pulsing with inner fire. Even from among the prisoners, Leopol sensed the magic from the fragile shell, and he held his breath, hoping the wizard accepted the fake as the real thing.

Hanzel's eyes blazed brighter, and his draconic wings spread slightly in anticipation. "Perfect," he breathed, the word carrying overtones of religious ecstasy. "Absolutely perfect. Bring it here."

King Aldric raised his hand, keeping the servant by his side. His diplomatic neutral expression clashed with rising horror as he sought a solution.

"Wait," he commanded, his voice steady despite shaking hands. "If I give you the prisoners and the egg, how do I know you'll honor your promise? What's to stop you from destroying Glathen once you get what you want?"

The wizard's expression darkened with annoyance, clearly unused to having his demands questioned. "You dare negotiate with me? You, a mortal king whose entire life is but a blink of an eye compared to my existence?"

"I dare protect my people," Aldric replied with growing strength. "Swear an oath—on all the gods, by whatever power you hold sacred—that if I give you these prisoners and the dragon egg, you and your army will turn around and leave Glathen without raising weapons against my kingdom or its people."

Leopol admired the king's nerve, even while fearing the futility of trying to bind a creature like Hanzel with words alone. Ancient wizards had ways of twisting oaths to their advantage, and this one had centuries of experience in deception and manipulation.

The undead army swayed in the afternoon breeze, their stench intensifying with the wind. The Dragon Claws Growlers paced restlessly behind the three riders.

Hanzel's scaled features twisted in rage at King Aldric's demand for an oath, his draconic wings flaring threateningly. The air heated up as his stolen magic fueled his fury.

"You insignificant old fool," he snarled, Bella's voice

turning hellish. "I am older and wiser than you can imagine, you insignificant worm. I roamed this world before your ancestors crawled from their caves."

The wizard glared at the prisoners, contempt in his eyes, his sharp teeth bared. "You think mortal concerns matter to me? Do you believe oaths hold meaning when the fate of the world is at stake?"

Leopol snorted and crossed his arms—a small gesture that cut through the wizard's bluster like a blade through silk.

The sound captured Hanzel's attention, his burning eyes locking onto Leopol with fierce intensity. Hanzel's gaze slowly went slack as he recognized who stood before him. Leopol was stronger now, more scarred—but his essence hadn't changed. Hanzel would know it anywhere.

Hatred dawned on Hanzel's face like a hateful sunrise.

"You," Hanzel breathed, the word carrying the weight of years of rage and frustration. His scaled hands clenched into fists, and the very air around him began to shimmer with heat distortion.

Leopol stepped around Knox, stopping beside the king and the servant with the egg in the box. He arched a brow and put a hand on his hip.

"Hanzel, you look terrible. What have you done to yourself?"

The wizard's voice rose to a shriek that made several horses rear and shy, their riders fighting to maintain control.

"Me? You caused all this! You cost me centuries of madness—trapped in that cursed mirror, watching the world through glass while my enemies and allies lived, died, and turned to dust!" He eased the nervous horse forward.

Leopol dropped his hands loose to his sides, ready for anything, and took an educated guess. "I'm not the one who stole dragonlings and died. None of this will bring your sister back, you know."

The wizard jumped off the horse and strode closer, eyes blazing with fury. "The contract with Asmoroth says it will."

He snatched the dragon egg out of the box, a look of triumph stretching the lips too wide. "Now, I will–"

Hanzel glanced down at the egg, then he looked up at Leopol, lips pursing as anger slammed into the wizard once more.

Leopol froze. The sound of the armies fell away, and not even the crashing of the nearby ocean could be heard in the stillness. *No, he couldn't know already.* They needed more time for reinforcements to–

"Lies!" Hanzel threw the egg to the ground, and it shattered in a thousand pieces. Inside–was nothing. No dragonling. Just emptiness.

Hanzel's rage peaked, spittle spraying. Hanzel's hand struck the servant's throat, dark magic amplifying the blow's deadly force. The man collapsed, eyes wide, neck twisted unnaturally.

Hanzel turned his bloody, dripping hand on Aldric, one eye never leaving Leopol's. Leopol had been too slow to save the servant, but the king's guard rushed forward, already stepping forward to protect their king.

King Aldric stepped backward to the safety of his guard, his face pale with horror as he finally understood the true scope of what he faced. "Wait, we can still–"

Hanzel's clawed hand pierced the king's chest, silencing his words in a gurgle of blood. With a spray of crimson, the wizard lifted the king's body effortlessly, as if holding a broken doll. "There will be no negotiations," Hanzel hissed, his voice laced with reptilian menace. "No bargains, no mercy, no escape."

He tossed the fallen king aside. It hit the ground with a wet thud that echoed through the stunned silence.

For a heartbeat, both armies stood frozen in shock at the casual brutality they had just witnessed. Then Hanzel's burning gaze fixed on Leopol.

"I'd hoped you lived. I dreamed of this moment, planned for it through every fucking day. Thought you fled to the northern mountains, but if you're with this rabble, you must've been in Hartsgrove this whole time. Today, you pay for what you did to me!" Then the wizard launched himself forward with inhuman speed.

The lunge carried centuries of pent-up fury, but Leopol had no more time to prepare. Leopol ripped the bracelet from his wrist and flung it aside. Golden energy exploded from his core, swirling into a protective shield that met Hanzel's claws mid-lunge.

Leopol growled, his voice carrying harmonics of ancient power that made the very ground beneath their feet tremble. "I've been waiting for this moment too, you bastard. Waiting for the chance to finish what I started."

The two forces collided, sending shockwaves across the battlefield, magic bending the air solid around him.

Hanzel's stolen fire struck like a comet—meeting golden lightning in a collision that cracked the sky and ricocheted off the ground.

Eryk and Merida rushed forward to their father, screaming and breaking the frozen moment.

Chaos erupted as both armies sprang into action. Glathen's soldiers charged with battle cries, their ranks slamming into the undead horde like a wave against a seawall.

Knox pulled Eirwyn into the protection of his arms, shifting to a bigger hybrid form to shield her, the rose, and the real dragon egg with his wings. Bracelets fell to the ground in quick succession.

Scarlet and Wulfric faced the Dragon Claws, rushing just ahead of the eight Growlers and Robins they'd brought. The alpha's roar of challenge echoed across the battlefield as he began his transformation, silver and black fur rippling across his expanding frame.

Prince Eryk had drawn his sword, his face set with grim determination as he moved to protect Princess Merida. The princess herself kneeled beside her father, weaving blue magic over his body in what Leopol recognized as an assessment spell.

At the center of it all, Leopol faced the creature wearing his mate's stolen flesh, energy crackling around him like captured lightning. Bella's spirit hovered nearby, her ethereal form glowing brighter as her own power responded to the magical conflagration erupting around them.

The final battle had begun. And before it ended, kingdoms would burn, gods would tremble, and the world would remember the day love and vengeance collided.

Chapter Fifty-Two

The Buspartan army surged across the battlefield like a black tide. Terror clawed at Eirwyn's throat. Her hands shook, sparks of light crackling between her fingers—but her body refused to obey. Even as power built inside her like a drawn bowstring, her knees buckled when she tried to step forward.

"I should be fighting, stop my people," she gasped against Knox's chest, her voice barely audible over the clash of steel and war cries as the two armies collided.

Knox's wings curved around her, creating a green cocoon of false safety. "Your job is to protect our babe," he said, his voice steady despite the arrows that whistled overhead. "Not this."

Rage flared alongside her fear. She wasn't some helpless princess to be sheltered while others died, but her legs trembled beneath her. The scent of blood and smoke filled her nostrils, and she found herself taking in every detail of the chaos surrounding them instead of acting.

To her left, three Buspartan soldiers had cornered one

of the Glathen guards. The man's sword work was elegant, deadly–parry, riposte, a spinning cut that opened one attacker's throat. Blood sprayed in a crimson arc, and Eirwyn's stomach lurched. She'd never seen death up close, never watched a man's eyes go vacant as life drained from his body.

Behind them, she could hear Eryk barking orders to his remaining men. "Hold the line! Keep them away from the princess!" His voice carried the authority of someone who'd seen countless battles, but she caught the edge of desperation beneath it.

A cry of anguish cut through the din of battle, higher and more terrible than the dying screams of soldiers. Eirwyn twisted in Knox's arms, peering around his wing to see Merida falling to her knees beside her father's fallen figure. Only a few feet away, she could see the spreading pool of dark blood beneath his robes and armor.

"Father!" Merida's voice broke on the word, raw with grief and terror.

Knox's grip tightened on Eirwyn's shoulders. "Don't look," he murmured, but she couldn't tear her gaze away.

The king lay motionless, no longer breathing. A gaping wound in his chest, and when Merida pressed her hands to the wound, blood seeped between her fingers, staining her blue dress.

"He's dying!" Merida screamed, looking up at Eryk with wild eyes. "I can see his heart! Eryk, what do we do?"

Eryk stood frozen for a heartbeat, his sword dripping red, four guards flanked around him in a protective formation. The Glathen army surged past them like a river around stones, most of the enemy soldiers focused on the main battle lines rather than this small group of defenders behind it.

The answer hit Eirwyn, and she sucked in a breath.

"Use the orb!" Eirwyn shouted back, her voice carrying over the clash of weapons. "That's what it's for!"

The orb. Merida fumbled with slick, wet hands for her pocket and pulled out the small apple-sized orb. Ancient magic, older than kingdoms, older than the wars that had shaped these lands.

Something shifted inside Eirwyn's chest, a loosening of the paralysis that had held her captive. She pushed out of Knox's protective embrace, her movements sudden and determined to help her friend.

He followed immediately, keeping his wings spread wide like a living shield as arrows continued to streak overhead.

Her hand went instinctively to her back, feeling for the reassuring weight of her egg through the fabric of her dress. Still there. Still safe. The knowledge steadied her, gave her something to anchor to as she approached Merida and the dying king.

Merida held it up to catch the weak sunlight that filtered through the smoke of battle. "Show me how to save my father," she whispered, then louder, more desperate: "How do I save him?"

The orb flashed with brilliant light, so bright Eirwyn had to squint as she kneeled beside Merida, setting the potted rose beside the fallen king. Images swirled within the sphere—a cave, tears falling like raindrops, a creature with scales that gleamed like pearls.

Eirwyn leaned closer, her breath catching as understanding dawned. "The siren's tears."

Both she and Merida said it at the same time, both gasping. But Merida was quicker to act, already reaching for her father's pockets.

"He had it on him. Where is it, where—" she sighed as she pulled it out.

Her fingers fumbled with the cork, precious seconds ticking away as her father's breathing grew more labored. The need to help her friend finally released the shock and paralysis that had swept through Eirwyn.

"Hurry," Eirwyn urged, shifting on her knees beside them, putting the potted rose down and pressing her hands to his chest to try to stop the flow of blood.

She couldn't look at the open wound. The king's face had gone gray, his lips tinged blue. She could see the slight rise and fall of his chest growing weaker with each breath, but refused to look down, to stop hoping.

Knox protected them on one side and Eryk and the guards stood on the other. The world muffled as her ears rang.

Merida finally got the vial open, the liquid inside shimmering with an otherworldly light. It looked like captured moonbeams, like starlight made tangible. She tilted her father's head back, prying his lips apart with desperate fingers.

"Please," she whispered as she poured half the siren's tears down his throat. "Please work."

For a moment, nothing happened. The king lay still, blood continuing to seep from his wounds.

Merida made a growl of frustration and pushed Eirwyn's hands away. Then she poured the rest of the vial directly into the open cavity of his chest where his heart pulsed, twisted and unprotected and punctured.

Then his body began to glow with that same sea-glass light, emanating from his skin like he'd swallowed the moon itself.

The transformation started slowly, a subtle shifting

beneath his flesh. Then his body twisted violently, contorting in ways that should have been agonizing but somehow weren't. Knox jerked Eirwyn back, and she grabbed the edge of the potted rose just as he began to flail.

Bones cracked—not in pain, but unforming, reshaping themselves into something smaller, more delicate.

Eirwyn watched in fascination and horror as the king's flesh tightened, warped, then softened. His weathered hands grew smooth and small, his beard disappearing as his features melted and reformed. His armor, suddenly too large, fell away piece by piece, clattering against the cobblestones.

The light intensified, and when it finally faded, a baby lay crying in the velvet folds of the king's cloak. Not a newborn though—perhaps eight months old, with chubby fists and clear, bright eyes that held no memory of the man he'd been moments before.

Merida stared at the child in shock, her hands hovering over him uncertainly. "Father?" she whispered, but the baby only cried louder, his wails piercing even over the sounds of battle.

Eirwyn's mind raced. The potted rose she'd been carrying—Bella's lifeline, somehow forgotten in the chaos beside Merida and the crying baby. Eirwyn grabbed the king's discarded shirt from the pile of oversized armor.

"Take him," she said, wrapping the shirt around the infant and thrusting him into Merida's arms. She pointed to the rose with its delicate petals and thorny stem. "You keep them both safe. We'll stand guard until your own guards can escort you safely back behind the gates. But take the rose with you and keep it safe. Bella dies when the last petal falls."

Merida nodded, some of her shock falling away as she

cradled the baby against her chest. The child's cries softened, perhaps soothed by the heartbeat, even in this smaller
form.

Something fundamental had shifted in Eirwyn during
those moments of crisis. The fear was still there, coiled in
her belly like a living thing, but it no longer controlled her.
She stood over Merida and the transformed king, no longer
the cowering girl who'd hidden beneath Knox's wings.

She had her own baby to protect. She had to fight to
save this world for him, so he could grow up safe and happy,
without the fear of the god of death coming back to destroy
it all.

The battle raged around them, but their small group
had become an island of relative calm. Eryk and his guards
formed a defensive perimeter, their swords creating a
barrier of steel between them and the chaos beyond.

An arrow whistled past Eirwyn's ear, close enough that
she felt the fletching brush her skin. Instead of flinching, she
raised her hands, light gathering between her palms like
captured lightning. The power felt different now—not wild
and uncontrolled, but focused, purposeful.

She sent the burst of light streaking toward a cluster of
Glathen soldiers who were trying to flank their position.
The explosion of light sent them stumbling backward,
temporarily blinded and disoriented. Not lethal, but effective—a defensive maneuver that bought them precious
seconds.

Another group of enemies approached from the right,
their weapons raised and eyes blazing with hatred. Eirwyn's
hand went to her back again, touching the egg through her
dress. She had something to protect now, something more
important than her own fear.

Shadows crackled between her fingers, pulling from

around her where the shadows of the wall were thickest. She threw it over the group of soldiers like a black blanket, and when it settled on them, they stumbled under the weight of it. She alternated throwing shadows and light, each one a controlled explosion of radiance and darkness that forced the attackers to shield their eyes and stumble under it. She wasn't trying to kill—she was creating a barrier, a zone of safety around her people.

"Well done," Knox said softly, moving to stand beside her. His wings spread as he shifted fully into his dragon form.

Knox growled low and reached through the mind link that bound him to Eirwyn.

I'll protect you, my queen.

She didn't answer with words. Instead, her jaw clenched, and she hurled another brilliant burst of light into the enemy ranks. He hovered, wings spread as arrows flew overhead.

She was a force of radiance—fierce, furious, and utterly breathtaking. Even with death all around them, he loved her more in that moment than he had the first time they touched.

I'd rather you take out the General... or the Chancellor. Her focus didn't waver, but her frustration pulsed through the bond.

But you—

She threw a glare over at him and her tone was steel. *I'll take care of myself—and our egg. I won't leave Merida or Eryk, if it makes you feel better about joining the fray.*

It didn't, not really. But he trusted her.

Knox inhaled, and thick green smoke rolled from his

nostrils, spreading like a plague across the battlefield toward the Buspartan army. He turned his gaze on the Chancellor, scanning for that smug, oily face among the chaos.

The bastard had dared to threaten Eirwyn, had tried to bully her into his bed when she was still just a terrified young princess. Knox had wanted to rip him limb from limb when Eirwyn had mentioned it.

His roar ripped through the air, shaking the very bones of the battlefield. Green fog churned around him as he surged upward, wings flinging dirt and blood into the air. His sharp eyes found the Chancellor astride a black steed, issuing orders with flailing hands while fire rained from the General beside him.

Bella's spirit fought beside Leopol, tossing objects at Hanzel from the ground, but her attention was divided between the General and Chancellor too. She couldn't finish them—not while Hanzel still loomed.

So, Knox would.

With a second roar, he dove. The General was a second quicker and jerked his horse back, barely avoiding Knox.

His claws snapped around the Chancellor like a vice, talons curling into rich velvet robes. The man screamed as Knox lifted him effortlessly into the sky.

"What are you doing?! Put me down!" the Chancellor screeched, flailing wildly.

Knox glanced down between his hind legs at the writhing man dangling by one foot.

"Disposing of garbage," he snarled, his voice thick and gravel-edged in his dragon form.

Then he let go.

The Chancellor's scream cut short when he hit the battlefield with a wet crunch. Knox didn't look back.

He circled once, high above the battlefield, and his

stomach twisted. The undead horde stretched beyond the horizon—a wave of death they couldn't hope to contain with sword or spell alone.

He opened his jaws and bathed the undead in a fresh cloud of noxious green gas. Nothing. They didn't even twitch.

Of course they can't be poisoned, he growled through the mind link, sending it to Eirwyn. *We have to disarm the horde. Leopol needs to use the core like we planned. He's the only one who can shut down the nekrotic magic.*

Her reply came fast, breathless. *We need a distraction—something big—to buy him time away from the wizard.*

He saw her shout something over her shoulder, but he was too high and too busy clawing the enemy lines to hear her voice.

Still, one eye never left her. She was his everything, and he would not lose her to this war.

Then Prince Eryk looked to Eirwyn, leaned over the transformed king—and rose, lifting something high above his head: another dragon egg.

He stepped into view from the blood-soaked stones, cradling the egg in one arm as he turned to face the battlefield. Light gleamed off its fiery scales, so real that Knox's wingbeat faltered.

He roared instinctively, wings tipping forward to dive—

Wait! Eirwyn's voice sliced through the panic. *It's another fake. Don't panic. I still have our babe behind me. Keep acting like it's real so the wizard takes the bait!*

Reluctantly, he veered off, unleashing a swirl of furious green fog across the battlefield as he circled the egg. The Glathen guards closed ranks around Merida and Eirwyn, forming a protective wall. Meanwhile, Eryk dashed across the open ground, waving the decoy like a lure.

"You destroyed my family for this?" he shouted, his voice cutting through the roar of war. He held the egg aloft. "Then take it, you scaly bastard—if you're willing to bleed for it!"

Hanzel's attention snapped away from his fight with Leopol to the prince—and Knox's heart seized.

One blast of corrupted fire hurled Leopol through the air. Almost simultaneously, another fireball slammed into Eryk, flinging him across the field like a broken doll.

The egg tumbled from Eryk's hands and rolled—straight into the heart of the battlefield.

Eirwyn's scream pierced the air. Knox twisted midair, thrown off by the sound—just in time for the General's spell to slam into his side.

He didn't have time to dodge.

The fireball hit with brutal force, ripping through his ribs and wing. He spiraled, wings folding, and fell hard—aiming instinctively for Eirwyn's side of the field.

He crushed enemy soldiers on impact, a blur of snapping bones and shrieks that vanished under the roar in his ears.

Knox! Eirwyn's scream reached him like sound through water.

Pain arced through every nerve—hot, sharp, unrelenting. He tried to lift his head, but everything felt wrong.

I'm alive—barely. Are you? What's happening? Panic pushed some of the haze of pain from his mind, sharpening his focus as he assessed where he was.

I'm alright! she said quickly through the bond. *I screamed to keep the wizard invested. Oh gods, you better not be hurt.*

He groaned. Of course, she hadn't done the expected and had just acted. He was already dragging himself toward her, heart pounding, instincts howling to get to her—to the egg.

Through blurry vision, he saw Hanzel grab the fake egg. Another fireball lit the sky—this one white-hot, aimed straight at Knox.

He couldn't move fast enough, not in full dragon form.

It was a solid hit. Pain exploded across his flank, and the world tilted as he hit the ground again, harder this time. Soldiers scattered beneath him like dry leaves, and the impact stole the air from his lungs.

Knox! Stay with me!

Her voice shivered through his mind like a thread of light, anchoring him.

She was above him now, her glow blazing brighter than the sun, hands flinging light like fireworks—shielding him, holding the line, even as tears streaked her face.

His body shook, and smoke curled from his scales as blood pooled beneath him.

Still, he growled low, a rumble from deep in his chest, a vow he would never break. *I'll never leave.*

He had to rise, heal, fight—for her, for their child, for the world they deserved.

Chapter Fifty-Three

Leopol crashed too far away.

"Leopol!" Bella screamed, her spirit streaking through the air like a comet toward his broken body. She dove low, hands glowing with magic, and cast a diagnostic spell mid-flight.

Broken ribs, fractured scapula, and a bruised lung. He was hurt—but alive.

Relief warred with panic as he groaned, his voice rough. "Hanzel?"

She whipped her head toward the center of the battle-field. Hanzel stood tall, her stolen body lit with infernal light, egg clutched tight in clawed hands. Dark runes spiraled around him, the magic thick as blood smoke.

"He has the egg—he's starting a portal spell. Please let that be the other fake one." Her breath caught, but she forced her gaze toward Eirwyn. There—kneeling beside Knox's massive fallen form. A clear bulge pressed against her back—not a petticoat or bustle.

"Thank the stars. The real egg is safe." Bella breathed

in–and gagged. The stench of rot and burning magic hit like a physical blow, now that she was touching Leopol and could smell.

"The wizard has a fake?" Leopol gasped, his voice echoing in the space around them.

"Yes, but that spell... I think he's really opening a portal to the hells, fake egg or not."

Fear gripped her chest. She reached for him instinctively, pouring her spirit into his–offering strength, just as he'd once done for her.

"We can't let him open it. We have to stop him." Leopol coughed, groaning as he rolled onto his side.

Helplessness ate at her because this was something she couldn't solve on her own. "Leopol, we can't take him on with the undead closing in. We're outnumbered. You have to use the bomb. Can you fly?"

He groaned again, dragging himself to his knees. "I think so. But the core will only block nekrotic magic for half an hour at best. It won't be long enough to stop him."

"Then we make it enough," she said, her hand firm on his back as she watched the battle unfold around them. "Half an hour to end the world or save it."

The General turned–and saw them. Bella rose to her feet, hands at her sides, sorting through every spell she knew.

Leopol stood beside her, and she glanced at him. He cupped her face, drawing all her attention to him.

His eyes shone with unspoken emotion. He licked his lips and kissed her swiftly, gone before she could fully taste him. That's when she knew–she didn't want to live without him.

"Bella, I–"

"I know," she said, her heart pounding as the sound and

stench of the battlefield crashed down again. She forced herself to pull away–it was the only way to mute the god-awful smell. Her hands dropped, pointing toward his waist, and she finally took a deep breath, the smell muted now.

Her voice firmed. "Save it for later. For now–are you sure you can fly with broken ribs?"

He rolled his shoulders and winced. "What choice do we have?"

She didn't argue, just prayed to the gods to watch over him.

He growled low, golden light spiraling over him in sacred runes and fire. Bones cracked as limbs twisted and stretched. In a rush of heat and wind, he burst into the sky in his full dragon form–magnificent and scarred, silver light gleaming across blue scales. In one talon, the Orythium core blazed like a second sun.

A blast of heat scorched past her shoulder, and Bella spun midair, barely dodging a flash of metal and stone.

The General advanced, sword crackling with fire.

She froze–just for a heartbeat–and thought: *What would Eirwyn do?*

"Stand down!" she commanded, rising higher, her voice ringing like a bell of judgment. "I am Bellatrix, Queen of Busparia. Call off your forces, in the name of your true queen."

The General gave a shallow bow, eyes never leaving hers. "You look like her," he said smoothly, "but you're not really here to give orders, are you?"

Her pulse thundered.

He opened a pouch from his waist and pulled out her crown. "My real queen ordered me to capture you."

The crown pulsed with dark magic that she could see now, thanks to her bond with Leopol.

"All I need is for you to touch it, then you'll be trapped." Then he hurled it at her.

She surged upward, dodging the cursed crown in a flare of rage. "Not a chance, you bastard."

With a thought, the air around her shimmered and swords lifted from the fallen. A shattered banner pole snapped into a spear. Knives skittered across the blood-slick ground like wolves on the hunt.

She unleashed them all at him and the undead around them.

Steel howled through the air, slashing and spinning, carving through the General's defense. He blocked some—but not all. A sword caught his shoulder, blood spraying. When another bit into his thigh, she dove, screaming and slamming into the sword, driving it deeper into his shoulder.

He staggered, and a final blow to the head dropped him into the dirt. She didn't wait to see if he rose.

Bella spun midair, searching for her family, for Leopol. Scarlet and Wulfric battled the Dragon Claws, teeth and steel locked in brutal combat. Hanzel's runes burned into the earth like brands, the very air warping with hellfire. Overhead, Leopol's golden lightning carved into the undead horde, dropping corpses in droves as he twisted the orb in his claws.

Her gaze flicked to the rose nestled near Merida. Its glow flickered—another petal curled at the edge. Time was up.

Hanzel must be dealt with *now*—with or without Leopol's help. She floated and aimed herself toward him, determined to end this nightmare. Through smoke and blood, through chaos and fire, she sliced through the sky.

She would not let him open that portal.

Fur, bone, muscle—Scarlet was the deer, swift and graceful, darting past slashing claws before they even struck. Then the rabbit, springing high into the air as jaws snapped at nothing beneath her. Then the wolf, all teeth and fury. Then the Hunter, human-shaped but far more dangerous, daggers an extension of instinct and will.

Blood flew in arcs around her. Claws clashed against steel. Jaws locked on jugulars, and shrieks rose as she spun and drove her blades home—every strike precise, every movement honed by grief and fury.

But the Dragon Claws didn't fight like warriors. They fought like cornered animals, wild-eyed and foaming, heedless of pain. Their fur was mottled, sickly, and their limbs moved with unnatural jerks. One leaped onto her back, snarling, and she shifted, slamming it down onto the stones. Her antlers drove deep, and blood sprayed. She shifted again, swiping at her own gash without flinching.

If they couldn't feel pain, they weren't going to stop or be easy to kill.

They had to hold the line, though. Leopol was out there trying to stop Hanzel. Bella needed to reclaim her body. Knox and Eirwyn would protect the egg. That left her and Wulfric to keep the rest of the army at bay.

They were doing it—for now. The narrow field gave them just enough of a bottleneck to slow the flood.

Then the shadow daemon appeared.

It slithered into view like smoke through cracks—lightless, shapeless, its presence warping the air. Scarlet faltered, remembering a previous shadow daemon battle. She couldn't track it by sight—none of them could. It was like trying to follow a nightmare.

"Don't let it touch you!" someone shouted. "It feeds on your life!"

"It can be killed, if you can find its body," Scarlet shouted back, voice fierce.

Then she dove, rolled beneath its formless swipe, and came up with her daggers crossed. The thing lunged again—pure hunger—and Wulfric leaped into its path, his massive body colliding with the void.

"No!" she screamed, as he hit the ground hard, the shadow clinging to him like oil and acid.

He didn't move.

Scarlet's heart cracked wide. She shifted mid-sob, her wolf form launching into the thick, choking air. Breath burned in her lungs, but she fought by feel now—pushing through darkness, stabbing at presence instead of shape.

There. Solid form beneath the smoke.

Her jaws clamped down. Her blades followed. The daemon shrieked, an echo of every nightmare she'd ever had. Still, she held on. Still, she *ripped*.

By the time it dissolved, her vision was going white at the edges. She dropped what remained, panting. The air stank of death and rot.

Wulfric still lay unmoving. She dropped to his side, shaking him, her hands bloody.

Wulfric. No answer.

Answer me, damn it. Still nothing.

She howled, rising with blades dripping, grief overtaking fury. The Dragon Claws surged, and she welcomed them. Let them take her. Let her burn the world down with her.

Across the battlefield, Knox lay still, Eirwyn casting bursts of light to shield him. Leopol moved through the sky with the glowing Orythium core, waving it like a burning lantern over the undead. Eryk's body lay prone, two guards protecting it. Merida crouched beside the rose—holding a baby?

Where had the baby come from?

The battlefield blurred—too many fronts, too many fallen. The General dropped and Bella floated like a vengeful goddess toward Hanzel, and Scarlet's heart sank.

She couldn't face him alone. They were all separated, all scattered. This wasn't war. It was a slaughter.

She looked down at Wulfric's still form, and something in her broke. She raised her daggers, shaking, lips pulled back in a snarl. "No, I won't leave him."

Ready to fight til her last breath, she braced herself. Then, the wall beside the gates shimmered.

Light flared, and a portal tore open, glowing with golden fire—and Lailant stepped through, skirts swirling in the unnatural breeze. The Seer looked around, calm and collected, then took one step to the side.

Dozens of Growlers poured from the portal, howling as they raced forward—her pack, her people, her family. They joined the fray with claws bared and fury boiling in their bones. The Robins followed, blades gleaming and slicing.

Cerci rode a battle eagle, light blazing in her hands. Ashur was just behind, sword in hand, his stone body leaping and gliding through the fray with the grace of a god. He was unbound by the curse that froze him in daylight, now that he'd taken the same ritual as the others back at Hartsgrove last week. He had been transformed by it, but the bond with Cerci had already changed his DNA, much like it had done to Scarlet all those months ago.

Above, more eagles screamed from the portal, talons snapping. They dove into the undead, ripping apart bodies and scattering the necrotic tide.

Alpha Growlers surged around Scarlet, forming a protective wedge that shoved the Dragon Claws back. Cerci dropped from her eagle's back and ran straight to Scarlet's side, a glowing vial already uncorked.

"Hold him," Cerci ordered.

Scarlet obeyed, unable to do anything else, afraid to hope, afraid to argue. Ashur stepped between them and the enemy, his sword a streak of afternoon light.

Cerci poured the potion between Wulfric's lips and pressed a glowing palm to his chest. Her brow furrowed, magic pulsing between her fingers.

Please. Please, gods. Please. Scarlet prayed to gods she'd long abandoned.

Finally—his chest rose. His hand twitched, and when his eyes opened and locked instantly onto hers, she breathed a sigh of relief.

Bunny, you're safe. His voice rang hoarse and tender through their bond. *Bella?*

Scarlet swallowed back a sob and helped him sit, her smile shaking and fierce.

"She took care of the General. She's headed for Hanzel now."

Wulfric groaned. "Gods, she's as reckless as you."

She laughed, the sound half sob, half snarl. "Takes one to know one."

Cerci stood and remounted her eagle. "I'll see if I can help Bella," she said, launching into the air.

Together, Scarlet and Wulfric rose. Together, they turned. Together, they *fought*—bonded, bleeding, burning with love and rage and the will to win.

Reinforcements had arrived, and the tide had turned, but the battle wasn't over yet. Not by a long shot.

Bella hurled blades, banners, broken bits of debris—anything she could animate—toward the wizard, her magic clawing through the air with frantic purpose. Each sword she flung slammed toward his body or the ground, trying to shatter the runes he etched into the earth with glowing fingers, but he barely looked her way.

One hand remained steady, tracing infernal symbols in ash and blood, while the other flicked lazily toward her projectiles, knocking them away with insultingly little effort.

She screamed—not aloud, but inside her own chest, where fury and helplessness battled like fire and wind. It was the Winter Palace all over again. The mirror. The tornado. The suffocating, sickening feeling of watching herself vanish while her body remained, wielded by a monster wearing her skin.

"No," she gasped, rising higher into the smoke-choked sky, spectral force beating hard. "Not again."

The battlefield sprawled beneath her like a broken painting, and her mind worked swiftly to break each piece down into manageable chunks. Through the shattered bodies, rivers of blood, and glimmers of resistance as Leopol worked to activate the core, an idea formed. What was meant for evil could be used for good, if she could work it right.

Toward her, sharp as a lance of light, flew the battle eagles. One swooped close enough to stir her hair, and on its back, Cerci twisted around to meet her gaze.

"How can I help?" the demigoddess shouted, voice ringing with divine clarity even through the chaos.

Bella didn't hesitate. "Find the crown," she called back, pointing toward the fallen General's body. "It's enchanted—

don't touch it. But if we can rip him out of my body, it can trap his spirit." Like he'd planned to trap her.

Cerci nodded once and vanished into the storm of feathers and fire. Knox was now up on his feet, blowing gas at the enemy, but Leopol hadn't activated the Sentinel's core yet to suppress the nekrotic magic.

But it'd be alright. When Bella's eyes returned to the wizard, she smiled as her plan came together.

"You're wasting your breath," she shouted down at him, staying high above the ring of glowing sigils. "The egg you're draining? It's another fake."

The wizard froze, hand hovering mid-sigil. His hand flashed with magic she could see now, and then, with a wordless growl, he hurled the egg to the ground. It cracked open like rotten fruit, spilling nothing but ash and dropping the illusion mimic spell. His fury twisted the air, and for the first time, his defenses dipped.

Bella struck hard.

She yanked the armored bodies of fallen undead into the sky with her magic, then slammed them into him like battering rams. One, two, three—steel and rotted flesh thudded into his frame.

He faltered, snarled, and tried to shield himself, but she wouldn't let up. She piled the bodies where he worked, slowing him just enough that his runes twisted slightly out of alignment—but not enough to stop him.

He sent a pulse of magic toward the circular symbol on the ground—black and wrong—and the ground cracked.

A black gash tore open at the wizard's feet, wide as a wagon and pulsing with heatless void. The smell of rot and brimstone billowed outward, and the sky darkened further as screams echoed up from below—souls or shadows, she couldn't tell. The portal wasn't to the lowest hell, not yet. But it was open. A threshold. A wound.

He stepped back, triumphant, his eyes glowing with madness. "It's done. Asmoroth will find the path. He always finds what he's called to."

Bella's fear and rage crystallized. She shot downward like a spear, snatching a broken flagpole from the rubble, and swung it straight into the back of his head.

The wizard's spirit tore free in a shriek of dark light, and Bella's body collapsed to the ground like a puppet with cut strings.

For a heartbeat, everything froze.

Then Bella lunged. Not for her body, but for his spirit.

Her spirit slammed into his, and for the first time in what felt like a lifetime, she faced him—truly faced him—as herself. No body. No enchantments. No stolen faces. Just two souls locked in battle.

He was older here, hunched and wiry, his hands like claws, but his strength remained unnatural. They grappled mid-air, ghost against spirit, magic and memory fueling every blow. She slammed her elbow into his face, yanked chains from the battlefield and wrapped them around his legs, tried to tear pieces of him away with every ounce of her hatred.

Every trick she'd learned growing up in a rough and tumble tavern? She used it, dirty or not. There were no second chances here. This battlefield was not a practiced gentleman's war, where battle line met battle line. It was a knockdown, drag out, fight with every tooth and nail battle to the death.

"Bella!" Cerci's voice rang out again, and this time, it was laced with panic. "You have two minutes to get back into your body before it dies!"

But Bella didn't stop.

The daemons slithered from the rift below, black shapes with hungry mouths and too many limbs, eyes glowing with the same sick light that had haunted her dreams. The wizard clawed at her, tried to drive them toward her with a beckoning flick of his wrist.

Bella ducked a swipe of spectral claws and called a broken spear from the field, driving it into his side. "You don't get to use me again," she hissed. "You don't get to win this time."

Below them, the battlefield raged on—but the center of the war was here, in this ghost-slick space between magic and flesh, and Bella wasn't leaving until she'd torn him down... or until time ran out.

Chapter Fifty-Four

The core's runes flickered like a dying star. Every second Leopol flew was another chance the wizard had to complete his spell, but he couldn't risk detonating it too close to Bella. Not with the rose still glowing on the battlefield. If the bomb disrupted the nekrotic magic holding the undead, it would hurt Bella too.

If Leopol severed Bella from her rose, he might kill her himself.

So, he flew wide, wings slicing through smoke, past the ridge where the undead pressed hard against Glathen's outer line, trying to flank from the east. They swarmed like ants–snapping jaws, rotting hands, glowing eyes fixed only on the kill.

There. A gap near the center, surely it was far enough away from Bella. He dove low, skimming just above the skeletal arms and half-armored torsos reaching for him.

The core pulsed again, and Leopol roared, launching it like a meteor into the thickest part of the horde.

Golden lightning erupted from the runes, pulsing out like a magical wave.

For a heartbeat, nothing happened. Then they dropped, *all* of them.

Every corpse hit the ground in a strange, synchronized collapse. One fell mid-swing. Another tumbled from a half-formed siege tower, crashing into the limbs below. A mounted undead crumpled into its saddle as the beast it rode buckled, bones flying as it too broke apart.

Silence rippled outward in their wake, broken only by the distant cries of battle still raging near the city gates.

It worked. At least–for now. At least, on the undead. There still remained the ragtag living Buspartan soldiers. Interspersed among the undead, mostly in leadership roles, they stood gaping at the devastation around them.

Then they began running toward the castle, where fighting still continued.

Leopol hovered, breathing hard, smoke rising from his nostrils. His pulse pounded too loudly in his ears–not with triumph, but with cold calculation. It had worked, but it wasn't permanent.

He circled once and scanned the wreckage. In the bomb's wake, magic bled from the undead like oil draining from a cracked flask. The Orythium core had nullified the nekrotic magic, purified it enough to cleanse the field–but only temporarily.

He scooped up the core's shell with one claw and inspected it as he flew. Already, the runes in the bomb casing had dimmed, the last ember of Orythium flickering low.

There wasn't enough for a second detonation. That had been the only shot to weaken the wizard enough to defeat him... or die trying.

He turned, wings straining against the wind from the sea, flying hard across the sky.

Where was Bella?

He ducked through smoke and swerved past the shadow of a daemonic bird-thing clawing at an eagle midair. The skies churned with chaos—battle eagles and their Robin riders clashed with winged daemons, arcs of magic igniting the clouds like firestorms.

And then he saw her body.

It lay still—spiritless—half-shadowed near a pile of zombified bones. His breath froze, but he dove to her side.

"Bella–" he landed hard, skidding across cracked cobblestone, claws gouging furrows in the ground. He shifted halfway down, grabbing her limp body while looking for her spirit. He'd never touched her body, but she needed it alive if she were to merge with it again. If they were to have a hope for a future.

"Please," he whispered, pulling a vial from his belt. "Don't be too late."

He poured the glowing potion between her pale lips. It slid down her scaled throat, but her eyes didn't flutter. Her chest didn't rise. Her spirit... wasn't there.

"Come back to me," he rasped. "You've got to come back."

There was no answer, no flicker of magic. Just silence from a body already cold as death. He searched the battlefield for her spirit, but his eyes landed on her potted rose.

There was one petal left now. They'd lost another one sometime between the prisoner exchange and now.

With trembling hands, he lifted her into his arms and launched into the air again, half shifting enough to fly her to the safest place he could think of—where the rose still pulsed.

A flash of magic drew his gaze to the portal by the gates.

The battle had shifted. The Glathen line still held. With the help of the Growlers and eagles, they'd pushed the Buspartans back from the gates. Merida stood with her father's cloak draped over her shoulders, cradling a baby against her chest and barking orders to the reinforcements.

She turned as Leopol landed beside her, her eyes wide with understanding as she saw Bella's body.

"She's not—"

"Not dead," Leopol said hoarsely. "But her spirit hasn't come back. Can you guard her body?"

Merida nodded, fierce and focused. "Of course, I'll guard her with my life."

He laid Bella beside the rose. The petal glowed faintly, as if waiting. He swallowed hard and turned to scan the courtyard.

"Do you have any healing potions," Merida asked, her voice tight. "Eryk—"

She gestured to where a Glathen healer knelt over the prince. Eryk was still unconscious, pale and slack jawed. Blood stained his shirt.

Leopol hesitated only a second, then pulled two vials from his belt. "Use one on him. Save the other for Bella."

Merida took them with steady hands, her eyes bright as she whispered, "Thank you."

He nodded and pointed to the portal. "Lailant's here. She'll tend the wounded once the portal stabilizes or she dismisses it."

"Good," she said. "I'll hold the army together from here."

"We have half an hour. When the core's power fades, the undead will rise again unless we destroy the source. If the wizard still lives..." His voice caught as he looked over the battlefield, then back to her. He took a deep breath and faced a truth he didn't want to admit. "Then we're out of options."

Merida's jaw firmed, eyes narrowing. "Then what are you waiting for? Go defeat the wizard. Bella's fighting him already."

Far ahead, half-obscured by warping shadows, he followed the point of Merida's hand to a shadowy blob in the sky.

Bella's spirit and the wizard's ghost were locked in a spiraling, shifting battle. Spells clashed like storms. The air twisted with daemonic energy, blurring the edges of their figures until they looked like one giant shadow, two souls wrestling inside it.

What he'd originally thought was a shadow daemon and giant eagle battle was worse. Much worse.

Leopol's heart nearly gave out at the sight. He'd never seen her look so powerful.

He should have been at her side—but she'd gone ahead without him, burning with purpose, fighting both death and destiny with nothing but light and fury.

He took off, and in two leaps shifted, wings beating the air, scanning the battlefield.

Scarlet and Wulfric had rallied near the eastern flank—Growlers at their side, Dragon Claws nowhere in sight. Eirwyn kneeled beside Knox, who stood panting clouds of green fog that kept everyone else far, far away directly in front of the castle gates. The real egg was still tucked close to her, glowing faintly like a heartbeat of hope with stronger magic everyday.

Then Bella cried out, a sharp pulse through his bond that stopped him mid-air.

He hovered, terror flaring in his soul. She was in danger.

A flash of silver blurred near him, and Cerci pulled into flight beside him, the breeze rippling across her white-blonde hair. She held something in her hand–gleaming and terrible.

A crown.

Leopol asked. "What is that?"

"Bella told me to recover it," Cerci said, her voice grim. "The General tried to use it to trap her. I think it's been bespelled to trap spirits, like you trapped Hanzel in the mirror."

"I'll take it," he said, eyes flashing with grim purpose.

He reached out a claw, and she hooked it on a talon, the enchantment still pulsing with the wizard's magic. He immediately recognized the spell, knew exactly how to break it... or use it.

"You lead the eagles to clear the skies. And Cerci–watch the rose."

She nodded once, then hesitated with a glance down. "I'm more worried about the portal than I am about the wizard, though."

He turned back toward the battlefield, holding the crown, the regulator tucked in his belt, and his breath caught. There at the edge of the cobblestone road where it met the dirt was a dark gash in the ground, surrounded by sigils and runes.

It was a shallow portal to hell, but even a shallow one let out creatures of nightmares. Cerci banked away, leading the eagle riders in a sharp dive toward the creatures flying out of the hell hole.

If he was going to trap a ghost, it had to be the right

one. Then he'd throw Hanzel inside the crown all the way into the Deep.

It was time for a permanent solution to this wizard problem.

Bella's arms trembled, fingers curled with effort, nose bleeding from the strain. Fuck, she was going too close to the Edge.

With a feral cry, she shoved Hanzel back, her palms burning with magic. He slammed into the dirt beside the hell-portal, a snarl echoing from his throat as glowing runes flickered behind him, pulsing with power. Fingers of daemons reached for him in the shadows, but he kicked them back and crawled away.

The Chancellor groaned, sitting up on one elbow, blood dripping down his temple, his other arm hanging limp and twisted. Before Bella could move—before she could shout a warning—Hanzel surged forward like a wraith and *entered him*.

The Chancellor's eyes went wide with horror. His mouth opened in a soundless scream as his soul was *ripped* from his body, flung backward into the waiting portal. A daemon rose from the edge—something ancient and cruel, made of bone spines and leathery wings—and *snatched* him mid-air, dragging him down in pieces. The Chancellor's soul never hit the ground.

The stolen body staggered to its feet, half-broken, the wizard within grinning through split lips and cracked teeth. "Interesting. This body can see auras of magic. What's this I see?"

Hanzel's laughter echoed from a throat that wasn't his,

too deep and too smooth. He turned-toward Eirwyn and the glowing dragon egg she protected.

No. No, no-

"*No!*" Bella screamed, but Knox was faster. The great green dragon lunged in front of his mate with a roar that shook the sky, his jaws closing over the possessed Chancellor's torso. Bone and blood erupted in a spray as he bit the man in *half*.

The wizard's spirit ripped free again, shrieking in rage, and Bella's own cry-of rage, desperation, and something that felt too close to terror-answered his as she shot toward him like a lightning bolt.

She hit him mid-air.

They tumbled, fists and claws and magic and teeth. Hanzel's ghost form was wiry and whipcord-strong, inhumanly fast, far more solid than he should've been. Every blow from him rattled her to the core, and every hit she landed came with blood leaking from her nose, her ears, her eyes. Her magic sputtered, and her limbs felt half-sunken in mud. She was dying. Or unraveling. Or maybe both.

He threw her off with a burst of corrupted power.

She barely caught herself, spiraling through smoke and screams, and by the time she turned back, he was already diving again-this time into the General.

"No-!"

The General, bloodied and limping, hadn't even seen him coming. The wizard tore into the man's body, and the General screamed, dropping to one knee with his sword jammed into the earth for balance. A daemon peeled up from the shadows, sniffing at the edges of the battlefield like it had caught a scent. Something darker than the rest. Not just a daemon-a *soul-hunter*, one of Asmoroth's leashed predators.

It lunged at the General's fleeing spirit—and *devoured it whole*.

Inside his new vessel, Hanzel threw his head back and laughed.

"This one's strong," he crowed, flexing bloodied fingers, gripping the sword like it was made for him. "Much better than the last. A true commander. I think I'll keep it and just use the egg to make this body even more powerful."

Bella's chest heaved, floating unsteadily above the battle-field, barely able to focus. Everything was *wrong*. The wizard shouldn't have been able to body-hop like this, not so easily. Not with daemons dragging the leftovers to hell.

And yet here he stood—stronger, faster, healing before her eyes with magic that pulsed black and sick.

He lifted a potion vial with casual delight and drank it like a toast. Bones shifted in his leg, righting themselves with sickening cracks, but it wasn't real healing—it was twisted and unnatural, propped up by the same power that kept the portal to hell open.

"No," Bella whispered, blinking back hot, stinging tears. "No, no, no..."

She turned her head, looking for Leopol, for solace and support—and there, in the middle of the battlefield, lay her rose.

With only one petal left.

One.

The glowing stem pulsed faintly, surrounded by ash, shattered shields, and the blood of everyone she loved. Scarlet was fighting with wild, wounded fury. Wulfric bled from the shoulder, still dragging himself toward her and fighting with his good arm. Knox's body smoked, half-collapsed near Merida and the child-king. Eirwyn's lights flickered as she shielded Knox and Merida with raw, shaking magic.

There, flying toward her, dodging shadow daemons and giant eagles, flew Leopol–

"Bella," his voice called, hoarse, trembling, and achingly real. "Come to me."

Her spirit tore through the sky, frayed and unraveling, until she was in his arms. She collapsed against the familiar shape of him—warm and solid and real, even in dragon form. His talons curled protectively around her incorporeal shape, even as one stayed away from her.

"You're here," she gasped, too drained to sob. "You stopped the undead, but I don't know how to win. How do we defeat him?"

He didn't answer right away. Then, he said simply, "I have a plan."

His magic wrapped around her like starlight and heat, and something deep in her spirit exhaled. She remembered what her fear had made her forget.

This wasn't over. Not while Leopol lived. Not while he stood with her.

When she was alone, it was too easy to give in to the intrusive thoughts and surrender to the darkness. But when Leopol was near, while he lived and stood beside her, even when he didn't say anything at all...

He gave her the courage to keep going. All she really needed to face the daemons was the man she loved beside her. Then she felt renewed, ready to face whatever came next.

The man she loved.

She wasn't alone anymore.

The realization hit with terrifying clarity, as if a storm

had broken within her chest. This wasn't fate or magic or duty.

It was love, a love she craved more than sunlight or breath, more than safety or sanctuary, more than life itself. Without Leopol, none of it mattered.

She clung to him, spirit wrapping tight around his ribs, afraid it would be taken from her too soon.

Chapter Fifty-Five

Leopol's wings beat hard against the smoky air, carrying Bella's ghostly form close to his heart. Her spirit was weightless in his arms, insubstantial yet vital—his anchor in a storm of chaos and fire. The battlefield below churned with screams and smoke, the air thick with blood and magic. But he had tuned all of it out except her and the crown pulsing in his other talon.

Its magic thrummed with potential, desperate to be released, but he held it steady, calculating, always calculating. The angle, the timing, the soul.

Below, Hanzel—inhabiting the General's body—surveyed the battlefield with stolen ease. His movements were arrogant, his expression pure hunger as he yelled, trying to rally the Buspartan army. What was left of it, anyway.

The soul-hunter daemon circled just beyond him, wings twitching as it stalked the edges of the chaos like it already knew where to strike next, lapping up souls as they died.

Leopol adjusted course, angling them higher, keeping them out of earshot.

"Listen carefully," he murmured against Bella's temple. "The crown can trap a soul, but only if the moment is perfect. We have one chance."

Her spectral fingers curled against his scales, just above the deepest scar across his chest. "I trust you."

That simple phrase filled him with so many emotions, it was hard to name them all. Determination to be what she needed him to be, and a driving need to protect the one he loved were the biggest emotions.

A thousand variables filled his mind—windspeed, angle of descent, magical interference, soul resonance, range. The battlefield below churned with chaos. Scarlet's blade flashing like sunlight on water, Knox's green poisonous gas rolling over the wounded to put them to sleep, the eagles screaming through fire-torn skies. But for Leopol, time compressed into one sharpened moment.

He held the crown gingerly, activating the runes on the side that would act like a suction tool.

A thunderbolt of crystalline energy surged from the crown. The tendrils unfurled like a living net, weaving through the smoke toward the precise sliver of soul where Hanzel's consciousness hesitated. The soul trap sang with the spectral lattice, anchoring its threads to the crown in his talon.

Hanzel's stolen eyes went wide. The enchantment constricted, focused in speed as it descended toward its target as the crown shook in Leopol's hands.

For a breathless moment, the entire battlefield stilled.

But then—Hanzel dragged a bleeding Glathen soldier into the trap's path, using the man's soul like a human shield, plucking it out of his body like ripping a piece of cloth.

Leopol's stomach sank as the soldier's essence was

ripped from his body—sucked into the crown in a swirl of quicksilver and grief with enough force to make Leopol stagger back a step.

The magic fizzled, the crown used, but Hanzel remained.

He laughed—jagged and unnatural, like rotting leather and broken glass.

"Not good enough," he snarled, cracking his stolen knuckles. Blood and corrupted magic dripped from his fingertips, burning fissures into the cobblestones. "Did you really think it would be that easy? After last time, of course I have a countermeasure prepared and ready. Care to try again?"

Leopol's wings tucked around Bella, protective and coiled tight with frustrated energy. One talon still gripped the crown. Its glow flickered now, unsteady. He'd calculated everything—everything but Hanzel's cruelty.

The daemon edged closer, casting warped shadows. Its eyes glinted, reflective and alien. It wasn't just here to collect. It was watching, waiting for the spoils of war like a scavenger.

"We need another way," Bella whispered.

His grip on the crown shifted. He'd been looking at this all wrong. He shouldn't target Hanzel. He was just a small fish in the pond, in the grand scheme of things.

If he trapped everything in the portal and kept them from escaping, it would defeat Hanzel's purpose just the same.

The crown pulsed again, answering the new aim with renewed purpose. He adjusted the magical charge on the crown with the help of the regulator. It was crazy enough, it just might work.

Its magic spun out like spider silk, spectral threads

searching, latching onto the jagged mouth of the hell portal just beyond the battlefield. It pulsed—wounded, ragged, but still open. The crown's enchantment trembled with an ancient, terrible purpose—not to trap a single soul, but to bind something far larger.

Leopol angled his wings and dove, positioning them directly above it. His talons gripped the crown with surgical precision, angling its magic like a weapon. The crown thrummed, synchronizing with the leyline fractures leaking from the rift.

And then he let go.

The magic struck the portal like silver lightning—piercing and unraveling. The enchantment didn't just close it. It unwove it, thread by thread. The portal's magical structure began to fail, light and shadow peeling apart like wet paper.

The daemon screamed—not with pain, but with fear. But it was Hanzel's roar of fury that drowned it out.

Bella felt Leopol thinking, his muscles tensing, and knew he was plotting a way out.

The hell portal pulsed. Dark shapes writhed at its edges—daemons sensing something was changing, something fundamental was about to shift in their universe of shadows and hunger.

Hanzel noticed too late, his scream making her ears pulse.

The crown's magic struck the portal like liquid silver lightning, spectral threads systematically dismantling the portal.

The daemon circling the portal shrieked—a sound that was more vibration than actual noise. Its leathery wings beat frantically as the magical architecture around it began to collapse in on itself.

More daemons rushed out, trying to escape the unraveling portal. She felt the shift in the air before she saw it—something pulling at the veil between realms.

Bella yelled at Cerci, "Put a dome over the portal. Nothing gets in and nothing gets out! Quick!"

"You're almost out of time! You have to get back to your body—*now*!" Cerci's hands were already glowing, the divine light of Illustros leaking from her fingers like blinding thread.

Bella pressed closer to Leopol's scales. Her body. Her stolen body was still somewhere on this battlefield. But her soul—her will, her love, her mate—was here. If the wizard escaped, there was no hope for any of them.

"We trap him," Bella said. "We push him into the portal and seal it. If my body dies—so be it."

Cerci spun toward her, white-gold magic illuminating the blood on her face. "No, your soul, your tether—"

Bella shook her head. "Then I die. I'm not letting him escape again. You saw the havoc he wreaked in less than a year—he'll just keep body hopping, over and over. We have to bind him, anchor him to a vessel, and drag him to hell ourselves."

Leopol growled low behind her. "No, I won't let you sacrifice yourself. There will be another way."

"Don't argue with me, Leopol, not now. We can't let him escape—and this will work. I trust you. But do you trust *me*?"

Leopol's wings tensed, his muscles coiling like springs ready to unleash. She could feel the storm brewing under his skin—he was thinking, weighing outcomes, searching for a version of this where she lived.

There wasn't one.

"I trust you," he said finally. "But I won't let you die alone."

She floated up beside him, and he met her gaze. A silent promise passed between them, and she didn't need words to know what he meant. If she died, he would follow.

Her chest ached as she shook her head. They'd talked about this. She opened her mouth to remind him, but Hanzel laughed below.

The sound echoed with multiple voices—the General's dying rage mingled with the wizard's malevolent glee. "You think you can trap me? I've escaped death a thousand times."

They didn't have time to argue about life and death.

Bella turned to Cerci. "Can you do it? Can you weave a dome around him and the portal? Keep the others safe—lock us inside?"

Cerci hesitated before nodding. Her eyes went white and power crackled in the air.

Then Cerci lifted her hands and shouted toward their family and friends, "Stop the fighting. We'll handle the wizard and the portal."

Ashur leaped, his stone wings fluttering as he shouted, "No!"

The magic that poured out wasn't just Cerci's—it was holy. Golden light shot through her like a beacon, divine threads spilling from her fingers as she wove the dome. Bella couldn't see past the edge of the circle once it sealed. The battlefield disappeared, and the world went silent.

Only four figures remained inside. Cerci. Bella. Leopol. And Hanzel in the General's body.

As the dome sealed behind them with a blinding flash of white, Cerci's voice rang through the battlefield, followed by Ashur's roar of panic.

"She's a demigoddess, Ashur. She'll be alright," Eirwyn said quickly. "She's lived through thousands of battles, if the history books are true. Trust her."

Ashur shook his head and raked a hand through his stone hair. "I do, damn it. I—I just need to know she's safe. She has nightmares about the hell holes, and I'm not there to fight the nightmares with her."

Her heart ached for Knox's best friend, but they couldn't see or hear anything from inside the dome. It was like staring at a pearl.

"How do we stop the fighting?" Merida asked, rocking her father-baby on her shoulder. Her eyes were wide—still reeling from the shock of the battle, the changes to her father, the worry for her brother—but she kept her head and was ready to lead. A true leader and friend.

The warmth and weight of the egg on her back sent her into action. Eirwyn took charge and glanced up at Knox, still in protective dragon form but almost healed. "How are you feeling? Think you can fly me around for a few minutes? I'll see if I can convince them with a light show to put down their arms."

He growled and spoke through their bond. *I'll never be too tired to fly my mate.*

She rolled her eyes and climbed onto his back, his talon giving her a hand up. When she was secured on his back, one hand on a scale and the other on the egg behind her, she tapped him twice.

Up they flew into the sky, coming quickly down to swoop over the battle lines that had been redrawn so many times in the course of the past hour.

Her hair snapped in the wind, the thrum of Knox's wings pounding like war drums as she glanced down.

Chaos still raged—Buspartan steel clashing with Glathen shields, spells lighting the smoke like lightning across storm clouds. Too many hadn't seen the shift of the battle, although it was hard to ignore the bones of the undead lying prone on the ground. Too many still thought they were fighting for their future.

Eirwyn raised both hands and let her magic fly.

Sparks exploded across the sky—fireworks in blooms of starbursts and fireflies, painting the air in hope and warning. With a sharp gesture, she shaped the magic into letters.

STOP.

The word blazed above the battlefield, pulsing with urgency. Eirwyn drew a deep breath and cast the amplification spell. Her voice rang across the field, echoing off ruined towers and bloodied stone.

"As Princess of Busparia and Queen of the Feral Forest, I beg you—stop!" Her voice cracked, but she pushed more power into the spell, let the light rise from her skin like dawn. "Glathen is not our enemy. You're fighting your brothers, your sisters—your neighbors. For what? To bring Asmoroth, god of death, back into our realm?"

With another powerful wingbeat, a hush rippled outward—like a stone dropped in a lake. Some soldiers paused, eyes turning skyward.

"Stop spilling blood and following a mad wizard bent on destruction. Who will you follow?"

For a moment, nothing moved but the two of them as they flew over the battlefield.

"This is how we end it," she called. "With light—not blood."

And then, like breath let out all at once, the clash of

weapons faltered. Blades lowered. Spells fizzled into harmless smoke. Buspartan soldiers glanced to their captains, confusion etched into every face. Some dropped to their knees. Others just stood, blinking—as if waking from a long, terrible dream.

Warmth flared at Eirwyn's back.

She turned, breath catching as she pulled her dragon egg into her arms, holding it close.

It glowed now—not just with soft magic, but with life. A pulse, strong and certain, beat against her palms—like a war drum softened into a lullaby. Then a crack split the shell with a sound like thunder and grace all at once.

She gasped, her heart beating just as hard as it had during the darkest part of the battle.

"Knox," she whispered, voice trembling. "I—I think the baby is coming."

A shard of glittering white fell away, and from the darkness inside, a tooth appeared, then a tongue swiped over it before moving. Then a single golden eye blinked up at her through the hole.

Hope had teeth now, and it was coming soon.

Chapter Fifty-Six

The dome sealed with a final snap of divine magic. The outside world fell away—no more screaming soldiers, no wind, no chaos. Only the wizard, the portal, Cerci's glowing hands, and Leopol's steady presence at her back.

Hanzel sneered, dragging the General's ruined body upright like a grotesque puppet. His shoulder slumped at an unnatural angle, and blood slicked his jaw, but the madness in his eyes burned hot.

Bella couldn't tackle him—not like this, when he had the weight of a body.

She may still be a spirit, but she had magic.

She raised her hands and summoned the swords scattered across the floor of the dome. The blades twitched once, then rose, jerking awkwardly as if surprised to be alive. She winced. They weren't graceful—nothing like when she'd commanded armies of chairs and candlesticks back in her tavern—but they moved and obeyed her.

One blade struck low, slashing Hanzel's thigh. Another cut through his side. He growled, staggering as he tried to bat them away. The General's body was already broken, and now it was slowing him down.

She pressed forward, sweat beading at her temples though her ghostly form shouldn't have felt heat. The blades surged with her will, her fury, her love for the people outside that dome—her love for Leopol.

She fought for him, for them, for their future. She grabbed one sword herself and sliced clean across Hanzel's chest.

He stumbled back, and she struck again, this time high.

His head tumbled to the ground.

For one horrible second, everything went still. She'd surprised herself, and she blinked.

Then the General's body collapsed, and the air ripped.

The wizard's spirit shot upward like a scream made visible—twisting and black, frantic as it tried to escape the confines of the dome. Cerci cried out as the portal flickered and unraveled, Leopol's magic guiding the silver tendrils of the crown toward the center of the hell hole.

"Hold it, Leopol. I can't keep the dome up and close the portal at the same time," Cerci said, her arms shaking. Bella worried her friend was already losing strength.

"Don't stop!" she yelled at Leopol. "Keep closing it—no matter what, close the portal!"

Leopol lifted the crown and regulator high, channeling their full force, determination flooding his face, and she sighed in relief. She really could trust him.

Bella turned toward the wizard's staggering soul, before he shook and launched toward the dome as if to punch through it. His soul brushed past her like a wind that didn't belong. Instinct screamed at her—catch him.

She lunged.

Her hands locked around the writhing soul of Hanzel,

and he fought—harder than anything she'd ever touched, harder than he had before the dome. It was hate and hunger and decay and triumph, slick and cold like oil poured over broken glass. Her grip almost slipped.

But she held on through sheer force of will.

Cerci's light exploded, a golden burst that arced toward the portal like divine thread stitching it shut. The woman gasped and sank to the ground, "It—it'll hold itself for a few minutes. I—I couldn't—hurry, Bella..."

She couldn't turn to check on Cerci, had to remain focused on the wizard. Bella reared back and gave him her best right hook, sending him back toward the center of Leopol's collapsing spell. The pull to the portal intensified, a roar in her ears matched the pulse in her hand.

As the wizard windmilled his arms, he caught her yellow dress and pulled her forward with him. Toward the center of the portal.

The heat of hells flared beneath her like an open furnace. She could feel the daemons swarming now, grabbing, clawing, claiming what wasn't theirs.

"No!" she shouted, twisting, trying to pull free.

Leopol roared, but the look on Hanzel's face gave Bella pause. He wasn't going there without her. He wasn't letting her go and would climb over her on his way back if he had to.

She tightened her grip on his arm where it clung to her dress, her nails digging into his wrinkled old skin. "You're not escaping this," she swore.

With that realization—the truth for both of them—the force sucked her down into the first layer of hell like gravity with a vendetta. The portal pulled her in, Hanzel locked in her grip, daemons clinging to them both. Her form stretched, ripped, unmade.

She looked up toward Leopol as the circle of light faded. She reached up for him with her free hand, screamed, poured everything she had into that single desperate motion.

He was right there—arms out, eyes wide. And his face—oh gods, his face—so stricken, so shattered. His mouth moved but she couldn't hear it over the wind and the roar and the crack of tearing worlds.

She reached—a futile attempt to escape fate.

As she fell, the last thing she saw was Leopol roaring in anguish, claws reaching for her, eyes blazing with everything she never had time to say.

This was it. This was how she died.

She expected pain, maybe fire or numbness. What she got was something else, something she was all too familiar with.

It was grief.

She hadn't told Leopol she loved him.

She hadn't told him that she'd dreamed—ridiculously, impossibly—of a future with him in a home somewhere green, a warm bed at night, and a child with his blue eyes. She'd tell their child bedtime stories about chairs that used to fight in taverns. She wanted to rebuild, to lead—not alone, never again.

She wanted him beside her, not as a protector or a savior, but as a partner, a mate, a true love unlike any she'd ever known.

The ache in her chest wasn't the tearing of the soul from her body.

It was the weight of all those dreams never spoken aloud. *That* was what made her soul burn in pain.

As the daemons wrapped around her like thorned chains, as the darkness swallowed her whole, as the heat of hell kissed her skin—Bella fought the wizard. She may be gone to the hells now, separated from all her family and her one true love, but she would not stop fighting this dirty bastard.

If she was going down, he was going down with her.

———————

Bella was gone.

One second, she was there—her fingers reaching for him, her mouth open in a scream he couldn't hear—and the next, the darkness swallowed her whole. Bella and the wizard, light and shadow, his nemesis and his mate. Gone.

Leopol's magic faltered. His grip on the regulator and crown slipped. The tendrils of the crown unraveled, the silver threads fracturing into chaos as his concentration shattered.

He let out a sound that barely resembled a roar—raw and broken, scraped from the deepest part of his chest.

"No, no, no, no—" The word became a litany, a refusal, a spell all its own. He dropped the crown and stumbled forward, claws scraping the stone floor of the dome. "Bella!"

He flung a burst of magic toward the closing portal—blind, unfocused. Useless.

The portal, now barely half the size of a door, collapsed.

He crashed to his knees beside Cerci, his claws gouging the earth as if he could dig her back, claw open the world and drag her out.

"Cerci," he rasped. "Help me, please—I have to bring her back, do something."

Cerci lay panting, her nose bleeding freely, divine light flickering and fading in her skin. Her hands trembled on the ground, the golden threads of the dome barely clinging to her fingertips.

"I–I can't," she whispered. "Too much, I held it too long–"

The bubble around the portal shuddered, then it too collapsed. And suddenly, the world returned.

Leopol gasped as air rushed in. His senses flooded, full of noise, color, pain, and people. He could see them now, his friends, his family, the army, the battlefield. Ashur ran toward them.

The fighting had stopped. He noted it like an out-of-body experience.

The field was silent, not in death, but in breathless, tentative life. Buspartans and Glathen soldiers alike stood in loose groups, blinking, shell-shocked. Knox flew overhead, his wings extended in warning, while Eirwyn hovered on his back, her hands still glowing with gentle light.

Merida stood next to the others, giving quiet orders that people were actually obeying. The war was ending, but Bella was gone.

A sharp bark of footsteps cut through the stillness, and he turned his head like an automaton.

"Leopol!" Scarlet screamed, Wulfric close behind. "Where is she?"

Wulfric surged ahead of his mate, panic radiating off him. "Where's my daughter?" he demanded. "Where's Bella?"

His throat closed, and his magic sputtered in his chest. He simply lifted one shaking arm and pointed toward the rift still yawning at the heart of the stone.

Daemon claws still scratched at its rim, but something had changed. The eagles were diving again, shrieking and tearing the things apart mid-crawl. Burned feathers drifted in the wind, ash and ichor mixing with the blood of too many kingdoms.

The soul-hunter daemon was gone, vanished. It hadn't left, though. It had followed them into the portal.

Leopol's stomach turned cold. It had followed her light, and how could he blame it? She was everything.

The only one who'd ever touched the parts of him that weren't meant to be touched. The only one who'd looked at the broken shell of a man, a beast, a dragon, and called him home.

His claws dug into the ground again, and this time he didn't pull back. He let the stone crack beneath him, let the pain anchor him because it was the only thing that felt real.

"She's gone," he whispered.

Scarlet staggered back. Wulfric dropped to his knees beside him, lifted his head back, and howled. It was long, low, and deep—a piercing sound of pain that Leopol mirrored in his mind.

But Leopol stayed where he was, kneeling before the broken portal, every breath a thunderclap of grief, his mind running a million scenarios as he tried to find one that would have even a sliver of a chance of succeeding.

His mate was in hell.

And if she thought he would stay here without her, if she thought he would just let her go—she didn't know him at all.

She was gone. His little girl, his daughter, his Trix, his Bella.

Wulfric dropped to his knees beside Leopol, but no sound came out at first. His body shook. The grief felt too big for his throat—like trying to scream through water. His hands clenched the earth, claws raking deep into stone and ash.

And then it came.

A howl tore out of him, deep and long, vibrating through the marrow of everyone who heard it. A father's howl. A broken man's battle cry.

But it wasn't enough. Nothing was enough.

Not when he'd already lost once—his wife, slipping through his hands from the fever no spell could cure. Now his daughter, stolen by a madman, ripped into the hells.

He couldn't protect her then. He couldn't stop it now.

But the daemons would bleed for it.

Wulfric surged to his feet, his eyes wild, the edge of his vision pulsing red. The ground still quaked from the dying portal, daemons crawling out in fragmented bursts of smoke and bone.

He met the nearest one with a roar. His fist crashed through its face. Then another and another.

He didn't care if they were fleeing. He didn't care if the war was over. His grief didn't want surrender—it wanted war. It wanted blood.

He ripped a jagged spear from the hand of a fallen soldier, spun it, drove it through a daemon's chest, and let the body fall smoking to the earth. His arms moved like war hammers—each swing an echo of every failure he carried in his soul.

His wife's dying breath. Bella's tiny fingers wrapped around his pinky when she was born. What he imagined was her smiling face when they'd crowned her queen. Her laugh in the tavern. Her scream as she fell.

"I wasn't enough," he snarled, driving his blade through another. "I wasn't enough for her."

Another clawed creature launched itself at him, but he

caught it midair and slammed it into the ground hard enough to crack bone.

If he had to fight the gods themselves to bring her back–he would.

He bellowed into the sky, flecks of daemon ichor splashing his chest. Wings flapped overhead–Knox's shadow passed once, then circled again–but Wulfric didn't look up.

He wasn't done. He didn't care that they were winning. He didn't care that the princess had taken command. His daughter was in the hells–and he would tear them apart, one daemon at a time, until he found her.

———

Cerci's legs tingled and her nose bled.

Her head lolled against Ashur's shoulder, his stone hand pressed against her ribs to keep her upright as they moved.

"I'll get you to safety, gorgeous, don't worry," he growled. His other hand fought–clean, precise blows that knocked daemons back into the dirt–but Cerci couldn't see them clearly. The world blurred at the edges. Her eyes were locked on the portal.

It was still open, still pulsing, still calling to her.

No, not again.

She whimpered, and Ashur pulled her tighter against his chest, his voice a low rumble. "I've got you. I've got you."

The portal pulsed like a heartbeat made of teeth, and panic gripped her. She tapped on Ashur's shoulder as the breath caught in her throat. "Put me down, Ashur, I'm going to–"

He paused, and she twisted away–vomit and snot and pain tearing out of her in heaving sobs. Ashur stroked her back and eased her to her hands and knees, but she could feel the pull of the portal. It was too close.

She spit up all her fear and terror until there was nothing left, until she was a shaking, miserable mess. Hair clinging to her sweaty brow, she wiped her mouth with the back of her hand.

Then Ashur sat, legs crossed, and gently pulled her into his lap—cradling her like she was something precious, breakable. He was her gentle giant, her gargoyle mate. He was home, something she'd never had before.

But one glance at the yawning black hole had her trembling, sucking her thoughts down and away from all the good that was Ashur.

She didn't realize she was whispering until the words became louder than the wind in her ears. "I won't go back. I won't go back. I can't—I won't get trapped there again."

Ashur's hand slid higher to cradle her head. "You're not," he murmured. "You're here with me. I'll keep you safe."

She couldn't look away from it, though. The smoke writhed at the edges of the gateway, oily and gray, laced with flashes of the red glow beneath. It curled like fingers, like claws, like chains.

She'd felt those chains.

No, don't remember, don't look, don't fall back in.

She blinked, hard, and the battlefield flickered. For a heartbeat, she saw flames instead of ash and a cracked sky overhead. Heard screams but couldn't see or help anyone. She was smaller, burning, trapped in something not human.

"No!" she choked out, and Ashur caught her face with both hands now, turning her away from the portal, even as daemons snarled in front of them.

"Look at me," he said, voice sharp now, grounding. "Cerci, look at me."

His eyes were glowing faintly, cracked around the edges like old stone, but warm and familiar.

"You're not in the hells anymore," he said. "You came back, and you're not going anywhere."

She opened her mouth, but no words came. She sucked in a deep breath, and that in itself was a victory.

Behind him, she heard wings—then Lailant's voice calling her name. Olive's footsteps pounded the grass, but she didn't turn.

She kept her eyes on Ashur, on the only thing holding her to this world.

Deep inside her soul, she trembled because the portal hadn't fully closed and something deep inside her knew, it would never close for good unless *she* was the one to seal it.

Chapter Fifty-Seven

Wulfric's chest ached like a drowning man chained to the riverbed—no breath, no light, only pressure.

He couldn't accept this—he wouldn't. There had to be a way to fix it. It couldn't be too late to save his little girl.

Every part of him screamed to fold inward, to disappear into the grief he hadn't yet made room for. Instead, the emotions burst out, and he roared, shattering the silence.

"How do we get her back?" he bellowed, launching to his feet and scaring the giant eagle back into flight. Olive and Lailant walked toward their group from where it had landed.

Scarlet's hand fell from his back, her eyes big and worried, for him, for his daughter, whom she'd once sworn to kill. They'd moved past it, worked through it, through blood and grief and guilt—but it couldn't have been for nothing.

She couldn't be gone. He turned to Leopol and jerked him up by the collar, dragging him to his feet as he growled,

"You're the smartest man in all the realms, dragon. You must know a way!"

Leopol didn't flinch. His eyes had the vacant look of a man who'd lost everything. Wulfric knew that look, had felt it himself when his wife had died. He shook Leopol, and the dragon slowly blinked.

He looked Wulfric in the eye and frowned. "There's nothing I can do," he said quietly. "Only the gods can give life."

Wulfric's face twisted, wild and desperate. He turned his gaze to where Cerci lay curled in Ashur's lap, dropping his grip on Leopol. He stepped forward, desperation clawing his chest.

"You're a demigoddess. What can we do? How do we get her back?"

Ashur bristled at his tone—or maybe it was the wild look in his eyes—and one wing flared as a shield. But Cerci only raised her head, pale and trembling. Her eyes were haunted, her voice barely a breath.

"There's only one way," she whispered, face crumpling in horror. She looked straight at Leopol and shook her head. "I can't go back. Not again, please. I can't—" And she tried to curl into Ashur, his wings folding over her now and protecting her from even the sunlight.

But at her words, Leopol jerked like he'd been struck by lightning.

He sucked in a sharp breath—like a babe taking its first cry. Not a scream, not a roar—just a shaky, raw, living breath. He muttered under his breath, pacing from one edge of the portal to the other—two long strides, back and forth, like a beast too smart for its cage. Thought buzzed off him like static.

Wulfric didn't move. Wulfric swallowed hard, heart

thudding like a war drum out of rhythm. He didn't dare interrupt as Leopol puzzled out a solution, afraid to hope.

Wulfric kneeled next to Cerci and Ashur, fury breaking into confusion. "What does that mean? What do you *know*?"

Leopol paced back to them, steps tight and measured along with his voice, answering the questions that weren't even directed at him. "It's a theory. Nothing more. In all the texts, scrolls, and books ever written, there was *one* line in *one* ancient book. A book in the Archives of the astral library that only the gods have ever seen... and me."

"Then try it," Wulfric growled, surging back to his feet, stepping into Leopol's path.

"I don't know if it will work," Leopol said. His face—his posture—still defeated. But calculation lit behind his eyes like sunrise through fog.

"All magic comes with a price," Lailant murmured, stepping beside the portal. She leaned over it, and the daemons clawing at the edge screamed at her presence and fell back. Her face was pale but unwavering. Olive stood behind her, silent, scanning the battlefield—checking Scarlet, Knox, Eirwyn.

Wulfric turned back to Leopol. His voice didn't rise this time. It cracked like a whip anyway—quiet, sharp, impossible to ignore.

"Is she worth the price?"

Leopol froze like prey, trapped by the words. Hopelessness flickered in his expression—and Wulfric knew this was it. Leopol loved his daughter, and she was worth every price, but it still wasn't going to be enough.

Wulfric felt it with a certainty in his soul, felt it in his fists, in his bones, in the tremble of the earth around them. A deep growl started in his chest, a warning.

Scarlet moved first. She grabbed his arm and yanked

him back, and Wulfric broke, turned into her arms, and fell apart. A sob wracked through him, shaking the whole of his frame.

She caught him, held him. This massive Growler crumpled against the one person who could hold the weight. She anchored him with that quiet, unshakable strength of hers—because somehow, she knew.

She knew exactly how desperate he was not to lose their daughter again.

Leopol's hands clenched and unclenched at his sides. A salty breeze rustled his rumpled jacket and blood-stained shirt. But inside, Leopol was all racing thoughts and a heartbeat too loud to ignore.

His mate, the only woman he'd ever loved, was in the hells—but he might be able to save her. Maybe.

The chance of success was slim to none, but it was the only shot he had.

Leopol's voice filled the silence, staring at the black hole at his feet then up at Lailant across from him. The Seer's eyes flashed solid white, reminding him of the woman he called mother, and he answered them all, his mind made up.

"I'm nothing without her. She's worth everything."

Lailant's whisper fluttered on the wind. "Even if you have to give up the body you fought so hard to get back? Are you willing to sacrifice your body to save her soul?"

Her words confirmed his suspicions, built on millennia of knowledge, and a spark of hope lit within him.

He met Wulfric's eyes as he was wrapped around Scarlet—saw the fury and helplessness barely hiding grief. Scarlet's jaw was tight, her hands balled on Wulfric's back where she held him close.

Knox landed with a gust of wind, tail lashing, his green gas already thinning on the breeze as Eirwyn slid off his back.

"Leopol, what are you thinking?" Knox's tone was a warning, a plea.

Lailant watched him with those white, god-touched eyes. She knew. She always had. Leopol had died before, but this felt different. This wasn't a death by failure or by war. This was a death by choice because some things were worth dying for.

Leopol jumped. He dove into the portal, the heat of hell swallowing him whole. The world turned black, but not empty.

He could see—barely—light flickering from the core of his chest. The Orythium scar pulsed in a steady rhythm, casting faint beams into the void. As if swimming through molasses, he swam down, his movements slow and exaggerated.

He searched the burning darkness, following his gut, his heart, the faint line of magic that connected him to Bella.

Slowly that line grew stronger, and she floated closer as if coming out of fog.

Bella. She wasn't broken or curled up in pain. Even here, in the first layer of the hells, she was fighting with all she had. A flash of her bared teeth, a cry of rage, a fist slamming into the wizard's spirit, she didn't let up or give up.

Gods, she was radiant. She was still herself, still his Bellakari, his Bellavore, simi dravak.

Hanzel's soul flickered with black fire, his grip fastened like tar to her arm, trying to drag her deeper.

A flash of something circled them. *The soul-hunter daemon.*

"No," Leopol snarled, pumping his arms and legs harder, faster. He had to reach them, had to save her.

He slammed into Hanzel's spirit with the full force of his fading magic, prying the wizard's fingers from Bella's arm. The contact scorched, ghost on ghost now. It felt like ripping hooks out of flesh, and Bella screamed in pain. But he didn't stop.

More daemons circled them, attracted to the pain, the fight. Somehow, the soul-hunter kept them away. It snapped at the others, baring jagged teeth before turning back to the three of them locked together.

Finally, he grunted and ripped Hanzel away from her, flinging him deeper into the void. The soul-hunter pounced on the wizard, swirling around him like a mini tornado. The wizard's screams were longer, drawn out for maximum pain.

Leopol didn't hang around to watch.

He wrapped both arms around Bella and kicked upward, toward the tiny pinprick of light above.

She clung to him, sobbing, her voice echoing through him like a memory. "Why did you come for me? I told you not to. You have to live for us both."

He looked into her eyes. So much light there, even now, and he gave her the only truth that mattered.

"There's no living without you, Bellakari. Where you are is where I'll be, always," he said, kicking harder. "Whether that's here in the hells or among the stars or on the throne of Busparia or in a ruined temple. You're my heart, Bella."

She shook in his arms, and he tightened his grip, burning through every scrap of his body's stored magic— stabilizing her essence, pouring his life into hers.

He felt his limbs slow, as if swimming through molasses. His vision tunneled. The Orythium in his chest dimmed, then flickered.

Bella's eyes widened, and her fingers curled around his face. "No. No, no, no–Leopol, your body, you're a spirit again. You–"

"It's gone now," he said softly, kicking again as if trying to rid himself of too many blankets. They wrapped around his legs, trying to drag him down, drag her down.

"It–your body burned up? You..." she gasped out a sob, clinging to him even as she started to kick with him. "Gods, we have to get back. I won't let you sacrifice yourself for me, not when–"

He kissed her. Softly, slowly, pouring every ounce of his love into it. She tasted like salt and ash and hope. Her hands trembled on his face.

When he pulled back, her face faintly lit by the barely pulsing Orythium in his chest, he said, "It's already done, Bella. There's no going back. I was a goner from that first touch, the first time you looked at me–not like you'd seen a ghost, but like a woman looks at a man."

He cupped her cheek with one hand, holding her close with the other as she sobbed his name, "Raelion."

"Don't you see? My body doesn't matter. Life doesn't matter. If we stay right here, in the hells, I'll be alright because I'll be with you. As long as you're in my arms, all will be fine."

And maybe that was the cruelest illusion of all–that even in death, he still thought he could protect her. That holding her would be enough to stop time, to stop endings. But he wouldn't let go this time. Not this time. Maybe never again.

Tears poured down her cheeks. She whispered, "Raelion."

He leaned in again, unable to stay away from her, from

this incredible woman that he'd been blessed to have in a sliver of his long life.

For one last time, their lips met, and all the screams in the hells fell away, muted. Breath tangled, arms locked tight, the burning heat that peeled his skin faded.

The Orythium pulse stuttered. Once. Twice. Then it stopped, and everything went black.

Cerci couldn't feel her legs. Her whole body buzzed with spent magic, caught between ice and fire. Ashur's arms wrapped around her like a fortress, his stone hand anchoring her against his chest. She could hear the battle's end, a few raging in bursts—snarls, metal, wings—but it all sounded far away. Drowned beneath the roar of the portal.

And then Lailant kneeled beside her, bringing a cool sea breeze.

A soft hand brushed her clammy forehead, and Cerci flinched at the sudden warmth. Lailant's voice was a whisper wrapped in steel. "You're the only one who can do it, child."

Cerci squeezed her eyes harder, refusing, unable.

"No," Cerci rasped, burying her face against Ashur's throat. "No, I can't. I can't go back—"

But Ashur was already kissing the top of her head, his voice ragged with emotion. "You don't have to. You're not alone, I'm here. I'll always be here."

She kissed him—fierce, desperate, clinging to the unconditional love he offered with no expectations in return. He just wanted to love her and take care of her. She'd never had that before.

What they had? *It was worth facing the monsters for.*

With a half-groan, half-sob, she broke the kiss, sat up, and shoved herself off his lap. His hands around her waist, he helped her up. Not arguing or trying to order her around. Just silently supporting like always.

Her knees buckled, but she staggered forward. Ashur pulled her to his side with a growl, but Lailant caught him with one hand on his arm. Her touch stilled him like a spell.

"Let her go," the Seer said softly. "This is her fight now."

Cerci didn't look at Ashur, couldn't bring herself to see the terror in his eyes at the thought of losing her. The portal was barely wide enough for her to jump through, and there was no way he would make it, hulking gargoyle that he was. He wouldn't be able to go in with her, couldn't try to rescue her like Leopol was doing with Bella.

She had to face the nightmares alone this time. No one could save her but herself.

She swallowed hard and steadied herself on her own two feet. She squeezed his arm, then spun to look behind him slightly. She had to distract him; otherwise, she'd not be able to do this.

Deliberately, she widened her eyes as if surprised, and he whipped around, hand barely at her waist now. While he spun to face an unknown threat that didn't exist...

She jumped into the portal, and it swallowed her whole, jagged edges scraping her skin and shadows licking at her. Her soul, spirit, skin, entire being crawled with the feeling of being back here.

It was like sinking in tar—thick, slow, every movement a war. But she pushed downward, divine light flickering from her palms, hunting for a thread, a flicker, a heartbeat—

There. Just a faint flash of light, but it was so far away. Her heart raced, hoping she could make it to them in time, hoping she didn't get captured again.

Daemons licked at her, but she swept her hands wide, keeping them at bay while simultaneously swimming through the soup toward that small blip of light.

There, through the dark and cloyingly black fog, she found Leopol and Bella, clinging to each other and surrounded.

Daemons circled them like vultures. The soul-hunter surged upward from the depths, a tide with jagged wings pulling shadow behind it like sails. It was headed straight for them.

She couldn't let him catch her again, had to rescue both of her friends.

"No," Cerci breathed—and lifted one shaking arm.

She blasted the nearest daemon with a shot of raw divine magic. The thing disintegrated into ash, howl cut off abruptly as the other daemons swarmed the pieces of it like cannibals.

Bella gasped, eyes wide as she spun to face the light. "Cerci?"

Cerci reached them as Leopol turned his head toward her, and she grabbed the stiff collar of his jacket. It felt more solid here, even though she could clearly see they were both spirits now, Leopol's body long burned up.

"Kick!" Cerci shouted, kicking her own feet and shooting another blast of light at the closest daemon. "Like you're swimming—come on!"

Leopol jumped into action, kicking hard, his arms wrapped around Bella.

Bella blinked at her, dazed. "How are you here? I thought you couldn't—"

Cerci was already firing again. Her breaths came fast and shallow, her arms shaking already. "The rules are different down here," she gritted out. "This place bends to truth, not power."

"What does that even–" Bella dodged a lashing claw.

"It means *we have to believe the truth*!" Cerci cried. "We have to mean every word, every action–hell knows when we're lying, what we fear. Don't give in to the dark thoughts. *Fight with me*–or we'll never escape."

Another blast, and another daemon fell back. The vultures swarmed it, but Cerci was fading fast. Her head spun, and blood dripped from her nose again, thicker this time. Her grip on Leopol's collar loosened.

Then–two hands touched hers, and she glanced down at Bella and Leopol. Brown eyes and blue eyes, both with the same determined expression stared up at her with hope and something more. They *believed* in her... enough to send a pulse of warmth surging into her where their hands clung to her arm.

It was just one blast of power, magic, essence, but it was enough.

It was like being caught in a current. Cerci surged upward, dragging them with her, the force carrying them like wings. Daemons shrieked behind them, clawing at her light.

Her magic was nearly gone. She could feel her edges fraying, her soul stretching too thin. She thought of Ashur– of what it would mean to lose him forever, and her breath caught.

Please, Mother, please. You gave me a mate, now let me live a full life with him.

The pinprick of light above grew closer even as she prayed, and then she saw him.

Ashur kneeled at the portal's rim, one arm extended,

straining and yelling, although she heard no sound. His face was wild with desperation.

Her hand stretched toward his, and for one moment, she felt doubt lick at her heels and whisper in her mind. *You won't make it. They're too heavy, all too burdened down by life.*

No! She shut down the thoughts and stretched further, believing like a mantra, a prayer without words, that all would turn out alright.

Their fingers brushed, connected, and he leaned further toward her, desperation and love giving him strength.

His stone fingers wrapped around her wrist and pulled.

She broke the surface like a drowning swimmer, gasping as the world exploded into color and light, sound and smell. Bella and Leopol's souls tumbled out beside her, sprawling across the cobblestones.

Ashur dragged her the rest of the way out and folded her into his arms. She clutched at him with bloodied fingers, pressing her forehead to his chest, his scent grounding her like nothing else.

Blood dripped, but he paid it no attention. Just smoothed the hair back from her face and spoke softly. "You're back. Oh gods, I thought I'd lost you. Thank the gods, you're back."

She sighed and her entire body gave a shudder of relief, the tension draining from her. "I love you, Ashur. I'll always come back to you."

"You won't because you're not leaving my side ever again," he growled.

She chuckled, a weak, broken sound, but it made his head pop up and his eyes widen. "I have to close the portal, Ashur. Help me up," she asked, wheezing and holding her breath, though her hands still clung to him like roots.

Ashur nodded, tears in his eyes, and braced her on her

feet, both his hands on her waist. He was as solid as a rock behind her, his wings folded around them like a crescent shield of protection as she lifted her shaking hands at the small hell hole.

The magic tore from her in a blinding wave, and she cried out at the pain of it. His hands bit into her waist, but she couldn't—wouldn't—stop now.

Light burst from her fingers like a sun, golden threads weaving through the portal's mouth, sealing it shut stitch by stitch, until all that remained was a ripple of dirt and cracked stone.

Silence settled around their group, and she looked at each of them. Wulfric and Scarlet stared at her from where they kneeled beside Bella and Leopol. Knox and Eirwyn stood, egg in her arms, as they watched the portal as if expecting it to open back up.

Over Olive's shoulder, she saw Merida walking toward them with her guards, arms full of babe and potted rose.

Then Cerci met Lailant's gaze, and recognition flared. She licked her lips and glared at her aunt. "Well? I did my part. What are *you* going to do now?"

Cerci swayed on her feet as she challenged the woman.

On this side of Leopol, the crown and regulator lay forgotten on the cobblestones, less than a foot from where the faintly pulsing Sentinel core bomb lay. He'd dropped them before jumping in.

Then the crown and regulator, still faintly glowing, fused up his spirit arm, the threads of the crown unraveling and weaving, looping around his arm like tattooed vines, wrapping his fading form in golden light.

The Orythium in his chest flickered to life, then glowed.

It wasn't a full resurrection, not yet, but he wasn't fading anymore. Tears sprung to Cerci's eyes, and she wobbled, only Ashur holding her up from behind.

Lailant stepped forward and cupped Cerci's cheek, brushing the blood from her face.

"Well done," she whispered, pressing two fingers to Cerci's forehead. "I'll take it from here, child."

Instantly, Cerci's eyes shut, and warmth flooded her, light sweeping over her, through her, filling her, restoring her.

Cerci collapsed into Ashur's arms, unconscious. He caught her easily, tucking her close, as if his arms alone could keep the darkness, nightmares, and monsters from ever reaching her again.

Chapter Fifty-Eight

Bella's spirit hit the cobblestones with a jolt, landing atop Leopol. His arms were still around her—tight and trembling—even though they were both just wisps of what they'd been, all spirit now, glowing and flickering transparent and barely holding together.

The moment her body touched the ground, magic shifted around them. Cerci's touch—so warm and present just seconds ago—faded from her skin like mist as she burned the portal closed with pure divine magic.

Now that they were spirits again, no one could touch them. And yet someone tried.

Wulfric dropped to his knees beside her, his face wet, his whole body shaking. He reached for her like a drowning man grabbing a lifeline. His fingers went right through her shoulder, making her shudder and flicker.

Bella looked up at him, her eyes glistening with unshed tears, her throat constricting painfully. "I'm still a spirit, Da," she whispered, her voice trembling with a mix of longing and sorrow.

"It's better than you being trapped in those hells, little girl," he uttered, his voice breaking and trembling with raw emotion. "That's more than enough for me."

She smiled, weak and wobbly, tears free-falling from her chin. Her limbs felt like air and ice and barely there, but she shifted, pushed off Leopol, and rolled to the side.

She glanced up at the bright sky above, idyllic clouds passing slowly as if nothing had happened in the past few hours, as if the realms hadn't nearly fallen apart beneath their feet.

Tears fell down her temples, and her father leaned over, blocking some of the sun.

She looked up at him, her voice a whisper. "Did we... Did we defeat the wizard? Are the undead still dead?"

Wulfric nodded, his face streaked with tears. "Yes, he's gone. It's over now. You're going to be alright. Tell me you're going to be alright."

She tried to smile, her lip trembling, her throat too tight to speak. She just nodded—because he needed to believe it. Because maybe, for one second, she needed to believe it too.

He pulled back, a cry of relief tugging him back and into Scarlet's arms. Still on his knees, he wrapped his arms around her waist and held her tight.

Scarlet looked down at Bella, then over at Leopol.

Leopol... Raelion... She turned her head so she could see him. Her spirit felt... wrong but looking at him felt so right.

His gorgeous blue eyes opened as he sucked in a breath. Relief flooded her as he turned to find her, mirroring her until they were both flat on their backs but heads turned to each other. Panting. Shaking. Staring.

Leopol looked... wrecked. The strong lines of his face drawn tight with pain, his hands twitching where they stretched to reach her. His hand was hot and clammy, but she gripped him tight and refused to let go.

His chest still glowed under the remnants of his tattered shirt, a faint Orythium light steady in rhythm, a heartbeat echoing the memory of one.

He licked his lips, cracked and dry, and whispered, "We did it. We're back."

Uncertainty made her gut twist because this didn't feel like a beginning. It felt like an end, like she was being gently tugged out to sea in a dingy without an oar or sail.

With a groan, he lifted onto his elbow and then it was him shadowing her from the sun.

One hand cupped her cheek, gentle and anchoring. "Everything's going to be alright now. You'll see."

She might've believed him—except she felt it. That tug, that pull of the tether.

Bella turned her head with effort, sensing the magic before she saw it. Merida stopped near their heads, silent and pale, a sleeping babe on one hip and the potted rose in her other arm.

She kneeled slowly, setting the pot down beside Bella's head like it weighed the world.

And Bella knew. Sun in her eyes once more, she didn't need to see the rose to know that the one, last petal was about to fall.

Tears spilled from her eyes as she turned toward it, and a shadow fell over her. Her heart thudded once, then went still. The petal trembled on the stem—

She wanted to scream, to beg the wind not to blow. But she just watched. The final petal fluttered free, dancing on a breeze. And then it fell.

Everything's not alright, she thought faintly. How many seconds did she have?

She turned back to Leopol, her breath catching on a sob. "You—you burned up your body for me?"

He didn't hesitate, hadn't looked at Merida or the rose, hadn't looked away from her, hadn't stopped touching her cheek, her lips. As if he could reassure himself she was still here by touch alone.

"Of course." He looked at her like she was the only thing worth saving. "You're my everything."

Her chest ached. Her whole soul trembled, and she couldn't look at him anymore. It hurt too much to realize the truth.

Bella glanced around, taking in each person—Wulfric still on his knees, arms around Scarlet's waist as she kept her arms around his head, holding him to her even as she stared in horror at the rose. Neither of them said a word or acknowledged what they both knew.

Eirwyn stood cradling the dragon egg to her chest, Knox behind her, bloodied and bruised but standing tall. Ashur, Cerci, Merida, Olive, Lailant.

She looked at each one like it might be the last time. There was no time left.

She turned back to Leopol. Her voice shook, but her eyes didn't. "I love you."

At least she got to say it. At least he knew.

Leopol smiled, soft and so heartbreakingly sure. "I love you too. We made it, Bellavore. We'll live like this forever, spirit and spirit, bonded and mated for eternity."

But she shook her head, pain wracking her entire spirit.

"The rose says otherwise," she whispered. "I can see the tether fading."

He glanced up, his eyes widening. "No, the wizard's gone. His spells should've broken with him. How are you still bound to the rose?"

She looked toward it, the stem curling in on itself as death already turned it colors. "It's not logical, but we were dealing with the gods. Perhaps it's my punishment for the part I played in setting the wizard free."

Leopol's expression twisted, panic flashing in his eyes. "No, no, that can't be it." He tried to sit up, his spirit-body trembling with the effort, nearly flickering out. "We beat him and stopped Asmoroth from finding the portal and escaping. You're free. You have to be."

She reached up, laid one trembling finger over his lips.

"Sh, it's alright," she murmured. "If this is the end... I'm grateful I get to die in your arms. Not as a queen or a weapon or a spirit."

He leaned closer, forehead brushing hers, his breathing labored.

"But just as myself. Bella. Your mate. The one who loves you more than anything else in all the realms."

Her breath shuddered, and her eyes fluttered, letting the last bit of strength slip from her soul.

The tether yanked tight. The color around her dimmed. Leopol's lips moved again, but she couldn't hear him. And then she fell.

Not through space or time, but through light itself, into the Edge and the Beyond.

Chapter Fifty-Nine

"She was just here," Wulfric said hoarsely, like if he looked hard enough, he could call her back. "She was *just* here..." Wulfric's voice broke on a howl–a sound so broken, so guttural, it shattered through Leopol's chest like a war hammer.

Leopol's spirit jerked upward, his hands reaching for Bella, but he passed straight through her.

For the first time since they'd met, he couldn't touch her. *No, no, no, no.* No time to lose.

"Drag her body over!" he roared, flailing to his knees in panic. His voice cracked, echoing like thunder through the still courtyard. "Now! Bring her to me!"

The guards hesitated only a moment before they obeyed. Three of them lifted her body–cold, limp, and life-less–and brought it to where her spirit flickered like a dying flame. Transparent. Fading.

The moment they set her down, her spirit shimmered, flickering between presence and nothingness. No, her ghost... The last petal had fallen, and the tether severed.

She was slipping.

No magic held her here except the faintest wisp of their mate bond—and that wasn't enough to restore her to some semblance of life. It held her close, yes. Anchored her to *him*—but not to her body.

She needed an anchor. She needed *life*.

Leopol scrambled closer, blood dripping from his torn palms as he clawed at the space between them, useless in this form, weaker than any other time he'd woken up on this god-forsaken planet.

"Open her mouth!" he bellowed at the guards, but they backed away. It was Lailant who sank to her knees with a groan. Lailant opened the scaled, twisted mouth of her body, and he dripped his spirit's essence inside.

Nothing happened. They were losing precious time.

"Where's the apple tea—pour the damned tea down her throat!" he demanded.

Scarlet's voice cracked from nearby. "No one has the potion—it burned up in your pocket when you were *in the hells*, Leopol." Her quiet certainty made him shake, trying to maintain control of the situation.

"No—no, I had it! I had it—" He clawed at his chest. His jacket was different than the one he'd had on this morning. Another body, another form, another jacket. He tried calling his magic to shift, to bring his jacket back, but there was nothing. No pouch, no pocket... No magic, only the seared echo of where it had been.

His scream tore the clouds apart, arms out and head thrown back like a Growler howling at the moon.

Cerci stirred in Ashur's arms at the sound, blinking sluggishly. "What? Oh, it's too late," she whispered hoarsely, her voice dry as ash. "Her body's been dead too long. She won't make it back in."

Leopol shook his head like he could throw off reality with will alone. "No, absolutely not. There *has* to be a way."

Lailant's voice cut through the air like a blade. "Look at the rose."

He did. He didn't want to, but that voice was a command he couldn't disobey. He turned.

The stem was curling in on itself, blackened and cracking. One second later, it crumbled to ash and floated away on the gentle sea breeze.

Gone, just like that.

Wulfric knelt in stunned silence, looking down at Bella's body like he didn't know what he was looking at anymore—like the air had been ripped from his lungs and there was nothing left to breathe.

Then something pulsed, a flicker of light.

At Wulfric's feet, where Bella's body had fallen, one last fragment of the Sentinel core gleamed like a dying star—forgotten until now. A sliver of Orythium.

Leopol's breath caught. "The core," he whispered, then louder. "*The core!* Bring it to me!"

He lunged, but his hands passed through it. He couldn't pick it up. He wasn't *real* anymore. Last time he'd woken as a spirit had been nothing like this.

"Stay with me. Don't leave me. Don't go where I can't follow," he whispered to her, his hands digging into the dirt next to her and the core.

Panting, trembling, he turned to Lailant on his knees. "Please," he begged. "Take the Orythium—anchor her soul to her body. *Please.* You have to try."

Lailant hesitated, her expression unreadable.

"Are you sure?" she asked softly. "This is Illustros' essence. It's not our place to tamper with it."

"I was made to protect knowledge," he rasped, "but she

642

is the only truth I want to guard now. Without her, I am nothing. There's still a flicker of Orythium left... not enough to heal a kingdom—maybe not even enough to heal a broken heart—but it might be enough to heal a soul."

She shook her head slowly and crossed her arms, her wrinkles deepening with worry.

Leopol's spirit trembled. Grief built to a roar in his chest, and he couldn't hold it in. With a cry, he surged into his dragon form—a silver-white spirit shape edged in gold, smoke curling from his snout as his body arched over hers.

Still, he was insubstantial. Still, he couldn't touch her. Couldn't feel her. Couldn't *reach* her.

He curled around her anyway, coiling like a guardian beast, and whispered every healing spell he knew—ancient tongues, broken syllables, forgotten lullabies of the old gods.

Lailant called out behind him. "Leopol, *stop*. It's over."

His voice shook the cobblestones. "No, it can't be over. I won't let her go. Not like this. We were meant to be together, to bring peace to the continent and prepare the world for the coming battle. Mother said—"

"Your mother is a fool," Lailant said, and Leopol's eyes widened.

Cerci said something in an ancient language, and the words tinkled his ear. *Did that translate to aunt?*

Then her eyes softened as they dropped to Bella, first looking at her twisted body and then her flickering spirit. Side by side, they hardly resembled each other at all.

"She hated that body," Lailant said, voice sad but firm. "When she took that nekrotic heart potion and did the ritual, that body stopped being hers. Living in it is not what she would've wanted."

"I don't care," Leopol snarled. "I love her whether she's a spirit, a drakin, or the wind itself. Please—by the Light—

bring her back to me. I cannot go another day without her, much less another *millennium.*"

Lailant's mouth trembled. "And if the Orythium isn't enough? What then?"

He didn't even pause. *"Then take what I have left and save her."*

He ripped his shirt, baring his chest and the pulsing scar across his tattooed skin.

Lailant stilled—everything stilled. No one moved, not even the wind. The whole world seemed to hold its breath.

Then Lailant simply lifted her hands to the sky, and the heavens cracked open.

Light began to fall—not lightning, not hail, not fire—but something softer, stranger, like a gentle rain made of stardust and memory. It shimmered as it came, slow at first, then thick and fast until the cobblestones blurred with it. It hit the ground in silence, each droplet a heartbeat, a whisper, a thread.

Everyone fell back instinctively—Ashur picking up Cerci to carry her, Scarlet yanking Wulfric by the sleeve. Merida took off running with her guards. Even Knox shielded Eirwyn and the egg as the magic surged, lifting them in his claws and setting them down a safe distance away.

Only Leopol stayed.

The light poured down on him—on her—on the body he curled around. It didn't burn. It didn't pierce. It wrapped around them, folding like wings, like a lullaby from the stars, like the protective barrier that was around his dragon body in the cave. He tried to hold on, tried to brace her closer—

But the light pulled at them.

A sudden wrench, and he roared as it separated him from her. "No! No, don't—!"

The cocoon closed around him first. Blinding. Sealing

him in light. It was warm. It was gentle. A thousand voices in harmony whispered his name—not the one he'd clung to for centuries.

But his true name. *Raelion*.

He stilled as comfort filled his soul. Breath caught in his throat. His dragon spirit form shifted into something more—less smoke, more substance. More *him*. Bones cracked, but there was no pain. Only warm, comforting light and a knowing presence. Someone was with him in this cocoon, but it was a good someone—soft and ancient, like the memory of a lullaby sung by the stars. Someone he'd known in his days as the Archivist.

When the light faded, the castle gates and walls came back into view—blasted stone, crumbled cobblestones, the hushed awe as everyone dared to look again.

Leopol gasped the breath of a newborn and looked down, weak as one too and unable to keep his head up. Then he blinked in surprise.

His hands were solid. Flesh and bone and blue skin laced with white and tipped in gold—warm and tangible. He flexed his fingers, stunned. This wasn't illusion or spirit trickery. It was real. *He* was real.

No longer a drifting Archivist in the ether. No longer a carved construct guarding sacred halls and an adopted family or even the body he'd just gotten back last month. He was restored to a better version of who he'd always been in his core.

And if the gods were just—if the light had heard his cries—then she would be too. His breath caught as he scanned the battlefield, frantic—until he saw her.

The light was lowering her gently to the cobblestones like a sleeping moonbeam. She lay crumpled in blue and white, her long hair spilling like ink across the ash where the rose had fallen and died.

He scrambled to her side, heart pounding, throat tight. The Orythium pulsed erratically in his chest, a frantic drumbeat urging him on as he pulled her into his arms.

She was still, but warm, the glow slowly fading from her. His hands trembled as he cradled her, one arm wrapped behind her back, the other supporting her legs like she might break if he wasn't careful. His head bowed to hers, forehead to temple, and he stopped breathing, just for a second, willing everything to be quiet—

There it was, a breath, barely more than a brush of air against his cheek, soft and warm and impossibly fragile.

He gasped and ran a diagnostic spell, felt the familiar tug of magic as it obeyed. He sobbed—that the magic worked, that the spell showed a healthy woman who was simply asleep.

The relief cracked from his chest like thunder as he buried his face in her hair. She was alive and breathing. Not gone. *Not gone.*

Tears poured from him, unchecked, unstoppable. No pride. No restraint. Just raw, ugly gratitude that he hadn't lost her after all.

Across the cobblestone street, three nations stood silent. Growlers, Robins, drakin, his dragon cousin—they all bore witness as a dragon warrior—guardian of memory, son of prophecy—held a fallen queen like she was the only truth left worth knowing.

"Simi dravak, Bellavore," he whispered, lips pressed to her brow. "Please wake up. I need to know this is real, that you're here and safe and alive."

He sat up, her body on his lap, cradled like the most precious thing in the realms—because she was. He didn't care who watched. He didn't care that the gods had already moved on. He had her back—and this time, he wasn't letting go.

Then her head lolled on the crook of his arm, and his breath caught.

In spirit form, she'd been a beautiful human with brown luscious hair that flowed halfway down her back and brown eyes that were so deep, he could stare in them while talking with her for hours.

After she'd taken the ritual with Gastone's heart, her body had transformed into a grotesque monster, becoming a morphed drakin with red scales, limbs that were too long, ridges on her spine and horns on her head. Her cute button nose had become a long snout that breathed fire, absorbed from Gastone.

But now—she was neither and both at the same time.

The ridges on her spine had softened into elegant whorls, like flowing script etched in pale gold he could feel under his hand. Her limbs, once stretched and jagged, had refined—strong and graceful, still built like the delicious woman she'd been but now a drakin queen whose form would be revered with statues, if he had any say about it.

Her red, harsh scales had vanished except for a faint shimmer of gold beneath her skin, like celestial runes just beneath the surface, catching the light when she moved. From her ears down her neck were ancient runes and sigils in golden Orythium ink, telling a story of power, magic, and wisdom.

Her skin—once red and raw—had returned to the warm golden-olive tone he remembered from her earliest spirit form, kissed by the gods now with a radiance that shimmered just slightly, like moonlight clinging to her even in shadow.

Where once horns jutted like weapons, now delicate spirals rose from her temples–ivory smooth, etched with glowing golden lines like ancient sigils. Her hair had grown longer, cascading around her like a waterfall of dark mahogany shot through with threads of gold starlight.

He lifted her hand and kissed her palm, resting it lightly against his chest as he took in the changes. No longer clawed or monstrous, but elegant and built to rule nations, her fingers were tipped with translucent golden nails that glowed faintly like the petals of her rose. The fine lines along her knuckles traced subtle sigils, almost like poetry written by starlight. When he brushed his fingers along her palm, power hummed beneath her skin–not dangerous, not wild, but focused. Chosen. Holy.

She wore no armor, no torn remnants of what she'd died in. The gods had dressed her in a simple robe of soft white and blue, cinched with a sash braided from threads of silver and pale gold. The fabric shimmered like mist and moonlight, the hem embroidered with barely visible draconic runes. Every time the light shifted, they pulsed faintly–like the robe remembered spells he hadn't yet read.

And in the center of her chest–where her tether to the rose had once lived, where the Sentinel's spark had been laid–there was no gaping scar like his or glowing core.

There was something better.

Fine golden ink traced a blooming rose over her sternum, each petal delicate and precise, the stem descending into her heart. From that center, Orythium threads spiraled outward across her collarbones and down to her ribs like living armor, like veins of starlight woven through flesh. The sigils there didn't just glow–they pulsed, visible through the fabric. Not with borrowed power but with *life*.

The gods didn't just return her. They had rewritten her.

She wasn't human, but she wasn't a dragon either. She was something new, a divine touched drakin. Whatever she was, she was alive and his, his mate, his miracle.

The hush on the battlefield shifted, and he felt it before he saw her. Her soft footsteps belied her presence and power.

Leopol looked up, arms wrapped tight around Bella's new form, her head resting in the crook of his arm, her breath soft but steady against his throat. The cobblestones still shimmered faintly where the light had rained down.

Lailant stopped a few feet away, backlit by the last rays of the sun as it set over the walls of the castle. Her robes fluttered in a breeze that didn't touch anything else. Her eyes—always sharp, always knowing—glowed solidly white now. Realization settled in his bones.

"You never really were just a healing hedge witch or a Seer," Leopol murmured, throat raw.

"No, Raelion," she said, voice softer than before, older somehow even as her wrinkles seemed to fade. "I was never only that, just as you were never only an Archivist."

He looked up at her, bone-tired and aching, his head hurting from too many emotions. "No riddles this time, Lailant. Say what you mean."

Lailant, now decades younger, stood taller, the cane for decoration instead of use now. "Your mate... yes."

He looked down at Bella again, at the golden runes etched into her skin like vows no man could break. "The Orythium was enough?" He couldn't hold back the question. His scholarly mind demanded an answer—and he knew Bella would want to know too.

"More or less. I took the sliver of Orythium from the core and what you had, then split it evenly between the two of you, remaking you both."

"She looks like—" He couldn't finish.

"Like herself," Fysica answered. "As she would have been, had no evil touched her. Her body is a new vessel—part human, part drakin, part divine. The Orythium you surrendered stitched through her soul like thread through cloth. The mate bond lit the path. And I... I wove the rest."

He glanced up at her, seeing how she radiated light now. No longer an old woman but one younger than Bella. A medallion hung around her neck, her dress the same style as Bella's but somehow more regal. Golden threads of godly essence flowed under her skin like glowing veins, and he finally recognized it—saw the resemblance.

"You're a goddess." It wasn't a question, but she answered anyway.

"One of the forgotten ones," she corrected gently. "I am Fysica, weaver of fates. Guardian of balance. I have worn many names, many faces. But this one... this one allowed me to watch over so much without interference."

"I remember you," he said softly. "With Analise and Feralt..."

Lailant—no, Fysica—nodded slowly, her glowing white eyes somehow sad. "My hands are often tied by the threads of fate."

Leopol's arms tightened around Bella instinctively.

"Is that why you let her suffer so much?" he growled. "Why you let me fail them?"

She sighed heavily. "Wisdom is not the same as fore-sight. Even the wisest among us—" her mouth curled faintly, knowingly "—sometimes miss the details."

"You mean Honifery, the woman who raised me?" He let out a bitter laugh.

"You no longer call her your mother?" Fysica asked.

He curled Bella tighter to himself. "She abandoned me long ago. No mother would do so."

"She was your mother, in her way. She gave you libraries and riddles and training and free will and doubt—because doubt sharpens the mind like nothing else. She did not birth you, but she was and is your mother, just the same."

Leopol blinked, emotions running high. "I was a construct, a slave to the gods in the astral library."

"You were carved for a purpose, Raelion. Forged by fate and sealed with a star's breath. Not born but made, as Bella has been remade."

Leopol's throat closed. "Why tell me this now?"

"Because the game isn't over. My sisters and I have delayed the end, but our uncle still stirs in the Deep. Hanzel was only the beginning, one of many sin lords that he's made deals with—all with the goal of coming to Celawyn to attack the rest of the gods. There will be other prophecies, other kings, other wars."

He stared at her, breath ragged. "Then what do we do?"

"You train your nation. You gather knowledge like blades and build cities of both strength and study. You let love be your compass and truth your torch... You live—and you prepare."

Her cane tapped once on the stone—and left behind a glowing rune that faded as quickly as it came. And then she turned, walking away without fanfare, each step morphing her more into the Lailant he knew until an old woman leaned heavily on her cane and disappeared through the gates, following straggling soldiers.

Live. He would *live*—with Bella. He glanced down at his mate, his heart in his chest as her hand twitched in his and her lashes fluttered.

His voice cracked on the next words, hoarse and

breaking open. "I love you, mibella. Gods, I love you. I need you to wake up now."

He leaned down and kissed her pale pink lips. Light and sound faded as everything stilled again.

He held her, clinging like a drowning man to the one thing that mattered to him. Maybe love wasn't a lifeline but a resurrection. Maybe it was the answer the gods had been waiting for all along.

Then her lips moved beneath his.

He jerked back to see her eyes open wide. Where solid brown had been before, they now reflected the golden essence of the gods.

"Raelion, my love." She sighed. Her voice rang with a timbre that didn't belong to this world alone—like music sung through time.

He sobbed and crashed his lips to hers again.

Chapter Sixty

Luvielle.

A soft, melodic voice called to her, repeating just one word as a soft wake-up call. She knew that word like she knew her own soul. It was her name.

She frowned, and a smooth hand caressed her cheek. She sighed, her frown falling away.

"Bellakari, will you wake up for me today?" His voice was melodic too, deep as the sea and promising adventure within the safety of his arms.

She wanted to please him, and her lashes fluttered.

The first thing she noticed was the feel of silk beneath her fingers. Smooth, soft, and so clean, she stretched beneath the covers just to feel it on her skin. Light dappled across the high ceiling above her, filtered through stained glass. Birdsong drifted faintly from the window, a sound too gentle to belong to the battlefield she remembered.

The battlefield. It all came rushing back.

Was she dead?

She shifted slightly—and realized her entire body ached.

She was stiff, and she groaned, sucking in a deep breath...
Breath. Her eyes flew open, wide awake. Alive.

"Leopol?" Her voice cracked.

"Bella." His voice hit her like a lightning strike of joy all
in one. "Gods, you're awake."

He was beside her in a heartbeat, his warm hand closing
around hers like a prayer come true. She turned her head–
and stared.

He was real. Flesh and bone and blue skin. The
Orythium glowed faintly beneath the edge of his shirt,
warm and steady. He was the same as before, but where his
scales had shifted from blue to white to silver before? The
silver had turned to gold now.

His eyes gleamed with tears he didn't bother hiding.

She lifted her other hand to wipe one away–and froze.
Gold. Not jewelry, not paint, but runes. Ancient, delicate,
woven along her skin like vines blooming in spring.

"Wh–what happened to me?" she asked, turning her
hands over as light caught different pieces.

Leopol just shook his head, choking on emotion.

"It worked," came a voice from the doorway. Bella
turned to see Lailant standing there–not hunched or tired
now, but tall and radiant. Her robes shimmered with
threads of starlight, her eyes deep wells of ageless knowing–
pure white that sent a shiver up Bella's spine.

"You're not Lailant," Bella whispered.

"No," the woman said with an achingly familiar smile. "I
am Fysica."

Bella gasped, struggling to sit up. "The Weaver? One of
the Fates. Guardian of–"

"The physical realm, weaver of what becomes. Yes, yes,"
Fysica said with a grin as she glided into the room. "I

guided you here, but it was you who endured all the years of training I put you through."

Leopol pushed pillows under her and helped her sit up slowly, the new strength and weight in her limbs foreign but familiar, like walking on land after ears of floating on the sea.

"Training?" Bella finally asked, her brain working sluggishly.

"Yes," Fysica said, taking a seat on the foot of the bed. "You're a key, child. I'm the fate who sees how it all ties together—and I'm the one who rewove you, stitched you into the fabric of the world's saving story."

"I—thank you," Bella whispered as Leopol brushed her hair from her face. Jaq and Gus hopped out of Fysica's dress pocket and across the bed spread. She stroked their handles and smiled a weak greeting. Then she asked the questions that were burning brightest.

"What am I now? Why the training? Why everything?"

"You are what we once called a *Divina Drakin*," Lailant said. "A being touched by the divine and anchored to love. Forged in the crucible of loss, imbued with Orythium, rebuilt from the essence of the gods themselves, and bound by the mate bond that you and Raelion share." She nodded to Leopol.

Bella blinked. "Raelion? You know him like this."

Leopol blushed and muttered, "Apparently, the woman I called my mother is Honifery."

She smiled at him. "You know her name now. I'm so happy for you." She squeezed his hand.

He took a deep breath and frowned. "Fysica says there will be more prophecies, more wars. We need to lead Busparia—perhaps the entire continent—into the future, find ways to learn and grow and protect ourselves for the coming fight."

Bella's shoulders stiffened. "I'm not sure I'm ready, but I'll be the best queen Busparia's seen in decades."

"Are any of us ready for responsibility?" Fysica countered softly, brushing her fingers over the golden script etched in Bella's free hand. "You've not just been changed so you can live. You've been rewritten into exactly what this world needs. Although technically, I'd already woven you into who you needed to be at the moment of your birth."

"But now I'm queen," Bella said with a frown.

"Now you're a queen, a mate, a true love. Now you're Queen Bellatrix of Busparia. Bella to those you love. But to the gods and your secret mission for me," Fysica said, her voice lowering with reverence, "you are Luvielle."

The name struck something deep inside her, a sound she hadn't known she'd been waiting for her entire life. It rang like truth in her bones, older than memory.

"What?" she whispered.

Fysica smiled, a familiar one that Bella had taken comfort in since she was a grieving child. "The soul bound to love, reborn in light, forged in grief, and bloomed in sacrifice. A rose of hope and wisdom when even the stars faltered."

Leopol's hand found hers again, grounding her. "You've always been more than a name," he said. "Now the world and the heavens will know it too."

Fysica patted her hand and let it go slowly. Bella swallowed, staring down at the golden script on her skin.

Luvielle.

"You have always been more than a name. Now the world and the heavens will know it too," Leopol said quietly.

It was fitting, she supposed. Luvielle and Raelion, secret

champions of Fysica herself. Bella took a deep breath and nodded gently, accepting her role with more than a bud of excitement in her stomach.

It was a chance to redeem herself even more. More than just reversing the curse that Gastone and the wizard had wrought. It was an opportunity to give her people tools and knowledge that would make their lives easier.

Fysica chuckled and stood. "Don't get too excited. You've years before the gods will call on you both. For now, you rest, rebuild, and love. When the time comes, you fight with the other champions."

"Against Asmoroth?" Leopol growled, his hand gripping hers harder.

Fysica turned, her face solemn as it morphed slowly back into the old woman she knew as Lailant. "He has not given up. The world still trembles at what stirs in the shadows. But you have a little time. Use it wisely."

And then, with a whisper of wind and the scent of roses and stardust, she faded through the door—leaving silence, and the weight of destiny, in her wake.

Luvielle, she repeated silently, letting it settle like starlight in her chest. A name not of shame or fear or curses—but of hope.

Bella blinked at the golden runes on her hands, still not quite believing any of this was real. Her skin shimmered faintly beneath the light, like the gods had painted prayers across her fingers.

She flexed them slowly, reverently, falling in love with how the light caught on the soft runed scales. "My hands are beautiful," she whispered, almost afraid to ask the next question. "But... what about my face?"

She looked up at Leopol, hesitant but watchful for his expression. He just tilted his head in confusion, so she added, "The wizard twisted me into something monstrous, but Lailant–Fysica–remade me. Do I still look like that? Will they fear me again? Or–will they listen to me like this?"

Leopol's smile was soft and immediate, like sunshine after storm clouds as he squeezed her hand. "Bella, you were gorgeous as a spirit. You were gorgeous when you were all snarls and fangs and fire. And now?" He leaned closer, eyes drinking her in as he kissed the back of her hand. "Now you're simply stunning."

Color bloomed in her cheeks, warm and flustered. "I'm not fishing for compliments. I know it's silly to worry about how I look, but–"

"Not silly at all," he said, setting her hand down and standing, holding both of his hands up in surrender. "I don't blame you. We're only human... well, sort of."

He winked and walked to the dresser. She saw the mirror above it and paused. Not an ounce of fear or worry hit her at seeing the simple gilded mirror. Somehow, facing the wizard had excised the fear of it out of her psyche.

He turned with a small hand-held mirror and handed it to her. "Here, see for yourself."

Bella hesitated, then took it with both hands. She drew a breath and tilted it up–

–and gasped.

Her face was no longer soft and human but sculpted– refined with elegant golden scales that gleamed like sunlit armor. She looked like herself... only more. Elegant, twisted horns curled from her temples like ivory, etched with gold. Delicate scales shimmered along her cheekbones and down her neck–like the petals of a rose reforged in starlight.

Her fingers trembled. "I'm definitely not human anymore." The words felt like a truth and a question all at once.

"No, you're something stronger," Leopol murmured, brushing her hair back from her face. "You were always strong, but before... The world just hadn't caught up to your ideals and plans yet. Now your body matches the strength you always carried. The strength the world tried to overlook."

"But you never did," she whispered.

Emotion rose fast in her chest. Her eyes burned, and she tried to speak, but only a sob came out. He took her chin between his forefinger and thumb, tilting her head up even as he leaned in to kiss her–

A knock at the door had him pulling back, and she sighed with disappointment as the door opened.

Merida swept in, dressed in crisp green and silver robes that shimmered with authority, a simple golden circlet on her head. She looked more like a queen than any royal Bella had ever seen, even more so than Eirwyn.

"You're awake," she said with a warm smile, her eyes lighting up. "Thank the stars."

Bella blinked back with surprise. "Princess Merida?"

"Queen now," Leopol murmured beside her with a slight bow. "Don't tire her out. She's just woken up."

"Yes, I won't stay long. I just wanted to see you myself." She stepped to the side, a proud light in her eyes. "How are you feeling?"

Bella glanced from the mirror on her lap to her hands and shrugged. "I'm adjusting to the changes. How are you? The armies? Your family?"

Merida sighed and sat in the chair beside the bed while Leopol bustled about the room, laying another blanket over her legs, bringing her a fresh glass of water, ordering food from the servants with the pull of a bell.

When he finally sat on the bed next to her and took her hand, Merida's summary was winding down.

"So, my father—we're just calling him Prince Aldi now—is in the nursery with a new nurse, happy, healthy, and whole. Just a normal griffion baby, really."

Bella shook her head. "Fascinating. All because he was given the full bottle of the siren's tears?"

Merida nodded. "The tears took him back to a time before pain. He was about this old when his own mother died." Her voice caught slightly. "He's just... a little boy again."

Bella was brimming with so many questions about the siren's tears, and she glanced at Leopol.

Later, she heard in her mind. She blinked, and her heart started racing. She'd heard a voice in her head before, and it had led to a battle with undead and a trip to hell.

Leopol squeezed her hand. *Bella? Are you well?*

Her eyes widened, and she sucked in a breath, suddenly able to breathe again. "Uh, yes, well, how's Prince Eryk?"

Leopol smiled, his hand anchoring and comforting her. "Eryk is ready to set sail. The only break I've had for the past three days was to go eat and change, taking shifts watching you with your father. As soon as I stepped out of this room, Eryk was asking all kinds of questions about the siren's tears, searching for the origin of them."

Merida nodded. "The plan at the moment is for him to find the siren. Maybe she's still alive. Maybe the siren will help him restore our father back to normal. In the meantime, I've been named queen."

Merida smiled as Bella beamed and congratulated her, then reached into a folder on her lap. "We sat down and ironed out the treaties. Signed them yesterday while you slept. Busparia's army began their march home under

Ashur's command too, but Cerci is still here for a few more days, helping Eirwyn and Knox. All we need now is the queen of Busparia's signature, and it'll be official."

Bella opened her mouth, her chest tightening again. She didn't know what to say, and she looked at Leopol with wide eyes.

He wasn't even looking at her though, even though his thumb went back and forth on her hand.

His brow furrowed. "There are food shortages in the Feral Forest, but reports say Busparia was hit worse by the daemon winter. We'll need to read through the treaty to see what it says about necessities such as food and medicine."

Bella blinked at the sudden shift—from affectionate mate to strategist in a heartbeat.

"Take your time and read through it. I and our council will be here when you're ready to talk it over," Merida said. "There's peace now. Trade routes can reopen. You're welcome to stay here and recover as long as you need. My castle is your castle."

She stood and curtsied—not deeply, but respectfully—and swept out, leaving the folder on the chair.

Bella exhaled slowly and glanced up at Leopol as he wrapped his arm behind her. She sighed and snuggled into his chest. "You're good at this," she teased, glancing at Leopol as her hand settled over his faint Orythium scar. "You always know what problem to solve next."

He snorted and covered her hand with his, color blooming in his blue cheeks. "It's what I was made for. Organizing, cataloging, moving puzzle pieces until they fit."

She paused and held her breath. "Are you sure you want to rule by my side?"

He kissed her palm. "Do you want me to?"

"I wouldn't dare even try it without you," she said.

He kissed the inside of her wrist. "I don't want to force your hand. If you'd rather live in a cottage in the woods, I'll make it happen."

Her heart warmed, even as her eyes wandered back to his thick chest. "I... didn't think I'd be ready to do this—rule as queen. With you. I guess a trip to hell will change a girl."

He chuckled and kissed the inside of her forearm. "I'll be here no matter how many changes you go through, Bellavore. We'll go through them together."

Her breath caught as his danced along her skin, her scales.

"I guess you've changed too," she murmured, lifting her elbow to his kiss. "Your scales—your tattoos..."

The silver that once tipped his scales now glinted gold, matching the glowing Orythium scar across his chest. His tattoos ran higher, new symbols curling along his throat in languages she didn't know but somehow understood.

He was still her Leopol, but now he was more Raelion than before. Reborn by love and sacrifice. Her arm curled up, her hand cupping the side of his head.

He turned to look down at her with those mesmerizing blue eyes, his lips slowly moving closer.

Her eyes stung. She opened her mouth to say it—I love you—but before she could, another knock on the door before it burst open. *Again.*

"Wakey, wakey," Scarlet called, slipping inside with a tray of food, her face calm but eyes bright with happiness and contentment. Wulfric barreled in after her.

"Sweetheart, you're awake," he gasped, crossing the room in two steps. He scooped her into his arms, her blankets half falling away to reveal a soft blue and white dressing gown and held her like a drowning man who'd found shore.

She cried—in surprise, in relief, in joy—and gripped his tunic. "I—I can touch you. I can finally hug you."

He didn't answer—just held her tighter. Tears streamed down her cheeks, and even though she had golden scales, and he was a hairy, black furred Growler, she closed her eyes and was transported twenty years into the past. Back when her father held her after losing her mother. Back when it was just the two of them, relying on each other and tackling the world together, one problem at a time.

Her hand reached for Leopol without thinking, and he stepped close, gripping it firmly. She sat there between them, her father and her mate, arm wrapped around one and hand in the other. Bridging the two great loves of her life.

This was when she knew—it really was all going to be alright now. She really was alive, had a future ahead of her, a purpose, a family to build and love and protect. Her sobs slowed to hiccups as her father rocked her gently.

Scarlet cleared her throat and shifted awkwardly, setting the tray of food on a side table.

Leopol squeezed her hand before letting go, arranging the tray to be secure. The smell of fresh bread and soup wafted to her nose, and she sniffed, pulling away slightly.

Scarlet patted Wulfric on the back, then reached for his arm, tugging gently with a grin. "Come on, Wolfie. Give them a second to settle into their new bodies together."

Wulfric scowled but didn't let her go. "I'm not letting them get comfortable with their new bodies. There'll be time for that after the wedding."

Bella squealed a gasp, "Wedding?"

"We're fated mates. That's deeper than any wedding," Leopol grumbled.

Scarlet laughed, but tugged on the scruff of Wulfric's

neck, a gentle reminder she *would* get her way, come hell or high water. "Either way, I'm hungry. Let's go eat something that isn't soup. You want a nice pot roast? I overheard the servants talking about that when I grabbed the tray from the maid."

He grunted again and sighed as he released her, standing beside the bed. Hands on hips, he glared at Leopol. "There will be a wedding. If nothing else, so the kingdoms will recognize your authority to back her up."

Bella rolled her eyes, but Leopol just quirked a brow as he held Wulfric's gaze. "Well, I won't force her. No one will. If she wants a wedding, then I'll gladly be the first one there. I'll even have some fancy gilded greaves made for my feet and shins. "

Bella sniffled as Wulfric beamed, nodding before bending to kiss her forehead. Tears pooled again at the simple gesture, and she wiped them away as the door closed behind them. Her shoulders shook with emotions.

Leopol didn't ask—just climbed onto the bed and pulled her gently into his lap. Her back settled against his chest, and his chin rested on her shoulder.

His fingers tipped her chin toward him. "It's not worth the tears. If you don't want a wedding–"

"It's not that," she said with a hiccup. "It's just all happening at once, and it's a lot to process and–"

He placed a soft finger on her lips and leaned in as he said, "We have all the time in the world now, though. No need to rush."

Her breath hitched. He was right. No wizard, no deadline of a dying tether, no idea when Asmoroth would rise, or the next threat would present itself. All they could do now was live their lives, one day at a time.

She licked her lips as he drew close enough to feel their breath mingle.

A shout echoed from across the hall.

A door slammed open. "It's time!" Cerci's voice rang out in the hall, wild and urgent. "Come quick!"

Bella blinked, heart thudding. "Time for what?"

Leopol groaned, dropping his forehead against hers. "We're never going to get that kiss, are we?"

But he was already helping her to her feet. "Come on. It's time for the dragon prince to make his debut."

Her eyes widened as he tucked her hand into the crook of his elbow. Legs still unsteady, she tilted her chin and walked with him across the room. The next miracle was already calling.

Chapter Sixty-One

Leopol helped Bella across the hall, his arm curled securely around her waist. She was radiant, golden runes catching the soft light, but she moved gingerly–still not used to the strength and weight of her new body.

She grumbled under her breath, "I swear, I didn't weigh this much before. I feel like I'm dragging a marble statue around."

He smiled. "A very graceful, beautiful marble statue."

She snorted but didn't pull away, her cheeks tinging pink. He watched her closely, catching the slight hesitation in her steps as they reached the door a second before her knees buckled.

"Got you," he murmured, sweeping her easily into his arms.

She slapped his shoulder. "Leopol, put me down. I want to see the dragon birth–I can walk."

"I know you can, and you will see the birth," he said, kissing her temple as he turned the handle to the hall. "What my queen wants, my queen will get. But I enjoy carrying you. Don't deny me the pleasure of spoiling you."

The little grin on her plump lips said she wasn't that mad about it. Her arms tightened around his neck as they paused outside the doorway, letting Scarlet and Wulfric pass them and go into Eirwyn and Knox's room.

She leaned in and whispered, "Well, when you put it like that, I guess I don't mind a little beastly behavior on your part now and then."

Then she licked the shell of his ear.

He shuddered and froze mid-step, his own knees buckling at the feel of her. It was like a shot of pure magic straight into his veins.

His eyes burned down into hers. "Watch it, mibella, or we won't make it to the birth. I'll throw you over my shoulder and have my way with you."

"Promises, promises," she murmured, golden brows arched in challenge.

He turned slightly with a growl, angling toward their room and ready to kick the door shut behind them.

But she shook her head, her grin widening. "Nope. Onward, my noble steed."

He laughed, full and hearty, his first as a living dragon, and the moment solidified in his memories where it'd live forever as one of his favorites.

He kissed her temple again and carried her across the threshold into the room, unable to deny her anything.

The chaos of the hallway fell away instantly. Inside, the chamber was warm and quiet, the hearth crackling. All attention focused on the nest of soft furs and blankets before the fire where the egg lay. Eirwyn knelt beside it, Knox's arm steady around her shoulders.

Leopol set Bella gently on her feet, sliding his hands

around her waist from behind. Her back pressed against his chest as they watched, both barely breathing in anticipation. He didn't realize he was holding his breath until she reached up and threaded her fingers through his on her hips.

And then—it happened. A clawed foot punched through the shell.

Eirwyn gasped. "Look! He has scales like you."

"He's a dragon, love," Knox said, though his voice cracked with emotion. "Of course he has scales."

Leopol's throat tightened at his cousin's tone. His hand reached forward and gripped Knox's shoulder without a word, offering silent support. He hadn't been there for Knox's hatching. He hadn't been there when the wizard poisoned hearts and turned the drakin against the dragons, wiping them out in a genocide masked as protection.

But he was here now. Witnessing the reversal. The beginning of a new chapter—for dragons, for magic, for the world.

The egg rocked again. A second foot burst through, and then—golden light flashed as a single gleaming eye peered through a crack.

Bella's hand tightened in his. Emotion radiated off her like heat.

He couldn't hold it in. He reached across the bond. *Are you alright, Bellakari?*

She jerked in surprise and twisted in his arms. "Did—did you just—"

Speak through the mate bond? he said again into her mind, warmth and amusement flowing through the thread that connected them. *Yes, I'd hoped... now that we're both alive again, whole again... we'd be able to speak like this, like it's recorded that fated mates can do in all the records.*

Her eyes widened, and she turned to whisper directly into his ear. "You can... hear my thoughts?"

He continued along the pathway to her mind, not wanting to distract from the moment of the birth. *Not exactly. It's like a thread between us. Most fated mates can access a mental pathway—it's more emotion than words, but we can speak, sense things, share when it matters. Try it?*

Her breath caught. *How do I know if it's working?*

He kissed her temple as she turned back to the dragon egg. *Tell me what you think of the dragon hatching so far.*

I think it's beautiful. I want to know everything—what's normal, what's not. I'm just watching you and hoping with a prayer, taking my cues from your body language. How do we know if the birth is going well? I hate going in blind.

He chuckled and squeezed his arms around her again, resting his head where he could watch and smell her at the same time. *It's going well, yes. I'll answer all your questions, show you all the books about it, if you'd like to learn.*

She sighed and leaned back into his embrace. *That's one of the things I love about you. You're always willing to share that big brain of yours—and all your books.*

She didn't say she loved him, but he knew she did, just as much as he loved her. It wasn't just fated. They'd fought for each other, died for each other... and now they were going to live for each other. Honestly, it might be the hardest thing they'd ever done.

Why didn't we do this before? Speak this way? Bella asked as a finger poked through the shell, tipped in a tiny claw.

I think we needed to be alive, tethered, healed. Now, we're truly mated, truly us, the way we were always meant to be, in the forms we were meant to share.

She glanced up at him, her eyes shining, and he kissed her softly. Just a light graze of the lips before a gasp echoed in the room. She whipped her head back to the dragon, whose entire fist had emerged, clenching and unclenching like he was testing brand new muscles.

The movements of the child grew faster, and tiny grunts echoed in the stillness.

And so, it begins. Soon, he'll be crying, and they'll never get a moment of peace again. What fun.

He tensed. *I can't tell if that's a good thing or not. Apparently, the mate bond mind link doesn't carry tone well. Was that sarcasm?*

He kissed her forehead as the egg cracked wider. Leopol stood with his mate at his side, a thread of light between their minds and hearts, knowing this was only the beginning.

Bella leaned her head back, content even with the extra weight her body now carried.

Not so much sarcasm as envy. I'd say it's a good thing for them. A babe changes everything, and this one more than most. The first drag-onling since Knox, and they're the first in centuries, since the drakin wiped out the full dragons.

Leopol kissed her neck. *It's the birth of a new era. Definitely a good thing.*

She held her breath as another tiny hand shot out of the shell, waving wildly. *Think we'll have one of those someday?*

It was still hard to believe it was even possible again—*a dragon hatching, a live birth.* The wizard had turned fear into fuel all those years ago before Leopol trapped him in the mirror, convincing the drakin to slaughter their own kind. Centuries of silence had followed. Until Knox. Until now.

His claws dug into her hips, and he spun her toward the door.

She laughed and wrapped her arms around his waist. "Leopol, wait. I didn't mean right now."

He paused near the door, his expression fierce, loyal, and loving. "You—you mean it though? You—"

She stood on her toes and kissed him—full of joy, love, and longing. She told him everything with that kiss: what she wanted, what she chose, what she hoped for. His love, for eternity.

She paused, then her lips widened even as she swirled her tongue with his, sending lightning of awareness through her.

I wouldn't mind a babe or two who looks like you. One who asks a million questions and dives headfirst into everything.

He sucked in a breath and deepened the kiss, his hands roaming over her back and hips.

I will give you all the dragonlings you want. Pure chaos. Dragons almost always have boys, not girls—the climate of this planet doesn't favor female dragons—but if you want a girl, we'll adopt one. Like you. One who lost her mama...

Raelion? Bella said softly through the bond.

He pressed her tighter, lifting her from her feet. *Yes, simi dravak?*

Shut up and kiss me.

His lips curved into a smile, but he never broke the kiss.

"You two are going to miss it," Scarlet hissed.

Wulfric groaned. "Gods, I'd rather you go back to your room than watch that. Wedding or not, don't make me watch."

Scarlet chuckled, but Merida's quiet shushing pulled all attention back to the hearth.

"He's almost here."

Leopol broke the kiss and murmured into Bella's ear, "I

don't think he'll be here for another few hours. We could sneak across the hall..."

She giggled, tucking close to him, her heart light. "No, I don't want to miss anything."

He sighed—*truly* sighed—and she cupped his cheek with a kiss to his jaw.

"Don't worry. I'll make it up to you later."

He growled, eyes glowing softly in the firelight. "Now who's making promises? You just say when you're ready, and I'll give you everything your heart desires."

Her laugh faded into a hush. *You already have, Leopol. Even that first day, when I was lost and tethered and terrified... you were there. My steady anchor.*

"I almost lost you," he whispered, his voice rough as his thumbs stroked the new scales of her cheeks. "And if I had... I would've lost everything. You're not just my mate, Bellakari. You're my world. I love you."

Tears slipped golden down her cheeks. "That's all I've ever wanted. To love—and be loved in return. And I do. I love you more than I ever loved anyone, more than I ever thought possible."

He kissed her—no tongue, no urgency. Just truth. A kiss that wasn't a promise or a fate, but a *choice*. The choice to love. The choice to stay. The choice to build a future— together.

She hesitated, then looked up at him. "You said earlier you'd never force me. But I want to give you a choice too. Do you want to help me rule Busparia? I know Hartsgrove is your home, but—"

He pressed a kiss to her horn. A seal. A vow.

Then tucked her close against his chest, right into the soft place under his collarbone. "My home is wherever you are. You're mine, and I'm yours. In every realm, in every form, from this moment forward."

Across the room, a grunt echoed as the dragonling kicked again. A soft squall followed–tiny and new, but full of life.

Guess we're official now, she murmured through the bond. *You and me, forever.*

Knowledge seekers. Truth bringers. Leaders of our people. Preparing the world for what's to come.

He meant Asmoroth. She knew. But for once, she wasn't afraid.

Together we've faced the odds–and together we'll triumph. I love you, Leopol. My Raelion.

I love you, Bellakari. Simi dravak. Mi Luvielle.

Rain pattered gently against the windows, and the fire snapped low. Together, they turned and joined their family by the hearth.

That night, as rain kissed the glass and firelight danced in the room, a dragon prince was born. Golden and glowing. Wet and winged. Squalling, brilliant, and alive. But that's another story.

More by Jane Poller

vinci-books.com/soldier-gets-his-girl

She doesn't have time for romance—until he walks through the door.

Single mom Cindy has no time for romance—especially not with cocky, charming Andy, her hometown's ex-military heartthrob. He's back for good, and despite her best efforts, sparks fly. But with demanding jobs and complicated pasts, is their attraction worth the risk—or doomed from the start?

Turn the page for a free preview…

The Soldier Gets His Girl: Chapter One

The scent of flour and cinnamon surrounded her before soft hands covered her eyes from behind. A light, tinkling voice said, "Guess who?"

Cindy didn't even have to guess.

"Maryanne."

"No fooling you, is there." Her sister chuckled as she rounded the bench and sat beside Cindy. "You ready for work?"

"Yep, just waiting on you." Cindy eyed her sister. An orange t-shirt with a smiling black pumpkin stretched over her chest and hung off one shoulder, showing her orange bra strap. Beside the pumpkin was a steaming cup that said *I'm a latte to handle.*

"Nice shirt," Cindy said with a nod. Compared to her own dark purple scrubs, her sister always seemed perfectly put together. The candy corn earrings, black choker, and black skinny jeans really put the look all together, and Cindy sighed wistfully.

"How can you wear those all day?" Cindy asked,

pointing at the high heeled, black open-toed shoes. Her baby sister always knew what she wanted and charged after it with abandon. If someone tried to convince her to do something else, she'd dig in her heels and do it anyway. She knew better than to tell her to wear something more practical while at the bakery.

"What, these? They're the most comfortable pair I own. You should try them on."

She kicked them off as Cindy shook her head. "Nah, I'm okay."

She looked at her sneakers, the epitome of comfort. Though comfortable, they still pinched her toes at the end of the day. She sighed as the timer on her phone went off. She silenced it and gathered her purse from her feet.

"James! Owen! I'm heading to work!" Cindy called to the boys on the playground.

Maryanne jumped up and strode with confidence toward the playground equipment. "I'll get them and meet you at the parking lot."

Cindy stood and stretched, looking for the oldest.

She smiled as her lanky boy ran over from the soccer field. Her brown-haired little boy wasn't so little anymore. He was only twelve, but already taller than her. But then again, she was barely five feet, so that wasn't saying much.

She smoothed the escaped curls back into her braid as she waited for him. "Good practice tonight?" she asked Cody with a smile.

He nodded and grinned, his teeth still too big for his mouth. "Yep. All good. Coach says I need to work on cardio at home."

She frowned, thinking out loud as they turned to the parking lot. "Okay, we can figure that out. I don't want you running in the neighborhood, though. It's not safe enough."

He rolled his hazel eyes, whining, "Mom, we live in like, the smallest town ever. There's only a few thousand people here! No one is going to do anything."

Maryanne and the other boys caught up to them at the fork in the sidewalk. They were talking a mile a minute, the two boys vying for their Aunt Maryanne's attention.

"Old habits die hard, though. Living in Houston, caution was ingrained into us," she reminded Cody.

Maryanne said something so low Cindy couldn't hear, then James fell back to walk with Cindy and Cody, tucking his little hand into hers.

Maryanne took off running, and Owen yelled, "Hey, that's cheating!" Then he raced after her, their laughter ringing in the air.

Cody sighed, "I know, Mom. But this isn't Houston. It's Crimson Creek, where nothing ever happens and everyone's happy."

Cindy grinned as they reached the SUV. Cindy was still helping James inside her SUV when Maryanne's little red car drove past, Owen smiling and waving from the backseat. Moving here had been the right choice, even though it was in the middle of nowhere. It was her hometown, a sanctuary that she was so glad to provide for her boys. They chatted about homework and their plans for the weekend before she dropped them off at their apartment with Maryanne.

She kissed them all before hopping back into her SUV to head to work. Every weekend, her heart broke a little as she had to leave them with her mom or her sister. Those few precious moments at the park during Cody's soccer practice were a balm to her soul and made her feel like maybe she wasn't totally failing as a single mom.

Working the weekend shift at the hospital was hard, but

worth the money. Cindy rounded the corner of the hallway of the hospital, humming *Walking on Sunshine*, bobbing her head, and trying not to think of the full moon tonight on a Friday night.

She shook off thoughts of missing so much in her boys' lives. It was going to be a great but busy weekend shift, then she'd go home and snuggle them.

Then on Monday, she'd start all over again with her second job as a physical therapy assistant. Juggling work seven days a week and the boys' school events was still better than the six years of hell they'd lived through. Moving here had been the right decision. She pushed thoughts of her ex-husband out of her mind too as she approached the nurse's station.

Resuming her song, she smiled and greeted Carrie. "Evening! How's it going tonight? You ready to get out of here?"

"God, so ready. I don't envy you the night shift. The full moon already has us busy as bees." Carrie bounced on her feet and leaned in to whisper, "But they just brought up a hunk from the ER. Girl, I am so jealous you get to take care of him. He's delicious, even rolling in on a gurney and hurtin'!" She passed off his chart, and Cindy skimmed it as they caught up on their lives from the past week.

"Kidney stone? Ouch." She wrinkled her nose as she turned to head into the room. The door opened, and she chatted with the two ER nurses before they left.

She entered the room and stopped. Normally, she'd be checking his IV, his chart, and the readouts from the ER. But Carrie had definitely been telling the truth about the hunk.

His jet-black hair was longer on top and short on the

sides. It looked like he'd been running his fingers through it a lot today.

Her heart skipped a beat as she glanced over his face. The nurse in her noted he was breathing deeply and methodically through the pain.

The woman in her noted the cleft in his chin and the crooked nose. He had high cheekbones and a five o'clock shadow on a firm jaw that was clenched in pain.

He wore a plain black t-shirt that stretched tightly over his chest. She sighed, catching sight of the huge biceps as he clenched his fists.

His icy blue eyes popped open at the sound of her sigh and captured her gaze. Her breath stuttered as he stared at her without blinking, then she straightened her spine and stepped toward him.

"Ma'am." His voice was deep and sent a tingle up her spine. But the pain clear in the tight, growly words sent her into action.

She cleared her throat with a smile. "Hello, Andrew. I'll be your nurse this weekend, if you're here that long. I hear you have a kidney stone?"

He nodded and closed his eyes again. "That's what they tell me. Had a CT scan already to confirm. And call me Andy."

"Nice to meet you, Andy. I'm Cindy. We'll wait for the CT results. Then the doctor will go over your treatment plan. On a scale of zero to ten, what's your pain level?"

"About an eight, I reckon, but I've had worse." He waved to his left foot, sticking out of the sheet.

He was wearing blue basketball shorts and his thighs looked like they could crush a man. They were so big.

She blinked at the running prosthesis attached below his

knee. How had she missed that when she walked in? Geez, some nurse she was.

"What happened there?" she asked, as she leaned over to check his IV. Hell, he smelled good. A combination of leather and wood smoke tickled her nose. She inhaled deeply.

"IED hit the Humvee in Afghanistan seventeen months ago." He clenched his teeth, her eyes dilating slightly with the pain.

"Thank you for your service," she said softly. "My father was in the Army for twenty-three years. What branch are you in?"

"Was… They kicked me out."

"Oh," she frowned, turning to the computer at his bedside and typing away. "I'm sorry."

He sighed and rubbed his eyes. "Not your fault. If I'd been injured twelve years ago when I first joined, I might have been able to switch my MOS and stay in."

"Twelve years? So, was it a medical retirement?" She checked the machines, then documented the information.

"Yeah," he said, seeming to melt into the bed in defeat.

"That's gotta be tough. Twelve years is a long time. Where all were you stationed? We moved a lot with the Army. The longest we were ever in one place was Fort Hood."

"Hood was my last duty station. You know what they say about Fort Hood, don't you?"

She grinned back. "Oh yeah. To leave, you either die or retire. So, I guess you got lucky, even with the bum leg. Medical retirement beats dead, doesn't it?"

He blinked rapidly, and his forehead wrinkled. "I guess it does."

She smiled and patted his arm. Jerking her hand back at

the spark of electricity that shot through her, she walked around the end of the bed to take his blood pressure. Her face heated, but hopefully her caramel complexion would keep him from noticing the blush. Still, she'd keep up a steady stream of conversation to distract him from the pain and her own awkwardness.

"We were stationed in several other places, but my favorites were the ones with trees. How about you? What was your favorite duty station?" She monitored the blood pressure machine and waited for it to stop testing him.

He groaned and clutched his side. "I was at Campbell first. The Land Between the Lakes was my favorite area. It was peaceful there."

She nodded and charted the results of the machine. "Peace is underrated. The world needs more peaceful places for sure."

He just grunted, so she continued. "The medication in your IV should kick in any minute now. You can rest until the doctor gets here, if you'd like." She unwrapped the blood pressure cuff, inhaling his earthy scent once more.

He licked his lips as though thirsty. "Can you talk to me until he gets here? You're a wonderful distraction from the pain."

She smiled and nodded, grabbing the plastic up of water with a straw from his bedside table and holding it to his lips to drink. "Sure thing. I haven't been to the Land Between the Lakes, but I grew up vacationing in the Arkansas Ozarks. I love the mountains! And trees. It's why I was so happy to move back here."

He stopped drinking and laid his head back on the bed with a wince. "How long have you lived here?" he wheezed.

She put the cup back on the table as she talked. "My grandmother lived in this part of Texas, so we came up and joined her about five years ago. She lost a foot to diabetes, so I'm quite familiar with prosthetics. Helping take care of her is actually why I became a nurse… How are your physical therapies going?"

He turned pale and whispered, "Been doing them on my own for the past week, since I moved into my house." He clutched his stomach and groaned, and she knew exactly what that body language meant.

She grabbed the bowl beside his bed in time for him to throw up. She crooned to him softly, telling him it was going to be all right.

When he'd finished, she hummed *Let it Go* while she cleaned up and grabbed him a wet cloth. She wiped his face, and he reached up, taking the cloth gently from her.

His lips twitched in a shaky smile. "Thank you, but I got it. Is that the cartoon movie? We watched that in Iraq." He wiped his face, and she grabbed the cup of water again.

Holding it to his lips, she couldn't help but notice how full they were. Perfect for kissing. *Wait, what the hell am I thinking? He just threw up! I shouldn't be thinking about kissing him!*

"It's a 'girly movie' according to my oldest, but he still watches it with us on movie night. My sister lives in town and loves the girly movies. She may be an adult, but not with Disney princess movies." She put the cup back on the table as he seemed to finally relax.

"Your oldest?" His eyes fluttered slowly, his eyes glazing over.

"I have three boys, twelve, ten, and four. Looks like the meds are kicking in. You rest until the doctor gets here," she said.

She felt pulled to him by an invisible string. It was more intense than how she normally ached to stop the pain of a patient. She left the door cracked when she left, not really wanting to go too far away from him. She snorted. What was wrong with her? Yeah, she could stare at his handsome face all night. But she'd never been drawn to a patient before. Or any man, really, since her ex.

She kept thinking of him as she checked the other patients on the floor, then went to the nurse's station. Movement from the corner of her eye caused Cindy to look up from charting at the computer. Dr. Jensen shuffled down the hallway. The sweet, old man's bushy white hair stuck up every which way. Probably should have retired by now, but she'd gotten to know him well when her grandmother had been a patient of his.

She sat back in her chair and smiled as he rounded into the nurse's station. "You pulled the short straw this weekend, huh?"

He cleaned his glasses on his shirt and shrugged. "Just another full moon weekend. Amanda sent some fried chicken, so I at least have that to look forward to."

He grabbed the chart from beside her desk, giving it a quick read. Groaning echoed through the hall, and a chill went down her spine. She jumped up and sped after the doctor into Andy's room.

He was tangled up in the sheets. Sweat poured off him as he moaned, his eyes closed. She grabbed the washrag and wiped his forehead, shushing him.

"No," he groaned, "No! You can't take it. No, I need it. It's fine! It's fine!" He shouted louder and louder with every sentence. Dr. Jensen was trying to untie his legs from the sheets.

"Shh. It's alright," Cindy crooned softly. His enormous arms grabbed her and pulled her half on top of him.

"No," he said, burying his head in the crook of her neck. Her curly hair had come mostly undone from her braid and spread over them. She gasped as his nose touched the soft spot where her neck met her shoulder.

"No, don't go. Don't leave me," he groaned.

She pushed off his chest, trying to sit up, certain that her weight was hurting his kidney stone. But he simply wrapped his arms around her tighter. She huffed and shifted sideways on him, drawing her knees up onto the side of the bed.

Feet hanging off the bed, her entire chest was on top of him, trapped in his arms. Dr. Jensen had gotten the sheets untangled and pulled away from his legs, muttering the whole time as he began to test Andy's groin and stomach.

"Yep, time to pass that kidney stone. Just a few minutes more," the doctor said.

"Andy, wake up," she said, trying to speak strongly, but hearing the wobble in her voice. He jerked back against the bed, and she pushed on his chest to see his face.

His bright blue eyes stared over her shoulder, unseeing.

"Andy," she mumbled, wiping his forehead with the washcloth. He sucked in a breath like a drowning man. The move pressed her breasts even tighter against his chest. It was like a chain reaction, making her gasp in response. It'd been years since a man held her.

Then Dr. Jensen spoke up with a strict, no-nonsense tone of voice that reminded her of how her dad used to talk when he went into military mode. "Andy, Andy, wake up. You need to pass this kidney stone NOW."

She saw Andy's gaze snap around, then lock onto her. He looked confused as he tried to place her, but his eyes were clearer.

"I'm Cindy, your nurse. You're in the hospital, and you need to pee to push this kidney stone. Do you hear me?"

His arms wrapped tighter around her as he whispered, "Yes, just—just don't leave me."

She nodded. "I won't. But listen to the doctor. You need to push, alright? You can do this."

He nodded, then buried his face in her neck again. His groans grew louder as his arms tightened.

She held onto his shoulder and wiped his forehead with her other hand. She couldn't move, even if she wanted to, could barely use her arms.

His breathing sped up, and she tried to get him to take a deep breath. He roared, squeezing her enough that her back popped.

But it must have been when he finally passed the kidney stone, because she heard a soft *plink* before he slowly let his arms relax. He breathed in deeply at her neck before letting her go completely and leaning back, panting.

She stood on wobbly legs, staring into his eyes. She was breathing as deeply as he was, but it wasn't from pain. Her cheeks burned as she glanced at Dr. Jensen as she climbed off the bed.

He handed her the cup with the stone in it. He rolled up the now soiled top sheet and disposed of it in the receptacle. Cindy glanced down and noted that his basketball shorts were still clean.

"Well done! You can stay in your clothes if you want, Andy. I kept it contained," Dr. Jensen said as he washed his hands. "You should be feeling better soon. Your CT scan only showed the one kidney stone, and that was it. You'll need to stay overnight for observation, but you can probably go home in the morning."

Andy nodded shakily. "Thank you."

"If you need me, I'll be down the hall. Just holler,

alright?" Dr. Jensen said as he grabbed the cup from her and walked out the door.

Cindy stood frozen, her gaze locked on Andy's. They both still breathed heavily. Even through the haze of pain, she saw awareness in his eyes.

She breathed deeply, glancing around in panic. Her eyes lit on the cup of ice water from earlier. She helped him drink. Putting it back, she checked his IVs.

"Well, you didn't bust an IV, so that's good."

He smiled wryly. "I'm sorry about earlier. I hope I didn't hurt you."

"No, no. It's fine. I've had worse in this hospital, trust me. I'm just glad that you got the job done so quickly!"

He rubbed his side softly. "Yeah, it doesn't seem like it's been quick. It's been hurting for weeks now."

"My friend Holly is really into natural medicine and such. We like to compare notes, so to speak. Her great-aunt got kidney stones after her house burned down."

She put the cup back on the table and turned the computer on to chart the incident as she continued talking. "Her aunt was scared to death of what would happen next. And that's what caused her kidney stone. Are you scared of something like that?"

She wondered if he had more than physical pain.

He looked across the room for a few minutes, staring unseeing. She thought he wasn't going to answer. So, she grabbed clean sheets and blankets.

After she'd made the bed and tucked the blankets around him, she turned to leave.

His soft voice stopped her at the foot of his bed. "I guess I'm afraid of what comes next. I've been gone for nearly two years. I didn't expect... Well, now that I'm retired? I don't know what to do."

She glanced at him as his eyes fluttered slowly. She grabbed the washcloth and smoothed the frown line between his forehead. The tension in his shoulders visibly released.

"Thank you," he whispered.

It made her heart flip over to know that she was helping. She started to reply but stopped. He was asleep, the deep snoring breath making her shoulders finally relax. He needed to sleep, especially after tonight's adventure in the hospital.

The Soldier Gets His Girl: Chapter Two

The rest of the night shift was just as busy. The full moon finally waned around one in the morning, and the floor finally chilled out enough for her to breathe through the rest of her shift. Before she went to the quiet room for her required scheduled sleep, she found herself outside his room.

She grabbed the breakfast tray from the chart and pushed the door open. "Good morning! How are you feeling today?"

He pushed the button on the bed to sit up, grimacing and rubbing his jaw. Covered in a five o'clock shadow, he looked gruff and a real man's man. Her dad would've liked him.

"I'm fine. Are you alright? I didn't squeeze you too tight, did I?" His voice was so deep, it made her stomach quiver.

She placed the tray on the rolling desk and pulled it to him, ignoring the attraction. It wasn't like she could or would do anything about it.

She smiled brightly and waved a hand. "Oh, I'm alright

too. Don't worry about it. Happens all the time around here. Were you having a nightmare about when they took your leg? My dad used to have nightmares."

He frowned and looked down at the tray, reaching for the fork. Typical guy to ignore a tough question.

She sighed and shrugged. "If you're not fine, you're not fine. No need to gloss over it. I'm a nurse. You can be honest."

He looked up, still frowning. But she refused to break eye contact, crossing her arms. He finally took a big breath and cocked one eyebrow up. "Fine. I'm not fine, but I'll be fine, okay?"

She nodded, "Sure. Fine." Her lips twitched, then a giggle escaped. He blinked before a chuckle escaped, making him clutch at his side.

"Oh, no laughing. Laughing is *not* fine!" he gasped.

Cindy laughed loudly but reached over to rub her hand across his forehead to feel for a temperature. She just wanted an excuse to touch him. "Oh, you poor thing. I'm sorry!"

He snorted as he grabbed her hand, holding it for a second too long. Butterflies danced in her stomach. "No, you're not. You're enjoying this."

She felt her face soften as she smiled again, cradling her hand when he released it. "Ha! You're right. I'm not that sorry. You should smile and laugh more, though. It's good for the soul."

He smiled at her. "Yes, ma'am. Whatever you say."

Dr. Jensen came into the room as Andy began eating his eggs and bacon. "Well, good morning! How's our fair patient today?"

"Fine, doctor," he said.

Cindy laughed too loudly, then fake coughed to cover it.

She caught Andy's eyes, and he winked. She turned and fiddled with the computer.

"Well, it looks like you can discharge within the hour. I can't let you drive yourself home, though. You'll need a ride."

Andy threw his head back against the bed and groaned. She hurried to his side, thinking he was in pain. But he said, "Can I stay here until I can drive myself?"

"Do you not have anyone?" Her chest lurched with the need to take care of him.

He grimaced. "No, it's not that. It's just… my aunt can be a bit much. And if she comes, then she'll smother me next week. I thought this first week home had been rough with her hovering…"

Clicking in the hallway echoed throughout the room, followed by a soft voice. She frowned as Andy froze, his eyes wide.

Suzie, one of the older women at church who still tried to be hip and fashionable, walked through the door. A friend of Cindy's mom, she didn't even glance at Cindy or Dr. Jensen as her poodle skirt swished from side to side.

"There you are!" she said, rushing to the bedside. "You weren't at home this morning, so I used that Find My Friends app, and it said you were here. What's going on?"

Cindy glanced between Andy and Suzie. Suzie's blond and gray hair was pulled back in a ponytail, accentuating the fine lines around her eyes. She didn't act like an older woman; she seemed to bounce and glow with energy.

When she moved to town, Suzie had been one of the church ladies who'd welcomed her. She'd been gone for almost two years but had been at the ladies' meeting at church earlier this month.

Suddenly, it clicked in her head like a puzzle.

Andy must be the injured war hero nephew that she had talked about at the meeting. They were all delivering meals to welcome him home, starting next week.

Andy sighed, pushing her hands off his face. "I'm fine, Aunt Suz. It was only a kidney stone. But the doc said I'm ready to go home."

Suzie placed her hands on her hips, her Dolly Parton t-shirt stretching over her thin shoulders. "Only a kidney stone! Good grief, Andy. Those are a bitch! Why didn't you call me?"

He sighed, rubbing his hands over his face. "I didn't want you to worry any more than you already do."

"Not worry! Not worry? How could I not worry? That's it. You're moving in with us today. You obviously can't be trusted to your own devices," she said, waving a finger in his face.

His eyes narrowed, and somehow his scruffy jaw seemed to grow firmer. "No. I'm a grown-ass man. I can do this, Aunt Suz. I won't have you hovering."

Dr. Jensen cleared his throat. "Suzie, it's good to see you back in town. You need to stop by Amanda's later. She's got some pumpkins about ready to pick."

"Pumpkins! Jensen, how can you talk about pumpkins at a time like this?" Suzie threw her hands into the air.

Dr. Jensen grabbed her hands. "Remember when Amanda first planted those pumpkins? She over-planted them. We had pumpkins on top of pumpkins. They couldn't survive. This man here is a pumpkin, darlin'. Let him grow."

Suzie blinked, staring owlishly at the doctor. Cindy caught Andy's eyes, who shrugged at his aunt's behavior. Suzie seemed to wilt as she breathed an enormous sigh of defeat.

Suzie slammed her hands back on her hips. "Fine. You don't have to move in with us. On one condition. Start physical therapy."

Andy threw his fork onto the tray, causing it to shake. "I don't need it anymore!"

Cindy would've been surprised by the sudden show of emotion, but it reminded her so much of her dad, she just smiled as the two argued.

Suzie waved a finger at him. "That's not what the doctor said, and you know it! You have to keep it up."

"I didn't work my butt off to let it all go to waste. All those exercises? I can do them myself. I don't need another doctor, another therapist, telling me what to do!" His jaw was clenched, his lips pursed in anger.

Dr. Jensen cleared his throat, saying, "Actually, I agree with her on this one. You need a physical therapist. In fact, Cindy can do it. Right?"

Cindy blinked. "Umm, I'll have to check the schedule, but I can call the office and see. Is that what you want?" She looked at Andy, his gaze glaring daggers at them all.

She waited. His fierce gaze gave her flashbacks to when her ex-husband would get angry. Her anxiety climbed as she waited for the tension to keep escalating. How strange, that when he acted like her ad, it didn't bother her. But the belligerent challenge in his eyes gave her pause.

Instead of arguing though, he gave a small nod and sighed. She took out her phone and called the physical therapy office, stepping toward the door to talk to her boss.

"They have an opening next Wednesday at two. Will that work for you?" She waited for him to nod, then she confirmed the details with them.

Suzie walked around the bed and said, "Here, I'll do that. Jensen, you get him ready to leave." Suzie took her phone, and Cindy's brows rose as she stepped into the hallway with it to go over the details.

Andy sighed and shifted on the bed. "Sorry about her. I told you she could be a bit much."

Dr. Jensen said, "Nothing we're not used to, son. I grew up with her." The doctor chuckled and went to the door. "I'm going to go finish up the paperwork. I'll be right back for your signature. Cindy, you can unhook him."

Cindy nodded, turning to him as they were left alone. "You alright?" She pulled out his IVs.

He sighed and nodded, "I'm fine."

She giggled. He smirked at her. That smirk haunted her as she went to sleep in the quiet room at the hospital.

On Sunday night, she wearily pushed through her apartment door. The sounds of splashing and little laughter echoed through the small space.

"Hey, sis! How was work?" Maryanne asked, ducking her head out of the kitchen. Cindy closed the door and kicked off her shoes.

"Not too bad," she replied, stepping into the kitchen and leaning against the cabinets as her sister finished stirring dinner on the stove.

Maryanne knew the weekends were brutal, but there was no point in complaining about it. She slept at the hospital on her mandatory rests for the forty-eight-hour shift. Missing her boys on the weekends was the worst.

"Oh, come on. It was a full moon. You don't have to lie to me. I'm your favorite sister."

Cindy chuckled. "You're my only sister. But seriously, the hospital was fine." Her cheeks widened in a grin. She seriously hadn't been able to say that word all weekend without thinking of Andy.

"Whoa, what's that smile for? Something good happen

at work?" Maryanne plated up some pasta. The noise in the bathroom grew louder, and Cindy sighed and stepped toward the entrance.

Maryanne's hand on her arm stopped her. "I'll get it. You sit and eat. You look like you're about to drop."

Cindy grabbed a plate and sat at the table, enjoying the warm garlic bread. Homemade food after hospital cafeteria food all weekend just hit differently. What would be good under normal circumstances became the most amazing meal she'd ever eaten every Sunday night.

Maryanne came back into the kitchen, wiping her wet hands on her black leggings.

Cindy shoveled another bite of alfredo into her mouth. "God, sis, you have no idea how good this tastes. Thanks for always helping. I—I don't know what I'd do without you and Mom."

Maryanne sat at the table with a plate, the sparkles on the orange pumpkin on her oversized shirt winking in the fluorescent light above.

"Don't mention it. You know we'd do anything for you. That's what family is for, right? And we have a lot of fun with the boys. They're no trouble at all."

"Speaking of, are they getting ready for bed?"

"They probably got more water on the floor than on themselves. But hey, It's better than nothing." Maryanne lifted the fork.

"How was the soccer game this weekend?"

"Oh, it was good! Cody had this really cool block in the last part of it. I got it on video! Here." She fiddled with her phone, then handed it over.

Cindy's heart lurched as she watched him check his opponent and sweep the ball right out from under him. The need to be there for him threatened to overwhelm her.

Cody joined them in the kitchen. "Hey, bud! Good game! Auntie M showed me the video of that block."

"Yeah, it was pretty sick," he said, as he grabbed a glass of water and leaned against the counter. He crossed his ankles and grinned so big it took over his entire face.

"Dude didn't even see it coming! Coach said I did good and might move up to JV next year. Wouldn't that be cool? I'd get to play against the eighth and ninth graders!"

"That'd be amazing!" Cindy jumped up to hug him.

He gave her a quick hug back before ducking back down the hall. Owen came running in, his socks sliding on the tile.

He hit her right in the legs and nearly knocked her down. "Whoa there! What's the hurry?"

"Mama, Mama, Mama! I have a loose tooth! Look!" he said, sticking his still wet finger into his mouth and wiggling his front bottom tooth. Her heart skipped a beat. *No! He couldn't be big enough to lose teeth already, could he?*

"What? Oh wow!" she said, bending down to get a closer look.

She overly dramatized looking down the hallway, before lowering her voice to a whisper, "I think you might lose that tooth before your brothers lost theirs. They didn't lose their first tooth until they were five!"

He grinned and whooped loudly, rushing down the hall to tell his brothers that he was going to beat them in the first tooth competition.

"They're growing up so fast," Cindy said, sitting back down at the table. She pushed the plate away and laid her head down with a groan. Maryanne picked up the plate and cleaned up.

"Yeah, but it's alright. Look how amazing they're doing. They may be loud and typical boys... but they're respectful and pay more attention than most adults. You're doing an outstanding job with them," Maryanne said, drying the last dish.

Cindy checked her phone emails and sighed.

"No interviews?"

Cindy shook her head. "I don't get it. Both Decatur and Denton hospitals have openings I qualify for. I've applied and there's been no word!"

"Yeah, but when do the jobs close?"

She frowned, "One closed last week, and another closes this week. The third... I'm not sure. I can't remember."

"Well, they either, have internal candidates that they were going to promote or they were waiting for the positions to close. You're going to be fine!"

"I just want to be home more. I'm so tired of missing out, M. I want to be home when they're home, go to soccer games, and be part of losing teeth!" Cindy swiped a tear out of her eye.

Maryanne drew her into a hug, the kind only sisters give.

"I know you want to be here. And they know that too. You'll get the job, don't worry. It's going to be fine."

Cindy chuckled at the word and squeezed her sister one more time before she headed home for the night. Monday started her PTA patients for the week. She already needed a day off.

The Soldier Gets His Girl: Chapter Three

"I can't believe I let you talk me into this. I'm already sore!" Landry complained as they walked through the parking lot outside the gym. Andy took great pride in smoking Landry in cardio, especially with his recent hospital stay. Dark eyes and a sweet smile haunted him at the oddest moments, but he didn't want anything to do with any doctors or nurses.

Andy wiped his face with a small towel and slung his gym bag over his shoulder. "Me? You're the one who wanted to go to the bar!"

"Yeah, because I have to. My brothers would kill me if I didn't." Landry sighed and ran his fingers through his still wet hair. The gym had been good for them both, but he wasn't so sure the bar would be.

Andy teased. "*Have* to go to the bar? Not want to? You getting tired of the bar scene?"

Landry punched him lightly in the shoulder before they split to go around the classic blue Ford. It was Landry's pride and joy, a keepsake from his grandpa that he'd kept in pristine shape for years. "Not so much getting tired of it as thinking there's something more out there. Weekends are supposed to be relaxing and fun."

"And playing at the bar with your brothers isn't relaxing or fun anymore?" Andy asked as he shut the door to the truck.

Landry's grin flashed white in the glow of the parking lot lights as he turned on the truck. It was only half hour's drive to the bar, which would give Andy a chance to get off his aching leg.

"Nah, it's fun enough. Can't and shouldn't complain, really. Not even Mom complains about it anymore. Ten years of playing in that bar almost every Friday and Saturday, and we've never once missed church on Sunday morning. We promised her, and we've stuck to our word." Landry's thumbs tapped a rhythm in time to the soft country music echoing through the cab of the truck.

"Aunt Suzie is already after me to go to church, but I can't handle all the little old ladies and their questions." Andy adjusted his prosthetic to scratch at a sore spot.

Landry glanced down at the floorboard. "You can't even tell, with your jeans on and that boot. Is the boot foot better than the one you were wearing yesterday or the one at the gym?"

Andy sat back on the seat and tried to stretch out more. "They're about the same as far as comfort level goes. The one I wore at the gym was the same one as yesterday. It's better for cardio and quick movements. Wearing a shoe or boot with this one is more restrictive. I feel like I limp more with it, but I've been told that it's all in my head."

"Well, I'll be watching you dance from the stage, so I'll tell you if it's noticeable." Landry's sly grin flashed in the lights from a passing car.

"Gee, thanks." Andy's voice dripped sarcasm as he shifted on the seat.

"What else are best friends for? Shootin' it straight and being a wing man is in the job description."

Landry was right. They'd been best friends for decades. He'd been the first one to visit when Andy had moved back to town just over a week or two ago. Andy looked out the passenger side window into the darkness, the trip home from the airport replaying in his head.

Andy groaned as Aunt Suzie pulled the truck up to the cabin. He kept ignoring her as she kept up a steady stream of chatter.

When the truck came to a stop, he pried his eyes open and rubbed them with the heel of his palms.

"We've kept it maintained so you won't have anything to worry about. You remember Herman?"

Andy shook his head as she pulled the keys out of the ignition and looked at him. She smiled and continued. "That's alright. He's checked on the cabin once a week while we were traveling and helping you. Have I told you how excited I am that you're home for good?"

He rolled his eyes and opened the passenger door as she kept talking.

"It makes my heart so happy. It could've been so much worse. I don't know what I would've done if you'd... if you'd..." she stuttered and he looked back across the bench seat. The fear flashing in her eyes made him pause and turn back to her on the seat.

He patted her on the arm. "I know," he said. "But I'm fine, and I'm home, so no need to worry. Can we go inside now? Is Uncle Mike bringing lunch?" He pushed the door and slowly stepped down onto the dirt drive. All the travel had left a dull, steady ache in his leg.

"Lunch should be already inside," Aunt Suzie said, closing the driver's door behind her and rounding the front of the truck.

He stared at the long, low wooden house. What had once been his oasis in the woods now seemed an icy prison.

Gathering his courage for this new life, he shut the door and limped to the cabin. "Leave the bags. I'll get them out after lunch."

Aunt Suzie bounced alongside him as they walked. "I'm so happy you're home, Andy. I've talked to the ladies at church, and we'll be starting a meal train soon."

"Wait," he frowned as he stopped on the front porch. "I don't want a bunch of strangers coming around. I can't... It's too soon." His gaze darted around the porch of the cabin before looking down the shaded dirt driveway, half expecting the little old church ladies to descend on him any minute.

Aunt Suzie sighed, "I figured." She opened the door ahead of him, and he limped inside.

The lights flipped on and a male voice boomed, "Surprise!"

Andy's chest twisted, and he dove behind the couch. He covered his head, listening to the silence as his heart raced. Blinking, his eyes adjusted as he realized what had happened.

A little blond curly-headed three-year-old came tearing down the hall yelling, "Prize!" Sitting up slowly, he peeked around the side of the couch. He hated surprises. His nostrils flared in frustration and embarrassment. Working hard to even out his breathing, he sat there until Mandy popped her head around the couch.

"Found you! Now I hide," she sang before skipping off back down the short hallway. Her smile and easy-going nature settled some of the frustration, and he sighed. This was just his life now, and he better get used to it.

He moved to his knees. Using the back of the couch, he pulled himself up onto his right foot. Waiting a few seconds, his heart not nearly slowed down enough, he stood.

"Andy! Are you ok?" Aunt Suzie squeaked as she jumped toward him from the doorway. He nearly fell backward as he flinched away from her. She stopped in her tracks with a stricken look on her face.

Then she spun toward the kitchen. "How about some food? We have a week of meals already in the fridge, but Mike made steak for lunch. He should have all the fixin's in the stove to keep warm. Just let me grab them…"

She kept mumbling to herself as she fluttered around the kitchen, her blond bun bobbing at the base of her skull.

Placing his full weight on both feet, he turned toward his Uncle Mike who shrugged sheepishly. "Sorry about the surprise. I should've known better."

"Don't worry about it. I have to get used to it, right? This is the civilian world." Andy's lips pursed. Not that he'd ever asked for this world. But that wasn't Uncle Mike's fault.

Uncle Mike walked slowly toward him and reached for a hug. Andy forced himself to stand still and pat his uncle on the back.

"It's good to have you home, son." His eyes glistened in the light with unshed tears.

Andy nodded as he trudged toward the kitchen. "It's good to be back." It was the right thing to say, and he did love this cabin. It was always good to be back here. He just never expected to land here permanently so soon.

"Better not sit down yet. You heard Mandy. You're supposed to go find her. Check the quilt chest in your closet. She likes it in there with her little lantern."

He shuffled past the kitchen on the right and the living room on the left to the hallway. When he reached his bedroom, his brows rose. There were some unauthorized updates to his room and the connecting bathroom. He'd only bought the old hunting cabin from Uncle Mike a few years ago.

Andy had joined them and his cousins every year as a kid and the memories here were all happy ones. Andy rubbed at the tightness in his chest. He hadn't planned on living here yet. He'd wanted to do the repairs and updates himself, with his buddy Landry.

A giggle from the closet had him peeking in. The lid of the quilt chest was barely open and light shone out from inside it. She'd definitely grown in the past year, if she could climb in there by herself. Seeing her in the hospital and rehab center wasn't the same as seeing her in his cabin.

"Oh Mandy? Come out, come out, wherever you are," he sing-songed in her favorite voice. Another giggle floated through the air, making him smile fully for the first time in months. He dragged the lid up, and his smile grew.

"Found you!"

Mandy giggled again. She was mostly laying down on a quilt in the bottom of the chest, a pink princess lantern beside her making her eyes bright and clear as she smiled at him. She had Sarah's eyes. Some of the tightness around his chest loosened.

"You found me, Unca Andy!"

"I sure did, princess. You ready to eat?" He reached down to lift her out. He paused, kneeling on his left knee to get more leverage.

Why couldn't things be simple anymore? If he wanted to lift something, he had to actually think about it. Lifting like normal didn't work anymore. He swung her up and grunted before he put her down on her feet.

She giggled again and pointed to the chest, "Light." He grabbed the lantern and handed it to her. She took off skipping out the door, swinging her lantern in her chubby little arm. He pushed himself to his feet and followed her out of the walk-in closet.

The light from the window landed on the silver prosthetic of his foot, bouncing light across the bedroom. It was a curved piece of metal for running and attached about halfway down his left shin.

He snorted. Calling it a foot was a joke. It was seven inches of carbon fiberglass, but it was a big milestone.

Getting this foot meant he had hit an Activity Level 4 in record time. He had worked his butt off in therapies and in the gym to maintain and increase muscle tone.

Reaching it had been his only goal for months. It meant he could go home and get back to normal.

But there was no more normal. The invisible weight pressed onto his chest once again.

A horn blared, bringing him out of the memory. He turned his head to glance at Landry.

"Fucking deer are everywhere. Can't wait for deer season this year," Landry grumbled, making Andy smile. His friend had shown up at the cabin the very next day, and they'd talked about everything and nothing for hours. He was also the only one who'd made the trip to the military hospital when Andy had been stuck there for months.

"Did I ever thank you for coming to see me in January? You're the best, you know." Andy's matter-of-fact tone rang with truth, but he kept it lighthearted.

"I know I am. I'm the best wing man around, remember?" Landry laughed. He was always good for a laugh.

Andy shook his head. "Well, I don't need a wing man right now. I don't think I could handle a woman. I'll barely be able to face the crowd tonight. Did I tell you that Aunt Suzie drug me to the mall a few months ago? She dressed Mandy up for some event. There were tons of people…"

Andy shivered, the cloying press of bodies, the smell of body odor and too much perfume had been a terrible mix with the loud chattering crowd.

"Got too close, did they? But hey. She loves you like a son. She wouldn't have made your Uncle Mike stay in Virginia practically all year to help you recover if she didn't. I rather pity your uncle sometimes. Being stuck in that RV with your Aunt Suzie and an energetic toddler?"

Andy chuckled, surprised already by how much he'd laughed since being home the past few days. "The man is definitely a saint."

They pulled into the parking lot of the Electric Cowboy. Turning off the truck, they could already hear the music spilling out the doors. A bouncer took cover charges at the front door of the large, over-sized barn.

"Don't worry about him. You're in the band tonight," Landry said as they got out of the truck. Andy forced himself to breathe deeply and evenly. He could do this.

"What am I supposed to be doing with the band tonight?" Andy smoothed his sweaty palms down his jeans as they reached the door.

"Hey, Hank! This is Andy. He's just returned from the sand pit and is helping with the band tonight," Landry said, shaking the bouncer's hand.

Hank tipped his hat and said gruffly, "Welcome home. Go right on in. Still quiet but it'll pick up."

Landry grinned at the ladies in line by the door, "I'm looking forward to it!"

They waltzed inside. But Andy automatically stepped to the left. He waited for his eyes to adjust to the light.

Landry scanned the room and waved at his brothers already on stage. "I'm going to go set up. You need anything, man? Want to hang out by the stage?"

Andy shook his head, his breathing evening out in time with the music playing from the jukebox in the corner. "I'll head over to the bar first. Quieter there."

Landry glanced at the bar and started towards it. "Hey, I see Nick. Come on, I'll introduce you."

His legs carried him toward the bar, but he couldn't tell if it was graceful or awkward. The loud music already overwhelmed him. Thankfully, the lights were dim but not blinking.

By the counter, it was quieter. Landry approached a hulking, short-haired blond man with a neatly trimmed beard. He shook Landry's hand, his biceps bulging out of his plain green t-shirt.

"Nick! Good to see you, man. This is Andy, the guy I told you about at poker this week. Andy, this is Nick. He's a vet too," Landry said. Andy reached forward and shook the man's hand.

"Nice to meet you," he said, as Landry gave them a thumbs up before swaggering towards the stage.

"Likewise," Nick said. "Welcome home. Heard you've had a rough year. Grab a stool, and I'll buy you a beer." He flagged down the bartender.

"Thank you. What branch were you in?" Andy tried to deflect the questions from himself.

"Marines for six years. Got me through college and then some. You?" Nick drained the beer he'd been nursing and swapped it for the new one.

"Army for twelve. Deployed?" Andy took a drink of his own.

Nick nodded, "Twice. You?"

"Three and a half," Andy grimaced. They swapped deployment stories and jobs, and it eased some of Andy's loneliness. The military was a brotherhood, and he didn't know where he'd find that kind of ready-made family now that he was out.

"How long have you been out?" Andy asked before sipping his drink.

Nick rubbed his beard thoughtfully. "Three years maybe? You never truly leave it behind... You grow up around here?"

Andy nodded, "Sort of. Spent summers here. I don't recognize you. You from one of the surrounding towns?"

Nick nodded, and they chatted about moving to small towns until Landry's brother, Gunner, did a mic check. Then they turned around on their stools.

Andy's gaze scanned the crowd, which had grown

considerably in the past few minutes he'd been there. The bar behind them stretched half-way down the room. To the left near the door was the side-room with the pool tables. The dance floor in front of them led to the stage on the right. To the right of the stage was the little hallway to the bathrooms.

"All right, all you cool cats and kittens. We're going to get feisty and kick off our Friday night right. Y'all ready to get this party started?" Gunner asked into the microphone.

People were already moving onto the dance floor as they struck up the tune to Miley Cyrus' *Can't Be Tamed*. Andy cocked his head to the side and chuckled.

"Seriously? This isn't a cowboy song," he said to Nick.

Nick nodded and grinned, "Yeah, but sometimes they grandfather her in because of her dad. Tonight is a themed night about lions, tigers, and taming the wild. I overheard them talking about it at poker night. Hey, you'll join us this week, right?"

Andy shrugged, "When is it? I've heard it mentioned but don't know the details."

"Tuesday at eight at Landry and Parker's. They'll grill out, and it's BYOB," he said, tipping his beer up to drink.

Grab your copy...
vinci-books.com/soldier-gets-his-girl

About the Author

Jane Poller read her way through middle school. Romance books got her through countless life changes... moves, degrees, having kids, deployments, teaching high school, international living, health coaching, running a wellness business, homeschooling, and more. She finally gave in to the characters in her head demanding their stories be told. She's an avid reader of historical romance but writes primarily fantasy romance and contemporary small-town romance. Look for the fantasy romance series on her website. The Crimson Creek series is a contemporary steamy small-town romance set in a fictional town in Texas. Speaking of, she lives in Texas with her middle school sweetheart. He's her real-life hero, Army veteran, and the inspiration for her stories. His interest in Role playing games inspired her love of fantasy romance too. Without him, the fantasy stories wouldn't exist. When she's not doing all the things, she's reading and writing. Or arguing with her characters, who refuse to do what she wants. But that's par for the course, since she's currently raising teenagers and two dogs. Those reviews really brighten her day and are much appreciated.